"Le diable rôde autour d'un monastère."

"The devil rides outside monastery walls."

the Devil

Smiths, Inc., Fort Worth, 1952

John H. Griffin

rides outside

Second Printing
Library of Congress Catalog Card Number: 52-9277

Grateful acknowledgment is made to Oxford University Press for permission to quote a portion of sonnet No. 69 from Poems *of Gerard Manley Hopkins, and to Chatto & Windus for permission to quote a passage from Edward B. Pusey's translation of* The Confessions of St. Augustine.

NOTE: *The characters and events of this novel have no basis in reality. The Monastery, the Village, and the Town are wholly imaginary, and the people who inhabit them do not exist elsewhere.*

TO MY MOTHER AND FATHER

the cloister within

within

1

Contents

the cloister within

"I am gall, I am heartburn. God's most deep decree
Bitter would have me taste: my taste was me;
Bones built in me, flesh filled, blood brimmed the curse.
    Selfyeast of spirit a dull dough sours. I see
The lost are like this, and their scourge to be
As I am mine, their sweating selves; but worse."

GERARD MANLEY HOPKINS

12 october

"But no, M'sieu," the driver groans, "since our fine government closed the brothels it's impossible."

The taxi moves slowly past outlying houses, following its headlights in the narrow cobblestone road. The front seat is cramped, and I cross my legs uncomfortably.

"It's the same in Paris," I say regretfully, "but there they've simply gone into the streets."

A cold mist blows in the window. As I raise the glass I look out at a passing night landscape of dim lights scattered throughout the Valley.

"Tell me, M'sieu—" His voice falters.

"Yes?"

The driver leans his heavy face forward over the steering wheel and with an effort turns on windshield wipers. "Not meaning to be personal. But the Monastery? You're going there for religious reasons? Maybe to become a—?"

"Lord, no," I interrupt flatly. "I'm going there to do some research."

"Ah well, then," he says with sudden relieved loudness, and settles back into the seat. "I wondered, you know. You tell me to drive you to the Monastery and then you

3

ask about girls. Couldn't quite make out the connection."

I laugh, "I guess it doesn't sound right, does it? Tell me, how are the monks?"

"Fine men, M'sieu. You'll like them. But," he chuckles after a moment, "it isn't there you'll find any young girls, eh?"

"I know. I'll just have to forget that for a while."

The driver puffs a cigarette hanging disconsolately from his lips. "Yes, the only thing our young men can do is keep themselves buttoned tight, M'sieu. Those damned sons-of-bitches in our government!" His voice changes, becomes more expansive. "I know how it is. I'm not so old as all that. Why, it's a terrible thing for our boys. Look at yourself, M'sieu—a fine young man like you—what can you do? It's impossible." He mumbles to himself for a moment, cursing all governments; then, turning to me, "You're American, aren't you? I can tell by the clothes. Did you have a girl in Paris?"

"Yes."

"How long you been with her?"

"Oh, a long time. Since before the war."

"You're going to miss her, eh? What's her name, M'sieu?" He lowers the window long enough to spit his cigarette out into the night.

"Her name's Lucette," I sigh heavily, "and I'm missing her already."

"That's a nice name, for example," he says, and nudging me in the arm, "I'll bet she's with somebody else this very night."

"Wouldn't be surprised. How far is the Monastery from that little Town back there?"

"About five kilometers, M'sieu. But I drive slow when these damned roads are slick. I put my last penny in this taxicab. You didn't expect to find a taxi in a little hole like this, did you? There's only one other car in the Valley."

I lean back, resting my head on the back of the seat, and watch the play of headlights cutting darkness. The train trip has tired me. The driver talks incessantly, recall-

4

ing his youthful adventures in Paris. He doesn't hesitate to admit that it was he, Salesky, who was instrumental in dotting this very countryside with attractively filled brothels until a stupidly misinformed government stepped in and ruined him. He explains with luminous pride how he personally, after having first explored each girl's potentialities to the fullest, saw to it that only the most interesting and accomplished of them stayed on to satisfy the physical needs of his clients.

"Nowhere, nowhere, M'sieu—not even in Paris—could you find such wonderful girls at such reasonable prices."

"Too bad I didn't come here sooner," I tell him.

I offer him another cigarette and he cranes his head in my direction. His face, reflected in the lights, is sober.

"Listen, my friend," he says urgingly, without taking the cigarette from his lips, "I know some girls in the City. Let me drive you there and we can each get one for the night."

"Wish I could," I answer, "but I spent nearly all my money on train fare here. I've only got a few francs left."

"Ah, that's too bad."

He turns into a narrow street. Headlights pass over the tightly shuttered windows and doors of many small houses lining the sidewalks. Salesky taps me lightly on the knee as the bright beams again pick up the street before us.

"That's really too bad, my friend. In any case I'll look out for you. If a nice girl comes to Town, I'll get her a hotel room and come for you. And," he adds with great friendliness, "I won't charge you a thing."

"Fine. After a week or so in the Monastery I'll probably be desperate."

"Naturally, M'sieu, naturally—you're young. It's the same with me, though I'm much older than you. But I trained my muscles well as a young man. You wouldn't guess me nearly sixty, would you?"

The car slows into a cobblestone square and pulls up before a high stone wall. A feeble street lamp glistens in

5

reflection from the wet stones, intensifying the blackness. "Here we are, M'sieu. Two hundred francs. Call me any time. If it gets too impossible, just call Salesky, eh? I'll find you something, even if it's only a washroom hag."

I step from the car into the deserted square and he drives away in a shifting of gears. I look up at the wall beyond which I am to live for a time, and in the mist-veiled darkness I can't tell where the wall stops and where the sky begins. A heavy door is thrown into relief by the street lamp. Reluctantly I pull the bell chain and hear it ring somewhere within. Salesky's taillights disappear in a turning of the road. I stand here in the sudden silence and wait. And as I wait, standing beside my suitcase, the mist becomes a light rain sifting flat level sound as it falls gently on the sleeping countryside. Wetness blows cold against my face, and I ring the bell again. It sounds harsh in the night. After a moment I hear approaching footsteps crunching. The door is opened by a black-robed monk who carries a lantern over his arm.

"Good evening, sir," I begin. "I'm expected, I believe. I am—"

The faceless monk nods his head violently and places a finger to his lips to stop me. Taking my suitcase, he motions me to follow him. The door is closed noisily behind us and we walk through a graveled courtyard. He walks with his head lowered against the rain, his lantern casting fantastic shadows about us. I am offended by his unfriendly brusqueness, but I try to hide it. Peering through the darkness to dimly outlined buildings, I remark amicably, "This certainly is an impressive structure you've got here. How many of you live here?"

My words die in the muffling rain. He doesn't answer and I feel uncomfortable and foolish. I follow him up exposed stone steps, staying close to the wall to guard against falling, for there is no rail. The yellow light from his lantern catches the outline of a squat, doorless opening at the top, through which we stoop to pass. The floors and walls of the door-lined corridor beyond are of rough

6

stone. There's no light except the flickering lantern over his arm. Our shadows, magnified and distorted, flit beside us along the wall until we reach an open door, which he motions me, with a slight bow, to enter. The door is closed behind us, and a lamp is turned on to reveal a small cell. The monk's robes rustle loudly as he bends over to deposit his lantern on the floor, placing my suitcase on the rough green blankets of a cot.

"Now, my son," he says shortly, impersonally, pushing back the cowl of his robe from a head of thin gray hair, "we have put you immediately above the chapel. The only way out is the way we came. On this night table is a card with full instructions as to your activities here. I think it covers everything." His words sound memorized. "You have arrived during the Great Silence which begins at nine-thirty each night, a time during which speech is supposed to be forbidden. If you have any questions please make them as brief as possible." He says this without stiffness, looking at me intently.

"I guess I can find everything, sir. If you'll just tell me where the bathrooms are."

"Ah, yes." The aging monk walks to the window and opens it, pointing out into the dark. "The water closets are in the courtyard. In the morning you will be able to see them from this window. But you are requested not to leave this cell after Compline. If you need it, there is a chamber pot to be used at night." He opens the door of the night table to show me the inevitable white porcelain chamber. "Let me see, the nearest water for shaving is downstairs to the left of the door. If you feel you can, we ask you to clean your cell every morning. Empty shaving water anywhere in the courtyard and water from the chamber pot into the toilets. Father Clément will visit you each day." He picks up his lamp and walks to the door, turning to bow slightly before leaving. "Good night, my son," he says with sudden gentleness. "May you find happiness here and may God give you peace."

The door clicks shut behind him. Without moving I

7

listen until the sound of his heavy footsteps dies to silence in the corridor outside.

After a time the wind blows in heavy drops of rain, chilling the cell. I turn away to close the window left open by the monk. No light, no flickering of light anywhere out there. In this maze of stone corridors and doors, nothing but my lamp burns at this late hour, weak in its nocturnal clawings against darkness. There are only the steadily falling rain, the terrible silence, and the knowledge that others sleep in other cells. Desolation of paralyzing loneliness, skeletal, as each passing moment brings thirsts for sounds and lights and noises left only a few hours ago. I must move about, light a cigarette, unpack the suitcase, do small things. The cell is cold and cheerless and smells of damp and mold and age. Unpack the suitcase. Blueness of pajamas, whiteness of underwear. The rain striking my window and running down, and from the corner of my eye, above the cot, the sheen of a carved-wood crucifix. White shirts neatly folded, and handkerchiefs and fresh green soap and rough towels. In Paris this morning, the kiss in the railroad station like all other kisses that follow woman's pleading for man to stay with her. Brown leather shaving kit and socks tied together in pairs with white string. Lips seen close with their fine ridges and their wetness, and the feel of a belly against your belly, of a belly beneath your mouth—moving, live, warm. Silence growing in the cold of these cells. I open the door into the blackness of the corridor and hear nothing. The door is thick, worm-pitted gray wood. I close it and continue unpacking.

Smoke from my cigarette curls floating on the air. I flick a safety pin from the brown satiny lining of my suit-case. I cough and the cough sounds loud and heavy on the silence. I look at the straw mattress of my cot and at its covering roughness of blanket, and I remember the good bed and white linens of last night, and how they covered a nakedness of breasts and navel and warm thighs, and smooth, sweet-smelling flesh of shoulder and back. And I am sick for wanting the safety of that bed, for wanting to

8

breathe the breath of another and to wake in the night and feel her against me.

But it's time to sleep. I unlace shoes and put them neatly to one side. They sleep in other cells; they sleep in their cots and never know the taste of another's pleasure. Socks are placed in the shoes. The stone floor is cold beneath my bare feet. With a dampened washcloth I rub caked dust from my ankles. Since there's no ash tray I crush the cigarette in the chamber pot.

I must swallow the night's desolation in small things. Tie and coat and shirt are removed slowly. The cell is small. It won't be difficult to clean. Undo the belt and step from the pants. It's a small cell with walls long since discolored and mottled with the dampness of countless winters. Fold the pants and put them over a chair. On the washstand a large carafe of water has been placed in a badly chipped porcelain bowl. Next to this on the marble table top is a soap dish in which there's no soap, and to one side, a towel rack on which there's no towel. Drop wrinkled white underclothing to the floor and reach for the blueness of pajamas. There is the night table with its lamp of small voltage and weather-spotted lamp shade. There are some books and the placard of instructions.

In the droning silence I sit on my bed and light another cigarette, hearing the match strike with hollow loudness. The instruction card must be read. It is hand-printed in ink, with a ludicrously shaky cross at the top, and it tells what I must do and where I must be at all times—from the first bells at four in the morning until the last bells at nine-thirty at night. It informs me that I must follow the rigid schedule of the Benedictines, and that I must neither do nor say anything that might provide a disturbing element or distract the monks from their work. And many other things.

Thunderless night of monotonous rain and of insomnias of newness and loneliness. I think of how her hair caressed my cheek and of how warmly she filled my arms with her sleeping nakedness. I think of the jovial face of Salesky

9

and of his world which is my world and which lies out there in the night somewhere, separated from me by the high walls of this Monastery.

Crafty, diluted-yellow light in my cell. Nausea of sleeping alone.

Sometime in the night I awaken and reach for covers which aren't there. In a half-dream I feel for the crease of her belly and find only the unyielding stiffness of evil-smelling straw beneath the rough muslin mattress cover. Sleep is a torture of discomfort.

13 october

I force myself from the cot. It is cold and my legs tremble as I feel about in obscurity for my shoes. It is dark as night. I turn on the dismal lamp. Sounds from below of chanting. I am late, my card informs me, for the early morning offices of Matins and Lauds.

The water in my bowl is covered with dust, darkening at the sides from last night's washing. I pour more water from the pitcher, watching it catch amber reflections from the lamplight. Sober, ascetic sight of water being poured into a white bowl.

My footsteps sound heavy in the gravel as I walk in the direction of the chanting. The air is chilled and clear after the night's rains and there is no hint in the sky that it's near dawn. An almost imperceptible light is filtered through heavily leaded stained-glass windows onto bushes beside my path.

Cold morning before sunrise, and I almost fall from

10

sleep sitting in the faintly lighted chapel. Impression of spaces and heights and heavy gray shadows in the vast interior. Sounds reverberate empty and the monks seem faraway. Hours of praying and chanting and praying. Unbearable dragging of time before breakfast. The bench grows hard. I am the only visitor in the chapel as monks sing their morning prayers. This morning there has been no waking slowly, no smells of coffee, no sleep-drugged belly beside me.

I wait for a long time in a sort of waking sleep, hearing nothing, until the hours have passed and it's time to leave. I follow the monks into a door marked REFECTORY, where breakfast is served on long polished tables. We are given large bowls of coffee which tastes as if it were made of ground acorn shells. It has a sickening flavor, a bittersweetness, that makes one cup enough.

Outside I find the bathrooms—many wooden doors in a rambling stone building, surrounded by hedges for privacy. I enter the first door into a clean little cubicle, where I find a sheaf of newspapers cut in six-inch squares nailed to the wall beside the seat. And above it a sign asks us to please conserve paper: nothing is plentiful in a postwar France. As I turn to leave I notice another sign tacked to the door. It is timidly printed in blue Gothic letters:

PLEASE LEAVE THIS PLACE AS PROPER AS
YOU WOULD HOPE TO FIND IT ON ENTERING

Leaving the place as clean as I should hope to find it on entering, I walk through an avenue of arched cloisters to the stairs leading back to my cell. No one has spoken to me.

There is a cool October sun of early morning. The Monastery rises high above the countryside, like some massive pre-Gothic fortress of stone.

In the corridor leading to my cell, the damp odors of age become almost suffocating. I glimpse back at the squat door, and beyond to jutting angles of stone stairs, worn low

11

in the middle by centuries of footsteps, brilliant in the white of autumn sunlight. The only sound is the sound of my footsteps and the closing of my door. Alone I walk to the one window of my cell to see a scene below that's like some unknown abstract painting: a foreground of gray Monastery walls cutting at an angle across clear green waters of the River; and on the opposite bank, flat pastures for grazing cattle, in the oranges and blues of early autumn; and far to the background, an undisciplined panorama of many small housetops clustered beneath the protection of high, wooded cliffs. A Valley extending as far as the eye can see. Small farms, fields of wheat and fall corn neatly arranged in level patterns. Lining the banks of the slow-moving waters, a uniform grove of poplar trees stands tall.

A countryside in which nothing seems to move, in which is felt the calmness of midsummer noon this cool October morning.

Immediately beneath my window the shining baldness of a tonsured head comes silently from one door to enter another, its owner not knowing he is watched.

The nerves detach. Cold wind, warm sun, dampness in the shadows, rain-washed countryside beyond the walls, and black robes in the courtyard below. Lazy honest pervading sound of stirring leaves, and a faraway cawing of field crows. Nerves detach in loneliness. They leave me in this cell and pay me no heed. Barren feelings must seek life this morning and remember other lives and lively smells of Paris and the comfort of a girl's smiling.

After a time the wind chills, and I turn away from the window. I sit on my cot and wait, for there's nothing else to do. Idly I pick up the placard of instructions and read it again, feeling that the crucifix tacked to the wall reads over my shoulder. It's an uncomfortable feeling. The thing is evil, shining, dark. It peers imperturbably.

I seek to escape it in straightening the green blanket on my cot, tucking it in and brushing out the wrinkles. My anger mounts as I grow to feel that they have no intention of admitting my presence among them, that they'll never—

12

My thoughts are cut short by a knock on the door.

"Come in!" I call out sharply.

The door is opened by a tall, gaunt monk. As he steps into the cell I quickly toss my cigarette out the window, hoping he doesn't notice.

"I am Father Clément, my son," he says, shaking my hand. His hair is sparse in texture, turning from brown to gray. And his face is warm, as if he expected to be amazed at every instant. "So you are my charge?" His voice is coarse. "Why are you here?"

"I'm a musician, Father—a musicologist. I've asked permission to do research in Gregorian chant from your manuscript collection."

"Many musicians have come here for short visits." He lowers himself stiffly onto my cot. "So you are interested in Gregorian chant?"

"Very interested, Father. I've spent several years studying the texts written by your monks. It's always been my ambition to come here. Will I be working with you?"

"No," he says smiling, "you will want to work with Father G'seau. I am here to be of help to you in other ways. Will you want to confess, to take the sacraments?"

"I'm not of your faith, Father. I wrote that in my letter."

"Of course. I had forgotten." The aging monk fingers the rosary beads attached to the belt of his robe. "Well, what do you think of this new home?"

"It's beautiful, Father. I think I'll like it all right once I get used to it. I've been reading the rules. Hope I don't make too many mistakes."

"If you just follow the instructions you will have no difficulty. But one thing, my son," he says gently, looking up at me—"I noticed you this morning: there is no need of your walking around with your head bowed and your hands folded in front of you. You can be perfectly normal with us, you know."

My face flushes with embarrassment and he looks quickly away. "I'm sorry, Father," I say impatiently. "I'm not used to this kind of life."

13

"You will be all right, my son," he smiles, getting to his feet. "I know this is all new and strange to you. Much of it probably seems unnecessary. I shall come for an hour each day to visit with you and to help you with any problems that may arise. But you may call me at any time, if need be. It is almost time for Mass. You will attend our offices, I suppose?"

"Yes, Father. I believe I'm required to live exactly as the rest of you?"

"With the exception," he puts in, "that you are free to come and go as you like. Our life is a great change from what you have known. You are young"—he smiles significantly—"you will undoubtedly need to dissipate some of your natural energy by exercising. You can break the monotony by walking in the countryside. Our Valley is quite beautiful this time of year. Now, is there anything else for the moment?"

"Yes, Father—I'm wondering if there's a piano I could practice on around here?"

Father Clément rubs his chin absent-mindedly. "I do not really know. The only good piano would be the one at a nearby château. How often would you need it?"

"I'd like an hour a day, Father. But I wouldn't want to impose. I thought perhaps—"

"No, no," he interrupts. "It is not a question of imposing. I shall make inquiries. Now is there anything else? Ah, but there are the bells."

From the tower, sounds of the great bells inundate my cell, so deep in tone they seem to evolve from silence. Metal striking metal—a physical, roaring, reverberating clangor vibrating walls and floor. They announce Solemn High Mass to the entire Valley.

I enter the chapel as the last bell sounds and then dies away to intense quiet. There are perhaps seven or eight others—people from the Village who come in by a public side door. After dipping fingers in holy water and genuflecting, they kneel. Each goes through the same motions, and I can't help but feel they are the motions of parrots.

14

I look through the gloom to see if there are any girls, instinctively seeking to pass the time by looking at them. But they are all old—old women and old men. I wonder what they think, how much they feel, or if they feel anything at all. I wonder when they bathed and what they had for breakfast this morning and how they slept last night. I've been here only a few hours, and already those on the outside take my interests. My affection goes toward them, and I think of their mumbled prayers and of how little importance such supplication must have in the counterpoint of a day's livingness—in preparing food, or in looking after families, or in putting on clothes over wrinkled, aging nakedness. And of their day outside, they come to spend an hour here. They genuflect and kneel with the wetness of holy water still cooling finger tips. They've done it always, and they'll go on doing it until they die.

Our smallnesses are lost in the heights and spaces of the long narrow chapel. Details which couldn't be seen this morning become clearer, although the interior is still heavily shadowed. Above us, in obscurity of poor light, overarches the vaulted ceiling—pale, cold, pure in its simplicity of line. It is dark where we sit, in the back, beneath the organ loft.

Halfway to front is a separating altar rail, and beyond, lighted by unseen windows at each side, long rows of ornately carved benches face center. The distance from altar rail to altar, sifted through slanting rays of morning sun, seems very far. Hanging tenuously on a long golden chain from the highest center arch, an altar lamp glows red in emptiness of stone and space.

Peculiar, indescribable odors of age and mold and humid rock: evocative, sweetened by a permeation of incense from untold numbers of Masses. Odor of timelessness.

From the silence of waiting, and these odors, a cough resounds, suspended lifelessly on air, to be destroyed by the bright-toned baroque organ above us, beginning a work of Landino or Frescobaldi; building sound on sound with a clarity of fresh flute and oboe tones echoing from bare stone walls of the unlighted chapel.

15

By twos, entering from the left, monks approach the altar. Without pomp, as naturally as if they were going home, they amble in. Heads, with cowls lowered, assume different positions: some are buried contemplatively on chests, some are held high, some look straight ahead. All move slowly, in pairs. At the altar, after a profound obeisance, they bow to one another and turn to take their places on the benches at the side.

Every movement is made in slow, measured cadence, producing an almost hypnotic effect as the rhythm of music is transferred to movement and back to music, until the entire Mass seems to take place inexorably, on a single basic pulse from the outset. Never-stilted, perfectly normal movement intermingling with sound, on the compulsion of a never-ending heartbeat. Ineffable grace of the ensemble— sober, severe, unhurried. This to the accompaniment of splendid organ sounds, heightening noiseless movements of the eye until movements stop and the monks are placed.

A final bright chord echoes forward through the chapel. But the sound is not allowed to die. Like a falling snowflake being billowed into the air as it touches earth, that tone, with a soft upswing of unisonal monks' voices, is carried forward into the opening phrases of the Introit. Voices answering organ tone at first in quiet beginnings, gradually intensify the melody line, allowing the chant to ride on this fundamental rhythm as a feather might float on the waves of a sea.

I forget the parrots. I forget the uplifted eyes and hollow faces. I forget the bitter taste of loneliness. This is my reason for being here. This, at least, I can understand. Many voices in perfect unison, breathing one melody, spreading in an ocean of sound without sharpness, to end again in silence. A fragility of black notes on white paper become tender, awe-stricken chant of adoration. Stunning contrast of plainchant cantilena after the contrapuntal organ processional.

Intoning voices and a Latin text. Medieval splendor— restrained, whispered, simple, final. Five white-vested celebrants before the altar, and on the altar a myriad of candles. Slow, deliberate, never halting, as a chanted *"Agnus Dei, qui tollis peccata mundi"* enters the filigree, entwining itself into the texture: "Lamb of God, that takest away the sins of the world" becoming a part of the fabric of sounds and sights and odors.

And to the right, smoke from the incense crosses rays of inpouring light and rises to lose itself in the grayness of the ceiling high above.

This is another dimension. It counterbalances the rudeness of the morning, the sadness of life which I read on the face of the Valley.

After Mass the spell of its music lingers with a lightness, a hush, as I walk from the chapel. At such times vision becomes precise and the sky is more vast than ever before and you can see each pebble of gravel at your feet.

I glance about at the Monastery. In this labyrinth of stone, monks spend the morning doing what they have always done—tasks of study, or writing, or physical labor. I think of Father Clément and his remark that I must exercise in order to dissipate the desires of my age.

The morning remains bright, with the air too crisp to be comfortable. I return to my cell where I may lie down and pull the blanket around my shoulders. Footsteps pass in the hall but no one knocks—and suddenly I come to know that this life is too great a change for me. Except for the music it's intolerable. I think of leaving. Something intangible—the cold perhaps, and many other things—fills me with great discomfort, with a nausea of newness. I think of sleeping alone in this hard cot and am lonely at the thought. If only I had money enough for the return fare to Paris! But another check from America isn't due for over a month. I reject for the moment a desire to write to Lucette for the money. If she can find it, she'll send it; I'm sure of that. But it will take a few days. I must wait. Perhaps the impressions of first hours will . . .

And it fades. It fades in a gyrating floating of all eyes and ceilings and sun on my floor. Last hints of magnified

17

pores of skin and of tiny curling hairs on my hand beside my face on the pillow. Remembered vomitings as people genuflect and bend naked and floundering over hideous rosary beads. Pools of white wetness beneath lustless prayer-fogged hearts. It fades in a dim scorching chill, curls like burnt paper, fades and curls of hair follicles and giant etched hand pores and cuticle floating against whiteness of pillow . . .

The clangor of small, high-pitched bells awakens me. My instruction card tells me that it's time for the noon meal, and that we have five minutes before entering the refectory. In a half-sleep of murmuring silence I push the blanket aside, cold and stiff from the chill of a trembling belly. The weather outside seems less bright, as if it were dusk already. A heavy yawn; sickness after sleep of mouth and stomach and lungs. I swallow the liquids that collect in the mouth upon waking.

I pour water into the bowl and wash with the soap I have brought. The water is like ice. It turns milky with dirt and soap congealing in a scum on the surface. I straighten my bed and wipe mud from the soles of my shoes. Movements are slow as the sleep of a few moments ago seeks to become wakefulness, as tissues of the body struggle from their torpor.

From the top of the stairs I look down into the court-yard. Seen from above, it's thrown into a strange perspective that focuses until I reach ground level.

An aged monk with a sympathetic red face stands at the door of the refectory, motioning me to hurry. In one hand he holds a silver urn, and over his arm is draped a small towel.

"I am the Father Abbot, young man," he says as I draw close to him. "Our original rule of St. Benedict stipulates that the Father Abbot must wash the feet of all who enter his monastery; but since it is cold today, perhaps you will be content if I wash only your hands?"

I reply that I can think of nothing more terrifying than having my feet washed by a Benedictine abbot, and that

18

I certainly won't report him to the powers that be, if he cares to wash my hands instead.

"Very well, my son, hold out your hands. Palms up. There . . ."

The small monk pours warm water over my hands, allowing it to drip on the already damp ground. Then he dries them with the towel. During this ceremony the other monks have walked quietly into the refectory and taken their places. Father Abbot takes my arm and accompanies me to my table. As we traverse the long, heavily beamed room, standing monks bow low from each side, holding the bow until we are past.

At a signal from the abbot, a prayer is started. On my plate a large bowl of amber-colored soup sends a fragrant steam to my face. Endless prayers recited in unison. Standing with head bowed, I wait with growing anguish as my soup cools and stops giving up its smoking aroma.

"Amen" is followed by a moment of silence finally broken by a peremptory tap, as Father Abbot strikes his table with a small wooden mallet. This tells us to begin. Sounds of scraping chairs, of silverware, of a conglomerate series of movements as the monks tuck large napkins under their chins.

I glance about me not knowing what to expect, but not expecting what I see. This is the first time I have observed at close range the assembled monks. Except for their tonsured heads and monastic robes, there was never a more ordinary-looking lot of men. Somehow I hadn't thought monks would look exactly like everyone else. Criminals, we think, look like criminals, and monks should look like saints. Aside from a certain repose of movement and face, these men are indistinguishable from any others. Some are bald and fat, as if they had stepped from the pages of Rabelais or Balzac; some are tall and gaunt; some are ascetic in appearance. All of them eat voraciously and noisily, occupied only with the immediate problem of consuming soup. Somehow it's offensive. The elegances of a feminine society have been long since for-

19

gotten and table manners returned to a primitive status. They are a simple-looking group of men each of whom is a specialist in some given field of intellectual endeavor. They bear none of the imprint such backgrounds are supposed to give. There is a coarseness, a matter-of-factness of manner. Virtuosic speed of eating. Since I am not hungry I eat very slowly.

"All meals except breakfast," my card had said, "are taken in silence. Each day during mealtimes a monk will read from works of special interest, after which he will be served in the kitchen."

We become aware of the reader after a time. He sits high above us in a raised pulpit and reads in a monotonous, chanting style that is at first almost unintelligible. Today he is reading about the missionary sisters in Canada and the cruel manner in which they were scalped by Indians.

With the most serious intent, the thing suddenly becomes uncomfortable. Wide grins can't be camouflaged behind napkins. The panic of laughter grows as the reader goes on. To hear him enunciating the horror of nuns being scalped by Indians in the wilds of that long-ago Canada, reading it in a trancelike, expressionless, singsong voice, as if he doesn't really give a damn who scalped whom, is inescapably ridiculous. In a sympathy of thoughts each of us is certain what his neighbor feels—a blasphemous, inadmissible affection for the Indians.

Monks of all ages, wearing blue-denim aprons over their habits, appear as a welcome distraction from the kitchen. Without interrupting the reader they gather our empty soup plates onto carts, and with quick movements disappear back into the kitchen.

As we wait, the reader enumerates in a voice of lethal boredom the exact dimensions of our Canadian nuns' first chapel.

Large, smoking tureens are soon wheeled in. The aproned monks dip great spoonfuls of an indescribable main course onto our plates. It seems to be a combination of meat broths, potatoes, yellow beans and onions, cooked

20

together and mashed through a food mill until it comes to us with the thick, lumpy consistency of gruel. With coarse brown bread we eat a great deal of this mixture.

After lunch we are allowed a thirty-minute free period during which we can relax and talk as we like. No one speaks to me today. The afternoon is spent walking about the Monastery gardens until I think I'm tired enough to sleep.

Now, after Compline, the Great Silence. I open my window and return to the unforgiving lumps of my cot. The countryside is black. Frosty night air penetrates. I lie alone in my bed, understanding nothing.

Somewhere there is a cough. In the dark of my cell I lie near sleep and listen. Above me the crucifix makes its ominous presence felt. I think of the old ones who came into the chapel this morning and of how their clothes must feel to them and of how they digest food and sleep safe this night. Patches of sleep come to me, but there is the brilliance of luminous torturing wakefulness, intermingling with turning blackness. My bed doesn't warm. Liturgy of dissonance against the coldness of night sky. Chants rise in my ears, screaming the passing of age into the vaulted ceiling of wakeful dreams. From a putrefying element to a place of maggots is the life of one man and all men. And it is today what it has always been. They sleep tonight as they have always slept, in their cells, never feeling the caress of pillow against face. Blessedness of mold. And when they are gone they don't go far, for their bones and foods and loves are replaced by others with the same hopes and prayers and wetness of finger tips from holy waters. They sleep and are never touched. And I lie buried in the blackness surrounded by living humanity. Out of all time.

15 october

For two days I've waited and this is the third day with no word from the Father Abbot. Father Clément came for only a few minutes yesterday. Otherwise I spoke to no one.

After breakfast I smoke a cigarette in the garden, then walk back toward the house in the grove. Father G'seau, the monk with whom I'm to work if allowed to stay, stops me. I tremble with gratitude for his friendliness. He is the classic monk, small, obsequious, smiling. I know of him as one of the so-called "great" Benedictines, a man respected the world over as historian and musicologist. We speak in English for a moment, and then he asks me in French if his accent is not "impossible."

Before I can reply, another monk standing nearby says loudly, in French, "My son, be honest. Father G'seau has a definite, an appalling accent in English. I know because I have no accent in English myself."

Father G'seau, humble, bowing, whispers, "Sin of pride, Father."

"It is not a question of pride," the other man says indignantly. "I simply have no accent in English."

"Really, Father?" I break in, puzzled at such boasting. "Then you must speak to me in English."

He turns to me with a large gesture of feigned surprise, quips, "Oh, I do not speak English," and bursts into laughter at my disgusted reaction.

As he walks away, head held high, Father G'seau steps nearer me and touches my arm. "Would it be correct to say that he is a 'goon'?" he whispers timidly in English. "Would that be correct American slang?"

"Where in the devil did you learn such English, Father?"

Father G'seau explains patiently, almost apologetically, that part of his work in studying social evolution is the understanding of contemporary slang. In order to facili-

22

tate his research, the Monastery has somehow procured for him a number of American gangster novels; but many definitions are not in the dictionary. Taking a luridly covered book from the folds of his robe, he asks me about the words he has marked. We dispatch to his scholastic satisfaction detailed explanations of such terms as *rod, gat, stool pigeon, slug,* and *mouthpiece.*

"Is that all, Father?"

"Yes," he nods. "Ah no, there is one more. What is a 'hot mole'?"

" 'Hot mole'? Why, Father, I never heard of that."

"Well, I cannot seem to find it here"—he leafs his book—"but it is used all the time."

"Maybe it's a new expression, Father. I've been away from America for several years now. How is it spelled? Do you remember?"

"It is spelled H-O-T M-O-L-L, I believe."

I explain *hot moll* to the Father, who notes it carefully and with warm thanks enters the cloister.

I go back to my own cell and wait, wait for Father Abbot to decide if I'm to be allowed to stay here and work. Several times I start a letter to my Lucette in Paris, intending to ask her for the money to return. My anger grows against the treatment here. I've come to work, but they pay no attention to me.

Outside the sun breaks through, dissipating clouds and mists. I open my window. A noise in the doorway, and I look about to see Father Clément.

"And how are you this morning, my son?" he greets me.

"All right, Father," I say impatiently. "But what about my work? If I'm not going to work there's no reason for me to stay on."

"Do you really want to work with us, my son?" He sits beside me on the cot, picking up a book from the table.

"That's what I came here for, Father," I say quietly.

"I see. Let me be very frank, my son. You are not of our faith and we have no desire to change you or to in-

23

fluence you in any manner. I think Father Abbot is waiting to see how you adapt yourself to our way of life. It is very hard, you know—little sleep, little food. Without a religious vocation to make it palatable, we must first see how you bear up under our regime. I think you will do well to read these books I have placed on your table and to try to understand the reasons for our life here. If I can, I will help you . . . Now tell me of your life in Paris. What exactly is your work?"

"You don't understand, Father," I say sharply. "I'm a musicologist and I'm interested only in doing some research in your paleography room. I didn't come here for anything else. I can stand your regime all right, but I'd like to be allowed to start as soon as possible."

"I shall speak to the Father Abbot again, my son. Do not feel offended if we seem not to give you the attention you think we should. You will soon learn that life within these walls is quite different from that outside. We are very much aware of your presence and all of us will do our best to help you."

We talk of my trip to the Monastery, of our interests in art and music, and of my background, first as a medical student and later as a musicologist. He draws me out until I become conscious that for one of the few times in my life, I am talking freely and with complete honesty. Instinctive realization that there's no need to exaggerate here, no need to cover one's faults. Father Clément talks easily and intelligently as a man. He is particularly interested to know of my life as a medical student. And when he prepares to leave, much later, my impatience is largely gone. As he shakes my hand, I ask him about their life. What makes a man embrace such a life? How can they accomplish what they do living under such a rigid schedule?

"You will need to understand these things gradually, my son," he laughs. "Tonight I will leave you some books. You may stay up as late as you like. Do you have everything? What about cigarettes?"

"No, I'm about out, Father."

24

"You can buy some this afternoon, or perhaps this evening after Vespers. Town is only a little more than five kilometers. Now good-bye—but first let me make one more suggestion. In your reading, you will do well to take notes about any questions you would like to ask me. Often the simple act of putting your thoughts on paper will clarify them for you. One warning, though: such things are valueless unless you write only what you think. Write nothing you do not feel. Make the clear distinction between what you think you should feel and what you actually do feel. It is very difficult, but unless you do that here, you are lost." He pauses a moment before the door. "You will immediately reach a conclusion of shocking immorality within yourself, but do not let that bother you. You will find I am not narrow-minded. It is the getting it down on paper with absolute honesty that is important. And do not hesitate to speak to me about anything that might help you." He opens the door and steps into the hall.

"Father," I call after him, "did you have a chance to ask about the piano?"

"Of course. I meant to tell you that the first thing. I spoke to Madame la Marquise de la Roche, and she agreed for you to have her piano for an hour each afternoon. Now," he says, walking back toward me, "I think with your piano, and with your work soon to begin here, you will be better satisfied. Is that not so?"

"Yes, Father," I answer apologetically.

Waiting for Mass, I read the book he has been fondling: *The Primitive Rule of St. Benedict.* And I carefully make notes.

Impossible to read for long. Nervousness of inactivity returns. I am cold unless I walk about my cell. The wind blows stronger in gusts. It's the waiting alone that destroys. The desire to leave, to go back to Paris, makes itself felt more strongly than ever. Still on my night table is one of the letters which I began to Lucette only a short while ago. Looking at it I know I can resist no longer, know I must make an end to this wretched existence before it's well begun—and sitting down I quickly finish the note, asking for the money to return.

Afterward I feel better; and I read all day, not leaving my cell except for Mass and Vespers and lunch.

And after Vespers I prepare to go into Town. It's a sensation of escape when I walk out the gatehouse door—sudden, happy escape back to my world.

Dusk comes early in the Valley and the landscape is gray and colorless as I make my way toward Town. The road, deserted at this hour, follows the River. Air chills rapidly with the fading day. Lights, yellowish lights, are turned on in irregular patterns across the River, reflecting as glittering headlights in the now-black waters. This is a time in France when odors become unique, when a pure coldness of evening air sharpens smells of roasting coffee and evening fires. Miracle of twilight sounds from those unknown shadows across the River where people live and eat and find rest.

Looking back, the calm silent Monastery dominates the scene, dominates the Valley. High, broken walls, massive stone battlements rise in serene silhouette above low ground-mists. From far away it's the same, a shadow of enclosed grandeur on the night landscape.

Welcome reality of lights and people as I enter the narrow main street of Town. Most of the stores are closed, their windows blinded with corrugated metal shutters drawn against burglars. Men and boys pass under the faintly glowing street lamps, walking their ways home with long loaves of unwrapped bread under their arms. They shout to one another and wave. In the cobblestone square near a bridge stands a large public urinal painted green. Children from neighboring houses play hide and seek in and around it before being called in for the night. You can hear the constantly running flush-water from across the square. There are no stars. A ceiling of low clouds hangs above the garish lamp on the urinal.

Farther on, a café; and inside, men who know one another have a glass of wine before going home. I go in, buy my cigarettes, and sit alone at one of the tables, a stranger drinking warming cognac. They look at me but go on with their conversations. A stranger here is rare. Because I'm alone and a stranger I leave a larger tip than I can afford, and walk out in search of something I don't know. I think with a sickening dread of returning to the specter of my barren cell.

After three days of monastic fare I'm starved, and soon it's too late to return to the Monastery for dinner. At a small hotel-restaurant leaning forward over the sidewalk, the proprietor and his wife serve me a good dinner, trying to persuade me that theirs are the cleanest, warmest, finest rooms in Town.

The warm fragrance of their kitchen trails me for several yards as I follow a cobblestone alley leading back to the main street. I wander through the streets, which are soon deserted, until I'm too tired to walk back to the Village. In the café they telephone for the taxi.

Salesky comes for me. He's been called from his dinner, he tells me, but is glad to come. He picks his teeth and talks with great friendliness as we drive slowly out of Town. And suddenly I realize the need I have for coarseness such as his; I need to hear filth and laughter, and to be nudged in the ribs, before stepping back into that barren cloister.

"And where's that girl you promised to find me?" I ask belligerently, offering him a cigarette.

"But, M'sieu," he grins, "it's only been three days. Surely you didn't expect—? I mean I didn't expect you to be so impatient. After all, you're not supposed to think of such things in a monastery cell. So I've been told. I'm shocked. What kind of a mind do you have, for God's sake?"

"The same kind as you. What're you trying to do?— wear me down so I'll be forced to accept your offer to find me a washroom hag?"

"M'sieu!" he says reproachfully—"please! I'm not a pimp, after all. Slightly tinged with pimpishness perhaps,

27

but never sinking to such depths, really. If you think—"

"What is this? Your pious night?" The car leaves Town and turns into the winding road.

"Yes," Salesky says, nodding his head exaggeratedly. "Each week I allow myself the luxury of one pious day. You will now please speak of more spiritual things."

"Good Lord," I moan, "you sound worse than the monks."

He accelerates the speed buoyantly, delighted with himself, and his voice returns to normal. "It's very amusing, M'sieu. Makes me feel so damned self-righteous."

"And tonight you'll chase Madame Salesky all over the bed, eh?"

"Exactly. Nothing tickles the passions so much as a good spell of piety. But you're disappointed in the Monastery?" he says, becoming serious. "I'm really surprised. The monks have always seemed like very fine men."

"Oh, they are—I'm sure of that. But it's so damned lonely, and the food is terrible. And then, what can you do? There's no way to amuse yourself at all." The taxi wheels sound loudly on a turn.

"Then why do you stay?"

"I'm leaving as soon as I get enough money to buy a ticket back to Paris."

"But your work?" he protests.

"I know. I'll really hate to leave that." I sigh unhappily. "But you can't imagine how miserable the life is. We have to get up so early. And I've always hated having to live on schedule. I can't stand for somebody to tell me what to do every second."

"And then too," Salesky adds, "I don't think you like to sleep by yourself. You're as bad as I used to be. I bet if I could find you a nice, sweet-smelling girl—"

"That would help," I agree quietly, "but it isn't really that. It's just that everything about the life disagrees with me. I can't stand sitting around in my cell like a damned hermit all the time."

Salesky looks glum. His cigarette, smoked almost com-

28

pletely, hangs from his lips. He pulls into the poorly lighted square and stops before the heavy door.

"Here we are, M'sieu. I'm sorry it's so bad for you. If you do leave soon, I wish you good luck, eh? That's two hundred and fifty francs."

"But it was only two hundred the last time," I argue.

"Very well, then," he says disgustedly. "Good night, M'sieu."

The night air is calm and without sound. The little Village sleeps. I stand a long time before there is courage enough to pull the bell chain.

20 october

No word from Father Abbot. I stay on waiting for the money that will allow me to leave this place. As yet I haven't told Father Clément of my decision to go.

But with the waiting, patterns begin to form, and with their formation, an involuntary absorption into this life which I don't understand, and which becomes increasingly difficult for me. I wait to leave, and in the waiting I live here and sleep and share foods with the monks.

Evolution of one week. A first realization of the true character of hunger and cold and discomfort. The patterns take me from Matins before dawn to Compline before bed. Hunger becomes a constant preoccupation, as does the cold. Each day I take more on my plate, surpassing even the most voracious of the monks, and always I leave the table hungry. Longing for warmth, and for foods that satisfy hunger, and for a mattress that isn't straw.

And yet, somehow, I grow to understand that for them there's a certain harmony into which these elements of physical discomfort and desire fit. It undoubtedly heightens the life they lead. There's a greater activity, a finer keenness of perception perhaps, as if these deprivations served as a tonic stimulating them to purifying alertness. Satisfaction, like sloth, would seem out of place behind these walls.

Every morning after breakfast, Father G'seau joins me in reading through early manuscripts in the paleography room. We work, rubbing our hands together to warm them, rarely speaking except with a sympathetically shared misery of eyes and motions. Occasionally one of us will arise from his workbench and stamp about the small room to restore circulation, while the other laughs at such weakness.

The patterns form. Solemn High Mass remains the climax of our day, and I live for the music during this too-brief office. During the free periods after meals, more monks speak to me. There is still great reserve but they speak to me. And each day after lunch I walk to the nearby Château de la Roche, where they allow me to practice the piano for an hour. This is one of the happiest interludes of the day, and to pay for using their piano I am giving a few lessons to Madame la Marquise de la Roche's younger son Jacques, a stiff-fingered young man of twenty-seven.

The afternoons and most of the nights I read. Somehow it's impossible to sleep with that eternal crucifix hanging above my bed. And when I do sleep, there are nightmares of such carnality that I'm ashamed to bring them into this cloister. So I read. I read everything about the life and the history and the reasons-for-being of these monks. And I read with growing fascination as Father Clément brings new books each day. Now that I wait only to leave, I pass the time learning something about the life I'm to leave behind me. I seek to understand abstractly the faith that allows men to embrace lives of such severity, to become monks. There must be a reason beyond the hollowness of the obvious, for these are intelligent men. So I read—St.

Paul, Fra Jacopone da Todi, Sister Katharina Emmerich, St. Benedict. I study in my cell or in the garden until the cold becomes unbearable and I must walk or run about the courtyard to restore heat to my body.

Days of calm desolation—of coldness without and coldness within. Days of great quietness. And always at night, the dreams, the nightmares of liquidness.

21 october

There's no sunrise this morning. Dense clouds furnish a dampness that chills us through heavy clothing.

Mass is magical, for the chapel is as dark as night. The gloom inside makes walls and high roof above seem nebulous and faraway. In contrast, many lighted candles on the altar and the red sanctuary lamp, swinging like a pendulum above us, show through the sallow half-light like living gems. Chants seem more vast, inevitably drawing us into the fabric of long melodic lines, offering escape from the gray heaviness of morning without sun. Mass remains warm, accepting us, and we know the comfort of forgetting ourselves during this brief hour.

Outside, delicacy of interior remains in our minds, and while we are under its spell clouds appear more forbidding, isolating us from one another in our silence. Wind stirs the autumn plants, baring branches of their last damp leaves.

After Mass, I walk to the château to give Jacques de la Roche his daily piano lesson. I'm surprised to find him waiting for me on the terrace.

"Excuse me," he says miserably as I climb the steps, "but we're in trouble."

"What is it, Jacques? If I can be of any help—?"

"The Chevissiers—you know, the family who work our farm—their little daughter is ill. I think she's dying, but they refuse to spend a penny to call a doctor. Could you look at the child? You told me you've been a medical student."

"But, Jacques, I'm no doctor. I never got beyond pre-medical work."

"But don't you see?—they'll listen to you. I may as well admit, I told them you were a doctor. I *had* to tell them that. Please, the child is very sick. You've done some hospital work, perhaps you can at least tell me if it's serious?"

I shrug my shoulders. "Of course it won't hurt to look at her."

His face looks relieved. "Thanks," he says warmly. "We'd better go on over there now."

We walk in silence through an acre of formal gardens which would have delighted a Ronsard, but which seem futile and ugly this dreary morning; down a rocky hillside into flatlands below. With a flutter of white skirts, a woman approaches across the field. We meet her in the pasture on a small, dung-pocked cow trail.

"Doctor," says Jacques—and at the word I glance at him sideways—"this is Madame Chevissier. How is the child, Madame?"

"I was just coming for you, M'sieu Jacques. She seems very nervous, but I don't think it's anything. She's been like this before, and after two or three hours she always gets over it."

"How long has she been 'nervous' today?" I ask.

"For over three hours, Doctor. The little smarty, she just does this to get her way."

"May I see her, Madame?"

"Ah, *no,* M'sieu," she says emphatically, worriedly shaking her head. "We can't afford a doctor."

32

"I won't ask any money, Madame. Come, let's walk over."

She doesn't move, looking uncertainly at Jacques.

"The doctor won't ask any pay, Madame Chevissier," he assures her. "You have my word for it."

She hesitates a moment longer, then reluctantly leads us down the path.

As we walk, Jacques whispers disgustedly in my ear, "These bastards! These ignorant bastards! They've made a fortune from the farm. I *know* they have plenty of money, for they sell everything on the black market— butter, eggs, meat—things very scarce in the Valley. Why, they get rich selling them at above market prices."

A little surprised at the usually mild Jacques, I say nothing.

"These people have children like flies. They'll break your heart."

When I still don't speak, Jacques falls silent, and we walk rapidly until we come in sight of a flat peasant hut made of stone.

"I'll wait outside," says my companion, stopping. "I'm afraid I'll get sick if I go in." He is trembling, his voice quiet with humiliation at his own weakness.

"Wait for me here then, Jacques. We may need a real doctor." I turn to follow Madame Chevissier. "Where is the child, Madame?"

The farm wife, dragging a black wool shawl across her shoulders, leads me hurriedly through a grove of boxwood hedge and around the corner of the low, sparsely windowed farm house. Across a flagstone courtyard is the open door. High stone walls enclose the courtyard, open at one end, and as we turn to enter, a flock of blue geese waddle in to be fed.

A room of stone floors, darkened beams, plaster walls, of the style built in the early seventeenth century. Monsieur Chevissier sits on a bench at the table. He is half the size of his wife, with the redness of face that comes from the incessant drinking of good country wine. His back is to

33

the door that provides the only source of light for the somber room.

"Is she better, Jules?" asks Madame Chevissier.

"No, Mama, she's still nervous," he says in a quiet voice.

"The little tease, we ought to give her a good spanking." This is the ironic, gritty talk of a woman who can't afford sick children, who will not admit sickness into her home; but the voice hints anxiety. Enigmatic woman—she has the look about her of work, of inherent goodness, and of the evil of ignorance. Like all such women, she probably dominates her family with a love and an efficiency that knows no fluctuation, no alteration. She is completely sexless— the sort of woman with whom one sleeps, with whom one makes love merely because she's there beside you and it's easy to do. Above all, the sort of savagely fecund creature who can't be breathed upon without becoming pregnant.

I feel commiseration for her husband, this little man with wooden shoes who farms all of France.

"Stand up, Jules," commands Madame Chevissier, "and meet this young man. He's a friend of M'sieu Jacques's come to see the Petite."

"Yes, Mama." He absent-mindedly shakes my hand.

"He says he's a doctor."

"Good. I'm glad you've come, Doctor." He looks up, and his face relaxes a little.

"But we can't afford a doctor," his wife continues. "How much will you charge, M'sieu?"

"I told you," I reply, "I'll charge you nothing. Now, where is the child?"

"She's over here, M'sieu. The little tease, she pulls this nervousness to get her way"—tough, easygoing talk, with a tremble of uneasiness.

Outside, a hazed October sun, breaking through the clouds, lights a square of stone floor at the door.

We walk to the darkest corner of the room, next to the fireplace. There against walls of ancient plaster a bed is propped high on bricks. On the bed, soundless, lies the naked skeleton of a child. A few dull-blond hairs straggle

34

atop a head bluish in cast. Open eyes stare wildly. The small face is colorless as if in death. Skin stretches taut over sharp cheek bones, and the lips are gray. Trembling, with violently jerking arms, she stares without seeing: hideous movements of a puppet, controlled only by a mad puppet-master—epilepsy.

I turn from the child. "How long did you say she's been like this, Madame?"

"For over three hours now, eh, Jules?"

"About that, Mama. Is it bad, M'sieu?"

Without answering I hurry from the house to find Jacques. As I run through the courtyard, startled geese scatter to each side. Jacques is waiting impatiently at the edge of the boxwood grove.

"Jacques, for God's sake get a doctor," I tell him in a voice I can't control. "The child's got epilepsy, I think. Anyway, she can't stand much more of this."

"Good Lord! Can you do anything?"

"I doubt it. Hurry, will you?"

He disappears, running down the path toward the château. Impotent ignorance, impotence of ignorance: I know nothing of epilepsy.

As I re-enter the courtyard the geese hiss loudly, craning forward long necks at my approach. Then turning, they walk away, their bills and feet a brilliant orange against blue plumage, against the grays and browns of the yard.

Monsieur Chevissier waits at the door. "It *is* bad, isn't it, M'sieu?"

"Very bad. You should've called a doctor immediately."

"She's had these spells before, M'sieu. My wife thought she was just putting on an act because we wouldn't give her the glass of wine she asked for."

"Your wife should be able to see that no one can put on an act like this, and that no child could live for long under such a strain. It's ridiculous."

Madame Chevissier, hearing us, leaves the child. "You better go now, Doctor," she remarks sullenly. "We can't afford to pay you anything."

35

"I don't want your damned money!" As she sulks I force calmness into my voice. "Your little girl is *very* sick. Can't you tell that?" I pause as she moves away. "Now go sit down—no, get me some clean towels and put some water on to boil. And I need to go to the bathroom. Where is it?"

She points to the door. "Just go in the courtyard, M'sieu —anywhere against the wall."

When I return I find two clean towels folded on the table, and a kettle of water on the black stove.

The child, in a seizure of frenzy, lies on her back. Naked, fleshless arms and legs dance with uncontrolled movements as if they were detached from her emaciated, colorless body. Gazing unseeing, terrified, she makes no sound. She is alone, not knowing we are there. A gyrating monster within her, sexless, makes you weep with the shame of it, makes you curse the cumbersome, murky wall of ignorance which tells you nothing, which can't be penetrated with the intensity of your desire to know what must be done.

Taking her hands in mine I pull a muslin cover over her body. Despite the chill her hands are moist with sweat, like snakes wriggling from my grasp. Moldy chill in that dark corner of the room.

The child's body quietens. Madame Chevissier moves to the bed, gently releasing two bodiless arms from the covers. They dance again, jerkily, in the obscure shadows— a ghost dance in the half-light.

The father, seated at the table, is silent. The room is silent except for the sounds of the child's mute struggle, the spitting of water beginning to boil, and the drone of flies aroused by the fire. Muffled outside sounds of the country deepen the stillness within as we wait.

On the blackened oak table, still smoking, dinner goes untouched—a large casserole of yellow beans cooked with blood sausages, onions and garlic, and two dusty bottles of red wine, streaked clear and dark where hands have touched them. The food smells of health and strength.

Monsieur Chevissier sits dejectedly with shoulders bent,

36

silhouetted against the incoming rays of dull autumn sunlight—a calm sunlight of halcyon October, making its way across the room as afternoon begins to pass, catching in its light floating particles of dust. Outside moves the slow parade of blue geese waiting to be fed. An hour has passed with no help.

"The water is near boiling, M'sieu." Madame Chevissier's voice breaks the stillness.

"Dip one of the towels in it," I tell her, "and the other in cold water, and bring them to me, please."

Sounds of water being wrung from wetted towels; drops falling to the floor spotting the dust. She hands them to me and I place the warm cloth over the child's desolating blue eyes, covering much of her body. Madame Chevissier again removes the sheet, exposing skeletal belly and legs.

"Put the sheet back, please."

"If she wets it'll be ruined, M'sieu."

"Put the sheet back," praying for patience as I work, my face close above the child's face, sweat dripping from my nose.

The child begins gritting her teeth, grinding her jaws together, always with the beaten stare of watering, unbeaten eyes that can't see.

"If I'd known you were going to mess up my clean towels, I'd have given you some soiled ones," complains Madame Chevissier in a resentful voice, masculine, nasal, irritating.

"Your child is very sick, terribly sick, and you simper about towels and sheets. Now go sit down and don't say another word until I ask you." Struggling, struggling against this obscenity of ignorance.

"Come sit down, Mother—the gentleman knows what he's doing." Monsieur Chevissier's voice is pathetic in its lifelessness.

An hour of compresses, alternating hot and cold towels. The doctor does not come. In mid-afternoon the spasms quieten, allowing the child's arms to rest, still trembling, on her chest.

37

Madame Chevissier, honest, expansive, broad, whispers, "Don't you think she's better?"

"Yes, she's still unconscious, but the spell seems to be leaving."

Against hope, I lift the warm wetness of rough towel from her eyes. They don't blink at the light—open, unseeing gaze of terror. Moment of hopeless hope, moment of intense affection for this ugly child who doesn't see me, with whom I work against the terror of death. Touching her, there is another dimension above the repugnance of moist, unconscious flesh. Struggling always to reach her somehow, to carry her back from this seizure.

Utter silence of a fly droning. Inexplicable occasional honkings of geese in the afternoon sunlight beyond our open door.

The food has stopped smoking, congealing its sweetness of odor in a greasy crust filming the top of the bowl. Into the vacuum created by the loss of these odors comes the smell of feed bins lining the room—oats, wheat, alfalfa, kaffir—warm, lively, clean.

Fine line of intensity, bending low over the child's face. Ageless face of age in the body of a ten-year-old. Eyes cowering, hurt. Quiet except for a trembling, a suppuration from the nose—feverish-smelling, fetid—as she exhales white foam. I clean her with a towel. We wait for help. We wait for some sign from the child, alone and far away from us. We are exhausted for her, and we have spent ourselves, for her struggle has been ours from the very beginning. Her teeth grind away until we fear they will crumble to chalk in her mouth.

On the cold air without, honkings of geese become more insistent: maddening animal sounds. From afar the desolating sound of a cock's crowing, carried into the room on a breeze from the west; lonely, lonely day when you hear a cock crowing in the afternoon, drifting over fields being plowed for winter. Nostalgia of sounds.

In the distance, glimpsed through the door, rain pours slantingly into a portion of the countryside. Trees seen

38

through the rain stand high in blocks of color, luminous and transparent as though painted there by Cézanne. Overhead the sky remains clear.

A gasp from the child as her left arm jerks into the air, to fall half-back and be pulled up again on some drunken, invisible, senseless string. Arms and legs tremble, slowly at first as in some macabre dance, becoming more frenzied gradually until the even rattle of her breathing grows labored, until the viscid mucus foams from her nose in gray bubbles to burst on the air. Her head moves slightly from side to side with great rapidity. Repeated short gasps come from her lips as we watch. The climax will take her. We know it but we work doggedly, hoping always that she may dance it out and still live. I heat the pads on her head and throat, wiping dampness from her colorless straw hair with a towel. Emaciated child against the strength of death. The dance continues.

Jacques must be driving all over the countryside looking for a doctor. I struggle with her, I fight; and in the frenzy of seeing us, the child and me, losing our hope, I close my eyes, changing towels and uttering wordless, formless prayers, pleading for—

"Do you think I should give her an enema, M'sieu?" Madame Chevissier's voice at my elbow shocks me back to reality.

"No, it would do no good."

"I gave her one before."

"No, I tell you, no!"—not looking at her, forgetting her for the child.

The child's eyelids tremble but don't close. She stares at something we can't know. The skull beneath the hair is deeply indented.

Another hour drags past with no change. The spasms come rhythmically in great heaves, with a gathering mucus rattling in her throat which the child can neither eject nor swallow.

No help arrives as the sun pours in a lateral, penciled line across the floor, reaching up and over the table with its

39

cold food, its dust-covered bottles of wine. As the sun penetrates, it casts into the dark room a lurid light almost festive in its gaudiness.

Hopeless fatigue, the ache of fighting against something unknown. The nose becomes congested and we try to clean it; but we stop, somehow feeling we are wronging this child. I raise her head, hoping to clear the chest of its caldron of mucus, but she jerks in my arms and I dare not force her frailty. I let her lie there in her imperious nightmare.

Flecks of saliva at the corners of her mouth. I feel the weight of my cheeks as I bend forward over the child, wiping foam from her mouth and nose. Awkwardness of convulsions, determined to rack her body still more before tossing it on the ash heap of death. Arms and legs take contorted positions, and these contortions become as natural to her before our anguished eyes.

Again the raucous, matter-of-fact voice at my elbow: "There, the little thing's gone and wet her bed. Shame on you, Petite. Ten years old and you still wet the bed."

"Love of God! Will you get away from here?"

"Come, Mama, she couldn't help it."

I clean her again with the towels.

Forty minutes more. Monsieur and Madame Chevissier sit quietly on each side of the table. After so long a time without help, without knowing what to do, gone is the intense desire to make her well, to enter with our bodies into her struggle against the dread puppet-master. Imperceptibly over the hours we begin wishing for it to end; no matter how it ends, we wish that it would end.

Madame Chevissier, alarmed with the passing of time, becomes grim and worried. My anger changes to compassion. We work together now, realizing that we're doing these things only because they must be done. The end of the dance has started. We change towels quietly, without further recriminations. The father remains slumped in his chair, and I sense his embarrassment at his helplessness.

Finally we stop applying the compresses. They're doing

no good. We sit and watch the child in her dance of horror. There comes a time in such things when all you can do is wait for the end, almost hoping for the death that will take a child from such murderous supplice. You don't cry then; you wait until death arrives. You wait for it, emotionless.

They know, and they feel as I feel an infinite tenderness for this child who is no longer a child, but merely live, suffering protoplasm on its way to death. In her agonies she has ceased being the Petite. Gradually with the loss of hope, she has become no more than a means of measuring the time before death-tossed flesh will cease being.

It is a vacuum, a waiting, and we can't understand it. The interim drags, and we wish for it to end. Without weeping we wait exhausted, suspended in time until death will turn this essence of suffering back to us. Then she'll become something we can understand. Then we can start moving and thinking again. Then this thing will be their daughter once more, real in death, allowing them to become normal in reactions of grief. For the moment we wait, wait for this thing to die and become real. And we are patient about it, as human beings are always patient about the inevitable.

The sun reaches across the room to the opposite wall, an amber, hazed ribbon pale on the floor—cold sunlight of late afternoon. Somewhere outside a hen chirps lazily—introspective, musing sound of a hen. And with another honking, geese crowd round the door, stretching long necks to look inside.

"Feed the geese, Jules, and drive them away," says Madame Chevissier in a weary voice.

Unnerving sound of mucus rattling in the child's throat; saliva pouring from nose and mouth.

Obviously relieved to move about, Papa Chevissier carries a wooden scoop of oats outside, geese noisily following. "Come on, geese," he calls—"Goosey, goosey, goosey, come on over here"—in a cajoling, intimate, nasal voice. Returning the scoop, dusting his hands on corduroy pants, he resumes his vigil at the table beside us.

41

After several minutes I break the silence: "You have beautiful geese, Monsieur. What kind are they?"

"Toulouse, M'sieu. Ah, they're nice birds. Look at them—that old gander thinks he owns the place."

We laugh, forgetting the child as a large gander chases one of the smaller geese away.

Turning to his wife, Monsieur Chevissier suggests, "Mama, perhaps M'sieu would like a glass of wine."

"Of course, M'sieu, let me get you a glass."

"Thanks. I am thirsty, and this looks like good wine."

"It's the wine of the country, M'sieu, but not bad. There."

She pours three glasses and we drink, refilling the glasses again and again, trying to ignore the soundless struggle. Late afternoon sun disappears behind the garden wall, and men begin bringing in heavily harnessed plow horses from the fields, their hooves clodded with fresh-turned dirt.

A short, gasping wail from the Petite brings us to her bedside; a pitifully human sound—the first human sound she has uttered—giving us hope. Her arms settle again to her chest.

"I believe she's coming out of it, Mama," whispers the father in a cracked, harsh, falsetto voice.

But the face, blue and ashen before, turns red with congestion. Her tiny body, rising from the hips, pulls up and forward as if she were trying to cough. Hands shoot out at crazy angles, to fall and rise back again. A heavy, inhuman sound comes from her lips, and liquid putrefaction pours from every orifice in her body. Her mouth opens as if to cough again, veins in her throat stand rigid, and her empty belly contracts deep under the rib cavity, sucking in. The mouth stays open, braying soundlessly. Toes, blue-veined, curled far to the back, double her dancing feet in the air. And the father, bending low to look into her staring eyes, sees them stop staring.

"She's leaving us, Mama!" he cries. "Our Petite is leaving us."

42

Twisted still, movement of a raging ocean gradually become calmness of the sea, as muscles stop trembling, as bubbles of evil-smelling foam burst against her nose and stop coming, as her belly rises slowly and grows quiet . . . as her heart stops beating.

In that instant of obvious death I put my hand on her chest, patting it unconsciously, grateful for her—this child who has never known me, whom I have known with such tenderness and intimacy, with such compassion. There is a frantic squealing from the mother, but Papa Chevissier, like me, is grateful that it's over, is filled with the peace of relief for the child. A steady stream of meaningless noise pours from the mother.

"Shut up!"

"Be quiet, Mother, he wants to do something."

Vainly I listen for a last heartbeat, my head on her chest; but the breast is still.

Again the terrible squealing, as if Madame Chevissier were doing it out of respect for the mystery of death rather than from grief. I turn to her.

"You mustn't behave like that, Madame," I tell her gently. "The child couldn't have lived long. She'd never have been well."

"But, M'sieu, she wasn't even baptized. She'll be buried like a dog!"

"She was innocent as an angel. Already she's in heaven."

"No, no, M'sieu"—with an agonized wail—"she'll be buried like a dog. They won't even let us put her in hallowed ground."

Papa Chevissier, patting the corpse, mumbles, "The poor baby, she never had any luck."

Others have heard. Children and farm workers come to weep. Deafening din. Only the father remains quiet. Unconsciously I walk to the table and finish my half-empty glass of wine. The others ignore me. I light my pipe and walk outside. I sit for a while on the steps of an open stable door. A cold autumn wind of dusk dries the sweat from my clothes. Fragrant winter smells of earth and hay. The

43

sounds of wailing, dying away to come again with renewed force, no longer bother me. The supplice has been too long and torturous to bemoan a welcome death.

Later, a new Citroën automobile with a physician's crest on the windshield enters the courtyard. The doctor steps out, and I follow him into the house.

They have moved the child from her bed to the dining table. Older children remove the soiled bedclothing, and a three-year-old, seated wisely and unembarrassedly on a chamber pot in the corner, watches with open eyes.

They wash the dead child on the table, letting her lie there in a pool of water. Her eyes have already been closed, and the skin is bluish in cast. Since she has died with her mouth open, they force the jaws together by tying a towel around her head with a large knot under the chin.

The doctor is furious. "That's right," he berates them, "you people won't call a doctor until it's too late. You're afraid to spend a damned penny, even to save a child's life. I can't guess these things. You have to send for me. Until all of you in this Valley learn to call when you need me, I can do nothing but sign your death certificates. The child is dead. Let that be a lesson to you."

The child lies there naked in the darkening room, the ridiculous dirty towel around her head. She is forgotten for the moment as the group listens humbly to the doctor. A tiny lake of water in her navel, where they have failed to dry her, holds my attention. I soak it up with a soggy towel.

The doctor bends efficiently over the table to sign the death certificate. No one moves in the room. Papa Chevissier's voice, almost inaudible, breaks the silence.

"What caused her to die, Doctor?" he asks timidly.

The doctor hesitates, glancing at the dead child. "It appears she died of brain congestion due to epilepsy," he says wearily.

The sight of the child lying there in a pool of water suddenly sickens me. They talk over her and about her as if she had never been human. The room becomes too much. Now others surround the doctor with tear-streaked faces, and

44

ask him questions about the death. I look again at the child, and unable to bear it any longer I slip out the door without a good-bye.

I walk back in a ravishing, low-keyed sunset—in a warm affection for the child. Exhausted from afternoon with a monster, now become child in death, and made beautiful in the small frame of the understandable. Across fields on a path between patches of fresh-turned soil, as cold evening air moves down. View far off of man and horse and plow on a rise beneath a giant oak tree, silhouetted against a background of last yellow sunset rising into pale- and then dark-blue sky overhead. And a first weak star. Odors of the earth. Clods, warm and soundless. Vast and tender peace rising from the firmament. Low ground-haze, warm to the feet, obscuring lumps of turned earth. Cold air, chilling face.

Jacques and his mother meet me at the château.

"Where did you go, Jacques?" I ask.

"I fetched the doctor but he was on a case, so I came on back here to wait for you. Is the child going to be all right?"

"She died only a few minutes ago."

Jacques's mother looks at me closely. "But, my poor boy," she says sympathetically, "you look exhausted. Come, we can go inside where it's warm, and you can drink a cup of tea while you tell us what happened."

Her words make me realize how unsteadily I stand on my feet, how complete is my exhaustion. I gratefully accept the cup of tea she pours for me, and take a seat near the fire. Briefly I tell them what has happened.

"The most peculiar thing, Madame la Marquise," I add —"and perhaps you can explain this—was Madame Chevissier's wailing about the child's not being baptized. Do you really think—?"

She interrupts frantically, "You mean that child wasn't baptized?"

"No, that's what all the fuss was about."

"Ah, the poor child. I must go to the family, they'll bury

45

her like a dog. Oh, why didn't I see to it that they had her baptized!"

After she has gone to weep with the rest, Jacques mutters, "I should have stayed. In case of a death like this one, anyone can baptize the dead person merely by putting a sign of the cross on his forehead, and saying, 'I baptize thee in the name of the Father, and of the Son, and of the Holy Ghost.' If you'd known that, you could have baptized her yourself. That way, it would have been accepted by the Church and she could have been given a decent Christian burial. Now they'll just bury her anywhere, without a service, and it's a terrible stigma on the family."

"Well, Jacques, couldn't we go back and baptize her now? I mean, if it makes such a difference—" I can't keep a feeling of derision for such superstitions out of my voice.

"No, it must be done within fifteen minutes after the death." He looks at me miserably. "You make me feel like a fool. You see, you don't have our beliefs. These things are important to us."

"Well, it's none of my affair—but it certainly seems terrible to me to deprive an innocent child of a decent funeral just because she hasn't been baptized." I think of the pathetic face of the child. "I never knew it went quite that far," I conclude heatedly.

"You mean," Jacques puts in, "you've been in France all this time and didn't know that?" I shake my head, and he goes on, "I wish I could explain it. Our Church just doesn't believe that anyone can get to heaven till he's been baptized in the Faith. You can't imagine the disgrace this will be for the child's parents. It's the worst thing that could happen to them, almost. Can you imagine having your child buried just any place, without proper last rites?"

"No, Jacques, I can't. And I don't think it's any credit to your Church that such a thing has to be. Oh, well, I don't mean to sound so disrespectful," I add, noticing how much my remark has hurt him. "I don't understand, that's all."

He murmurs patiently, "I'm sure it must be hard for an

46

outsider to understand. You should ask the monks about it."

Seeking an excuse to end this conversation, I look at my watch. "Guess I'd better go now. It's almost time for supper and I have a long walk." I rise, and Jacques walks with me to the door; I remember to ask him, "What about your piano lessons? Shall I come in the morning?"

He looks at me almost apologetically. "I'm afraid I don't feel much like piano lessons since all this has happened. Perhaps we'd better postpone them for a while."

I nod. "That probably would be best. At any rate, I'll see you soon."

As I walk down the road, late dusk turns into night. The River and the Valley are quiet and indifferent to my presence. I cross the River with the ever-phantasmagoric vision of snakelike struggles with death which I have shared with a little girl this afternoon. Large drops of rain begin falling in the Valley, and in the hint of my thoughts I know that people about me must be reaching out of their windows to close shutters against the night and the rain. The sense of aloneness becomes more acute as window after window is thus blotted from view. Quietness of scattered rain, and of low clouds and night. I stop to knock ashes from my pipe against the bridge rail, when suddenly the bells of the Monastery, calling us to our evening meal, give a life of welcome sounds to solitary night.

Welcome sounds of bells from the Monastery, and my footsteps hasten in their direction. There is a strange compulsion to hurry. My body is eager to flee the blackness of falling rain—to ease the aches of the day by returning to the cloister. I feel hungry for food, but even hungrier for the light of the refectory and for the sober happiness of eating with the monks. And suddenly I know that I want their company, no matter how silent. I want to escape the abstraction of unreal death that lingers still, in the reality of eating prosaic food with the monks this evening.

Rain begins falling heavily as I enter through the small side door. I run across the outer courtyard into the cloister with its sign, ENTRY FORBIDDEN, and I am safe.

47

The monks are standing, reciting the opening phrases of a long benediction, as I quietly take my place in the lighted refectory. After the long prayer we begin eating. Above us the voice of tonight's reader drones the never-ending story of nuns in Canada. My shoulders are wet from the rain, but the relief of seeing familiar activity, of seeing denim-aproned monks wheeling their carts of steaming food from table to table, makes me forget this discomfort. I wonder at my joy in being back; at the peace which fills me as I eat the food that I have detested before. Even a week ago I should have wanted to get drunk or to get a girl to help me forget this terrible afternoon; but now I want nothing but the warm food and the hard bench and the surrounding monks, and later the rest of sleep in my cell.

We eat. We eat swiftly, devoting our best attentions to this task of consuming food. And we listen to the high, chanting voice of the reader. Tables of black-robed monks eating noisily, alive. And somewhere back there in a peasant hut, a child on her bier, with candles; and farm women talking of how natural she looks; and children being put to bed who want to stay up and hear again how she died.

With food in my belly I learn anew the completeness of my exhaustion, of my desire for sleep. When we have finished evening prayers in the chapel, I stay only long enough to be told that the Fathers already know of the death of the Chevissier child, as everything is always known within a monastery. Relief that I won't have to relive the experience in the retelling of it.

Without taking advantage of the free period I return to my cell, wash, and put on my pajamas. It is nine o'clock. The signal for Compline has just sounded—a tinkling of small bells, not carrying far beyond the walls.

But the day was too much. I hear the rumble of feet below me, and the beginnings of the night's last service. My legs ache as they relax beneath covers. The rain pours against my window now, and lightning intermittently floods my darkened cell. The child, and sleeplessness of too-great fatigue, and other rains . . .

48

I remember such rains as this during my school days in Tours, when I returned to my room after dark to find the only light that of a wood-burning fire. Beside my fireplace would be hot milk and rum, and in the fire a few chestnuts and apples in a long-handled skillet. I remember the hour before dinner, with rain spattering against the windows of my room, sitting before the fire with a warm drink.

Now without these accoutrements, stripped of all but the rain outside and the warmth of a bed, which is the only refuge from the damp chill of these early winter nights, I feel the same deliciousness a thousand times magnified. It's as though the fire and hot drink had served merely to introduce me to the feeling, and were then taken away to make the feeling grow in intensity as it became more direct in its nakedness. Love of feelings, love for an unidentifiable object, fills me with an ecstasy of the moment and of the time and of the place.

For here there is an intimacy. In the poverty of comfort and surroundings the small richnesses become more acute. In this bed, in the midst of living humanity and of centuries of livingness, the introspection of inner feelings delights as it lives in the bare ground of my being.

But the dissonance of such a day can't be resolved in a few moments. Before the completion of Compline I sleep, to awaken sometime later in the middle of the greatest silence of sleep which surrounds—silence vibrating in soundless intensity from the stone that shelters us. I awake feverish and sick from the wetness of disjointed dreams that fumbled away at crazy angles. In the half-sleep of the torturing dreams, I feel the tightening putrefaction of my chest, and the ache of muscles. The wetness becomes cold, and I roll away from it to the edge of my cot. Momentary thought of the child lying on her bier, with a candle at each end for company. She is alone this night, and with overwhelming suddenness her loneliness becomes my loneliness, and I feel lost and afraid in the dark. Fears become desolation, and I grope in the confusion of inner night for sanctuary, and strange and frightening words half-form them-

49

selves in my consciousness. For the first time, a mumbled *"Ave, Maria, gratia plena . . ."* But my face blushes in the dark with the embarrassment of a begun prayer. The words become obscenity in my mind, and I can't go on. The blessedness of mold. Acrid smells from ancient *Kyriales,* my chest tight with the foul air of nightmares. I pull the pajamas from my wet legs to fall this time into a sleep without dreams.

Later, the night swirls with long, reverberant thunder. In half-consciousness I think of a fairy tale of Pushkin, lying open beside hands that are dirty. Fleeting, fitful images fleck the night. Notker the Stammerer, long dead, binds his manuscript and plods the flagstone way to the frozen River, preoccupied with the chant, and knowing. And later, Gastoué and Mocquereau. And beyond walls topped with moss, in a house of sanctity, a lone cough, and the snoring. In the corridor a flute dies away to the final sounds of chants echoing against stone in darkness. Perotinus dreamt of the wax embryo, trying to thrust the dream from him.

No longer a pouring rain, but a drizzling monotony, as sleep restores the sanity of dreamlessness to the madness of dreams.

22 october

It is not yet dawn. My window is a square of dark gray against the blackness of interior.

Filtered through walls of stone, muffled sounds of monks at Matins in the chapel below. The first bells didn't wake me, and now, as I lie here in the dark, the wonder of this early morning office awakens me with cadenced gentleness.

With nothing to see, with no sound except these delicately flavored chants, time is once again an ever-present *now*. This is the Middle Ages, or any time. Alone in this cot, in darkness, I know a hidden intimacy of delight more complete than any before.

There is a chill in the predawn air. I savor the moment of night before morning. "Guests are requested to attend all offices in the chapel." By the accident of not being awakened in time, I live a high moment in my life.

Chants fill my small cell. Turning on my side I draw the blankets about me, pull the pillow close under my head. There's no thought, only sensation. The terrible night is dissolved in the singing of Matins casting rays of light into the early dawn—a pure joy of living the moment of first waking. Stringent rawness of cold striking my nose and ears, and warmth beneath the blankets; animal sensations, waking of stirring muscles, as the office continues its sublime unfoldment. Again I become aware of the crucifix hanging there in the dark, but this time it's not ominous, this time it enters into the coloration of the chant below.

How many others in centuries past, moving more deeply beneath the covers in this same bed, have heard and felt what I hear and feel this morning? Man becomes attuned to something infinitely perfect in these rare moments—to a completeness of physical well-being on a plane above morality.

The chants stop. A single intoning voice reads the office of Matins below. The words, the text are lost in distance; only the inflection penetrates to my cot. The voice ends on a high-pitched cadence, and as from the very age and cold of morning, expansive quiet chants float again to my ears.

In this cell, alone, hidden from the world, no one knows of me in this bed; no one knows of me here, buried in darkness, listening to sounds which soar from the hearts of men for all centuries to go on forever.

It's unreal, made real only by the nagging undertones

51

of my breathing magnified by the pillow on which my head is cushioned. Breath steams clouds of gray in the early air that dissipate themselves in the window's silhouette. Bedclothes smell of soap, fresh, over odors of stone and chill in my cell. Absorbing commixtures of odors, tempered and gentle with the inevitability of age, form a moving counterpoint to the outside sounds permeating my cell and my being from the choirs below. Other sounds, intimate: my hands stirring beneath warmth of blankets; my ears rasping against the white of muslin pillows.

The music of Matins becomes the music of Lauds. Vast and undulating chants rise with edges rounded through the filter of stone floors, reduced in distance to the perfect proportions of quietness. They continue timelessly as windows grow light with the nearness of dawn, at last dying into silence as if they had never been.

Without wetting my face I dress, and hoping to give the impression that I have been up for hours and was sitting unobserved in the rear of the darkened chapel, I stroll nonchalantly into the refectory.

At breakfast the monks can talk. There's no reader, and everyone eats when he wishes. An elderly Father sits down next to me.

"Did you sleep well last night, my son?" he asks.

"Yes, Father, very well."

"At least you slept long enough, my son"—chiding without malice, as though he felt it was all right for me to oversleep as long as I didn't pretend I had been awake since the first bell. In a monastery, somehow, everything is known.

I smoke a cigarette in the garden, then visit the house in the grove. This time I find myself in a bathroom boasting the added elegance of a washstand with a small cracked mirror. In this cubicle, too, is the sanctimonious little Gothic sign, an abbreviated version stating simply:

PLEASE LEAVE THIS PLACE PROPER

The mirror tells me what I'd forgotten, that I need a shave.

52

I return to my cell, and after only a few moments Father Clément comes to join me. He nods briefly to my greeting, his face serious as he takes the place I offer him on the unmade cot.

"You did not tell me you were a doctor, my son," he says without preface.

"I'm not, Father," I reply, slightly confused. "As I told you, I went to medical school but never finished. Why?"

"It has spread all through the Valley that you are a doctor, and that you let the Petite Chevissier die. The tales are very ugly."

I stare at Father Clément, dumbfounded. "Why, Jacques de la Roche told them I was a doctor, Father, to make them listen to me—and a real doctor did come after she had died. But I did everything I could to bring the child out of it. Who's telling these stories?" Nervously I light a cigarette and sit beside him on the cot.

"The Chevissier family, apparently, and a Madame Renée, who is one of the most respected women in the Village." Father Clément looks worried, as if he can't entirely believe me. "I do not understand it. Can you think of anything you might have done to turn these people against you? Such stories can make it impossible for you to stay on here. Her funeral is this morning, and you must go. Otherwise I fear you will be ruined in the Valley."

"I don't get all this, Father. Do you mean there's to be a public funeral? But where is it to be?"

"Of course there is to be a public funeral. What do you think we do with our dead?" He looks at me curiously. "It will be from the parish church at ten."

I exhale smoke in surprise. "But I didn't think you could bury anyone from the church who hadn't been baptized?"

"The child has been baptized. I went to the house last night with Father Sauvac, the parish priest, and they told us she had been baptized. Do you know something about this you are not telling?"

"No, Father"—avoiding his eyes—"I don't know what

made me ask such a foolish question." I hold my tongue instinctively, wondering at the daring of the family to lie to the Church.

The reason behind their tales of me becomes obvious. They hope that I, the only outsider and a person living at the Monastery, won't stay in the Valley to tell my story. They live in the fear that at any moment I may reveal the truth that would wreck their lives here.

Thinking what monsters can grow from ignorance and superstition, I regret having mentioned this to Jacques; and I'm grateful for the fatigue that sent me to bed before I could speak of it last night. Involuntarily I've averted disaster for these people, and I can see no reason for exposing the truth. It means little to me—I'm glad to have the child buried from the church. Surely one little heathen smuggled into heaven can do no harm.

Father Clément talks in the background in lulling tones, expressing the hope that this unfortunate incident will not cause Father Abbot to send me away. But my only thought is that I must get to Jacques as quickly as possible. I'm not supposed to know about these things; I misunderstood. But I must waste no time, for already he might have told the story in defense of my dwindling reputation in the Valley.

"Now, my son," concludes Father Clément, rising, "I think you had better go."

I flick the cigarette out the window, and Father Clément helps me spread my bed. Neither of us says anything more, and in a moment I am outside the walls and walking fast down the road.

Before I go far I'm stopped by the macabre funeral cortege. The body, in a small, newly carpentered wooden box, is riding on a two-wheeled cart draped in black, pulled by a pair of weeping men. Bouncing over the rough country roads, it is followed by an ever-increasing group of Villagers. The immediate women members of the family wear black veils over their heads which completely cover their faces. People dressed for the funeral wait in open doorways. When

54

the cortege reaches them they join the group walking behind the cart. Stores are left empty as owners and workers swell the dreary parade. Only the sick stay behind in the deserted Village.

Thunder roars in the distance, and the weeping group grows larger. The gray sky, the immense fertile Valley dwarf us; and we must appear no more than a small knot of animals creeping along the road. We rumble across the bridge. Jacques and his mother, standing beside the road on the hill above us, wait to join the silent crowd. The hill is too steep, and the procession stops as more men go to help pull the cart up the rough cobblestone incline. Seeing the Marquise de la Roche, Madame Chevissier floats a screaming wail upon the cold air—her childish way of showing the Marquise that she is especially sad and honored to have her join the group of mourners. The Marquise, her veil flowing over her shoulders, steps firmly into the head of the procession with the bereaved family. Jacques waits to take his place at the end.

Many Villagers have joined the group behind me. I stand aside, allowing them to pass, and wait for Jacques. We drop back several paces. When we are out of earshot I mutter, "Jacques, I must have been wrong about the baptism. I hope you haven't told anyone else what I said?"

Jacques glances around. "Mother thinks you were wrong too," he says rapidly, "and it's best that way. But I know what really happened. They called in a Madame Renée after everyone else had gone, and it was she who baptized the child."

"She did? But why, I wonder? Father Clément spoke highly of Madame Renée. Why would she do such a thing?"

"I don't know—out of kindness for the family, I suppose. She's very good to these farm people. Anyway she did baptize the Petite, four hours after she died."

"The baptism's no good, then . . ."

"I know, but when Father Sauvac asked if the child had been baptized, they told him yes—he didn't ask when.

So now they're terrified for fear you've told the truth."

Far to the front, a second falsetto wail informs us that another person of importance has joined the family. Jacques continues, whispering hurriedly in short phrases, "I don't know what's right. But I can't ruin these people. It must be our secret."

"That's pretty much the way I'd imagined it," I tell him. "And they want me out of the way, even if they have to accuse me of letting the child die. But why," I add, "did Father Clément insist that I come to the funeral? Surely Satan himself couldn't be less welcome."

"He probably thought you might avoid some talk by being here. It clears you in a way. At any rate I'm glad you came. The family will try to find out if you've told anyone, and you can reassure them. If they think they can trust you to keep your mouth shut, they may stop spreading these detestable stories about you."

Doubtfully shaking my head I ask, "Do you really think they'll stop after going this far?"

"Perhaps. They're ignorant people, but shrewd at a bargain. Let them understand their secret's safe with you, if in turn they stop trying to drive you from the Valley . . . Or go still further and make them recant what they've already said—make them admit they were mistaken." We walk in silence a few more yards; Jacques adds, "That sounds shockingly like blackmail to you, doesn't it? But you must do it, it's the only language they'll understand. I got you into this, I hope it doesn't cause you any real harm. Now we must get back to the procession. They're watching us."

We rejoin the group just ahead. But our conduct has been noted, and the family must be in terror, wondering what we may be planning. An immense feeling of pity overwhelms me. I want to go to them, to calm their apprehensive hearts. But it's impossible. I can't reach them, and there's no way to give a reassuring sign.

We approach the church through a grove of large oak trees bared of leaves. I watch the parents, seeking some opportunity to speak. The procession stops, and four men

56

lift the cart up rough stone steps. Jacques leans toward me and whispers that this is the moment: if the story is known a priest will appear and denounce their hoax, denounce their sin against heaven before all the Valley people. I look at the parents. They are trembling, holding to each other, waiting . . . But no priest appears. They exchange glances, and their shoulders drop a little as tension leaves their faces. Again I wish for some sign, some word I could pass to them to take from their minds this dread; to allow them the luxury of simple grief for their lost daughter. But the crowd is impenetrable—and hostile.

In the church the box is placed on a table near the altar rail. It is surrounded by four large candles. The people file into pews to await the Requiem Mass.

I look about me in the small, packed church. Men of the country, dressed uncomfortably, stare into space, or at their hands—hands which are never really clean; hands which are beautiful in their crudeness and in the harsh designs of their wrinkles. Hands which have known everything. Hands which have felt the earth at planting time, and washed the udders of cows before milking. Hands which have known bodies—their own, and some girl's in the country after a dance in the square. Hands which have known their wives in every emotion from experimental feverish fumblings to the no-longer-excitable manipulations of experience. Hands which have known their children, until the children grew. The faces are bored, with a sadness that is social duty, anxious for this stuffy respect to be paid. But the hands are at home in their calmness, reposing in laps that don't feel their weight.

A single note sounds from the harmonium, played by a hideous little woman leaning myopic eyes forward to read the notes she can't play. Around her neck is the desolating cheapness of a ragged fur scarf. A bored, extremely sanctimonious-looking man sings the Introit, head held high, swaying out of rhythm. He is fat—and evil. In this Valley where the chant is sung so beautifully, this unsympathetic man sings for his fifty-franc fee. And it's not worth it.

57

I shudder with horror at the thought that I may some day be buried with such ugliness, with such a sad, mean ceremony.

It drags on, for hours it seems. The marvel of the words, *"Requiem aeternam dona eis Domine: et lux perpetua luceat eis,"* becomes base and avaricious sound, desecrated by these envoys of the devil who play and sing. Finally the last phrase: *"Requiescat in pace."* She is resting in peace, but only because she is dead and can't hear this abomination in her and God's name.

In relief we leave the church. The box is dumped once more on the cart and we follow it to the cemetery. Body heats have warmed us in the chapel, and we carry tiredness and sleepiness outside. It is warmer, the calm of stillness before expected rain. Jacques and I walk together, agreeing in whispers that the Petite was the luckiest one there to miss the obscenity of such an ugly service.

When we reach the tombstone-crowded cemetery, picking our way carefully between graves on a narrow, graveled walk, the body has already been deposited. We stand in line to walk single file past the weeping parents. A light rain begins to fall, and umbrellas appear. Madame la Marquise shakes hands with Monsieur Chevissier, kisses Madame Chevissier on both cheeks, and walks quickly out the iron-grilled gates. This is the time for tears. Passing before the parents everyone weeps. The child in her unfilled grave is ignored. Each woman embraces the parents, and all the men shake hands. I arrive next in line and look beside me to see spatterings of rain splotch the unpainted wood of the Petite's casket lying in its hole.

The father, shaking my hand, says humbly, directly, "Ah, M'sieu, we know things, you and I, don't we?"

I bend my face close to his. "Yes, my friend," I murmur. "But no one else need ever know."

His timid eyes almost close for a moment, to open wide in unbelieving relief. His face relaxes and he breathes heavily, allowing his head to fall slightly to one side, and he clasps my hand with great pressure. His wife hasn't

58

heard me; she is being comforted by other women, and her laments fill the air: "Ah, poor, poor woman that I am! Pray for me, have pity on me! I am lost . . . lost . . ."

Monsieur Chevissier is speechless with relief. He does not release my hand. After a moment he asks, "You have told *no one*, M'sieu?"

"No one, my friend. It's none of my business."

"Ah, thank you, thank you, M'sieu. We've been so worried. Thank you a thousand times. We thought you might've mentioned it to someone less good than yourself." He looks at his wife, but she is far too busy with her mourning. Turning back to me, he seeks to reassure himself: "Will you be careful, M'sieu, to tell no one?"

"Yes, of course. But you must in return do something for me."

He withdraws his hand, and his face becomes coarse with suspicion.

"You must stop these stories about me," I go on. "They're doing me harm. If you'll promise me that, and if you'll correct the bad impression you've given about me, I'll forget all I know."

He makes no denials, his face clear and sympathetic. Again he takes my hand. "It's understood then, M'sieu," he says slowly. "The whole thing will be forgotten . . . Come, you're getting wet—get under this umbrella."

"No, my friend. I've spent too much time away from the Monastery and I must get back. Good-bye and good luck."

I arrive back in a soaking rain, hang wet clothes on my washstand, and dry myself with a damp towel. We stay indoors; but the Monastery is full of drafts, and it's impossible to keep warm. The courtyard is pocked with holes of water, and the steadily falling rain streaks the window of my cell.

In the afternoon it becomes so cold that I take my work to bed. As I pull back the covers my face flushes red, for the linens have been changed while I was away. Instead of the stain of last night's dream, there is the brightness of freshly washed and ironed sheets. One of the monks has changed my bed and knows of the secret dream, and of the fever of the night.

Monastic formality gives way to brief visits from many of the monks. There is a loneliness of rain and a somberness within, that makes us feel the fringes of night during the day. Father G'seau knocks on the open door and bows his smiling way in, followed shortly by Father Dutfoy. We talk of the monastic life and its history. Father Dutfoy, who is from the Midi, constantly mentions the tropics. He is always wiping his brow, on which there is only imaginary perspiration, and sighing, "Oh, how I should love to live in those places—to be warm once again."

The books come, are read and digested, and replaced by other books. The spell of the Monastery begins to enter my blood, and the years of study in the outside world grow more remote. The reasons for the monastic life become more apparent as time passes. But a man is unable to live this way unless he believes, with St. Benedict, that God makes suffer only those whom He loves. For in his *Regula* Benedict states that we must not only accept all hardships, but give thanks to God for giving us hardships; and that above all we must never "murmur" against anything which arises in our monastic life, as such discontented murmuring is a sin. To live like this under the stringent vows of a monk, requires either a religious vocation of the highest order, or an interest, such as I have, in research. And yet I know that no amount of interest can give me the strength to continue this life for long . . .

30 october

The days have passed with a growing dissatisfaction. The nausea of doubts. A questioning within me. A nervousness of waiting. Disintegration of logic. Desire to run from this place now, while I can. But Lucette has sent no money, and for the time being at least, I must stay on.

We have our standards, our criteria of judgment; but the sight of death purifies the spectator of any "modern" emotion, and the Monastery destroys from within, the hardened nuclei of external values, reducing you to a sort of pure sentiment at which we have taught ourselves to laugh.

If we could only conserve the clarity given by great emotion! In the presence of death we do unashamedly, things which otherwise we would consider intolerable. In love we are even worse. Imagine the misery of a man in love who insisted on keeping his love-making in the perfect taste of our elegances! To escape the maudlin, we invent barriers against sentiment. We emasculate emotion. We become despicable.

Worst of all, we can't distinguish between these superficial social niceties and the true mental inventiveness that goes far above, such as that of art and music and literature. We confuse the copy with the original. Trends of importance always attract parasites, and we are content with the almost-as-good. One thinks of Cézanne, Gris, Miró, Modigliani, and the host of their imitators . . .

Father Clément interrupts this, entering my cell to find me in bed completely clothed. "Excuse me, my son," he apologizes. "Are you resting?"

"No, Father," I reply resentfully, "I'm just trying to keep warm."

"I know all this is very hard for you, my son. Why do you not go away? Our life, now that the newness wears off, becomes increasingly difficult. Or is that it?"

61

"I guess so, Father. As a matter of fact I've been thinking of leaving for some time, but I must wait for some money. It annoys me to see all of you with your pious little beliefs. You have everything figured out—what's good is God, and what's bad is the devil. I'm sick of the whole mess."

If Father Clément is surprised at my outburst he doesn't show it. "I am very sorry," he says simply. "If only you knew how little we have, as you say, 'figured out.' How much these same doubts come to torment us. How often we awake at night wondering if this is real. We live on faith, my child, not on concreteness of fact. We content ourselves not to ask for proof. It is a gift of ourselves we make, and if there are doubts, the gift is that much greater." He sits on my cot, looking at his hands; I lie to the far edge behind him. "And if the gift is great enough," he continues almost to himself, "sometimes God lets us know His love . . ."

"There, Father," I break in, "that's what I don't get, that's the reason I can't stand these books of piety. They're full of such dogmatic phrases—God's love, the devil's evil, and all that muck."

Father Clément looks at me. "It is a good sign to see you like this, my son," he remarks very quietly. "If you were sure of your own disbelief, our beliefs would not annoy you. It is because you become uncertain that you are troubled. Is that not it?"

"I guess so"—disconsolately—"but I could never accept."

"Will you let me say something that may appear very naïve to you?"

"Say anything you like."

"Do not fight so hard to hold on. The moment the devil sees a sign of belief, he causes that belief to become so painful to you that you are in reality suffering from the devil, and not from God. Know that you are not essentially different from any of us here. None of us is struck, none of us is 'enlightened.' We struggle, and sometimes we lose. Few men have an unquestioning vocation. Like you, we

62

are filled, day after day, with unremitting temptation."

"But unlike me, you resist it, Father. I've never resisted—never."

"Have you ever wanted to? Have you ever tried, my son?"

"Yes, Father. But I can't—it's impossible for me."

"It is impossible for *anyone,* my son. We can convince ourselves of our own prowess, we can substitute the satisfaction of one temptation for the resistance of another, and thereby believe we are morally strong. But no man can really say no except with the grace of God. There is no other way . . . But I have talked too much." He rises stiffly to his feet. "Oh incidentally, Father Abbot says you may stay as long as you like, attend any of the classes, and work freely in the paleography room and library."

I receive the news apathetically. "Thanks, Father. But I'll probably be leaving soon, as I told you."

"Well, perhaps now that you can busy yourself with these things, you will be more content. I hope so."

I throw back the covers and walk with him to the door. "I'm sorry I talked so impertinently to you, Father," I say to him as we shake hands. "Please forgive me."

He laughs, "Remember the parable in the *Chroniques* of Joinville?"

"No, Father, what parable is that?"

"Suppose I ask you the same question a wise priest asked Joinville. If there were a war, and I were placed on guard at some castle far behind the front lines, whereas you were placed on guard in a castle at the very front, which of us would more deserve a medal?"

"I guess I would, Father," I reply, "since I'd be facing all the danger."

"Exactly," exclaims the monk. "And as the priest pointed out to Joinville, it is the same with your faith. I am so certain of mine that I guard a castle far from danger of doubts. Yours is a much more dangerous castle, and therefore if you keep it safe and intact, how much more is your merit in God's eyes."

63

When I don't speak, Father Clément says, "One thing
more. Your life is not an active one here. It might be
easier on your nerves if I asked Father Abbot to assign you
some sort of physical labor—perhaps working in the garden."

"Ah, no," I groan. "Frankly, that's not the sort of physical exercise I need."

Father Clément chuckles, "I understand, but I cannot
approve. Gardening would be infinitely preferable. An
hour a day, eh?"

"All right, but don't blame me if the Monastery has a
vegetable shortage. When do we start?"

"Perhaps tomorrow—I shall let you know. Good-bye
for now."

He leaves behind him two books which I spend the
afternoon reading: *Paludes* and *Thésée* of Gide. Extreme
facility, almost lightness, virtuosity. A rhythm which carries
sentiments over the border of satire into the realm of the
truly serious. Gide's ability to take on the coarseness of
a Thésée on the one hand, and yet in the same work to retain
the nobility of style on an entirely different plane.

Now in my cell preparing for sleep, the assuaging
process of Compline from the chapel below, relentlessly
spoken, monotonous—like a warm bath, relaxing by the
intonation and rhythm rather than by the text.

2 november

It is a dark rainy day. At noon I'm at work in
the paleography room with Father G'seau. We turn on

lamps to see the manuscripts before us. Our long work-tables are covered with faded pages, bottles of ink, and writing paper. The room smells of paper—of old paper and dust.

Outside the open door, stone corridors seem vast in the darkness. I am so accustomed to associating the chant with the purity of silence, that I often feel I hear it in moments of great quiet such as this.

Father G'seau rises, stretches, stamps his feet on the rough floor. He lifts a cardboard box of hand-copied manuscripts from one of the shelves, and mutters, "What is this? Come here, my son—see what I have found."

I look. It is an album of Bach preludes and fugues, so satisfyingly recorded by Cumpson.

"Now, how do you suppose that got here?" he asks.

"I don't know, Father, but it's a very valuable album. Do we have a phonograph?"

"No, but you might take it to Jacques's if you want to hear it." He yawns. "How much longer till lunch?"

"Nearly an hour. Getting hungry?"

"No," he groans weakly. "Brrrrr—these drafts."

"While we're talking, Father, how does one go about bathing in this place? I'm getting filthy."

"It is too cold to bathe, my son. Just wash a little. The showers have no hot water, you know. But that reminds me, I have been reading a most amusing book. Wait—let me fetch it from my cell across the way."

He returns immediately, leafing the pages of a tattered and yellowed book. A page falls to the floor and I pick it up. After a moment he finds his place, and glances back at the cover for the exact title.

"This is from Blondel's *Les Causeries Médicales de Dios-coride*—the part about baths. He says: 'Taken even as often as once a day they can do no harm, provided you keep a thermometer in the tub at 95 degrees, and continue adding warm water, so that when you have finished, the temperature is 102.2 degrees. The bath should last exactly ten minutes.' Now, my son"—feigning seriousness—"you

65

know how to bathe in the most advanced scientific manner."

"It hardly seems worth it, does it, Father?"

"We have evolved, my son, even in monasteries. Under our original rule Benedict strongly discouraged baths not only as being unhealthful, but also as a device of the devil. Only the sick could bathe promiscuously in our early order."

"But if baths were considered unhealthful, it seems odd that the sick should be given them."

"The sick are always pampered. Baths are a luxury, and it was felt they did more good than harm in such cases."

Father G'seau returns the book to his cell. We resume our work until one o'clock, when the bell calls us to the refectory. For lunch: soup, potatoes, cauliflower, apples and bread.

Again the disarming physiognomy of these monks attracts me. There is a simplicity of expression, a childishness, which one finds on the faces of virgins. Here you must develop a new standard of facial judgment, for these are men of great intelligence without appearing in any way intelligent, according to outside standards.

We work, our activities interrupted throughout the day for services; and the afternoon becomes colder. But in working, in physical fatigue, satisfaction returns, and with it a calmness of spirit. I come from the garden before Vespers, my feet frozen and covered with mud. Changing shoes, I wait for the Vesper bells. The late afternoon sun appears momentarily, filtered through bare branches into my cell. From the chapel below, organ music of spell-binding loveliness: Couperin, *Messe pour les Couvents,* played by a visiting organist. The spell catches me, drawing from me a tension of thirsts and hungers which finds satis-faction and rest in these sounds . . .

And now the Satie *Messe des Pauvres* sounds cleanly through the cold autumn afternoon. My entire being, con-ditioned by new life, becomes distilled in this moment to a point where the music I am hearing reduces me to the quietness, to the hopelessness of tears.

The opening chants of Vespers fill the courtyard as

66

I enter the half-lighted chapel. I sit in the back, in obscurity, listening. My ears ache from the chilling dampness.

The counterpoint of ancient conductus, as experienced when two voices recite—it is here, perfuming the air. The monks' choir sings the Vesper chant, endless, unchanging, exquisitely evocative. The ear hears this as a single voice: indefinable plainchant, fusing with the foggy half-colors of the interior. And one hears in the imagination a second voice, intoning on a single note the *"Ave, Maria, gratia plena; Dominus tecum: benedicta tu in mulieribus, et benedictus fructus . . ."* repeated again and again in the minds of the kneeling, silent figures . . .

The rest is lost in change and transition, and no one disturbs the hours until dinner.

And for dinner, there are boiled celery, bread and water.

There develops here a nakedness which alternates between extremes of unhappiness and calm. I long for Paris— to be warm, and to get drunk, and to be happy and shallow, and to know a bed and a woman, and to hear noises and see lights . . .

Instead I attend Compline, staying in the chapel a long time after the monks have gone to bed. Doing nothing, thinking nothing. Sitting alone in the dark. Staring at the votive candles and the red altar lamp. Watching them flicker in the stillness . . .

I stir myself and walk outside. Damp freezing mist penetrates my clothing. The night is blackness without silhouette. I feel my way to the corner, find the steps, turn and walk back. And standing there enclosed in darkness and light rain, I leak on the ground. It makes a terrible noise; it seems I shall never finish.

I go to bed fully clothed, with a burning fever and the beginnings of a chill. During the night I wake to draw on more covers, but there are no more. Somehow I need the sickness. I need the sickness and the fever. Somehow, I know I need them . . .

9 november

The fevers break, and I awake in a strange cell in a bath of sweat. I am alone. A small fire spits in a long-unused chimney. And I am in pajamas.

After a while Father Clément appears, accompanied by a young friar in a brown sackcloth robe. He is anxious about me.

"This is an old story with me, Father," I reassure him. "It's malaria. I caught it in Tours during my school days, and it recurs suddenly like this. Now that the fever's broken I'll be all right. Tell me, though—how long have I been unconscious? When was I moved into this cell?"

"You have been in a coma almost a week, my son," he murmurs, bending over me. "When we found you, Father Abbot suggested we move you into this cell where you could have a little fire. Brother Placide here has been caring for you. Your things are still in your old cell, and you may move back whenever you feel strong enough. Tell me what you need—food, a bath, medicine?"

"I'm soaked, Father—I'd like some dry clothes and a bath, if possible. You can find clean pajamas in my cell. And I might be able to eat a little, too."

"How do you feel, my son?"

"Just fine, Father, but awfully weak. When the fevers leave, they leave you feeling good. But I think I'd better get on some dry things before I catch cold."

They leave together, Brother Placide walking behind. He is a small man with sand-colored hair and a lean red face. He has the look of a man who is profoundly good and simple, but not very intelligent.

In a few moments they return with Father G'seau and Father Dutfoy. They enter without knocking, rubbing their hands together and blowing from the cold. The three monks go immediately to the fire, nodding to me over their shoulders, but Brother Placide lingers near the door.

68

My spirits are light after the fevers, and I roar at the monks, "Ah! so you come to see me in order to get warm by my fire, eh?"

"Such an ugly suspicion," retorts Father Dutfoy, pretending to be insulted. "We come only to be of help."

"Then come away from that fire and help me. I'll catch pneumonia if I don't get some dry clothes and linens."

Father G'seau throws clean pajamas at me and grumbles, "Such an ungrateful being. Here—here are your clothes." He turns to Father Clément. "Our friend would make an excellent Father Superior for the Trappists, eh, Father Clément?"

The latter agrees. "Indeed," he adds, "I am surprised to see such a low, suspicious mind. We leave our work and come to help him, and merely because we stand away from him for fear of catching the dread disease, he thinks we are here for the fire. Move over a little, Father Dutfoy."

There is a nonplused grin on the fine face of the young friar Brother Placide, who doesn't know if we're serious.

Father Dutfoy calls to him, "Brother Placide, come and warm yourself. Not till our friend has the kindness to fall ill again will you get this close to a fire."

"No, my Father," replies the other softly. "I must help him, and change his bedclothes."

The friar comes to my side and helps me onto my feet, then pulls the linens from the bed. Father Dutfoy pours a bowl of warm water and hands me a bar of soap. Father Clément unbuttons the clean pajamas while Father G'seau stirs the miniature fire.

I wash with a cloth about the face and neck, trembling from the cold room. Feebly I grumble, "If you Fathers will be so kind, may I have a little of the fire that was originally started for me?"

"Of course," says Father Dutfoy—"if you feel you need it."

They make no move to give me room by the tiny blaze.

"What a disappointing lack of stoic abnegation," Father Dutfoy continues. "His soul is as weak as his body."

69

"Surely, Fathers," I complain, "you've luxuriated before my fire long enough."

Father Clément shrugs his shoulders and draws up a chair, and they let me sit between them. There's a momentary silence as Brother Placide beats on my bed to get the wrinkles out of the clean sheets.

I remove my pajamas, folding them into a soggy bundle, and drop them on the floor. Father Clément hands me the fresh pajamas. With two fingers Father Dutfoy retrieves the others and holds them at arm's length.

"Here," he mutters disgustedly, "I will take these disease-ridden, sin-ridden, filth-ridden, leprous shrouds, and burn them."

"Don't you dare!" I say sharply. "Pajamas are too rare and expensive to lose even a pair like that."

They go to help Brother Placide, turning their backs so that I may finish my bath in privacy. I dry and put on the clean pajamas, which are cold to my skin. As I crawl into bed I dismiss them with a final peremptory gesture.

"Now that you're warmed you may go," I say haughtily, "for I must have complete rest in order to recuperate from this terrible malady. When you return, you may bring me a small bowl of chicken broth, some *pâté* and a green salad, with a bottle of dry white wine, to help me in my recovery."

"Ah, what a wonderful Father Superior he would make!" Father Dutfoy murmurs ecstatically.

With mockingly profound bows they walk humbly out the door. Wind catches their robes as they step outside. Brother Placide remains with me.

Without speaking he folds the dirty sheets, carefully sweeps the cell, and pours from the door the water in which I have washed. Momentary glimpse of the frozen garden. When he has done all this to his satisfaction, he comes to my bed and in the softest, most gentle of voices asks, "Does Monsieur wish me to go too?"

"No," I tell him, "I was only joking with the Fathers. I'm grateful for your company, Brother Placide. But you mustn't let me keep you from your regular work. What would you be doing today if you weren't here with me?"

"Father Abbot told me to stay with you at all times, Monsieur," he answers timidly—"but my regular duties are attending the hogs."

"I didn't know you had hogs here."

"Oh yes, Monsieur. I will show them to you when you are well again."

Feeling that Father Abbot might have chosen someone other than a hog specialist to look after me, I ask, "Tell me, Brother, would you rather stay here and take care of me, or be back with your hogs?"

His face lights up with a glowing smile as he replies earnestly, "Ah, Monsieur, I would *much* rather take care of you."

And I am assuaged.

Brother Placide—simple, scrupulous little man, fearful of the luxury of warmth—takes my chair from its place near the fire and sits in the opposite corner. Through half-closed eyes as I pretend to sleep: the angelic vision of a young friar clad in brown sackcloth, seated in the low chair, reading with obvious difficulty his breviary. The room is quiet except for an occasional spitting as the small blaze penetrates green wood. Brother Placide sits facing the sallow light that enters the dirty window glass, his blond hair making a sand-colored aureole. Shadows are heavy and diffused in the small cell. He squints his eyes, moving his lips in silent pronunciation of the text, but the mouth retains its persistent smile. He turns the page and I know there must be a picture, for he smiles delightedly, turning his head from side to side to view it from every angle. Losing himself in admiration, he studies the picture lovingly, seeming to talk to it. The reality of his intimate love and delight in finding the picture, is a little shocking, as private acts of devotion often are.

"Brother Placide"—I address him softly lest I startle him—"sit with your back to the window, so that the light falls on your book. You'll ruin your eyes trying to read that way."

71

"How, Monsieur?"

"Just turn your chair around . . . There, that's the way."

"Thank you, Monsieur, you are very kind."

The Brother's words make me wish they might be true. In his simplicity—almost stupidity—the goodness which radiates from him seems infinitely dear.

I sleep most of the day, dimly aware that figures which speak to Brother Placide in hushed voices, come and go in my cell.

11 november

Days of convalescing: much reading, interrupted by the loving cares of Brother Placide, and occasional visits from the monks. The room remains cold, for I'm allowed only a small fire in the early mornings and late evenings.

There is a lightness after the fevers which persists, which makes me thirst, feeling the strength of desires without the physical health to satisfy them. My cell is clean and light and smells of the fire and fresh bedclothes. It has the positiveness of convalescence, the gaiety of weakness becoming strength. Enthusiasms become exaggerated, as do discontents, as does desire—animal and pagan, and superbly lustful . . .

"Are you asleep again, Monsieur?"

"No, Brother Placide."

"Good, then I will leave you for a moment. Here are some books Father G'seau sent you from the library." He places them carefully on my table and walks out the door, pulling his hood over his head.

I read because there's nothing else to do; I read as an animal eats. The top book is a paper-backed edition of *Notre Foi Contemporaine,* a study of contemporary religious and philosophical trends, which contains a section devoted to refuting Gide's *Corydon.* Every faculty tells you that Gide is wrong in his reasoning, but it will take an argument much more profound than this to appear anything but moral prattling. It has the pseudo-coldness of a shocked old maid. It's a risk to take sides against Gide, even when you know you're right.

Fabre, I recall, gives a fascinating account of the life of the praying mantis. The female of the species, after the sex act is over, tends to develop a violent hunger; and since her mate is there, weakened and exhausted, she simply eats him.

Certainly there can be no moral drawn from such a biological fact, but we immediately observe the pragmatists who label it cannibalism or sadism; and it's the same tendency in Gide which forms the principal weakness of his argument, in *Corydon,* for licensed homosexuality. Gide contends that because dogs, cats, and other higher vertebrates can satisfy their urges only at certain specified times with the female of their species, and as a result have recourse to members of their own sex, pederasty is the normal state among animals and heterosexual love the abnormal state. He applies this as a parallel to man. But can we give animals human stigmatic names—sadist, homosexual, pervert —when no question of moral will is involved? Can instinct ever become a moral quantity when intelligence and freedom of will are not present? Conversely, can animal behavior ever, in any way, apply to the human being? . . .

Returning, Brother Placide enters quietly, his face red and raw from the cold. He stirs the fire. I sit up in bed, propped high on borrowed pillows, with a blanket around my shoulders. He takes his place away from the fire, trembling and rubbing dry hands together.

The day passes quietly, and I sleep early.

73

16 november

Three a.m. It is cold at this hour—obsession of cold, cursing cold; nightmares and sleep to be renounced—and outside, I know the River is dark and frozen.

The blinds are closed in this sick cell. I turn on the lamp.

The fevers have left an execrable taste in my mind, and I detest everything I have been doing and thinking. Things that fascinated me before my sleep seem trashy: the *avant-garde* composer Kotzebue, playing the cultured clown, giving a cultured lecture to the cultured clowns of Harvard; Viardot burning his candles at the altars of Stravinsky and Valéry. A genius becomes ordinary when he steps from his proper frame: Einstein on politics, Stravinsky on psychoanalysis, Beethoven on sex . . .

With the light still on, walls seem impersonal, cold, forbidding, clean. They ignore me. I push farther beneath the covers. From the hall I hear a cough; someone turns in his bed, sleeps . . .

In this great silence I long for sound, more beautiful sounds than exist.

There is nothing to occupy the insomnia. Walls disapprove: unsympathetic walls, wanting me to turn off the lamp and sleep. A polished sheen of crucifix above my bed looks down, disapproving also: unsympathetic crucifix, accusing stick of carved wood . . .

Mind turns confusedly—Dada, surrealism, cubism, plastic form, atheism, plasticity of rhythm, mysticism, existentialism, rationalism—words filling me with terror. Strip each of these things to barest essentials, and the answer is always the same. After all the intellectual searching one is offered only two obvious solutions: the *néant* of daily life on a level plane of mean juices, or the grace of mystical renunciation of the ego, opening floodgates of satisfaction in the denial of satisfaction. The true course of intellectual

74

research must end in mysticism or in dust, if carried to its final stage. For the nonintellectual, mysticism is a grace; and the only completely happy man, from the purely quantitative viewpoint, is he who arrives at this goal without the search . . .

All of which is damnably dull and pedantic—and unimportant. For with the passing of fevers and the forgetting of flashes of nightmare logic, there is in this early morning of sharp disgusts the bitterness of something good which in this moment, in this place, becomes evil. The fevers give the good feelings, the place denies their consummation, the nightmare makes them insomnious. Thus the feelings find no object, and remain pure . . .

I am in love—that's the feeling. I am in love hopelessly, passionately, desolately—alone in this frozen cell. I am sick, sick—and I am in love. I know it, I am sure of it. But tonight it can be centered in no person, in no object. There are no bowels, no intestines, no moistures. Tonight it's pure, as an emotion: the sensation of loving . . . nothing . . .

The first bells for Matins come from the silence. It is three-forty-five. My stomach aches with the desire for food or for a cigarette, and my feet are frozen in the bed. Gradually, as night passes, I begin to feel better. It's good to be alone. My mind clears. The Monastery is still silent; everyone sleeps until the second bell at four o'clock. There is a secret joy in being awake alone, early in the morning, even in being uncomfortable from the cold in one's bed. There is a detached voluptuousness in desiring a cigarette when there's no hope of satisfying that desire.

I wait, listening for the second bell. Idly I begin to count the number of times a cock crows in the Valley.

But this is never finished, for I drop off to sleep again, and this time a dream finds me walking with a buxom young girl who says, "You have been so kind, Monsieur. You've done so much for me. If you'll return home with me I'll do anything, anything to please you."

I put my arm around her waist, whispering, "You're

75

sweet," and pat her on the behind in a suggestive caress.

She looks at me surprised and moves away, murmuring, "Ah, no, Monsieur—nothing like *that*."

The image is shattered. I sleep dreamlessly until noon, when Father Clément brings me some soup.

"You are feeling better," he observes, handing me the tepid bowl. "You slept a long time."

"I was awake much of the night, Father." I tell him of my dream, and it sounds idiotic in the broad light of day.

He laughs—not at my dream, but at my crestfallen disappointment that she refused me. "It is nice to know that your dreams, at least, are populated by people of a higher morality than you appear to have."

"I shouldn't mind so much, Father," I sigh, "if it had happened on the outside. But in a monastery it's a shame to miss the only chance I've had in weeks." With this I begin to eat the watery broth he has brought, holding the bowl close under my chin, manipulating an enormous spoon.

Father Clément talks in the background, standing beside my bed. "I shall see to it," he remarks, "that Father G'seau takes these books back and brings you something a little more edifying, my son. But I am glad you had your dream, for it is a sure sign that you are once more on the road to health."

The fire has been lighted. After I finish my soup Father Clément leaves me alone with Brother Placide, my silent, lovable companion. He sits near the window, at the proper angle this time, reading his breviary. I reread the poems of Mallarmé, Rimbaud, and Reverdy—insatiably. They seem completely foreign to my surroundings, but the sickness is pagan in me and I can't stomach the books of piety which Father Clément insists on bringing.

Brother Placide drowses in his chair. I watch him as the book in his hand gradually, in small jerking movements, drops into his lap; as the hand relaxes, letting the breviary fall to the floor. He raises his head—to have it fall to the side, resting on his shoulder. Suddenly he awakens with

76

a violent snore, stares about embarrassedly, and gets up and moves about the room.

"Why don't you sleep, Brother Placide?" I suggest. "Come, you take my bed and I'll sit in the chair near the fire. You're dead on your feet."

"Thank you, Monsieur—no, I cannot."

He sweeps the room, smiling. He is nothing, but already he is in heaven.

19 november

The cold becomes unbearable, with temperatures below zero and no more heat. I have moved back to my cell. Our life has become a huddling against cold. We can think of nothing else. It reaches the brain after a time, seeming to freeze thought.

The compensation is that we share this extreme discomfort together, and in some inexplicable manner this alleviates it for each of us. There's no complaining—one doesn't complain alone. The monks place their discomforts as a sacrifice to God, giving thanks that He allows them to make these involuntary offerings.

This cold which blots all other considerations from our minds, increases the intimacy of our life together; for discomfort eventually becomes pain, and in pain protocol is lost, and modesty is lost, and self is lost. Only the essentials remain, and work is reduced to skeletal proportions. We huddle in corners out of the wind, standing close together to draw heat; and when one of us must leave the cold cloister for the freezing outside, the others commiserate with him in his heroic deed, and commiseration lessens the pain.

The monks don't wear gloves nor a hand covering of any kind, not even accepting mine when they have to go out. Their hands are blue and puffed, with scabbing cold sores around wrists and fingers. Life here, for most, becomes almost superhuman. Outdoor tasks must be done—water must be drawn—and we take turns.

Looking out frosted windows of the great hall downstairs, we watch the one whose time it is to draw water as he runs with black skirts flying, sloshing water from the pails he carries. The path to the well is a series of small lakes of ice, for the water freezes on the ground before it can dry.

Skies are always gray and overcast. The background of the garden has taken on the colorless oranges and blues of sleeping winter. The River below our walls is frozen, intensifying our chill as we glance in its direction. We call it the "Refrigerator."

We work in the paleography room, Father G'seau and I, covered with a heavy weight of clothing. We work until our hands become so numb that we can no longer hold books and pens. Until this morning we could restore circulation by walking arm in arm about the courtyard, but now even that is no longer possible. A fine mist has frozen during the night, making it impossible to walk fast enough to generate heat. Running about the corridors is out of the question, but we try it until Father Abbot corrects us.

Feet sweat when it's cold. Nothing else is as bad as this; nothing bothers us so much as feet which are frozen and wet in our shoes. It doesn't help to change, for clean dry socks become instantly soaked.

Our strict regime suffers many setbacks. Yesterday morning our toilets were frozen, throwing us into a momentary panic. One of the Fathers who was an engineer before entering the Monastery, ordered that the disks at the bottom be taken out, allowing the water to drain through before it could freeze. This was but a temporary solution, however; now we find that we can flush the toilets only by pouring warm water into them—but at least we can flush them.

The little bathroom signs are replaced by larger, hurriedly printed signs informing us that, until the freeze has ended, we are requested to use the bathrooms only when it is absolutely necessary. We are instructed to please urinate outside, and if we must use the toilets, to go to the kitchen where we will be given a carafe of warm water with which to flush them.

The experience is accepted, and it becomes highly amusing when we see ourselves walking precariously across the frozen courtyard carrying bottles of hot water which steam like trains in our wake. At least for this little journey we can warm our hands.

Bathing is out of the question, as is changing clothes. I wear two pairs of socks, underwear, two pairs of pants, three sweaters, a wool shirt, a jacket and an overcoat, with hat and gloves, which I never remove even for sleeping. The water in my washstand is frozen and my hands become filthy, smelling of leather and sweat and dryness.

Fathers Clément, Dutfoy, and G'seau incessantly remind me of my sickness. "Do you not feel a little feverish today, my son?" one of them will say.

And I reply, "In this weather fever would be a blessing, Father."

"If you feel you could stir up a little coma, we would put you back in the sick cell with a nice fire, and the three of us would be happy to watch over you."

"I refuse to get sick just so you three can be comfortable."

When this fails, they approach me with other suggestions: "My son, we were wondering how long it has been since you last had a bath?"

"About six weeks now, Father, since I had a real bath."

"How can you bear to live with yourself? Come, we must see to it that you bathe now, this very day."

"In this weather? Why, Father, I don't even take off my clothes to go to bed. Don't think I'd take them off in an unheated monastery for a bath. Besides, all the water is

79

frozen hard. I couldn't take a bath even if I wanted to."

"We will heat some water, and I will pour it over you while the others stand by with towels."

"I'll catch pneumonia."

"It is worth the risk. Think how wonderful it will be to feel *clean* again. Does it not tempt you? Come now, no more talk. And if you *should* get sick we will put you in the sick cell with a fine fire, and watch over you devotedly, never leaving your side until the weather warms up."

"Why don't *you* take a bath, Father? I'll do the pouring. How long has it been since *you* bathed?"

"My son, you are indeed a person without taste. Come, Fathers, we will leave."

They walk out grumbling about being insulted by such personal questions, and about the bad taste of so many foreigners.

23 november

After breakfast this morning a young novice brings a packet of letters to my cell. It's the first mail I've received. I note that most of it has been forwarded from Paris. Lucette's small handwriting covers the envelopes of the readdressed letters, but there's no word from her. My good, faithful Lucette.

Quickly I tear open each letter to see if there's money from America. Two of them contain checks. I feel my heart begin to pound. Now I can leave this place. I can leave the frozen nights in my cell. I can leave the silence and the bad food. I can go back to Paris and all that Paris means to me. And the very feel of the checks in my pocket raises my spirits, warms me.

But the checks must be cashed. Stopping at the gatehouse on my way to Town, I tell Father Dutfoy I'm spending the day away from the Monastery. A sharp wind bites through my heavy clothing as I step out into the street. Chimneys are smokeless all about me. The snow-covered countryside is dreary, inescapably monotonous and dreary.

Walking along the road I think of the fire, of the small black stove that warms the room in Paris. I think of sitting by it late at night with the smell of tea and cigarettes to delight my senses. I think of sleeping warm sleep, with an arm thrown across the soft belly of my Lucette.

Town is as cold and stark as the countryside. The streets are almost deserted. People huddle in doorways.

Finding the bank, I watch the teller turn my checks into cash. I stay there a long time, for the building is heated. It's the first time I've been warm in weeks. Again and again I count my money. I have money in my hand. I can leave.

But as I look at the roll of bills, the sight fades. The sight loses its clear focus. Paris and warmth and foods and a bed shimmer in myopic hollowness. There is noise, a deafening constant noise in Paris; and there's greater loneliness with a woman you no longer love than there is in solitude. Paris and its image shriek harsh and shrill, now that I have the money to go there. The picture of it becomes inverted in my mind, filling me with doubt. It's inverted. I had wanted Paris and the outside world because it represented warmth and mediocrity and comfort. Now that I can have it for the price of a ticket, it seems suddenly cold. The warmth of the mind and the peace of that warmth float visions irrevocably back to the Monastery and my cell, and to the monks whom I grow to love. It is the outside which seems blunt and harsh.

I am drawn back. I'm thunderstruck to be so drawn back, but it's there like some invisible umbilical cord of the soul which won't release me except in pain. I stand by

81

the stove in the bank and look at my money. Warmth seeps through the clothing around the calves of my legs. I look at the gray-smocked clerks with their sallow faces and their dull eyes. They know homes and newspapers, and they're dead while still alive. The very heat seems contaminating.

I am drawn back, but I'm sick at the thought. From within comes a pinpointing of desire to fight this attraction, to leave now and never return. An elderly man behind the counter smiles at me. The pinpointing remains as I ask him to call the taxicab, as I wait. I want to return to the spaciousness, to the tranquillity, to the warmth of my Monastery. And to its safety.

My old friend Salesky, wrapped to the eyes in a fur coat, roars a familiar greeting when he sees me standing in the dirty snow. "Come sit in front with me, M'sieu. And how are you?"

His coarse voice makes the outside world loom closer, more tempting; half-reluctantly I get into the car. "Pretty well, thanks," I tell him—"or at least so numbed by the cold I can't feel any pain."

"I haven't seen you in so long, thought you'd gone back to Paris like you planned."

"I gave up that idea," I explain, as though the decision had been made weeks ago. "I'm going to stay on at the Monastery awhile."

"Fine. You won't regret it."

The car moves slowly down the street. Puffing his pipe, Salesky leans far back in the seat. I know what to expect, and I prepare myself.

"And the other, M'sieu, how is it?" he asks expansively. "Still impossible?"

"No," I reply casually, "I almost forget it these days."

"No! Have you been sick?" His voice is full of concern.

"As a matter of fact I have, but it isn't that. There's something about living in a monastery that makes such things seem unnecessary." I look away, out the window to the snow-covered fields and bare trees. "I'm not obsessed by girls any more," I go on sanctimoniously, trying to ignore the disturbing images projected onto the landscape by my mind.

"I'm sad to hear that, young man. You're strong. I'm old, but I could never stop thinking of girls."

"Neither could I, usually. But I never think of them here."

There follows a long silence, giving Salesky time to contemplate my untruths. Then he brightens, takes the pipe from his mouth, and asks, "What's your favorite way of making love, M'sieu?"

"Ah, Salesky," I groan helplessly, "you get me talking about that and I won't be able to go back to the Monastery."

He nods his head delightedly, driving very slowly. "Isn't it the truth? It's a fine thing to make love. Tell me, do you ever hear from that girl of yours back in Paris?"

"Not a word."

He grins. "Just like I told you, she's probably with somebody else. How long you been without a girl now?"

"Six weeks, about."

"Oh, la! that's a long time. You must be bursting."

"It's too cold to burst, Salesky," I laugh.

He leans his head close to me, grinning. "When you were in Paris, for example, did you ever go to the Bois de Boulogne at night?"

"Naturally. What student hasn't?"

"The best in all Paris is in the forest there. And free, too," he nods. "A man can get any kind of girl there."

I say nothing. The road is covered with ice and Salesky's cab moves still more carefully. He stops for a moment to relight his pipe.

"Tell me, M'sieu," he says above the shifting of gears, "while you were with your girl did you fool around with anyone else?"

"No!" I answer sharply. "What kind of a person do you think I am? She was a nice girl and I never thought of going to anyone else."

"Honest?" He sounds incredulous.

"Honest. I was absolutely faithful to her. Oh, occasionally when she was spending a week end at home I'd find myself another girl, but not often."

A skeptical "Hmmm" is all that comes from Salesky.

"Now let's talk about something else," I suggest. "Tell me about the Valley. It's beautiful this morning, isn't it?"

"Except for the Monastery, M'sieu, a terrible place. Beautiful, yes—but a hell of a place to live in. I may as well tell you now, for you'll hear it anyway. I have a girl friend on this side of the River—Madame Rouen, she runs a little spice shop. She's given me two children, which is more than my wife ever did. Is it bad for a man to love his wife and yet want children by another woman?" His face becomes serious. Opening the window he empties pipe ashes outside.

I don't answer.

"Anyway," he goes on, "there's not a woman in the Village who wouldn't like to have me in her bed—or you, M'sieu, or any other man. But they're mean. They dream of it and condemn me, Salesky, because I've done it with somebody else. I tell you, it's a devil's paradise here."

"I can't believe that, my friend. These people seem all right. Besides, you'd be talked about anywhere in the world for keeping two women to sleep with."

"Would they run and tell my wife?" he says angrily. "Would they keep watch on my mistress's house, and count the times, and run tell my wife? No. But that's what they do here. They're bitches. Oh, there are a few good ones here, but they keep to themselves."

"Do you know Madame Renée?"

"Ah, yes." Salesky's voice changes. "Now there's a strange one. She's one of the Village 'great ladies,' but she's democratic. She never spreads tales and she's good to the poor."

"Why do you find that strange, Salesky?"

"Because with all that," he explains, "she's still one of the 'great ladies' here. She associates with the other bitches without being a bitch herself . . . Ah, look at that

84

pretty girl there. Don't often see one that good-looking."

He jams on the brakes. The car skids to a halt near a young girl walking with her back to us. She turns and walks hesitatingly toward the car.

"Look at that, M'sieu," Salesky whispers rapturously. "Those little breasts—how'd you like to have a handful of that, for example?"

The girl approaches his open window and he asks, in an exaggeratedly lecherous Parisian accent, if we can't take her somewhere. She giggles a flushed refusal, and we drive on.

"Salesky, you fool, you embarrassed the poor kid half out of her wits."

"But no, she was pleased. Couldn't you see that? She'll be lost in daydreams all week now, thinking of a big hulk of a man like yourself. At night she'll lay against her pillow, imagining it's you. We did her a favor, I tell you."

"You bark loud, my friend," I taunt. "But I bet you'd have been lost if she'd got in with us."

"Oh, it wasn't for myself, M'sieu," he grins. "It was for *you*. You could've cooled her off a little in the back seat. You could've sprinkled her little garden for her, eh?"

"Of course, of course. Are you trying to get me run out of the Valley? I'm too well known for that sort of thing now."

We arrive in the clean snow of the Village, our tires making the first blue tracks. Salesky sighs deeply. We look about at uneven, icicle-fringed housetops leaning out over the sidewalks. It is quiet. The street is deserted and the chimneys are smokeless. The air is very clean and pure, for there's no fuel for heat in the Village, no smoke to perfume the morning. Trees have been cut and stripped bare. Every twig has been a moment of warmth; but now there are no more. Snow and ice are everywhere—on window frames, on lamp-posts—muffling sounds into perfect quietness, reflecting grays of sallow morning. The Village street winds before us, an unbroken ribbon of frozen white fading into morning mists beyond the last houses.

85

"Ah, for the sun again," Salesky says softly. He brings the car to a crunching halt several yards from the Monastery. "Here we are, M'sieu."

I start to get out and he lays a hand on my arm.

"Look," he says, "be a good boy and do me a favor."

I hesitate, holding the door half-open. "Sure. What is it?"

"My girl lives across the way, and I don't get to see her often. I'm always watched. But the streets are deserted now. If you were to stay in the car while I went in, none of these bitches would suspect. I'll make it short, M'sieu, just a few minutes."

"I couldn't do that. What do you think I am?"

"Please, M'sieu," he pleads. "If I'd asked you to sit in the car without telling you why, would you have done it?"

"Yes, I suppose so. But this is—"

"No, M'sieu, because I'm honest with you you should be even more willing. *Please* stay with the car. Here, I'll give you a package of cigarettes and you can keep them."

Salesky, saddened by the morning of cold, touches me with his plea. "Very well. But make it quick."

I stand guard, lighting a cigarette. Confusion of sentiments. Here a few feet from the high Monastery walls, I who grow to find nourishment in the virtue, in the saintliness of these monks, to a point of hinting it for myself, play the decoy for my friend as he performs a hasty, peremptory act of fumbling love. Too late, regret and guilt surprise me, revealing the change of a few weeks. And I curse the introduction within me of these long-dormant feelings.

I haven't finished the first cigarette when Salesky, wrapped in his fur coat, reappears. He lights his pipe, glances in both directions with a broad grin, and gets into the car with a profoundly contented exhalation of smoke.

"Wasn't she there?" I ask.

"Yes, she was there."

"Was something wrong?"

"Not at all, M'sieu. Didn't want to keep you waiting in the car. Thanks a thousand times for helping me. It was wonderful—but quick, eh? Quicker than you could have handled it, young buck that you are. I didn't even take off my coat, M'sieu."

He laughs proudly, and as his language becomes coarser my guilt and regret become good-natured envy and regret of another sort.

"Yes, without taking off my coat. 'Onto the bed with you!' I shouted at her. 'Onto the bed, my belle!' And zoom! her needle was good and well threaded. Wonderful how these things work, eh?"

"Oh, shut up, shut up. No one else could've talked me into such a thing. But if you need a witness let me know. I'll swear you were under the car all the time."

I enter the cloister, closing the door behind me, closing out the moments before entering. My dread of returning is dissolved in the relief of being back. For a moment I lean against the door, two inches of wood separating two worlds. Outside is my world: lubricative, warm to the senses, free in comfort of debauch; allowing one the time and the place in which to seek pleasure. Inside is their world: cold, ascetic, pure, detached; allowing senses to sleep safe from all things; giving a safety of happiness, a comfort of cleanliness within bodies covered with filth; destroying gnawings of guilt; destroying all small things; clearing the spaces for growth. I can work here, for there's nothing else to do. Work holds greater happiness when the nagging lines of street-prowling sensuality are no longer a possibility dividing your attentions. And there is another kind of sensuality, a roaring of the insides, a drunkenness in this inner quiescence, that makes you work like a god, in long phrases, with giant-like gestures.

The rest of the day is spent at my table copying manuscripts of Zachau, Walther, Pachelbel, and Lübeck with the energy of a trembling belly which hasn't forgotten that there are other bellies. Stacked beside me are Titelouze, Grigny, and Frescobaldi manuscripts waiting to be studied and analyzed.

When I think of the outside the word "mediocre" haunts

87

me, and it is the same everywhere, in all things. My longing is divided. For mediocrity is warmth, and commonness, and healthful coarseness—and an escape, and a paleness. And the longing is for those. But it's also for the greater warmth of trembling insides when strength is left; for the perfection of this naked bone of happiness which grows and which has no blemish. In the background, a flowing beauty of monastic life; in the foreground, small considerations that occupy us and will be forgotten—leaving the whole an ensemble of rhythmic patterns.

How can one deny the mysticism, the calm, the inevitability of deep satisfaction infusing those who accept? By degrees, imperceptibly, man becomes his surroundings regardless of habits or beliefs, until the evolution makes itself known. Despising these beliefs, these superstitions, these mocking abstractions, I realize my deception; for I don't despise their results. The realization becomes that food I would never touch, becomes my nourishment, insinuating itself into my blood and my flesh. The taste may be evil, I may vomit it; but it's inescapable.

I think of my life in Tours and in Paris, and it seems pale and sad—and hopelessly futile. My nourishment becomes a part of me, feeding emotions I don't want. But that, too, is inescapable. And I go to sleep sick with the knowledge that I'm no longer above, that I can no longer look down and sneer. Sickening, sickening undercurrent. Mysterious chemistry of environment.

I sleep, removing only my shoes. During the night wet socks dry on my feet and become warm. And my clothing suffocates me.

24 november

I awake in time for Matins. When we leave the chapel for warm, bitter, ersatz coffee, it's beginning to be daylight. Somber dark day.

Day of sighs and discontent after the discovery of yesterday. I return to my bed, seeking to swallow this dissonance of emotion.

A book of *Laudes* by Jacopone da Todi, a Franciscan spiritual monk of the thirteenth century. This "Second Francis" lacked the sunlight of the first, but the *Laudes* lying on the pillow close to my face, static black words on yellowed paper, bring indefinable clarity in their reiterations of my fear.

I lay them aside for the more impassioned *Soliloques* of St. Augustine, a work strangely similar in tonality to *Les Nourritures Terrestres* of Gide. This is a love of the man, a love of sweat, and a passion which I can understand—the hands folding nervously. A passion of man for God, but of man nevertheless, with man's littleness and heats.

I open my window, for there's no wind today and it's no colder outside than in my cell. Flatness of the Valley, calm and peaceful in its snow. Long lines of poplar trees lost in gray mists of morning. Restrained delicacy of sound and color and smell. But the mucus freezes in my nose, sticking to cartilage, irritating the nostrils when they distend to breathe. I close the window.

Sounds of dishes being washed, of pans and of silverware, as I pass the kitchen on my way to Mass. Exquisitely chanted Requiem Mass in harmony with the day.

In the paleography room we make photostatic copies of the organ works of Cabezón, working until Vespers without speaking.

And tonight, in my cell, the pendulum swings back. Tonight when bitterness could become an aberration, it swings back. After days of restless calm, possession of self

89

returns; returns to the emotionless balance of quiescence.

Clouds of the day give up their rain tonight. The delightful sound of it pours against my window, striking from the outer blackness as crystals of light that dissolve instantly.

The St. Augustine *Soliloques,* upon rereading, cleanses me momentarily of the ever-present web of doubts and turns me into a growing happiness. My head sings like an ancient harmonium. A purity of flute and oboe stops becomes equal purity of thoughts, separated, clear, well arranged to the accompaniment of the pouring rain.

My faculties return, and I realize that this peace which seems to have invaded me is, rather, a momentary relief from the bewildering crisis through which I am passing in this year of great change. A distending of nerves. Rest, for an hour, from the crushing and sinister aphrodisiac that deadens my senses, that kills within me all moral sense. Transition with the same strength, with the same exaltation, with the love no less fierce; but changed now to become love of the daylight, of the sun, and of warmth, as opposed to the other, to the older first love of night and of stars and of the clarity of blackness.

But the insides don't change. There is no charity, no real desire, except that which is hypothetical and autosuggestive. Left is the emotion . . . and the actor . . .

Now it's late night. The rain has become a storm, with winds clamoring at my loose-fitting window. The monks sleep. Surrounded by blessed, consecrated, complete men, I realize how profoundly implanted is my smallness within me. There must be a way to feel what they feel, to feel this cleanliness, this cleanliness of a pure soul. But for me there is only knowledge of its existence—no hint of its reality.

Every faculty opposes it, but the desire, timid and ashamed, stutters and will not die. Experience it. Experience it as an esthetic emotion, perhaps. Lines form, the undulation begins, and like Perotinus I attempt to thrust the dream from me. *As an experiment:* words in my dream. And I think of another experiment that was per-

90

formed not far from here a few years ago; an experiment that did not fail, but at which we laughed. The experimenter was René Schwob. Suffering the ridicule of his friends, he was told that his experiment would be a definite cause of the death of his intelligence. Such human vanity in the face of a possible temporal sacrifice leading to sanctity —a sanctity surpassing all the intoxications of the earth— seemed to him a terrifying thing.

But it's safer to laugh than to be laughed at, and the world of my world is a world that laughs. Like Schwob, I already hear the arguments: "You're capable of something better than a life of love for God." "You're above that ridiculous sort of thing, which is all right for some, but not for you." "You aren't the 'religious type.'" "It would wrong your intelligence to take on such naïve beliefs."

The rain stops, as suddenly as it began. And like a crayfish I hastily backtrack. But the hint is there. I think of my Lucette, of my Paris. And I decide that I must go— soon. For my going will be a retreat, and retreats are less painful.

But in this vast, night-filled silence, in the enormousness of my solitary cell, the thought of leaving and of returning to Paris is a rebuke, a pinpoint to nerves. The long line settles into repose. I cannot bear to leave.

The moon streams through the frosted window. On my night table the lamp flickers weakly. The hysterical ticking of my clock is the only sound. Occasionally the wind stirs, freezing crystals of water on the windowpane. I sit here in bed, knowing that tomorrow these things will make no sense.

25 november

*Remember San Juan de la Cruz, poet of the
night, of the dark soul?*

But the day is bright, with a clear sky and a first sun
blinding on the snow, making it yellow-opaque with blue
purity of shadows.

*Is not Christian mysticism worth the striving? The
pain?*

Ah, no! leave me in peace. Think of the ball, think
of the fete. Of tight pants and tight dresses. And a perfect
mole in just the right spot on your shoulder—not a mole
but a beauty spot.

*Think instead of the concretion of ideas on the elemen-
tary but necessary sexual conciliation of the true Christian
mystic.*

No! To hell with the must and musk of sanctity! The
sun is shining, and it's whiter than any white on the snow.

*For the specialists, whom we must believe, assure us
that the only manner of achieving this fantastic refinement
of sensation known as exaltation is in total chastity—*

Or the bed, or the sunlight, or a frozen raindrop. And
your voice is harsh, my beauty.

*—in total mental and physical purity, without which
God will not accord us this intoxication greater than all
the intoxications of the world combined.*

You're off key, my fine tightness of bodice. We sing
out of tune.

*This is the elementary plane, upon which other planes
must be built—like an abstract painting—until the conscience and the heart have reached a purity pleasing to
God.*

Must and musk of sanctity! Be quiet, you little fool,
you're disturbing my thoughts. For your voice—

*We must choose either the fire of total purity—more
dangerous to the spirit than earthly burns to the flesh—*

92

with the hope of its ultimate reward in God's favor—

Enough! The day's still bright, but the fete no longer matters. It's infinitely better to walk alone in the frozen garden, to knock ice from bushes with a stick, to hear it tinkle in the clear breeze. It's better than the mole, or the tightness. We must become one, singing in the same key . . .

—or impurity with its more tangible temporal reward of pleasure. We do not think of purity's reward in heaven, for that is too remote for man on earth, but rather of its physical, earthly reward in the ecstatic union of man with God.

I can do nothing but follow. Your way seems distant and impossible, but desirable—heartbreakingly desirable.

And this there is then—

". . . who takest away the sins of the world, have mercy upon us."

". . . who takest away the sins of the world, grant us Thy peace."

Father Clément enters without knocking. There is no must and musk, but rather a livingness, a movement of black robes, as he sits in the sunlight on my cot. He brings me a glass of warm water with which to brush my teeth. We talk of the day, of the sun. And I stamp nervously the length of my cell.

"You are like a caged animal, my son," observes Father Clément. "What bothers you this fine day?"

I turn to him. "I don't know, Father, I've been thinking. I feel rotten inside, thinking of all the things I've done. Why can't I be more like you people here? Why not? For what little reason? Simply because I can't overcome the flesh, that's why. I can't get my mind off of it. And I know that once I leave here it'll be the same as before. I really need help." The words have shot from my mouth like bullets, automatically, for I couldn't help myself.

Father Clément, startled, looks away from me, studying patterns of moving shadows on the floor where sunlight is filtered through branches. "My son," he begins hesitat-

93

ingly, "I scarcely know what to say. You talk as though non-chastity were the only sin. Why this sudden stressing of the sins of the flesh?"

"It's not the lack of purity, Father. That's only a symbol, a symbol of my entire weakness. If I've never once been able to resist temptation, how can I—? I don't know how to say it."

"Understand this simply, my son. Do not judge the present by the past, for then you saw no reason to refuse these demands. Remorse was dead, and I believe it is being reborn. Remorse, my child, is the symbol—and it is a very grateful one I find in you. Nothing is consistent, nothing. We here know that better than most. I have never discussed this with you before; but now that there is within you this spark of discontent—But would you rather I did not talk of it?"

"No, Father"—disgustedly—"tell me what you think. If it's remorse you want, maybe we can stir up a little more. I have the wherewithal."

"Now do not think this little upset is a change, my son. It is natural that you should feel it here, and it is an ephemeral thing, a very ephemeral and fragile thing. It is upon entering—even superficially as many of us have—this way of life that we begin to sense the duplicity of our characters, the inherent double life of our very beings. In destroying by force all things opposed to our love of God on this earth, we end up with two violently contrasting characters. On the one hand there is a nakedness of the soul, striving for the richness of a total eclipse in God; and on the other, a nakedness of physical desires which grow into proportional violence. It is only by the grace of God that we live with any degree of purity. It is through His sacraments, my child."

I walk to the window and gaze unseeing at the countryside. "You have those sacraments, Father." My breath faintly fogs the glass. "I don't, and you are the chosen ones."

"There are no classes among believers, my son. The

poor bread of the Host enters the body of any who will receive it. And it makes a great change in him, a mysterious physical change for the believer. When the Host enters his body it enters as a source of purity, making him conscious of the filth of his physical receptacle." He pauses, then, "If only this feeling could exist for more than a few moments," he muses.

I turn slowly from the window.

"It strikes you physically, my son," he continues, "to receive the blessed body of Christ into your own rottenness of body." He stares at the floor, and I know that he no longer speaks to me; he confesses his love to the air. Floats of steam come from his mouth more rapidly as he speaks. "It is something like climbing into a clean bed with a filthy body. It is with an overwhelming sense of guilt that we allow ourselves to take the Host, and with a blessed sense of relief that we receive it; for the desires, the ignobilities cease and become quiescent, and a rapture of the most intense physical and moral peace fills us."

"I didn't know, Father. I had no idea."

He stirs, rises stiffly to his feet. "It is worth it, my child. It is infinitely good to be in love with God. He is severe, demanding, but more gentle than can be dreamed. When you fall in love with Him—completely in love, with all your being—nothing else matters. Your only desire is to be faithful, as a husband desires to be faithful to his wife." He leaves walking quickly, bent and brown, not caring to let me hear more.

"Love"—detestable, shattered, misused and exhausted word—becomes strong again in the mouth of Father Clément. But another voice may create emotions which die when the voice leaves. And if I desired before, my desire is a confusion after his departure. My greatest personal enemy is the imagination of pleasures never yet felt, a poison occupying too much of my mind too often. But now there is the feebly felt antidote of remorse.

But I'm too deeply implicated in the lives of too many; for Lucette waits for me in Paris. And the ideal of Marie

95

des Vallées haunts my day: "My God, substitute Thy will for mine." It's a precipice over which I dare not step.

Casting it from my consciousness, I work without rest until I fall from sleep, to awake and work again. Bending remorse, suffocating it, losing it in the cold, in the health of cold and work.

7 december

A lighter sickness this time, but a nightmare for all of us. The doctor says that I must get out of this place until the weather warms; that I must have better nourishment and more sleep, and a fire. After the fevers the cold becomes a greater burden, for the blood is anemic and can't be warmed.

The monks assure me that I may stay on, but they see no reason why I should subject myself to their regime if I can find some other place to live. And I feel I can no longer ask them to care for me during these frequently recurring attacks.

"Tell me, my son," says Father Clément, having come to my cell to discuss what I must do, "why do you want to stay on here when our life is so bad for your health? Why not go back to Paris and return here in the spring?"

I hesitate before answering. "I know it sounds foolish, Father," I tell him after a moment, "but spiritually I'm too uncertain, too weak. It's not my work that keeps me here now, it's the hint of your life. I don't believe in it, and yet I can't leave it—at least not for a while. I still have no strength on the outside, but my desires are changed. It's just as if I were watching a chess game and didn't want to leave before learning the outcome."

"You are afraid to go back to your life in Paris? Is that it?"

"Yes. I know myself too well. I haven't been here long enough to make me want decency, just long enough to know I'll *some* day want it. So far, my separation has only made me miss what I left in Paris. If I should go back now I'd end up on the worst spree of my life. And this time it might be spoiled by doubt and regret."

I stare at my gloved hands. I am sitting next to Father Clément, and something within him, unspoken, makes me complete the story. I tell it not to him but to his warmth, and to the texture of his robe, and to the sores on his hands—and to all that he is.

"Also, there's a girl in Paris, Father. We lived together as students years ago. And when I returned after the war we got a flat together. It's impossible for me to be in Paris without eventually going back to her."

From the warmth sitting beside me the voice asks quietly, "You do not think she would understand, my son?"

"Yes, she'd understand," I reply, "and approve. It's not her fault. It's mine."

"Perhaps you could marry her?"

"I suppose I could, but it's not like that, Father. We aren't in love. We're just used to each other. We pool our money, and she does the cooking and washing. She's still in art school. It's always been a convenience for both of us. Two poor students can live well that way. We're good comrades, we sleep well together. But she doesn't want me for a husband and I don't want her for a wife."

"Have you had no children with this arrangement?"

"No, Father. We've been careful."

"My son, it is not in running away from this thing that you can help yourself. There is no merit in purity when there is no opportunity to be impure. There are only two ways to purity—either by marriage, or through the grace

97

of God. Since you have no vocation, you must marry. And as soon as possible."

I shake my head. "I'm a student, Father. I've gone too far with my studies to quit them now. I can't afford to marry till I finish this research." I pause a moment, choosing my words. "Actually it's not the flesh that bothers me; I've done that too much. It's something intangible—a question of honor, of basic honesty. My life might go on as it was, but if I left you now I'd always wonder if I hadn't missed something infinitely precious. And I know I can't live decently without help. Can't a person like me have such help?"

Father Clément sighs, "Not only do you not have our beliefs—which is relatively unimportant—but apparently you do not even believe in God. However, you have been honest with me. Tell me the truth"—looking at me gravely—"do you really want to renounce these impure habits now, this minute, and for all time?"

I walk about my cell, waiting to answer. "No, sir," I say at last, "I must admit I don't. I should *like* to want it, but I don't really. That's why I can't go all the way. I know I'll fall as soon as I get a chance—and with great willingness. If I stay here with you people, I'll have neither the chance nor the time to think of it. Don't you see? It's a question of time now. I have to have time in safety."

"Your experiment is impossible, my son. The two ways to purity which I mentioned are the only ones. There is no third way. And why this *one* sin? You seem to ignore others which are as bad."

"This one is more real to me, Father. And it's a test. If I can overcome it, there might be some reason to think I could become free of others."

"If only you could say no just once, is that it?"

"That's it, Father. Just once. And I don't even know why—except that I see all about me what it produces. And what I see is so much better than what I am, I can't help wishing it for myself."

"Ah, my son, my son," Father Clément says suddenly,

98

earnestly, "if you could only believe! What is this persistent peg that holds you so? If you could one time go into the chapel and pray to our Blessed Virgin. Why not try it—blindly, on faith? You cannot imagine what wonderful things will happen, what questions will be answered that cannot be answered."

I look at him frankly, shaking my head. "I couldn't do that. It would be embarrassing. The thought of it makes me sick in advance."

Father Clément doesn't force me. With an effort he gets to his feet, unconsciously picking at the cold scab on the back of his hand. "We pray for you here, my son," he says softly. "Many of our Fathers are men of great learning, and their learning was got on the outside. Surely if they can believe, you might wonder why you do not? God will come to anyone, but you must give Him the chance. Now I must go," he adds wearily. "It is my turn to draw water for the kitchen."

I imagine the aging monk straining to carry the heavy pails. "Let me help you," I say without thinking.

He laughs, snorting, "No, I can carry water as well as the next."

"Of course," I mumble, flushing. "Before you go, Father," I add quickly, to smooth over my mistake, "do you think I might move into a house in the Village, where I could have some heat and extra nourishment, and still spend my days at the Monastery?"

"Perhaps. We shall try to find you something. In the meantime I think you are right; you will do well to stay with us. But let me warn you: when you go out into the Village, you will find that the devil surrounds a monastery. You cannot imagine the things that go on in this innocent little countryside. You will have free opportunity to practice every sin in the book if you want to. Your only refuge will be here, for you will suffocate from temptation when you are alone in the Valley . . . But there is no hurry. You must stay on for some time. Next week we will have two distinguished visitors from Paris whom I want you to know."

"I don't care to know anyone from Paris, Father."

He ignores my ulcerous statement. "The one," he continues, "is a celebrated young monk of the Dominican Fathers on his way to become a missionary in the desert. He was converted here some years ago, and has since achieved a sanctity of the most extraordinary reality. He is accompanied by a Dr. Rafael Castelar from Central America. I have not met him, but he must be a man of interest to travel with Father Marie-Ornoux. We will see about your house when they have gone."

Alone in my cell, I think of our conversation. For the first time I have had the courage to be honest. I have told the story to Father Clément—simply, with no self-righteousness or boasting. In the face of this confession the hypocrisy of man overwhelms me.

For the moment the flash is there in conception. For no reason I write in my notebook, "Never tell Father Clément a lie, no matter what he asks," knowing that these things never last.

Someone knows—knows the worst. For the worst is not the act but the humiliation of acknowledging it as wrong. In Paris they know, too. But there they say, "Lucky devil, that Lucette should be a fine thing in bed," and there is a pride in the sound of it, with no acknowledgment or hint of wrong. That is the humiliation—my niggardly little desire to "do better." In this I have placed myself in the sore hands of Father Clément.

I read St. Augustine, and this time there is a drawing-out, a compulsion to read and to discover my malady. I am struck by this passage, so like my own remark to Father Clément: "O God, I want to be chaste, but not yet for a while."

Putting down the Augustine, I take up a little book from which the cover has been torn. It is a volume of spiritual exercises which seem insultingly naïve until I read:

I cannot know what is the conscience of a murderer or a thief, but I do know that the conscience of an honest man is a thing of hideous ugliness.

With what self-hypnosis do we persuade ourselves of our virtue as something merely had for the wanting!—like a woman become beautiful in a gown which hides the horror of a putrefying cancer. It must first be admitted within us before it can be ferreted out—if it is desirable that we ferret it out. But it must be recognized in order to be either cured or embraced. At least let there be no hypocrisy in admitting to ourselves that it is there.

9 december

Somber days again. Days without sun. The snows of a month have become the frozen filth of many footprints, reddened in the courtyard by gravel sprinkled there to keep us from falling.

Since Matins the morning has been spent working out a problem in morality, given us by Father Clément in his spiritual conference last evening. It is concerned with whether the renunciation of spiritual riches is a legitimate part of the vow of poverty. In some of the severer orders, tastes in music and art and literature are eschewed by the monks, who feel that their vows of poverty are not complete unless they include poverty of the spirit as well as of physical considerations. It contradicts the parable of talents. I arrive at no solution, hoping I won't be called upon in class today.

The cold becomes unbearable and I take my work to bed with me. The bed warms. Words imperceptibly detach themselves from the page. Words pulse in consciousness of eye near the page. Walls sweat. Wetness dribbles from steamed walls. Is a vow of poverty, does a vow of poverty legitimately include poverty of spiritual riches? The words focus into warmth beneath covering blanket. Move deeper into the bed. Poverty and richness of spiritual riches. The room turns. Dark outside the window of morning. Sweat on walls running down. Breaking away and running down. Hermetic rigidness and a tightening of smells. Smells and a tiny square of bareness on covered flesh. A coughing. Wheezing. Swallowing. Snorting. Head returns to its pillow. Back to the other. No class. In poverty there is. Walls dark with shadowed crucifix. Walls near bed. Turning from walls. Grit and musk and floor of mold. Pornography of. Sanctity in. Poverty. Back, back. The return. Footsteps in the hall. Approaching. There. Fading. Heavier breathing of rattling palate. Back. And back is return and behind. Either one. Back is return to questions. Of poverty. And ass. Either one. Black-robed nun with skirts and kindness of face. Kindness of all in poverty. Aching at nape. On and on and off to the other. Smell of bareness. It draws near and. It recedes. Kaleidoscope. Back is poverty. Legitimate. Night of all nativities. Phantasmagoria of back. On and on . . .

Class and a flood of light as I look up. Startled to look in the direction of a ticking clock. It sinks into the mind and touches something which makes me leap from bed. I have slept. It's past time for the noon meal. I have slept through the time of my morning classes, and now I run to the refectory.

The monks are seated. The reader reads. Their meal is almost over. No one looks at me as I walk quickly to my table. Food is brought, and bread, and a glass of water. I can't eat with the guilt of my sleep. I nibble the bread and drink the water. Atmosphere of fault. I have violated the rule under which we live.

After lunch I am called to the Father Prior, who suggests that I spend the afternoon carrying water from the frozen well into the kitchen, and when that is finished, scrubbing the toilet bowls with warm water. No reason is mentioned, but the coincidence is obvious; and I do my penance without question.

Water sloshes on my shoes, freezing instantly, and the effort makes my breath come in short gasps. Later, on my knees in one of the bathrooms, I scrub the toilet bowl with a long brush. The door opens behind me, but before I can turn, it is closed and the door to the next cubicle opened. I hear sounds of urinating, and take comfort in the knowledge that I'm not the only one who breaks rules. Footsteps crunch away into silence. I go next door to clean the yellowed, evil-smelling bowl, still steaming from the body warmth of unflushed urine. I sprinkle cleansing powder into the yellow liquid, and it bubbles a gas which drives me out. I scrub and rinse with hot water from the kitchen until the toilets are as clean as I can make them.

Since I work fast the penance takes only two hours. Father Prior tells me to utilize the rest of the time in cutting a stack of newspapers into six-inch squares, then placing them on the nails in each cubicle. This sober task is accomplished, but it takes longer than I had anticipated; for I can't resist scalloping some of the papers and cutting others in folded designs. Nevertheless, it's a humiliating job, and it's with a profound distaste for myself that I return to my cell to change wet socks.

Father Clément meets me on the stairs. "My son," he says, "I believe I may have some good news for you." The expression on my face makes him pause. "Was this afternoon that hard on you? I remember my first time. But you must not feel that you have been humiliated. It was not for that. Any work here is work for all of us; and each takes his turn."

We enter my cell, where I remove shoes and socks.

"I believe we have good news for you," repeats Father Clément. "I have talked to the Countess de la Villesverte, who has a small villa here in the Village which she occupies for only a few days each summer. She leaves it in the care of Madame Renée, and she assured me if Madame Renée approves of you as a tenant you may have the villa for

103

the winter. You may see Madame Renée this evening after Vespers if you like."

I am elated, instantly forgetting the water and the toilets and the squares of newspaper. "That sounds almost too good, Father. Tell me, what must I do to make Madame Renée approve?"

"It is hard to say. She is a strange woman. But I do not think you will have any difficulty. We have known her here for many years; in fact her son Michel is a monk at another of our Benedictine monasteries. Her younger boy was killed in a plane crash in England at the beginning of the war. From what we know, she is a woman of the world who has retired to this Village to take her place among the other so-called 'great ladies' here. These women cause us a great deal of trouble. They literally run the life outside. If they do not like you, they can make it impossible for you to stay. No store will sell provisions to anyone of whom they disapprove. I think Madame Renée is probably the best of them, for she is essentially a good woman and has shown great kindness to the farmers and the poor. But beware of these women, my son. Be nice to them, but try to have as little to do with them as possible. They are clever, and often vicious."

"If only I can rent the villa, Father," I tell him, putting on dry socks, "I'll spend my days here. That way I'll have no time for them."

"And remember what I said before, my son. You will have the opportunity to do anything you wish. Work as hard as you can here, and if a temptation arises which you cannot overcome, return to the Monastery and I will stay with you until you are safe."

"I hope I can make it to the Monastery, Father. It seems I can't set foot outside without having the opportunity—and the desire—arise." I tell him of the Salesky episode.

"Salesky is unique," remarks Father Clément when I have finished. "We know him well here. But do not feel so discouraged. You must know that you have made some progress. Your very desire not to do this, your repugnance

104

toward the Salesky favor—these are sensations which you would not have experienced three months ago. The very fact that you are trying means a great deal."

As he talks, I take the heavy blanket from my cot and spread it over our legs.

"You must know that as God works within you, the devil will work that much harder to keep Him out. You have only opened the door—and that involuntarily. You may as well expect what is to come. The devil will work overtime to undo the good which you have done yourself. You will be plagued with desires, with temptations, until this fragile sense of remorse is once again lost and sin becomes only a word as it was before." His words take him. His voice becomes a lulling caress of words and thoughts that he loves. "And this is so easy, so very easy, my child. The first time that you lie, that you do something selfish, that you fall with a woman, that you refuse to give charity to someone more in need than yourself—that first time you will feel a deep sense of loss. You will feel that something in you is no longer whole, that you have lost a precious part of yourself. That is what we call remorse. Remorse is not guilt, but loss. You will regret it as if part of your being had died within you. But the second time the remorse will become less, and the third time still less, till finally, to save yourself the torture of your loss, you will seek out occasions to sin; you will hypnotize yourself into a philosophy which, for some intellectual reason, by some logic, destroys remorse and places a belief in God and a love of Him into the category of superstition. For God must be destroyed in your make-up if you wish to sin with impunity. With this death of remorse, the devil will have won." His voice has died into a whisper.

In the same whisper my voice answers hoarsely, "I know you're right, Father. And I'm afraid that's exactly the course I'm going to follow. I'm not strong enough to keep myself from it." We talk to the walls in dead voices.

"You say," he goes on, "that you have been happier here, despite the hardships, than ever before in your life.

105

You will lose that, you know—you will lose it unless something is done. But it can be made to grow if you will *only* ask for God's help. Force yourself to go into the chapel. Beg God to have mercy upon you, and to help you by destroying the temptations which the devil will throw in your path—to destroy them until you have the strength to face them and to overcome them yourself, with His help. Then when you are stronger be thankful for those temptations, and pray for the ever-growing will to overcome them. That is a part of the health of our battle, my son. We do not seek the destruction of temptation, but only the power to destroy this potentiality for sin. All of us have been, and still are, ravaged by the conflict which you face. Most of us have had no more strength than you. You must get away from the idea that chastity, humility, and charity are virtues practiced by 'nice people' and not practiced by 'bad people.' No one can overcome these immense forces for evil without the help of God, and 'niceness' as such has nothing to do with it. Niceness is generally a lie necessary to our present-day civilization. Our society demands that we act 'nice,' no matter what we are. In here there is no necessity for that. In here the contrary is true."

Without smiling Father Clément looks up into my face, and straightens his legs beneath the blanket that covers us. I light a cigarette. He bends over, placing his elbows on his knees.

"As for the other," he says slowly, "I have thought much about that too, as have all of us. Look at it this way. When you do not eat you long for food, and when you do not have sexual contact with a woman you long for the flesh. But that longing is never satisfied merely through the satisfaction of the flesh, my son. Hunger can be satisfied by food, but the hunger of the flesh is in reality a longing for a sublimation above the mere act. That yearning, which takes the form of a physical search for ever-more rarefied pleasure, is a complex thing in which the spirit plays a more important role than we realize. If we look to a final solution, it is satisfied only in God. The spirit, the soul, needs that love, and the more it can burn you the greater is your happiness on this earth. For we can give our love to God— even our physical love, our sexual love. When the offer of chastity is made to God; when we can lie in our cots tortured by the desire for some physical object and pray to God, asking nothing, but giving Him this desire—then our love blossoms and bears a fruit of bliss and delight more health- ful and more ecstatic than all the sensations of the flesh combined. When the offer of our worldly goods, of every- thing which we consider important, is added, as it must inevitably be, then we begin to live with God; and He grows within us until the devil—and what is the devil but a dissonance of conscience?—is dissolved. That is the ideal, or very near the ideal, my child. And it is an ideal which you can have, which you can achieve without any calling, with no vocation to the religious life. You can achieve it in the measure in which you want to become that most blissful of earthly creatures—the man who lives in near- unity with God."

His words create an uneasiness within me. Conflict of ambivalent emotions. My cell is quiet. All things conspire to make his explanation seem plausible and real.

"If only I could be with you always, Father," I say to the cigarette in my hand, "I might hope for that. You make it sound so desirable and so easy to achieve in spite of the way I live. But the minute I meet a Salesky or some- one like that, I forget you and everyone else. I start look- ing forward to my next opportunity. Don't you see? I get a great deal of satisfaction out of that."

"I see, my son. You mention that you forget me and everyone else and start looking forward to your next op- portunity. And that is the answer. By that you mean that the idea of getting a girl, the first approach, the uncertainty of not knowing whether she will accede, and the experi- mental fumblings are usually the actual climax of your de- light. For does not the accomplishment often—nearly al- ways—come as an anticlimax? Of course it does. You think that each time may be the perfect one, and it never is. It

107

may be good, it may be fine, but something will always enter the picture as a disappointment—a word out of place, perhaps, or an unpleasant odor. It is only when we are hardened enough to take pleasure from aberrant coarseness that these things resolve themselves. The miracle, of course, is that all such things are nullified by great love. When a man loves a woman, then—and only then—will the climax come in the performance of the sex act and not in the contemplation of it. Why, then, do we continue to seek women? Because of the pleasure of anticipation, and because we are incurably optimistic about it. With God, my child—forgive me for mentioning Him in such context, but I wish to speak a language you can understand—with God the procedure is reversed. Our hopes, our contemplation of His love can in no way compare to the actual joy of becoming one with Him. In seeking the consummation of our love, when God gives us of Himself the wonder of it is a thousand times more profound than we could have dreamed. It is this bliss, the very hint of which causes many of us to spend our lives in the renunciation of earthly pleasures, that makes any sacrifice seem unimportant when compared to the hope that we may please our Adored Saviour, that we may merit His grace within us, and above all, that we may live with Him in heaven one day. Is it any wonder, then, that I beg you as a friend at least to open your heart to the possibility of making God a greater part of your life, as you see fit, and as He indicates to you?"

His voice has remained calm, and I am deeply moved by his simplicity. I hesitate, embarrassed at my ignorance of such matters.

"Frankly, Father, I never realized it could mean so much to you. I never knew that God—who's just an idea to most of us—could become so real to any man as He has to you."

"To all of us, my son," he says gently. "You see, we live in an unbroken line from St. Benedict. We live in the faith of the early centuries of Christendom, when Christ was still fresh in men's minds. People are inclined to think of us as frostbitten, sour old men, who come here to escape the world. Some think of us as men born in some special way, or who have been struck by lightning. Actually you find here, my son, the earth's most ardent lovers—ordinary men drawn into community by their common love of God. We come here not to escape the world, but rather to deprive ourselves of it. There are many vocations among the various monastic orders. Some preach, some do nothing but pray, some are missionaries, some care for the parishes. In the Benedictine order our place is largely contemplative adoration. We devote ourselves to the worship of God on earth. That is primarily why our rule is made so severe—because we wish to deny ourselves any pleasure not in God. But it is also made severe because some men persuade themselves of a vocation by autosuggestion. They enter the monastery with highly romantic ideas. We believe that only a true and powerful vocation can stand up under our regime."

"Do many of those who try, fail?" I ask.

"Not many, for we examine them thoroughly and advise only the strongest and most well balanced to come with us. But occasionally one will leave before the seven years' trial period is over—before he takes his final vows of poverty, chastity, and obedience. If a man has not the vocation, it will generally become manifest after the initial year or so of this life. Then he cannot go on, and we allow him to return to civilian life with no regrets; although we ourselves feel profoundly the great loss of him who might have been our brother, sharing this life with us."

The cold seeps through our covering blanket. Father Clément's jaws begin to tremble. We need to move about. I grind out my cigarette on the floor.

"Before we go, Father, I need to ask one more question. Why do you people seem so—? How can I say it? So—?"

"Commonplace? Ordinary? Is that what you mean, my son?"

"Yes, sir. You neither look nor act like mystics."

"How does a mystic look or act, my boy? But I know what you mean. We look and act like what we are—men

109

who *are* both commonplace and ordinary. Perhaps we are different from others in that we have fallen in love with God and seek always to please only Him. But there is nothing about that, that changes a man's exterior chemistry. Most of us are essentially students, researchers, and the like, so aware of our own deficiencies and shortcomings as to have an honest humility that destroys elegances . . . Now we must go. It is almost time for Vespers. We shall talk again whenever you like. Ah, my feet are numb from all this sitting still."

We tremble violently as we get to our feet. My back and ears ache from the cold. The five o'clock bells ring us to Vespers.

Darkness of early evening and a heavily overcast sky, at once separating us and drawing us nearer together. Loneliness of dark evening and frozen snows, dirty and sad in the courtyard. And a quietness that terrifies. I walk more closely to Father Clément in order to feel his robe, to assure myself that I am not alone. He leaves me at the chapel door, whispering but not urging, "Try a little prayer tonight, my son. I shall be praying with you."

"I've never felt like this before, Father," I confess. "When I talk with you everything seems possible. Look back at me during Vespers and I'll try."

Vespers begin in the foggy chapel, with the opening chant rising to settle over those present. We are not more than five or six in the darkness.

Long lines of Latin phrases take me, but feet wet and numb in my shoes can't be forgotten. Monks stand and chant, moving their bodies imperceptibly with the felt rhythm. But the cold draws us in and the movements are small and cowering, without freedom.

Another sense tells me that the chapel door is being opened silently by a young woman. She genuflects deeply to the candle-lit altar, then kneels in a pew in front and to the left. I can't see her face, but she is young and wears a Mexican shawl over her head.

Thoughts leave Vespers. In a twilight of forgetting

110

cold, I note her slenderness and the curve of her back in kneeling. The fever comes to my face, but my eyes won't look away from the heavily shadowed nothingness of buttocks.

Counterpoint of her prayers murmured in counterpoint to the chant, and floating somewhere above and about us. Evocation of incense of tonight and of all ages.

But you nourish the body, and from beyond, the voice of age declares hoarsely that there are indecency and common depravity involved. They slash you from yourself and it is abuse we don't name, little knowing it's a favor we bestow. Then it's a cutting and a searing and a burning; a violence of right that is known to be wrong through the judgment of many. And it is called evil—this which cannot in any way be.

The eyes that look down from above are sad. There is no sound left in the chapel except a choking of the insides struggling hopeless against a craving that has no being, a craving infinitely stronger than emotion. In its stomach is the heat of ice and the pain of wanting.

But those eyes are not here. And mine are the eyes left. They seek to penetrate the darkness, to know her back and the dream of her breasts. Flecks of struggle close my sight to this, and from somewhere remembered there drifts a pair of breasts imagined to be hers—Mexican breasts, dark, and softer than any other softness, and webbed with tiny blue veins near the surface; dark and splotched, and a drunkenness leading down from throat and up from belly. The vision returns whole again and again, as I try to thrust it from me.

Vespers move on. It is time for the adoration of the Blessed Sacrament. White-clad priests add candles to the altar. Calmness of movements and a fleeting image, and a badness of taste in the mouth and in the heart.

Unconsciously I go to the back of the church. Without thinking I put my gloved fingers into the font of holy water and bring the cold wetness to my lips, to kiss and to taste. Impersonal taste of wet leather.

111

The moment comes. The Sacrament is taken from the sanctum sanctorum. The priest raises high this body of our Lord. Quickly, as the sanctuary bell tinkles bravely throughout the chapel, I take another seat across the aisle. The bell rings again, and the Host is offered to the congregation to glimpse and to adore.

I look across at the Mexican girl. She is in profound obeisance, leaning forward on her knees. At the second bell she raises her head. Through frightened, timid, half-closed eyes she stares at the Host with the greatest longing, with the most ravished adoration. Only for a second she looks, for the sight is overwhelming. She closes her eyes, sways forward as if to faint, catches herself as her lips murmur a wordless prayer. Her hands close, tightly clasping the black beads of her rosary. It is the same with the others. Only I remain without feeling.

Father Clément glances in my direction. His eyes search, but they can't penetrate the gloom. I go to my knees, for I have promised to try. And the cold returns, and prayer from my lips becomes a natural madness.

"My God, my God, forgive me. Forgive me and have mercy upon me. Make me love Thee, make me love Thee despite myself. Force me, I beg Thee, to want *Thy* love." I lie in my prayer, but the words come, and I cringe from them. "Make me want Thee above all other things. Forgive me for my coldness. Let me learn the impossible grace; a faith, a belief, a love which is pure; a love which asks no questions, which expresses no doubts. Let me know why these other things are wrong, why they are really wrong. Let me, O God . . . "

The prayer dies in my throat with the chill—suddenly— as I wonder to what I've been praying. I waste my breath seeking an image that is false. No, no, they say it is real; it *has* to be real. But the doubt is there, and I cheapen myself and become a fake. I pray to a wall in which I have no belief because I think it may warm my belly with some trifling goodness of feelings. I utter idiotic prayers to a darkened vein of the soul. There's no help there. My

112

disgust is deeper now that I've done it—deeper than ever before. Fake, fake. If I were honest, if I had the blood of knowing, I would cleanse myself of this halfness in debauch. My lechery is purer than my prayers, and more respectable . . .

But in retrospect the pendulum of immediate disgusts swings to relief. It was the principle that destroyed, the principle of praying to a God I didn't know. No better than if I had prayed to the sun or to the moon or to a she-wolf. My brain is twisted against the wall of my ignorance. Father Clément will say it is infinitely better that I didn't pray to the sun or the moon—things which are known—but to the Maker of the sun and the moon and all the stars.

I stand in front of the chapel smoking a cigarette. After a moment Father Clément joins me.

"Come," he says with much warmth, "Madame Renée is waiting in the gatehouse. I see you tried our prayer, and that now you are disgusted with yourself."

"How in the devil did you know that?"

He laughs. "It happens to everyone at first. It happened to me the same way. Prayer of that sort is said to be highly aphrodisiac, but it is the devil himself who fights to make us recant, who puts the stutters in our prayers. You were obsessed by visions of the flesh. Ah, the cosmos is a strange thing. The devil makes his last stand in our weakest spot." He laughs again, a short, snorting laugh of grudging admiration for such diabolic strategy.

We stroll slowly in the direction of the gatehouse.

"All of us want the animal flesh," he says to the night air. "We know our way about on that plane. Every man instinctively wants it as a source of pleasure. As a last resort the devil will choose it as his battleground, filling us with heats that make us put off knowing God. We put it off, like St. Augustine, in the hope that some day when we are too old for such pleasures, we can piously renounce the devil and the sins of the flesh and devote ourselves as remainders to God. Remember, it is not the awakening of something new in you that causes this terrible urge. It is what often happens, and you must know about it. If now you can continue praying—blindly at first, against every disgust and discomfort—you may win."

I make no reply, turning over in my mind what he has said.

We enter the conference room in the gatehouse, where a beautiful woman awaits us. She appears to be middle-aged, with prematurely gray hair framing a youthful, unwrinkled face. Her skin is white and fine, and her expression, dominated by clear blue eyes, is relaxed. She is obviously a woman of the world who knows exactly what she's doing. In a glance we find each other sympathetic. Here is a woman who has had the courage to baptize a dead child. My doubts are resolved with the meeting; and I feel sure her reasons for baptizing the little Chevissier girl were open and honest and good.

I know immediately that I may have the villa. I tell her of my sickness, and of my need for good nourishment. She suggests I give her my ration cards and take my meals with her, sharing expenses. She is the finest cook in the Valley, she admits without hesitation.

"I am sure, Monsieur, that the Countess would want it that way. I live just across the street from your villa, and you'll see, my cooking is excellent. Of course I've never cooked for anyone but myself and my friends, but in France, you know, even those of us who come from the best families are taught to cook and sew."

It is quite clear that if I'm to have the villa I must agree to this arrangement. I tell her it will be satisfactory, and we decide on the first of January as the date of occupancy.

"It's understood, then, Monsieur," Madame Renée smiles. "You will move to the villa on the first. Come for lunch if you like, and I'll have some of the other ladies of the Village in to meet you."

As gently as possible, I sound the first warning. "I must tell you, Madame, that much as I'd like to be able to visit with the ladies of the Village, I can take off only enough time for my meals each day. I must spend the rest of the time either here at the Monastery, or at the villa. I think you should understand this from the beginning."

"I quite understand, Monsieur. Until soon, then . . ."

The news is known instantly. Father Dutfoy smiles when he sees me. "Well," he beams, "I understand you are to be a Villager now. Congratulations—but we shall hate to lose you."

"Thanks, Father, but you won't be losing me altogether. I'll have all the advantages of the Monastery without its disadvantages. I'll be here all day, and yet have a chance to warm myself and get some good food at noon and at night."

"Be careful of the outside, my son," he cautions, sounding an echo from Father Clément. "Stay clear of Madame Renée and the other 'great ladies.' They think they have been given some divine power to run Village life. They are clever, and often ruthless. Stay with us as much as possible and do not become entangled in the sordid affairs of the Village."

13 december

The Feast of St. Hilaire. This day of great celebration in honor of our Village patron saint, brings the obsession of cold to our first consciousness. We prepare for a pontifical High Mass, and after the Mass there will be a feast in the refectory for many invited guests.

With warm water from the kitchen I shave for the

occasion, but I haven't the courage to remove enough clothing to wash. Clean-shaven, I feel I've saluted the day to limits beyond those expected.

The atmosphere is festive as a great many men, wrapped to their chins in coats and scarves, stand in the little room of the gatehouse waiting for Mass to begin. Salesky is there looking uncomfortable. He too is shaved for the occasion, and there is about him an obviously rehearsed air of piousness and soberness. Nodding unsmiling in my direction, he looks virginal, as if a smile would be a sacrilege undreamed of in this holy place.

A first timid bell is immediately drowned by other bells, until the Valley is alive with clanging sounds calling Villagers to the feast. Grayness of skies reduces the Valley to a smaller plane—a vacuum between solid sky and frozen, snow-covered earth—as if we were together under the low ceiling of some large room. The Valley is peaceful, with the calm pallor of a Sunday death about it floating as fragrant smoke on the still air.

In the houses which line the River, one imagines meat and vegetables left simmering on the wood-burning stoves as entire families prepare to go to the Monastery. Children are dressed and sent to the outhouses for a last time, and given firm instructions to behave in church. Father tells them to hurry, he's been dressed for an hour. But the children argue and tell tales on one another until Mother —eternal Mother—inevitably announces, "It does seem to me that on this one day of the year we could have a little peace in the house."

Father laughs, for it's the same story every church day. He sends the children out to play.

Mother pulls her good hat to the proper angle on her head. "Do I look all right?" she sighs. "I never have time to get myself dressed."

"Yes, you're fine. Come on."

She walks past him to go out the door. He pats her on the back—a touch that once meant something but which has, with the years, become automatic and unfelt . . .

116

We enter the chapel until it's full, and those who are left go to the parish church. This beautiful Mass with its color, with its rhythm, with its slowness of movement, becomes commonplace confronted by the coughing, noisy Villagers. Calm, measured cadences grow static beneath the paralyzing desire of those present to have it finished, a desire felt by everyone and communicated into the very atmosphere. In such a crowd, body heats warm us. The children behave. Those of us who have been alone in the chapel for daily Mass, feel a jealous anger that our beauty has been taken from us, that our privacy has been destroyed. Briefly I notice the veiled head of the Mexican girl, but this time the visions are quiet.

The service lasts too long, almost till noon. We pour from the chapel, some to return home for comfortable clothes and a good meal, others to stay for the feast in the refectory. The calmness remains on the frozen air. Our beings are permeated by a contagious awe of the day.

Possessed by an overwhelming desire to be alone, I walk precariously up the ice-covered steps to await lunch in my cell. The room is clean and bright in its smallness. Decrepit gray walls appear warm, and the crucifix above my cot surveys the scene with its fixed wooden sheen. This ugliness of cell welcomes me, infusing a calm into every portion of my being, spreading into the narrow backwaters of my very self. I am home. I take off my shoes and lie on the bed. It is a physical outpouring, an extension of sensation—desiring nothing, devoid of all thought—in the vacuum of the moment . . .

Father Clément drops in. "Are you resting, my son?" he inquires.

"No, Father, come in. I'm not doing anything. Won't you sit down?"

"Thank you," he says smiling. "I have been thinking about you. You are too much cooped up here. What are you going to do this afternoon?"

"I don't know, Father. I don't seem to be able to read or put my mind on anything today."

117

"Then how would you like to walk into Town? There will be no classes and you will miss nothing. You should enjoy the walk. Take an afternoon off, go to the tea shop for a cup of hot chocolate, buy yourself a good dinner. I believe it will be good for you."

"I think I will, Father. Might even go to a movie. But this is a feast day for the monks. Mightn't I bring something back for you?"

"Not for me, my son. But since this is an important day in our lives, perhaps you could bring back a sack of dried dates and prunes which we can divide among the other Fathers and Brothers. I am sure the Father Abbot would not mind."

After a feast-day lunch of oysters and lentils and cake, I walk swiftly the three miles to Town.

The enchantment of the Valley is felt everywhere. The streets are almost deserted, and there's no noise. A few children play in the snow-covered square near the public urinal, in which water no longer flows. Their shrill voices echo in staccato phrases from the hollowness of early afternoon.

And it crashes, this security, giving way to a trembling of loneliness. The day is somber and cold, and the streets are deserted. I am seized by a desire to go into the first store and buy something—anything—so long as I can speak and hear another voice answering.

I walk past windows closed against winter; windows on the sidewalk, curtained, hiding interiors where people read the newspaper and smoke and sleep after a good lunch. And I know exactly how they are inside. I know the carpets, and the chairs, and the tables, and the fringed lamps. And the comfort of comfortable clothes and of cleanliness and of the puffings of full digestion after food. Things of this life which make it ordinary and wonderfully real. Things no longer a part of mine. Dusts and fatty foods and smells of this morning's paper. Stuffed chairs with worn nap, and pictures of the family. All closed from me behind windows and curtains. All in a world out of reach. Their

118

feet are warm and mine are cold. They live big and I live little. And I want it now. I want these things which go to make our lives ordinary and real . . .

I stop at the open door of a shop. Sweet, pungent odors of spices and soaps on the cold air of the unheated store. And she is there, an ugly woman behind the counter. I look at her and I want her. I want to have her in a filth as great as the filth of my feelings. But she leans forward, and I know the stink of her fat folds. Without speaking I leave.

But the harm has been done. My legs become weak, and my face burns with the uncontrollable desire to find something to take into a bed. This is played in dissonance against the complete consciousness of what I'm going to do, and of the admonitions of Father Clément. It's too far now—the voice of it is cracked and weak and it knows it's too far. My entrails ache to be back in the safety of the Monastery, and my every wish pulls hopelessly against the inexorable line of my body as it becomes a detached thing ignoring my hopes, my prayers, and my pleadings. I no longer have control over it. The body drags me through the streets despite the sickness of my realization that it is subverting all I've done. I watch it drag me through the snow in quest of its prey; brutal in its thirst, in its fever; giantlike in its strength of purpose.

Let there be a first time, the weakness moans, *let there be something to stop this.*

I turn to walk back to the safety of Father Clément, who will know the right things to say to kill this force so much greater than my force.

But the body laughs. The body has no ears and no intelligence, and it refuses to move in my direction. Carrying me along the streets, it seeks its own goal. Through the glass window of the tea shop I see a lone woman seated at a table. Before entering I know in every part of my being that she is there for me, and that it's too late and too far.

I take a table next to hers, and order a cup of chocolate

119

from a woman I don't see. My ears burn. I light a cigarette with shaking hands. I am sick, and my legs ache beneath the table with two refrains: *Know her warmness—Go back, go back.* But the last refrain is weak and faint, and the first is of a strength that fills me with the impulse of a beast.

This woman is mine already. Already I know how her body will be; how the navel will fold in her belly, and how her legs will have the buttermilk markings of used flesh which has once been firm. For she's not young and damp. About forty, with blond hair swept to the top of her head, and a small Parisian hat. She will know already. And hers will be the answers to questions forever asked.

I smoke and stare, calm on the outside, and she asks, "You're the young man staying at the Monastery, aren't you?"

"Yes, Madame. And I suppose you're here for the Feast of St. Hilaire?"

"That's right. I have a son named Hilaire. The service was beautiful this morning, wasn't it?"

We talk, we look at each other, and as people who want the same thing always do, we let our desires be understood. I play the youth honored to attract her notice—somewhat awkward, seeking to understand these things, honest to a point of high crudeness, and deeply sincere. And she is the perfect counterpart, a widow from Paris—intelligent, helpful, but wanting someone to lean on. A woman confused and alone in the world, who is trying to find the solution to her problems here at the Monastery. A woman profoundly unhappy and at a loss for companionship. We are both absurd; but we need each other.

"It must be very difficult, Madame," I say to her, fighting to keep my voice even, "when once you've been married, to get used to living without love."

"Ah yes, Monsieur," she says softly. "It is—very difficult."

"That relationship between a man and a woman can be made such a beautiful thing," I say musingly, and then,

120

forcing deep sympathy into my voice, "I've never been married but I've had many girls, and I know what it can mean. I've always thought of it as a great privilege."

My stomach prods me to hurry. I know my way on this ground. I am at home with such disconcerting inanities. But this is too rushed, too obvious—too laughably obvious.

She smiles, looking at her cup. "You're quite a Don Juan, Monsieur. You embarrass me."

"Not a Don Juan at all, Madame. I'm just giving you credit for being what you are—a beautiful woman of the world. But you must forgive me. I'm being honest. I think we both want the same thing, and I think we can help each other. If I'm wrong I apologize."

"You're really very nice, Monsieur"—nonchalantly, with ease and grace of manner. "Perhaps we could have dinner tonight?"

"That would be fine. But look, I must return after dinner and we have an afternoon before us. Let me get a room at the hotel where we can be warm. We can visit there until dinner time."

My eagerness catches her, coloring her throat into a blush with the beginnings of desire. She smiles a yes without answering.

I pay the two checks, take her arm, and we go to the hotel. The hotel keeper and his wife, who remember this young man, smile openly, delighted at my luck. They give me a room with bath and have the grace not to mention that we have no bags. My warmth toward them grows.

The room is heated—blessed heat. I help her off with her wraps, with the touches such closeness indicates. We sit on the bed and light cigarettes, feeling frozen feet beginning to come to life. The actors of the play continue acting, for it's not yet the time when acting can cease. With a loud but honestly felt sigh, I take her hand in my own to study it, and her pressure answers mine.

"You don't know what it means to hold someone's hand again," I tell her.

"I feel the same way. You're very sympathetic, my

121

friend." She glances up at me—quickly, half-tentatively. "And you're very beautiful."

We fondle hands and then arms, until words die in a vast, sobbing, all-engulfing joining of our mouths. The approach is forgotten as the kiss becomes its own fever. Burning outpouring of her tensions into me and mine into her, resolving all tensions into the health and strength of ministrations from a common source. Our breaths catch like two people who drink too long after great thirst. The feverish intensity of starvation flows out from us and we relax our bodies, fainting against each other in relief as muscles melt and the kiss insinuates itself as a pure line of pleasure between us. Now the cauterizing initial healing has taken place. Now the therapy of a needed kiss is accomplished. Now we can take pleasure one from the other. The dissonance, the ugliness leave, and a clumsiness of beginnings gives way to the ineffable grace of animal responses. As the soul is purged of its hermetic smallness, of its grit of modesty, the demands of our bodies become more powerful.

Breathless I lift my face from hers. "I can't believe it," I gasp. "I've never felt like this before—never. It's almost like we're really one. Do you feel it too?"

"Yes, yes," she murmurs passionately. "Yes."

I hold her there in wonder, tenderly stroking her cheek, brushing the fine blond hair back from her forehead: small movements of waiting, movements suspended dimensionless. And at last her breathing subsides against my breast, and my hands stop trembling. Reality slowly returns to the room.

"Now, my sweet," I urge gently when I feel I can speak, "you must let me go and take a bath. I should have done it before, but I didn't know we'd meet. You can rest here on the bed."

"Can't I help you?"

"No, I'd never get through if you did. And I'd rather come back to you here in bed."

Leaving the bathroom door open, I throw my clothes on the floor. While the hot water is still running I step

122

into the tub. The soap spreads and cleans. The nearly forgotten luxury of soap bubbles on wetness of skin is enchanting. I soap and rinse again and again in the warm water. There is no longer any struggle between my two selves. We're both very happy. Poor Father Clément! I smile, imagining that he imagines me in a movie.

"You're awfully slow, my dear," comes her voice from the bedroom.

"Are you in bed?"

"Yes, and I'm lonely."

"But I haven't had a bath in three months."

"Oh, la! Then take plenty of time."

I splash about in the water. "Come in here, won't you?" I call to her. "I need some help."

She enters the steaming room, with a sheet around her, to find me lying in the tub. "Ah!" she exclaims, "that's pretty, for example."

"Would you please wash my back?"

"With pleasure, M'sieu." She says this in imitation of the broad patois of the farm women. "But how can I wash M'sieu's back unless M'sieu turns over?"

I turn on my stomach in the warm soapy water. In silence she scrubs the length of my back, seriously, as if I were a child. I turn back over, splashing water onto the stone floor.

"Thanks very much, my sweet."

"Not at all. And I was good about it, eh? No tricks."

"You were wise. It's been a long time since I last made love. I'm very delicate."

She changes the subject: "Tell me, how do you bathe in the Monastery?"

"In a little tub—a foot bathtub—a little at a time. But the cells are unheated and it's impossible to bathe in this weather. But I would have anyway, if I'd known we were going to meet."

"Today is the Feast of St. Hilaire. You wouldn't bathe for him, but you will for me. I'm flattered."

"I doubt if he'd have appreciated it as much as you

123

will. Now if you'll please leave, Madame, I'll dry myself."

"Strange—you let me wash you, and you don't have anything on in the bathtub; and yet you want me to leave while you dry. Why is that?"

"I don't know. It just seems to work that way."

The smiles stop. With the end of my bath approaches the instant of consummation; the beginnings of nervousness in both of us. She returns to the bed.

When I am dry I turn to go to her. Breath catches in my throat, and I run to the bed. Without looking, without thinking, I draw myself into it, under the covers and into the oblivion of her body. We lie close, discovering in blind embrace the secrets of the warmth within us. There's no time and no reality as arms bring tightness to our embrace, as our stomachs press together until they dissolve into one. No longer do we kiss only with our mouths drinking each other—our arms, our legs, our stomachs join in the kiss, becoming fused in a caress that envelops all. Hands descend the length of warm flesh, till they come to rest in the fleshiness of buttocks, the very feel of which fills us with profound drunkenness. Hands search further into our innermost selves, and without losing the thin fine line of sensuality that floats through closed eyelids . . . we become slowly united.

No longer a man and a woman, but a revolving bodiless emotion. Deeply, more deeply into the liquidness of her, into the void of swirling sensation. Slowly like the waves of a warm ocean, inexorable, undulating out of space and time. Blackness and silence in the roaring of two become one. Angles, brilliant behind eyes that swim in detached body, floating in space. Richness and warmth and coolness of the wet on one's lips. Lips against her face feeling skin pores. And smoothness of soft cheek and shoulder. Squares mist milkily, and from the stillness and the dark the curve mounts immutably rhythmic, in ever-mounting intensity. A new gathering of momentum. And through the darkness an occasional glimpse of concentrated white. Now it begins to grow, this strangeness, turning over and over. Slowly,

124

slowly, turning steadily, and the rhythm follows ever growing. And now from the very bottom of a faraway numbness is the quivering beginning of trembling. It's unbearable. The numbness is punctured. Momentum gathers. And the long sigh, unheard, pouring forth from the edges of consummation. From a distance, far within, curving swiftly now, a fast sighing swaying motion curling over and above and around. Beating, beating against the drum of the being, pounding louder and louder till there can be no more loudness, but increasing steadily into the very pulse of the blood. And now before the eyes, the before-hinted, now-brilliant flashing white, growing and expanding to break spattering against eyelids. And from without, a fog of ever-thickening intensity, sparkling and harsh to imagined sight. Simultaneous welling-up of the heaving exploding brilliance, and the beating, now-pounding rhythm piling sound and muffled obscenity, ever expanding above and around, turning faster and faster above the moaned "No! No!" Tightening of the heartbeat, drawing-up of the ribbon. Ecstatic point between life and death when all becomes hermetic and rigid. The pause in space without pausing in movement. The waiting without breathing. The muffled upward surge of the entire being to the crest of the wave, to the very top. Up and up, soaring high onto the peak of noise and heat. The whirling gyrating splash of warning to the mind. Louder now into the head and the brain. Upheaved violence of the belly. This is the flashing of the stars, the cleansing burning of the insides into fervent ash. And the taste of blood grows stronger on the rigid tongue. Finally the broad expansiveness of union, of man's warmness without pain. Sounds descend thinner, slower, draining away to sighing quiet. And the felt pulse of the rhythm faints away to enveloping blackness. The slow easy downhill slide with a final unheard catching of the breath, leading onward and downward until the curve slows to stop against the dark. And down, down again slantingly, quietly to a depth beneath the seas. Beyond movement to stillness. Then the loosening, the resumption of

125

breathing. Gratitude, and the serenity of silent waters.

Heads fall apart. Light returns. There is rest now without moving. Rest with the body spent, the head facing down on the pillow of her shoulder. Rest for a long time without becoming separated, feeling only the warmth of her breathing and the stir of her hair against my cheek. Life returns. The room becomes real. Without moving away we roll to our sides, still tightly clasped. And we sleep.

For how long I don't know. Without awakening I find myself awake, still enclosed in her arms. She breathes heavily in her sleep. We are no longer united. The room no longer moves. It remains quiet in its smallness, telling the tale better than we could tell it.

The gray light of winter's afternoon filters through the dusty lace curtains beside our bed. A rug on the floor has lost its color through wear and the accumulation of dust. It is a thin, pathetic covering for the blackened wood floors. On a gold-fringed overstuffed chair near the window, her clothes are draped—pinks of underclothes and darkness of hose hung neatly over the arm. Through the bathroom door can be seen my clothes, in a filthy pile where I left them. And on the tub a roughness of damp towel hanging at a thrown angle.

Room of heavy shadows lighted only by somber afternoon, and soundless. A room which would be intolerable if I were here alone, but which has taken on a fattish, conniving atmosphere because I am in bed with something human, with something that lives and breathes and sleeps.

In her dreams she turns on her back. My head rests on her shoulder beneath the blankets. In the microscopic perspective of nearness the coarsely woven pillowcase, white and wrinkled, is brought into clarity of focus. Every thread can be seen, and minute portions of brown starch-stain streak the pattern of freshness. The eye shifts to shoulder flesh and focuses on an inch of skin, seeing pores and smoothness and oiliness and one speck of dryness that irritates— white, flaky, dead. Moving my cheek against it I brush

126

it away. My head cradled on her shoulder is half-covered with the blanket. We lie here warm and drying—and she sleeps.

Smells from under covers, smells when sight grows tired. Odors of neutral nakedness of flesh. Odors of shoulder and belly and of the dried hint of frenzy, mingling with those of blanket wool and coarse linens. Odors of the sweetness of unperfumed being, captured in a warmth of darkness beneath covers. Profound satisfaction of the senses by touching and breathing, and the sleep of a body in the arms of wakefulness. I raise my leg across her thighs and lie close to her, with the inside of my leg, above the knee, resting on her stomach.

Without opening her eyes she murmurs drowsily, "You're suffocating me, my friend."

"Oh, I'm sorry. I didn't know you were awake." I raise my head.

Her eyes open to see a face that has lost its strain, and she smiles. "Are you happy, my darling?" she asks.

"It was marvelous. Shall we go again?"

"No—some other time perhaps. The next time wouldn't equal the first and we'd both begin to regret it."

"But I want you."

"No, please—don't." She reaches down and moves my hand away.

"All right, my dear," I say coolly. "Then let's get up. I can't lie here with you without trying."

"Yes, go into the bathroom and dress," she says almost apologetically. "I'll spread up the bed and get dressed myself."

"Fine—so modesty returns. Very well, my sweet, up with you."

I go into the bathroom, sickened at having to put on my filthy clothes again. We continue talking as we dress. Gradually with the ebbing of desire, my resentment leaves. I become conscious of a growing gratitude toward this woman who has given me so much.

I call through the door, "I'll treat you to the best dinner

in Town—all you can eat. This hotel has excellent food."

She joins me in the bathroom, standing before the mirror combing her hair. "I'm supposed to take dinner in the Village," she says through a mouthful of hairpins. "Maybe we'd better go back."

"Nonsense. Don't tell me you're the sort who likes to make love and run?"

"No, but food is high here. There's no need for you to spend any more on me."

The thought that I have bought her only a cup of hot chocolate strikes us both as ridiculous, and we laugh like two children.

"Ah," I chuckle, "two and a half francs. You're an expensive woman. But I'm a perfectionist, my sweet. Unless I fill your stomach from the *top* this time, I'll feel my work is only half-done."

"You *are* a pig . . . But really, let's eat somewhere else. These people would think me brazen. They'll suspect what we've been doing."

"And for once their suspicions will be justified. No," I grin, "we'll eat here and give our friends the pleasure of being right about us."

"But I'm not a brazen woman."

"I know you're not, my dear. But the point is, you've been doing all afternoon just what a brazen woman would do."

"You embarrass me." She is offended. I have gone too far.

"Come now," I say softly, "I'm only joking. You know that. We'll eat wherever you like. And believe me, I want to take you to dinner because I like to be with you, and not just because I'm grateful."

She lifts her face and smiles. "All right."

"Now, shall I keep this room for a few days? We can come here every afternoon."

"But what about your work at the Monastery? Surely you can't leave that? Didn't you tell me your work was your life, your only passion?" The suggestion of a smile is

128

at the corners of her mouth. "Isn't that what you said?"

"Yes, but not *all* my life," I mutter, feeling like a fool. "And I find I have other passions, too."

"Even so, I don't think we'd better keep the room. I must tell you, as much pleasure as this has given me and as wonderful as it's been, I'm here for another purpose. I'll confess what we've done, receive penance, and make every effort not to do it again."

I shrug my shoulders. "You're probably right. This couldn't be helped today. I know what you're trying to do and I respect you for it. I'm afraid I've set you back. But it's easy to be virtuous once passion is satisfied. I feel pretty Christian right now, myself. But what shall we do when we feel it again? Can what we've done be so terribly wrong?"

She is silent a moment. "I don't know," she hesitates. "But I'll do as the monks say."

We walk down the carpeted stairs to the lobby. I stop to pay the bill while she waits in the hall near the entrance.

The proprietor feigns surprise when I approach the desk. "But, M'sieu, you arrived only a few hours ago. We can't charge you for a room you've scarcely used. No, there'll be no charge. We'll just put someone else in the room, and since you haven't slept in the bed we won't have to change the linens."

I put some bills on the desk. "Here, take the money and an extra twenty-five francs for the chambermaid."

"But, M'sieu, I don't understand. Since you haven't slept in the room, what will the chambermaid have to do?"

"Believe me, my friend, the room has been well used. And the chambermaid will more than earn her twenty-five francs."

He would like to know more, but I turn away and join my companion at the door.

"Now for some good dinner, Madame," I smile. "I'm famished."

After dinner we walk back to the Village together, in the specter of ever-more chilling dusk. The Valley is de-

129

serted. Everyone has been driven in to families and lights and food. Not touching, we walk slowly under the heavy grayness of almost-night, through a countryside crisp and covered with snow. Our footsteps crunch the icy path. Around us is the colorless landscape of winter, empty and intolerably sad.

"Thank heavens you're with me," I tell her quietly. "I'd die of loneliness if you weren't here."

"And I feel the same, my friend. I'm glad we're together."

We walk on in silence, unhurried. First stars appear, seeming to bend to the snow, and the scattered covering of luminous skies fills me with the chill of longing. There's a growing awareness that we are but two brief moments of life, suspended apart in the frozen purity of night's beginnings.

"Tell me what you're thinking?" her voice murmurs from the darkness beside me.

I feel for her arm. "I was just thinking," I say slowly, "it's like we'd never slept together now. We're just as we were when I met you in the tea shop. I've known you in the most intimate way possible, and yet we're like strangers. With other women it's different. Afterward you get more and more intimate, till finally it's no longer exciting. If you were anyone else I'd stop right now and take you in my arms and kiss you. But I don't feel like doing that with you. It wouldn't seem right."

"It's only the night and the cold," she reassures me. "It's so lonely out here in the dark we get wrapped up in ourselves."

I shake my head. "No, it's more than that. It's a feeling I have for you. And yet it's nothing like love. If you should leave tomorrow I wouldn't miss you in the slightest. I don't know, I'm terribly confused. This afternoon I hated you for being there to tempt me. I just wanted to have you and get it over with as quickly as possible, knowing how much I'd regret it later—not because of what I'd done, but because I hadn't been able to resist the temp-

130

tation. You see, I'd persuaded myself that that was the sin—not ever being able to resist temptation."

"But you're wrong, my friend. The sin is in us, in what we've done. Like you, I can't feel it was really wrong, but I know it was. We're no different from anybody else."

"We feel the same, don't we? Neither of us understands."

She moves closer to me: instinctive seeking of warmth. Her voice is softness, accompanied by the loudness of footsteps breaking through crusts of snow. "Yes, we do feel the same. You might always have been my lover, for we seem to be much alike. But it's dangerous for us to think like this—very dangerous. We mustn't persuade ouselves that it's right. We have to play by the rules of the game even though we don't understand them. We can't presume to think that we're right and all society wrong."

I say nothing, and she draws still closer to me.

"We're cool now," she whispers, and the night takes her words. "Our passion is spent. While we're in our senses let's make up our minds not to see each other again."

I am silent a moment before answering; but I know there's nothing else to be done. "If you wish," I acquiesce. "Maybe some day I'll learn the reasons. Do you really believe either of us would be better off right now, if we hadn't been together?"

"I don't know—I really don't know. That's what makes it so hard for people like us."

"At any rate I'll never forget you—or what you've done for me."

We are close to the bridge. We walk a few steps farther, then I lay a hand on her arm.

"I think we'd better separate here," I say gently. "You go where you have to go and I'll return to the Monastery. Good-bye, and good luck. Let's hope we're doing the right thing."

It is dark night. She moves from my touch without saying anything more. Her footsteps take her into the shroud of obscurity, fading away. I stand here until she is out of

131

sound, this woman who has answered my questioning numb-
nesses. The delicate scent of her face powder remains to
die on the air. I know nothing of her, nor of her destiny,
nor in what bed she'll find sleep and warmth this frozen
night.

A half-chill brings me to my senses. I feel a sudden
gladness that the day is gone with her footfalls. I pick up
my step and my spirits, and find myself laughing with
pleasure and relief as I enter the darkened mass of stone
that is home. I walk carefully past the faintly lighted
chapel: muffled sounds of Compline, which will be followed
by the Great Silence. For tonight, at least, I am safe. No
explanations can be asked till morning.

But with my return, returns a remembered promise. It
stops my steps and my heartbeat, burning my face in the
dark, striking my consciousness and my conscience. The day
has made me forget my purpose in leaving the Monastery.
They chant their prayer of night and of rest, these monks
to whom I'm more devoted than I know; these monks who
would have taken such pleasure from the dried fruits I was
to bring them. A prune or a fig, with Father Abbot's permission, would have meant more than can be imagined to
these men who have so little. It would have been a celebration in keeping with the day. In my happiness of the afternoon, I have forgotten *their* happiness.

As dust in my mouth become the pleasures of the bed,
the good dinner, the night of stars, the woman's arm—those
things which only a few moments ago filled me with such
peace. Stripped of its suggestive elegances, I have done
nothing more than sleep with a woman. Nothing more
than that. Only my guilt remains. In the chapel below, as
I undress, many men pray. Men who have cared for me
when I was sick. Men who share their food and goods with
me. Men who are my brothers. Men who have awaited
my return and the small pleasure it might bring to a day
of celebration. Men who have waited and whose waiting
was futile. The pleasure of the many sacrificed for the
pleasure of self. All that thrown away for the filthy little

132

heats of holding a woman's naked buttocks in my hands.

I take off my clothes and throw them in a heap on the floor. I am freezing, and sick with guilt at having forgot. In my pajamas, trembling violently from the cold, I crawl into my cot. Its hardness calms and forgives. I shall return to Town early in the morning. I shall tell the monks I forgot my package in the tea shop. Father Abbot will let his monks eat today's gift tomorrow.

Compline ends in the chapel below. In the silence which settles heavily over the Monastery, I hear the shuffling of cautious footsteps finding their way to my cell in the dark. I know it is Father Clément coming to see if I've returned, before seeking sleep himself.

The door opens, and a hand scrapes across the wall feeling for the light switch. Light floods the room to reveal the ruddy cheeks and the hands blue from cold of Father Clément. The rest is a blackness of his robe, and a blackness of hall beyond the door. A few gray hairs straggle onto his forehead from under the cowl.

I pretend to sleep, looking at him through partly closed eyes. He approaches, glances at my clothes on the floor, and looks into my face. I breathe heavily as in sleep. Walking carefully he retrieves my overcoat from the floor, and spreading it over my feet and legs, tucks it under the straw mattress. There is a firm tugging at the cot as he makes certain I am covered. Finally he turns to go, looking back once again before pressing the light switch.

Without opening my eyes I grin broadly. Father Clément, surprised, snorts in disgust that his tendernesses have been watched. Then he smiles just as broadly, and returns to my bed to shake hands—the only way we have during the Great Silence of saying that everything is all right, and of bidding each other good sleep.

After the room is dark again, thoughts of the afternoon become confusing. Right and wrong intermingle, and I force my mind away from them. Some of the feeling has returned—the sensuality of tired muscles, and the emptiness inside the stomach. My sleep is dreamless, profound.

14 december

It is seven o'clock, and I have slept through Matins and Lauds. Rain and sleet pour against my window as if the elements were determined to prevent my going into Town for the dried fruits. But if I could forget them for yesterday's pleasure, I can certainly suffer weather's discomforts to get them today. I put on every piece of clothing I own, and take my umbrella from the corner. In the corridor I pause for a moment before stepping out into the rain. I am just opening the umbrella when Father Clément's voice causes me to turn. He is coming rapidly down the hall, and I walk back to meet him.

"Where are you going in this weather, my son?" he asks.

Instead of answering him I suggest, "Let's go in my cell, Father. I have something to tell you."

"My son," he begins, when I have closed the door behind us, "I am not going to ask you what happened yesterday. I feel, as a matter of fact, that I may have been too forward in pressing you to do what I have believed to be right."

"I'm terribly sorry about yesterday, Father, and about oversleeping this morning. But please don't lose interest in me. You've done me a great deal of good."

"But I have not lost interest in you, my infant—not in the slightest. I only meant that I do not want to lead you where you do not want to be led. I never want my enthusiasms to make you uncomfortable."

"Father, I can explain about last night. In Town yesterday I met a young couple I'd known in Paris. We had dinner together, and simply talked till it was later than I realized. But I did buy the fruit for you—only I left it at the hotel where we had dinner. I was just going for it when you caught me."

"Are you out of your mind, my son? None of us would
134

permit you to go out in this weather for a bag of dried fruits. You exaggerate their importance, it seems to me. Oh, yes—and I am surprised—you slept in your pajamas last night for the first time since the freeze. Father Dutfoy will be impressed by your newly found stoicism. Now, why not get some breakfast and begin your work?"

He leaves, breaking the conversation short. It passes easily, the explanation, and I'm relieved that I don't have to go for the fruit. I have lied to Father Clément for the first time.

We work in the paleography room, a loudness of swirling sleet against our windows. At ten o'clock we turn on lamps. Dampness penetrates the paper manuscripts, roughening them between our fingers. Father G'seau enters late, his robe covered with crystals of sleet and frozen rain. The ice doesn't melt.

We work, but my work is poor this morning. I am distraught with my lie, unable to forget a penciled notation in my notebook: "Never tell Father Clément a lie, no matter what he asks."

Uneasiness can't be swallowed. It ruffles beneath the skin and grows as a nervousness throughout the morning of outside storm. It is a barrier, and barriers are intolerable in this place; barriers isolate and separate, and loneliness becomes its own obsession. With no explanation to Father G'seau I close my books and walk out the door.

It must be done quickly, while the heart beats in the throat: quickly and simply, and with assurance. I find Father Clément writing in his cell. It pours from me as renderings boil from a caldron, flowing over onto the floor of my being.

"Father, I must do something that takes away my last ounce of self-respect. I must tell you the truth. If I don't, all the good you've done me will be ruined."

His mildness turns to concern. "What is it, my child?"

"The whole thing is a lie—everything I told you."

"That is all right, my son. You have done me no wrong, only yourself. And now you have the courage to undo the

135

wrong. That is very difficult, I know. Do not tell me what happened. It is much simpler that way. And do not let this embarrass you. To undo a lie is perhaps the most humiliating thing we can know."

"I'm so confused, Father," I tell him. "Things don't fall into the neat little pattern you've described. I got a woman yesterday. We spent the afternoon in a hotel room. And I forgot all about bringing back the fruit for the monks. That too was a lie."

"The fruit is of no consequence, my son. Now you are sorry for the other, is that it?"

"No, Father, this was different. If it had been with anyone else, I'm sure I *would* have been sorry. I was sick with remorse before it happened, but afterward . . . it was so different. We agreed not to see each other again, but simply because we knew what we were doing was wrong, wrong from the outside—although neither of us felt it, really."

Father Clément shifts in his chair and stares out the window. "You are in a very delicate spot, my son. You are trying to be something too advanced for your present stage of spiritual development, and I believe you may succeed for the simple reason that you are willing to do things. You are willing to give up this woman who is obviously not ordinary—not because you understand, not because you *think* it right, but uniquely because something in which you do not even believe forbids such actions. What a marvelous step forward, this trusting blindly something in which you *want* to believe!" He turns to look at me. "I am indeed pleased."

"You find virtue where none exists, Father. It seems to me all the good's been undone." I shrug my shoulders disconsolately. "Well, now at least you know. I'll leave you with your work."

"No, no," says Father Clément, rising from his chair. "There is no need to go." He motions toward the bed. "Sit down and let us talk for a while."

"What's the use?" I say, disheartened. "I'll behave

136

myself for a time and then fall again. There no longer seems any reason to try if I can't make progress. I may as well go back to Paris and forget all about it."

"Do not talk so, my son. Here, sit down. You alarm me with your short-sightedness. Your values are strangely out of place. If a lamb falls into a mud puddle, he struggles to get out; if a hog falls in, he stays there. It is not the number of times the lamb falls in that is so important, but the fact that he always struggles to get back out. It is the same with you in God's sight. The mud of yesterday and of the yesterdays before is less important than the struggle to leave it. God forgives those who climb back; and His forgiveness makes us clean. But do not mistake His forgiveness for a convenience, as some do. Conscience does not lie and cannot be tempered. You have struggled back this time. That is undeniable, and it is what counts."

"You people have all the answers, don't you, Father? I can't imagine myself in the role of a lamb. It's difficult to despise this mud, to want to climb out of it, when it's such a comfortable resting place for me. Well, all I can do is put myself in your hands. I'll do as you say. But don't be surprised if you come in to find me rooting up the floor of my cell instead of eating clover."

"You must not let all this become an obsession, my son," he admonishes. "To be obsessed with chastity is also to be obsessed with the flesh; to be obsessed with humility is to be obsessed with self-righteous pride; to be obsessed with food is to be obsessed with hunger. Until you have studied more, become more advanced, try only to find help in God. You are a type who needs answers. I am not strong enough for you. I wish I could do more. But the answers will come to you, my child."

"I must confess that all this has the allure of a new game now, Father. Like trying a new drink or a strange food, just to see how it will be. But it's not an obsession with me. I only want to feel something of what you men feel. It's little more than a question of self-respect. If I could just say no to temptation, especially physical tempta-

137

tion, I wouldn't be so persistent. But it gets me, it's beyond me."

"You cannot really judge," he frowns. "For us it is an act against natural law. For you it has become a natural function. For us it is detestable in God's sight like all other acts against His nature. In the spring you will study our course in natural, ecclesiastical, Christian and canon law, and you will learn that illicit and promiscuous satisfaction of the senses is an abuse of those senses away from God's intention. However, great force toward sex is often a very good sign, my son. We think of it as a pendulum: the lower a man can swing, the higher is his potentiality for goodness, and the higher he can swing, the greater his ratio toward evil. Those of us who stay in the middle, going neither very high nor very low, make up the rank and file of the world. The others, those who swing in a greater arc, have much the same physical make-up; but circumstances, chance, environment make the ones into men of great creative force—saints, artists, doctors, but all very great—and the others into conquerors, criminals, miscarriages of morality. Sanctity is something, you see, which must be achieved more often than not. Rarely is a man struck, like St. Paul, with the inspiration of God. We must work for it; and those who work the hardest, who are the most creative, who have the widest arc, achieve the goal of which we dream."

"Do you believe that, Father?" I ask skeptically. "It seems to me a man with highly developed sexuality would find it almost impossible to overcome the senses without some direct inspiration from God. I'm a person in the middle of your pendulum arc, and yet my sensuality is almost a sickness with me, as you've seen."

Father Clément stands up, pours me a glass of water from his carafe, and walks to the window of his cell, staring at the steadily falling rain. "Ah, but you are completely confused, my child," he says gently. "I speak of *sexuality* and you speak of *sensuality*—realize that and do not misinterpret what I have just said. The one is a great force within us, which makes us strong or weak according to its

138

strength or weakness. It is rarely the cause of sin in itself. It is almost the exact opposite of sensuality, which is a debilitating thing developed within us as tastes are developed within us—a thing which should be crushed out. But you must not associate the two, for it is certain that people with highly developed sensualities—that is, the ability to draw ever-finer lines of pleasure from lustful flesh, and from food and drink—are rarely people of great sexuality. Sensuality develops in an undisciplined mind. It grows as a hunger for ever-more exquisite pleasures, and it is a weakness, like cancer. We have long since learned that it must be killed within us before we can hope for any purity of God's grace. That is one of the reasons for the strictness with which we repel pleasure of the senses. Be certain you understand this difference, my son. Sensuality is the mincing little froth which we despise, devised by our smallness to make up for lack of sexuality—to create a littleness of emotion when the wellsprings of our being are not blessed with bigness. The one is a force, the other a weakness—always—and the measure of a man's ability to play the Don Juan is much more often a criterion for judging his sensual development than his sexual strength."

"I believe I understand, Father," I say, putting the glass on the floor at my feet. "But I've always heard of the two as parallels, not as opposites. This makes much of your regime clear to me now."

"I explain badly. Our strictness actually is not so much for the tearing-down of sensuality, as for a simple sacrifice of earthly pleasures for the love of God. We want nothing which is not in Him. Now, as for you—I think you had better not leave us any more for a while. As I told you the other day, Father Marie-Ornoux of the Dominicans and a Dr. Castelar are due to arrive this afternoon. I feel that you have need of a help less ordinary than mine, my son. With your permission, I shall put Marie-Ornoux in a cell across the way. He is possessed of a sanctity such as we rarely see in a man. Since he is only thirty-three, much nearer your age than most of us, I believe you will find his company

139

rewarding. He was a Trappist for many years, but is on his way now as a Dominican to carry on the work of Father Foucauld in the desert country. I shall ask him to spend his spare time with you, if that is all right."

"If you think you should, Father. But I must confess that the prospect of meeting a saint is a little rich for my blood."

"You must tell him everything, my son, just as you would tell your symptoms to a doctor. Tell him of your former life, and of your Lucette if you like, for you will need to return near her one day. Tell him everything."

"Now I must get back to my work, Father. I feel much better."

I turn to leave. He walks with me to the door of his cell, and laying his hand on my arm, hesitates.

"One thing more, my son," he says slowly—"and I do not wish to embarrass you—but if you must commit these indiscretions in Town, do not be quite so obvious about it. Do not walk back with the lady, for your own sake. It does you great harm in a village such as this where everything is known and freely discussed. I should not tell you, I suppose, but it is known here what you did. Some of our nicer ladies of the Village saw you entering and leaving the hotel. They saw you walk back here together."

"Oh, no!"

"I have no doubt they timed you," he laughs. "It is a shame we have such people. But no harm has been done. It was quite amusing this morning. They felt it their Christian duty to come to the Monastery at six and report their findings to Father Dutfoy. According to them we are harboring a true fugitive from Hades in our midst. Father Dutfoy, who has a good head and a poor temper, told them that such tattling was extremely distasteful, and that perhaps God in His great mercy might give us the strength not to be perverted by another man's sins."

"Love of heaven! Bless him for that. What did they say?"

Father Clément smiles. "When they objected, he assured
140

them that if anything had transpired—which he doubted
very seriously—between you and the blond woman from
South Africa, then you had more right to be here to receive
help from us than they who are so stainless. As they left,
Madame Vincent herself came to confess. It was I who
heard her confession. She stayed to receive the sacraments
at my private celebration of the Mass."

"You knew all the time, then!" I say, amazed. "And
the other Fathers know. Why, you know more about it
than I do. I didn't know she was from South Africa, and
I didn't know her name was Madame Vincent."

"You just . . . uh . . . did not do much talking apparently, son."

"Not much." I burst out laughing. "Sounds a little
callous when you put it that way, doesn't it, Father?"

"I trust you had the grace to say hello and good-bye, at
least?"

"Now, it wasn't like that at all. But you knew all the
time! Ah," I sigh, "I'm glad I confessed my lie."

He becomes serious again. "Not all the other Fathers
know, but it cannot be kept for long. Do not worry about
them. We do not feel qualified to judge another man here.
But it will be known. The good ladies will have it all over
the Village and it will return to us in a thousand different
ways."

"I might as well have done it in the square. I never
heard of such a ridiculous thing. It isn't so bad for me, but
Madame Vincent will have a bad time, and she doesn't deserve it. She's a good woman, Father, I know it."

"Fortunately for both of you, my son, it has the weakness of conjecture on their part, so no real harm is likely to
result. I am the only one who knows the truth, and of course
no one else will ever know. They do not really believe it,
they just want to—but they will watch the both of you now.
I told Madame Vincent what I am telling you. She hopes to
stay on indefinitely. It would be best if you treated her naturally in public, as if you were old friends and nothing
more."

141

"Thanks for telling me all this, Father. This is a new world here, and I'll have to get used to it. I'll never be so careless if the occasion should arise again, heaven forbid."

"It will arise, my infant, never fear. But we will hope you are better armed next time. Now back to your work. We forget this, eh?"

Pulling his hood over his head, he walks rapidly down the corridor. He is bent, and looks older than he is. I watch him disappear around the corner, hear his footfalls sounding beyond the turn—and wonder at the misery I cause him. He understands, and his kindness is infinite, as infinite and touching as the names he uses for me: "my son," "my child," "my infant." Rain pours against the long window at the end of the door-lined corridor. My affection moves with him, following as the sound of his steps on the stone floor. The game is no longer a game; for the hurt flows out, and now it must flow back to its source. In a moment, a catching of the nerves, we see these things, and understand them, knowing that complications within self become abuse when the grimace is felt on the face of another.

I stand in the hall and it becomes easy, this thing which was so difficult an hour before. For there's a dimension over and above self, seen in another's eyes, heard in another's whisper, felt in another's pain. It's a sort of love above loving, and it dissolves you with the shame of yourself. Father Clément's heart is old and it deserves its repose. And you can accomplish things quickly and simply for another's ease of heart which you can't dream possible for yourself. You have only to know it.

My own footsteps echo before me. I walk back to my work, glad that I know now these things which are never known, but only felt. It's almost as though I had been here always.

In mid-afternoon my work is interrupted by a young novice, who comes to whisper close to my ear that the guests from Paris have arrived. I am requested to return to my cell, where Father Marie-Ornoux is waiting.

Approaching my open door, the thought that I'm about

142

to meet one of the great Christians of our day causes me a momentary qualm. But it's needless. As I enter the room, white robes rise from the cot and walk to meet me. As if we were old friends the voice says, "So it is really you?"

"Yes, my Father . . ."

We talk in smallnesses, as two strangers do. His habit is the white robe of the Dominican, now faded and poor and patched heavily with unmatching white squares. The face is not young, nor is it old. It has no age. The eyes, clear and immense in the skeletal head, dominate the figure. It's impossible to escape them. His skin is dark and leathery, with deep wrinkles at the corners of the mouth. He smiles continually, like Brother Placide, and his eyes compel me to look at his face. There is a look of fear, almost animal fear: a cringing as from something unknown, like a dog which has been beaten. I instantly feel that it's because he lives in the awe, in the mystery of his great love of God. His is the most ordinary of faces made living beauty through years of seeking nothing but God's will. In society without this luminous transformation, he would go unnoticed; but here his very presence radiates like a living light. To be near him is a moving experience. His is poverty, and simplicity, and instinctive knowledge of things.

"So you are a musician, my son?" he says finally. "I fear you will find me inadequate. However, I am in a cell down the hall, and Dr. Castelar is in the room adjoining yours. I must go for the moment, but I have Father Abbot's permission to spend all my free time with you. Until soon, then . . ."

His leaving takes with it his great warmth. Afterward my cell seems chillier, more impersonal.

Sheltered under my umbrella, I walk through a deep softness of freezing rain across the courtyard to the bathrooms. As my hand touches the door of one of the cubicles, it opens from the inside. A short, heavy-set man steps out, looks about distastefully at the weather and the rain-drenched courtyard. He stands under the eaves, the book he has been reading tucked under his arm, and finishes buttoning

143

his pants. Though well dressed in an American overcoat he is obviously Latin American, with thick black hair streaked heavily with gray. Fumbling with his buttons he looks beyond me into the rain, glances up at icicle-edged eaves, and mutters in disgust, "Filthy weather . . ."

Stepping past him, I enter the bathroom and turn to close the door behind me. He steps forward into ankle-deep slush, groans a curse, and returns under the sheltering eaves.

Speaking loudly to be heard above the rain, I suggest, "If you'll wait a few moments, Monsieur, you can walk back under my umbrella with me."

"Thank you," comes in a thick, unsmiling accent, but with a slight bow. "I'll go in the next cubicle and smoke. Call me when you've finished."

When I come out he joins me. We walk back hurriedly, in silence except for his eloquent, half-muttered curses; up the stairs into my cell row. Without thanking me he bows again and enters the cell next to mine.

There is a compulsion to talk with someone, so I leave my door open. In a few moments he stands outside my door, looking in and knocking. A cigarette hangs from his thick lips, and he has a black beret on the back of his head. Asking him to come in, I introduce myself. Shivering, still unsmiling, he takes my hand.

"And I am Dr. Rafael Castelar, from the *warm* countries of Central America. How do you stand it here?"

"You are a doctor—of philosophy?"

"No, of medicine, though at present I'm in France with the ambassador from my native country of Guatemala."

"But you have a very fluent French, Doctor. Won't you sit down? I'm sorry I can't offer you something. Even our drinking water freezes in these cells."

"That's all right, young man," he says, settling heavily onto my cot. "As for my French, I was educated in France and Belgium, and my wife is from Bordeaux."

"Are you here at the Monastery on a case, Doctor?" I sit down beside him.

144

"No, I've been at the Dominican monastery in Paris. My wife has taken our children to the South of France to visit her relatives, so I stayed with my old friends the Dominicans. When Marie-Ornoux decided to make this trip, he urged me to accompany him. I jumped at the chance."

"You're interested in the Benedictines?"

"In all the monastic rules. I know the Dominicans and the Trappists well, and I'm very curious to learn about the Benedictines. Questions of morality are a passion with me, and your Benedictines are noted scholars. You'll help me to answer questions, eh?"

"If I can, though I'm here mainly to study the music. But tell me about Marie-Ornoux? I'm anxious to know him better. Father Abbot has given him permission to spend his free time with me."

"But he knows nothing about music," says the doctor, scratching his head under the beret.

"Like you, Doctor, I'm very much interested in questions of morality. It's for that I want to know him."

"Then you're indeed fortunate, young man. Marie-Ornoux is the most magnificent man I know—and I'm not easily impressed. He instinctively knows more than those of us who spend all our lives studying."

" 'Instinctively' knows more? What do you mean?"

"He's that rare phenomenon," the doctor goes on, "a person who clearly sees the difference between right and wrong, and who can explain that difference to another. They've never allowed me much of his precious time, but I am his doctor, I know a great deal about him. I envy you."

"But you can join us here in my cell, Doctor," I tell him, having already taken a liking to this man. "You can be with him as often as I."

"No, that wouldn't be allowed," he answers bluntly. "Father Marie-Ornoux still lives under the Dominican rule, and that rule is very strict. If they allow him to spend his time with you, then your needs are obviously considered of great importance." He pauses. "But tell me, is there

145

any objection to our having visits together, you and I?"

"Not at all. We don't often have guests, and I'd welcome your company."

"And I yours, Monsieur. This place has a sadness about it. I'm used to noises around a monastery. It's very quiet here, and cold. *Madre de Dios!* it's cold."

"It's always cold, but the impression of sadness should be gone by morning, Doctor. We're next-door neighbors, so feel free to come in whenever you like. We can't talk after Compline, but during the day there's complete freedom—and we're the only two guests."

"Good. Now I must leave you to your work."

For the first time a smile softens his face. We shake hands, agreeing to leave our doors open if we want company, to close them if we don't wish to be disturbed.

The bells sound for Vespers, and we walk down together. Dr. Castelar dips his fingers in the holy water, crosses himself, and turns to offer me the wetness on his finger tips. I touch them and carry the moisture to my forehead, mouth, and chest.

We separate, sitting in different pews to await the beginning of Vespers. The chapel is dotted with people of every poverty, come to say their Ave Marias: people who enter, stamp the mud and ice from their shoes, and kneel to pray. Each time the doors open behind us the sound of steadily pouring rain becomes alive, entering as a chill until the doors creak slowly closed again.

Opening Vesper chants, and for the first time since morning I am alone, and very tired. I sit numb amidst mumbled prayers and chants, resting, looking about. The doctor is on his knees, leaning forward on the cradle of his arm against the pew in front of him. The Mexican girl with her shawl is not there, nor is Madame Renée. Monks stand and chant, long rows of black robes punctuated by the white robe of the Dominican, in the sallow vesper light of a storming outside.

Again the sound of opening doors. A gust of damp air and rain. I look about unnoticed in the dark. It is

146

Madame Vincent, removing a glistening raincoat. She kneels on the last row. Persistently I look back, seeking to catch her eye. Once looking at me she closes her eyes halfway, but makes no other sign of recognition. At this hour yesterday we woke in the same bed from a naked sleep; and now it might never have been. At this hour twenty-four hours ago I smelled her shoulder beneath my head, and my hand cupped the naked smoothness of her sleeping belly. Tonight she is cleansed of this and it's never really been. She prays there now—but can she forget a kiss in the small of her back? . . .

Lips become dry and I wet them, exhausted. Turning, I listen and forget this bodiless emotion clutching a blackness of rosary beads back there near the door.

Vespers conclude with the singing of the *Salve Regina*. When I turn to go, Madame Vincent's place is empty. It must already have started for her then—the cold stares, the shaking of heads, the prudish looks of disapproval. Poor woman, her worship is haunted with caution.

I wait at the door for Dr. Castelar, but he stays on his knees in the empty chapel. I leave without him.

Marie-Ornoux joins me in the corridor. "Come," he says, "I will walk with you back to your cell."

"And how does our chanting here compare with that of the Dominicans, Father?"

"Oh, it is without comparison, my son. We do not chant well. But there is a reason for that, too."

"What possible reason could there be for not chanting well?"

"The atmosphere of our two orders, like their purpose, is entirely different. After all, a people who are preparing themselves to work with the dregs of humanity can scarcely be expected to devote enough of their time to music to make it anything more than adequate. Our mission is much less esthetic, much less glamorous than that of the Benedictines, who are concerned primarily with the cult of the worship of God. They must sing like the angels. Ours is a more active order; and when you send men into the slums

147

of the world, you must be wary of giving them too great a sensitiveness to beautiful things. They need, on the contrary, a very great thirst for the ascetic, and a much more highly colored mysticism, to survive."

We enter my cell, and at my invitation Marie-Ornoux sits on the cot. He refuses a cigarette. I open my window, wiping ice and frozen mist from the glass so that more light may enter the room. Below I see the doctor as he runs from the chapel into a corridor and out of sight.

Father Marie-Ornoux moves, giving me a place beside him on the cot, and looks at me quietly for a moment before asking, "Now, what shall we talk about? First, tell me of yourself. Are you in trouble?"

"By your standards, Father, I'm at this moment being seared by the devil's warm breath; but by my own, I must confess I don't feel it."

"How is that? Father Clément has told me something of you, but I should like to hear more."

"It's simply that I'm all right, and happy enough, as long as I stay in the Monastery—and that every time I leave I get into some sort of trouble. Father Clément, whom I've done nothing but disappoint, suggested a man like you might help me. Frankly I don't feel it was the thing to do. You're too busy for me to take your time, and I'm ashamed to be shunted like a sick child from one member of the family to another. However, I promised Father Clément I would do exactly as he asked. But I feel you might be doing something much more to your credit than worrying with my dirty linens."

He laughs. It sounds throughout the corridor, giving a health to somber dusk. His figure beside me becomes a specter in the growing dark. "I can think of nothing more to my credit," he assures me, "than, as you say, 'worrying with your dirty linens.' And I thank the Good Lord for the chance. But it is difficult, you see: I am in no way qualified. According to Father Clément you are a man of many knowledges. You have culture and intelligence, whereas I am only a man of average learning." He hesitates.

148

"But I believe you have a mistress or something here? Is that correct?"

The thought that two months ago I would have resented such a question makes me smile. "I have a girl in Paris, Father; and I got a poor woman into trouble here only yesterday. But how did you know?"

"Unless there is some reason not to have one, an unmarried man of your age very often forms such liaisons. We will talk of this later. For the time being, I shall ask you not to leave the Monastery for anything. Have you met Dr. Castelar yet?"

"Yes, Father, we introduced ourselves this afternoon."

"Good. As you will discover, he is a man of great learning, and most important, a Christian of the caliber that shames all of us. Like many of the really outstanding Christians this is not obvious at first, for he is very rough in speech and much of his conversation is devoted to un-Christian subjects. But we are devoted to him, and he has helped more than one of us past a bad hurdle. You will get more from him than from me." He rises from the cot. "I must hurry now. But here, I have brought you a little book which I hope you will read. It is called *La Vraie Dévotion à la Sainte Vierge,* by Grignon de Montfort, and it outlines the procedure followed by many of us in giving ourselves to the Blessed Virgin. I am an oblate of Mary, as are many of my brother Dominicans. You may find it too naïve for your tastes, but try to read it through. Incidentally, Grignon de Montfort is soon to be canonized in Rome. He will officially be recognized as the saint he actually was." He turns his head to the door. "Wait a moment, I think I hear the doctor now." He opens the door and steps into the hall, glancing in the direction of Dr. Castelar's room. "Ah," he says, "I thought it was you, Doctor."

"Can I do something for you, Father?" comes the other's voice from the corridor.

"Are you busy?" Marie-Ornoux asks him. "I thought you might like to visit with Monsieur for a little while. I must run along."

149

"I'd be very glad to."

He appears beside Marie-Ornoux, his overcoat turned up around his neck. I stand and offer him a seat as he follows the monk back into my cell, but he shakes his head.

Marie-Ornoux smiles. "Since you gentlemen have already met, I shall leave you to yourselves. I feel sure you will find much in common."

When he has gone the doctor hesitates a moment, standing near the door. "We have almost three hours till dinner, Monsieur," he says. "You're an American, but from your French I judge you've spent much time here. I don't know America well, but I do know you're a highly moral people who sometimes consider drinking a sin. However, I've brought some wine from my native country, and if you'd care to share a glass—?"

"I'd be delighted to, Doctor," I tell him. "I've been in France too long to feel that way about alcohol."

"Good. Come to my cell, we'll have a glass. I should like you to taste the wine of Guatemala. It's strong and crude and full of the devil, like my people."

In his cell, he pours two water glasses of the thick red wine. But I am lost in admiration of the painting, unframed, that leans against his night table. It's a magnificently conceived rendering of multicolored abstract designs on a black background.

"You like it, eh?" says the doctor, handing me a glass. "You have taste for one so young. It's a Maria Blanchard of the early cubist period. To me it's the most beautiful painting in the world. And I've finally saved enough money to buy it. It's a great work, don't you think? And it gets better as you get drunker."

He laughs, and I cringe from the noise. I close the door to his cell.

"It's a wonderful thing," I agree admiringly. "I think I've seen it at Kleinman's in Paris. Some day I'll buy it from you, Doctor."

"Come then, drink up—we're sympathetic. But drink slow, the wine is very strong. You must drink enough to

150

put you to sleep; otherwise you'll go crazy for a woman. There's no half-way about the wine of my country."

We drink, and talk—mostly of art, and literature, and music, and women. We drink glass after glass of the heavy wine. Our talk becomes quiet and intimate. Noises outside become remote as night falls. We struggle against the silence within. The wine warms us, destroying the barriers of ordinary formality.

"Doctor, tell me of your family. You mentioned children."

"Yes, I have ten children—in fourteen years of marriage."

"Too much wine?"

"No. Too good a Catholic, and too fond of my . . . uh . . ."

He walks stiffly to the wall and pushes the light switch, groaning against the sudden light. We drink quietly, and we're warm with the wine. My question about his children has obviously put him in a bad mood.

"Doctor, how much of this stuff does it take to make you go roaming the streets? I feel more religious than. . . that way."

He laughs at our clumsy attempts to find substitute words for words that come naturally in drunkenness—and he no longer tries. "For me, I prefer walking the streets. I've been one month now without my wife. That's a long time, eh? Only once have I had a woman, and that was because my friend the ambassador wanted me to go with him. We got two girls, good-looking girls, and I examined them. The one he had chosen was eaten up with syphilis, so he didn't get his after all. I managed mine all right, but it wasn't any good."

"Tell me, you're a doctor who knows everything there is to know about women—doesn't that very knowledge make you desire them less? I mean, there's no longer the element of discovery, of the unknown." Breathing becomes more difficult as the wine soaks into my being, and the words must now be sorted.

151

"But no, not in the slightest." The doctor's accent becomes thicker. "I've been married for many years now. I have ten children, at least nine of which were unwanted. But now I enjoy my wife more than ever. I'm much the bull type, my friend. When I was in medical school at Montpellier I kept two mistresses."

"Oh, and changing the subject," I put in, "I wanted to ask you one thing more. We recently had a child to die here in the Valley. I was at the house when it happened. Now, she was in a fit for almost eight hours—an epileptic fit, I think. The doctor arrived after her death and called it congestion of the brain due to epilepsy. Is that a medically sound diagnosis?"

The doctor smiles at my unprofessional presentation of the case. "It doesn't sound right to me. How old was the child?"

"I think she was about ten, Doctor."

"Here—drink some more wine."

His words become fuzzy, his accent thick. I shake my head with a violence that surprises me and hurts my neck. Stomach begins to ache. The words become fuzzy and the doctor talks. He talks long lines of words in the background. Cheeks swallow a turning of the stomach. Hands numb, and the face feels a tiny pinpointing of underskin movements. Doctor talks. I look up at window and door and back at window under drooping eyelids, forcing eyelids to open bright. Doctor talks. Inner winds rise to be stifled by a lowering of the head and a pursing of the lips. Window and door black, staring back holes of black to dim sallow yellow faded diluted light of lamp in cell. Benign smiles trace face muscles and become set. I listen to the doctor and his thick accent and understand little and breathe out heavily, opening lips, whistling silently upward into my nose. Window black hole stares reproachfully. Look down and the glass is held in alcohol relaxing at an angle almost spilling. Words and smiles and chromatic crawlings of warmth under the face skin and the doctor reaches over to straighten my glass in hand. I drink. He talks.

152

". . . and this dangerous condition, called *status epilepticus,* very occasionally does result in death. But in the child's case I should think—Ah, watch the wine. There."

Words come in pulsings to drink-lulled senses. I listen intently. Doctor leans far back on the cot.

"You understand that much?"

"No."

"Well"—he pauses, straightening beret—"I'll see if I can tell it clearer."

"That's all right," I exhale wearily. "Phew—this stuff's strong, isn't it? I'm sleepy, Doctor."

Doctor raises his head. "Ah, poof. There's the bell for dinner."

"T'hell with dinner, Father—I mean, Doctor. We can't go down there like this."

"T'hell with dinner, then. Here we are starving to death, and we say to hell with food. Good wine, eh?" Out of corner of eye. Doctor with glass to lips. Gurgling of wine down throat and a red glistening drop on chin. "Now, about this poor, poor, *poor* little girl. How old did you say she was?"

"Sixteen, I think."

"And you caught syphilis from her. Is that it?"

"No, I never. Caught syphilis from anybody."

"Well, don't be boastful. I hate boastfulness, don't you?"

"Oh, I remember now. The little Chevissier. She was *ten,* Doctor."

"And you abuse a girl ten years old? Ah, really . . ."

"Didn't abuse her. I tried to save her life."

"*Mierda!* Of course. Forgive me. I got off the track because, you know, syphilis will very often cause convulsions similar to those of an epileptic seizure. But there's no connection between the two." Belches loudly. "I would guess offhand—very offhand, you understand—your child died of congenital syphilis."

Mumbled. Pauses. Gather wits. Focusing fuzzy lights. Sad cell. Rough floor. Pauses. Focusing words. Words

153

and concentration and focusing. Words fall to patterns with shimmering inner dissolving of tissues sweeping like chill through chest, and they clarify the sharp light. The clear outline of things. The doctor becomes coherent. He leans forward and stares at the floor. His dark skin is reddened from drink.

Seeming to forget the light and the floor and the window and me, he mutters again and again, "*Spongia, spongia, spongia, spongia,*" until it dies in a whisper. Then, turning to look at me, "You're not shocked at my language, young friend?" Voice soft and deep from his throat swallowing.

"How can I be shocked? I don't know what your language is."

"You don't know *spongia*? Forgive me"—and he bows—"it's bad manners to swear in a language you don't understand. I shall explain. Do you want me to explain?"

"Please do."

"*Spongia*"—voice becomes eloquent as if giving a lecture—"*spongia* is an ancient Latin word meaning 'sponge.' I must explain that. In the days before the height of the Holy Roman Empire. A sewage system of intriguing . . . uh . . . ingenuity. Existed in Rome. But perhaps you know more than I about this period in history?"

"No, Doctor. I know nothing. Of ancient Rome. Except I believe there was also an ancient Carthage."

"Correct! But this is in Rome I'm talking about. Well, I'm very much interested in social customs. I want to know everything. About daily life in ancient Rome. Well. As I said, this *spongia* is a Latin curse word. Of remarkably satisfying eloquence. This sewage system you see. Was in some ways more modern than our practices of today. For toilet paper they used a perfumed woolen cloth. Which was washed and used again and again. And in the urinals for men. Sponges tied to long sticks were used to . . . uh . . . wipe the urine from themselves. After they had finished urinating. In every bathroom these sponges were to be found. One sponge being used for many men. As you know it was considered great sport in those days to

154

throw captured prisoners into public pits. To be destroyed by wild animals. This was a death often very slow. And very torturous. In many of the public arenas enclosed bathrooms built of stone were placed somewhere near the center. For the convenience of those about to die. Death of this nature was horrible. You can't imagine how horrible. So it became a fashion for men thus thrown to the lions to go into these bathrooms. And in a desperate attempt to take their own lives. Quickly. They chose the only means possible. They would cram these urine-soaked sponges far into their throats. Opening their mouths wide. Holding to the long-handled stick to which the sponges were tied. In that way death by suffocation came quickly. From this practice. So unimaginable in its connotations. Came the ejaculation *spongia* signifying not only this physical function. But death by suicide. And profound disgusts. It's a slang word still used in some Latin countries. Although its original meaning has long since been lost."

"That's very damned interesting, Doctor. Those were the good old days."

"Good days! Hell! People make me sick who speak of the 'good old days.'"

"Uh. I'm sleepy."

The doctor ignores me. Stares at the floor. Eyes pursed. "Tell me, young man"—finally, quietly—"what is your passion? What is your great passion?"

"Well. Let's see—"

"You're a weakling. Aren't you?"

"I am drunk, my friend"—bitterly. "I am nothing."

"That's what I thought. You have no passion. And without passion you're nothing."

"I can rise to heights."

"Like hell! I know you. Better than you think. And don't be offended, eh? Here. One more glass of wine. No, just one more. And then we go to bed. It's getting late. There. Now back to you. To what heights can you rise, my poor friend? You like my Blanchard. But you don't love it as I. For it makes me live. You like women.

155

But you don't know how to go to the very heights with a woman. Because there are some things your culture and your intelligence. Tell you are wrong. You're good in a small little mean way. And what's worse. You're bad in a small little mean way."

Eyes averted. Words swim in background. Taste of stomach behind lips. But words make themselves felt. "I think you're right, Doctor"—miserably. "I'm the type who'd make. An impeccable clerk. Or a good politician. I write a nice neat hand. I can speak several languages. I'm soft. Where I should be hard. I know this. And I loathe it. I'm the sort of person. I can't tolerate. What do I do but take up space? Fill the sewers? Vote like everyone else? Some day produce my share of children? Who'll be like me? Without understanding. Without ever understanding."

Bells for Compline clang. Feeling of emptiness. Doctor arouses himself. Speaks more loudly over dyingaway sounds. "Don't get maudlin, eh? I had you well typed. Though I didn't know you were smart enough. To realize it yourself." Voice becomes bland. And gentle. "You must learn to love God, my boy. In people like you. Who have everything else. Ability, training, knowledge. An immense love of God. A passion for God. Can make these things come to life. It's the only thing. That can do that."

Below in the chapel. Rumbling of feet. Monks entering for Compline.

"Do you really believe that, Doctor? Wouldn't any synthetic passion? Do as well?" Head sings drunkenly. But words come. And won't be forgotten.

"It's very difficult to know. I don't believe these things come from parental blood. I think rather they come from an education that stultifies. That kills man's own compulsion within himself." The urgency of the doctor's words sobers. "How many promising talents are ruined in the schools of learning! The conservatories! How much is our moral tendency toward right killed by parents! And a society which doesn't allow us to *choose* right, to make our

156

own mistakes! Mistakes aren't permitted us in our youth. So we grow into this shell of little moral righteousness without having made the choice. And it becomes a core deeply imbedded within us. But the body makes demands that can't be denied. As a result we satisfy them in mean and little ways. And the hard core of our beings remains as a confusion. As a death of individual compulsion. In order to free ourselves from these traits which become intolerable once they are known, drastic steps must be taken. I feel this very strongly. We can't do it in rebellion, which does nothing more than stack confusion upon confusion. Two negatives don't here become a positive. The core must be destroyed. And it's never destroyed in rebellion. If a man is eaten with pride within himself, he doesn't overcome that pride by detesting all others who have the same sin. If a man is drawn too much to the flesh, he doesn't overcome it by detesting all whores. That's confusion upon confusion. And a pattern of behavior, of standards which are not understood, can only be destroyed or brought to understanding by something infinitely more powerful."

The doctor's reasoning is persuasive and clear. And from the chapel below, sounds of monks reciting Compline rise to us, coloring his words.

"As a doctor, I can assure you there are many ways of accomplishing this. I could get you drunk enough to release you from this bondage. It could be done with opium, with any sort of narcotic. But you can see that it takes an agent strong enough to soften, temporarily, this deeply imbedded core which is planted there for society's good, by society, as a block against the moral freedom to choose for yourself. There are many narcotics, and each is debilitating. That's why I tell you to develop this passion for God, for that too is a narcotic. It will accomplish the same thing within you, without the harm of the others. It's as though you wished to open wellsprings. With opium you may take an ax and chop, and destroy the retaining wall. With alcohol you will take a hammer and break the wall. With each of these you destroy. With God, you merely

157

turn the spigot; and as love for Him grows, as the passion for Him and only Him spreads throughout your belly, the wellsprings flow and the being understands. And it keeps you whole. And it destroys only the bad within you. It's a narcotic in that once you possess it, your happiness can never again be without it."

Chants rise from below. We sit in the half-light of the doctor's cell. The chants cease, and the monks recite again. The doctor, his face flushed, leans to me, drinks sideways from his glass, and becomes more intense.

"You say nothing, my young man, my pale young man. I tell you, I know I am right. That's what these existentialists are doing. Exactly that. Without God. They speak of essence and existence. They make an easy route for people like you. People with brains and nothing else. Logic, logic. And it will end, as the Dadaists, in nothing. It's laughable and heartbreaking to see them, these brains without bodies, these queers, these pederasts who find logical explanations for their sicknesses. Theirs is the negative cure of the negative malady. And it's not strong enough. It's a plaything, like the pillow of an adolescent boy at night."

He moves away. Turning, he pounds his fist on the table and glares at me. Sounds of Compline, ocean of sound from below, and the doctor's staccato voice.

"You have no passion, no passion. Forgive. I am drunk. I—I have the passion. I'm an intellectual only by excessive effort. I'm a man of action. And sin. And love. I've done everything, Monsieur. I've committed adultery. I've seduced other men's wives. I've cheated and lied and stolen. But with all that"—his voice whispers, choking—"with all that I'm less bad than you. You and I know that, tonight, in this place. I'm sorry. I don't dislike you. But I hate what you are. I hate littleness in a man. And weakness."

"But if you don't believe, Doctor? . . . If a man doesn't believe? . . ."

"*Madre!* Look at yourself. Look at your piggish little objections. You're not interesting. Sacrifice yourself! Men

158

of your type of weakness are often capable of sacrifice for another that people like me can't envision. It's this which can make you strong. Which can make your miserable little belly worth something. But you must be proud of it, my friend. How I laugh at those who mock me for my love of God! You must draw yourself up to your height and pity those little bastards who question your 'good taste' in loving God. It isn't something to hide. I'm a doctor, I know what men are made of, and the little ones snigger easily; but they always have headaches or stomach ulcers or some equally justifiable disease to bring them back to reality. They're generally obsessed with keeping their intestines cleaned out, and their pleasure is in a good laxative. Don't let their derision be yours. Don't imitate them. Imitate these men here, whom we love and admire. In them you will find strength. Otherwise you may do valuable research, you may do good for the community, but you'll die without ever having lived."

The chants of Compline become a last prayer. Dr. Castelar rises, slaps my drink-numbed shoulder, and says, "Your glass is empty again. Here, empty those dregs so I can fill it again."

I no longer try to protest. He laughs. Forcing my hand with its full glass of wine to my mouth and filling it again. I choke, spitting sifts of pinkish moisture onto the cold air. Tiny beads of sweat form with inner congestions seeking to accept full swallowings. And it disintegrates. He sits beside me. Quiet and muffled noises from the chapel. Loneliness of night and stones and long darkness of empty corridors. Overwhelming. Locking muscles and jaws. And sharp catches of breath. Another glass near tears. Coming back in revulsions. Rising. Fighting foams. Breathing pulses of temple and head and vision. Coming going. Coming going.

Dr. Castelar stands. Towering. Shadow bending over. Hands. Fine pores etched microscope of dark skin. Pulling. Jerking dead weight of my coat. Pulling bundle. Laughing. I don't move.

159

"Come!" Shouting. Pounding on eardrums. "We'll go. I'll find some food. One of the cafés. It's early. And we'll begin by destroying you. With the most decrepit and disgusting whore in Town. You will make love. To her. I'll watch." Arms raised. Voice prophetlike. "Then we shall build something new on the junk heap of your purged disgusts."

I don't move. "No, no! I promised Marie-Ornoux."

"Ah, forgive me. I'm too drunk. To know what I'm doing. I just wanted to shock you. Out of this spiritual. This spiritual vacuum."

"Not tonight. I'm drunk. Do you realize we're drunk? We've got drunk. My friend. Both of us are drunk. I get drunk because I'm sad."

"About what? My poor friend. Tell me of your sadness."

"It's my Lucette. Dead these many years of epilepsy."

"Ah, you *are* drunk. Your Lucette's at this minute. Forgetting your weight beneath the weight of another."

"Good for her. I'm going to bed."

I rise. Groaning. Noise of footsteps. Noise of breaking ice outside. Monks returning. Coming back to fill emptiness.

"You'll dream of Lucette tonight, eh?" says the doctor. Chuckling sound.

"Hope so. Lord, I hope so. And believe me, Doctor. Never will she be so magnificently . . . uh . . ."

"Yes?"

"Ah, this wine. This wine. It heats. And in the wrong places. Good night, Doctor."

Noises coming closer. Labored step away from cot. Head falls. Arc of light bulb in the ceiling. Sweeping sight. Moving there in heavy lowering step. Blackness of door there. With laughter somewhere behind. Angles of light and dark changing. Adjusting. Changing. Forward. Falling. Clutching. Falling. Thump and eye seeing cemented seam of stone floor. Smelling it. Twirling twisting floor under eye. Hard against cheek. Racking pain over numbness . . .

160

During the night I awaken sobered with nausea. My body is numb. I am well under the covers in the dark night. It's quiet, deathly quiet. Someone has removed my clothing and put me without pajamas into bed. There are no dreams.

15 december

A hand shakes me roughly from sleep. Father Marie-Ornoux is bending over me.

"People who get drunk in monasteries," he says without anger, "even under a doctor's supervision, are indeed very low."

"I'm sorry, Father, I—"

"But you are hurt, my son! What is it?"

"My arm, I can't move my arm." I groan with pain. "Serves me right. Are you going to send me away, Father? I'm sick with shame. Never have I sunk so low."

"Of course we are not going to send you away. And if you have never sunk so low, then you are better than most of us." He straightens up. "But I must fetch the doctor. He told me early this morning what you did, taking the blame on himself. You were apparently caught off guard by his wine, my son. He assured me, however, that he looked you over after the fall and could find no broken bones."

I laugh, but the movement hurts. "We were so drunk he wouldn't have known it if I'd had a broken neck."

"You *are* a pretty mess. I shall run get him."

His wooden-soled shoes clump through the door and sound echoingly down the hall. In a moment I hear them returning. He re-enters the room with an expression of con-

161

cern on his fine face, closing the door softly behind him.

"The doctor is not there," he says. "Are you in very much pain?"

"No, it's all right." I smile wryly. "I'm afraid your doctor's a little rich for my blood."

"You must not judge him by this one incident, my son. When you get to know him better you will see."

I shake my head skeptically. "I don't know. His methods are too advanced for me."

"You do not like him?" asks Marie-Ornoux, walking back to look out the door.

"Yes, I like him all right. But he's not at all what you led me to expect. You said he was a great Christian."

"And he is. I told you that he was rough, that he talked a great deal about un-Christian subjects. It is hard for people like us to understand him, I know."

"It's certainly hard," I concede, "for *me* to understand him."

"But he *is* a man of immense worth," the monk goes on. "A true mystic and a great Christian. There are not many like him in the world. When you get to know him you will see that I am right." He looks at me anxiously. "But perhaps I had better try to find him so that he can examine your arm?"

"No, he'll be back in a minute. Sit down, Father." I pull the injured arm to a more comfortable position. "What a night! Did we make much noise?"

"A little, but do not worry about it." He smiles, then chuckles amusedly. "You know, it is quite obvious that the doctor shocked you. He shocked me too, at first. But I hardly think it any credit to us that we *are* shocked."

"What do you mean?"

"I have come to look upon him as almost Biblical: the type of powerful Christian who made the early centuries of Christianity a period unequaled in history. We really have become weak, you know. All of us. We place too much importance upon exterior qualities—upon niceties of language and behavior."

162

"Probably."

"Look at a man like St. Paul, or St. Augustine even. Either of them would make the doctor look like a lamb. I often wonder just how shocked some of our nice ladies' groups, some of our civilized Christians would be if one of the early saints should walk into their midst. They would never recognize him, I fear! For a man's exterior actually has nothing whatsoever to do with his love of God, with his passion for God. The strength which often makes him seem uncouth is the very strength with which he adores. Such a man is—" He pauses, listening to the sound of footsteps outside. "But I believe that is Dr. Castelar now. Wait a moment, my son."

He walks out into the corridor, leaving the door half-open. The voices of the two men, the one so gentle and the other so rough, come back to me clearly; and I think over what the young monk has told me, understanding little.

"He seems to have hurt his arm," I hear Marie-Ornoux say.

"Then I'd better take a look at him," replies the doctor thickly.

I glance up as they enter the room. Marie-Ornoux waits at the door. The doctor comes straight to the bed and, without speaking, reaches down and pulls back the covers. He examines my arm and shoulder in silence, then pushes his fist into my abdomen.

"Everything's all right there," he mutters. "Now let's see about the legs."

"It feels like you've just rearranged my insides, Doctor."

"The legs are right. Now turn on your stomach."

But the effort is too much. I wince and reach for the pain in my shoulder.

"Well, it's the shoulder all right," the doctor announces regretfully. "But only a little break. The bone may be cracked, but it's not out of place. I'll put your arm in a sling till it gets all right." Looking very sour, he covers me again and reassures Marie-Ornoux that my injuries are

163

only minor. "He'll just be uncomfortable is all," he adds.

"Then you really think he is all right?" asks the monk. "I must leave you now, but I shall return this afternoon. It is after eleven. Try to fix him up, Doctor."

We wait until his footsteps sound no longer. The doctor appears very uncomfortable.

"It was unforgivable of me, my boy," he begins. "Here, let me check you again. I was terribly worried about you last night. You took a nasty fall."

"I'm really not sorry for it, Doctor. We might have chosen a better place, but otherwise it was worth it. We got a lot of things said last night that might never have come out."

"It had its good points. Here, take off the covers again. I felt a lump inside the knee. No, I guess it's nothing. Does it hurt there?"

"No, I don't feel a thing."

He grins. "Did you sleep all right last night?"

"I guess so."

"No Lucette?"

"No Lucette." I shake my head sadly. "Tell me—was that why you didn't put me in pajamas?"

"Of course not. I wasn't in much better shape than you, young man. Consider yourself lucky to have been put to bed at all. I never wear pajamas myself, and in my stupor I suppose it didn't occur to me that you would either. Here, I'll put that arm in a sling. And as penance for my bad shepherd act, I'll be your nursemaid. Where are your clean clothes? In this bag?"

"Yes, sir—some clean socks and underwear."

I get painfully from the bed, but it's impossible to move my left arm. The doctor makes me stand as he puts my clothes on me. When I am dressed he places the arm in a sling, then stoops to tie my shoelaces. He does this simply, impersonally, efficiently, not speaking except for soft mutterings to himself. I look down at his head with its dust-covered beret.

"Such undistinguished work for a man of your repu-

164

tation, Doctor," I smile. "Your patients would be shocked."

He laughs, still kneeling, bending his head back to look at my face above. "Not at all, my friend. It's man's greatest health to help the helpless. And the lower the task, the greater its value." He gets to his feet slowly—dark, stocky, impersonal—the doctor again. "Now, let's see. You're dressed. Try unbuttoning your pants. Now take them down—and then the underwear. That's fine. Now see if you can put them back."

"What the devil is this for, Doctor?"

"I want to see if you can manage it. Otherwise I'll have to take you to the bathroom. But no, I think you can make it all right by yourself, can't you?"

"Sure. It's slow but I can do it. I think I could get dressed except for the shoes and socks."

"All right. If you need me you can knock on the wall separating our cells. Now, how do you feel after last night?"

"Pretty well. A little drawn in the back of the neck—slightly washed out—but no headache."

"No nausea? The stomach feels all right?"

"Yes, sir."

"You look bad. Come, we'll go for lunch. After that you can sleep."

"I have to go downstairs first, Doctor. Wait for me here."

Yesterday's rain has frozen in the courtyard. Pools of slick ice. The sky is overcast. I go to the kitchen for a carafe of warm water. Activity of lunch preparation—cooking foods, noises of cutlery and silver and dinner plates. Concern and questions about my injured arm. An old monk offers to carry my water to the bathroom, but I refuse. The water warms my gloved hands. Father Dutfoy, entering the kitchen as I leave, bows low and smiles, his red face clear and amused. Without speaking he raises his hands and moves the forefinger of one across the forefinger of the other, shaking his head from side to side.

And then I am alone in the court, alone with my steaming pitcher of warm water. I walk slowly, stepping carefully

165

on the ice-covered ground. The sky is gray—unbroken, low-hanging clouds. Naked tree branches wave stiffly, made twice their size by a covering of transparent ice.

Drops of water spilled on the stone floor of the bath-room cubicle are frozen. Water in the toilet bowl is frozen. Crystals of amber urine, like costume jewelry, dot the scrubbed whiteness of the toilet. They melt, dissolve, flow to other ices in the drain as I waste warm water to be rid of their sight. Steam pours from the drain, gradually dissipating itself.

When I have finished I return the empty but still-warm water carafe to the kitchen, and rejoin the doctor.

He leaves me after lunch, and I close my door. The shame of last night's guilt forces me to begin the little book by Grignon de Montfort which Marie-Ornoux left on my night table. But the day is dark outside, and coldness will not be forgotten. The book reads as if it were written by a child, and I lay it aside. I return to my bed to sleep.

No one disturbs me as the long afternoon passes. There are no noises until the heavy shoes of Marie-Ornoux sound outside my door. Voices. The doctor quietly opens my door a few inches. Drugged by the desire to sleep, I don't move. The door closes imperceptibly, and I hear his voice suggesting to Marie-Ornoux that I'm in no shape for a spiritual conference—that I should be allowed to sleep as long as possible. The clogging footsteps leave more quietly than they came, walking slowly and carefully down the corridor outside.

The weight of last night's drunken conversation returns, filling me with dread, for I know that the doctor was right. I have known this a long time without admitting it even to myself. Something must be done, now that knowing puts it into movement. But it's the dragging of it into public, like a leprous social disease, that repels, that becomes physi-cal repugnance.

Strangeness of a world within walls separated from the world without by the thickness of a door. Here there is a clarity of intention that strips the most casual acquaintances

166

of all need for tact or diplomacy—as suffering strips a hospital's inhabitants of modesty. Men become brothers in their search for the infinite. Impurities are purified and become without motive. In the outside world, the relationship between Dr. Castelar and myself could never be. It could never happen that after twenty-four hours, barriers of years would be destroyed. There develops here an intimacy of speech and manner, a safety of emotions, as if we had been here always, as if we had known nothing else.

The monks are too busy with their own lives to feel qualified to judge my acts of last night. Instead of the high pedestal of indignation which I had expected, they seem to feel that I've had an unfortunate accident, a momentary illness. Their patience is endless, demanding nothing in return.

I climb from the bed fully clothed. It's not difficult to put on my shoes with one hand, but it's impossible to tie them.

Dr. Castelar is in his cell, reading in a chair by the window with his black beret on the back of his head. He looks up as I enter. "So you're awake?" he says quietly. "And how does it feel now—the hangover?"

"Oh, it's about gone, Doctor. Will you tie my shoes?" I sit on his bed, looking again at the top of his head as he ties the laces tightly.

Without looking up he murmurs, "You know, I've been thinking about last night. I'm really more sorry than I can say. I always get smart when I drink too much. In any case, now that I know you a little better I'm convinced I was wrong in much of what I said." He gives the shoelaces a final jerk. "Now, there you are."

"No, you were right, Doctor—and you know it. Don't start looking for things that aren't there. Don't be dishonest out of kindness to me."

"In spite of everything I said last night, I find you very sympathetic, young man." He sits beside me, pulling gloves of brown knit wool over his stiff fingers.

"Thanks, Doctor. I was just thinking the same thing—

wondering if two people as different as we, could ever have become friends on the outside. Why is it so easy in here? Because of the cold we share? The discomforts? I just met you yesterday afternoon and yet we're already like brothers. But why? How?"

"You pose a difficult one, my boy. Let me think . . . Of course, the fact that we got drunk together could have had something to do with it."

"But I've been drunk lots of times, Doctor. It's not the same. Barriers may be destroyed while you're drunk, but they're there again as soon as you sober up. No, I think it's a change that takes place inside the Monastery."

He rises to spread a blanket over our legs. "You know, the relationship of man to man is always a peculiar one," he says slowly, with much concentration. "So many intangibles are involved. It's difficult to explain what I mean. Man is basically an entity, complete unto himself, who has become dependent on society. Man needs and seeks woman, and we've learned to think of the couple as an entity. But physically this is not true. Man is afraid of solitude and of darkness, both natural to him. We pity the blind, not because they can't see, but because their blindness makes them live in darkness and as solitaries. And yet we often find that the blind man develops a happiness which astonishes us, because he's been forced to revert to a single unit of himself, to live in a manner more natural to his basic character. He becomes an entity instead of remaining part of an entity. Man carries within himself these seeds, which are physical and involuntary; and as he's attracted to woman, he is in his innermost self wary of both woman and man. It's this wariness, this never-complete trusting, that keeps man from knowing friendship. But there's also an undeniable element of physical attraction or repugnance involved. Study the great friendships of men on the outside—that of Montaigne and Etienne de la Boétie, that of Joinville and St. Louis, that of Hallam and Tennyson. In each of these there must have been a total sublimation of the physical to a point where doubts could not possibly exist. These friendships were

168

deeply felt. They were a sort of love above love as we think of it. And they were clear and clean and lucid. Once man is sure, this physical barrier developed in society, by society, for the good of society, is destroyed and he can taste something which few of us ever know. Such a depth of moral union between men is almost nonexistent—and we shy from it. In a monastery, of course, the barrier is destroyed. It's understood that man's interest is purely moral once he enters these gates. There's no possibility of physical ramifications. It clears the ground . . ."

"But, Doctor," I interrupt, "you think the physical has that much to do with it? I find that hard to believe. Surely—"

"Wait a moment—let me ask you a question. Have you ever made what you thought was a close friendship with another man? Then have you been separated from this man for a long period? And have you been disappointed to meet him again, finding he has lost the qualities you once found in him?"

I think this over for a moment. "Yes, I believe I have. But on the other hand, I've been separated from other friends to find them exactly as I remembered."

"That's the difference. A youth is a hero worshipper, and hero worship, no matter how innocent, how spiritual, is a sign of physical immaturity. It's rooted in the physical."

I make a movement to protest.

He laughs, "You don't believe that? Let me finish . . . Each of us has known this emotion in his life. I remember as a student I formed what I believed to be a deep and real friendship for an old professor of philosophy. Never was I so happy as in his company; and I was actively jealous of other students who took his time. Now there was nothing, nothing dreamed of between us; and yet jealousy is a disease of passion, no matter how dormant that passion may be. On my return I revisited the old man, only to find him stripped of his former qualities. Time had changed him and me. I left quickly, so great was my disappointment in finding him ordinary and like other men. That's a characteristic of this youthful, and often adult, hero worship. It mingles its roots in the passions, and it will always disappoint."

"I've had a similar experience, Doctor," I admit. "And yet since the war I've revisited former friends who were in school with me, and the feelings between us were unchanged, as if we had never been separated."

"Oh, yes. But that's a sort of comradeship, developed in adolescence, which has no illusions. It's an entirely different, and much better, thing. And those friends will never change. A good criterion is the emotion of personal jealousy. When that enters the picture there's something wrong, and it can result only in fruitless disillusion. When passion enters, no matter how subtly or inoffensively, any permanency is lost. You see, that's why I say there's a fundamental caution between men on the outside which has no place here. Now, is that point clear?"

"I guess so, Doctor."

Marie-Ornoux stands in the doorway. It is late afternoon. The doctor's cell is dark, and the corridor forms a blackness of background for Marie-Ornoux's patched white robe. He comes in and sits with us on the now-sagging bed, and the doctor explains his theory. The young Dominican monk listens carefully.

"That is very astute, Doctor," he says when the other has finished. "My opinion would be a much simpler one. Of course that barrier, which is undoubtedly a very great one, is forcibly destroyed here. But you know, I think it is something else too. On the outside, man's privacy is preciously guarded. It is his business, and only his, how much money he has in the bank, how successful he is, and so forth —and these are things by which he is judged. Man always seeks to make a slightly better impression on his fellow man than his condition merits, and he is afraid to let his private tastes be known. Here, of course, the moment you step inside these walls those outside standards are lost. It makes absolutely no difference to us what you wear, how successful you are in business, or whether you are a pauper or a

170

rich man. There are no classes here. How can we, who live in poverty, who seek poverty, be impressed with temporal successes? No, that is lost here. The only standard left is man's goodness or lack of goodness, and lack of goodness is regarded as no more than symptomatic. It is understood that we seek the same thing, and only in the purity of our intentions can these barriers fall and man learn to love his brother as clearly and as quickly as it is accomplished here."

The doctor leans far over toward Marie-Ornoux. "That, Father, is probably the real explanation," he agrees. "Goodness to you is the same as health to a doctor. Badness is your equivalent of illness or disease. When we come here our sins, which are our disease, must be explained as symptoms. And as sick people in a hospital will discuss their maladies, so do we here discuss our moral deficiencies. They are no longer to be hidden, but, rather, exposed to care. Is that it?"

"Yes," answers Marie-Ornoux, "that is essentially it. Our young friend here was worried for fear we should ask him to leave. His behavior, bad as it was, is nothing to be hidden. Sending him away would be to us exactly like turning a patient who developed a fever from one of your hospitals, Doctor. And it is this, certainly, that destroys most of the barriers. For as you two discuss your faith, your life, and your sins and weaknesses, with a view to understanding them impersonally and honestly, you automatically discuss very intimate things. You discuss pride, lust, anger; and you expose yourselves as simply as one of the hospital patients would expose his fevers, his pains, his scars. Nothing is hidden—nothing needs to be hidden. There are no illusions to be destroyed, nothing that is forbidden. Is that not the real explanation?"

"Yes," mutters the doctor, staring at the floor. "You explain much better than I, Father. It's a combination: destruction of the physical element of doubt between men; destruction of a standard of values which exists on the outside; destruction of man's hesitancy to let himself be seen as he is, naked, spiritually naked, so to speak . . . But I'd

171

better leave you two. I know I'm not supposed to intrude on your spiritual conferences."

Marie-Ornoux rises quickly. "No, Doctor," he protests. "I had only a few moments. I must go now. Remain as you are."

He walks out, leaving a thoughtful silence behind him. Dr. Castelar settles back and leans against the wall.

I am not satisfied. "But to get back to this for a moment," I suggest. "If a man thus exposes his sins to another, isn't respect likely to turn into disgust? I don't feel that way with you. But if another man came here—if he were, say, eaten up with stinginess—I should detest him regardless of the intimacy."

"No, young man, I don't think you would. On the outside you would, but not here. You would detest the fact of stinginess, as I might detest cancer. You never detest that which is seeking to better itself, which is seeking cure. You may despise sin, but never the man who provides the receptacle for sin, the man in whom sin finds its repose."

I sigh deeply. "These are days of great change for me, Doctor. I've decided to do exactly what Marie-Ornoux asks —even to try reading that book by Grignon de Montfort about *La Vraie Dévotion à la Sainte Vierge.* Do you know it? It's an impossible thing."

"Of course I know it. And I love it. You can't afford yourself the luxury of such sophistication, young man. It doesn't become you. For these monks, and for me, this is very real. I pray to the Blessed Virgin every night. She's my greatest happiness."

"I can't make you out, Doctor. One moment you're a mystic, in love with something intangible to the point of being poetic, and the next moment you want to get me the worst old whore in the Valley."

"Forget that, won't you? I was wrong—completely wrong. But you see, you're obsessed with chastity to a point I can't understand. Why are you putting such emphasis on this particular sin? Is it worse than pride, or avarice, or anger? I confess I take great pleasure from love. I've per-

172

haps committed this sin so often it's no longer important to me. It's impossible to be chaste without the grace of God. I can't do it, and neither can you nor anyone else. I must have it—and I'm so accustomed to it that I can't hope to put myself in the watery eyed category of those who say they don't need it. God will give purity; but this I can't ask. Do you understand?"

"No. It doesn't make sense, Doctor. I know a man can't do without physical satisfaction. Maybe that's why I'm so determined to overcome my slavery to it. But you're a believer. With God's grace you could hope for purity."

Dr. Castelar, his face pursed with distaste, lights a strong French cigarette. "I know it doesn't make sense," he continues, talking as if to himself. "You with your fine mind seek consistency. But things are rarely consistent. I've prayed for purity. I worship God as a great sinner. I've begged Him to take my sins from me, no matter at what cost. He's the one sure thing I have, and I love Him to a point of self-annihilation. How I long for this! But I'm too little within God to merit it, to be what I so desperately want to be. But I do know His love, I know it; and with that, my friend, nothing is wasted. Nothing on this earth can harm me. That's why I'm happier tying your shoelaces than I would be between the legs of the most beautiful woman in France. That's why I'm a doctor. If I had been chosen by God I'd be happy as a monk or a priest. But I'm an ordinary man with the blood of my country, which is a savage blood. And God has been content to give me this love without the grace to be sinless. He has left me ordinary . . . ordinary . . ." He looks away, out the window, mumbling to himself. "There, now, there—my heart is bared. I'm without defense against the scorn of an unbeliever. You see, I'm a man of great strength, but in this I'm more helpless than a newborn infant. I have nothing to be proud of except my love for you and all the 'yous' of this earth. And my love for God. And my hope to give of myself in His name. To help the helpless. To find my place in heaven one day."

His face is immobile. He looks at me, breathing a deep sigh of profound discontent. I say nothing.

"Humph—it's too bad these concrete dreams come so seldom. I—I wonder at my place in the world. I love God like the saints, with all my passion and my happiness. I should have been chosen. But the thing doesn't make sense. It must not be in the measure of our sin, but rather in the measure of our love, that we base our hope. That's not theologically sound, perhaps, but it's my only reason for living. What's wrong with this?"

I can't answer. He goes on speaking slowly, or rapidly, or angrily, or cajolingly.

"No one knows. No one questions God's way. I wait. I wait to find out. But my love is no less great. I produce children without actually wanting them, to pay—and to pay strongly—for the love I give my wife. I could prevent this easier than many men. But I can't bring myself to do it. It's against nature, and anything that's against nature is detestable to God. I'm not a good father, not a good husband. I don't know—we see these things, as now, and they become clear. But look, my friend, there are other things more important. My family is a convenience, the result of my libido. I married a woman because we slept well together. I married her for physical satisfaction. But my happiness is not there—my happiness is in my sacrifice. I have everything most men want—money, social prestige, success in my field, a good bed—but these things are as dust to me, for I know what I am. I remember that the Indian women with whom I have lain were born as I and will die as I, and that the children they have by me can never be my equals. What makes these changes? I understand nothing of them. No, my only hope is that the chance will come. We stand around and wait for it, wait for the change to take place, for a man to become his pride. My obsession is with death—to die a martyr, a Christian. It's so easy that way. And my only gift, the only moment of this life which is really happy, is when I can make the gift of myself—my knowledge, my education, my comforts—for another in the

174

name of heaven. If I pervert you to drunkenness it means nothing—the passing of a few moments no more bad than good." He begins to speak with great rapidity. "But if I, who have performed the most delicate of operations in the most modern of hospitals, who know the secrets of human anatomy—if I can give you a bath, or dress you, or do the most menial tasks for you while you are without the use of your arm, then I am happy and my life begins to make a little sense. For here I give of myself, and I am humbled; and both the giving and the humility are sweet to me."

The room is dark. Pulling the blankets from his lap, the doctor rises to turn on the lights. The sound of Vespers reaches up through the floor. The glare hurts our eyes. In another voice, a voice brought into reality, he asks, "Do you want to go to Vespers?"

"No, Doctor, I think not. And why don't you turn off the light?"

He presses the switch, again throwing the cell into the half-light of an early winter's afternoon. Snow, frozen to his window, obscures any view. He crosses the dim light and sits heavily beside me, covering himself again.

"This is a new world here, Doctor," I say to the dark. "One I've never known—more real, more sharply defined. And I envy you your life, my friend. No matter how confusing it seems, it's straightforward and clear—and it makes sense, somehow. Whether or not I ever believe, I'll never forget what you've told me."

There's an embarrassed silence. I stir my numb legs beneath the blanket.

"Ah yes, young man," Dr. Castelar recovers himself. "I wish I had something to offer you to drink, but I'm afraid of the wine for you now. Have one of these terrible cigarettes with me . . . We sit here, you and I, we sit here and we're absorbed in each other, seeking warmth, sharing a closeness of body heat; and the interests of each are in the other. Suddenly I think of my wife, wherever she is, and wonder about your family. It's very strange how they can be forgotten. This life *is* a new one, isn't it? It's clear; it

175

changes your entire standard of values. But you will go far beyond me, my friend—far beyond if you'll open your eyes and forget all the bylaws of life to learn again from new foundations, without the stultifying background of tailored opinions of behavior. People who can go straight to God, and who know what they're doing, become a law unto themselves—much more severe, but also much more real and satisfying. It's for the emotional, the instinctive, the unenlightened men that we must pass rigid social laws, for like the cenobites of early days they would have their cake and eat it too. These people—and each of us is in part such a man—will have a certain amount of concrete virtue, but the virtue is generally lost in the pride of it. The world is full of them. It's they to whom we refer as 'unenlightened' or 'instinctive.' They take responsible positions and are considered people of virtue, because they so consider themselves. But is sin in a man nullified by simply ignoring it, or by replacing it with another? Can there be any virtue in not committing fornication if you masturbate in its place? And how many who stoutly defend their ability to remain chaste out of strength of will, delude themselves by this substitution of the one for the other? If such were chastity it would indeed be a simple matter. That's the great sin of many of us, I think. We have a convenient criterion of morality which is not basically honest. I've seen people show marked admiration for a woman who doesn't smoke, or a man who doesn't drink. It appears to make little difference how stingy, how uncharitable that man is. If he doesn't smoke or drink he is a nice man, one to be admired. And we're even more dishonest when it comes to ourselves. Anyone who has a sense of perspective, and who lives with himself, must know of the countless private actions and thoughts which plague all of us daily—unspeakably pornographic and unnatural for the most part. We have them unless we convince ourselves differently; they are ours. And yet we would condemn them in another. It's like the old swimming pool story. You urinate in the pool without any qualms, and yet you'd report anyone else you caught doing such a

176

thing; you'd have him thrown out of the pool and fined for committing a public nuisance, when you had just finished doing the same thing with perfect impunity yourself." He laughs, looking at my confusion. "So I hit you with that one, eh? Who hasn't done the same thing? It just never occurs to us that anyone else would do it. We're geniuses for excusing ourselves. It's pretty much the same with everything. You say to yourself, as does everyone else, 'Well, it isn't right, but it won't hurt if *I* do it.' You see, that's what I meant by clearing the mind. Urinating in a swimming pool is primarily harmful in that we delude ourselves into placing the act in a category of innocence within ourselves, while condemning it in others. When the blame is placed elsewhere, the thoughts cannot be clear."

I squirm on the cot, and he asks, "What's the matter? Am I talking too much?"

"No, not at all, Doctor." It is dark in the cell. His teeth show white in the anonymity of obscured facial features.

He continues, "I was going to say that one of the primary values of confession is that we confess simply to our Father in charge, with the firm instruction never to offer mitigating circumstances, never to place the blame on another's shoulders. This is very healthful in making us see our part in the system of guilts. You must learn to think this way. Either you do a thing or you don't, but if you do, then accept the fact without excuse. A great step forward which is always made in these monasteries is the realization that we ourselves are so inadequate, so imperfect, it would be a presumption to judge another. It's a clarity of perception more than anything else, I think, that you get here. These men, who seem almost saintly to us, have reached a point of such scrupulous purging of every fleck of sin, that they regard their souls with microscopic consciences; and since they strive for a perfection which is above the human, their humility must forever grow as they see that the ideal is always far beyond their potentiality for realizing it. They never say, 'This is good, I did not hate Brother So-and-so quite so much today,' or, 'I did not

177

gorge myself at noon, I am doing better.' No, they don't occupy themselves with the little goodness they've accomplished, but instead with the deficiencies that remain to be cleared up. That's why humility is one of the keystones of the monastic life and why pride is one of the most detestable of sins; for pride implies a lack of basic honesty, a blindness of the spirit. Pride is indeed nothing less than spiritual self-abuse. It shouldn't exist in any man, and when it does it should be stamped out at all costs. It's little, debilitating, and cancerous."

The doctor throws these words to the now-complete darkness, his voice acid with disgust. We sit in a black void, feeling only the immediacy of each other and of the cot and the blanket.

I ask, "Do you really think pride is the worst of all sins?"

"Yes, I do. It destroys the soul more surely than any other sin, for it's an intangible, and those who have it are rarely conscious of its existence within them. You know when you commit the others; you know when you sleep with a woman, or when you become angry, or envious, or stingy. But pride blinds you not only to itself, but to all other sins as well. What's the most despicable person you know? Why, it's the man who can never say simply, 'No, thank you, I don't care for a drink,' but instead declares with a flush of superiority, 'No, thank you, *I* don't drink,' or, '*I* don't fool with women' (heaven help him), or, '*I* don't smoke.' He's a paragon of virtue who's reduced to a nothing by the moral castration of pride—pride in the ability he has to stand alone and above poor devils like us. That same man is also 'good.' He's good because on page four of his little spiritual codex it says that 'goodness' must make up so much of his life. He'll help anyone in his class, and give an occasional basket to the poor but 'deserving'—always *deserving*—people of his community. And he'll return home to his good wife and say, 'Ah, but it makes a man feel good to help others.' But if you're drunk, or if you're some poor beggar who's got himself rolled by a whore, then he won't soil his hands on you, he won't weep

178

or waste a prayer on you. He'll despise you, despise whoredom and drink, and forget his own inadmissible fevers of the past. As long as that pride exists he can't love God, he can't be *in* love with God abjectly and profoundly. No, he gives God a firm handclasp and goes on not doing the things that are done. He's happy in a mean way, for he denies what's always there."

"I think it goes beyond that, Doctor," I object. "You've painted a true picture of me. I'm exactly like that. But it's simply that such things don't enter the heads of people with backgrounds like mine."

"I paint a true picture of myself too, my friend. It isn't pretty, is it? But we're striving for something so sublime that it takes a clear view. No man can love God who despises the least of his own. When we can learn to see that this pariah, or that beggar, is of our clay, and is better than many of us, then we've taken a long step forward in the conquering of pride . . ." He stirs on the cot and gets slowly to his feet. "But I've talked too much. It's easy to talk with you. Come, my feet are frozen. Let's go to dinner."

This, then, is the man whom Marie-Ornoux called one of the great living Christians. Only now do I begin to understand the fire of his rightness.

We stoop through the low door and walk slowly down the ice-covered steps into the courtyard. It's a still night which probes instantly to bone marrow.

"Wait a moment," I tell the doctor. "I'm going behind that tree and melt some of this damnable ice."

"Better hurry. In this weather your water will be frozen before it hits the ground. Listen . . ." He spits, and the saliva strikes loudly in the dark, become ice in the air.

When I return he says, "Now we'll go in to our feast in the refectory. What would you like for dinner tonight?"

"Oh, I'd like a nice thick beefsteak cooked very rare, some French fries, some *crêpes,* a good bottle of red wine, coffee and cognac—and a buxom, giggling, brainless girl."

"Remind me to give you a bromide," says the doctor drily, "before you go to bed. You have as much chance of

179

getting the giggling girl as you do of eating beefsteak and French fries."

"How well I know it!" I sigh. "My stomach is aching for food and we'll have soup. Couldn't you give me the bromide now, before we eat?"

In the refectory, after a long prayer, we eat thin, tepid soup made from the water in which cabbages have been boiled. It smells strong on the cold air of the refectory. It has a bitter taste, no more satisfying than tainted water.

The reader's chanting voice is pitched high in a desperation of hunger and cold. He reads from Daniel-Rops's study of the Bible, and his words come as billows of steam in the bald light. He describes the beheading of St. John the Baptist, and in the description is a passage devoted to Salome. His voice falters, steadies itself, becomes another singing monotone as the author tells of the unwrinkled firmness of Salome's body and of the fullness of her milk-white breasts, intoxicating to both hand and mouth. The passage has only begun, but Father Abbot raps the table with his mallet, and the reader stops. There's a momentary silence as he loudly turns the pages to a more edifying chapter—and commences reading again.

We stare at our plates, not daring to look up. Slowly the flush settles. Silently the doctor reaches across the table and places two small white bromides in my palm, shaking his head hopelessly. In a single gesture I swallow both the bromides and my laughter.

The doctor stays for Compline. Since I can't undress alone I go to bed fully clothed, removing only my shoes. I fall asleep before the end of this last office of the day.

17 december

Face down on my pillow, I lie awake in the dark. There's the movement of a black robe in the cell. It is Father Clément placing something white on the floor.

"Is that you, Father? What time is it?"

"It is time for Matins, my son—not yet dawn. I have brought you a foot bath and some very hot water, thinking you might wish to bathe while the others are in chapel."

"It's so terribly cold." Our voices are hushed in the dark. The only sound is a wind outside.

"I know, my son. But if you bathe quickly and return to your bed you will not suffer. However, if you prefer not to . . ."

"No, I'll try it. I'm filthy. I'll do anything to be clean again. But I slept fully dressed."

"I can help you off with your clothes, and when you have finished Dr. Castelar will be glad to dress you. But can you bathe with your arm like that?"

"Yes, sir."

I crawl from the bed. Father Clément carefully pulls the sweaters and shirt and underwear over my head. I sit down, holding a stockinged foot in the air.

"Now, Father, if you'll just help me off with these socks, I can manage the pants with the help of gravity."

He removes my stiff socks, spreads the wrinkles from my cot, and leaves me hurriedly as opening chants of Matins rise from the chapel. I undo my pants, letting them drop to the floor, and step out of them. The cold is not much worse naked than fully clothed, and the water is very hot. With soap and a cloth I squat in the panlike tub and wash myself clean. When I have dried with a thick towel I sit on the bed, place my feet in the tub, and finish the bath.

Gradually, lying again beneath the blankets, a half-warmth returns to my body. I wait without sleeping, trembling, for Matins to become Lauds, for the doctor to return

181

and dress me. My impatience makes the chants seem endless.

He arrives soon after the final chants, as dawn begins to turn the sky to a soft gray. Bracing myself against the pain, I let him dress me quickly. We talk quietly of nothing, and hurry to the refectory for breakfast. I eat nearly all my day's ration of bread, knowing that tonight I'll regret it.

The wind becomes strong, menacing, creating drafts through the closed windows. The somber morning is spent at work in the paleography room, holding manuscript pages in place with my left arm and writing with my right.

To the craving for food and warmth is added the need, felt by each of us, of manual labor, of physical exercise. It's impossible to walk with any freedom on the ice-covered ground. There are no outside chores to be attended to. We do inside work, but it doesn't satisfy. We sweep the corridors, we polish brass, we wax pews in the chapel; but there are many of us and only a few jobs. I ask Father Prior if I may clean the bathrooms again or carry water; but these tasks, which become highly desirable as ways of expending energy, have been asked for and assigned many days in advance. Scrupulously, in our spare time, we clean and reclean our cells. We carry our blankets outside and help one another shake the dust from them.

The courtyard is now an ugly roughness of dirty and discolored whites. The snow is tinted red where gravel has been thrown, and gray where bathwater has been splashed onto the ground and left to freeze. It is speckled with dust from numerous blankets, and dotted with countless amber spots where urine has melted snow, mingled with it, and become frozen again.

We live in smallnesses, waiting for Mass and Vespers and Compline. Our thirst grows for these moments of forgetting, of worship, of great beauty. They don't change. As our life becomes more paralyzed with the elements, with the deprivations, these things remain unchanged and we cling to them.

At noon Marie-Ornoux comes to my cell. Covered with

182

blankets, we sit and discuss the warmth of abstraction to escape the coldness of reality. His face is red and clear and frank, with an openness about it that makes you forget exteriors, that invites you to immediate intimacy. He asks me what I think of the monastic life by now.

"I don't know, Father," I reply, wanting to choose my words carefully. "Life here is a strange new experience. You people bandy God and the Blessed Virgin about so freely, you make them real. I can't understand it. To me it's as though this entire Monastery were made up of puppets being worked by strings from heaven."

"I wish that were true, what you say," he murmurs, "but it is not. Ours is a struggle more severe and more constant than any struggle known to man, and we never reach our goal. But tell me, why do you persist in this determination not to accept us?" His voice is quiet, almost joking.

"I do accept you, Father," I protest. "And I admire and love you as a people on a plane far above me. But it's simply not in me to accept your strings from heaven. At least I'm convinced it's I who am wrong, and not you. That's what keeps me here. If I weren't convinced do you think I'd go through all this just to learn how Tutilo invented tropes, or how Notker set words to difficult cantilena passages?"

"Look, I am a fairly sane man," he says matter-of-factly. "Let me tell you something. I have been a convert for only ten years myself. In fact I was converted right here in this Monastery under the direction of Father Clément. I am a Jew, my son, brought up in Egypt and educated at the École Polytechnique in Paris, with a degree in engineering. That does not make for a background which willingly accepts the intangible. I am not a strong man—I never have been—and no man had less respect for morals than I during my school days in Paris. But strength in these things comes from the desire for it, and from the initial acceptance of God as a real and living thing within us. By force I achieved this initial step, and ever since then my path has been the crawling of a man dying of thirst, who seeks an oasis in the desert."

183

"But, Father," I interpose, "how much of that is auto-suggestion? That's what I don't get."

"Probably a great deal at the outset," he confesses without hesitation. "But we make the proof very real and practical. If it is caused exclusively by autosuggestion, by a momentary upsurge of the soul, it will last only until the spell dies. You can see the severity of the monastic life. In other orders it is even more severe. We are postulants for seven years before taking our final vows. The human body cannot long stand such privations unless it desires them as a sacrifice to God. For those who have an immense desire to strip themselves of all earthly pleasures, there are orders like the Trappist or Carthusian. The point is, we make our lives together so difficult that no man without a true religious vocation can stay with us for long. But this is a progressive thing. God becomes more real to us daily, as we in turn do our best to make Him the only reason for our lives. The door must first be opened, however. We can do nothing until the initial act of faith is made—no more than a grocer's clerk can fill your order before it is formulated. It is very easy to say, 'Why, the vows of poverty, chastity, and obedience are not so difficult'—but try them for yourself. When I was a Trappist I lived only three miles from my mother, but in the seven years I was there I never once heard from her. If she had died, I probably never would have known. That is a poverty which embraces everything, my son. We sing our offices badly in Paris, at the Dominicans', because our sacrifice must include even the spiritual richness of beauty."

I nod my head. "I can understand that, Father. But tell me about the Grignon de Montfort book on the Blessed Virgin. I can't understand how a man of your background can accept such childishness."

"As a matter of fact, my son, much of our faith makes us seek childish simplicity. But to explain the book . . . For some of us the vow of poverty is the most difficult to embrace. We cannot so much as keep a photograph of any member of our family with us. We cannot spend a penny

184

unless our conscience tells us that it is absolutely necessary. We must not eat one bite more than we feel will keep us alive and in health. When you are tortured with hunger it is easy to forget this vow. For others of us the vow of obedience is the most difficult. You cannot be obedient, blindly obedient to a superior, unless you desire humility and a suffering of the spirit such as our Blessed Saviour suffered. And for nearly all of us the vow of chastity is very severe, because it is not only a spiritual exercise, but a physical phenomenon which is always with us, which grows in force. We are never free from it, you see. And a vow of chastity means, of course, *total* chastity. In the world of today chastity is considered little more than refraining from sleeping with women—something to be had for the wanting of it. But a monastic rule cannot be based upon such niceties. In the original rule of St. Benedict, you will remember, he makes careful provisions against any contingency which may arise. It is obvious that if a man, in a moment of weakness, cannot have release in the normal way, the tension will mount within him until he finds satisfaction of some sort. It is also obvious that if you take a youth in his adolescence, before the object of his passion has crystallized definitely into the form of a woman—if you take this youth and never let him see a woman again, then his passion will assume a new and unnatural object and turn toward anything which provides a potential fulfillment of this function. If that object can be God, then the result is a chastity which embraces God with human reality. But in the adolescent this does not always happen, for the simple reason that a concrete and stable love is found only in the balance of adulthood. We took care of the problem in the early days of monasticism in the only way possible—we simply never gave it a chance to happen. St. Benedict was very specific in his rule pertaining to it. All the monks had to work so hard and undergo such privations as to lessen the urge, that when they did sleep they were so exhausted that nothing but sleep mattered to them. However, all the monks slept, as do the Trappists today, fully clothed on the floor. They lay head to foot,

185

with an old monk sleeping between every two young monks. In addition to this precaution a light was kept burning during the hours of darkness, and one of the old monks stayed awake to watch over his sleeping brothers. If they became uncomfortable in their sleep he soothed them with a touch, or with a few words spoken quietly. You must remember that this rule was written during a period of great coarseness, when such problems were faced with absolute frankness and a touching reality. Never were these early monks left alone. Every instant of their lives was passed together, on a schedule of such rigid minuteness that a time was set even for answering the needs of the body. Although this is considered a little overcautious, even unnecessary nowadays, the nature of man has not changed one iota since that time as far as this phenomenon is concerned. We must face it in all its multicolored phases. The same rule, of course, still applies in the more severe orders."

He hesitates before going on, and I say, "I can see that, Father—there are after all a thousand hidden ways to destroy chastity. But what's that got to do with the Montfort book?"

"I was getting to that. You must not think that we give this undue attention. For many of us chastity is the severest vow to take, merely because the breaking of it can come with so little warning and produce such terrible repercussions within us."

"Tell me one thing, Father—what happens if there's an accident? Surely a man shouldn't be dismissed for just a momentary weakness?"

"Of course the breaking of each of the vows is of equal importance and must be confessed. If I break my vow of poverty, or of obedience, or of chastity, it is a terrible thing. No, we are not dismissed. We are helped, watched more carefully, and placed doubly on guard against a repetition. Generally if a man breaks a vow three times he has to leave. And three times during a lifetime is very little allowance, my son."

"Lord, I can imagine!" I exclaim. "I'd have to be given

186

about a thousand. I think I could stand a vow of poverty the easiest of all. That wouldn't bother me."

Father Marie-Ornoux looks at me highly amused. "You are superb, my son. But the vow of poverty is just as complete as that of chastity in my mind, in my interpretation of it. It depends on your conscience. To me poverty means total poverty, the same as chastity means total chastity. And it is every bit as difficult if carried to its logical conclusion. If you who love fine things knew that you would never again hear a Mozart sonata, nor look at a painting by Braque, it would be very difficult for you not to lie awake thinking of them at night. I have that trouble a great deal, and often the only thing that can drive them out of my thoughts and dreams is for me to sleep on the stone floor, or wear a hair shirt. When discomfort enters the picture it drives these other things out, and for me the vow of poverty would be broken if I allowed myself the richness of remembering a Juan Gris painting or a Monteverde madrigal. I cannot, you see, share my love of God with anything else, for it is all His, and I cannot allow myself the pleasure of sharing it with a feast for the eyes and ears. This is my greatest temptation, as it would be yours, I think."

"Don't you think, Father, that you're carrying this thing to the ridiculous? After all some of the great Benedictines, and Dominicans too, are specialists in fields of secular music and painting and literature."

"Ah, yes. But you see, that is their work, and it is all done to the glory of God; whereas my work is infinitely more humble and I must answer the fine lines of conscience. I should indeed be happy if I had been directed to do research in the arts or literature; but I love them too much and it would have been a source of unmerited richness which would have made a mockery of my vow of poverty. Each man has his niche, and that is not mine, alas. Satisfaction of this sort is lethal to my conception of my role in God's work. I am not worthy of it, for I have a much more menial work to do."

"But that's what I don't understand, Father," I say emphatically. "How in the devil can you actually know what

187

your work is? I'm sorry, but all this is confusing to me."

"Why, God tells us, my child."

"Yes, but that's what I don't get. *How* does God tell you? Does He come to you in a vision? Does He speak to you? And if you answer yes I'm getting out of this place right now."

He relaxes, looking at me uncertainly, smiling at my almost desperate confusion. "Not exactly," he says calmly. "I do not have visions, if that reassures you. But you see, this life is on another plane, and as you get into it certain things become clear. God tells us what He wants of us in many ways, and often they seem diametrically opposed to what we actually think and feel. He speaks to us through our consciences and there is no mistaking or changing His word. He speaks to us through our thirsts and hungers, thirsts and hungers so great we cannot ignore them. I may thirst for ever-greater humility in my mission. I may thirst for God through work with the downtrodden. My hunger may be to live among the most miserable of His creatures. Others may desire within themselves merely to adore God in perpetual prayer. Still others may wish to take on themselves the sufferings of those who do not believe. They long to suffer on this earth in order to expiate the sins of men who disbelieve, who lead lives of evil and thereby do harm to God's will. They are among the greatest of the world's Christians today, for their sacrifice is total and they live in the depths of ugliness and pain. You see, men who devote themselves to God do not differ greatly from those in our outside society. There we need bakers and carpenters and artists and doctors. Here also we need men to fill many different roles, and what is right for one is not necessarily right for another."

"And what exactly is your role, Father?"

"I am too weak and unimportant to do much, my son. I cannot offer myself in suffering for the sins of my brothers because I am already given to the Blessed Virgin. No, I hope to go among the derelicts of the world—not to convert them, but to live with them and to help them; and if God

188

is willing, to let them see how He can work through the poorest of vessels, such as I. I have asked permission to go, as did Father Foucauld, into the Moslem deserts to live among the greatest enemies of our Church. I know the country and the language."

"But the desert country is the worst place in the world for a Christian, Father. They're vowed to kill all Christians. You wouldn't last two weeks before they killed you just as they killed Father Foucauld."

"I know—they told Father Foucauld the same thing. But he stayed on for years before they martyred him. I have followed in his footsteps, and I am the only one to take his place now. If I am killed then someone else will come after me, and they will keep coming forever. It took a saintly man like Father Foucauld to open the way. Now little men like me can do our part, for I have by the grace of God this one longing in my heart, and it will see to it that I do my best."

"What is this strength you people have that lets you do impossible things?" I ask in wonder.

Father Marie-Ornoux stares uncomfortably at the floor. "You exaggerate, my son." His voice remains firm. "We are the least of men, and our sins are that much greater; for we have before us examples of the saints whom we wish to follow, and within us a weakness that makes our steps falter."

"You make me feel like so much trash, Father."

"I had hoped to make you feel a little above that, my son."

"I didn't mean it that way. When I talk with you and Father Clément I feel as if I were consumed with filth, but that it's possible for me to do the impossible. But when I'm away from you the other comes back."

"That is because you depend on human beings for inspiration, my son. You must go beyond us to the Source which is God."

"But I've gone so far in bad habits!" I protest. "I've become so hardened to pleasure it's above me to overcome

189

it. You can't imagine how much these things bother me."

"But I am the same way, my son—all of us are. That is the reason we must have help constantly. But the first act must be made by you. Let me tell you of the reasons why I became an oblate of the Blessed Virgin. When I first began to realize the mystery of this life I was hardened, like you, into bad habits. I thought that I might learn to keep the vows of poverty and obedience, but that it was not humanly possible for me to take a vow of chastity. You see, I was converted. I believed, but I did not make the famous initial step. How many times have I got up from my prayer to walk about the streets of Paris and pick up the first girl I could find! You can imagine the torture to my self-respect, to my mingled beliefs. But I kept on. I begged God to give me the hope of one day being His. The shell of habit is hard to break, and although a remorse was born within me, I could not control my desires, I could not stop my quest for the flesh. The night before I entered the Church was the most carnal of my life, but I decided to go ahead. Things did not change as I had hoped they might, even though my conscience did become more acute. I promised in the confessional that I would make the effort not to do it again. Each time I fell, however, until finally the act of confession became little more than a lie. I was convinced that no matter how hard I tried, how sincerely I promised, this was a part of me which could not be conquered. But my love of God was established. The two forces pulled me apart, destroying my being. One day I asked my priest if I could not perhaps try entering a monastery. He assured me that I was not ready. He told me that the test for chastity was to remain six months without stain—that if a man can remain six months he can remain a lifetime. I soon reached a point where there were only two possible solutions: either to give up my hope and enjoy what I was doing, knowing that with the destruction of remorse I would regain my health; or to leap wholeheartedly into the unknown and do something definite to stop my periodic relapses. I spent many days worrying, until one day the book

190

by Grignon de Montfort fell into my hands. Finally, knowing that what I was doing was impossible, a false dream, I went to my Father Confessor and took a vow to the Blessed Virgin and became her oblate, giving myself and all my life, now and in the future, to her. I could never have anything again, because everything I would ever possess would be hers—my life, my money. I took the vow to her because I had learned to love her. My feeling for God at this time was one of fear and awe. It was not comfortable, not real. But she was real, and I knew that I would not harm her if I could help myself. That first night I lay in my bed promising her everything—my life, my chastity, my adoration, and all my prayers. I promised never to spend another penny on myself except for absolute necessities, never to think lascivious thoughts again. It was easy then, for it seemed so terribly final. I slept on my back with my hands outside the covers, so that in my sleep they might not touch my body. It was truly unbelievable. Every time that I would forget and begin to think of forbidden things, her voice—a lifeless, soundless voice—would speak inside me like the point of a memory, the cry of conscience. I do not know what it was, but it would be there, interrupting my thoughts with only three words which never changed: *You promised me,* it would say. And the peculiar thing is that it never failed. Each time I forgot, each time I noticed a girl in the street this strange voice within me would not forget; it would say, *You promised me,* and I would stop, for I knew it was her voice reminding me. These were the happiest days I had ever known, for it never failed. At the first hint of something wrong she reminded me that I had promised, and I would never hurt her nor break the promise."

"Do you mean you actually heard a voice, Father?" I ask incredulously. "A woman's voice?"

He shakes his head. "No, it was not that exactly. But it was very acute. It seemed as though she had taken me, had entered my very being, and speaking through my conscience, warned me every time. Even when I had forgotten, or was not thinking about her at all, it would still be there—

always the same three words. It is like your own conscience. If you were to steal some of the wine from the shop across the street your conscience would, in some nebulous, unintelligible manner, let you know that it was wrong. Well, the Blessed Virgin speaks to you through this same medium, but she sharpens it and makes it more precise."

He pauses. Gusts of strong wind sound monotonously outside, isolating us in my cell. There is the false brightness of noon in winter. We sit quietly, covered with the coarse blanket.

"I fell completely in love with her that first week," he says after a moment. "Every day I said the rosary, singing it at my work, happy in the knowledge that I had taken the step and would never again sink from her sight. I knew she would turn her face away if I broke my promise. You cannot imagine the joy of lying in bed at night thinking only thoughts I knew would be pleasing to her. Nor can you dream of the joy in walking home with her from work. Gradually things I had considered necessary became unnecessary, until finally I wanted nothing more and most of my pay check was going to the poor. But you know, after a couple of weeks I began to worry about the experiment, for I was beginning to be filled with the need for a woman, a need so powerful that nothing—not even my promise—could stop it. It was beyond me. Despite my every wish I had to turn my back on her. I went into the streets, my lust driving her voice from me. There was soon no more indication that she might still be there. I was sick. I was taking money that I could have given to the poor and planning to spend it on a woman, to buy myself satisfaction; and worst of all, my fidelity to the Blessed Virgin was gone. I walked on and on determined to find myself a girl, until finally I came to a quiet little side street off the Place de l'Opéra where I knew there was a brothel. But the lights were poor, and I had walked only a few steps when I found myself falling into space. My hands grabbed the air. I fell to the bottom of a stairway which led from the sidewalk into a cellar. I remember just one thing before losing consciousness—I

192

remember murmuring, 'Thank you,' to the Blessed Virgin. She was back with me again. She had answered my prayers and kept me from reaching my goal. I was, miraculously, not badly hurt, but the fall had left me enough bruises and pain to take away all desire for a woman."

Interrupt. This leaves a bad taste in the mouth. It's offensive in a way, and I ask, "Father, do you really expect me to believe the Blessed Virgin was responsible for all this?"

"No, and I did not either, at first. It is very difficult to make another understand, but it is real enough. However, as I say, I gave it little thought myself, although I was glad it had happened. But you must know that in another week, when I was well once more and had got my pay check, the thing happened again except in a different manner. There were the same tortures, the same inner apologies, and I thought she had left me as before—so I went directly toward the brothel. But this time I was accosted by a pretty girl in the street, and I accepted her quickly before anything could happen. We went into a hotel near the Bibliothèque nationale and got a room. She seemed very nice and I knew that nothing could happen this time to stop it. First, however, she took all my money—every penny of it. When she had the money she took off her blouse and chemise, but to my horror her body from breast to hips was swathed in heavy tape. She told me she could not do it in the normal way. For some reason I cannot explain I burst into laughter —I roared with laughter. Here I had spent all my money, built up my hopes and my sins, and she destroyed my desire with her broken ribs and her unnatural suggestions. I asked her for my money back, but she refused to give me even car fare home. You see, of all the women in Paris, is it not strange that I find the one who can do nothing for me, and who robs me of every cent I have to make the lesson more severe? In spite of it I was happy to escape . . . I could go on and on with such stories, each one becoming more drastic —until finally I no longer tried. Never, never since I took that vow to the Blessed Virgin, my friend, have I been able to do this thing, and I tried it many times before my own strength to resist it was established. Do you wonder, then, why I passed you the little Montfort book? It is childish, but is not our love for God always a childish thing? Would I tell this story I have just told you to anyone else? Does not it too sound childish? And yet I assure you now that my life has become more concrete, she is no less a force in it than before, although now I doubt if she would be quite so drastic. If I fell now it would be a terrible thing, for I know better, I am armed against it—and she would not interfere. That is why this is such a haunting, such a continually terrifying possibility. And it is why I understand you so well, my young friend. You see, I believe our Blessed Mother staved this thing off for me until I had built up my strength to enter the Trappists, where of course there was no further possibility of falling. We are all plagued with it, but we are out of the habit, and we struggle to stay in the grace. This is an intimate story, my son, which is true in every detail. I may be wrong in telling it to you. If others were to open their hearts to you as I have, you would find that the same thing has happened to many of them. If I had been told this several years ago, I confess I would not have believed it myself. You should understand that we are not struck by bolts of lightning. It is a long and often-sordid path we must travel, but the love which we have for God makes it an enchantment." With an effort he rises from the cot. "Now I must go. Forgive me for talking so much, but I wanted you to understand our character—that we are not different from the least of our brothers on the outside. It is almost time for the noon meal."

I get up and stretch the tightness out of my muscles. "Your visit has meant a lot to me, Father," I tell him. "It goes much further than you know. Next time you must tell me of the work you plan to do in the desert."

"Very well, my child. And do not bother with the Montfort book if it is that annoying to you."

"I'll try it again, Father."

I accompany him to the door. He smiles a good-bye and

194

walks slowly away in the direction of the stairs. I stare after him, for his movements are dominated by a heavy limp which I haven't noticed before. I hesitate a moment, then hurriedly catch up with him.

"What's wrong, Father?" I ask. "You're limping."

"Just a little sore knee, my son."

"But it looks bad. Can't I help you down those slippery steps?"

"No, thank you, I—"

"Ah, there's the lunch bell now. Wait a moment, I'll walk with you."

We make our way carefully to the refectory. Marie-Ornoux obviously walks with difficulty, but he volunteers nothing more and I don't ask. With a slight nod we separate at the door. After the prayer I eat quickly, anxious to have done with the sadness of my food, my mind racing with thoughts of the young Dominican monk. Dr. Castelar is not there.

Back in my cell, I read again the Grignon de Montfort, forcing myself to concentrate on his outline. I fight off sleepiness, and the time drags slowly by. In mid-afternoon there's a welcome noise in the next cell followed by creaking footsteps of wet leather, and the doctor stands at my open door.

"Well, Doctor," I exclaim, laying my book aside, "where've you been all day? I can take my clothes off, you know, but it's impossible to dress myself. I've been marooned here since lunch because I couldn't get my shoes back on."

The doctor is wrapped in his heavy overcoat. He leans against my night table. "Go on with your reading. Don't let me stop you."

I rise to sit on the edge of my cot. "No, I've done my duty to this impossible book."

"I was sorry to leave this morning," he says, "but I forgot all about you. How'd you make out with Marie-Ornoux?"

"Fine. We had quite a session. You see the result—I'm reading what he wants."

195

"Good." He glances about the cell. "Where are your shoes? And do you know you need a shave? You're beginning to look like a tramp."

"Well, I can't by any stretch of the imagination shave myself, and Marie-Ornoux has forbidden me to leave the Monastery. I can't even go to a barber." I reach under the bed and pull out my shoes.

The doctor leans down to put them on my feet. "Here, hold out your foot."

I ask, "Incidentally, did you know Marie-Ornoux has hurt his leg? He's got a bad limp today."

"Yes, I know about it."

"What's the trouble?"

"Tuberculosis of the bone," he replies flatly. "He's had it for some time now. I'm awfully worried about him."

"Tuberculosis of the bone?"

"Yes. It's a terribly painful secondary form of the disease—and very dangerous, of course. Yet he wants to leave the relative safety of his monastery for a hazardous life in the desert. But they feel they can't clip his wings by making him stay." The doctor's voice reveals his weariness and he doesn't look up.

I sit staring at the top of his beret, for words aren't needed. Silence seems loud in the cell. Silence broken by the doctor's breathing, and the rubbing of leather against wool as he puts on my shoes, and the wind of afternoon outside.

"But he doesn't seem to be in great pain." My voice sounds harsh on the stillness. "Do you give him drugs, Doctor?"

"No, he won't allow it. And the pain is constant and very severe. He'll never have relief from it either, because total rest is the only thing that will give relief. Ultimately the knee joint will be destroyed, and he'll be certain to die after a few years." The doctor gives my shoelaces a final tug. "But Marie-Ornoux is a true vessel of grace, a child of God," he says in an expressionless voice as he rises to sit beside me. "All of us who are with him know we're in the

196

presence of a man so much above us, we'll probably never meet his equal on earth. That's the reason they'll let him go even if it's to die. Such a vocation as his is beyond temporal consideration."

"But you know," I reflect, "he doesn't seem so different from the others to me."

"The difference isn't apparent at first, he's so humble. But his worth, his sanctity are of the highest caliber."

"Does he know what he has, Doctor?"

"Of course he does. And he gives thanks to God that it happened to him and not to another who might not be able to bear the pain. Yet he rarely shows it. He seldom winces and never shows fear—except the fear that he prove unworthy of this cross which God has given him." He gestures impatiently. "Come, I don't like to talk about it. Let's see if we can get you shaved. Where's your razor?" There is a forced vivacity in his voice.

"There in the case," I reply as lightly as I can. "But are you sure your nerves are well enough under control?"

"My friend, I'm without nerves. I've been out slutting all morning." He makes an easy gesture with his hand, smiling, as if he'd just finished with a woman. We're both satiated with sanctity. Our beings cry for relaxation in the comfortable atmosphere of ribaldry.

"Was she a blonde?" I ask, carrying the upswing of good feelings. "A blonde with hair combed on top of her head, and a Parisian hat?"

"Precisely. She was your friend from South Africa. Ah, and you ask me if I have nerves . . ."

"So, you forget your duties toward me to go after my women! And I thought you said you'd rather tie my shoelaces than be between the legs of the most beautiful woman in Paris?"

"Tying your shoelaces, my friend, is one thing. But don't overestimate its aphrodisiac qualities. There are degrees of happiness. I'm happier tying your shoelaces or shaving you, but I'm certainly not unhappy sleeping with a woman. The happiness is less, but I can bear it till time

197

to tie your shoes again. You see?" He explains this with mock seriousness, his voice becoming very loud.

"Don't tell it to the whole Monastery, Doctor," I caution him. "I'll bet you weren't anywhere near Madame Vincent this morning."

"I wasn't. I was calling on a case in the Village." He lathers the shaving bowl mechanically. "Hold still while I perform this delicate operation. Otherwise I may cut your throat." With magnificently clumsy gestures he covers my face with soap.

I cringe, spitting, "I hope you're more skillful with your scalpel than with that shaving brush."

He shaves me quickly without answering. Loud scratches echo in the quiet cell as the razor cuts cold, brittle whiskers. He stands at an uncomfortable angle shaving with small strokes. Globules of white lather, gray-flecked with whiskers, fall on my washstand. The wetness is cold and chaps my skin instantly. After wiping my face with a towel he stands back and tilts his head appraisingly.

"There you are," he says. "Clean-shaven as an expensive whore."

I run my fingers lightly over the raw skin. It is smooth and hardens uncomfortably beneath my touch. "I wouldn't know. I never went to an expensive whore."

"You don't know what you've missed," he grins. "But then I guess it's not too different from your cheap ones."

He looks behind me toward the door. His eyes open wide, and then he bursts into laughter. I turn around to see Marie-Ornoux standing in the open doorway.

"How long have you been there, Father?" asks Dr. Castelar.

"Not long enough, apparently, Doctor."

The doctor assumes an air of innocence. "This young protégé of yours started it, Father. He's a sex fiend. You can tell it by the curve of his head."

I start to protest, but Marie-Ornoux holds up his hand. "You know," he says, "it really is amazing. The average layman comes here seeking spiritual guidance, and whether

198

or not he gets it he acts as if he does. He never speaks, never laughs. He prays well and goes about in silence with his hands folded in front of him. But look at yourselves. You really carry it a little too far. You talk loud, laugh loud, smoke in the corridors, use filthy language, and the very first night you celebrate by getting drunk. Never have I seen such Rabelaisian conduct nor heard such unseemly language." A slight smile of despair lifts the corners of his mouth. "What am I to make of you?"

The doctor is in high good humor, enjoying himself, but I feel uncomfortable. He asks, "Now be honest, Father, would you rather have us or the others, the ones who're inspired?"

"Why, we would much rather have you," Marie-Ornoux laughs. "You present much more of a challenge to us—to our patience." But seeing our crestfallen disappointment he adds gently, "No, it is a relief to find people who remain normal with us. So many who come here develop a sort of sadness which they mistake for piousness. Perhaps you go a little far in the opposite direction, but we take great pleasure from your presence"—he looks at the doctor with warm affection—"and we know that goodness such as yours does not have to be worn like a mask so that all can see."

"Father, I'm reading the book like you told me," I weakly excuse myself. "And I haven't forgotten our conversation this morning, despite the doctor's evil influence."

He turns to me slowly. "We will talk of it again later. And, Doctor," he says to the other, "would you care to join us?"

The doctor nods his head in agreement, and the young Dominican limps out.

20 december

Having become twisted in bed, the pain in my arm awakens me to an early morning quietness of freshly fallen snow: silence of covering snow frozen on my window, cleansing past filths. I straighten myself, then lie motionless in the dark cell. Assembling thoughts. Untangling threads of this new life. My talks with Marie-Ornoux and the doctor have brought into open view things which were never more than surmised. Accept what can be accepted, and discard the rest.

There is the weight of background, first in America and then in a little French village school. And there are the two people who grow so imperceptibly within every man, that in the bright light of day one forgets the nakedness of night. The idea that in *me* some things do exist which can't exist, and which must be neither named nor accepted. This nakedness is covered in outside backgrounds. And it must be.

These things—pride, lust, anger, lack of humility—which have evolved in our lives outside as more or less fashionable, certainly as natural, become within a monastery's walls symptomatic of a disease; and the disease must be diagnosed completely and honestly before it can be cured. On the outside the doctor will ask, "Are the functions normal? Is there a pain in the chest? Does it hurt when I touch this?" But here the disease, which is impossible to diagnose elsewhere, must be determined by asking, "Do you sleep well? Are your thoughts at night lustful? Did you commit a sin of the flesh? With someone else? With yourself? Do you desire to amend the lie you told?"

On the outside there are things more valuable than truth: diplomacy, delicacy, and the outright denial of personal shortcomings. Man must be his own advocate, and totality of truth is a coward's device, a detestable and self-elevating repugnancy. Here there is nothing more destructive than the lie. It would be as faulty to tell a lie behind these

200

walls as it would be to tell only the truth outside. For it is automatically presumed that truth is a naked and healthful cell; while in society it is automatically presumed that truth is merely the nucleus of the cell of politeness, a cell around which unlike personalities may revolve and mix.

In the world without, all of us must have certain acceptable desires. In the company of men we must first have a desire for women, indicating a fair amount either of real or of simulated success with them. In the company of women we must desire whatever it is that interests the woman—painting, architecture, some fascinatingly risqué joke—and possess a readiness to comply with hinted lechery.

We must have our ounce of piety and belong to some church, from the Catholic at the bottom, to the next high, the Baptist, and on up the ladder of Methodist and Presbyterian to the very stratosphere of the Episcopal. We must smile rather embarrassedly when we say, "Well, I've been made a deacon in my church—can you imagine that?" or, "Junior's been appointed first acolyte. He has such a lovely manner, really, and he's so graceful at the altar. We're rather pleased."

We adapt ourselves, for there must be a constant modulation of character in accordance with the different planes of social strata. Our opinions must fluctuate in the company of Catholics, Jews, Negroes, and other inferior peoples. And in circles dominated by very advanced thinkers we must be able to express sincere and admirably balanced platitudes about segregation, birth control, premarital physical relations, and man's function in the cosmos. All very important topics.

In other circles—the ultrahigh type—we must have been to Europe, and we should have a store of slaughtering, slightly sexless insults: "She's absolutely cadaverous. She's my choice for the depilatory queen of the year." We must keep a few such choice remarks on hand, and afterward they'll say, "He's got the quickest wit. He's merciless. I certainly hope he never gets it in for me"; or, "You simply *must* get him to your dinner party, my dear. Get a few

201

drinks in him and he'll do a screaming take-off on *La Traviata* in Italian. Or you may get him to talk about those stuffy old monks he used to live with. He sings that funny Gregorian stuff like a real abbot."

And in lower circles we adapt ourselves. We laugh at all that crap. We agree that niggers are just as happy as if they had good sense, and that they were a lot happier before people started putting ideas in their heads about human rights. We agree that whoever happens to be president is either a son-of-a-bitch or a godsend. We laugh and admit it's not normal for a young man to be without his little ass every once in a while, and that the girls are just waiting to go out behind the barn with us. Or we stand upright and announce that this younger generation is wild as hell, that we weren't brought up that way. We're serious, and we want to make just enough money to ask Rosalie for her hand. We want to work up from the bottom till we're chief clerk and can have an automobile and a television set.

And in the spirit it follows, and we adapt ourselves again: "What church do you go to?" "Well, I really don't go to any church. I suppose I'm pretty much of a heathen, but hell, I figure a man can get to heaven by just being good. My wife's a church-goer, but damned if I like those bastards slapping me on the back and calling me 'brother.' I figure I'll get there my own way."

And in the social substructure of the arty group we must know something about somebody big, and we must have a vocabulary of confusing clarity: "Oh yes, my sonata was played by Roger Moff at the Woman's Club last year." "Of course I know Kotzebue. He visited me last winter when he gave his concert here." "You know Latmar, the great critic? He's one of my best friends. We had dinner together last year, and he told me Rosza Leachebach had to leave the Opera on account of her sickness. She's a syph, you know." And we nod significantly—sure we knew. "Tell me, what do you really think of Schönberg's tone row? Doesn't it seem to lack plasticity?" "Not so much harmonic

202

plasticity as rhythmic plasticity. Now, you take the classic sonata form . . ."

But it all fits in, complicated, successful. As we go up and down the scale we're convinced that we're an individual: we are *we,* and we can hold our own with anybody. We're democratic, too: we like the low as well as the high.

It's out there beyond the walls. And it's good and generous and beautiful—and a delusion of reality. For out there is the warmth of bellies and hearts, become glorious in the small frame of the unreal. And when we die, the moment we die, everyone says, "The community has suffered a great loss. He is irreplaceable." But who remembers our grandfather any more? We *have* to be replaceable and on the outside we always are, even with all the saliva we waste on the dead. Our success is measured by whether we were rich, civic-minded, generous, and by the number of children we so splendidly brought into the world by merely indulging our passion.

It has all evolved, rough at the edges, empty in spots, until the chance comes—beginning with nothing, splashing, rising—a cellular entity disorganized to end in nothing. Is it true? Is it worth it? And what is there at the end? How much longer does the taste of pheasant stay on the palate than that of boiled potatoes? How much longer does it nourish the body? For out there the climb is up the ladder, and it is automatically presumed that what we get at the top is worth the climb.

And over and above, we are offered the freedom of choice. God, they say, gives us the freedom to choose. But this is a thing of the mind; these qualities of the outside are things of the mind. Can they legitimately be ugly, or even delusions? Can there be freedom of choice when the emotion, not the mind, has the thirsts? And aren't all these things tempered within us to a point where man lives his outside life with no need for consistency of ideal? Are not the smells of wet flesh, the comfort alternating with discomfort, the street sounds, the healthfulness of licentiousness to warm blood, the wonder of our miracle of livingness, enough?

There's no freedom to choose until other knowledges insinuate themselves into the heart and the emotions, until other knowledges become other thirsts not to be denied. Then, and only then, can a choice be made.

Return to the inside, to our poor cloister and its world of the interior, its second portion of every man: the fog-filled interior known as man's health of soul. It too is a thing of the mind not yet ready to become a choice. Instead of riches we seek poverty, instead of the reeling insides we seek chastity, instead of sources of pride we seek sources of humility. But these aren't the end, as are wealth and success on the outside. They are the means to an end—the end being the destruction of all obstacles standing between us and the love of our life, which is God.

Immutable standards of interior criteria. The paradox of destroying individuality to become whole, of forming the irreplaceable link of a chain knowing that that chain makes of us a portion of living time; knowing it will go on forever with our pinpoint of breathing as one of its links. It isn't done for self but for the many, and for God. And it creates a rapture within that grows into completeness.

Two pictures, and a choice. The one which most of us know is brightly colored—brilliant, splashing—and satisfying to every cell of the human body. And over its hues death throws the shroud of an undetermined end. The other picture, the one within, is rather the color of the sun, white: the source of all colors before it is passed through the spectroscope and divided. It consumes the satisfaction of each cell of the body, so that the heat of many colors may become the Source of heat; burning the spirit into such a bliss as man may never know, but which, if we believe, is filtered through to us here on earth. It must not be contemplated lightly, for we shall never recover from it once it has seared us within. And the struggle is brief, for its fire becomes a process inside: first a cleansing process, and then the curing of the intangible maladies of reserve and modesty, and with them the stinginess of our desire to remain individual unto ourselves . . .

204

Light turns the snow on my window into a gray which will become white with the morning sun. It is early dawn. Half-sleep becomes wakefulness. Cold. Sweat-streaked walls. And outside, another pureness of gently falling snow.

No one moves in the long halls. I want to get up and walk about. I want to understand these things, to go into the chapel and understand why these things are wrong and right. But I can't dress myself, and the doctor sleeps in the next cell—like an animal, I imagine, heavily snoring.

And pagan thoughts return. For somewhere out there in the early morning, not many miles away, she sleeps too, the girl who has slept in my arms so often. But I no longer think of each time. The only memory worth having is of our beginning together, after I first came to Paris—a young and inexperienced student in the ecstasy of first discovering the City of Light. My affection flows warm for our beginning. Lying here in the early dawn I pass the long minutes in a tracing of heats to coolness, because the fevers we shared became as cool and pedestrian as the functions, to take or not as we desired.

I remember how I used to sneer at my friend Louis for sharing his flat with a girl student.

"But it's the only way," he would explain. "No one in school away from home can afford much by himself. But if you can get a nice girl, together you can live well. Monique and I pool our money. She does the cooking and washing, we both do our studying, and we sleep together. It's the best possible arrangement, old man. Together we live twice as well and a lot cheaper."

"But, Louis, how can you get any work done? Or do you neglect that part of it?"

"No, no, you don't understand. We're students, our studies come first. We don't fool around with each other till we go to bed, and then just once each night. And tock! we're happy and content. You must try it too. I'll ask Monique to find you someone."

Paris is lonely at night, and I was very young. Almost

205

every evening I went to my friend's flat for a visit or for dinner. Monique was friendly and we talked freely.

"Listen," she told me one night, "I know a nice young girl at art school who can barely get along. She's from a good family, but they're opposed to her studying art in Paris and don't give her much money. They hope she'll get discouraged and return home. Louis tells me you're just barely making it too. Why don't you let me bring her here to meet you? If you get along we can have a fine time, the four of us. You tend to your business, she'll tend to hers. That way it'll work, won't it?"

"But, Monique," I protested, "I just haven't been brought up that way. In my country we don't do those things."

She asked bluntly, "Tell me, are you a virgin?"

I hesitated, and a flush rose slowly to my cheeks. "No . . ." She and Louis exchanged glances while I looked at the floor. With his laughter in the background she shook her finger mockingly in my face. "Why, you are too," she cajoled. "Now tell me the truth."

"Well, all right." I smiled sheepishly. "Don't rub it in."

"Seriously," Monique went on gently, "you say you haven't been brought up that way. Well, neither have I and neither has Louis, and neither has this girl at school. But it's the only sensible thing, and it's worked for us. Now, let me bring her here to meet you. She just came to Paris a few months ago and she's never been with a man."

"All right, Monique," I acquiesced with a sigh. "May all my maiden aunts forgive me."

"What about tomorrow night? Shall I ask her?"

"I guess so, if you want to."

The following night my friends were jubilant. Louis met me in the hall. "Good news, my buddy!" he announced, clapping his medical-student hands with glee. "We've talked to one of the students who lives across the hall. He can't afford his flat and he's agreed to trade it for your room at the pension. That way we can be neighbors."

Eagerly he led me inside. The girl was already there

and he introduced me to her—Lucette Chanoine. She was as timid as I. We both seemed to feel we were being carried along by enthusiasms not entirely our own. She was medium in all respects: the type of French girl who doesn't attain full beauty until she's much older. She was small and uncertain and her uncertainty gave me the assurance to ask, "Well, Lucette, do we take the flat across the hall? Do we try it? I'm not much, but I'll be as good to you as I know how."

"Very well," she murmured hesitantly, "let's try it for a while. I think we can get on together."

"Bravo!" shouted the irrepressible Louis. "We'll celebrate the nuptials. But first I'll tell you the rules. Remember you're both students, so studies come first. If you start making love three times a day your studies will be ruined. So you make love only once, and that's at night after all the work's been done."

"Oh, shut up, Louis," I laughed. "We'll work that out ourselves." We laughed easily, for there were four of us.

But the next morning, when we had finished moving into our flat and were alone together for the first time, there was a heavy timidity between us. I tried to overcome her doubts—which were also mine.

"Now look, Lucette, we're going to try living together. Neither of us has been around very much or had much experience. I'm willing to do whatever you like as long as I get my work done. If you want to make love I'm here; if not I won't bother you. It's bound to happen sooner or later because we're sleeping in the same bed. But I promise I won't do anything against your wishes."

"But I have no right to refuse you," she said. "After all, you're taking me in."

"No, I'm not. You don't owe me a thing. We're sharing the flat and the work, that's all. I think boys probably like this sort of arrangement better than girls do. That's the reason I don't want to do anything you wouldn't like. Shall we just let things work themselves out?"

"You're very nice," she said gratefully. "Yes, that

would be best." And my own relief, unspoken, matched hers.

That night I was the first to return, since she had a late life class at art school. The flat was indeed a sallow little place—a bedroom, a sitting room furnished with fringed black furniture, and a miniature kitchen. The bathroom was down the hall, but there wasn't a bathtub in the building. Nevertheless the flat was intimate and alive. I placed my books and writing materials under the sitting-room table, which would serve as my desk; and for Lucette I borrowed a smooth kitchen table from the proprietor.

Feeling very big and domestic I sat down to work, for it seemed the thing to do in my new role as man of the house. I decided I must learn to smoke; there was the need of a pipe and a pair of slippers. The sensation was delicious —the first discovery of being master of my household, of being a man with responsibilities, of having a mate who would need me. Animal sensations flooded me in the anticipation of possessing again and again this other body which would be mine, and which would look to me for its wants.

There was a knock at the door; it was Louis. "And where is your wife, Monsieur?" he inquired with mock formality.

"She hasn't come in yet, she's still at school." We burst into laughter, shaking hands. "Ah, this is marvelous, Louis. I can never thank you enough."

"There's nothing like it, is there? Having your own place, paying your own bills, doing your own shopping, and—"

"Having your own babies?"

"You haven't got to her already, have you?" he asked with concern.

"No, but look—I'm as dumb as anything about these things. What must I do to keep from getting a baby?"

"You dumb bastard, it's a good thing you asked." He reached in his pocket. "Here, take one of these and use it tonight. Tomorrow I'll get you some pills for her."

"You don't think she'll mind if I use this thing?"

"If she's as ignorant as you she won't even know it. Anyway it'll only be for one time. The pills are a lot better. Do you think things are going to be all right?"

"I don't know. She's awfully nice, but from the way she talks I don't think she's too anxious to go to bed with me. I promised not to touch her unless she wanted me to."

"Oh, no!" Louis moaned, holding his head. "A girl like her isn't going to come right out and ask you to do it. You've got to make the try, and then if she's not quite ready, why all right. One thing, though—a little advice. It might hurt her. If she acts like it's hurting her, just stop. That way the pain'll go away and she'll enjoy it."

"Thanks, Louis. This is a complicated business. Why don't you and Monique come and have dinner with us tonight? I think it'd be a good idea. We get embarrassed when we're by ourselves. I'll call you when Lucette comes in and gets it ready."

"Good boy. And if I don't get a chance to say it later, good luck tonight, eh?"

We laughed again, for no reason except that we were enchanted with our new lives as family men. We felt like grownups but we laughed like children. There was a lightness, an undercurrent of joy without stain.

When Lucette returned, carrying a fiber sack of groceries, I showed her what I had done. She was delighted with her new table. She could get a piece of heavy cardboard, she said, and make a fine drawing board just the right size. She was beautiful after all with her short, gasping breaths of pleasure, her cheeks flushed from cold and excitement, and her eyes which had become alive with the realization that she had a flat—not a room but a real flat—where she could cook and keep house for the both of us. We didn't need Louis and Monique. Much of the barrier had fallen. But we had invited them, and Lucette was glad to celebrate her new kitchen.

As an impertinence, a shared intimacy, a fleck of daring good spirits, we decided it was absolutely necessary to change clothes for the dinner party. But first Lucette had to start the chicken. I removed my shirt, tossed it on the floor, and

209

went into the kitchen to wash my face at the sink. With a fine quickness of movement she ignored me, talking to herself. She rubbed the chicken with garlic and put it in a casserole to simmer, adding onions and white cooking wine.

Each scrupulously ignoring, but carefully watching, the other, we changed our outer clothing in the bedroom as nonchalantly as an old married couple. Our small talk was casual and full of delight. Without embarrassment she gathered up my shirt and pants and put them on a hanger in the wardrobe, murmuring something about washing them the next day.

There was an animal comfort in both of us, shown in the miracle of these small newnesses. To have her examine my shirt collar where it needed turning. To comb my hair, wetting it with water from the kitchen faucet. To smell the food on the stove. And not to be alone. The luxury of not having to pick up my clothes from the floor. Of not having to go into a dining room full of strangers. Hundreds of small things, new and rich and appealing. And above all, the nearness of a fellow being of flesh and blood and clothing and hair and warmth, sharing parallel emotions which were the more poignant for her; for hers was the giving nature of woman who finds more nourishment than man in doing for another; who is the embodiment of tenderness in countless ways. And she was there and she was mine, and my youthful arteries sang with the joy of it.

It was almost seven o'clock when Louis and Monique arrived. They were washed and powdered and dressed for the important dinner. We counted our money and decided that between the four of us, we could afford a bottle of sparkling wine with which to salute the occasion. Arm in arm Louis and I walked out into the cool night air of Paris in search of a bottle that wouldn't cost too much.

"You know, my friend, I was just thinking," said Louis, serious in his role of confidant and adviser—"when did you last have a bath?"

"It's been over a week now. What do you do for a bath in the flat?"

"We bring a tub into the kitchen. But you can hardly do that in front of Lucette when you haven't even slept with her. It's very important, you know. She won't like it if you aren't clean and good-smelling. It'll spoil it for her." He stopped and turned to me. "Why don't we go to a public bath right now and get you cleaned up? Later on, when you've got used to each other, you can bathe in your kitchen."

"But I can't afford those public baths, Louis. You know that."

"Nonsense. It's only three francs, or two and a half if you get the shower. I tell you what: you go to that bath across the street and I'll get a cheaper bottle of wine. Here's two and a half francs. A shower will be good enough and it won't cost as much. But take a good one. Wash several times with plenty of hot water. I'll come for you when I find the wine."

At the entrance an old crone collected my money, complaining because I didn't have enough to tip her. When I had finished my shower I pounded on the door of the stall and she brought me a clean towel, suggesting that a youth of my obvious qualities should have a girl and she knew just the one. Laughing, I chased her out, telling her that if I couldn't have her I'd have none of her protégés.

By the time Louis and I got back to the flat, dinner was on the table. Finding four suitable chairs, we began our marriage feast. In addition to the chicken, the girls had prepared a good noodle soup, French fries, and a green salad. Lucette remarked that it was a good thing she had bought the chicken, for it was so large we could eat on it all week. At the thought I groaned like an old man, chuckling to myself at the picture I made.

Suddenly Louis asked thoughtfully, "Have you two kissed yet?"

"Not yet."

"Then you must do it right now. Go on, go on. I pronounce you man and mistress as of now. A nice kiss."

Monique agreed laughing. And because we were so happy, it was an easy thing to do. I kissed her lightly on

211

the cheek, but Louis shook his head and held up a hand. "No, no, on the mouth. A real kiss."

It was a natural and graceful thing with Monique and Louis there. While they looked on and applauded, we giggled and kissed a real kiss. I was grateful to Louis: I knew that now it would be easy to do it again, without timidity or clumsiness, when we were alone.

Later, for no apparent reason, Monique burst into laughter.

"What's so funny?" I asked her.

"I was thinking of our poor maiden aunts."

"Oh, no!"

Louis raised his glass. "To the maiden aunts," he proclaimed, and took a long swallow of wine. "Think of them," he went on, wiping his mouth. "They are, I imagine, warty and bulbous old things, at this moment asleep hugging much-battered water bottles. No, no, wait, let me think—that's no fitting desecration of maiden aunts. They're probably covered with stiff hairs in the wrong places." He turned to me. "When we're doctors, my friend, we must pledge each other we'll pluck out all the hairs from wrong places on warty old maiden aunts."

"Louis," Monique admonished, "you're impossible and unrefined. Why do I stay with such as you?"

"Because of the children, remember?"

"Oh, of course, because of the children we'll have one day. Did you know, Lucette, that Louis and I have decided we're in love? Yes, we'll throw away the pills one day and become respectable married people."

"You may not be married," Lucette said quietly, "but you're two of the most respectable people I know. I'm very fond of you—both of you."

Louis looked at his watch. "Before we can get married," he sighed, "we have a little thing like school work to do. It's almost ten. We'd better get busy."

After telling her how nice it was, and that we must come to their place for dinner the next time, Monique warmly kissed Lucette on both cheeks. Louis and I shook hands,

212

and they left. I carefully locked the door for the night.

Lucette cleared the table. I followed from sitting room to kitchen. "That was fun, wasn't it, Lucette?"

"Yes, it was. Monique is so nice. We'll have good times together."

"I must start on my lessons. Shall I help you with the dishes?"

"No, go ahead and work."

I sat with an open book before me without seeing it. I imagined her looking at me from the kitchen and feeling, as I, that we were well started in our new life together. I was intoxicated with the thought that I wouldn't be alone again; that I'd share with her a much better life than either of us had known before.

After a while, flicking off the light in the kitchen, Lucette went to her table to begin work. I looked up from the page I hadn't been reading.

"Oh," she apologized, "I didn't mean to disturb you."

"You're not disturbing me. Are you through in the kitchen?"

"Yes, and now I *must* get to work." She announced this firmly, and we burst into laughter again.

"We sound like old married people already, don't we?" I said.

"Yes, I guess we do. But that's what we are—practically, anyway. But I do have a lot of work to do before I can go to bed."

"Well"—I faked a yawn—"think I'll go on now. How long will you be?"

"At least two hours. You go on to sleep."

My cheeks were on fire. She didn't want it. She was studying late so that I'd be asleep when she came to bed. Controlling my disappointment and embarrassment, I murmured, "Tell me, Lucette, do you want me to stay awake and wait for you? I must know. If there's a chance I'll stay awake, but if you say no, I'll forget it and go on to sleep."

She didn't lower her eyes. "I'm awfully sorry. I have an assignment of drawings I've got to get in. What shall I do?

213

Do you want me to wake you up when I come to bed? If you want me to I will."

"No—if you're worried about that you won't be able to work. Maybe tomorrow night would be better anyway, when we've known each other a little longer."

I walked into the bedroom, half-closing the door, and changed into pajamas. From the other room came the rustling of heavy drawing paper, a deep humming sigh, the scrape of a chair. I was relieved. I was glad we had decided to wait. Returning to her side, I stood near the lamp and watched her make the first strokes of her drawing.

"You're ready for bed?" she asked, looking up. "You seem taller in those pajamas."

"May I kiss you good night?"

"Of course."

I kissed her cheek, and then her mouth—lightly, timidly —thanking her. And leaving the door open, I crawled into bed.

Later, in the middle of the night, I awakened to hear her quiet breathing beside me. She was asleep, and we were in the dark, in the warm dark night of our new home. We were alone—two people breathing in a single smallness of surroundings with only the intimacy of our bed and our sleep-drugged bodies. And outside, all the city of Paris lived its nocturnal life in a million different ways. In the flat all was lost. There was no longer a living room and a kitchen. All was lost in darkness except what we could feel, except the immediate *now* of bed and covering and air. I lay there not touching her, happy to hear her even breathing, to know that beside me this living warmth of a stranger—a young girl with breasts and belly and knees and heart—was mine without my having yet possessed her; a stranger of whom I knew nothing but who was with me in the same bed, safe from the desolate loneliness of the world of humanity about us. We occupied our tiny space within the cellular framework of a great city. Others lived and slept and ate and wept above and below and on all sides; but we were there alone, hidden from them as they from

214

us, with our own steams and pains and joys and inner liquidnesses.

I rolled against her in the dark. She allowed her body to relax in my arms. She did not turn nor pull away. She was warm. A warmth of sleeping flesh covered with night clothes, drugged by sleep, without thought or intention. The night was a vacuum permitting instincts to dissolve the counterpoint of background and timidity into pure feeling. Our arms found one another and we lay a long time face to face, with nothing but the softness of her breasts to give me consciousness. We slept again fitfully, automatically clasping each other against the unknown which lay beyond our bed in every direction. Finding delicious quenching safety in the embrace. Breathing pure smells of clean bedclothes and clean night clothes and tiny spots of bareness. Again we slept, and awoke twisted. The bed creaked as we straightened clothing with an understood union of movement, and settled once more into the sleep from which we hadn't really awakened. Comfortable, fitting close. Warmth of arms under arms, of legs between legs, of the nothingness of stomachs separated only by wrinkled cloth.

Gradually through the night—imperceptibly somehow, without beginnings—clothing which separated us was unbuttoned and pulled aside. In a dream, unconsciously, legs found their comfort. The wetness of too much covering formed where flesh heated against flesh. Lips touched lightly, growing stronger but never really strong. Hands fumbled with flimsy night things. In the dumbness of night the tension of these half-gestures grew. We tightened our clasp and soon were pressed side by side. There was a stabbing of liquid warmth. Nerves and muscles relaxed to become tense again. I knew the waiting, the inevitable seeking of man's insides to become woman's insides as the embrace brought us without touches into greater tightness . . . until we were united. Until there could be no more pressing of stomach to stomach. Until the fullness of one became the fullness of the other. Clasping with no need of movement, with an inner deliciousness of drunken newness that throbbed

215

and was concentrated, that searched and was feverish. The brain descending from head in a giant curve, deserting head to take its place in a contracting belly. All lines of feeling leading into the darkness under covers. All life dying except the one consummated in an animal ecstasy of nerve against nerve, of nerve nourishing nerve, of nerve ravishing nerve. Till it could no longer be borne and nerve must assuage nerve with its heavy balm, its warming sedative of liquid gratefulness.

She pulled her head away, breathing heavily, and slowly her breathing returned to normal and her heart stopped pounding against mine. We did not draw apart after it was over. We returned to the close plane of sleep from which we had strayed only a few emotions. Still clasped together, I remember murmuring, "Thank you," close to her ear, and feeling her head move against my mouth in wordless nod of acknowledgment. Later, perhaps only a moment later, a last fleeting thought that I'd forgotten to use the thing Louis had given me in the afternoon. But the thought held no worry. The brain was back in the head. My happiness was unblemished and complete.

I remember the days following, each day becoming more complete with night. And then the pattern, when experimentation became refinement, when timidity and modesty were lost, when I knew her every respiration and fever. In time the pattern grew to be regular and natural and unimportant, a convenient habit which has never stopped. I know that if I wanted to, I could leave this bed now and go to her bed and have her—not in the little, modest way of our ecstatic beginning, but in the quenching, satisfying way it has become.

But I'm content not to move from my cell. I stare at the walls sweating from cold. I wait for Dr. Castelar to come and dress me. For once there's a longing to go to the chapel for Mass—a warmth unlike other warmths. I hear a cough from the next cell and I knock on the separating wall. His muffled voice comes back sleepily: "Right away."

Moments later he opens my door dressed in slippers and

216

a thick bathrobe, scratching his head and yawning, "How are you this morning? Been awake long? God, isn't it cold?"

"I haven't been awake too long," I tell him. "Thought I'd like to go to Mass with you this morning. But go ahead and get yourself dressed."

"God! it's cold," he moans, his mouth twisting into a grimace. He impatiently pulls the blankets from me. "Here, get out of bed. Stand still. Now put your leg in there. Good." He dresses me hurriedly, breathing hard. "So you're going to Mass with me this morning? What's that supposed to mean?"

I ignore the tinge of sarcasm in his voice. "I just felt I'd like to go with you."

"All right," he dismisses me, "go wash up. I'll finish buttoning you when you come back."

When I return I find the doctor ready to go down to Mass. He looks haggard and tired. On the way I tell him briefly of my recollections this morning, and of my contentment to remain here instead of going in search of Lucette.

He asks, "Did you remember all this in a dream, or were you awake?"

"It was almost like a dream."

Without taking his eyes off the stairs we're descending, he says matter-of-factly, his face heavy and unmoving, "Was it wet?"

"No, sir."

"And you actually felt you'd rather stay in your cell than go to her if you had the chance? Did you feel that? That you'd rather be alone in your cell than in bed with her?"

"Yes, sir, that's right. It's something I'd never have believed of myself."

He sneers, shaking his head wearily, and looks at me in disgust. "So you're happier here than you would be kissing the breasts of your Lucette? I don't believe you. Your piety is a milk-fed thing. It disgusts me a little."

Humiliation flushes my cheeks. "It's a beginning." My voice trembles but is calm. "I know I don't show up very

217

well, but I told you the truth. What do you expect—a bolt of lightning?"

He walks more slowly, not looking at me. His face is heavy and sullen. "You're a type, young man," he says impersonally. "You have a certain interest when you go out of yourself. You're tolerable when you're drunk or in pain or foaming for some woman's behind. But when you come to me with your little goodnesses I begin to—"

"To hell with it, Doctor!" I stare at him in rage, then turn and stamp back up the steps to my cell. I am sick at his derision.

The room is hideous, unbearable. I lie down feeling I shall degenerate into tears, alone and detesting all this. Longing for people who don't have to be big and real and authentic. Longing for people who share in weakness. Longing for my world. I get off the cot exhausted and sick. My legs, which only an hour before had felt the lightness of exuberance at my progress, now drag beneath me.

And in another dimension beyond the loathing of here and now, lurks the knowledge that the doctor is right. Had the situation been reversed, I'd have had his reaction. It's that which sickens me: the revealing of oneself in such a private, intimate weakness of goodness. Our conversation comes back, worse in memory and reaction. The man is stupid who peddles his cheap wares before a connoisseur. It's not their cheapness that hurts, but the fact he thinks them quality merchandise and tries to persuade another of their value. My anger is my own humiliation. I blush at the transparency of my attempt to impress the doctor with my progress. The pain of being found out is too great.

Surrounding empty cells begin to taunt me. I need the warmth of people. I can no longer bear to be alone.

Mass has already started when I enter the chapel. An aged monk is chanting the *Kyrie,* answered by other monks singing, *"Kyrie eleison."* It goes on. There are almost a hundred people from the Village this morning: women clutching their rosary beads, men unmoving, and young schoolboys, the same ones who write four-letter words on

218

the outside walls of the Monastery. Dr. Castelar, looking up, makes a place for me on the last row. I take it, knowing I'm defeated even in my hopes for companionship.

I sit or stand, emotionless and miserable, as Mass continues. I hear none of the music, none of the texts. I wait. Dumbly I wait for it to be over. We stand and I look at Dr. Castelar standing beside me, unconscious of my presence. Somewhere, somewhere in that belly is a derision that taunts me.

"*Oremus*" echoes through the chapel, and there is a rustling of clothes and a creaking of benches as those standing kneel to pray. I sit in my pew and stare at the doctor's kneeling figure. Sullenly I think of this morning. I too could have prayed then. But now it's impossible. Every gesture, as seen through the eyes of the doctor, would become false. He would look at me and know—know I was playing the role, acting the player. But the thirst is there. I look about me. In the somber chapel everyone bends his head forward in prayer. I am the only one who remains seated.

But the desire grows within me and is carried forward by the very fact that his presence denies me prayer. The thirst becomes unquenchable, unquenchable. It's what I want, what something within me wants. For the first time in my life I really need to pray.

A dullness of weight drags me to my knees, and my head falls forward into my hands. Behind closed eyelids I forget. Somewhere in the background is the unintelligible upward swing of a chanted "*Agnus Dei, qui tollis peccata mundi . . .*" And the coughing, the smells of incense. They are there, forgotten except in fact of existence. The darkness within takes me farther away in a swirl of forgetfulness. Formless words, concrete thoughts pour from me into the isolating space: "My God, my God, forgive me for what I am. Change me, change me . . ."

In the darkness of prayer my eyes close more tightly. My head turns slowly with the concentration, seeking its God.

219

"I beg Thee—"

A hand touches my shoulder and I'm paralyzed by a contraction of nerves. Surprised and shocked I jump uncontrollably, clutching the pew in front of me. Mass has ended and Dr. Castelar, saying nothing, has awakened me. He takes my arm. We walk out together and I tremble from the sudden arrival back into sounds and sights and odors. My heart is gone and I am sick. But I have prayed.

We say nothing until we're at the door of my cell.

"May I come in?" the doctor asks, without looking at me.

"If you like."

"Would you care for a glass of wine? It's a bit early but perhaps it would taste good."

"Yes, sir, I think I would." Despite myself my voice is cold. My bitterness toward the doctor is hard to dissolve. The violence of my feelings amazes me. When he shook me from my prayer all rancor was gone, but now the prayer is ended and we must face each other again. I can't be humble forever.

"Here you are, my boy." His voice is a whisper, as if he were talking to a dying patient. The eyes beneath the black beret are sober.

We drink in silence, but the opening words must be said. I can think of nothing to say and wait nervously for him to begin.

"Why did you do it?" he asks at last, wincing from the answer. "Why did you do it? Why?"

My nerves leave me with no further control. The virulence of my humiliation returns, pouring from me like vomit. "Because I had to, that's why. I did it because I was hypnotized. Is that weak enough for you? This time I couldn't help it. This time I prayed. You could see that." My voice dies away; with no expression I force words from my exhausted brain. "I prayed till I lost consciousness and then I kept on praying. It's a sacrilege for a little person like me to pray, I know. Only *great* Christians like you should do it. But take it for what it's worth. And may your nasty—"

His face blanches. I can't go on. Everything empties from me. I have struck very low. There's no remedy for the filth I've thrown in his face. The violence of my shame makes me turn away. I want desperately to hide, and I fall face down on the cot, grateful for the sharp pain in my shoulder which forces me to be conscious of something other than the moment. Bitterness fills me drop by drop. I make no attempt to straighten my arm, to remove the pain that's like a screen covering the specter I shall always carry of the white, drawn face of the doctor, looking as if I'd struck him across the mouth.

He makes no move, no sound. The bed doesn't help. It causes a tension to mount, rising to a point that can end only in tears or the loss of consciousness. I fight down the tears, but it's no use; sobs swell in my throat to be swallowed again and again till they can no longer be swallowed. And with no further effort I forget everything in the balm of pouring out my loss and guilt into the blanket rough against my face. Idiocy. Relief of something concrete and wet and banal beyond all other things. From this whirling of thought and sensation I hear the cracked voice of my friend, forcing itself, saying slowly, "I didn't know. I was wrong. It's not that bad. Turn over a moment. Let's finish our wine. Come, turn over. Look at me, won't you? You couldn't help yourself. It was my fault. Come, turn over." He continues talking in endless, choppy little phrases, until my senses return.

Exhausted and dizzy, I pull myself to a sitting position. The doctor bends over me and straightens the cloth sling around my shoulder. His face shows the emotion he's had to bear.

"Do you want me to help you?" he asks. "Can I get you some water?"

In a voice I don't recognize as my own, I answer wearily, "Please. I'd better wash up." And as he leaves with an empty water pitcher, I add, "You know I'll never—I mean—I'm sorry. I won't try to—"

"Forget it, son," he replies, trying to lighten the situation. "Nothing's happened as far as I'm concerned. I'll fetch

221

you some water and when I come back we'll finish our wine, eh?"

We drink our wine, and it returns strength to bodies emptied of emotion and poorly nourished in food. The day remains dark. Seeming normalcy returns between us, but I know that only time can make us forget the brutality of this morning. We are wary of each other while trying not to be, while trying to make it seem as if nothing has been changed. But the freedom, the camaraderie are gone— gone because man must spring to his defense against the one thing clear enough and truthful enough to be of help to him. We're two people intelligent enough to know what has happened, to understand and accept without rancor; but we're not intelligent enough to nullify it.

Our meeting ground now is in the free use of filthy and suggestive language. It serves as a covering for the serious. The doctor describes in detail his medical experiences— primarily those involving sex cases—and we joke coarsely, not daring to venture on unsure ground again. We no longer argue. Only time will let us argue again.

22 december

Looking very downcast, Father Marie-Ornoux comes into my cell before I am out of bed. In his hand is a yellow telegram.

"What is it, Father?"

"I am recalled to my monastery in Paris," he says sadly. "Permission has finally been arranged. I leave for Jerusalem and the desert countries in ten days."

222

I smile, rising to sit on the edge of the cot. "I can't tell you how glad I am for you, Father. But you don't seem very happy?"

"Oh, but I am. I only hate to leave so soon. We must take the morning train tomorrow."

"And I hate to have you leave. Your visit's done a lot for me. I'll miss you and the doctor."

"You should try to persuade him to come back, my son. He has nothing to hold him in Paris until his wife returns, and you will need him to help you with your arm. He tells me that you have made progress in the right direction. Once settled in your house, you will be able to understand in time what you must do with your life. And your work will soon be resumed. I have no fears for you now."

"I think I'm beginning to understand already, Father. Will I ever see you again?"

He smiles warmly. "Probably not, my dear friend, probably not. And I shall not write you; although if you are in trouble and I can help, you must write to me. I will say good-bye now, for there is much for me to do before leaving."

"I really do hate to see you go."

"But no, I will see you in heaven. God bless you, my child."

He turns and is gone, gone with the clump of his shoes down the corridor; gone from us to the life of his hope, to the newness of adventure, to his flaming fulfillment. And there is a great cold in the room. It becomes small and chilled and lusterless—and very empty. Waiting to be dressed I lie down again. My shoulder aches. I feel a tremendous longing for something I can't understand, a longing somehow connected with the patched whiteness, the burning happiness of Marie-Ornoux's immolation.

Dr. Castelar, wearing his usual beret and a heavy robe, opens the door. Beneath the robe his legs are as dark as stained wood. "I couldn't help overhearing," he says.

"I didn't expect you and Marie-Ornoux to leave so soon," I tell him.

223

"You really hate to see him go, don't you?" he observes. "He's a humble little man, but he leaves a great emptiness behind him. Before he dies he'll have a period of intense living. It's a wonderful thing to see." He reaches for my clothes. "Here, let me dress you. And tonight I'll help you take a bath."

"We needed more time, didn't we, Doctor?"

"You've given me a great deal, young man. But tell me, how will you manage after I'm gone? I can dress you in the morning before I leave, but after that? . . ."

"I can manage. I'll sleep in my clothes, and I'm sure Father Clément will help me with my shoes. When I move to my villa I can hire someone to come in and help."

"You won't have any servants?"

"No, there's only Madame Renée, and she's a high-born woman. I can hardly see her stooping down to pull up my underwear pants, can you?"

"Not exactly, though I imagine it'd do her old heart more good than harm. You'd probably be hot as a poker."

"Not after that. She's got snow-white hair."

He laughs. "She'd be so grateful, and in the dark you'd never know the difference."

"Why don't you stay with me, Doctor?" I suggest hopefully. "I know if we separate now, after our misunderstanding the other day, we'll never see each other again. So why don't you stay with me for a while? I'll move into the villa where you can have a nice room. You can stay as long as you like."

He scratches his head. "I must go with Marie-Ornoux, but maybe I can come back—in a week, let's say. I may come back in a week or so and see how you're settled. By then Madame Renée should be pregnant."

"Will you really come then, Doctor? I can get along for a week without any help."

"If I can. My wife won't be back for several weeks."

"Good. I'll save Madame Renée for you. She ought to be just about right for a man of your age."

"*Mierda!* we'll see. And wouldn't you like for me to

224

deliver a message to Lucette while I'm in Paris? Be glad to, you know."

I shake my head. "Thanks, but I'm afraid she'd never be satisfied with me after that. I can already hear her saying, 'Rafael did it this way,' or, 'Rafael did it that way.' But tell me, will you stay at the monastery in Paris?"

"No, think I'll return to the hotel where I can rest and have the luxury of a real bath. Think of me there next week while you're squatting over your little foot-bath, trying to rinse the soap from your immense behind with a liter of cold water."

Half-laughing I groan, "Ah, I'm tempted to go with you. A real bath in a real tub with warm water! Lucky devil!"

"Will you have a bathtub in your villa?"

"No, but I'll have a big metal tub and all the hot water you want—a tub large enough to sit in comfortably."

We suddenly realize that we've got back almost to normal; we realize it at the same time.

"This is much better, isn't it, Doctor?" I smile.

"Much. We'll have a good visit together next week."

24 december

Yesterday work was resumed as usual. After dressing me for the last time, Dr. Castelar left with Father Marie-Ornoux. Tonight they will celebrate Christmas in Paris.

Many visitors have made the pilgrimage to the Village for Christmas Eve services at our Monastery. Throughout the Valley there's a lightness, a hurrying of movement, as last-minute preparations are made; and one knows that farm wives are dragging out hidden cheeses, and cooking special dishes, and cashing saved ration tickets to buy meats and sugars and condiments for the feast. In the Monastery, monks move about sweeping floors, polishing woodwork, pouring new wax for candles. I am impressed by the restraint of Christmas here, a Christmas without the carols and the lighted trees. A Christmas of heavy clothing, of good food long hoarded, of overcast skies, of calm. Isolated in this Valley, far from other Christmases, the spirit of the season is no less contagious. Men become good—all men become good this day—and there's a greater nobility of heartbeat.

Alone in the paleography room, I lose myself in work. My feet are wet and frozen in my shoes. There are no presents, no cards, no decorations, no smells of pies and cakes and cooked meats; but only a small room with sweating walls, and rough-edged manuscripts that smell of timelessness. Outside, the world moves in its greenery, in its shaking of hands, in the happy redness of its cheeks. In this room only my pen moves, scratching against damp paper. I hold my head close to the paper to see what I write. The table is dark, polished, and cold to its innermost grain. I'm as alone in this room as if the outside world didn't exist. And yet I feel no loneliness. I recall other Christmases spent alone, when I walked aimlessly in search of exhaustion that would let me sleep. When I wept at the sound of a Christmas carol. When the day was an unbearable separation from those I love. Here it's not like that. I am alone, but alone among solitaries; and there is a deep, serene joy in looking on while others prepare. In hearing cries in the street. In knowing that below, the chapel is being swept and dusted and polished. In the certainty that all men carry a charity and a generosity in their hearts these last hours before Christmas, having somehow cast aside meanness and cynicism and hatred.

I work quietly with Tutilo and Notker long dead,

226

remembering past Christmases that live only as notes on faded paper here before me. It is a happiness of dormant sadness that I know, a happiness full and unmoving and always there. A happiness not shouting but whispering, whispering its thin little tune in a high-pitched voice, but quite beautiful in my ears this dark day of light.

I walk to my cell. We expect a change all about, but the cloisters, the corridors, the stones are the same. Yet different, too: different in the way we look at them, different in us. They have more light, floors carry an unreflected-sand quality, echoes return more lively: imperceptible changes seen from within us in exterior things, seen as the goodness of feelings makes our view gain warmth. We smile for no reason except that everyone smiles. Work becomes play. And that something, that something every man knows, which is somewhere there inside him like a large artery or vein of emotional reaction—that thing curves upward exciting the chest and the heart, exciting the insides.

My Christmas present is in my cell. They have changed my bed, putting on freshly laundered linens that have been turned back from the pillow ready for sleep. In this maelstrom of activity someone has changed my bedclothes, and it's a finer gift than I ever got.

On the night table is a new card containing the schedule of Christmas services. Dinner is earlier tonight, it informs me, so that the dishes may be washed in time for all to attend Christmas Eve High Mass at nine o'clock. "At 8:45 you should go to the kitchen for a hot drink": this is scribbled on the schedule in Father Clément's hand. Mass will last from nine p.m. till three a.m., after which we may sleep until the bell at five-thirty. At six a morning High Mass will be given, and another at ten. The card also suggests that since we'll get no more than a maximum of two and a half hours' sleep, we nap for an hour after the noon meal.

I try to sleep, but in mid-afternoon it's impossible. Though there's no noise, no sign of activity, the activity is there and it is felt. Finding the Father Prior, I ask him if I can't help by carrying water. He reminds me of my injured shoulder, but I insist I can make twice as many trips. All afternoon I carry bucketfuls from the well into the kitchen, and, when they have been heated, upstairs to the cells so that the monks may wash and shave before tonight's celebration.

Supper, eaten hurriedly, is solid and satisfying—soup, extra bread, and a thick mush of potatoes, beans and meat broth. We swallow great mouthfuls, anxious to eat as much as possible before Father Abbot's mallet calls us to a halt. There is no reader tonight—no noise except forks and spoons loudly striking plates in the desperate effort to consume food.

At eight-forty-five I return to the kitchen for the hot drink. I find several other laymen there who have been invited to share in this little festivity. The drink, served in large cups, is the same as we have for breakfast. We stand about sipping the warming liquid, until one by one we put down the cups and go to take our places in the already crowded chapel.

Darkness outside, and rough-frozen snows. But the chapel is well lighted. Two monks serve as ushers. They place me far to the front, near the altar rail.

Noises of waiting for Mass to begin: whisperings, the blowing of noses into handkerchiefs, deep coughings reverberating like wind in the trees. Low, level sounds of waiting. A crowd of overcoats and gloves and scarves and galoshes. We sit leafing through the order of service, overcoated shoulder pressed against overcoated shoulder. Eyes are different, resting clear and calm. In the eyes of those who believe, is a mixture of tenderness and excitement that erases nineteen hundred-and-more years. They're not celebrating an anniversary but participating in the original. Eyes are generous, and offer space for you on the kneeling-pad, and volunteer to pick up the rosary beads you drop. Eyes are quick and kind, as they were meant to be.

We draw into ourselves from the chill. Feet are silently stamped to warm them. Shoulders are held slightly raised in a perpetual cringe. Drafts find their way into hidden places around the neck and above the belt, and up trouser legs to the knees. Movements to arrange clothing are a

228

constant preoccupation, a glacial tenderness shared by all.

From far to the back comes a first pedal-tone of the organ, and movements die to the stillness of expectancy. Other tones sound in quiet beginnings, with a warmth of harmony closely knit. It is the calm and radiant *Magnificat* of Frescobaldi. No trumpetlike announcements, no blasting of Christ's birth, no loud choruses of jubilation; but a serene, infinitely tender organ prelude telling emotions to hush, to accept, to know a joy of humility more akin to tears than to shouting. A fine little rhythm moves tones into the treble flute register. Joy becomes an inner intoxication, breaking through to lift the spirit high within the body, creating an adoration from mood; and the emotion of adoration is prepared for its concrete fulfillment in the beginnings of a chanted Introit. The emotion was created in a vacuum by pure sound combinations. Now it is given spirit and meaning with the opening words rising slowly, almost whispered, carrying upward to tenderness for Child; words chanted in exquisite inner ravishment by black-robed monks swaying with the unisonal rhythm: *"Dominus dixit ad me: Filius meus es tu . . ."* Soaring bodiless sound permeating the chapel, filling our beings: "The Lord said to me: Thou art my Son . . ."

Candles and smoke, and incense floating up like smoke, gently and inevitably lift man to worship, lift him above worship to a plane beyond and within: a plane of intimacy and inner movements of the soul ascending high inside the throat. Unbearable poignancy of restrained joy, for in such restraint there is no horizon. Its dimensions begin and end in the vastness of silence, and its light is the Source of all light. These many people crowded side by side lose their shames and their fears and their very identities in a common subordination of all else to the moment. They are here, all of them, and they are clean. They who know mutual hatred embrace a oneness of Source and for a few hours become clean.

Madame Renée, kneeling across the aisle, gives me a warm smile of fine-looking teeth. Madame Vincent is lost

229

behind closed eyelids. Nearby, Madame la Marquise de la Roche kneels with head deeply bowed. Salesky, whose knees are not so ardent as his capillaries, rises to sit hunched forward beside his wife. The Chevissiers, more humble, are placed far to the back. The beautiful Mexican girl leans forward, her black shawl falling across her face. They are all here, the people who tomorrow will tear at one another again.

And in Paris, Father Marie-Ornoux and Dr. Castelar know this affinity of feeling. And in every corner of the world it is the same.

A delicate "Alleluia, alleluia" floats through the chapel. More candles are lighted. Seated in a fringed and canopied chair at the side, Father Abbot asperses his monks. And Mass goes on and on, unchanging in texture, slow in movement. Vestments of white and black mingle with robes in celebrating with infinite grace the loveliness of Christmas.

It moves timeless until the end. The chanted *"Ite, missa est"* empties the chapel—too soon. It is too soon. It is almost three a.m. on Christmas Day. We leave the chapel. We walk in the snow outside, not speaking, not shaking hands, not wishing to destroy our inner tendernesses. The night is black and still and frosted, with clean, unmoving air. I walk past the chapel, where lights from stained-glass windows reflect across the snow in long, inverted Gothic patterns, broken here and there by a frozen bush. There are no stars.

Without undressing I crawl into bed. I am gripped by a momentary violence of trembling as the covers warm. We sleep like angels this night. The chants, the cold, the incense, the reverberant night of Christ's birth—calm, filled with adoration—become sleep's dimension. We sleep alone, surrounded by walls, trembling in our beds. The sleep is pure and the night holy and the world better than before. We sleep heavily sprawling, faces buried in pillows. We sleep well, for our sleep is its own Christmas Night.

25 december

But in a moment, when night breathing becomes its heaviest and rest the sweetest-smelling before dawn, walls and floor and bed vibrate with the great bells calling us back, beating in our ears, surrounding and overwhelming us. We wake, staggering from sleep, and we go to early Mass.

Masses throughout the morning. Masses and emotions and growing fatigue. And a good meal at noon: oysters lentils, a dry cake.

Christmas Day is its anticlimax. Following the celebration there is a Sunday quietness of afternoon, of great weariness and of welcome rest, when too much food finds its digestion in sleep. I sleep all afternoon. And tonight, at Vespers and Compline, we become as we were—simple, skeletal, clear.

Tomorrow will be yesterday. The fete is over.

We feel the loss. We seek to prolong the heights of hours gone until another year. But we sleep again as always, surrounded by the Great Silence. And we are glad, in a way, to be back—to be back in our lives.

"Whence is this monstrousness? and to what end? The mind commands the body, and it obeys instantly; the mind commands itself, and is resisted. The mind commands the hand to be moved; and such readiness is there, that command is scarce distinct from obedience. Yet the mind is mind, the hand is body. The mind commands the mind, its own self, to will and yet it doth not. Whence this monstrousness? and to what end?"

ST. AUGUSTINE

the devil

without

1 january

The compromise with health and the physical needs of warmth and food finds its first consummation this late night of the New Year. Only my sleep is changed. I shall sleep in another bed. But there are fears; and the leaving, the breaking away from my little cell, has been difficult.

At the last moment, when my clothing had been moved into this villa, I faltered and asked Father Clément to let me stay on in the Monastery.

"But, my son," he answered, "you are not leaving. You have permission to stay. Only the manner of your staying is changed. You will come to us each morning and do your work as always. And at night after Compline you will return to the comfort of your warm house. It will be as if you walked a little farther to your bed, that is all."

"All right, I'll try it. But there's a difference all the same. I may still be close to the Monastery, but I'm not *in* it; and I don't trust myself on the outside. Can I come back if things don't work out?"

"Of course you can. If your health permits, you may return whenever you feel the need. But you will be all right.

Keep your life here, have as little to do with local affairs as possible, and you will be safe and happy. We shall visit every day and you will tell me of your life on the outside. It will not be so different."

"What about my work here in the garden?"

"You will need physical exercise more than ever now, my son. When the thaws come you should return to your work with the Father Gardener. We will discuss it later. But for the moment let us be frank. Your chastity will be more difficult to guard now. Why not try to make this a period of particular watchfulness?"

Other conversations flecked the day. Madame Renée helped me unpack. But she is a timid and correct woman, and her visits are short.

My villa is perched on the cobblestone sidewalk, but there's no door to the street. Both front and back doors open into a small, bricked courtyard surrounded by high stone walls. Lining the walls are tiny flower-beds and a few young pear trees. To the rear, on the opposite side of the courtyard, is the outhouse, enclosed by strategically planted shrubs for privacy. The courtyard's only entrance from the street is an iron-grilled gate, contrived to ring a warning bell when it's opened.

The house is better than I had hoped. Each room is on a different level, and each has brightly tiled floors. From the front door, a long, well-lighted hall extends the length of the front of the house. To the right, a half-glassed door opens into the salon. Beside the door is a table with a silver platter for mail and calling cards. At the opposite end of the hallway three steps lead to a master bedroom, then curve upward to other bedrooms on the second floor. The house is comfortably furnished in English country style, and there are formal fireplaces in all the rooms.

I shall live and sleep in the salon, for there's only enough wood in the garage to heat one room. The salon is lighted by two windows, and contains a large table and a quantity of stilted furniture which doesn't seem out of place. The room's most outstanding feature is the bed, to the right of the fireplace. It is the most lurid couch I've ever seen outside a brothel: a bed with no head or foot, but framed instead at end and side by twenty brightly colored cushions propped against the wall. I remember a girl in Bordeaux who lived and practiced her trade in a tiny little room. She called men her "little ones," and she smelled of strong, cheap perfume. She would do anything for twenty francs, and in the corner of her room was this same couch with these same cushions, identical to the last tarnished fringe of gold. Looking at it tonight—the couch upon which I'm to sleep—it seems I can still smell that blatant perfume. Madame Renée apparently had none of these reactions, for she fluffed the cushions before she left.

At the rear of the salon, two steps lead to a door opening into a large, airy kitchen. I am very fortunate, as Madame Renée observed this afternoon, for I have a water faucet in the kitchen: there are only three houses in the Village with running water. In addition to a sink and a stove, the kitchen is equipped with an electric hot-plate with which to warm water for shaving or making coffee. Above it is a freshly penciled reminder to "Please remove cord from socket each time you have finished using hot-plate. Thank you!"

While I was inspecting the kitchen with Madame Renée, I heard sounds of invisible cattle in the room with us. She explained that this is a very old house, and that the wall behind the kitchen sink serves also as the wall of a neighboring barn. I am delighted: it's intriguing to be under the same roof with cattle.

Alone now in the salon in a completeness of privacy, with the courtyard gate closed for the night, I taste the first differences of the return to life on the outside—a return made extravagant and poignant by long months of monastic deprivation. There is no sleep to be had: feelings, the return, the freedom are too much. I celebrate alone. I waste precious wood in a fire of superb warmth. Sitting before the flames I take my time. I have all of time tonight, and there's a happiness in rediscovering nearly forgotten sensations.

237

The Valley sleeps frozen and deserted beyond my drawn shutters. And there across the way, my beloved Monastery with its sleeping monks. And an empty cell. And my own house enclosing its single living occupant for the night. The house is rich but simple, and I am poor tonight; for there's nothing to eat or drink and on my table only a half-pack of cigarettes.

But it's impossible to contain myself so great is my joy. And the poverty of my larder does nothing to hint its distraction. I think of this morning. I think of sleeping and of struggling to dress myself, and flecks of other conversations return. Father Clément tying my shoelaces: "But you have changed, my son. In these last two weeks you have changed, you speak differently."

"Father, I was wondering if you knew of some man in the Village whom I could hire to help me dress till the doctor comes back?"

"I am sure we can find you someone, my son. Let me think . . . I know—the postman. He passes your house every morning at seven-thirty, and he needs a little extra money. His wife, like all the females in the Valley, is expecting a baby soon. I imagine he would be glad to dress you. You can go to the post office now and ask him. He is one of our favorites here—an iconoclast, an atheist—but a fine man. He should do nicely."

When I found the postman he had several letters for me. He was small, fat and jovial, his cheeks perpetually reddened by wine. His speech was colored with the thick, beautiful accent of the Valley country.

"But yes, M'sieu," he agreed readily, "I'll be glad to help." He sounded as though he were constantly shrugging his shoulders. "Shall we have a glass of wine on it?"

We had our wine—two glasses of ersatz war apéritif, served by a young girl in the local store. I enjoyed his company. His conversation was intelligent and amusing.

"And how did M'sieu get his arm broken like that?" he asked me.

"To tell the truth, I got drunk and hurt it in a fall."

238

"M'sieu is joking!"

"No, that's the way it happened."

He swallowed the last few drops of the wine. "Well, take my advice, M'sieu—invent some other explanation for the people here."

I think over his words as I stir the fire, scorching the back of my hand. But the deliciousness of feelings crowds all else from my mind. There should be food and drink on a night like this—a night of such pointed poverty. Knowing I shall find nothing I go through the kitchen cabinets in the hope of discovering something with which to celebrate the occasion—perhaps a few leaves of tea, a bit of coffee or chocolate. The shelves are empty. But in a poverty which knows relief is on its way—in a poverty which is intentional—there is much that delights man to the very roots of his being. It is sharper and more exquisite than the banality of plenty.

I remember days of like poverty in Paris. After school I would walk to a local parish church to practice on the little reed organ. I allowed myself only two and a half francs each day, and no lunch. Between hours of practicing I would try to decide when to spend the meager sum. And the cup of tea or coffee or chocolate, when finally it was ordered, had all the delights of the waiting and the desiring. It became real, every taste, and precious as only poverty can make little things precious.

So it is tonight. Warmth is a rapture of senses long denied, and I know that a cup of tea or coffee would taste as it has never tasted because I can't have it, because there is none to be had in this war-rationed Valley.

The fire warms my feet, warms them miraculously until I have to move back. Such a thing becomes more intense in silence and in solitude, and I must sing, or throw something, or laugh aloud at nothing, so great is my wonder at being alone and warm and poor.

Curiosity takes me on another tour of the house as the Monastery bells toll midnight. I look in every room, in every dresser drawer and closet. Beside each bed is a night

239

table with its lamp; and in the little compartment beneath shines the enameled whiteness of the chamber pot, like a large cup. Each pot is turned upside down with all the charm and thoughtfulness of the French chambermaid who overlooks nothing, not even the law of gravity.

In the Countess's closet I find a package wrapped in tin foil. I smell it. It is tea, real tea, with a thick green mold on top. No matter . . .

Without a single twinge of conscience I requisition the package. It must have lain there since the beginning of the war and will probably make me sick, but that is of no importance now. A fitting celebration must be held. I boil water on the hot-plate and throw in some leaves from the bottom of the package. I fill a cup brimming with the liquid, then carry it in by the fire. The tea is hot and bitter and I savor it a sip at a time, filled with introspective pleasure. After a while the fire burns low, and a chill rises at my back.

Now, at last, I can go to sleep in that terrible bed. I turn back the covers and drop my clothes to the floor. With the smell in mind of a perfumed room in Bordeaux, I crawl in; and there's a feeling that despite my aloneness that same high-smelling girl will somehow appear. It is strange, sleeping alone in a bed so obviously intended for something more recherché—sleeping alone on a whore's couch.

2 january

Soon after I awake, the postman arrives to dress me—somewhat diffidently this first time—and I hurry to the Monastery. The morning, like all other mornings, is spent in the paleography room with Father G'seau. Before noon I go to the gardens to see Brother Placide's fine white hogs. He is very proud of his charges, patting them affectionately with cold-stiffened blue hands.

I return to the villa early. Madame Renée helps me arrange my worktable with books, writing paper, and other equipment for my studies. Despite my protests she has had an ancient, blackened wood-stove installed in my beautiful fireplace.

"It's less romantic, Monsieur," she tells me, "but it will heat twice as well with half the wood. When your present supply is gone there'll be no more. This is one of the three rooms in the Village with heat, and only because the Countess bought wood when it was more plentiful. You must use it sparingly."

Along with my regular ration ticket, I give Madame Renée my doctor's certificate for extra rations. We arrange the price of my meals. She asks two hundred and fifty francs a day, which is reasonable enough, but I refuse to pay more than a hundred and fifty. We settle for a hundred and eighty. Warned by the monks, I decide to have my way from the beginning, and it's not difficult with a woman of such good manners and charm.

She offers to get me a maid who will come each morning to clean the house while I'm at the Monastery, and who, if I wish, will also return in the evening to light my stove. But I tell her that I'd like to keep house as a relaxation from my other work.

"Then too, Madame," I conclude, "I want absolute privacy, even when I'm not at home."

"Very well, Monsieur. But would you mind if I kept my potatoes and other staples in your cellar? My little house across the way has no space. I can come and go without disturbing you."

"That's perfectly all right, Madame. I don't want to be disagreeable. You're free to come and go in this house whenever you like."

I feel sorry for this woman so helpful, and in a way so

241

pathetic. She who has known plenty is reduced to a cheap black dress and a black beret. She smiles easily and laughs often, as if she were as delighted as I with the arrangement. I feel that we shall be good friends, good comrades. Her conversation, which was somewhat stilted at our first meeting, is now relaxed and free like that of a woman of the world. It has a slangy quality, intermixed with a few highly elegant words to make the coloration complete and self-assured.

"Now you're installed, Monsieur, and may your stay be a long and happy one. I'll go fix lunch."

"Thanks very much for your kindness, Madame."

"Don't thank me, Monsieur. Both my sons are gone from me. Caring for you will give an old woman a new interest in life."

After Madame Renée's lecture I feel frugal enough not to light my stove until tonight. The room is like I left it, but clean. Dirty clothes have disappeared and the bed has been spread. The day is lighter: calm, noonday light through curtained windows. And a great silence of surrounding snow.

After a while Madame Renée returns. "Lunch is almost ready," she says quietly, fingering a button on her black woolen sweater, "and I have a fire in my dining room. If you like, you can come over and enjoy the fire while I set the table." She smiles a warm cordiality. Her cheeks are red. Wind from the open door blows the fine gray hair escaping her beret.

Closing my gate behind us, we walk together across the street to her house. She clasps my arm tightly, gasping and stepping carefully in the frozen snow, looking up and laughing at our slow progress. I feel the beginnings of affection for her spirit and gaiety.

In her salon is a stingy fire. I stand close to it half-warming myself, while she finishes the preparation for lunch. The room is small, with floors of tile and beams of darkened wood. The dining table is near the fire. There is an easy chair, and a couch. On the mantel, flanking a photograph

242

of her son in uniform, stand small vases of artificial flowers beneath a gold-framed mirror.

The table is quickly set with a white cloth and gleaming blue china. Madame Renée walks with quick steps from kitchen to table and back to kitchen, trailing small talk and laughter.

"Lunch is ready, Monsieur," she announces in a few moments. "Would you like to sit next to the fire?"

As I sit down, she puts before me colorful hors d'œuvres of tuna and beets and onions marinated in oil. It is food such as I haven't seen for months. It is followed by a large gigot cooked rare in dry white wine, garnished with mayonnaise and served with French fried potatoes and a green salad.

"Such a feast, Madame!" I exclaim. "I've never eaten better food. You must buy all this on the black market, eh?"

She laughs, looking away. "Monsieur mustn't ask embarrassing questions. I know many of the farmers in the Valley. We shall manage, I think."

"But you must teach me how to make mayonnaise like this. And the gigot—how did you cook that? It's superb."

"Very simple, Monsieur. It's a true peasant recipe—and there's no better cooking in the world. You take a leg of lamb and remove the bone—Do you know how to do that, by the way?"

"I've seen it done."

"Well, you fill the cavity with small whole onions—and oh yes, add a clove of garlic for each pound of meat. Then put it in a hot stove and render out the fat for fifteen minutes. All you have to do then is pour a cup of good dry wine over it and let it cook in a moderate oven for fifteen minutes to the pound, if you like it rare."

"Sounds easy enough," I remark. "You don't use any seasoning except garlic and onions and wine?"

"That's all, and maybe a dash of salt. And always be sure to let the gigot stand for about twenty-four hours before you slice it."

243

"What about the mayonnaise?"

"That's easy, too. It's made from egg yolk and oil and wine vinegar, with salt and a little lemon juice. And for the finishing touch I put in some of the wine from the gigot."

"You must let me watch you, Madame. I can't leave without learning to make this."

"Any time you have a free moment, Monsieur. I'm flattered you like it."

I take portion after portion, assuaging past hungers. Madame Renée eats sparingly, watching me. Looking up I ask, "Am I eating too much, Madame?"

"No, no," she answers quickly. "We can afford to celebrate this time."

For dessert there are cheeses, a custard aromatized with kirsch, and coffee—real coffee with sugar. After the second helping of custard I lean back in my chair. For the first time in weeks I am full and satisfied.

"That was truly wonderful, Madame Renée," I sigh. "You can't imagine how good it tasted after eating at the Monastery all this time."

"It was a pleasure to watch you eat, Monsieur." She pauses a moment, stirring her coffee slowly and carefully. "But I'd like to ask you something."

"What's that?"

"You've always lived in big cities." She hesitates almost imperceptibly. "May I suggest that life here is very different? I know you don't realize it, but everything you do in the Valley is known. You're a foreigner and the center of much talk."

I blush, thinking she refers to Madame Vincent.

"You were seen in the store yesterday," she goes on, "having a glass of wine with the postman."

"Yes," I readily confess, "we had a glass of wine together. Is there something wrong with that?"

"But, Monsieur, here in the Valley, people of your station never appear in public with their postman."

"Oh, really? I'm surprised. And for what reasons, may I ask? He's going to help me get dressed every morning.

If he's good enough for that, surely we can drink together."

She laughs, "I agree with you, of course. But these are local customs. I only wanted you to know. You see, you're more or less on trial here, as it were. The better people are certainly on your side, but this sort of thing is an indelicacy which can give you trouble."

"I appreciate your telling me this, Madame," I say politely, "but I must admit I find it irritating. I like the postman."

"Oh, so do we, Monsieur," she protests. "But that doesn't make him socially our equal."

"I've always made friends where I like, Madame. What could this better class of people do about it? I resent being, as you say, 'on trial.' When they find out that the monks and Madame la Marquise are my friends, I dare say I'll be acquitted."

"But they can do you great harm. They can make it impossible for you to receive ration cards or provisions. They can make it impossible for you to live in the Village. I like you very much, and I carry a little influence here. But don't forget that in allowing you the hospitality of my house I'm more or less responsible for your behavior."

"But such unreasonable standards of behavior can't be dictated," I say evenly. "And let's get one thing straight at the outset, Madame. I don't mean to offend you, but I'd like you to understand that you're in no way responsible for me or my actions. I eat with you, that's all. If you feel you owe it to your friends to make me act as they do, then we'll call the whole thing off right now."

There is a strained expression on her face. "If you can do nothing but make fun of us," she says in a voice becoming angry, "I certainly can't continue to receive you in my house."

I look at her a moment before speaking. "Very well, I'll be as discreet as possible," I agree. "But don't forget one thing—I'm here to study with the monks. That's my only interest. Please don't think you have to teach me how to act. I know how to kiss old ladies' hands and which fork to use.

As far as I'm concerned I like you and I'll enjoy my meals with you. I don't imagine you'll have many apologies to make for my conduct."

Her face softens. She pours fresh coffee. "I didn't mean to insult you," she apologizes. "Please don't take it the wrong way. You see, I understand you. I've known your kind of life but you've never known life in a small village like this. I only wanted to—"

"Of course, Madame—it's very foolish of me. You must always tell me these things." I get quickly to my feet. "Now I must go."

"Where are you going?"

I chuckle. "I'm going to take the postman into Town and get drunk."

"I don't blame you," she laughs. "See you at supper."

I stroll toward the Monastery in the clear winter air of the sleeping afternoon Village. Past doors, walking in the street where cars never pass. I am disturbed because of the scene at lunch. Already a hinted domination of the "great ladies." My only weapon is to ignore them, to have nothing to do with them. It's a poor start I have made. The vultures begin to hover, and to tear.

Low terraces leading down to the River bank make a peaceful winter scene. I walk slowly. Ahead, closing a door, I see a gray wool suit and upswept hair and a Parisian hat. My heart begins to pound. It is Madame Vincent. It is the first time I've seen her since our walk back from Town in the snow.

"Good afternoon, M'sieu," she says in the patois of the Valley, speaking cordially as if she remembers what she's tried to forget.

I shake her hand, glove against glove. "I'm glad to see you, Madame Vincent. I didn't know you were still here." We are alone in the deserted street. She smiles. Like so many French women she has only begun to be beautiful. From forty to sixty will be her years of greatest loveliness.

She whispers, "I've kept up with you through Father Clément. Did you enjoy your friends from Paris?"

"Very much."

"And how is your shoulder? I was so sorry to hear you'd hurt it."

"Doing fine, thanks. But did you know that I have a villa here now? That I'm a Villager?"

"You're lucky," she says, shaking her head. "It's hard for me to live in this pension. They don't approve of me in the Valley, you know. And we mustn't be seen talking together. These people have eyes in the back of their heads. They all agree that we did what we did in Town."

"To hell with them!" I tell her of my conversation a few moments ago with Madame Renée, realizing that I exaggerate to my own advantage. We walk slowly toward the Monastery. I try to take her arm, but she moves away.

"Don't let them get their teeth in you, my friend," she says. "They're poisonous—I know. One of your 'great ladies' runs my pension, and the remarks she hasn't made about both me and my friend Mademoiselle de Castro! You remember her—the girl who ruined your prayers once. You told me about it that day in Town."

"Of course. But she had nothing to do with that. She seems like a lovely girl."

"She is."

We turn into the Monastery, stopping at the gate.

"Well, good-bye, Monsieur," murmurs Madame Vincent. "I wish we might be friends."

I hesitate, putting my hand on her arm. "Look, you can trust me," I say slowly. "I know I shouldn't ask, but we're two of a kind, surrounded by uncongenial people. Now that I have my villa, why not come and see me? You could go into Town and let yourself be seen there, then return to my place late at night. We could have a couple of hours to sleep together and no one would ever know. I have a good fire, and we could—I mean—"

She smiles regretfully. "I *am* sorry. You're very sympathetic, and as you say, they're all cold to us. But it would be foolhardy to take such a risk. We mustn't be seen together any more. Your Madame Renée would have me

247

chased from the Valley. And besides, I don't want such a thing to happen to me again."

Sighing, I observe jokingly, "You say that as if I'd given you the worst time of your life."

"You know better than that. I'd just like to forget about it, that's all."

"I find that a hard thing to do. But couldn't we still see each other? Not for that reason, but just to get a little relief from these paragons of virtue around here? Maybe I could have you and Mademoiselle de Castro to tea. No one could misjudge that."

"We'll see. But I'd better go now. I have an appointment with Father Clément."

"Poor Father Clément!" I groan. "At least he can hear both sides of the story this way. Just tell him the truth. That's what I do." I grin. "And will you tell him I tempted you today? Will you ask him to pray for you not to fall into my clutches again?"

"I certainly will," she laughs.

"Then we're both lost, for I'm going to ask him to pray for me to have the strength to resist you."

She smiles merrily. "You know, if we ever do fall again it's going to be terrible. It'll be a foot race to see who gets to Father Clément first. This is a strange triangle, isn't it? We're mutual friends who hide nothing from one another, and Father Clément's in the middle."

"I'm glad," I put in, "I'm not in his place."

"Wouldn't you love to hear his prayers? 'Dear God, lead Thy humble servant Madame Vincent away from that terrible young man who has already caused her to fall.' And then, 'Dear God, please give this boy, Thy humble servant, the strength to resist that terrible woman who has already caused him to fall.' "

"Bless his heart," I chuckle. "We must behave."

"Yes, we must. Now I really do have to go." She warmly shakes my hand. "Good luck to you in your new life."

"Thanks—the same to you."

248

I watch her walk away, standing there a moment without moving. The stirrings of desire are strong within me, and it's only with intense effort that I succeed in fighting them down.

When I enter the paleography room Father G'seau and a younger monk, bending over manuscripts, scarcely look up. I quietly take a chair at the same table. I force my mind onto my work, reading, copying. But I am relieved when, much later, the great bells announce the beginning of Vespers.

There are fifteen or less in the chapel for Vespers. These people who before were nonentities or abstract temptations to me, begin now to fit into a pattern. Madame Vincent and Mademoiselle de Castro are kneeling when I enter. Shortly after the opening chants, Madame Renée walks softly down the aisle, makes a profound genuflection to the altar, and kneels in one of the front pews. Despite her age she is the most beautiful woman there.

In the gathering dusk of early evening the empty chapel echoes the measured beauty of the chants, dissolving the day's pettiness. We draw into ourselves. It's impossible not to go to my knees.

Satisfaction lingers and lulls after the office is over. The Valley is a quietness of dusk become magical. Returning to my house I walk past other houses: past doors, past decrepit, crumbling outside plasters, past curtained windows, past frozen cells of livingness hugging the sidewalk. I walk contented to be away from the world of Paris, the world of the world beyond. Satisfied to be here in this corner of the earth with its one street, its undisciplined houses large, small, leaning, where values become clear and happiness comes with no effort to seek it out.

I find my room already warm. Madame Renée has lighted the fire. Windows are closed and blinds drawn. Lying down across my bed, I wait for dinner at eight o'clock. The new stove spits and warms. Red reflections from the grilled opening dance magnified on the opposite wall.

The Monastery bells wake me from a doze—bells calling

the monks to their evening meal, and me to mine. The night is dark, closed out. My gate screeching iron against iron destroys a silent purity of huddled, deserted street.

Madame Renée, clutching a heavy shawl, is outside closing her blinds with rapid movements. She greets me warmly, with the reserve of good taste. "Come in, Monsieur."

I follow her into the house. She tosses her shawl across the couch and goes to rub her hands over the fire. I sit at the table removing my gloves, and I apologize for my brusqueness at noon—"I'm not used to the ways of a small town"—moving my feet close to the stove and touching it with my shoes. In the heat the snow steams and melts.

"I know that, Monsieur. It's perfectly all right. I'll have dinner in a moment, so make yourself at home." She walks into the kitchen. "That's a good radio," she calls back, "and there should be a concert from Paris soon." Her voice sounds alive and at ease. "I have a surprise for you for dinner."

"Oh, really? What is it?" I ask eagerly, knowing eagerness is expected.

"You'll see—I said it was a surprise, didn't I? No, now—go sit back down and listen to the concert."

She laughs, and there is a goodness in being together. And our talk remains light and companionable through the excellent meal which she serves on the little table by the fire. Again I eat heartily while she watches, unable to resist the tempting dishes she has prepared. Until at last we are ready for dessert.

"Now," she says, "the surprise for Monsieur."

From the kitchen a tray is carried in with grandness of manner, and I stretch high in my chair to look over the edge as she holds it elaborately above me. The "surprise" is a large platter of *crêpes*.

"Wonderful!" I cry. "My favorite of all desserts. But how did you know?"

"Do you really like them?"

"There's nothing I like better. This is a *real* surprise."

She is pleased as she sets the platter on the table and serves me. The *crêpes* are indeed delicious—as outstanding

250

as the rest of her food. My months-old hunger for such things won't let me stop, and when I put down my fork the platter is empty. I think of the monks getting up from barren tables, and my full belly doesn't envy them.

Madame Renée removes the dishes, then returns with a small coffee filter. The easy chair is moved near the fire. She sits on her couch heating coffee on the wood-stove between us. The white demitasses wait on the table's edge. We talk and drink cup after cup. We talk with a concert played by the Orchestre Colonne turned on low volume. She asks about my life in America and in Paris, and she contrasts it with life in a tiny village such as this. Slowly, delicately, she carries the conversation to Madame Vincent.

"I may as well tell you, Monsieur," she says at the appropriate time, "you were seen with Madame Vincent in the street this afternoon. She's not very well thought of here. One of my good friends runs the pension where she lives. She overheard her speaking to you in the patois of our district. It seems very rude to me to make fun of our way of talking."

"I'm sorry," I apologize for Madame Vincent. "She didn't mean to be rude. Madame Vincent isn't that type at all. It was a private conversation. She wouldn't have talked like that if she'd known someone was listening."

"In any case, Monsieur, we don't consider it proper for a woman to approach a man on the street." She pours more coffee, stirs in a lump of sugar, and hands me the cup.

I ask, "Tell me, why isn't Madame Vincent well thought of here? I find her very sympathetic. Is it because she's a beautiful woman, perhaps?"

There will be no argument this time. She laughs. From the radio comes a roar of applause as the concert ends. I turn the dial, finding more music.

"You're caustic, Monsieur," comments Madame Renée. "No, I agree it might well be her beauty, but that isn't it. She's considered a woman of rather easy morals. It does you no good to be seen with her. She's obviously after the rich American."

251

I look at her in astonishment, then burst into laughter.
Madame Renée stiffens.

"Is it so amusing, Monsieur?"

"Forgive me, Madame. I know it's impolite, but you're
a woman of the world." I hesitate. "What would you say
if I told you that actually Madame Vincent's an old friend
of mine, and that she's not after either me or the money I'm
supposed to have and don't?"

"But where did you know her, Monsieur?"—guileless,
leading, making it easy to share confidences. "I've heard
talk, but I didn't believe it."

"I'm not ashamed of it," I say without thinking.

"But no, of course you're not"—still leading, cajoling.
"After all, you're a young man, and young men aren't supposed to be made of steel. You're wise to tell me. It all
becomes clear now. She isn't young, she knew what she was
doing. Obviously she led you on. What inexcusable conduct
for a woman her age! Why, I think—"

"No, Madame. It was just one of those . . . uh . . .
situations. I was to blame, not she. Proof of that is, she'll
have nothing intimate to do with me now."

"Have you tried? And did she refuse?" Madame Renée
is serious and sympathetic, and the night and the fire and
the room with odors of cigarettes and coffee and sachet, destroy barriers.

"Yes, I may as well be honest," I answer without reserve.
"I have tried, and she's refused me. Isn't that strongly in
her favor? Anyone can fall once, but to keep from doing it
again seems—"

"Perhaps," she interrupts. "I know young men do these
things. It's natural at your age. But for a woman of her
age—ah, no"—shaking her head—"ah, no, Monsieur, really.
She's little more than a strumpet, and we know what to do
with strumpets in our Valley."

"You're not going to tell what I've just—?"

"I must, Monsieur. There are other young boys and men.
She's been here too long already."

"You *must not*," I say desperately. "Now listen—if I

252

hear of it I'll never share a confidence with you again. Promise me you won't do this, promise me it's—"

"Very well, if you feel that strongly about it. But please don't see her again. As a service to me. I think we could be good friends. In this short time I'm already fond of you. But you must realize my place in the community. I can't receive you in my house if you continue to show such open indiscretion."

"I understand, Madame."

"I hope you do. You see, I'm from another world myself. These petty little things don't occupy us there, but unfortunately they have to be considered here." She draws the shawl about her shoulders and leans back against the pillows. "Now let's speak of more pleasant things. How's your work at the Monastery?"

"I have more than I can handle, but Father Abbot's very lenient with me."

"I'm glad to hear that." She smiles tolerantly. "I suppose he's a good man at heart, but those of us who know him, who have had dealings with him, consider him somewhat uncouth and unpolished—almost a brute at times."

"No, not at all," I protest, mildly shocked. "You mustn't say such things, Madame. I'm very fond of Father Abbot. No one as gentle as he could possibly be called a brute."

"That's because you don't know him well enough," she returns. "I may as well tell you, he wouldn't take my son Michel because he didn't think he was good enough."

"I can understand how a mother would resent such a thing," I tell her. "But don't you know that's official policy? I believe they always send young monks to monasteries where they won't be too close to their families. Isn't that the reason your son was sent some place else?"

"Perhaps."

I decide to return to my room. Something about this good woman irritates me. Is it her superiority of manner? Her lordly derision of local people? Her tendency to find meanness in everyone we discuss? Only toward me does she appear genuinely kind and tolerant.

253

I rise and make my excuses. She accompanies me pleasantly to the door, taking my hand to bid me good night. Her hand is warm and dry and gritty. I release it quickly.

In my house, I close the doors behind me. I have a great deal of work to do before morning. But studying is difficult in new surroundings. Above and on all sides are dark, empty rooms. Solitude and the completeness of privacy invade my first thoughts. The room is warm, so warm that I can remove clothing with no discomfort. These are happinesses of gesture, doing for myself alone in my house. In the Valley outside, the others sleep. Lateness of hour and isolation add to the warmth. Clothes are dropped, movements intercutting desultory study until study becomes dullness and obligation dampening, like a prudish person, spirits of more delightful warmth.

There are many small things to take me from my open books: small features of newness and a warm house which beg me to leave learning. There are lateness of night, outside cold and inner warmth, and wakefulness amidst sleeping. These things call to me to stir the fire, to get a glass of cold water from the darkened kitchen, to turn up the lights—no, that only glares—to turn down the lights. Brown and white tiles beneath my feet and scattered rugs lure my gaze from volumes of apologetics and history. And soon the books are left with pages open, staring white and unseeing at the lamp above.

Indecision. Time is there. Indecision of movements to take up time's surplus. Until decision. Definite, not changing delight's plane. Decision is intimate. It must be something intimate this night. Decision to bathe. Bathing is intimate and small and a joyous taking of time's surplus.

Remaining clothing is dropped and kicked into a corner. I leave for errands in other rooms, running quickly on bare feet. Into the kitchen for a carafe of water, upstairs for the small, pail-like bathtub. In other rooms it is damp and unapproving lateness. Other rooms stare at my nakedness clothed only in the sling of a broken shoulder. They stare and purse their lips; they are coldness and formality. I

254

apologize to them, I didn't know. They are women, old women who are shocked. With tub, soap and towel I return to my salon. There's a difference. The salon, like a fine mistress, welcomes me and is warm. And chill of stone floor gives way to comfort of rug before the stove. No need to apologize. She likes me like this. She smiles and approves.

I wait for the water to heat on top of the stove. I retrieve clothes, hang them neatly on a chair. Anything I do becomes a pleasure tonight. Madame Renée has left a small basket of firewood beside the stove. I put most of it in, opening the top and pulling back my head to escape sparks and sudden gushes of smoke. The extravagance of fire roars up the long stovepipe, blazing and tossing out sparks that will die on the frozen stillness without.

Despite the spitting and popping noises of the stove, late bells from the Monastery penetrate the thick walls, more felt in vibration than heard. The silence, the silence of an empty house, of empty rooms above. The disgusted silence of hard-arteried old rooms. They didn't know their salon was that kind. Humph—they had always thought her above that sort of thing. Theirs is a silence of lonely, haughty spaces. We forget them quickly. Ours is a silence of warmth and small things. Silence is our companion. We ignore other, more eloquent silences.

Fire lights the stove window. There arises the new sound of steaming water at the boiling point. I half-fill the tub with cold water from the faucet. Gingerly removing the carafe from the stove, I add hot water till the temperature is correct for bathing. I decide to wash face and arms first, so I place the tub on top of the stove, lifting it by its bail with my good arm. English prints of elongated horses hang on the walls and admire. But I'm clumsy with my stiff arm, and water runs splashing on the floor. I dry it by pulling a rug over it. We take a certain satisfaction in being untidy, my room and my elongated horses and I. When I have rinsed myself, and rubbed my neck and face and arms almost raw with a heavy towel, I put the tub on the floor and sit in it. The water begins to cool, becoming heavy with soapy

255

filth. Now despite rinsings thin films of soap remain on legs and feet. I stand in the tub to wash my feet, and almost fall trying to dry them without getting too much water on the floor. When this is done—when time has passed a little —I bask in cleanliness.

I pick up the soap and towel and lay them on the kitchen table. I open the back door and run barefoot into the courtyard to urinate on the frozen snow. Limping from the cold ground back to my fire, I put on more water for tea. And this time I'm prepared with a sack of dry cookies.

Night moves on. I eat cakes and drink tea, both of them vile, but tasting tonight like food for the gods. I read and drink tea till I can no longer hold my eyes open. And I sleep like a child. The lives of the saints is my work for tomorrow, and I sleep dreaming for a moment of St. Theresa of Ávila—and then of nothing.

3 january

"Here's some mail for M'sieu." The postman awakens me standing beside my bed, pouring letters on my chest. He laughs at my startled reaction.

I ask, "But how did you get in here? I didn't hear you ring."

"The door wasn't locked, M'sieu. Am I supposed to ring?"

"No, no, of course not. Excuse me, I'm still not awake." I force myself to a sitting position on the edge of the bed. "There, I got out clean clothes last night. If you'll please help me . . ."

"With pleasure, M'sieu."

He holds my clothes as I awkwardly step into them, then he buttons them up for me. I wince when he pulls the shirt over my shoulder.

"And how're you making it with Madame Renée?" he asks.

"All right, I guess. But I'm not used to villages. The customs here are different."

He nods his head, stooping to pull on my heavy socks. "Madame Renée's a good woman, better than most. But they're all—if M'sieu will excuse the expression—they're all bitches. They don't think a poor postman's good enough for them. For myself I don't care, you understand, but it's hard on my wife. You'll be criticized for having a drink with me, M'sieu."

"I know, my friend—I already have. But frankly they can put their criticisms in the lace of their patched panties. I don't care what they think."

He rises laughing. "You'll find little lace among them," he says as he lights a cigarette.

"I wouldn't look for it."

Moving back he flicks ashes on the floor. "There, you're dressed. I'll be back tomorrow. And, M'sieu"—opening the door, half-joking—"be careful of the bitches. If you let them, they'll bruise you where it hurts the most."

"I can imagine."

"The best thing to do is keep yourself above them. Make them come to you. Be aloof—they can't stand that. And don't tell them a thing."

"Thanks for the tip. We'll have our way yet."

As he steps out I hear another door in the hall. I know it's Madame Renée returning from the cellar with provisions. She walks quietly out after the postman. From far away their voices come back to me.

"Is there any mail for me this morning?" she asks.

"Yes, Madame." A slight pause. "Here you are. Well, the weather looks a little better this morning, doesn't it?"

"Yes, perhaps the worst is over. And how's your young

257

wife? She's having a hard time with this first pregnancy, isn't she?"

"Yes, the poor thing. It's not easy for her."

"The second one won't be so bad," Madame Renée says easily, with kindness and sympathy. "Can I do anything for her? I have a few old dresses—perhaps she could use them for maternity clothes."

"You're really too kind, Madame Renée. I'll tell my wife. Thanks a thousand times."

"Not at all, Monsieur. Good morning."

I join Madame Renée as the postman continues his rounds. She looks up from her letters and smiles.

"Ah," she greets me, "you're up early—a good serious beginning."

"The postman," I chuckle, "is better than an alarm clock."

"How does your shoulder feel this morning?"

"Seems to be steadily improving, thanks."

"Good," she says cheerfully. "It'll soon be well, I'm sure. Would you like some coffee?"

"Love some."

We cross the narrow street. I open the gate into her yard, holding it for her.

"I couldn't help overhearing what you said to the postman," I tell her. "That was very kind of you."

"But how, Monsieur?" she says shruggingly. "He's a fine young man. We're fond of him here in the Village. He's most obliging, really."

"Then why do you object to my having a drink with him? Here, I'll get the door."

"Thank you. But you don't understand," she explains, as we enter the salon. "One simply doesn't drink with one's postman. We have little in common, but we don't dislike him or abuse him as you seem to think. You'll see. When his baby is born, all the better people here will do whatever they can to help." She pours a large cupful of coffee and warm milk.

"Thanks. That really smells good." I sit down and

258

gratefully sip the hot liquid, its steam rising damp and fragrant in my face. "Incidentally," I say between swallows, "I can't expect you to go on helping me with my housework. There's much more to it than I'd imagined. Do you suppose you could still get me that maid you mentioned?"

She laughs, joining me at the table. "I knew you'd change your mind. These old houses aren't like your American homes. Yes, I have just the girl for you—Germaine. She does some work for me occasionally. And she can take care of your laundry, too. Just leave your soiled clothes on the kitchen floor every morning, and she'll wash them and put them back in the dresser for you."

"That sounds like a perfect arrangement. Could you please tell her to start right away?"

"Of course, Monsieur. But I must warn you of one thing —don't leave any letters or personal papers lying around. These people will read anything you don't hide, and they'll soon spread it all over the Village. You'll be careful, won't you?"

"If you say so. You've helped me a great deal."

"It's nothing, Monsieur. You'd do the same for me, wouldn't you?"

"Certainly. But it isn't necessary for you to go so much out of your way. It isn't expected, you know."

Smiling broadly, she refills my cup with black, smoking coffee. "It's a pleasure, Monsieur, to do things for one's friends. I can tell you now that I didn't want to take you at first, that I took you on trial. But you remind me so much of my poor Jean-Julien"—she looks at his photograph on the mantel—"I feel I'm really doing this for him. He would have been your age. I know what young men like, and I want to make your life here as pleasant as possible."

Too soon, and with reminiscences; I know it's time to retreat. I say firmly, "I'm not a grateful person to have as a friend, Madame Renée. I'm afraid I'll disappoint you if you look on me as you would your Jean-Julien."

She ignores me and injects lulling affection into her voice. "There, there, that's exactly what Jean-Julien would

259

have said. He was blunt and hard just like you, only he didn't have your polish, your manner. He'd say to me, 'Mother, you're fluttery as an old hen. Stop treating me like a baby.' He was so much franker than his brother Michel. Michel's too sweet. But I must let you read Jean-Julien's war diary, poor thing. They sent it to me with his effects after his plane crashed."

The tears start. How very much she wants to talk of this Jean-Julien; but the words of an adulating mother become intimate profanity. I can't bring myself to encourage her.

Falteringly, to break the silence, I mutter, "I'll consider it a privilege to read his diary, Madame."

She gets up and opens a drawer beneath her wardrobe, taking from it a small pocket notebook so bent and folded as to be pathetic in its lack of sheen. She thumbs the worn pages as she sits down again. Then leaning far forward she hands it to me.

"There are some bad words in it," she whispers, half-smiling. "Jean-Julien was always a little . . . uh . . . free in his speech. But he was a real little man. You'll see."

I feel an instinctive repugnance for this boy, this boy whom I know only in the mouth of his mother; it makes what I say false, and it sickens me with myself. "I'll be very interested to compare his reaction to the war with my own," I recite glibly. "I was nearly killed several times myself." Howling self-laughter—detesting self, sneering at little, little hero of self. Her son is dead—dead for his country. You shame him in yourself. Furtive, discordant shame.

But she doesn't know: "You're the only person besides Michel I've allowed to read it. Others might not understand. But you will, won't you? Promise me you will." She takes my hand in hers. It is dry and feverish to the touch. I resist an urge to draw back.

"Of course I'll understand," I assure her. "And I appreciate your confidence in letting me read it."

I take the diary and walk back to my room. Lying there near the window I read. It's not long. It tells of Jean-

260

Julien's escape from France, and of his emotions, very real and touching, as he stood crowded with others watching the last lights of his country fade from sight, knowing that somewhere back there he left his family and everything he loved. A few pages later the realness of his feelings is lost. He learned English, filling the diary with slang phrases and simulated emotions. There's his lip-curled desire after some English girl whom he didn't have the courage to approach, and such stanch manly phrases as, "Heave to, up and at 'em, my poor ass." "Ass" is spelled with one *s*. For several pages he is intoxicated with it: "my poor as"; "my sad as"; "my aching as."

I think of the glory, the heroism of the first few pages of his diary. His chance came, his great chance—the one Dr. Castelar mentioned. He died. With that in mind the rest falls into place. His mother's open love and my reaction both seem incredibly cheap beside this mousy, frugal attempt of a youth to be a man; beside his involuntary success in the flames of a death which he probably didn't merit. He did everything badly. He tried too hard. When he forgot his lycée journalism, when he ignored his wincing loins, the diary is moving experience. Otherwise it's like all others, raised above the level of the commonplace only by his immolation. He died perfectly, cleansed by the magnificence of his terror.

I read the last pages written in the childish hand of the dead man. Written as hairs and scalp and digestion and nocturnal fondlings and temperature and brushed teeth and swallowed saliva. Written by a man alive and unimportant. Words that remain as life wrote them, but given luster by the perspective of death. His last entry is openmouthed banality: "I spent the week end with the McCombs. They complimented me on my English." That's all. That's the last word written before he died. Of the entire week end, the only incident he thought worth recounting to his diary, which was himself, was that they told him his English was good. No premonitions of the end, no worth-while observations, no final gasp of clarity. Nothing but a touching necessity to pat himself on the back before hairs and scalp and digestion and nocturnal fondlings and temperature and brushed teeth and swallowed saliva became ashes and tears and earth's silent dimension of memory.

I put the diary aside. It's not interesting, but it pushes to the foreground thoughts of the strange relationship of characters, and the persistency with which we play a role. How much has our literature led us to believe in man the stereotype! If he is strong, we think, then he is strong; and so it is with goodness and badness and weakness. But with the doctor I was a weakling because I was in the presence of greater strength. The role of strength is usurped by the strong. While reading Jean-Julien's diary it is I who am changed; it is I who am strong in the presence of weakness. Is all this purely quantitative? Confronted with greater badness a man is less bad, although he may possess in full every attribute of badness.

Can a man forget these attributes to delude himself into a consistent role? Can goodness actually be had, even with the grace of God, and can strength become a constant thing? Or is it not rather a potential, like money in the coffers, to be utilized only when needed, to be discarded a thousand times a day? Is not consistency of behavior the blindness of delusion?

I think of backgrounds, of standards of conduct inculcated deep within every child. A man knows what they say is right and what they say is wrong; but he must also know that there's a fixed means by which to measure these things within himself. Man becomes me, and I know what man knows. I know the value of morality, and yet I find health in immorality. It's not discovered in me, for I hide it. It's only hinted in others, for I can't imagine that they are what they are—exactly like me. I know the value of hygiene, but I don't hesitate to urinate in my kitchen sink if it happens to be raining outside. Like his nocturnal fondlings, a man will never admit such things; and if I were told that a man walked in and found another man urinating in the sink because it was raining outside, my disgust would be complete.

262

I would forget my own culpability. My delusion would make me overlook the fact that I had done the same thing myself. And I would be sincere in my reaction.

For a man is himself only when he is alone, completely alone; when he can act without the risk of another's judgment. He may not be good, but for perhaps the only time in his life he is real, a realness lost in a sort of other-dimensional amnesia when society becomes his conscience. He is real because in his intimacy he becomes all things simultaneously: an instantaneous commixture of goods and evils and sanctities and lusts each playing in counterpoint to the other, each more stringent, more violent, more naked in its character than at any other time. It's then that a youth revels in his most delicious thoughts; that an older man returns again and again to the memory of things never forgotten, never divulged; and that a woman draws phallic symbols and feels the sickness of sweating flesh beneath breasts that now hang a little. It's then that a man knows himself and his inconsistency in all things—in acts and thoughts and self-forgiveness.

And it's not good.

It's not good unless all these private little meannesses and goodnesses are focused to a point where he is hopelessly in love with the stomach of another. For in no other way can self-love be nullified. A man's thirst must find satisfaction in the belly of another, into the very entrails of whom he can never really reach. That or a simulated love of comparable force is the only equation mark in the mathematics of his being. A simulated love is the love of a St. Francis which grows into grandeur, which must be sought if one has the courage to thirst for it. A man can always find his thirst, but the will to find it must be set purposely in motion in the privacy of his being, for it rarely exists there as an indigenous part of himself.

Answers, hints of poorly formulated answers to questions one doesn't ask. They are symptoms which inevitably arise when a man lives for the first time among other men whose only breath is in God. He attempts to understand them, and in the attempt he must begin himself to breathe of the

263

same air. His unworthiness, the privacy of his actions and hopes may not change; they may even deteriorate. But he can't escape the questions, nor the answers . . .

There is a knock at the front door which I hear too late, followed by a glimpse of a black-robed monk passing my window, and another knock at the kitchen door. I walk to the door and open it, nodding my head casually in greeting. He is large and plain and middle-aged, looking like a thousand other monks.

He bows. "Good morning, Monsieur. I am Father Sauvac, priest in charge of the parish here. Since you're now my parishioner, I've come to see how this part of my flock is settling himself."

I invite him in, and we take chairs near the fire. He glances about appraisingly.

"Ah, you have a nice place here, young man," he says in an approving voice. "You're indeed surrounded by comfort."

"I'm glad you came, Father," I tell him. "You're my first real guest."

"Is that so?" he smiles. Folding his hands over his stomach, he settles more deeply into the chair. "Well, I'm always interested in my parishioners."

"I'm sure you already know I'm not a Catholic, Father Sauvac. But I'll be glad to fulfill any duty toward the parish that's expected of me."

"Fine, fine." He nods his large head, accepting a cigarette. "There's one thing in particular I wanted to ask you— Ah, but here is Madame Renée."

I twist in my chair. She stands in the hall holding a large tray with cups and spoons and a coffee filter. She is half-laughing.

"Good morning, Father," she says brightly. "I saw you enter the courtyard and thought you might like a cup of hot coffee."

The gesture annoys me, and annoyance becomes anger when I notice there are three cups on the tray. Without being asked to stay she sits on my bed, and she and Father

264

Sauvac carry on the conversation. I drink my coffee in silence.

The priest smiles knowingly and asks, "And how is your son Michel, Madame Renée?"

"Just fine, thank you, Father."

"I understand you're helping care for the newest member of our community here?"

"Yes, we're going to be good friends, I know. He teases me a little about some of our local customs, but he's a good boy." She looks at me with distasteful affection, flushing. Seeing my grimace, she turns back to Father Sauvac. "How's the Carnot baby, Father? Has it arrived yet?"

"Not yet," he replies. "The poor woman's already lost her waters." He pulls at the hairs in his nostrils. "The doctor thinks the child's been dead inside her for about ten days. That's one of the things I wanted to talk to Monsieur about."

"But what on earth could this boy do to help? He can't give any money, if that's what you want."

She stretches herself into a half-prone position on my bed, smiling at both of us, obviously trying to give Father Sauvac the impression that she'll handle all these more banal details of my existence. I am deeply embarrassed. Only a wife or a mistress sits on the bed when chairs are available. I feel certain Father Sauvac is thinking the same thing, wondering at the intimacy of our relationship after only a few days.

He says resignedly, "It was quite something else, Madame Renée."

And she pursues, still smiling, "But what was it, then? Or do you prefer to discuss it alone?"

"Not necessarily. It can wait." His voice is of a gentleness that at once understands and rebukes. "There's no hurry, and I'm late in my rounds this morning. Now, if you'll excuse me? And thank you for the coffee—it was delicious."

I walk with him to the gate. "I'll come to your house this afternoon, Father," I whisper. "And believe me, I'm as surprised as you are. Why, I scarcely know her. Please accept my apologies. I can't imagine what she had in mind."

He laughs, kicking ice from the gate. Reaching up, he pulls my ear close to his mouth. "She's protecting your interests, my son," he murmurs sarcastically. "Until this afternoon, then. Better make it after Vespers. As for her, I know how to handle these things. I haven't been a parish priest twenty-seven years for nothing, eh? I'll fix her in the confessional. She'll wear out her beads after this, I can promise you."

I stare after him, not believing what I've heard. Then I walk slowly back into the house. Madame Renée is replacing the cups on the tray. I thank her for bringing the coffee.

"I knew Father Sauvac would like a warm drink," she answers innocently. "I've known him a long time, *that* one. You must get some cognac in the house for his next visit. He'll be back"—she smiles and nods her head—"he'll be back since I stopped him from trying to get money out of you."

"I dare say," I remark bitingly.

She looks up at me. "You didn't mind my coming in like that, did you? He's a good man, but a man without culture. You'll find you have nothing in common with him. And *don't* start giving him money. He's always begging for money, and I don't think you should feel obliged to give him anything."

"But you're mistaken, Madame Renée. Just because a man isn't cultured doesn't mean we have nothing in common. I detest 'cultured' people—the kind you're talking about."

"Then you're going to see him again?" She stands in the doorway holding the tray of empty cups.

"But of course—this evening after Vespers."

Her face becomes sober. She glances down, but quickly raises her eyes in half-hurts, half-smiles, to say, "I'd rather you wouldn't."

"I *am* sorry, Madame. I've lived my own life for many years, and I feel my decisions are my own. Rest assured I know how to say no just as well as the next man."

266

Her face contracts slightly. "Now I've hurt your feelings," she simpers, staring at the floor, "and I was only trying to be of help." Instinctively we both know—we know that her coffee has been wasted and that she has lost.

"I know you were only trying to help," I seek to placate her. "Surely there can be no harm in visiting the Father?"

"Will you tell me what he says? Particularly if he has anything to say about Michel?"

"But we're strangers, he and I. I'd never permit a discussion about either you or your son, and I'm sure Father Sauvac would never even think of it."

"Oh, wouldn't he? Do you think it was appropriate for him to discuss Madame Carnot's losing her waters, and her baby dead inside her, in front of you? No, it must be something strange or he'd have asked you while I was there. You must tell me what he says. Remember everything."

I keep my voice normal. "You have the wrong idea, Madame, and you may as well know I have no intention of explaining my actions to anyone. My life's my own. If I think you should know what he has to say, I'll tell you; otherwise, no. You're making a great deal out of nothing, it seems to me."

"Very well," she sighs. "I should have realized I was a meddling old fool. You as much as imply that, you know. But you can't doubt the goodness of my intentions, no matter how ungrateful you are."

"I imply nothing—and I *am* grateful. Now it's time for High Mass. You must excuse me."

She smiles sadly, like those pictures of eternally heroic women, unappreciated, smiling to hold back the tears. I thrust away the uneasy impression that she has rehearsed this expression before a mirror. Again she takes my hand in that dry, warm grasp of hers.

"You're a hard man, but good—so much like my Jean-Julien."

Ugly suspicions. Her voice broke exactly right, as I feared it would, when she mentioned her dead son.

She recovers herself and whispers, "Go now—I'll have
267

a good lunch for you at noon," ending the statement with a bright smile.

Again the smiling-through-tears motif. I'm ashamed of my suspicions, but there's nevertheless a compulsion to applaud.

But as I walk to the Monastery my shame becomes her advocate, taking her side, convincing me that I'm wrong. And Mass cleanses me, dissolving the remaining dregs of doubt, destroying debilitating misgivings that she is false. Her advocate reads the list of her qualities, and a Gregorian cantilena, floating above us in the darkened chapel, nods its affirmation. Her emotions are real, it says, her self-sacrifice almost noble, her interests selfless and touching.

Mass is sublime. The same few are there, Madame Vincent and Mademoiselle de Castro kneeling side by side in front of me. Their realness is above doubt. I think of the realness of Dr. Castelar kneeling there a few days ago, and I hope for news of his early arrival.

I spend the remainder of the morning with Father G'seau in the paleography room. We work well together. For a given chant we compare in detail every known example of early manuscript, studying the differences, seeking to arrive at an authentic restoration. It's a type of research to which each of us is well adapted. I have become attached to our little study with its writing desks, its photostatic equipment, its early editions. Each day before Vespers Father G'seau fetches a broom and we clean the room, putting it in order for the following day's work. With my one good arm I manage to dust the tall desks and replace most of the reference books.

At noon Madame Renée makes no mention of the morning. She is gay and at ease, and I enjoy my lunch with her. She informs me that we're to have a guest for dinner tonight —an elderly spinster called Mademoiselle Marthe, who was once a professor of literature in the university at Nantes.

"She's one of the wittiest women in the world," she goes on to tell me, "and yet she's so poor she never gets enough to eat except the one night a week she comes here. I think you'll find her very interesting. You'll like her a lot."

"I'm sure I will, Madame," I reply. But my mind is filled only with relief at the knowledge that, with this Mademoiselle Marthe in the house, there can be no possibility of a scene when I return from my visit with Father Sauvac.

The afternoon's work is soon over, and after Vespers I seek out the house of the parish priest. It is he who answers my knock, and as I step inside he begs me not to remove my hat. His house is dark and evil-smelling and glacial: an odor of sanctity, and sober things, hidden inner things of the entire Village.

He leads me down a long hall to his private sitting room. He motions me into a chair and sits down facing me. Leaning forward, he places a beefy hand on my knee, his robe rustling at the movement. There's a momentary tightening of his clasp on my knee until I almost wince, and his voice asking if I'd like a little glass of alcohol. With the clear liquid fire of a drink in our hands, and a cigarette for each of us, he leans back sipping slowly, inhaling aromas. We talk of the drink. I compliment him on serving such an excellent liquor. He is warm and open now, enjoying himself, laughing easily but sanely.

His heavily wrinkled face is softened by a perpetual expression of good-natured piety, the eyes half-closed with the benign look of a man absolutely sure of himself, of a man studiously masking inner fires. Inner fires of what, I don't know. Of fanaticism? Of passion? He is coarse and refined and studied. The pool appears clear, but one doubts.

I crush out my cigarette and say, "I'm still puzzled about what Madame Renée did this morning, Father. Didn't you find it strange?"

"A little. She was protecting you from the long and mercenary arm of the Church. But isn't the real reason obvious to you, my son?"

"I'm afraid not. I know there must be one, but I have no idea what it is."

"I will speak freely, then. We're men, I trust your discretion. You see, I know all about you from the Monastery.

269

I know you're not rich. But here, every American is rich. You're the proverbial rich American, and the very fact you're a foreigner makes you highly acceptable socially. Madame Renée has told the entire Village she's an old friend of your family's, and that you were sent here to study with your parents' request that she watch over you."

"But I don't even pretend to be rich. Madame Renée knows that."

He leans forward, refilling my glass. This time I furnish the cigarettes. His face clots with a cough and a repressed belch. He nods his head vigorously, spitting into his handkerchief without apologizing, clearing his throat.

"I know, I know," he says when he can speak. "But it makes no difference, you see. You're a very bright feather of social prestige in her cap, and she wants it to look like you'll have nothing to do with anyone in the Village but her, or some of her fortunate friends. She's playing you, my son, to her own advantage. You're in a showcase, jealously guarded. That's why she watches you so carefully, to make sure none of the stories she tells gets back to you. That's the reason she sat on your bed this morning—like a mistress or a substitute mother. That's the reason she wants you to behave yourself. It's an unfortunate situation."

"I'm amazed, Father," I say incredulously. "I had no idea. May I ask you a question?"

"Of course. There, just flick the ashes on the floor. No need to get up each time."

"Since we're being frank, may I ask why you tell me all this? After all, your fidelity belongs more to her than to me. She's your parishioner."

His face reddens again with a chest cough. His hand clasps my knee once more to make the point. "I have fidelity, my son, *only* to God in heaven, and to *right* on earth." His voice is strong and strident. "You are a child, walking blind. Madame Renée has put herself in the position of a protectress and made out your relationship to be something it's not. And I know once the lie is started, she'll do anything to make certain the truth's never revealed. It's not a healthy thing,

270

and it will lead to disaster unless you stop it right now."
I smile skeptically, exhaling a cloud of smoke.

"You don't think so?" Father Sauvac shakes his head.
"I hardly envy you, my son." His voice is quiet now, becoming a whisper of impersonal affection. "I'm a priest with
much experience and few illusions about God's children.
Madame Renée is holding you up as something you have
no desire to be, and when the time comes she'll show you
off like a performing animal. Yet basically she's a good
woman. You were simply her chance to lord it over the
others, and she's taken it. A friend from America can be
a glamorous asset in these small communities." He shrugs
his shoulders.

There is a silence. The chill of the bare room makes me
shiver. From one wall a large crucifix stares at us blankly.

"You make it sound like a hell of a situation, Father,"
I say slowly. "But what can I do? I certainly don't intend
to let her dominate me."

The smile returns. He leans far back in his chair,
sprawling heavily shod feet in front of him. He looks large
there in the half-light. "There are a few things you can do,"
he says without removing his cigarette. "But first, try not
to judge her too harshly. She has a very real affection for
you, I think. She believes you were sent her by Providence
to replace her lost sons. Caring for you gives her a new
interest in life."

"Which I don't want to be," I put in.

"You might break with her, true—but if you did she
could write the Countess and have your house, and you'd
be forced to leave. The choice is yours. But you can stay
and still keep a firm hand on your independence, if you're
stubborn enough. She won't force your hand, never fear:
how could she explain in the Valley what had happened to
her old friend from America? No, her lie might work to
your advantage in this. You can control your own life, if
you take a stand *now*."

"It's infuriating!" I exclaim. "But I don't have any
choice, do I? I can't lose my house . . . Damned bitch!" I

271

add half to myself, thinking of her conniving sweetness. Father Sauvac's smile broadens. He looks at me quietly through nearly closed eyelids, cigarette smoke curling upward from his nostrils. "Gentlemen of the world," he remarks in an amused voice, "never describe a woman as a 'damned bitch,' my son."

"I'm sorry, Father. I forgot myself."

"It's nothing. But I do hope you'll be kind to her. Try to accept this as our Saviour accepted his cross. Being a Christian is often a subtle and difficult thing. You must be humble under your burden, accepting it as a service to God, yet keeping your distance and your independence."

"I'll try, Father."

"Good. Now before we move on to what I really wanted to see you about, I must warn you of one thing more."

"What's that?"

"Tell me, does Madame Renée hold any physical attraction for you? Have you thought of her in that way? After all, she's a handsome woman."

I stare at him in amazement. "Lord, no!" I snort. "I have just the opposite reaction. She nauseates me. I don't even like to shake hands with her."

"I see. That *is* another danger, you know. Be careful not to let her affection for you get out of hand. She's ripe for such a misadventure. I know it seems impossible, but these things are inevitable when contact is constant. Be careful of it."

I can find no answer. Father Sauvac, stretching, rises from his chair, settles back again, and asks, "Tell me, are you happy here?"

"Yes, completely."

"Fine. But if I may ask, what do you do for the flesh?"

I stare hard in his direction. Late dusk in the room obscures his exact expression. It is cold. Mixed feelings within cause me to hold my tongue. After a moment his figure moves to the accompaniment of heavily rustling robes, and he rises to switch on a dim lamp.

"You're surprised, my son?" he says gently as he resumes

272

his seat. "Forgive me. It's a priest's duty to learn these things. But if you'd prefer—"

"That's all right, Father. As a matter of fact, I don't do anything for the flesh here. Somehow I manage to behave myself."

"Good. At least you make the effort. Is it difficult for you? Tell me the truth."

"It's so difficult," I tell him frankly, "I'm sometimes afraid of myself—afraid I'll harm some girl or commit a public indiscretion."

"My poor boy," he smiles sympathetically. "You're large and full of life's sweet youthfulness. It makes itself felt, I know. Be thankful for it and use it wisely. But we have other things to discuss, things more"—he glances at me sideways, smiling slyly, his look destroying the grace of his words—"more pedestrian, eh? There, good boy. Now, do you have enough wood to heat your house?"

His face changes as he slowly realizes the ambiguity of his question after what has gone before. We're both conscious of it, but try to ignore it.

Confused, I answer, "I have enough to keep my downstairs warm most of the day, Father. Why do you ask?" Each word becomes another double meaning; I blush deeply.

He leans his thinning gray head forward, ostensibly lighting a cigarette; hiding the smile, repressing the smile. "I have a very unusual request to make of you, young man," he says. "Madame Renée will certainly think I'm imposing on you." He falters before going on. "She'll think I'm lowering your social standing."

It gets worse. He stops, his face serious. We're embarrassed, embroiled in regrettable hints of other meanings.

"I'm sorry, Father Sauvac."

"I am sincere, my son—I'll be direct. Do you know there are only three heated rooms in the Village, and that most of my poor sheep must walk to the square to get their water from a public well? I'm quite vexed at this comedy we've just shared, so I'll not beat about the bush. Would you consider letting some of them into your heated *down-*

273

stairs occasionally"—glaring, speaking loudly—"where they might warm themselves, and perhaps even bathe? They would be mostly old women, or women with young children. They could come in during the day while you're at the Monastery. I know them well enough to assure you nothing would be harmed, and they need warmth so badly—"

"Of course, Father," I interrupt him. "You know I'd be happy to have them."

"—so badly many of them are half-sick all the time."

His voice has grown calm. Eyes have lost their glare. Our faces carry understood apologies for the shared obscenity of our misunderstanding.

"Do you think the Countess would approve?" I ask him. "I wouldn't want to use her house without her permission."

"She's a fine woman, the Countess. She'd object only if she thought it was going to impose on you. I ask you to think it over. These are common, poor, uneducated people. Madame Renée will be angry, and she'll be certain to write the Countess an exaggerated story. But it will be a good thing for you to do. People here hold you in awe, and if you do it you can prove to them you're human and kind and one of them. Your life here will be a more grateful one, I think. Don't decide now. Think about it, and I won't be offended if you find you must refuse."

"But I don't need to think about it, Father. I want to do it. Anyone who wishes can come in any time during the day. They can get water from the kitchen and make themselves at home. I'm not there anyway."

"Good for you," says Father Sauvac jubilantly.

"As for Madame Renée," I continue, "she must be made to understand I owe her nothing. I pay for the house and I pay for my meals. I can't see she enters into this at all."

"Wonderful!" cries the priest. "May I suggest we phone the Countess before mentioning it to Madame Renée? She's in Nantes. You can explain everything directly to her and nothing Madame Renée writes will make any difference."

"Can we reach her from here?"

274

"Of course—I'll put through the call."

While I light another cigarette, he goes to the telephone and asks the operator for a number in Nantes. Then he turns to me with the receiver to his ear, waiting.

"Now when you talk to Madame Renée," he instructs me, "just tell her I asked you to let some of the Villagers use your downstairs during the day"—smiling at the "downstairs" reference, jovial, delighted—"as a place where they might come and warm themselves. And if she objects, which she certainly will, tell her you're surprised; that you were under the impression the villa was rented to you and you were responsible to no one for your actions, which are, after all, designed to help the needy. She can't go far without exposing herself." He speaks rapidly into the telephone and turns back to me. "Ah, these country phones . . . You must pretend ignorance of the story she's spreading. Tell her you have the Countess's full approval of this good deed. She's intelligent enough to know there's little she can do." He laughs, his voice rising to tenor. "After all, she'll hardly tell you she wants you to herself, or that your glamour will decrease greatly if you open your house to any and all comers. In turn I'm her confessor, and I'll give her the right kind of advice. How can she win from two such brilliant—? Hello, hello, is this the Countess de la Villesverte? This is Father Sauvac. Yes . . ."

He explains our plan and introduces me, passing the receiver so that I may hear her answer. In a coarse, unaffected voice the Countess assures me that not only is she in favor of such a plan, but that she'll try to send us more wood at her own expense from the City, where she has a brother. I tell her I feel certain Madame Renée will object.

"Madame Renée's always objecting to something," comes from the other end of the line. "Don't let that worry you."

"But what if she should write you and make it sound like we're ruining your villa?"

"Believe me, it wouldn't make a bit of difference. Now, go right ahead and do what you can for these poor people. I think it's a wonderful idea."

275

I replace the receiver, filled with a warm liking for this woman I've never seen. Father Sauvac is jubilant. He slaps me hard on the shoulder and offers me another drink.

"There, my son!" he almost shouts—"there's the real aristocrat for you! She was born to it. She doesn't have to fear having the poor in her house. Both she and the Count are among our best people. They belong to a generation that was taught simplicity and good manners instead of snobbishness."

We drink another glass of the liquor. It helps to warm us.

"I just happened to think, Father," I say after a moment. "We're having a Mademoiselle Marthe to dinner tonight. Wouldn't it be a good idea if I broke the news of our venture at the table? I've never met Mademoiselle Marthe, but she'll probably be in favor of it; and Madame Renée won't be able to say very much without hurting herself."

He swallows and nods rapidly. "Excellent, excellent! You're not stupid. Mademoiselle Marthe will be sure to like the idea—she doesn't have enough heat herself."

"That's what I'll do, then."

"Fine, and I'll announce your kind deed to the Village. Now you must run. You understand everything? You have it all clear in your mind?"

"I think so. I must remember to let the Villagers into my *heated* downstairs and keep Madame Renée from my *other* 'downstairs.'" I grin broadly.

"Excellent, excellent! Good-bye, my boy. Good-bye and God bless you. Refreshing to have met you." In high spirits he urges me out down the hall.

"Tell your parishioners," I say to him in parting, "to use my house whenever they feel like it, Father. And thanks for helping me share what I have with others. It makes me feel very Christian."

"Excellent, my son, excellent! Good-bye again. And do come back soon." He closes the door with insulting enthusiasm behind me.

My house feels cold and damp as I enter the front door,

276

but a rush of warm dry air greets my face when I walk into the salon. It tells me that my "protectress" has once again cleaned the room and lighted the fire. Except for the glowing stove window the room is dark. Relief that I can be alone for an hour before dinner. Since I have no more cigarettes I begin smoking preciously guarded butts; and after each one is smoked I save for my pipe the little tobacco that remains. Turning on my desk lamp I sit down to study. Books and papers have been neatly arranged so that I can find nothing.

I realize there must be a readjustment of thought. I must remember that she cleans the room, makes the bed, and lights the fire out of the generosity of her affection for me. But it annoys me; it's a meddling which I resent. I begin shuffling the papers, cursing eloquent and satisfying obscenities, when I hear the bell on the front gate, then the front door opening. It's impossible. Is she going to follow me about like this all winter?

Writing meaningless Latin phrases, I pretend to be deeply engrossed in work. Madame Renée stands for a full minute silhouetted in profile against the glass portion of the door. Finally the timid knock, and the harsh reply: "Come in!"

"Good evening, Monsieur. Did you find all your things all right? I took the liberty of washing out some of your clothes and handkerchiefs—you really mustn't use your handkerchiefs till they get so dirty. Here, I put them in this drawer. But your pajamas? I didn't find anything but clean ones. If you'll just tell me where you keep your soiled—"

"I never soil pajamas, Madame," I break in. "I've quit sleeping in them. Thanks for washing those things, but I really must insist you leave that to the housekeeper. I don't mean to be impolite, but I've got some work here I must finish before dinner, or I'll be up till dawn."

"Do they give you so much work at the Monastery?" she asks sympathetically, with wide-open eyes.

"Yes, more than I can possibly get done."

She makes a move to leave, but stops at the door to

277

ask, "Did you have a nice visit with old Father Sauvac?"

"Yes, we got on very well." I lower my head and write; she remains standing there.

"Did he say anything about me?" Her face becomes red and there's an obvious fear that he might have told her secret.

"No—as a matter of fact you weren't mentioned."

"Then what did he want?" A sudden softening. "Oh, forgive me, I shouldn't have asked that."

It's impossible to hide my disgust. I say wearily, "No, you really shouldn't have asked that. For one thing, he wanted my annual contribution to the Church, which I gave him. The rest was personal."

She is impervious to my hints; superbly impervious and insistent and self-assured. "I told you he wanted money. Ah, how well I know him. You aren't obliged to give him money."

"I wanted to, that's all"—looking into my scattered papers, assorting them, ignoring her.

"Did he want to know if you had any girl friends? He always asks that—always something about the flesh. I think he's got a filthy mind."

"No, he didn't mention that. I suppose he knows already. Now if you don't mind, I must get this work done."

"But of course"—the radiant smile and coy whisper. "Will you be over in half an hour?"

"In half an hour."

Her gloved hand grasps the door knob. "Oh, but I almost forgot," she says. "I have a surprise for you. Don't ask me where I got them, but here are three packages of cigarettes I *managed* for you."

"Oh, really? That's luck. Tell me, how much were they?"

We argue about my paying for them. She wants me to have them as a gift, but I refuse; I refuse to become obligated to her even to that extent. The minutes slip by while we settle it, and when finally I have paid her, to the accompaniment of much small talk, it is time for dinner. With a sigh

I switch off the light over my untouched work. Madame Renée smiles and takes my arm as we walk carefully across the slippery street to her house.

Mademoiselle Marthe is already there, being helped with her wraps by a young maid who is new to me. I am introduced to the older woman and am conscious of making the properly polite noises, but I don't see her. And when Madame Renée mumbles something about the inexperience of the maid, I don't hear her.

For the girl and I are looking at each other like two young animals, aware of the presence of the two older women and, in a way, detesting them. She is a loosely hung blonde, about seventeen I imagine, with a shrugged-shoulder attitude toward her mistress and her training in domestic service. She smiles easily. We understand each other. Her eyes know heats and the pleasure of rutting, and they're rich with the devil's own richness. You think of such a girl as smelling strong of the female. Intoxicating warmth of lithe muscles and firm young hips. She knows it. She knows nothing else, this girl. She would laugh easy and tickle easier. She moves about setting the table, but we look at each other and understand.

A man's vision is colored by a woman, and he sees things instantly. Instantly some tension above tension tells him what he'd like to do with this girl or with that girl, and it's clearly graved in the mind. With Madame Renée's maid the picture is there, a single picture. It's of a man standing upright holding her in the air. She rides high in the picture, her hands clasping his head, and he kisses the fine transparency of her side beneath the ribs. He bends his head at an angle to achieve the taste, reeling from richness of odor. I wonder if the girl is to be my housekeeper. If so I shall know this picture, and many others.

She knows it too, she knows how it will be; for she swallows loudly and finishes setting the table. And her movements betray an awareness of arms and legs and breasts.

I suddenly flush and drag my eyes away from her. What have I been saying since I arrived? I have been talking to two old ladies, yet I remember nothing I've said. But a glance assures me that they've not sensed the undercurrents in the room. They probably think my cheeks are red only from the cold, and that my discomfort is from the tightness of my clothes; that my breathing is deep in response to the odors of cooking.

For the first time I look at Mademoiselle Marthe. She is small and very decrepit. She has a large mouth with thin, mottled lips which smile constantly, and a tendency to bend forward almost double when she stands. There is but little hair left on her skeletal head: she spends idle moments caressing it with gnarled, heavily veined hands. But her eyes are alive, and her speech is clear and precise. Her thoughts are expressed in a language of great beauty. She talks in long phrases with a placidity, a serenity of age borne lightly. She is dressed in black—the color of the Village—made frivolous by a touching accent of amber glass beads about her throat.

"I'm really delighted to meet you, Mademoiselle Marthe," I say to her at last. "Madame Renée's told me all about her friendship for you. I know how much it means to her."

Her smile deepens. "Madame Renée is too indulgent of an old woman, young man," she replies graciously. "But tell me, you're a musician, and I always ask musicians a certain question—and never yet have I received a satisfactory answer. There are many works of music that express the depths of the soul's grief: the late quartets of Beethoven, some parts of the Bach Mass in B minor, among others. But do you know of any score, Monsieur, expressing the real and true interior joy of the soul, the lightness of spirit that fills a man possessed of the grace of God? For most of my eighty and odd years I've hoped to hear such a piece of music. Does it exist? Perhaps in some obscure work?"

I stand in front of her chair. She looks up at me with the plainest of faces. The answer comes without thinking. "Of course it exists, Mademoiselle—and in a setting that ought to satisfy even a person like you. In fact you've heard it many times. I myself came to the Valley to hear it.

280

Haven't you forgotten to look right here in the Village?"

"You mean the chants? Which ones, to be exact? I admit I was thinking of other music."

"What other music compares with it? Let's see—I'd say offhand the Easter Alleluia is one of the most perfect expressions of the joy you mention. And then there's the *Dominus dixit* from the midnight Christmas Mass."

She strokes her hair a moment, then, "I believe you're right, I do believe you're right." She laughs a reproach to herself. "Isn't it incredible? Right at my very doorstep! I wonder why I never thought of the chants myself?"

"It's always hard to appreciate the things closest to home."

"It is indeed. Well, I can't begin to thank you, young man. I only wish I'd met you long ago."

Dinner is served as an intrusion upon our conversation. Madame Renée takes command of the scene, placing us at the table. Mademoiselle Marthe and I share intangible distastes while our hostess plays a role to impress us. She heard the end of our discussion on music, and when we are seated she asks me whom I consider the greatest composers of the age.

"Well," I begin, "I think first of all Stravinsky, Bartók, and Honegger—"

"I know Honegger, of course," she interrupts smiling, busy serving her plate with hors d'œuvres.

"You *do* know Honegger, Madame Renée?" I reply. "I know him too. I must speak to him about you when I see him in Paris next time." It's a shot in the dark: I have never even seen the composer. My glance catches Mademoiselle Marthe looking slyly up from her plate.

"Oh, he wouldn't remember me," Madame Renée says quickly. "I shouldn't say I *know* him—we merely met one evening in Paris at a reception."

It's time to change the subject. Chicken is served, a superb bird beautifully prepared, and red wine. I think of how we pay for this fine food by compromising our tastes, by listening to Madame Renée. But she has the food, and we'd starve without her. I surreptitiously watch the maid as she waits on us: firm young breasts and small waist and slenderly muscular legs. She subtly flaunts her charms as she moves back and forth between table and kitchen. My throat is tight and dry. I have to force myself to listen to what the two older women are saying.

After a while, choosing a lull in the conversation, I turn to Mademoiselle Marthe. "I have a very interesting idea, Mademoiselle," I remark as casually as I can. "I'd like to know what you think of it. Father Sauvac told me this evening there are lots of poor people in the Village who don't have any heat in their homes. Did you know there are only three heated rooms in the entire Village?"

"No, Monsieur," she answers sharply—"only that mine isn't one of them."

"When he told me about it," I go on, "I decided maybe I could do something to help. I've been cold too long myself, and I realize what a little warmth can do when it's needed."

Both Mademoiselle Marthe and Madame Renée look at me closely, waiting; each portraying a different kind of intentness. I pause to swallow a bite of chicken.

"At any rate," I say as I wipe my mouth, "I phoned the countess who owns my house, and she's agreed to help furnish enough fuel to heat my salon during the day." I continue to look at Mademoiselle Marthe, but I can feel the tension rising from Madame Renée. "I thought perhaps some of the Villagers might like to come in and get warm. I've decided to leave the room open all day for anyone who wants to use it."

Mademoiselle Marthe smiles warmly and eagerly. "I think that's a remarkable and splendid idea, Monsieur," she says immediately. "A most thoughtful gesture—and I'll be among the first to take advantage of it."

From the corner of my eye I can see that Madame Renée isn't smiling. She isn't trying to hide her feelings, only to control them. She looks at me poutingly, understanding all, and I know she wonders how much I understand. Avoiding

282

her gaze, I nibble innocently at a piece of chicken. She faces Mademoiselle Marthe.

"But you don't mean," she says rapidly, "that you'd go into this young man's house as if it were public property and associate with the riffraff? They're the only ones who'll take advantage of the offer, you know. Certainly none of the better people would lower themselves to accept such obvious charity." She stares at me coldly.

"The high, my dear, can get as cold as the low," is Mademoiselle Marthe's angry retort, while the maid grins. "I'm sure I'll not be contaminated." And turning to me, "I know these Valley people, Monsieur. They deserve this kindness. You won't regret your decision."

Madame Renée is struggling for composure. "You were certainly ill-advised, Monsieur," she states haughtily. "The house will be a shambles within a week, what with all the children they'll bring in. I can't imagine the Countess agreeing to such a thing."

"She was really enthusiastic about it."

"Well, I can assure you," she says in measured words, "*I'll* never get cold enough to avail myself of your somewhat childish offer."

"But you don't need to," I tell her. "You're one of the three in the Village who have enough wood to keep warm."

Delighted, Mademoiselle Marthe rolls her eyes, urging me on. I sense that her friendship with Madame Renée is probably at an end.

"I'm sorry you find my plan so objectionable, Madame Renée," I add as an afterthought, in a tone of innocent mildness. "If these people need heat, I certainly can't see anything wrong in letting them use my house. I've even decided to furnish hot water so they can bathe, if they like."

At this, Mademoiselle Marthe chokes on her coffee; she very concentratedly sets the cup back on its saucer.

Madame Renée looks appalled. "That's wonderful!" she moans almost tearfully. "Just wonderful! He not only wants to warm them, he wants to clean them, too. Can't you realize that in this part of the world"—her voice trembles with a sense of outraged propriety—"people of your class simply don't receive peasants and such in their homes? Consider my feelings for you. I'll be the laughing stock of the entire Valley."

"But who can laugh at you, Madame? You don't have anything to do with it. It's my house and my idea, and you're in no way concerned. If they want to laugh at me, let them. I don't care."

"I thought you wanted absolute privacy?"

"I'll have my privacy at night. Besides, that doesn't matter much if some of these people can get warm."

Madame Renée blows her nose. "Well, I suppose there's no use discussing it," she says resignedly, "if your mind's made up. I just hope you won't try to make friends with them."

"It'll work out all right," I reply noncommittally. I stir uncomfortably in my chair: there's something suddenly pathetic in the sight of this woman wiping her nose and staring at her plate in defeat. I feel a surge of pity in my belly. I add quietly, "And I'd very much appreciate it if you'd look after things for me while I'm at the Monastery. You could give them soap and show them where to warm the water."

Mademoiselle Marthe glances at me reproachfully. I've become soft. Tides have been released, carrying me with them. Madame Renée raises her face. The rancor has all but disappeared from her eyes. She is smiling again.

"Of course," she agrees eagerly, "I'll be glad to. You're a good boy, you have a good heart. I'll help all I can."

Mademoiselle Marthe throws at me the subtly quick suggestion of a grin. I raise my cup and take a swallow of lukewarm coffee. Sitting erect in her chair, Madame Renée once more commands the scene.

"Shall we have another cup of coffee?" she says politely —and calling toward the kitchen, "Christianne, bring some fresh coffee, please."

Christianne—I record the name in my mind as the girl reappears from the kitchen. Again the eyes seeking eyes,

284

and the tightnesses. She leans over me refilling my cup, and I feel the stinging touch of a breast against my shoulder. Blood rushes to my face, and as nonchalantly as I can I stir sugar into my coffee. I press the spoon hard against the bottom of the cup to keep my hand from trembling.

"I believe that will be all this evening, Christianne," Madame Renée says to her, when she has refilled the other cups. "You may go on home now."

Before she leaves the room, Christianne and I exchange a final meaningful glance. We both know we'll see each other again—and without the two older women.

I'm aware of a slight twinge of loneliness after she has gone, but it passes quickly. Lingering crosscurrents of antagonism demand my attention. Sipping our coffee, we try to chat casually as though nothing had happened. Madame Renée plays her role with embarrassing insistence, and Mademoiselle Marthe and I are the reluctant audience. We wink at each other when our hostess admits that perhaps my plan will work after all—that she'll see.

"If only you won't let people take advantage of you," she concludes. "You're too generous."

We finish our coffee, and Madame Renée carries the cups into the kitchen. Mademoiselle Marthe looks me full in the face, laughing silently. She too must wonder how much I understand, how much of this was planned.

Bending across the table she whispers, "Since she couldn't win, she's now on your side."

I grin. "I know. And she'll be as much *for* it now as she was against it before."

The back door opens and closes. Madame Renée's bladder is carrying her out of earshot. My companion laughs out loud.

"You're quite observant, Monsieur," she chuckles.

"I had some expert help, Mademoiselle."

Her wrinkled face looks very wise. "Madame Renée reared two doltish sons, but she won't know how to handle you. This is going to be interesting to old Marthe. Come to see me, won't you? I'm sure I'll never be invited here

285

again. The two of us are much more than she can digest."

"It's my fault, Mademoiselle. You shouldn't have agreed with me."

"Nonsense. Now that she has you, she'd have got rid of me anyway, and I must confess it's something of a relief. But do come to see me. What about Tuesday evening after Vespers? I'm too weak to go to church, so Father Sauvac brings me the Blessed Saviour in private Mass every Tuesday. I always clean house to receive the Good Lord."

The door latch clicks. I nod in acceptance as Madame Renée comes back into the room.

"What were you two whispering about?" she asks gaily, beginning to clear the table.

"I was just telling Mademoiselle Marthe," I reply easily, "what magnificent food I think you serve."

"You're too kind, Monsieur."

"Yes, the food was indeed magnificent," Mademoiselle Marthe concurs—"and the company more than stimulating. But I'm afraid I must go. This is late enough for an old woman to be away from her bed."

"Please don't go yet," I beg her, against the ominous background of Madame Renée's silence.

"Thank you, young man, but I must."

I jump up to help her, and she rises shakily to her feet. With cold politeness she and Madame Renée bid each other good night. No mention is made of her returning for dinner next week. I start to leave too, but Mademoiselle Marthe insists she can walk the few steps to her house alone. I hold her coat for her and go with her to the door. A warm handshake, a warm glance reaffirm her approval. Then reluctantly, I turn back to face Madame Renée.

Neither of us says anything. While I rub my hands over the fire, Madame Renée clears away the remaining dishes and folds the tablecloth.

"I certainly do like Mademoiselle Marthe," I remark to break the silence. "A charming woman."

"Yes," she says indifferently, "she's been one of my best friends here. There are so few people in the Valley who

286

can converse intelligently." She turns off the center light, leaving only a lamp burning on the radio, and loudly stirs the fire. "I must talk with you a moment, Monsieur. I know you have a lot of work to do tonight, but won't you have one more cup of coffee?"

I shrug my shoulders and settle myself in a chair by the fire. We are silent as she brings fresh coffee from the kitchen and takes a chair facing mine. Outside the windows it's dark, and late. I know of the cold, the deep snows there, and I'm grateful for the warmth within.

"There's something I feel I must say to you," begins Madame Renée, mechanically stirring her coffee. "When you first took the villa there was a certain amount of talk—talk that should have discouraged me from recommending you to the Countess."

She pauses, and I realize she expects an immediate reaction; but an ambiguous "Yes?" is all I give her. The disappointment on her face is almost imperceptible.

"First," she continues, "there were the unfavorable stories that you let the Petite Chevissier die, and then came the gossip about you and the Vincent woman. You can see I accepted you at a certain personal risk."

"I see."

"Well, in order to minimize this risk"—she chooses her words carefully—"I let it be known that your family had long been associated with mine, and that they had specifically requested me to provide your meals. As you can see, it's necessary for you to know this before the real story gets out. I hope you don't mind? I didn't do it for myself, of course—though some people might have frowned on my taking a stranger into the house—but for you. No one would dare question your right to be here as long as it's known we're friends. That's why I slightly altered the facts like that. You haven't told anyone anything to the contrary, have you?"

"No, I haven't. But I must admit I wondered about your reason for—how shall I say it?—for treating me with a great deal more personal interest than you would an

287

ordinary boarder. You can imagine how strange it seemed."

"Now you know, and I'm glad."

"Now I know. Well, it does help me understand several things. I'm sorry such an exaggerated report had to be circulated, but I suppose you did what you thought best."

She leans forward urgently. "Yes, Monsieur," she says quickly, "and that's why I feel so responsible for you and your actions. You must be very careful. Any misconduct on your part would reflect on me and ruin your chances of staying here."

"Very well, Madame Renée," I say just as quickly—"since you've been frank with me, I'll be the same with you. I want to stay here very much. But let's not make the mistake of living your version of the story. Let's not forget I'm here to study and that I only take my meals with you. It's not worth it to me if I have to be treated as a sixteen-year-old. I'm not interested in what the Valley thinks of me. I just want to be left alone so I can work. And if I may say so, you have one habit that's *very* irritating."

I am surprised at the sympathy in her eyes; she leans back unoffended. "But what is it?" she inquires sweetly. "I've certainly tried to be as I should. Tell me honestly and simply what it is?"

I go on without hesitating, for it has to come out. "You insist on treating me like I was your son. You feel obliged to tell me how to act and whom to see. I'll certainly do my best not to jeopardize your standing here. But you must realize, Madame, that I'm not here for your pleasure. I must be left to choose my own friends and do as I please without any interference from you. I know you mean well, but I'm not used to close relationships. I think you're too forward in trying to take over my affairs. In other words try to remember I'm nothing more than a new acquaintance, and act accordingly."

I have been too strong; but it was beyond me to speak more kindly. Her eyes become a sadness near tears. It's quite perfect—too perfect. It destroys shame within me, and compassion. Already I feel that she's planning something a little less obvious. But why? For what possible reasons?

"I'm beginning to see, Monsieur, that I've been guilty of a certain lack of taste"—slow words, quiet words, understanding words without rancor. "It's so easy to think of you as a youth, you must forgive me if I've tried too hard these first few days to make your life here pleasant. I've done it simply because I wanted you to have complete freedom from outside worries."

"That's not—"

"But certainly you give me motives I don't possess," she goes on inexorably, in the same voice. "Yes, I must admit I was beginning to look upon you as a son. But that's an older woman's weakness which you can forgive. And I didn't realize my sons were such as to be offensive. It hurts, Monsieur, it hurts a little." Her voice breaks—tears and the wincing face of tears.

Despite myself I begin to feel uncomfortable. But this time I remain quiet.

"As for your liberty," comes from her in a moment, "believe me I had no thought—none whatsoever—of interfering with it. I've been trying to think of you and your work first, and not of my own 'pleasure,' as you put it. Humph. The pleasures of my life are gone, Monsieur, gone with my husband and son. I've waited years for the end of this misery, and I can assure you the only pleasure I get is in helping other people. When you came I said to myself, 'Now there's a fine young man who's alone and trying to do important work. He's been sent to me so I can devote my empty life to making his stay here comfortable.' You can't say I haven't tried these few days, Monsieur—you just haven't understood. You've resented me and thought I was meddling in your affairs." She dries her eyes, and her voice steadies its courage. "I'm humiliated that in trying to help I've done harm. But my intentions are still the same. You're in no way obliged to account to me for your actions. I'm an old woman whose feelings don't matter. I'll try to be as helpful as I can without being too *forward*." Twisting her head away from me, she begins to cry again.

It is wrong. The line turns, falsifying my intent, using my intent against me. Her speech was that of a noble woman. What I say can be nothing but spermless ignominy —but it must be said.

"I'm terribly sorry, Madame Renée. I was wrong. Please! I didn't understand, that's all. I told you I was an ungrateful person to have as a friend. But I do appreciate everything, nevertheless."

The line turns, and my intent is falsified. Words have been said, mean, niggardly, male words less strong than the nobility of tears. Tears and gray hair and contracted face of misunderstood woman dissolve man's heart and ribs and genitals into nothingness. She looks up, raising hair and tears and quivering mouth.

"And we'll be friends?"

"Of course, of course."

The eyes are dried again, but conversation remains broken and sobbing. Now the explanations, now the surplus. Woman explains simply, honestly, with a sighing smile, why she castrates man and how much better it is for him. Such things as: "You know, you led me to think there was some misunderstanding between us after you told me about Madame Vincent. I interpreted that as meaning . . ." And off into a lengthy analysis of meanings and countermeanings and ambiguities; until at last, "You see, that's what gave me that impression, which I know now to be false. But I wasn't wrong about the other, now was I? There *is* a sympathy between us or you wouldn't have told me about it in the first place, now would you?"

"No, no, of course not. Just don't think about it any more. Now I must get back to my work. I'll see you in the morning."

She rises wearily and walks with me to the door. I wonder if it shows—if there's a suppuration, and blood. She takes my hand and holds it a long time. I feel the groveling of defeat at the hands of a clever woman. She holds my hand comforting me, making my surrender a sweetness of charity; and her clear blue eyes assure me of her understand-

290

ing and, most painful of all, her forgiveness. In a low, intimate voice that I can scarcely imagine coming from a so-called "old lady," she whispers, "We've cleared up many things tonight, haven't we? You see, you must always be frank with me. It's much better to discuss these things in a calm way. You understand now, and I'm glad. I want you to know you've got a good friend in me. You mustn't make such a mistake again. If you ever do, promise you'll tell me. You see how wrong you were tonight, don't you?"

"Yes, and now it's forgotten—right? Good night."

I open the door and step outside. Darkness and cold air and the crunching ice of a starless night, making me laugh, replacing dissipated hormones, chilling face and thoughts and reliefs with cleanness. And there is no suppuration or bleeding. I feel myself and know I'm all right. I cross the dark street singing in English:

> "The bitch has won,
> the bitch has won,
> ta-da, de-da,
> ta-da, de-da.
> And my tada's bruised,
> and my tada's abused,
> and she's mangled my poor
> ta-da de-dum!"

Night and a bath and tea and laughter. How wrong I was and how right she was! And hers is a willingness to forgive. Hers is a fineness and a generosity of heart. And in her darkened room is she not nodding her head violently in affirmation? It was so easy, with tears and nobleness and a spermless recipient.

In my sleep I dream of the maid Christianne, and the dream is the earlier vision. It *is* possible to hold her like that and kiss her beneath the ribs. And the dream is such that *she* will know, that fine grayness of hair and unwrinkled face across the way; she'll know and consider me more hers for the knowing. It's an intimacy unspoken, an intimacy

291

vicariously shared when she makes my bed in the morning.

But perhaps—always the "perhaps"—I am wrong. I could be. I could be completely mistaken.

10 january

The week has passed quietly, a week dominated by Madame Renée. A week of draining confidences and of petulance, of small irritations coloring the design of happiness.

Despite myself I can't keep my distance; for she is the questioning woman, and proper questions require the telling of confidences. Her desire for intimacy is winning—a desire entailing forbidden subjects and personal conclusions to nourish our "friendship." She wants to feel that I'll discuss anything with her, that no barriers exist. She employs clever insinuations; and the nights, the cold, the food, the loneliness succeed in opening my lips to expose past memories and guarded knowledges. I talk freely, enmeshed, growing ever more weary of her nightly remark that ours is truly a unique relationship. I try to fight the deadening hypocrisy of her attentions, but I haven't the skill. She accepts only reactions that bind us together, clinging to them, cataloguing them, remembering them. At the rest— the efforts to stand away from her—she laughs, turning their meanings to her advantage.

We do have our understandings, our small debilitating heats; for I know that if she's angry or hurt I have only to share another confidence, or make another suggestive remark, and she'll laugh with sweetly indulgent disapproval.

292

The sordidness of my discovered self is beginning to grow into a consistent pattern of behavior of the cut and fit that Madame Renée likes best. When I'm with her I change into a swaggering, socially acceptable man of the world, retaining a roughness of speech which makes me an individual in her eyes. Certain remarks become fetishistic. Thus a few days ago I muttered that I was "horny." I explained that it was American slang, and told her its meaning. Every day since then she has asked me, pursing a sly smile, if I am horny—and I always laugh.

Looking back I can see it has been a week of imperceptible changes, become great change in the aggregate. Intangibles have been accumulated by the kindness and beauty of a woman who repels. Only now is their collective weight beginning to be felt.

I often think of Dr. Castelar, trying to imagine the advice he would give me if he were here. He could readily tell me how to handle Madame Renée—what to say to her, what to do in order to extricate myself. But imagination alone must serve, for yesterday the postman delivered a telegram from him. His wife and children are already back in Paris and he'll be unable to return. Disappointment sharpens the feeling of loneliness. The news has made me realize how much I was depending on his visit, how gratefully I had anticipated his support. I recall our conversation in my cell the day before he left with Marie-Ornoux. I remember remarking that if we had to separate so soon after our misunderstanding, we'd probably never see each other again. Now I am sure of it—but it really doesn't matter. The bitterness of our misunderstanding was dissolved in his leaving. I know now that the years will make little difference, for ours is the kind of friendship the doctor himself defined—the kind that doesn't change.

He would be relieved to know that my injured shoulder, the embarrassing reminder of that incredible first night in his cell, is at last almost well. The postman came for the final time this morning. I no longer need help in putting on my clothes. And today, without the hindrance of a disabled arm, I accomplished more than usual in the pale-ography room with Father G'seau.

But my work at the Monastery has lost some of its clarity, for the knot of inner dissonance is always with me. Only the conferences with Father Clément remain the same, and we don't mention Madame Renée: there's nothing concrete to discuss. I pray a great deal. The offices of Mass and Vespers allow prayer after prayer to flow from me—prayers asking, ever asking for guidance in my personal life. For a moment I know release. But when I return to Madame Renée's house the earth is there, the grunting earth.

There's no consistency in our conversations. She can discuss all subjects with authority. And when I ask her to see the good in things and in people rather than the evil which always meets her first glance, she becomes a momentary mystic, rebuking herself while praising me for my inherent goodness. Thereupon she is likely to extol still further my idea of giving warmth to the poor, again remarking what a generous heart I have. For just as Mademoiselle Marthe and I predicted, she has devoted herself to the scheme since our dinner a week ago. She tells everyone what a blessing it is to the suffering Villagers, and she carries wood and provides soap and helps them with their baths.

There is indeed much to be done, because our plan has been received with pathetic enthusiasm by the Villagers. The bitter cold continues unrelieved, the temperature remaining below zero most of the time. During these few days my house has become a sanctuary from the weather. Each day I return to find several neat rows of wooden shoes in the hall. In the salon their owners—old women and young women with children—sit visiting and knitting, their shoulders covered with black woolen sweaters and shawls. When I appear they prepare to leave, murmuring polite good-byes in their beautiful patois. I ask them to stay, but with soft, aged voices and toothless grins they remind me that they have homes to keep. Their smiles are the smiles of age for youth—confident and delighted. In a single week's time I have grown to love them as a healthful relief from Madame Renée. They are strong with the strength of the country. Their language is for the most part crude and uncouth, and their conversation, primarily concerned with abortions and miscarriages and illegitimate pregnancies, rarely leaves the plane of obscenity. I hear only a few words of such discussions: when they see me they stop talking and commence tittering. During my absence I'm sure my most intimate merits and demerits make for high conjecture in their gossip, and I would give a great deal to hear what they say.

Each day their numbers have increased. Tonight the salon was crowded. Every piece of furniture was utilized as a seat, and numerous children played on the floor among the legs of the older people. I exchanged greetings with several whose faces I've come to recognize. Then they were gone, leaving the room remarkably neat and clean.

And now, as I dress for dinner, the house is quiet and warm with the livingness of people no longer there, of people who cook dinner in other houses. I feel caught in a confusion of sentiments that sterilize me and drive me to seek the repugnance of intimacy with Madame Renée. But tonight I'm prepared for a change: I'm determined to dissolve the disgusts in my belly. For despite everything, I know that within me is a very real affection for her; very real whenever I think of losing her; real enough to soften decisions. Her generosity, her sadness, her aloneness—even her dregs—have insinuated themselves into my existence. She really is superb, in a way.

I cross the street and let myself into her house. As I enter she looks up from a newspaper, her eyes kind and gentle above horn-rimmed spectacles which she quickly removes. While she finishes the preparations for dinner we talk and we are friends.

"Did you have a good day at the Monastery?"

"Yes, I worked hard today. I'm tired and hungry."

"Ah, good"—gaily—"I have a fine pork roast for you."

295

We eat slowly, but the conversation is too calm for her strong appetites; presently she asks, "Did you see Father Clément?"

"Yes. He says I'm learning." It's only a pinpoint, but it opens a tiny wound which I'm afraid she won't let heal. She has hinted before that she'd prefer my not discussing personal questions with Father Clément.

"Here, take more meat than that." She smiles pleasantly. "So Father Clément thinks you're learning? Why, you know more in your little finger than Father Clément will ever know."

"Don't say that, Madame Renée," I gently reproach her. "Father Clément knows goodness, and that's what I want to learn."

"He's just as weak as the next man, I tell you. I know things about him." She is still smiling, feeling her way.

"Well, please don't tell me about them. I love Father Clément."

"Come now, you haven't been around him long enough to make such a statement. You're just defending him, aren't you?"

I eat without looking up. "I love Father Clément," I repeat, "well and simply. He's been my—"

"Oh, be sensible," she interrupts. "What can you find in him? Why, he's not even considered one of the great Benedictines."

"I realize that. As monks go maybe he's ordinary. But I'm completely devoted to him. He's given me a great deal. Is anything else important?"

She grins, chewing, merry in her destruction. "Don't start talking to me about his goodness. I wasn't going to tell you—I'm not that indiscreet—but they had to send one of the Sisters of Charity away from here, that's all. She was seeing too much of Father Clément in the confessional. Don't talk to *me* about him. I could tell you some other things, too."

Filled with loathing, I lean far back in my chair. "Even if what you say were true it wouldn't make any difference to me. But I don't believe a single word of it, not one."

"Humph. If you don't believe me then you think I'm lying, is that it?"

Nerves falter, degenerate; control is lost. "Yes, I think you're lying," I say in a flat voice—"deliberately and maliciously. I think you made up this story. How I detest the filthy little minds in this Village! You've gone too far."

"Then you will kindly leave my house, Monsieur!"

"With pleasure, Madame."

The chair falls as I rise suddenly from the table. I am sick with disgust. We look at each other a moment. But Father Sauvac's wish that I accept this woman as a service to God—that I treat her with kindness—returns to my mind. And in the background lingers the fear that she might force me to give up my villa. Picking up the chair I sit down again.

"No, I won't go," I tell her firmly. "The other day you asked me to be frank, so I'll be just that. I think you're lying, but whether you are or not I want you to keep a civil tongue in your head when it comes to my friends. I wouldn't tolerate such talk about you, and I won't hear it from you about anyone else. Do you understand?"

Her face swells, growing red with the smile she gives me. Now that her work has been done she'll remain quiet. Controlling her temper she continues serving the meal. But her glance contains nothing but hatred. I can't eat.

"You're not eating, Monsieur," she mocks. "Surely what I said about your precious 'spiritual father' didn't ruin your appetite?"

"No, no, it's not that. I know Father Clément's worth. The unpleasant atmosphere of this house ruined it."

"You'd better watch yourself, Monsieur. Don't forget you started this discussion." She begins clearing the table with the abrupt movements of an offended woman.

"I didn't—but it makes no difference."

"You're *always* right, aren't you? You must always have *your* way."

"I suppose so. Good night." I stand up and turn from

297

the table, determined to end this maddening conversation.

"Where are you going?" She follows me. "You haven't had your coffee yet."

Reeling with repressed anger I lean against the door. "If it's any of your business," I mutter, "I'm going to Town and find a good, healthy, simple-minded peasant girl who'll sleep with me and make me forget what's happened. And what we do will seem clean compared to what you and I have just been through."

Madame Renée's anger vanishes. She pulls me away from the door and stands with her back against it. Her face is now full of concern. I am trembling so violently from the repugnance of inner silts that I can scarcely stand on my feet.

Rapid phrases pour from her: "Oh, I'm sorry, I *am* sorry. Oh, my dear boy, I didn't know you'd take it so seriously, I didn't know you were so sensitive. Here now, sit down"—softly, with cajoling tenderness. "There. Now a good cup of coffee. I was only joking with you. No need to get so upset. *I'm* the one who should be hurt. *I* should be leaving, not you." She pats me on the shoulder and laughs uneasily. "There, there, drink your coffee. I promise to forget everything you've said this evening. Now look at me." She places her hand under my chin, lifting my face to meet hers. "You know and I know you didn't mean it, so don't think about it any more."

"All right. Let's forget the whole thing. I'm worn out."

She watches as I finish the coffee and put the cup on the radio. She stands against my chair, leaning into me, her hand on my shoulder. Bending forward with her face close to mine, she peers at me with all the warmth of her soul.

"It's sometimes hard for me to understand you," she whispers, "when you're wild and savage like this. But I do try. Tell me"—I cringe away as she nudges my arm, her breath warm on my cheek—"isn't it because you're used to having girls regularly? You've lived like a saint here, and I know it must make you awfully nervous at times. Isn't that it? And you can't help yourself, you take it out on

298

me. You see, I do try to understand. And that's what's wrong with you tonight—you need a girl, don't you?"

"Think what you like," I say wearily. "You will anyway. I don't know what I need. A little rest from this constant nagging, perhaps."

She ignores me; she is certain she has found the answer. "I wish I could help you."

The unspeakable intimations of silence. I glare at her. She lowers her eyes.

"If it's so bad, why don't you send for Lucette?" she hastens to suggest, changing the substance of her remark. "I don't want you playing around with these country girls. I'll make sure no one knows. You see, I'm willing to debase myself to make you happy. I'm a terrible woman."

"You know I wouldn't do that."

"I didn't think you would. It wouldn't be treating me right, so you wouldn't do it. Beneath that rough exterior of yours you really *are* fine. You're so fine you try to hide it—even from me."

I laugh—a sick laugh. "You're maudlin. Do you know the one reason I wouldn't do it? Not because I'm so fine, not because of you—but simply because Father Clément wouldn't want me to."

"Now, now"—pulling away from me, smiling, understanding—"you're feeling much better, I can tell. I know you better than you think. But let's talk about something else." She takes a seat on the sofa. "Do you know who called on me today?"

"It wasn't the Holy Trinity asking for counsel, I suppose?"

"Silly, it was Madame Marceaux. You've met her, haven't you?"

"I've seen her."

"I'm not too fond of her, but she did bring some amusing news. I'm sure you've heard of Salesky, the taxi driver? Well, there's a girl here, Madame Rouen, who's his mistress. She has a little spice shop."

"I've heard that. What about it?"

"We believe she's pregnant again. Poor thing, I feel half-sorry for her."

"Where's her husband?"

"Oh, he was a prisoner of war for several years, and during that time she bore Salesky two children. Of course when her husband came back and found out about it, he left her."

"Too bad." I light a cigarette and wait for her to go on.

"Well, the girl's been getting large again, but this time she denies she's pregnant. She claims it's a tumor and says she's going to the City to consult a doctor." She leans forward eagerly. "You won't believe this, but two or three days ago she said she was suffering and sent for Madame Marceaux. When Madame Marceaux got there Madame Rouen was in bed, and on the floor by the bed was a blood-stained cloth. Naturally Madame Marceaux asked about it. The girl explained she was menstruating, and pulled another bloody cloth from under the covers. She apologized to Madame Marceaux for being in such a condition, and begged her to get a young girl who works in the store to carry the rags out and burn them. She also asked for a clean cloth. By doing this, you see, she knew Madame Marceaux would be convinced of her innocence."

"And wasn't she?"

"She was until today. Now this will amuse you. Today an old hag—who's the mother of your domestic, by the way—this old hag was cleaning the store, and she found the half-burned carcass of a cat in the stove." Madame Renée laughs piggishly; she seems to think it excessively funny.

I play with a strand of tobacco hanging from my cigarette. "And I suppose you good ladies pumped her for all the gory details?"

"Of course not. I knew nothing about it till I saw Madame Marceaux this afternoon. But obviously Madame Rouen's pregnant. She planned it, don't you see? She killed the cat and soaked the rags with blood, then sent for one of our better-class women. She didn't realize how soon

300

she'd be found out. Now it's all over the Village and the poor creature's in more disgrace than ever." She chuckles and shakes her head. "Really, did you ever hear of such a trick? Can you imagine such audacity? And apparently Salesky hasn't been near her—in that way, I mean—for several months. At least he hasn't been staying long enough to do *that*." Madame Renée is in good spirits. She leans back with a pillow behind her head, looking for my reaction.

"I think," I remark, staring at my feet, "that's one of the saddest and most grotesque things I've ever heard. I don't mean the poor girl's trick, or the fact she's pregnant; I mean the fact you ladies could think it amusing. Why, it's absolutely offensive. And I imagine you really take pleasure in discussing it, don't you?"

"It *is* amusing."

"Sure, you're smug, and you laugh, and you even try to find out the day and hour Salesky gave her the child. You ought to be ashamed, all of you. You consider yourselves so far above her, and yet you delight in her tragedy and get a sort of perverted sexual thrill out of discussing it."

"You're just like my husband!" she retorts sharply, rebuffed. "He thought all a woman dreamed of was the flesh, too. Well I can assure you, you're mistaken. If we discuss it among ourselves it's to see that something's done to keep a girl like that from influencing others. We're hoping to be rid of her soon. I'll have you know that most of us consider the flesh rather repugnant."

"Nonsense. You all want it." I mash out my cigarette in emphasis.

She laughs with what is supposed to be bitterness. "Oh, I know you men. You're all alike. My husband was the same way. Do you know he talked very much like you? And when I was a girl of sixteen you can imagine how quickly I fell in love with him and his fine words. He was twenty-nine years my senior, of course, and he had the glamour of the artist about him. Oh, I know you men. I was completely ignorant, and he filled my ears with that stuff about beauty."

"Did you believe him?"

"Of course I believed him. I was from one of the great families, and he was only an artist. I loved to slip away from school to go visit his studio. That's how he took advantage of me. But he did love me. And he was honest enough to divorce his wife and marry me."

"Aha!" I grin. "So there's a blemish even on the past of such an aristocrat as you!" This is the first time Madame Renée has seemed willing to discuss her earlier life. "Go on," I tell her, "I'm very much interested."

"It's the same old story," she says with a shrug. "My family didn't consider him our social equal. And of course he was a married man. They wouldn't tolerate a marriage. Our only hope was for me to bear him a child, in which case my parents would be forced to consent." She pauses. She is serious now, and I know she's reliving old pains and old pleasures. I let her dream them undisturbed. "When I became pregnant," she continues, "my father helped us financially, and we were married in a civil ceremony. But my mother never forgave me. She disowned me, and thanks to her I have nothing today. It wasn't right, Monsieur. She died only a year ago, after I'd given her a home here during the war years. She abused me, she never forgave me. She died with hate in her heart. At her request I wasn't notified till she was already buried. My only consolation is that she'll spend eternity in hell."

"Please, Madame," I protest, "you mustn't say such things. You can't mean—?"

"But it's true, Monsieur," she puts in calmly, rationally. "She was never a mother to me. The happiest day of my life was when the Good Lord delivered me of her. She didn't leave me a thing."

"But don't you think you're headed for hell yourself? Isn't there hate in your heart too?"

"Not at all. I've forgiven her, I've made my peace with God. But the facts don't change."

"Even so, it's an ugly story no one likes to hear."

She looks at me anxiously. "I hope you don't despise

302

me for this confession about my husband? I thought it might help. You've told me so much about yourself, I wanted to show you we're a good deal alike—that I'm not proud of my past either."

"I'm hardly in a position to despise anyone," I answer wearily. "But remember that past of yours the next time you start to deride somebody else—the next time you're about to make fun of a pathetic subterfuge like Salesky's mistress used."

Madame Renée rises and approaches me. "You'll hold it against me," she whines. "I shouldn't have told you."

"No, I won't." I get to my feet and stand looking down at her, buttoning my coat. "I think I'd better go."

"But I haven't finished the story."

"Couldn't you tell me the rest tomorrow? I'm awfully tired, and I have a lot of work to do before I can get to bed."

She walks with me to the door. "Incidentally, Monsieur," she murmurs diffidently—"and I hope you'll forgive me for mentioning it—but I'm afraid you've forgotten something."

"What's that?"

"The week's wages for Germaine."

"Oh yes, I *had* forgotten. Thanks for reminding me. She's never around when I come in. How much do I pay her?"

"Twenty francs a day. That's a hundred and forty francs for this week's work. If you'll give it to me I'll pay her in the morning."

"Tell me, who is Germaine? I've never even seen her. Is she anything like that pretty young girl you had last week? Christianne, I think her name was."

"Monsieur!" she says reproachfully, but with joking finality. "I'm not so naïve as to hire a girl like that for *you*. There'd be talk."

"She seemed nice enough."

"But not serious like Germaine. No"—laughing—"there's no danger with Germaine. She couldn't by any

303

stretch of the imagination be called an attractive woman."

"Well, tell her to come at noon tomorrow. I prefer paying her in person."

"But there's no need of that. Just give me the money." She holds out her hand.

I pause to light a cigarette before answering, "I have some extra things I want her to do for me."

"Then tell me what they are, Monsieur?" she says impatiently, with an annoyed insistence. "I hired her for you. Isn't her work satisfactory?"

"Her work is fine—but it's my house and she's my servant. I insist on paying her myself." I raise my head to keep from blowing smoke into Madame Renée's face. "In fact, I intend to run my own household from now on. Remember what you said about freedom and liberty?"

"Oh, very well, if you're going to be stubborn. I'll give her your message." She studies me through half-closed lids. "There's something behind all this, isn't there? She's not pretty, if that's what you're thinking."

"No, the thing that's behind all this is very simple— my desire to run my own affairs as I please, without being responsible to anyone. And I'm sure Germaine would prefer having only one master. Tomorrow I'll tell her what I want done, and I'll appreciate it if you'll leave the running of my house up to her, and her alone."

Madame Renée falters. "Of course, of course, young man," she says in cold anger. "You needn't worry. Next time I'll let you *ask* me for help. You can be most annoying when you set your mind to something, and I must say this is pretty childish. Maybe you'd like for me to stay out of your house altogether and leave it to the old peasant women?"

"No," I say sincerely, "you're doing a fine thing there and I'm truly grateful—though I wish you wouldn't bother them so much. I've heard the way you speak to them—not unkindly, I don't mean that—but with that flush of superiority. Can't you just be helpful, like a nice girl, without having to run the show?"

304

"I'm not a domestic for a bunch of evil-mouthed old hags. I have my pride. You'd like to see me humiliated, wouldn't you?"

"Not at all." I exhale a plume of smoke. "I'd like to see you behave like a normal human being. They may be evil-mouthed old hags, but none of them's laughed and told me about women who soak rags in cat's blood to make it look like they're not pregnant. None of them's ever offered to get me a girl. No, I don't want to humiliate you, but I'd have a lot more feeling for you if you humiliated yourself. If you don't, something or someone else will."

Madame Renée turns away and sits down near the table. She is grinning at me sarcastically. "Well, well," she says bitingly, "how superbly you wear the robe of St. Benedict! Or is it St. Augustine? Did you suddenly get enlightened?" I have sounded false, and she has caught me.

"I think it's your meanness," I say to defend myself, "that attracts me to you, Madame. When you make the effort you can be the most detestable woman I've ever known." She makes a move to speak and I hold up my hand against it. "And this time don't try to use my words against me. Can't you see it? Are you so full of yourself you can't see it? You've lived a good life. With your beauty and intelligence you could be a remarkable woman. Why fool around with these niggardly little self-deceptions? You know what I mean, and with very little effort you could change. Now good night."

She says nothing until I've opened the door and am about to step out; then, "You'll be sorry you said these things one day. You'll see."

I flick my cigarette through the door and trace its orange arc on the night air before it hits the snow. "I'm sorry already. I wasted my breath." I glance back at her, my hand on the knob.

Swelling with anger she asks miserably, coldly, "Will you be here for breakfast?"

"I suppose so." I hesitate a moment, undecided; then I close the door and come back into the room. "Now

listen," I say earnestly, "why don't you *try* to change? Why
don't we finish this thing now, honestly and frankly?" I
sit on the edge of a chair speaking rapidly. "You can't
win, you know. You got a good start before I realized
what was happening, but now—now you can't win. You
may as well stop trying. You've got everything to lose and
I've got nothing. You consider it a defeat, a personal defeat,
because I insist on paying Germaine myself. It's just a little
thing—I don't give a damn who pays Germaine—but little
things make big things and I'll *always* insist. And I don't
care how much you talk about self-sacrifice or anything else,
you know deep down inside that everything you do has a
selfish motive. Friendship can't be based on cunning, you
know. I like you but I won't let you win. When you've
decided to quit being so foolish, why then we can have
a little respect for each other."

Kaleidoscopic changes of expression on her face: anger,
denial, resignation, and now a masochistic superiority that
reproaches and defends. "For the first time you're being
honest," she observes. "If that's the way you feel about it
why have you led me on? Why have you confided in me
when all the time your friendship was just a show? You're
wrong—wrong in every contention."

I force myself to be patient. "You don't understand,
Madame Renée. My feelings for you are awfully hard to
put into words. My friendship's real enough—you can be
sure of that. Otherwise why should I waste my time with
you? I've confided in you because you've wheedled things
out of me. You've done it deliberately and you know it."
I lean back in the chair and fold my arms. "No, something
must be done, and it's for you to choose. You know I'm
not imagining all this. You're interesting for what you
could be rather than for what you are. And things will
never be different unless you take a good look at yourself
and stop criticizing other people."

"You're wrong, wrong!" she protests bitterly. "I've never
listened to such talk! What could possibly be my reason
for doing such things? I'll have you know I've got friends

all over the world who can tell you I'm not the monster you make me out to be."

"There's nothing monstrous about it. It's a little thing and I should never have brought it up, but now that I have, let me finish. I have the impression that for some reason— God only knows why—you're obsessed with the idea of dominating my life here. Maybe it's because you've been able to dominate everyone else you've ever known, except possibly your mother. But you find I don't dominate and it drives you crazy. I'm a challenge. Your nature, your pride demand I be conquered. For proof of that look at what happens every time I make friends with somebody else: you try to destroy them in my eyes. You've turned against Father Abbot and Father Clément, and now against Mademoiselle Marthe. You deny even your own friends."

She looks startled. "My own friends? Why—"

"Oh, not obviously," I go on, straining for control. "But you haven't had Mademoiselle Marthe back to dinner. And another thing: you lose your temper unless you know all about what I'm doing and where I am. You must admit that's hardly the behavior of a woman who wants only the happiness of her friends. But you can't see it. You mask every ignominious trick with that glorious word 'self-sacrifice.' And it's ruining you—you who could be so fine. Face it. Admit it."

I catch my breath. Madame Renée is staring at the fire. Her face, in profile, reveals nothing. She doesn't say anything and it wells out of me again.

"Oh, I could easily give in and then you'd be happy. But I'll never do it. Don't you know you can't succeed the way you're going? You'll not only lose me, but what's more important you'll lose all your old friends, people like Mademoiselle Marthe and Father Sauvac and Father Clément. You don't seem to be happy except when you're with me. I feel you'd turn on anyone who tried to join us. And some day you'll end up alone. But you can't see it; no, you have your own little logic that denies it. You convince yourself of something that's not true. It's just like young

307

boys and girls fondling themselves and imagining it's like the real thing when they can't possibly know. You're indulging in the same sort of self-abuse, only yours is mental instead of physical. You depend on your family name and your social position. You persuade yourself of your virtue and your honesty. And you deceive yourself. It's actions that count, not accidents of birth. Can't you realize that for your own sake? Won't you believe at least part of what I say?" I stop exhausted. I have emptied myself. There's nothing more to be said. Only my anger remains, pressing up inside.

Madame Renée continues to gaze at the fire. Then she turns her head and looks at me. Her eyes, stunned and dead with shocked humiliation, speak before her lips. "Have you quite finished?" she says expressionlessly. "Have you said every filthy thing you have to say? If so, then get out. I've been a good wife and mother. I've given one son to my country and another to God. I've suffered as only a mother can suffer, and you dare accuse me of self-abuse. Your conduct is unspeakable, unspeakable. I can't believe it. I'm not angry, I just want you to leave. I won't give you the opportunity to say such things to me again. You may find your meals somewhere else."

Her words shame me. Her words kill the hysterical fevers of my resentment. Neither of us says anything. A log burns in two and shatters in the grate. Lights seem dimmer.

"I'm sorry, Madame Renée," I murmur after a moment. "I don't blame you if you're offended. I guess I lost my head."

She says nothing, staring again at the fire.

"Please let me come back for breakfast. If I was wrong I'm truly sorry. I'll say a prayer for you at Mass in the morning."

"A prayer from you, Monsieur, would be sacrilege," she announces quietly. "Come for breakfast only if you're prepared to apologize and retract everything you've said." She bows her head slightly. "Good night, Monsieur."

"Good night, Madame."

I rise, bow stiffly, and opening the door, walk out into the snow. And the word "slut," repeated, chants at angles from all quietnesses.

My certainty vanishes. Victory is defeat. I must know. I must know if I am wronged, if I have wronged.

11 january

"Monsieur, Monsieur, wake up! Monsieur!"

Madame Renée shakes me from sleep. I am on my back. Shadowed darkness of early morning.

"Wake up, Monsieur, I must talk to you."

She turns on a lamp. She is dressed only in a heavy wool bathrobe. A lacy nightgown is revealed at the neck. Half-awake, I am conscious of my nakedness beneath the bedclothes.

"Do you have to come into my room," I mumble, "at this hour of the morning dressed like that?"

"Michel's leaving his monastery," she says in a stunned voice.

"What?"

"Michel's leaving his monastery," she repeats. I notice that her hair is uncombed and her face stupid with bewilderment. In her hand are the pages of a letter.

"What's happened?" I ask her, suddenly alert.

"I just got this letter from his Father Abbot. Michel's leaving. And after taking his final vows, too. He's leaving —quitting. We're ruined, ruined." She is dazed from shock.

"But what happened? Why is he leaving?"

"The Father Abbot says he doesn't have a true vocation

to the religious life. He threatened to commit suicide. And he's already taken his final vows. Here—here's the letter. I can't believe it." She sags into a sitting position on the side of my bed. "I just can't believe it."

Shifting under the blankets, I glance over the letter. It is brief. The Father Abbot carefully tenders his regret at losing one of his sons, but explains it's best for both Michel and the monks that the boy has decided to take up a normal family life. The letter is gentle and unmistakably sincere, but vague: the Father Abbot obviously prefers Michel to present in his own way his reasons for leaving. He goes on to say that Michel will need the money to return home, requesting that his mother send it to him at the monastery.

"Well, if he hasn't the vocation," I observe, handing the letter back to her, "he *should* leave. At least he's tried to make a go of it. His threat of suicide proves that. There's no scandal involved."

She puts her head in her hands, staring at the floor. "To think my boy could do such a thing!" she murmurs. "Could throw away his life like that! It seems like a bad dream. I can't believe it. I simply can't believe it."

"You mustn't let it upset you, Madame Renée"—hollow words that echo hollowly in my ears.

She raises her head to look at me. "Mustn't let it upset me? How can I help but let it upset me? Michel's ruined his life, that's all. We'll be disgraced—absolutely disgraced."

"It's not that bad."

"I don't understand how he could do it," she bitterly tells the air. "You'd think he'd have a little more consideration for his mother, wouldn't you? After all I've done for him!"

I can think of nothing to say. In her eyes is the first hint of tears. I stare at the opposite wall as she begins to cry: moist quietness rising inevitably to the urgency of sobs. The discomfort and the restlessness. I push myself farther up on the pillow. She pushes her fists into her eyes and weeps.

"That won't do any good, Madame Renée," I say as

gently as I can. "Is there anything I can do to help? Are you going to send him the money?"

She shakes her head emphatically, wiping her eyes with wet fingers. "No, no, he can't come here," she says tremulously. "And please, Monsieur, you mustn't mention this to a soul. I don't want anyone to know about it till I've tried to persuade him to stay. You understand, don't you?" She looks at me pleadingly.

"Yes of course, I understand. Then what are you going to do?"

"The only thing I *can* do is go to him right away." She dries her eyes again, this time on the sleeve of her robe. "If I can't reason with him I guess I'll take him to Paris."

"To live?"

"Yes—for the time being at least. I'll have to get him some clothes and find him a place to stay."

"Well, can I be of any help?" I inquire again.

Madame Renée hesitates, sniffing. "I'm embarrassed to ask you, Monsieur—but there's still time to catch the early train and the bank's not open yet . . ." She pauses. "Do you suppose you could let me have enough money for the trip? Say three thousand francs? I can get more in Paris."

"Of course, be glad to." I motion toward the chair near my bed. "There, look in my pants pocket. Take what you need from my wallet."

Her movements are slow, like those of a grief-stricken child. "I'll be gone perhaps a week," she says, replacing the wallet. "Can you make out alone?"

"Certainly. Go ahead, now, and don't worry about me."

"I'll put some tea and coffee on your hall table."

"Fine. I can take my meals at the Monastery."

She fondles the money nervously. "Oh, but you won't eat well there. I hate to leave you."

"There's not a thing to worry about."

In a wearied voice, recalling tears, "I hope you don't think I'm too terrible. About last night: I know now you were right. This proves it. My sins are being visited on my son."

311

"Don't even think about it," I answer, pitying her. "Michel's the only important thing. You must get to him as soon as you can."

"You want me to go, don't you? You're happy to be rid of me."

"Nonsense, Madame. You don't believe——?"

"Oh," she interrupts, forgetting, "there's one other thing: would it be all right if I borrowed your suitcase?"

"You're welcome to it. Just let me know if there's anything else I can do."

At the door she falters. "You do have some affection for me, don't you?"

"Certainly—you know that now."

"I'll fetch the tea and coffee, they're in the cellar. There are some eggs and a little butter there, too. Be sure to eat them. Just help yourself to anything you can find."

"Thanks, Madame. Good luck on your trip, and I'll see you in a few days."

"Good-bye, Monsieur."

"Good-bye."

She leaves sadly, closing the salon door behind her. I almost hold my breath as I listen to her footsteps fade down the hall in the direction of the cellar—and then, in a moment, return. There's a faint rustle, and I know she has put the tea and coffee on the hall table. Then comes the double click of the outside door opening and closing, and she is gone.

She is gone! I remain in bed relishing the sensation. She is gone, she is gone! The house seems to relax, to rest for the first time since my arrival. It becomes alive and happy. I silently ask forgiveness for the pleasure I'll take from her painful absence. A week! A whole week without her! Every moment must be counted, must be savored. Calmness in the half-light. Silences of ease and health. Release from a bondage of which there was no knowledge. But release comes as a flood of light to the soul. A lingering sickness has vanished. There must be more light. There must be a country dance with a bumptious, buxom, giggling girl. There must be none of the austerity of febrile night things.

The cold in my room, so malevolently sneering before, becomes strong and clean as I run from my whore's bed to open the blinds. Early morning sun: sweet-smelling morning in the Valley. A week! A week alone to waste firewood, to visit my unknown guests, to seduce all the old-maidenly rooms upstairs, to live as I please. Trembling with delight and cold I start the fire. The beginning warmth soothes my bare arms.

Clad in nothing but slippers I go through the kitchen and out into the courtyard. The air is clear and still, freezing my breath into a fog. No one can see me—only the sky and the morning sun and the vines sleeping on the garden walls —and they've seen it all before. The act of urinating joins the festival. Before, it was a furtive thing done against the wall; a thing to be finished as quickly as possible with eyes shifting self-consciously in every direction. Now it's a joyful, unashamed thing aimed high into the open air; a part of this pagan canticle to the earth, to the winter, to man's ephemeral return to earth from the heavens above and the hells below. Alone, inundated with exaggerations of lights and freedoms and fine level lines, even this lowly function becomes a song taking on the joy of the moment; becomes an impertinence which the natures above and below tolerate in these rare moments when man rises to their own heights of godlike drunkenness. Here we are equals. I embrace the cold air, the crystal ices, the clear skies. I no longer fear earth's dark terror. I insult it. I water it and wet it and melt all its snows—and laugh at the dead beneath. And may someone some day desecrate my sleeping remains with like waters and like jubilations; for I shall know and be happy for it.

Shock back. Shock back with the sound of the gate bell's ringing. Shock back to senses and today and now and being caught naked in the courtyard. In a breath I'm back in my room struggling to cover myself. The door opens and I cry out, "Wait a minute, won't you? I'm not dressed."

"It's just the postman, M'sieu," comes from the hall.

He waits whistling outside the door. After I've hastily buttoned my underwear I call for him to come in. He looks at me smiling with no cause, as one smiles at a child.

"Good morning, M'sieu—your mail. And how's the arm this morning?"

"Still stiff, but I can use it pretty well." I continue dressing. "I'm glad it was you out there. The bell surprised me. I was in the courtyard."

"You were in the courtyard naked on a morning like this? You're joking!"

"No, I didn't have time to put anything on."

Understanding lights his jovial face. "Oh, so that was it. But why didn't you do it out the window? I often do."

"It could be seen from the street, my friend."

"Just stand far back. *It* might be seen, but you couldn't be. You can always say it was Madame Renée. She's here often enough." He says this in mock seriousness, and the conjured vision brings unrestrained laughter from both of us. He helps me into my coat.

I say gratefully, "I want to tell you again how much I appreciate your helping me dress these past few days."

"It was nothing, M'sieu. This is my last mail stop and I've had the time."

"It was a big favor to me."

"You're handsome again dressed," he remarks. "You know, it's a funny thing, this modesty. It's often senseless. I was thinking about it while I waited for you."

"How's that?"

He deposits his empty mail bag and reaches into an ash tray for a cigarette butt. "Well, look at us now," he answers deliberately. "For almost two weeks I dress you every morning. Each time you crawl naked out of that bed without a sign of embarrassment in either of us, because it's something that has to be done. And yet this morning when I open the door and glimpse that same bare ass, I instinctively draw back in the hall till you cover yourself. And you feel the same thing, for you tell me to wait while you struggle to hide what I've already seen so many times."

314

"That's quite true," I agree, adjusting my tie. "I've never thought about it before. I suppose modesty's too deeply ingrained in us to be overcome, except by something like sickness or an accident."

He nods. "I've thought about it often," he says slowly. "A study of the philosophy of modesty should be made, for I believe it's something more than mere background or training. It seems much more fundamental to me. It's like, say, the fireless cooker—a necessary part of the evolution of a society that's become ever more closely drawn together."

I stare at his heavy face in astonishment: these are words and thoughts not expected of a postman. "But I didn't know you were a philosopher, my friend," I mutter admiringly. "You amaze me."

"Every man has his petty little interests, M'sieu. I'm not a philosopher—not even an educated man. But I read, and I try to think. It's an interesting subject, modesty. You're educated, you know what I'm trying to say." He smiles.

"Then you think"—giving him a fresh cigarette—"that modesty's not a purely psychological trait, but rather a physiological reaction that's involuntary? And that it's more highly developed in advanced societies? But why?"

"I see it this way, M'sieu. We know that a duck, for example, has webbed feet because it must swim in the water. We know that among primitive peoples physical modesty's seldom known. I've read that immorality in primitive societies is often severely punished—sometimes, even, by death. It seems to me they don't need modesty, that it hasn't had to grow as a part of their physical equipment. But we civilized people, as we relax more and more our social and moral laws, as immorality becomes highly acceptable—as it has in all past civilizations—we grow this modesty like the duck grows its webbed feet, as an agent to counterbalance the laxity of our social laws. It's not, as I used to think, something false ingrained in us by our parents, but rather a normal physiological part of ourselves. That's proved by our return to it this morning; for otherwise there'd be no reason for me to stand in the hall while you dressed yourself."

"I think I'm beginning to see what you mean," I put in. "In other words if modesty were only to keep people from being exposed to each other, then it would disappear between two people the minute its purpose was defeated— the minute one of them discovered the 'secrets' of the other."

"That's right. You and I've both slept with nice women, M'sieu, and seen and felt every part of their bodies. But have you ever tried to pat one of them on the behind the next day? Chances are she slapped you to heaven. I think modesty's a natural preservative for a minimum of physical morality in crowded societies. When it's destroyed, as it is in the sex act, then the act itself becomes a rampant thing leading to misuse, perversion, and the destruction of society. Look at the Greeks, the Romans, and then look at us. We're headed the same way with our relaxed laws, our intellectual freedom from moral principles, our filthy little communists and the like. Any agent which cuts us off from the growth of modesty must be an agent harmful to our very lives. Look at M'sieu Gide—our greatest writer, and yet he'd like to see marriage between males made legal as it was in ancient times. And all this destroys our civilization, our great France, drop by drop. Modesty may end up as an unnecessary growth, like an appendix or a tumor." He stops long enough to inhale deeply from his cigarette. "You must think about these things, M'sieu, and tell me the answers."

"You seem to have them pretty well thought out yourself. It's an interesting theory you have." I lean against the mantel. "But speaking of modesty, have you heard my good luck? Madame Renée's been called away for a week."

"No!" He grins through a cloud of smoke. "Well, now you can have some freedom. You can even get a nice girl in here to stay with you, eh? Maybe Madame Vincent's beginning to—"

"Not her!" I laugh. "She's like your nice modest lady. We're good enough friends, but that's all."

"Tell me, M'sieu—I'm not trying to get personal—but is the talk I've heard true? Did you really have an affair with her? Somehow I've never thought of her as being that type."

I smile: it's a question I would resent anywhere but in France. "The talk's true, all right," I readily admit. "But she's really a fine woman, better than most. And she's making amends, you know. She wouldn't let me touch her now."

"Too bad," he sympathizes. "Sometimes they'll treat you that way, though." He glances toward the kitchen and adds abruptly, "I was wondering, M'sieu, if I might shave again while I'm here? Haven't had a decent shave since you let me borrow your razor the other day. This is the only place I can get hot water, you know."

"Help yourself," I tell him. "You'll find my razor in the same place—there by the hot-plate. And heat enough water for some coffee too, will you? We can have a cup before the ladies start coming in."

"I'll fix you some coffee, M'sieu, but don't believe I'll have any myself, thanks. It's too rare—like cigarettes." He draws once more on his cigarette, now about to burn his fingers, and reluctantly crushes it in the ash tray.

"To hell with it. Let Madame Renée worry about it. I suspect she shakes her fanny for about anything she wants around here anyway. We always seem to have plenty."

"Plenty of what? Surely you don't—?"

"No, hardly that."

He laughs as he walks into the kitchen. "And has she shaken it," his voice comes back, "at you yet?"

"Not yet," I reply, sitting down at my worktable. "But she's too damned friendly. It may come to that one of these days—not that it'll do her any good."

"No?"

"Hell, no. If I had to I'd rather take one of these old hags."

"Then if one of them starts looking younger all of a sudden, I'll know, eh?"

"That's right—you'll know I had to make the choice."

While he shaves I gather together the books and papers I'll need for my work at the Monastery, then get up and build a fire with the wood already beside the stove. Soon

317

the chill begins to disappear from the air. I stand close and let warmth seep through my clothing. The postman, his face smooth and fresh-looking, sticks his head through the kitchen door.

"I can't find any coffee, M'sieu," he says.

"Madame Renée left it on the hall table. I'll get it for you."

I rummage for clean cups and saucers as he finishes making the coffee. We carry our steaming cups in by the fire, letting the hot liquid pleasantly scald our mouths and throats.

"Has your wife been in to take advantage of the fire?" I ask him.

"Not yet, M'sieu. She doesn't go out much these days— just rests in bed. Ah, this coffee's good."

I give him another cigarette and he settles back with his feet close to the stove. But the gate bell rings and he sits up quickly, glancing at me.

"Your ladies come early. I'll finish my coffee in the kitchen."

I look out the window. "Don't bother—it's only Salesky."

Closing the salon door behind me I meet Salesky in the hall. He is wrapped to the ears in a fur coat, smoking a pipe which seems to be a part of his face. Every time I see this man I feel the beginnings of laughter.

"She's gone!" he announces as if to the vastness of an auditorium. "Gone bye-bye, M'sieu! I just took her to the station."

"You did? Well, she'll—"

"I hear she's been giving you a bad time. What's the matter, won't she let you have it? Or won't you let her have it? Which? She's a good looker for her age. I could tear up her—"

"For God's sake don't talk so loud!" I caution him. "I've got a visitor in the salon."

He looks startled, covers his mouth with both hands and says in a loud stage whisper, "No! Who is it, M'sieu? Not a lady, I hope?"

318

"No, you fool!" I answer, feigning tearful embarrassment. "It's the Bishop of the City."

Salesky's eyes roll skyward in horror. "God!" he explodes with a half-groaning inward laugh.

"What do you want to see me about?" I whisper.

"Sure he can't hear?" he whispers back.

"Yes, he's having coffee. Go ahead."

"Well, M'sieu, you've got a big garage and no car. How about letting me park my cab there while I go down the way to see my girl friend? Or better still, let me find you a nice girl and we can all have a party here tonight."

"No, thanks. Use my garage whenever you like, but leave me out of your plans."

"Maybe I could rent the garage permanently? People wouldn't suspect a thing that way. Why don't you come on and relax and have a good time with us?"

"Take the garage, Salesky, but keep your girl friend away from here. My house is open to the public, but I don't want to come home and find the two of you together upstairs. You know I can't risk such things, much as I'd like to."

"All right, M'sieu," he says resignedly. "But I'll pass you an occasional pack of cigarettes. And say, do you need anything else?"

"No, I guess not . . . Oh yes, I can't find any toilet paper in the stores. You wouldn't—?"

"I got some. I'll bring you some the next time I come. We stocked up not long ago." He turns at the door. "One other thing, M'sieu: if you need spices or anything like that I wish you'd buy them at my girl's store. She needs the money and I don't have much to give her."

"Be glad to, my friend."

"Thanks."

Rejoining the postman in the salon, I pour us each another cup of coffee. "Did you hear all that, Monsieur le Bishop?" I inquire grinning.

"Yes—Salesky has a loud mouth even when he whispers." We laugh as we hear the creak of garage doors being opened.

319

"I can't make him out," I remark between sips of strong coffee. "He seems to love his wife and yet he's unfaithful to her every chance he gets."

"Salesky's a type, M'sieu," the postman observes seriously—"a character. But he's a good fellow at heart. He and I have had more than one good time together. He's funny when he's got a girl."

"He's funny all the time."

"Yes, but you ought to see him on a party. Now there's a man without a shred of modesty. There's nothing he won't try to do—and right there in front of you—to please the girl he's got. I think you're crazy not to let him find you a girl like he suggested—but that's your business, of course."

I shake my head. "I'm too tied up with the Monastery. Can't afford to take the chance . . . What's his wife like, by the way?"

"You'd get along fine with her. She's much too good for him and he knows it. He loves her and loves to show her off." He swallows the last of his coffee. "You know, you can't help but like Salesky even though his main reason for living seems to be below his waist."

The gate bell sounds again, interrupting our conversation for the second time. Through the window I briefly glimpse an aged face above a stooped body. "Looks like the ladies are beginning to arrive," I say to the postman. "It's an old woman I've seen here before."

"Well," he says, pushing himself up from the chair, "I'd better be running along. Thanks a lot for the coffee and cigarettes—and for the shave too." He picks up his mail bag and slings it over a shoulder.

"Come whenever you want to," I tell him as we walk to the door. "And I hope your wife will be all right. Let me know if I can do anything."

"Thanks, M'sieu."

In the hall we find the dour-looking old woman cleaning her shoes on the doormat. The postman politely nods to her.

"Good morning, Mother Nourrie," he greets her cheer-

320

fully. "Didn't know it was you out here. You're up early."

"Good morning, young pup," she gruffly replies. "And how's that pretty squirrel of a wife this morning, eh?"

"She seems to feel fairly well this morning, thanks."

"Aha! Soon the new little beauty'll stick its head out of her and squall and you can begin to make another one on her."

The postman chuckles, opening the front door. "I'll do my damndest, old Mother."

"What?" she croaks.

"Nothing." He winks at me before stepping outside, and from the cold air without his low laughter drifts back into the hall.

The old woman turns to me, and I smile at her. She is broad and dumpy and bent with age, but there's an impression of great physical strength. She has a mean face and her eyes are slightly crossed. In one hand is a large oilcloth shopping bag.

"Please come in—Mother Nourrie? Is that what they call you?" And to the nodding of her head I add, "You're the first one to come this morning."

She doesn't move. "I'm the mother," she states resolutely, "of your housekeeper Germaine."

Things click in my head: this must be the old woman who found the dead cat in Madame Rouen's stove. "Oh, really?" I reply. "Well, I've never seen Germaine but I'm glad to know her mother. Germaine's a fine housekeeper."

Her stare is sullen as she asks sharply, "Then why'd you let her go, M'sieu?"

I look at her questioningly. "Let her go? Where'd you get that idea, old Mother?"

"Madame Renée came to our house not an hour ago, M'sieu, and told Germaine you'd have no need of her till further notice. She told her not to come for her wages— that she'd be paying her herself when she got back from Paris. Why'd she go to Paris, M'sieu?"

"On business," I say, puzzled at what I've heard. "But she certainly had no right to fire Germaine. Why, I'd never

321

let a housekeeper like her go. They're too hard to find."

Mother Nourrie gazes up into my face, squinting. "You mean you didn't tell her to fire Germaine? Why, the old bitch! She's got a tap loose, M'sieu. Yep, there's something wrong with that sour prune . . ."

Against the background of her chatter I think over what she has told me. Despite her grief Madame Renée hasn't overlooked a chance to dominate my life. But it was a ridiculously childish attempt made in apparent desperation. Otherwise she must have known I'd discover it immediately. I feel a sudden urge to laugh, but restrain myself; instead I say, "Look, Mother Nourrie, could you go tell your daughter I know nothing about this and that I'd like her to come back to work for me right away?"

The old woman has paused with her mouth half-open. "But of course, M'sieu."

Gathering her heavy wool scarf about her head with the awkward nervousness of age, she steps carefully from the front door and makes her way through the thick, crusted snow to the street. I stand in the doorway. She stops at a house only a short distance away, and her shrill "Germaine! Germaine!" comes back to me. The morning is bright and the echo seems to rebound glistening from the icy street. When her daughter opens the door the old woman gesticulates explanations to her—movements without sound. Then a second black figure emerges from the house and they return together, their heads lowered against the cold. In my entrance hall they remove scarves and stamp snow from their feet with sighs and half-smiles and muttered complaints about the weather.

Germaine is large and dark and placid, with none of the mean look of her mother. Such a woman makes explanations seem unnecessary. She appears unconcerned that Madame Renée released her from service. I give her the week's wages and receive in return a slight smile and a low "Thank you, M'sieu."

I pick up my things to leave. The two women are lost in subconscious images of bedclothes being spread and gar-

322

ments being retrieved from the floor. But as I walk from the room Mother Nourrie comes back into focus, giving me a friendly grin, ancient and crooked. I smile back at her, chuckling beneath my breath.

At the Monastery the day merges into a pattern: a pattern made up of work in the paleography room, of a meager lunch in the refectory, of offices in the chapel. It's a happy pattern enriched by the sense of freedom left behind by Madame Renée. Work assumes new dimensions, and I welcome the silent company of the monks at the polished tables. And when finally before going home I enter the chapel for Vespers, there's no feeling of dread at the evening stretching ahead—only anticipation of the long silent hours alone.

There are three or four Villagers scattered through the chapel. I immediately recognize Madame Vincent kneeling in a pew to one side. Unnoticed, I take a seat behind her. Her hair is swept up and held in place by a small hat. Through heavy clothing the form of her body is more imagined than seen. Vespers provide dissonance as my thoughts for the thousandth time conjure up a hotel room and that same body warm-pressed against mine: buttermilk markings of used flesh, and gasping breath, and blond hair moving against my cheek. I grow tense. Fatigue of mind strangely stirs the ferment of desire, and chants add lascivious contractions to the neck muscles, making them ache. My buttocks burn into the wood of the bench.

When the service is over Madame Vincent walks quickly by without noticing me. I get to my feet and slowly follow her outside. The cold air seems to shear heat from my face in layers, to be replaced by other heats in other layers. I stand near the entrance, and Madame Vincent's heels crunch through the snow. A square of dim yellow light momentarily throws back the afternoon gloom as she passes into the gatehouse.

Uncertain, I continue to stand there in the fading day. I am aware of a pulsing in my throat, and on my face the flashes of heat and cold. But the line of intent stretches taut.

I know I must speak to her. Quickly I cross the small span of frozen ground to the gatehouse and, unthinking, enter.

I hesitate just inside the door. The room, lighted by a small lamp, at first glance appears empty. Then I notice a movement behind the grilled cage, and Father Dutfoy bows his bald head in my direction. Madame Vincent is behind a bookrack across the room, leafing through a religious magazine. She doesn't see me approach, and my voice startles her.

"I'm sorry, Madame," I say, taking her hand. "Guess I shouldn't be seen talking to you at all, but Father Dutfoy's the only one here."

Her hand is dead weight in mine. "It makes no difference now," she replies. "They know anyway, your good ladies. I'm leaving."

"I don't understand," I say after a moment. "What do you mean? What do my 'good ladies' know?"

"Very simple—about us, of course. They've asked me to leave the Valley. You had to talk about it, didn't you?"

I stare at her, unable to answer. She looks large in the half-light. Her small stylish hat seems suddenly incongruous and pathetic. On the silence comes the sound of a door closing. Father Dutfoy has left his cage and gone into another room.

"You don't have to say anything," she remarks dully. "They've also asked Mademoiselle de Castro to leave. Funny, isn't it? She has to leave because she's my friend. She's done nothing, you know, except come here and pray."

My stomach turns sick. Face tissues dissolve and burn as I realize what she is saying; as I realize that my own weakness—my weakness in telling—is forcing her to leave this place which has become so important to her. I can say nothing. The shadow of the bookrack falls diagonally across her face, protecting it in part from the lamp, making it wrinkled and sallow.

"How'd it get out, do you know?" I bring myself to ask. "I thought they were beginning to forget their suspicions."

324

"They were, my friend. It could have come only from you. I'm sorry you had to do it. This is the only place where I feel perfectly—I don't know. But I was making progress. You can ask Father Clément. And I was just beginning. All those things we didn't understand." Her face is expressionless. She presses a hand against her temple, ruffling her hair. "I can't stand to think about leaving. For the first time my life makes sense. I don't know where to turn. If only you knew how lost I'll be, how—" A sound makes her turn her head: Father Dutfoy is back in his cage sorting papers.

"Can I do anything?" I ask miserably. But Father Dutfoy is there, a third person damping the need to speak; the fact of his presence fills the room.

"No," she murmurs, "there's nothing either of us can do now." She opens wide her eyes; she looks me full in the face, her face faltering.

I ask, "When are you leaving?" dreading the answer.

"Right away. I'll say good-bye now."

Lines of aching strain. I am sick. I want to stop her. Father Dutfoy shuffles papers. My arms are tired, and cells of the face seem to be held in place by props. She turns, walks over to the cage and places a magazine on the counter.

"How much is this, Father?"—opening her purse.

"Thirty francs, Madame. But it is not the latest issue."

"That's all right. Thank you"—as he returns her change.

She opens the door and walks out. I hear her crunching steps as the door swings slowly closed behind her. Nostalgia of her footsteps in other snows: unbearable sound muffled at last by the thick wood clicking shut. My hand feels the rough plaster wall at my back, rubs hard against it, feels the knuckles bruise. I raise the hand tremblingly. It is splotched with white flakes of plaster. Over the knuckles the skin is broken, revealing translucent raw underskin and tiny points of filtered blood. I put it to my mouth and, without looking at Father Dutfoy, walk quickly from the room. The cold air stabs the open places and makes them ache, and I suck them. Unseeing, I trudge through the

325

snow to my house, dreading all feeling, killing all feeling.

The house is empty and immaculate. There's no indication that many people were here during the day. I prepare a supper of toast, soft-boiled eggs and canned peas which I bought at Madame Rouen's store. But I can taste nothing. I can't forget that I have harmed Madame Vincent for the meanest of reasons—for the pleasure of laughing and boasting of my conquest.

Thirst for solitude—disturbed solitude. Calmness. And in the hermit evening of roughening guilt, hopes show the first possibility of being realized. Madame Renée has gone. Prayer flows and asks and begs. Outside it is dark bleak winter; inside, lamplight and quietness. I think of other families, far away, gathered about evening fires. I think of young wives and their children and their full, bustling lives. Here the skeletal vastness of silence, architectural, overwhelming, makes me seem infinitely small as I putter about the cleanness of my house.

I wait. There is a waiting within, a waiting for something to happen, something unknown—unknown fate at an unknown time. I wait calmly for what must be, to happen.

Desultory work before the fire. It's impossible to sit still for more than an hour. I wander outside and walk for a long time beside the River. Behind heavy clouds, the diffused light of a full moon. Lights from the other bank reflecting across the ice. Avenues of trees losing themselves in low night-mists.

Always in the back of my mind there seems to lurk the potentiality of understanding; but it remains deaf to every call. The knowledge that it's there, that I could understand it if I really wanted to, makes me think and feel things opposed by logical conviction.

The cold drives me back to my room, and I turn on the radio. From London, the Beethoven Violin Concerto played by Francescatti. I know it from memory, but I hear it for the first time tonight.

It grows late. Nothing satisfies. I open a volume of Rilke, but I can't read. I stand at my window, nose pressed against the pane, breath fogging the glass, and stare down the street. Strange brassy tonality of the full moon, now breaking through the clouds onto clustered housetops: more abstract, more frozen than abstraction. We strive for warmth in color to forget these scenes, these moments, these liturgies of dissonance, these cold angles lost in heavy shadows, just as we try to live warmly to escape death. Bitter lives—hard, nasty, guilt-nourished—to escape the hypothetical sweetness of death. But we die in pain.

Fitful sleep and other escapes and the madness of casting off the present ache of throat muscles. Think of other nights—there, there in your bed—think of other nights. Think of other nights when it was warm and you could sleep and there were no frozen eaves. Other nights of adolescent fury when you'd take the puffed English girls and lie with them on the grassy banks of the Cher River, shading your face from the moonlight beneath blossoming lime trees. Autumn nights; and the delight of sleeping cool under a light cover. Nights in a city; and oysters and white wine after a concert, when you had the money. Nights of interminable late walking in search of a woman who would look at you that way, who wouldn't rob you, who would give you sleep.

Other nights and newer remembrances. Nights alone in the Monastery cell, the chants of Matins and Lauds waking you before daybreak, the ravishment of lying in the dark listening to chants filtered vaguely through stone walls and floors. Nights of exhaustion when sleep comes immediately. Sleepless nights, when the bed becomes a woman and the pillow her lips. Nights alone, of fury. Nights of disgust.

A cock crows distantly. It is not yet dawn. From the silent mass of this sleeping Valley a cock, awakened, crows. It is tonight's night past, a beauty of early morning sound destroying quietness; inundating you with relief that morning is here and you're no longer completely alone; heralding the light of day while it's still dark.

And now the great bells of the Monastery announcing the beginnings of wakefulness. Only a few yards away

327

someone else is awake, and wakes others. A monk prays through chattering teeth as he rings the bells. And there must be a light and the smell of cold incense. In the darkness of their cells other monks, rubbing unbrushed heads and sleep-caked eyes, yawning and stifling the escaping airs of a night's sleep and empty stomachs, force themselves to crawl from their cots and with a trembling of violent movements to put on shoes. They daub their faces with towels wetted on the ice covering their washbowls, and they spread their beds. They know the earth these first few moments of wakefulness as bells again sound. They know unshaved faces and the inner rumblings of digestive juices that have nothing to digest. They cough and swallow night's acid evil collection of saliva, and they scratch where it itches and yawn again, and they stamp their feet and know completeness of chill. And they walk slowly, with deep clawings of hunger, into the chapel. And sleep retreats from them, giving way to warmths and loves and inner joys and mumbled prayers of heart-fullnesses. The other is forgotten. Badly begun chanting becomes adoration, rising vivacious, tender, angelic, killing night's puffings and swellings and snorings. The deadness of incense odors is revived with new smoke.

Here, in my room, is old smoke. The cold dry air is heavy with the acrid odor of cigarette smoke. I open the window, see that the sky begins to lighten in the east. Housetops become the black angles of silhouettes.

Exhausted by my vigil of the night, I fall into a dreamless sleep. Last thought of upswept blond hair and a Parisian hat—and tears and guilt.

12 january

"Fat boy, young boy! Hey, hey, wake up, M'sieu! Going to sleep your lazy life away?"

I look up; I look up into the crossed eyes of old Mother Nourrie and groan at the sight. A hag with crossed eyes shakes me from sleep.

"Come on, come on, out of bed! I've already lit your fire." Grinning she throws the blankets from my body, bursts into cackling at the sight. "Oops, why the young pup's naked! Ha! Come on, up with you!"—grabbing my ankle, jerking me over, slapping me hard on the behind.

I roar angrily, "Get out of here, old woman!" and try to cover myself, embarrassed and indignant.

She leans back, rocking on her heels with laughter, coarse, dark, laughing like a man. "What's the matter, hey? Ah, he hides himself, for example. Come by the fire. You got nothing to hide from old Mother Nourrie. I seen men lots bigger'n you, and lots uglier. Why, my Papa Nourrie—" She squints and moves her hands to show me how Papa Nourrie is made.

"All right, all right," I interrupt impatiently, "I didn't ask you for an estimate of my sleeping qualities."

"What?"

"Nothing." I crawl disgruntled from the bed, but already my anger at the old woman's familiarity is beginning to subside under her barrage of good-natured ribaldry. She hands me socks and shoes.

"There, young turnip, and here's a chair. How come you sleep by yourself? Why, you're young and full of sap and you're a fine beauty of a thing."

"You're old, Mother Nourrie, anything would look good to you. Now leave me alone."

She grunts and tosses her shawl across my shoulders, a grinning, half-surprised expression on her cramped face. "The blood runs good in you, sweet child. Ha! it does me

329

good to see you. Stand up. No? In my day a man stood up for me. It's good to see youth even when you can't feel it any more."

I tie my shoes. "You're pagan, old Mother."

"What?"

"Nothing. Hand me my underwear, will you?"

She retrieves my underclothes and examines them carefully, shaking her head slowly from side to side.

"What's wrong?"

"Ha! they're filthy."

"Here," I sigh, "I'll get some clean ones just to please your ignoble old heart."

She gazes at me, clasping her hands. Quickly I put on clean underclothes. She steps close to me, her face serious.

"Tell me, fine boy," she says loudly, "you look good and full and nice-sized, and your whiskers grow healthy and the behind is broad—are you sick?"

"No . . ."

"Then why do you keep a lonely bed? Why waste young muscles this way? It's sad—none of my business— but sad. You ought to be locked to somebody else. Ah, look at you! You got blood and your skin's rich and rosy. You'd be better letting another's hands know you."

"If you don't stop talking, miserable woman!" I tell her—but now I am laughing.

Standing back, she applauds. "Aha! the young garden begins to grow and bud and blossom. Good! Go, young beauty, the country's full of girls who smell of fresh straw. In winter they're green and warm like young plants. Leave this old hag and find them. Break their backs and fill them with children."

I am dressed; I go to her, and bending low I kiss her whiskered cheek. She becomes paroxysms of laughter and her eyes draw closer together. She looks at me.

"La, he's dressed," she mutters toothlessly, "he covers his beauty from my sight. If he was my lovely sweet I'd hide his clothes and pass the day watching all his movements. I'd sit in my chair rejoicing at such a happy sight."

330

The gate bell rings, and she becomes jubilant. "Ha! there come some of the others, but too late, eh? Only Mother Nourrie knows the charming sight. Mother Nourrie got here early and saw."

"And," I remark drily, "she'll probably tell the whole Village."

She grins. "Mother Nourrie, young kitten, is not stupid. If she told, they'd all be here in the morning. Now only *she* will come. I light the fire for you every morning, eh? And help you dress. And sing at the sight of you."

"You're impossible, old hag, impossible. Don't come early and don't wake me again."

She feigns deafness. "What?" she says, as footsteps sound in the hall.

"Nothing." Looking up, I am surprised to see the tall thin figure of Jacques de la Roche, hesitant, appear in the doorway. "Well, Jacques!" I exclaim.

"Hello," he says. "Are you supposed to just walk right in?"

"Of course—come in, come in. This *is* a surprise." I shake his hand.

"Been a long time, hasn't it?" he observes.

"It really has. How've you been? And how's your mother?"

"Just fine."

"Here, let me have your overcoat."

"Thanks."

As I help him out of the coat, I vaguely wonder at the suddenness of this early morning visit. He glances smiling toward Mother Nourrie, who makes no move to leave.

"You'll see nothing else today, Mother Nourrie," I tell her. "Run along a minute, won't you?"

"Where to, M'sieu?"

"Why not go in the kitchen and boil some water? Perhaps Monsieur Jacques"—turning to him—"would like a cup of tea or coffee if we have any?"

"No, thank you," he replies. "I can only stay a moment."

With a snort Mother Nourrie waddles into the kitchen

anyway, closing the door loudly behind her. Jacques and I take chairs near the fire. He looks quickly about the room.

"You have a nice place here."

"Thanks, I'm glad you came to see me." We talk pleasantly of his family and of my life since leaving the Monastery; but he appears uncomfortable and I sense that he has something else on his mind.

At last he says cautiously, "I've found out something I think you should know about."

"What's that, Jacques?"

"Remember the Chevissiers?"

"Of course. How're they getting along?"

"I'm not sure, but—well, I do know something's wrong." He pauses awkwardly. "I thought perhaps you could tell me about it." He stares at the stove and his voice is sharp. I watch his long fingers nervously fondling a button on his coat.

"What are you trying to say, Jacques?"

"Don't you know?"

"Haven't the slightest idea."

His face relaxes and his dark eyes study me in relief. "I'm glad. I couldn't believe you'd be—" The sentence dies in a shrugging of his thin shoulders.

"I'd be what? What's this all about?"

"Well," he sighs, turning in his chair to face me squarely, "it's hard to say. But—well, you know the Chevissiers were making a good deal of money off our farm a few months ago. I told you all about it."

"Yes."

"Well, now they're penniless—completely penniless and in debt."

"But how—?"

"Doesn't it seem strange to you," he goes on rapidly, "that Madame Renée is suddenly the only woman in the Village who always has ample provisions? How does she get them?"

"I—I don't know," I stammer, feeling somehow guilty. "I suppose she buys them from the Chevissiers. At least

332

that's my impression. I certainly am paying her enough."

"It doesn't make sense. If she *buys* them from the Chevissiers, why should they be penniless?"

"But," I counter, "how could she get the food without paying for it?"

"I don't know. I had to pay some of the Chevissiers' bills for them, so I went over and tried to make them tell me what the trouble was. They were terrified. Couldn't get a word out of them. But something's terribly wrong, I'm sure of it."

I wait a long time before saying, "And you think Madame Renée might be mixed up in it? I can't believe that."

"Perhaps not." He rises suddenly. "But see if you can't find out for me, will you? I'd appreciate it a lot. I must run along now."

"Look," I say, walking over to retrieve his overcoat from the couch, "why not ask Papa Chevissier to come and see me? Maybe that way I can learn something."

"Do you think he would?"

"He knows he can trust me. Insist that he come, will you?"

Jacques slowly buttons his coat. "Well, all right," he agrees. "That may be the best solution."

"What about today at noon?"

He nods. "I'll try."

"And come see me again, Jacques," I add at the door.

"Thanks. Good-bye."

Closing the salon door, I search my brain for a possible explanation of what he has told me. My thoughts are interrupted by Mother Nourrie's flat gray head peering in from the kitchen.

"Has he gone?" she whispers hoarsely.

"Yes, you can come back in now."

She putters about the room, muttering, singing, dusting with a dirty towel. I put on my overcoat and hat.

"Good-bye, Mother Nourrie, I'm going to the Monastery."

She grins. "Bye-bye, sweetness, bye-bye, young fatness,

333

bye-bye, nice thing, bye-bye, pinkness, bye-bye, prettiness, bye-bye, fresh garden, bye-bye—"

"Oh shut up, won't you?"—laughing.

She stands solid, hands on hips, glaring. *"You* tell me to shut up! Wasn't even talking to you."

"No? Then who were you talking to?"

"I was talking to your you-know-what, young boy. I was telling it bye-bye, sweetness, bye-bye, nice thing, bye-bye, prettiness—"

"What?" I ask, mimicking her.

"Nothing."

Her chuckling follows me out of the house; her old woman's singing chuckling laughter and crossed eyes follow me all morning. They form a blessed relief from the doubts raised by Jacques's visit, from the disgust of his suspicions. During the morning they fade away, this laughter, this pagan health. I withdraw into myself, huddling over my workbench in the silent paleography room, ignoring the monks who come and go.

My eyes, poring over the stained pages before me, find magnificence in the *Diferencias* of Cabezón, an astonishing organ composition; and later, in the *Clausulae* of Cabanillas. Quietness of morning. Penetrating cold and losses of re-membered laughter become confused with ancient notes on faded paper, notes that somehow live and linger as deli-cately hinted sound heard only in imagination.

At noon I return to my house. It is empty. The salon, warm forever and cluttered with chairs drawn up around the stove, is full of the sweet odors of old women's talk, of old women's black wool.

I sit at my table and wait for Papa Chevissier. Ringing silence throughout the house. A globule of sweat slithers down the wall. Other globules. Spattered globules striking the new wood of a child's coffin, being absorbed into the grain, being absorbed into the soft felt of men's hats. Papa Chevissier does not come. Globules of water slither down the wall, down the wrinkled cheeks of the screwed-up face of a peasant mother. I stare at the stained streak. Soft eyes under soft gray hair, and a soft voice saying, "There, I baptized the child. There, the child is buried in hallowed ground. There . . ."

"No, by God!" I kick the chair into a corner. Silence, and no answers to my questions. The fire warms my feet through thick-soled shoes. Outside it's cold. But there are answers outside. I put on my coat and pull it tightly around me. Leaving the house, I head for the Chevissier farm.

The countryside is bare and somber. At the Château de la Roche I lower my head against the wind and trudge through the formal gardens, now dry and dead; down the rocky hillside into flatlands below. An ocean of snow, unbroken, stretches before me. In the distance can be seen a clump of trees and colorless buildings and a thin column of smoke, white against the gray sky.

My footsteps break the silence. They lead me at last through the grove of boxwood near the Chevissiers' house, and around the corner of the low stone hut. I turn to enter the courtyard. A flock of Papa Chevissier's Toulouse geese sleep in clusters on the snow, their heads drawn up under their wings—lumps of blue and gray against the white ground-cover.

My feet are wet and numb and I stamp them on the doorstep. I hear a chair scrape inside. The door opens.

"How are you, Madame Chevissier?"

She eyes me coldly, fingering the black wool shawl around her shoulders.

"May I come in?"

"What do you want?"

"Just to visit a little while," I smile.

She reluctantly steps aside to let me enter. Little Papa Chevissier, half the size of his wife, rises from his bench at the table. I shake his hand cordially, hearing his wife slam the door behind me. I glance about at the same room of stone floors, darkened beams, plaster walls. The room is silent except for the familiar spitting of water beginning to boil on the stove. On the blackened oak table the same

335

dinner is set—a smoking casserole of yellow beans and blood sausages, with dust-streaked bottles of wine. There is something mocking in this re-creation of another scene, as though time had refused to elapse since that terrible day the Petite died. It seems strange not to hear her pathetic strugglings in that dark corner of the room, strange not to see her lying on the table with a pool of water in her dead navel.

The parents remain ominously quiet, watching me, as I walk over to warm myself near the stove. "Cold today," I remark pointlessly, rubbing my hands together.

"What do you want, M'sieu?" demands Madame Chevissier again.

"Well—I hear you're having some trouble," I remark softly, deciding to come straight to the point.

"What do you mean?" is the suspicious rejoinder.

"I don't know. I just heard you were having some trouble. Thought perhaps I could help."

She picks up a spoon and plunges it into the casserole, dumping a large serving on her husband's plate. "Here, Jules, eat," she commands, "while it's still hot."

Papa Chevissier stares at me uncomfortably. "We hear Madame Renée has gone?"

"That's right."

"M'sieu Jacques wanted me to come see you," he mumbles almost apologetically, "but . . . I don't know, M'sieu." He pauses.

"What, Papa Chevissier?"

"Hasn't M'sieu ever wondered," his wife breaks in angrily, "how Madame Renée always manages to serve such good food? She's always got plenty of meat and eggs and butter."

"I don't know much about her arrangements," I answer. "I've wondered, yes, but I supposed she bought them on the black market."

"Black market! Humph!" she snorts, tearing a piece of bread from a long loaf. "I'll tell you how she gets them —she takes them from us. She makes us give her every-

336

thing. What she doesn't use she sells to all her friends."

"We become poor, M'sieu," Papa Chevissier puts in timidly, and she nods her head violently.

"What are you talking about?" I say sharply, to cover my uneasiness. "Madame Renée wouldn't do a thing like that. I know her. Besides, how could she make you give her anything?"

Papa Chevissier's eyes grow unexpectedly hard. "You know she baptized the Petite," he whispers. "Well, when you began taking your meals with her she didn't have any money for provisions—"

"She did too!" I protest. "I paid her in advance."

"Well, she said she didn't. At first she borrowed from us and promised to pay us back when you gave her the money. But then she just started taking everything . . ."

"That bitch!" exclaims Madame Chevissier spontaneously. "That dirty bitch!"

"It doesn't seem possible," I murmur. "Why don't you refuse to give her anything more till she pays up? She's got the money."

Madame Chevissier rubs her arm against her nose and sniffs loudly. "She's a dirty bitch, that's what she is."

"My wife did refuse," Papa Chevissier goes on, "but then Madame Renée threatened to tell everyone about the Petite—about her being buried without really being baptized." He looks at me pleadingly. "If she did that we'd be ruined, M'sieu. We'd be run out of the Valley. No good Catholic would ever give us work again."

Stunned, I fumble for a cigarette; it tastes foul. "Still doesn't seem possible," I repeat after a moment. "When was she here last?"

"Only last week, M'sieu. She takes more and more all the time. It's the truth!"

There's a silence; thoughts collect nervously in contradiction, confusing logic and disbelief.

"You really didn't know about it, M'sieu?" Madame Chevissier's voice sounds gritty and faraway.

"Had no idea."

337

"I was sure you didn't, M'sieu," her husband says quietly, picking at his food.

"Well," she sighs presently, all trace of suspicion gone from her voice, "what can we do?"

"One thing's sure," I say slowly, "you can't let this go on. She'll never stop if you do. If I were you I wouldn't give her another thing regardless of her threats."

"But she'll tell!" Papa Chevissier says almost desperately—"and we'll be ruined. Maybe it'd be better for us to leave the Valley now, while she's gone."

"No, no, you can't give up everything you've got here. Besides, where would you go? What would you do?"

He says nothing, his shoulders sagging in despair. Madame Chevissier sighs again, heavily.

"Look," I say as gently as I can, "you've got to stand up to her. Maybe she's weak, maybe she saw a chance to make some money and couldn't resist the temptation. But I don't think she's really bad. Explain to her that she's making you poor"—Madame Chevissier shakes her head derisively—"and if that doesn't work, why then threaten her in return. After all, *she's* the one who baptized the child. Tell her if she exposes you, she'll be in more disgrace than you."

They look at each other for a moment; slowly their expressions change. "Of course," Papa Chevissier mutters excitedly, "of course! We hadn't even thought of that."

I add, "No matter what she threatens I don't believe she'll risk disgracing herself."

"Of course she won't!" His face is flooded with relief. "Why, she won't dare tell! Of course she won't! Why didn't we think of that?"

His wife gets up from the table, smiling. "Here, M'sieu, have a seat, you must eat something. Get him a plate, Jules, and some wine."

"No, thanks just the same." The thought of eating at the same table upon which the Petite lay in death, is too much. "I've got to get back."

They chatter together excitedly while I warm my hands

once more over the stove, dreading the cold walk back.

"One other thing," I tell them finally, as I move to the door—"it might be better if no one else knew of this visit, especially Madame Renée. If she gives you any further trouble I'll be there to see what's going on from the inside. We can work better that way, I think."

They nod eagerly, hovering near me like two children.

"And you must forgive her," I feel compelled to add. "She isn't really like that, I'm sure."

"When will we see you again, M'sieu?" Papa Chevissier asks.

"Soon, I hope—but if you need me for anything call for me at the Monastery. And don't worry, we'll work this thing out."

I leave the house with their thanks lingering in my ears, with their smiling faces lingering in my mind. But other images intrude: a rain-splotched coffin of new wood, and the ghoulish fingers of Madame Renée. The walk back turns my forgiveness into hate; I suddenly hate Madame Renée viciously and bitterly—and I know that the afternoon will be too long.

I am hungry and tired when I open the door to my house. I pause in the hall. The old women have returned: from the salon come the hoarse raspings of their voices, and the laughter of children. A salon crowded with women and children; and down the street, the Monastery where there's work to do. No, no—not now, not now. Impossible now. I'm exhausted, and the afternoon will be too long.

Aimlessly I wander down to the cellar, where I remember having seen, over in one corner, a single dust-covered bottle of wine. I open it automatically and begin to drink—long, cool, gurgling swallows. I drink until I'm drunk, and drunkenness becomes a wail of loneliness. Morning words return. Drunkenness drawing face taut, and cravings for the girls. Warm wetness and cold. Greenery. Girls smelling straw and fresh.

Salon full of old women. Take down your pants for all old women. "Young boy," "nice boy," "sweet boy," and long howling wails of desire. Escape now. Escape all nows. Upstairs, away from them. One of the bedrooms. Upstairs and onto the bed. You hard-arteried old rooms, you stare at me. What's so damn' wonderful about you? Blackmail under the baleful eyes of piety. Blackmail. You rooms. You sweat and you're cold, you're not green and your behinds aren't broad. You frown, Great Ladies. Great blackmailing bitches with your noses turned up . . .

Noises downstairs, laughter. I awake trembling, frightened. Utter desolation of early afternoon, terror of cold afternoon that's too long, and stiffening drunken sleep. Light sifts through dusty lace curtains. I get up. Staggering down the steps I enter the kitchen the back way and drink a glass of clearest coldest water. Every sense is rampant. Sober loneliness of fright. Always the sensation of waiting— for what? I decide I must go where people are; I must find Father Clément.

The aging monk succeeds in calming me, although I can't tell him about the Chevissiers: he is a priest, his duty would be to the Church. We talk instead of Madame Vincent. There's no reproach in his tone; his voice is regrettable and regretting forgiveness.

The day somehow passes, and at last it's evening before the fire. I can't read tonight. The heavy volumes of apologetics, theology, lives of the saints, repel me. I execrate the world. Exhaustion. The wine and the confusion. I feel, and that's all. Nothing, nothing pleases me. The light blinds. I stare at the stove window till my eyes cry out against the torture.

I find music on the radio: the Brahms Third Symphony brilliantly performed by the Vienna Philharmonic. Idly I turn the dial in favor of the unbelievable tension Bach could put into a sonata for unaccompanied violin. Tensions within me relax under Bach's tension, pouring out as passions pour out in a first frantic kiss. But my hand turns the dial before it's finished.

The desolation of "Asa's Death" played on a theater organ drives me to the greater sadness of an English Protestant church service. "The Lord be with you," and dials again turn.

Inner sinkings, to the very bottom. Glimpses of glazed eyes turning to death in a ten-year-old. Glimpses of the smile and the charming beauty of Madame Renée. Glimpses of a night in the snow and walking with Madame Vincent; and later her tears and the telling in the Monastery gatehouse.

Again on the radio from England: after a few tremolo chords on the organ a manly voice proclaims, "I am Love," and is answered by an unaccompanied women's chorus singing madrigal style, "The voice of Love is light . . . bright . . . right!"

13 january

There's no more coffee, and in my wallet only twenty-five francs for the purchase of bread tonight. For breakfast I prepare tea. Father Sauvac, smiling, bowing, congenial, comes in as I am sitting down to an unsugared cup.

"I don't have any sugar, Father," I say, when the greetings are over, "but I can offer you a cup of tea."

He leans far back in his chair, fumbling a large hand into the recesses of his robe. "Thank you, my son. Er—I always carry a little sugar with me. There it is"—straightening folds, bringing a small brown sack into sight. "I'll share it with you in return for a cup of that nice-smelling tea." He drops, with exaggerated gesture, one small lump of sugar into my cup.

I bring another cup from the kitchen. The tea is hot.

341

He leans forward over it, blowing and sipping it loudly.

"It's good to see you again, Father," I tell him. "Has our experiment been going to your satisfaction?"

"But of course—this is awfully good tea—admirably so, my son. But tell me, why did Madame Renée leave so suddenly? You haven't quarreled, I hope?"

I nod. "We've quarreled all right—that's about all we have done. But she left for private reasons. Sorry, I promised not to tell."

"That's all right, expect I'll know soon enough. Are you enjoying your little vacation here alone?"

"Very much—but I have so much work to do I can't get enough sleep."

"I see." He leans forward in his chair, grasping my knee, and asks cordially in an offhand manner, "Tell me, my son, do you shop at Madame Rouen's spice shop very often?"

"Sometimes. In fact I went there the other day to buy some prunes, but they were too expensive. Seven francs a prune—can you imagine it?"

"That's the reason I came this morning," he smiles. "We can talk freely as man to man, I think. I must ask you not to buy anything more from that woman."

"Why not?" I look at him in surprise. "She does charge high prices—but I can't see what difference that would make to a priest."

"But let me explain." His clasp on my knee tightens, and he looks intently into my face. "That young woman is a disgrace to our Village. She's the taxi driver Salesky's mistress. Even now she's carrying another one of his children. It's certainly my place to see that such a blatant example of adultery be forced from our Valley, and the only way I can do it is to deprive her of her ability to make a living here."

"You're not serious!"

"Of course I'm serious. There's no alternative."

"But she has two of Salesky's children already, Father. She's been his mistress for several years. Why have you

342

waited till now? Why didn't you run her out to begin with?"

"Out of pity—purely out of pity. But now she's done some very foolish things. The talk's loose and sinful."

"But even if you deprived her of her living," I argue, "Salesky wouldn't stand by and do nothing. He can support her well enough."

"No, Salesky doesn't have a thing—his wife sees to that. And he'll never leave his wife, either. I know best, believe me. Won't you help us drive this bad influence from our Village?"

For a moment I don't answer, staring at him distastefully; but I know that unless I comply, I too will be driven from the Village. "What else can I do, Father?" I say, shrugging my shoulders. "But I don't like it a bit, I can tell you. It's against every principle I have."

"You won't regret it." The priest leans back and smiles self-complacently. "There's another thing too. You rent your garage to Salesky, don't you?"

"Yes."

"Don't you realize that every time he puts his car in there it's for the express purpose of going to see his mistress?"

"Look, Father Sauvac," I say impatiently, "I made a simple business deal with Salesky—I rented him my garage, which is perfectly legitimate. What he does after he leaves his car there is no concern of mine. Surely you don't think I'm trying to make things easier for him and his mistress? It's just none of my business."

"Very well, my son," he says testily, "we'll leave things as they are. But it does you no credit in the eyes of the Village."

A retort is on my lips, but I restrain myself. Instead I ask, "Can I get you another cup of tea?"

He accepts another cup and drinks it rapidly, our conversation drifting into the safe neutrality of small talk. I think of the price I have to pay to remain in the Village, and I fight down repercussions of conscience. It's with relief that, a few moments later, I bid Father Sauvac good-bye. He

343

invites me to come to see him again, but I reply only with a noncommittal grunt.

As soon as he's gone I walk to the Monastery. In the streets this morning are red-faced Villagers: the butter vendor making his deliveries; a small crowd in front of the bakery shop, each person holding his ration ticket and his money, awaiting his turn to buy bread.

Throughout the day: German, Latin, musicology, moral theology. The thought of this work is paralyzing. Steady work, including classes, for about sixteen hours each day. If I don't keep up, I am lost.

On my way home after Vespers I stop to buy bread; but seeing two people drinking wine in the shop next to the bakery, I too order a glass. It takes my last twenty-five francs. No bread, no coffee, no butter, no sugar until Madame Renée returns. A few cigarette butts and some tea. With nothing to supplement my noon meal at the Monastery, and no food for the night, I grow depressed. Even the monks are eating better than I.

I try to forget my hunger in the reading of poetry, first picking up a volume of Reverdy. Hidden in the shadows of more brilliant talents such as Éluard, Cocteau, and Apollinaire, he remains for me the purest poet of our age; on a plane with Mallarmé, infinitely above the intellectual dust of Valéry.

Today Father Dutfoy gave me a collection of the poems of Mistral, written in the heat of the Midi. They are in Provençal—warm, clear, sunny words. The beauty of a series of words as rhythmic sounds, producing an over-all impression which can legitimately contradict the meaning of the words. Mallarmé does this superbly.

On the radio begins a concert of the Ars Rediviva from London. I stop my work to listen to the newly discovered Triple Concerto of Telemann, with Dominique Blot as one of the soloists.

On my table, other books: an analysis of Fra Angelico by Huysmans. He is a remarkably unsympathetic writer, and although his study of Fra Angelico is probably false, it is none the less fascinating and I can't put it aside.

How much in these happy solitary days am I obsessed with the abstraction of purity! How ardently I love the feet of this condition so far removed, standing so haughtily above me! But the liquid images of sensuality crowd out the cooler capacity for pureness. For weeks, since the last fevers, there has been within me the niggardly, diluted purity of overwork and insufficient food. How much I admire the giant massive chastity that destroys all little things, that comes from a force of desiring, from an emotion of *detached* voluptuousness! No courage even for the fleck of its possibility. Affections and warmths for little impure sweats and toothless grins and fine pink things.

Exhaustion: at least *that* is a straining on the outside, and the experiencing of it becomes a source of pride.

14 january

A heavy morning fog outside my window. German lessons with Father G'seau before lunch. Work, unending work in the paleography room.

There are now two sanctuaries in which I feel completely happy: the Monastery where I spend my days, and the room where I spend my nights preparing lessons for every next day.

Since we'll have no classes this afternoon, Father Clément, worried about my health, suggests that I work with Father Gardener to obtain some exercise. Joining Father Gardener after lunch, I help him set off charges to loosen the frozen ground. He works without gloves in the icy mud, packing dirt around the explosive. And when he has set the fuse he hastily pulls off his glasses and we run back, sliding on the ice-covered ground, turning about and covering our ears for the explosion. After an hour my feet are covered with mud and I am shaking from the cold. The monk sends me inside.

I am tired. Muscles sing. First feelings of health. I stay till the end of Vespers, which grow more miraculous each day as weakness becomes the ardor of adoring.

On the way home Madame Rouen stops me at the door of her shop and gives me a package of cigarettes. They'll say I didn't obey Father Sauvac, but it doesn't matter. She is heavy and unbeautiful, and her belly shows round. She carries Salesky's grunting weight. She has sensitive parts and little understanding. Bloods and corpuscles grow within her and become fondlings. I eye her pityingly, but I buy nothing.

My room reveals a cleanness of tile floors, of good smells, of warm air. While it's still early I prepare supper. There are tea, a little grease, some salt, a handful of dried cookies—and hunger. I boil water for strong tea and pour it into a large soup bowl. A tablespoon of grease is floated on top. Salt and the crumbs of cookies are added. There's enough for two large bowls of this unnamable concoction. My hunger makes it taste surprisingly good, although the grease is slightly rancid.

Tonight the fog thickens. The street is empty. All sounds return muffled. It's good to have a light and the dry warmth of a room behind closed blinds. For an instant I think of the straw mattress of Father Clément. How he'll tremble this night, his hands clutched between his thighs for warmth!

Desultory work. Open-faced sleepiness and the fatigue of physical labor drag me into a coma of excitement artificially nurtured by strong tea. A numbness of sense bathed in the enchantment of this transitory solitude. Time becomes counted, more precious than any in memory. My pulse quickens when I think of some day having to leave.

346

And now, in this early evening, I think calmly of desires felt while I was in my cell; desires for noises and lights and a flank to caress; remembering moments of physical passion when I murmured, "If only this would never end." Tonight the murmurings are the same, only for an opposite emotion. The night becomes words—from walls, from the sensitive young girl of my room bending forward to smile and brush her hair so that I may see. Other dimensions speak, and she, not understanding, smiles and winks at me. She's polite and she listens, but she understands nothing of what they say. Walls sweat, and my stove spits its airs of green wood turning into ashes. My room listens to silence become words— total words of mental and spiritual ecstasy.

We never experience such ecstasy in our ordinary lives, as a man who has not heard music cannot experience the magic of a Monteverde. But we must know that it exists, and that it is a giant sublimation of all littlenesses and all bignesses and all hungers and all thirsts of the flesh and of the spirit. For in the perfect fusion of all sensory and intellectual faculties into an abstract ideal, the sensual is completely satisfied after having first been crushed within us, as a seed must be bruised before planting and growth. It is satisfied in serving as a parallel function to an emotion which we generally consider exclusively spiritual.

But my room combs her hair, she doesn't understand. Another voice, dusty, clean-bellied, with a wart on its chin, takes her and tries to explain.

With this phenomenon, and only with this phenomenon, the misnamed sex urge is utilized and satisfied in a flame of purity which in no way compromises the condition of chastity. It serves, rather, as a fundamental base, a pigment, of proportionally great and abstract beauty.

My room glances at me where I sit by the fire, shrugs her shoulders and stifles a grin, then looks back innocently into the eyes of this night speaker, nodding her head politely as if she understood. But wart-on-chin leaves, and another speaker takes my room on his lap and pinches her navel, laughing.

347

You see, it is a shame that the word sex *inevitably must carry connotations which never allow it to be considered in this most logical and legitimate connection.*

She giggles, and another takes her on his knee, an old man with a beautiful face. He sets her squarely on his knee, looks at her, and his speech is without meanness.

What he meant, that other one who pinched you, was that the joys of the spirit, the ecstasies of the true religious mystic, are not divorced from the sexual function. It does not disappear, as I fear more than one fine lady knitting for the guild auxiliary is inclined to think. How they would frown upon a St. Francis, or a St. Theresa, or a St. Augustine! —for they think sexlessness is a virtue. They have never been thirsty with their bellies, as have the saints—only with their bladders and their mouths. Why are seekers of sensations content to by-pass this most satisfying of all sensations—the complete physical and spiritual union of ecstasies?

My room shows a glimmer of insight, climbs down from the strange knee, and walks over to sit in my lap. The speaker, ignoring her, looks at me and continues.

It is a sad thing to see men who have once known this bliss, and who have for some reason lost it, spending their lives searching for it again, renouncing all the things of this life in the hope that it will come back to them. And there are many more than we realize who go blindly through hell in praying for its return. For those rare ones who have it, life itself means nothing. Hunger and physical hardships become graces. Few will pass from this to go to the more advanced austerity of Juan de la Cruz, into the hypothetical heights which remain only a dream for the rest of us: Marie-Ornoux, Father Foucauld, Lydwin of Schiedam perhaps— and a handful of others.

All this is very interesting, but my room grows heavy in my lap; she sulks for caresses and wants to play; she has understood almost nothing. I drop her to the floor and she again becomes walls and ceiling and plaster and tile. But she still smiles and approves of me.

348

Canons, German lessons, and past-midnight hours. Two more cups of strong tea, stringing my nerves on the fine wire of a struggle against fatigue. A good fire and the silence of long evening, punctuated by sporadic attempts to work. No longer the hope of understanding man, of judging the self by man's standards.

I am conscious of the differences between the civilized desire for consistency of thought and logic and behavior, and the reality of inconsistency in all things. Consistency and order are social growths invented outside of man, and they're abominable. In a single breath we breathe many airs—happiness simultaneous with grief, love simultaneous with hate. In a globule of ink on paper we change from prayer to obscenity. But *we* don't change. We're all goodnesses and all badnesses and all sensualities and all chastities at each moment.

Lateness turns into exhaustion of legs beneath the table. Delight of desiring sleep, drunkenness of not having to think, cataloguing of physical sensations growing from exhaustion—holding off, holding off with the bed beside me. Emotions filter from night to a plane of early morning health. Wonder of fatigue. Wonder of approaching sleep, dimly aware that outside, mist freezes on the ground, that here it's warm. Every house in the Valley is dark, every room filled at this hour with odors of heavy, open-mouthed sleep. Somewhere out there a woman turns in her bed, rouses from a dream trembling, moves closer to the sleeping flesh beside her and falls again into the sleep from which she has never really awakened. A husband unconsciously throws covers from the foot of the bed and crawls nearer the softening flank and veins and inner rollings of his female.

Never has night known such happiness; never such awareness of the nourishment of these vast dark silences reflecting into me from the cobblestones of this Village of age.

I rise, falling to sleep on my feet. There's only time to undress. Despite every effort, my eyes close in heavy sleep. And there's the fruitless grin of a woman in heat, rubbing

349

her inner thighs. *"Ave, Maria, gratia plena; Dominus te-cum . . ."* But prayer does no good. The hideous smirk remains, lowering one side of her mouth, making her look like a specter of Madame Renée.

15 january

The remarkable goodness of Christians!

The targets of their virtuousness: Madame Vincent because she seduced me, and Mademoiselle de Castro because she is Madame Vincent's friend. They whitewash me and despise Madame Vincent because they are Christians with a profound sense of decency. And this morning they applaud justice and feel relieved, for their targets walk to Town to take a train somewhere.

You must pass the test here; you must elevate yourself to their high moral plane or they force you to seek your own level elsewhere. "If they can't respect our ways we know what to do," they say, and smile.

Two women walk in the snow-covered road, carrying heavy suitcases. And the air of our Village becomes perceptibly less tainted. The leaders of society and the humbler women of equal spotlessness feel deep satisfaction that, in seeing justice done, they have returned the rightful atmosphere of halcyon peace into the Valley.

Two women walk in the snow-covered road, carrying heavy suitcases. And I remain behind by my comfortable fire.

16 january

Father Clément has told me to set aside one night each week when I must do no studying, when I must occupy myself with something other than my usual work. To pass an evening determinedly opposed to others is difficult. It's impossible to forget the day, to forget that this afternoon at the Monastery we began a new course in natural, ecclesiastical, Christian, and canon law—the course Father Clément mentioned to me before Christmas. I am anxious to read through my notes, to try to understand these still-obscure concepts; but with an effort I force my mind away from them. Instead I idly pick up a volume of Mozart's letters. They are interesting but poorly translated. Whereas in German, Mozart is frank enough to call a behind a "behind," or more frequently an "ass," in this watered version the word is simply replaced by dots.

Dissatisfied, I open a study of primitive art given to me by Father Dutfoy. The text is too pedantic to hold my attention, but I am fascinated by the illustrations—photographs of carvings from Africa and the South Pacific. Looking at them I become aware of the retrogression of my mentality toward ancient attitudes. Primitive modes of thinking and believing, in which I've bathed myself for so long, have become as natural. How much my tastes return to Roman and pre-Roman architecture in preference to Gothic and post-Gothic! How much they grow to love the primitive in preference even to the classical! And in art, abstractionism and cubism must be a return. Surely they must have existed at one time as the basis of all art.

It's the same with Gregorian chant, written in a language that the world has lost, of which today there remains no hint. I don't mean the spoken language, nor even the musical language of modality; but, rather, that spiritual conception of such restraint, such directness, that all succeeding music seems to have declined until our very beings, brutalized by the obvious, can no longer hear the tension of whispered emotions; until we require climactic sounds to express climactic, stereotyped emotions.

I think of Psalm 118, containing the line: *"Haec dies, quam fecit Dominus: exsultemus, et laetemur in ea."* We translate it: "This is the day which the Lord hath made; we will rejoice and be glad in it." How many times have I heard this intoned in a restless voice by a minister!—when its logical accompaniment seemed to be summer's droning of flies and the sighs of corseted women and bilious men and restless children, all waving cardboard fans to stir the warm air. Listening, yes—and being gentle and kind and uplifted. These are only words, and not very beautiful words; they fit well into the drone of flies, the occasional cough, the half-closed eyes of those being spiritually uplifted. And the minister reads, sometimes with a quiver of emotion taught him in the seminary, but never in the right place, never on the right word.

If the line is set to music it is set to music which rises to climax, for of course there must be a climax in all good, *really* good music. And we will, when we write the music, make the climax fall on the word "rejoice," which possesses a certain poetic grandeur. We will discriminate; we will choose a musical scale in a very bright key to express the bursting joy of the text. We will write a grandiose melody with a stolid rhythm. And the result will only add one more piece of trashy emotion to the already immense repertoire of such hymns.

Looking into the *Gradualis* we find a difference, for here there are no surroundings, no fans, no sweats, no impatience. The Gregorian version of this psalm, unknown, taking a most modest place in the cloister of anonymity, is one of those rare, perfect creations that go beyond the accepted realm of the human. It is a simple setting of a text consisting of only two sentences, and yet it reveals more than volumes of history, philosophy and art. The mode chosen for the music is the second, perhaps the most subtle of all the eight modes. It expresses a slightly dissonant

352

mood of contemplation, a very delicate sadness. It is introvert: not the joy of the obvious, but the far greater, more intimate joy of those who don't profess to understand the marvels of God's creation but who, rather, stand aside in awe, scarcely daring to breathe for the wonder of it. And it is, above all, the sideways glance of a people who are so much in love with this mystery as to be ill at ease, fearful of a gesture that might destroy the affection of their great love. The chant is an intimately personal expression like the surging of a pure joy within, a joy so profound it fills us with quietness, calling up tears instead of laughter or shouts. Such is this music felt in the heart of some anonymous monk in the early centuries of Christianity, when the memory of the Lord hadn't yet become the diluted thing it is today: the expression of a joy so intense, so profound, so tender, that it makes us participate for the moment in something out of our time and our life.

My eyes devour the page again and again, hearing it in memory. Over the word *"Dominus"* the caress of the melody is a little unsure, to indicate that, although we have seen these things for ourselves, they are miraculous almost beyond belief. And on the word *"exsultemus,"* an admixture of emotions with but few notes: exultation too profound for coherent expression—repeating, folding back upon itself. And next: *"Confitemini Domino, quoniam bonus: quoniam in saeculum misericordia ejus."* This becomes a true love song, a personal love song filled with the tenderness and bliss of a real, physical love of the heart, breaking the bounds of human feelings to enter the realm of the divine. *". . . quoniam bonus"*—". . . for He is good": here is the high point, the outpouring of adoration in which the very soul rises to ecstatic heights, falling back and repeating without the exquisite sentiment, burning the listener with the fire of the unreal become real. Art of the past, revealing a consummate emotion with a few touched-in notes.

I put it aside, thinking of how sickeningly the memory of other religious music insinuates itself into the mind. For there's always the glamorous murk of a Parsifal in search

353

of the Holy Grail, casting bewhiskered eyes at the skies to an accompaniment of brasses and trembling vibrato strings; causing the bosoms of the old school and the nineteen-year-olds to burst with the beauty of it and then to roam the weeping wilderness of self-worship. The flies return, the fans, and the heated, corseted, wattled women. And the boys dream of the swan of *Lohengrin,* the Kundry of *Parsifal;* open-eyed, promising, never suspecting that this is abominable, that this is the dregs of chest-beating; nor that Kundry, the mad witch, would make a better piece than most. But it's there in the music, in the text. Wagner himself was frenzied night-wetness converted by genius into music. His was a genius of the lower belly, and somehow his music excites upper tears from lower-bellied people. Bayreuth, and a married woman at Zürich, and an illegitimate grandson of Liszt fall through the roof onto my head, and the Metropolitan throws bolts of hatred into my bleeding stomach. But somewhere, long ago, Tutilo of Saint-Gall and Odilon of Saint-Amand had already cleansed the blood.

A new fever rises quickly, accompanied with the beginnings of violent chills. I must reach the bed now, while I can still move. Burning blistering fever, drying lips, parching eyes. Impossible to get to the kitchen for my quinine tablets. My head aches throbbingly as I crawl into bed. The touch of sheets accelerates the fever, and their pressure against my back is exquisitely painful.

Finally, sleep; and later I awake in the dark weeping and screaming, "No! no! no! . . ." until no more sound comes from my throat.

17 january

Roomful of hags watching me. Murmurings to Mother Nourrie for quinine. Sleep and chills, and cold glasses of water with quinine. And a circle of black women knitting, sewing on white things. Faraway muffled talkings. Sleep, and later emptiness of room and evening. Awaking to dark. Pain and black darkness. Fevered sleep.

18 january

From the wash of this horror a nightmare last night, clearly drawn. I dreamed that I was alone in a shabby hotel room, and that beside my bed a window was hung with dusty lace curtains, limp and yellowed with the sadness of too-long use. As I was dropping off to sleep in my dream, I heard the padding of naked feet in the darkened room. From somewhere a strange light revealed a woman. She had upswept blond hair, now disheveled and beginning to fall about her shoulders, and she wore a torn Parisian hat. Blood streamed from her nose and mouth, and her eyes were black shadows in her face. She approached my bed with clawed hands. Screaming with fear I threw my arms over my head, trying to ward her off; and this gesture awakened me, for my hand struck the wall above the bed. I lay there in the dark trembling, afraid to sleep again, conscious of empty rooms surrounding me.

Now the strange light of early dawn, when pain, become hypnosis, is no longer felt; when the heats of fevers and dreams break into sweats and urine. After a while I retire to an upstairs bedroom, leaving my salon to the women and children seeking warmth. I know that Germaine, thinking me gone, will make the bed below me.

I sleep again, but during the day the pains grow more intense. Holding my head I run to Mademoiselle Marthe and beg her to help me. She gives me three aspirin tablets in hot water and two large tumblers of cognac. I return home and fall into a drunken slumber, unconscious of any activity downstairs.

When I awaken hours later the headache, along with the fever and the nausea, is gone. With the return of normal sensations I go down to the salon, empty now in the late afternoon. I shave, put on clean clothes, and search vainly for food. There's only a musty box of oatmeal left in the cellar. My cravings urge me past the first repugnance of sight and smell, and I boil the cereal. But I have no butter or milk or sugar, and stale oatmeal by itself is sickening. To kill the weevily taste I pour over it the remainder of some cold black coffee, then hastily swallow a bowlful.

After one of these attacks, good feelings return more quickly than strength. The joy of having the fever terminated fills my evening; but I can't forget the hunger of three days without food. Desiring fresh air as a relief from the stuffy room, I open the door to go into the courtyard; but I'm repulsed by a strong wind thick with snow.

A book of drawings by Klee enchants me tonight. All feelings become good—better than in health—for there's a weakness which satisfies itself in small things, in a slowness of actions. And how vividly the diffuse writings of Claudel come to life!

On the radio, a typical performance of English church music: a soprano warbling her domination of the choir. And in imagination I see the congregation like all other congregations, with a Sunday look of posed, paused goodness.

Night passes. The gnawings of hunger stimulate all

356

faculties, all passions. Somewhere out there asleep, sheltered from the heavily falling snow, is the peace of the Valley. In other valleys, Madame Vincent and her friend, safe from the barbs of our good women. Across the River, Salesky in the arms of his wakeful, tortured wife. And in a single room behind the spice shop, his mistress sleeping with her children, safe only until morning.

Weakness becomes a sort of tentaclelike force when passion pushes it—cramped, crablike, with claws that won't release. Its force roars in my ears with the passing of night. I can't sit still; I can't believe that this could carry me screaming in my temples, bruising my head with the happiness of it. I stamp about the room filled with the mounting strength of detached passions, feeling the resurgent drunkenness of exaggerated strengths. The being, with night and lateness and emptiness, freed from blistering fevers, surges upward like a dervish, whispering growing to roaring, continuing until I become the embodiment of a laugh, a cry. I storm from the room, and the falling snow cools me. Flakes dissolve on my ear, down my neck. We celebrate the return of health. Purity of snow.

Again dreams. Dreams of carnality, never realizing themselves. Rack of predawn sensuality.

20 january

Days of waiting and of the return of strength. Days sharply divided into hours of light and darkness. Quiet, uninterrupted work at the Monastery, going from lesson to lesson, from spiritual conferences with Father

Clément to the offices of Mass, Tierce, Sext, and Vespers. Beginning to live these offices, beginning to feel their imperceptible hold on me. Days and nights of contrasting happiness blemished only by the dread of Madame Renée's return.

Life here becomes a hallucination of perfection, austerity, and learning during the day. And an enchantment of kaleidoscopic raptures at night. All the between things have left me. On the one side, only the physical functions of hunger, thirst, elimination, rest—nature stripped to nakedness. On the other, manuscripts yellowed and spotted with age, books, the reasons why. In between, nothing, nothing at all. Nights of ever-growing carnality growing like a physical function into a source of happiness after days of calm work. The fire diminishes steadily, for I can no longer afford to be free with the fast-disappearing wood supply.

Lessons are prepared—German, harmony exercises, law, and history. But I can't sit still for long. After an hour I must turn on more light, walk about the room; for there's an inner trembling of sensuality which can scarcely be borne. I must move about to quiet it, that slow-undulating abstract curve of voluptuousness: pure feeling without object, but no less torturous. The feeling grows constant and frustrating. It seems as though I could destroy myself in outgivingness, in loving the air, the solitude. Sensations. Fear of sleeping.

I bought tea today, and now after innumerable cups I stay awake working all night. The monks gave me lunch, but hunger punctures. There's no longer any need to go to the outhouse every day, for my stomach hasn't enough food to make the trip necessary.

Nerves reach a high point of tension at which laughter is almost uncontrollable and tears follow too easily. A Handel Concerto Grosso on the radio sets me walking about my table, singing, stamping my feet.

To keep energy at a point of focus, books must intercut my work. And in this agonizing emotional overflow I turn to the highly recommended Francis Jammes—and I should have known better: never read highly recommended books. In a poem about finding a "simple" wife, for example, he prays that she guard a gentle chastity in her heart so that when they are united they may smile but not speak.

Laughter swells from outrage. What an exciting, stimulating thing to have in bed! The obscenity of gentle things, the unspeakable obscenity of diluted bloods and higher smiles and good dull peoples! What degrading abuse of self does man manufacture!—civic leagues, honor societies, dinner speeches . . . carcasses. How much more appealing is Henry Miller's dream, in which they choose the most carnal moment to smoke cigarettes and discuss life. It's less gentle but it lasts longer, and under no circumstances does a cigarette taste so good, does talk about life flow so freely.

Cigarettes, and sudden rushes of desire to escape this; somehow to escape the paralytic thoughts of this evening; to escape Francis Jammes and Henry Miller and civic leagues and dinner speeches and honor societies and youth's uplifted eyes and thanks to the Saviour for their purities.

Thoughts of Christianne—thoughts drowned in turning up the radio to a full-volume playing by Bachaus of the Brahms D minor Concerto. Stupendous riding of man on piano. Lulling moments when man discusses the philosophy of Brahms. But my mind can't cool to the adagio. It dreams of walking through doors and outside in quest of Christianne and rutting and animal things. It dreams of the possibility of the impossible, of the young flesh of young breasts, of young girls young in night of cold and how warm they'd seem. But no, it can't be: I'm too well known, too conspicuous. The consideration isn't moral, only social.

The cleavage of night and day is complete, without betweens. In the day I love, in the night I lose myself in loving; and both are naked and clear, and magnificent in their strength.

21 january

I slept little last night; thoughts danced until dawn. Now at the Monastery I wait in Father Clément's cell, wait for Mass to begin. From the maze of our conversation comes my admission of the emotions which occupy me at night. Father Clément listens attentively, nodding for me to continue.

"The strange thing about it," I say slowly, "is that this desire seems almost—well, almost detached. It's sort of disembodied. I was wondering if maybe it couldn't be something important? If it couldn't be—?"

"Yes, go on," he urges.

"Well, if it couldn't be God's way of drawing me to Him?" I can't find the words with which to express myself.

Father Clément looks at me quizzically, half-frowning. The room echoes a monastic silence that seems never to be broken. "I do not know, my son," he says finally. "How can you arrive at such a conclusion as that? It does not look to me as if you were being drawn to God at all, but rather to something much more immediate in your mind—to sensuality. You must not let yourself become confused: nothing can be further from God than the feelings you describe to me. If you could love God with this same passion you would know it. You would want only to do His bidding. You would thrust such carnal thoughts away from you by force. And yet you embrace them, seeming to take health from them."

After a moment's hesitation I say, "Perhaps I don't make myself clear, Father—but for the first time since I've known you I think you misunderstand what I'm trying to tell you. Is it fair to disagree with your spiritual father?"

He smiles at me. "By all means. You disobey my orders, you do not rest properly, you are in a state of the most detestable sin, you do not study with any discipline—disagreeing with me should be the next logical step."

"I'm sorry, Father—I guess these feelings I have destroy discipline. They're diabolic, but I'm sure they're not the devil. There's something clean about them."

"Perhaps, my child," he says patiently. "But you may be deluding yourself. You present a most difficult case. What am I to do with you?"

"Tell me once more," I murmur contritely, "what you want me to do. I'll do it this time—I promise."

"You must try to live on a smaller scale until you learn more, until you can channel this passion into something a little less dangerous." The black-robed monk sighs wearily. "You are a problem. We have all been through what you are going through now, and we know you must have it out with yourself."

First bells sound for Mass. Father Clément stirs himself, and I rise to my feet.

"Now listen, my child," he says harshly, "you will—and this is an order to be obeyed—you will eat properly, you will sleep from midnight till eight in the morning, and most important of all, you will accept Madame Renée as a lesson in humility. I am sure I do not know what is between you, but I do know that you must destroy these feelings of distaste you have for her. You can help this poor unsympathetic woman. And one thing more—you will say a simple prayer every day. I do not care what it is, nor where you say it; but you will say it as a matter of discipline. And you will try to keep these physical outbursts at a minimum."

I nod my head and say nothing.

"I must admit, however," he goes on, "that I think you do very well for one so young." He pats my shoulder. "At least you are not giving these passions full sway. You told me once, weeks ago, that you could not resist temptation, that you had never once resisted temptation in your life. Do you feel stronger about that now? If the chance were offered do you think you could refuse?"

"No," I answer miserably, "I feel even weaker that way than before. It's very humiliating, but I don't think I could even begin to refuse . . . But you must get to your place in the chapel, Father. See you this afternoon—and I'll do exactly as you say."

As I find a pew in the chapel I think of how balanced his life is, how clear in every conception. How undisciplined and turgid seems my own by contrast! And a change in my feelings for Madame Renée, promised. My prayer, which will have little meaning, must be for her. For a moment I think of a young girl knocking on my door to test my strength. I force the image from my mind, closing my eyes against it.

Peculiar lightness after fevers, made lighter by hunger. Remarkable wellness-of-being. Love for this place and for Father Clément, who finds in me so much to distress him. But the comparison the monks make is with the ideal. This happiness must have a reason, a reason in something we can't understand; in something they can't understand until the tide turns.

I leap with surprise at the first brilliant organ tones above, ringing clear throughout the chapel: the Prelude in E flat of Bach. I forget everything, inundated to the edge of tears by the introspective tenderness of the opening measures. When I look up, black-robed monks are entering by twos, bowing deeply to the altar, going to their places for the beginning of Mass.

It's hard to pray. I pray resentfully for Madame Renée, forcing myself till that part of my prayer is ended and the Mass takes me with it, praying for me easily. And this time every cell of my being echoes the texts.

Time stops. Then for a moment I'm aware that from somewhere within me I am giving words volition, words that find voice in the mouths of these monks. But they come from me: *"Sanctus, Sanctus, Sanctus . . ."* And later, with how much more affection, how much more warmth, the words to the Blessed Virgin from the dregs of this same inner darkness—the light of one phrase: *"Dei Genitrix, intercede pro nobis."* And with this melody, fearfully written by some poor one better than I, in the anguish of

362

his love—humble notes on paper pleading from the soul's profoundest recesses—the Virgin Mary becomes startling reality for the time of a breath. We suddenly feel it all about, this warmth, this permeating presence. She has this instant heard something spoken to her centuries ago. Voices chanting tendernesses repeat, *"Dei Genitrix, intercede pro nobis."* And somehow, by some inner chemistry, by some brief changing of matter into the nothingness of delight, physiologically, imperceptibly, inexplicably, this phrase has been touched. The caress offered to closed eyelids of concentration has been touched by something ethereal. In the intense darkness of prayer I seek her whose name is on my lips, and . . . we become slowly united.

No longer a man and the Mother of God, but a revolving bodiless emotion. Deeply, more deeply into the liquidness of her, into the void of swirling sensation. Slowly like the waves of a warm ocean, inexorable, undulating out of space and time. Blackness and silence in the roaring of two become one. Angles, brilliant behind eyes that swim in detached body, floating in space. Richness and warmth and coolness of the wet on one's lips. Lips against the pew feeling wood pores. And smoothness of stained polished wood. Squares mist milkily, and from the stillness and the dark the curve mounts immutably rhythmic, in ever-mounting intensity. A new gathering of momentum. And through the darkness an occasional glimpse of concentrated white. Now it begins to grow, this strangeness, turning over and over. Slowly, slowly, turning steadily, and the rhythm follows ever growing. And now from the very bottom of a faraway numbness is the quivering beginning of trembling. It's unbearable. The numbness is punctured. Momentum gathers. And the long sigh, unheard, pouring forth from the edges of consummation. From a distance, far within, curving swiftly now, a fast sighing swaying motion curling over and above and around. Beating, beating against the drum of the being, pounding louder and louder till there can be no more loudness, but increasing steadily into the very pulse of the blood. And now before the eyes, the before-hinted, now-brilliant

363

flashing white, growing and expanding to break spattering against eyelids. And from without, a fog of ever-thickening intensity, sparkling and harsh to imagined sight. Simultaneous welling-up of the heaving exploding brilliance, and the beating, now-pounding rhythm piling sound and muffled obscenity, ever expanding above and around, turning faster and faster above the moaned "No! No!" Tightening of the heartbeat, drawing-up of the ribbon. Ecstatic point between life and death when all becomes hermetic and rigid. The pause in space without pausing in movement. The waiting without breathing. The muffled upward surge of the entire being to the crest of the wave, to the very top. Up and up, soaring high onto the peak of noise and heat. The whirling gyrating splash of warning to the mind. Louder now into the head and the brain. Upheaved violence of the belly. This is the flashing of the stars, the cleansing burning of the insides into fervent ash. And the taste of blood grows stronger on the rigid tongue. Finally the broad expansiveness of union, of man's warmness without pain. Sounds descend thinner, slower, draining away to sighing quiet. And the felt pulse of the rhythm faints away to enveloping blackness. The slow easy downhill slide with a final unheard catching of the breath, leading onward and downward until the curve slows to stop against the dark. And down, down again slantingly, quietly to a depth beneath the seas. Beyond movement to stillness—

Startled. Startled into a hard convulsive contraction of muscles. A hand on my shoulder and a raucous imperious voice: "Well, Monsieur, are you sufficiently frozen?"

Trembling, without rising, I mutter, "Yes, Madame."

It's Madame Marceaux, great, sacred lady oblate. She talks loudly for a moment then leaves me still kneeling, miserable and bewildered. She hasn't felt what the rest of us have felt. Disappointment is on the faces of those about me. All of us sense that she's had the greatest possible presumption, that in reality she has, with her hideous loud voice and merciless calling-to-mind of the cold, chased the intangible whisper away from us. Now there's nothing to

364

do but leave. There's no longer any reason to stay, for the place is suddenly bare and we realize that we are in truth sufficiently frozen.

Standing in the door of the gatehouse, Father Dutfoy sees us walk out. He motions me to him, smiling questioningly. I explain what has happened. My hands tremble as I light a cigarette, and I feel sick.

His red face becomes serious, clouded. "It is a disgusting shame, my son. To be visited by a sensitive grace may occur only once in a lifetime, and to have it interrupted in such a vicious manner—it is a great shock to you, is it not?"

"Yes, it is. I don't know what happened exactly, Father," I tell him hesitantly, "but I feel—"

"I know," he nods, eyeing me almost pityingly. "It is indeed a shock. Come, we will go back into the chapel and you must stay there till it has returned you to peace. That is the only way to undo the harm."

He enters first, dipping his fingers in holy water and touching my outstretched fingers with his. We kneel side by side for a long time. He prays silently. I say and think nothing. A hand touches my shoulder lightly, this time with no shock and no voice, and passes on down the aisle. It's Father G'seau, who kneels to the front, coughs, takes out his beads and begins his prayers. Father Dutfoy leaves without speaking, without looking at me. The chapel is dark now, heavily shadowed and obscure before noon, and I know that snow must again be falling outside. I kneel here watching the flickering altar lamp until the silence, the emptiness of spaces replace trembling with calm. And when I leave it's because the bells call us to lunch. I'm sorry to leave, finding it difficult to rise to my feet, to force myself away from this magical quiet. The breath, cooling in the dark air of the chapel, remains—the breath of the Virgin Mary. I'm no longer alone, and the chapel isn't empty.

In the refectory a burdening exhaustion possesses me. Now I want only sleep—but many hours remain before sleep may be had. Lessons all afternoon. Eyes set in the head, fighting sleep.

At last, rapturously chanted Vespers—and soon there'll be rest. It remains, the spell. Past insomnias dissolve, become hushed. Pressures are removed. Only sleep—only the magic of sleep after such feelings, after such profound breathings.

Snow continues to fall heavily as I trudge toward home in the near-darkness of late afternoon. But my hunger hasn't been assuaged; I must eat something before sleep will come.

I stop at the store, hoping the proprietress will sell me an egg or anything else I can eat. She looks at me sharply. "But, M'sieu, aren't you taking your meals with Madame Renée any longer?"

"Yes, of course, but she's in Paris."

"Oh, then you don't know—she's come back. She's already been here for provisions."

Father Clément's order: "You will accept Madame Renée as a lesson in humility . . . You can help this poor unsympathetic woman." But his words aren't needed: other things, inexplicable things that happened in the chapel, have destroyed their need. I walk home quickly, happy that she's back.

The house is empty, immaculate; and there's a fire and the touch of Madame Renée's hand. She comes from the kitchen, her eyes glistening with the joy of seeing me again, and my heart responds.

"And how was your trip?" I say warmly. "I'm so glad you're back."

She shakes my hand, her face flushed with pleasure; then she becomes serious. "It was awfully sad, Monsieur. My poor Michel's lost—but he's my son and I'll have to help him make the best of it. We bought him some clothes and he has hopes of a job." She looks away, shaking her head in discouragement, faintly shrugging her shoulders. "But let's not talk about it now."

"All right," I agree pleasantly. "But don't let it worry you. It's not so—"

"You don't know," she breaks in sharply, "how deep it goes, Monsieur. It's more serious than you imagine. I

366

can't think of it now, I don't dare let myself think of all it can mean . . . But that's enough about Michel. Just don't mention him again, will you? Please?"

There's an awkward pause; but after a moment her beautiful smile returns.

"Well anyway, it's good to be back," she remarks. "I understand you haven't been eating so well—and I can see by the house that Germaine's been inexcusably sloppy in her work. Just let me leave and things go to pieces. The Countess would be horrified if she could see the dust under this bed. And the outhouse—it hasn't been touched since I left. Where'd you get the toilet paper, by the way?" She looks at me sweetly.

Disgusts puff and swell inside me, but I hold my tongue.

"You're really getting clever," she adds—"toilet paper's hard to find here. But you should have asked me, I could have let you have some."

Her incessant return to the functions! She will know me, even my most intimate me, and I can do nothing to keep myself from her: she's been through all my things.

"And look at these books and papers. I tell you, these girls don't know the first thing about housekeeping."

My nerves begin to organize defenses against her renewed encroachments. "I asked Germaine, Madame," I say quietly —"in fact I ordered her—not to touch my worktable, and I hope you'll respect my orders to her. She's answerable only to me, if you don't mind."

Her eyes set, the smile vanishes—vanishes wonderfully fast. "Are you going to start that again? Really, I thought you got it out of your system the night before I left. I haven't forgotten that little scene. This is all very well, but if the Countess returns to find her villa a shambles it's I who'll be blamed. But you're the *master* here. I'll return to my position as just another of your domestics. Like me to prepare your dinner now, *master?*"

I chuckle. "Yes, *mistress*, please do."

"That," she snaps, "isn't amusing, Monsieur."

I grin. "You can send the darts, can't you? But you can't

367

take them in return. I was merely answering in kind. I—"

"There's a little difference. You're a young man, I'm an older woman: I deserve at least a minimum of respect. You're more than a little impolite, you know." She glares at me.

"Sorry," I say, lowering my voice. "But let's settle this thing sensibly here and now, like two intelligent people. I've been happy here alone this week; I'm just as happy alone as I would be with you. As for respect, I respect the person and not his age. And as for our argument the other night, I'm truly sorry for it. I've decided to try to change. My intentions were all good when I heard you'd returned, for I can't see why our relationship shouldn't be pleasant. Now, don't be so suspicious—nothing's going to happen to this precious house. I've instructed Germaine to follow only my orders. If you stay out of things here and tend to your own business, we'll get along."

Her face softens; she hesitates, forcing herself. "Very well, Monsieur—if that's the way you want it I'll make the effort too. We'll forget the past and start over again. You need food, I can see that. I know it hasn't been too pleasant for you." She looks at the floor. "I hope you'll understand—this is a trying time for me."

"Of course," I sigh deeply. "We just got off to a bad start. I'm sure we'll both feel much better about it now."

At table in her newly warmed salon we eat and talk easily. I enjoy my dinner, and afterward the *crêpes* and coffee.

"This coffee tastes wonderful, Madame Renée."

"Doesn't it? There's a secret to making good coffee, Monsieur. You'll find that no one else can make it better than I." She refills my cup. "Now tell me all the news of the Village. Have you seen my friend Mademoiselle Marthe? And how is she?"

"Fine, I think—but like everybody else she can't get the proper food."

"Poor thing, I must have her to dinner again soon. At least she can eat her fill here. Would you like that?" She asks this very pointedly, wearing a disarmingly sweet smile.

"Yes, I would, she's a fine woman." I turn my chair to the fire. "But tell me, you're really amazing, you know—how do you do it? While you were gone I couldn't buy anything to eat, and no one else in the Village does more than survive. Yet you always have butter and eggs and plenty of meat, apparently. How on earth do you manage it? What's your secret?"

She laughs and shakes her head, looking at her plate. "Aha, my friend, you found it difficult without me, eh? Well I'll tell you, it takes a head on your shoulders. The truth of the matter is, I've done more than one favor for the local farmers and they're very kind. They pass me enough food to live on and don't charge me exorbitant prices. I go after what I want and I treat them right. They'd do anything for me." She looks up and smiles kindly. "It's simple as that."

"Oh." I can't bring myself to say anything more.

"Not to change the subject," she goes on, "but are your vermin-ridden house guests still surviving the winter with your help?" Her voice remains pleasant, without rancor.

"Think so. Father Sauvac says they are. I seldom see them myself."

"Father Sauvac must feel very Christian about his exploitation of you—Oh, but excuse me, that's one of the things you don't like, isn't it? I'm not to say ugly things about others."

I lean back in my chair. "Precisely, Madame. You've caught on beautifully."

She remarks, "Do you know I wouldn't tolerate such behavior from anyone else? But there's a frankness about you I like; it's refreshing. Actually you were right about letting them use your house. I can see that now, and I'm truly ashamed of my opposition to the idea. I was only thinking of the fact it would be an imposition on you."

"Yes?" I say noncommittally. "Well, there's one other bit of news you should be happy to hear—Madame Vincent's been driven away."

369

She stares at me with an almost genuine expression of concern on her face. "Oh, but I'm not happy at all, I'm very sorry, believe me. I know how fond you are of her, and I've grown to think of her rather sympathetically myself. I can understand such a woman, Monsieur. I can understand how she might fall with a man like you."

"Well, she's gone now," I say wearily, anxious to change the subject, to escape. "Guess I'd better get back to my room. I have some work to do and I promised Father Clément I'd be in bed early."

"Before you go," she says quickly, "I did want to talk to you a little about Michel."

I settle back in my chair. "Certainly, Madame."

"I'm profoundly disappointed in my son," she begins, "and it's not good for a mother to feel disappointment. I suppose I should understand, but I don't. It's a shock, Monsieur, when a mother discovers that her son is a weakling." Carrying her coffee cup she moves to the couch. Her gray hair is freshly brushed, and her eyes are clear. She is beautiful in the half-light of a single lamp.

"You're too hard on him, Madame," I tell her placatingly. "Judging by the letter his Father Abbot wrote, the fault isn't entirely Michel's. You'll just have to believe the whole thing's an act of Providence, and be thankful he left the monastery before he took his priestly orders."

"He'd never have left if he hadn't been so weak."

"No, he merely decided such things as parenthood, sexual love, and so on—all the things that go with normal manhood—were too attractive. He couldn't reconcile himself to a celibate life any longer. Too bad he waited so long to find it out, but there's nothing bad or even weak about it."

"But why after all these years should he find it out? Other monks have the same desires and they lay them at the feet of God. No, he's a weakling, a weakling. He's brought me the sneers of the entire community—for they'll know soon enough. And worst of all, he's no longer mine."

"Why, he's more yours now than he was before; before,

he was completely subservient to his superiors—he was a child of God."

"I know," in a voice of regret. "But he poured out all his earthly love on me. You should see the letters he wrote, filled with tenderness for his mother. He kept nothing from me. But now he'll have no time for that—he'll have other interests. He's beginning to change already. I know what will happen," she adds, nodding significantly.

"Well," I say awkwardly, "I'm sure Michel will turn out better than you think. It's really too soon to know. If I were you I wouldn't think too much about it till we see how he fits into civilian life."

"I do have that power, Monsieur," she tells me in a voice of determination. "When Jean-Julien was killed I simply didn't allow myself to think about it. I realize now I must do the same with Michel. It's too much for me, coming so suddenly. I don't know what to think."

"Let's let this thing work itself out. Michel may not be happy in this life at all, you can't tell. And you know I'll do whatever I can to help you." I rise from my chair.

"You're right, Monsieur. I'm really more disappointed than I am angry. And now you must get to your work. I'll be better tomorrow, you'll see," she says bravely, stirring from the couch to accompany me to the door. "I'm tired from the trip but it's good to be back. Good night."

I walk slowly from her house through the deep snow. When I open my door I've already forgotten her and her troubles. The excitement of the week has left me stupid with fatigue. This morning returns, chanting softly to deep calmnesses. I'm no longer alone, I'm no longer alone. The remembrance of morning in the chapel fills me tonight: I feel that I'll never be really alone again.

I fall into bed, and it's as though I could sleep forever.

371

27 january

Six days have passed, and imperceptible changes become perceptible. With time, insinuations of changes become changes.

And it's the same with the days. The betweens have returned. Days are divided into three parts once again. The first and last parts remain the same, alternating between the Monastery during the day and my salon at night. The between is the time I spend with Madame Renée.

Six days, and she does everything possible to thrust Michel from her life. We always eat lunch and dinner quietly, avoiding dangerous subjects—but each day they return, they invariably return. She seems to crave their return, to draw some inverted nourishment from her pain.

Today, sitting down to lunch, she asks, "Have a good morning at the Monastery?"

"Yes," I answer carefully, looking beyond her out the icicle-framed window, looking beyond her to the cold white of a snowy outside. "I'm at last beginning to catch up with my lessons."

"Tell me, do you think the monks know anything about Michel?"

"Probably, since he was at a sister house—but they haven't said anything to me about it. Why don't you quit hiding it, anyway? There's no reason to be ashamed of your son. After all it'll have to be known one day, and seems to me the sooner the better. When Michel comes to see you everyone will know—and they'll probably surmise something worse than the truth."

Reaching across the table, she takes my hand and stares at me pleadingly. "Michel *can't* come to see me," she whispers. "I'm so ashamed of him I'll never allow him to return here." She shakes her head violently and I know she's seeking an argument.

"It's your affair, Madame, though I can't understand

372

what makes you persist in this—this blind martyrdom."

"You're cross with me, aren't you?" she whines, squeezing my hand. "A little? Just a little cross with me?"

"No, not at all. But it hurts me to see you like this. You exaggerate out of all proportion."

"You can't understand me, that's all. How could you? —you're only a young man. But I realize these last few days haven't been very pleasant for you, so I have a surprise for you: I've invited a charming young lady from the City— an old friend of the family's—here for dinner tonight. We might also have Mademoiselle Marthe if you like. We'll celebrate—you can dress up and I'll fix a wonderful dinner. How does that sound?"

"Fine!" I exclaim, with genuine enthusiasm. "It'll be nice to have company—and it'll do you good to occupy yourself with something besides your own troubles."

Still holding my hand she leans forward. "You know the only reason I tell you my troubles," she says sincerely, "is because of my great affection for you, don't you?"

"Yes, yes, I realize that."

"Then why aren't you a little more responsive?"

"I just don't have a very responsive nature, Madame— I've told you that before. I see no reason to advertise my feelings to anyone."

She releases my hand and leans back, smiling offendedly. "Let's change the subject. About this girl: be careful of her, she needs a husband badly. It's almost pathological with her. When I invited her she asked me all sorts of questions about you, so be on your guard."

"Ah, this may be interesting."

"No, no, now, no foolishness, or I'll tell her not to come."

"Don't worry, Madame Renée—I was only joking."

The day drags slowly by in anticipation of the evening. After Vespers I dress carefully, looking forward to a change from the usual lugubrious conversation.

When I arrive they are already there, Mademoiselle Marthe and the girl—and a flustered Madame Renée. The girl's name is Marguerite Désormière, and I smile at the sight of her. She is beautiful in a large way, with gray eyes and a mouth that smiles unmistakable insinuations. Forgetting the old ladies we look at each other, speaking wordless desires with our smiles, completely blatant on another plane, knowing that our spiritual flirting can't consummate itself. She wears a perfume so obvious it almost makes me laugh aloud. Immediately we call each other by our first names, and we savor Madame Renée's flushed discomfort. Mademoiselle Marthe looks on disapproving but amused.

When we sit down at the table Madame Renée is hawklike; she realizes her error and knows she can't correct it. Pleading stares, angry stares, hostile stares. We ignore her. Strained gaiety thinly disguises the unspoken reproach of the two older women. Madame Renée rides the crest of high conversation, using the right words, laughing at the right times. She interrupts everything we say. She plays the fool, the authority on all subjects, the bluff—and the rest of us try to hide our embarrassment. Finally, to carry the conversation to safe ground, I mention Claudel. Marguerite's eyes brighten.

"My favorite poet," she remarks.

"Claudel? Pooh!" snorts Madame Renée. "Let me tell you something about Claudel. First he writes an apostrophe to Pétain, and later he writes another praising De Gaulle. Nobody can admire the one without hating the other. Is that a man who knows his own mind? Why, no, use your heads; he writes to curry favor."

"You miss the point, Madame," I put in. "We're discussing his work, not his character. And I for one am able to admire both Pétain and De Gaulle."

She dismisses me as if I were a child who shouldn't have spoken. "You're an American—how can you judge a Frenchman's feelings? I lost a son in this war. You learn something when that happens to you."

"Then, Madame Renée," interjects Marguerite, smiling, "you don't like Claudel?"

Madame Renée glares at the girl. "No, of course not. He's not in what I like to call the 'Great Tradition.'"

Mademoiselle Marthe, eating a chicken leg, mutters disgustedly, "What about his religious poems? The *Jeanne d'Arc*, for example?"

"Maudlin, absolutely maudlin." I choke as she adds, "It's written in such a little style." She rides on, gay and charming, kind to her more ignorant companions. How proud she must think I am of her! Her self-conviction exhausts us, but there's a grudging admiration for her nerve. Christianne cringingly serves the meal under the constant rebuke of her mistress.

"Here, now," she says to me after a while, "you haven't eaten nearly enough." And to the others, "He loves his meat with the wine sauce. No, Christianne, put a little sauce on his potatoes too—he loves lots of sauce on his potatoes."

I'm tempted to reach back and pinch Christianne on the leg.

"Oh, I have a time with him," Madame Renée goes on. "He gives me a little talk once in a while, but we get along, don't we?" She glances at me possessively, with the utmost tenderness, her head tilted to one side.

I swallow my humiliation and look pleadingly at Marguerite. Amused at my redness, she directs an imperceptible twitch of distaste at Madame Renée.

"I really tease him a bit too much, though," our hostess says. "Is the coffee ready, Christianne? Well, stupid girl, don't just stand there—give him some coffee with his dessert. That's the way he likes it, that's the way they do it in America. I'm learning about American ways, I can tell you. About the teasing, though—it's one thing he can't always take. Just like my Jean-Julien. Marguerite, you knew Jean-Julien. Aren't the two alike?"

I roll my eyes heavenward. Mademoiselle Marthe glares at Madame Renée, who devours me with her open smile. Marguerite looks at me over Madame Renée's turned shoulder, laughing to cover her obvious disgust. "Yes, very much alike," she answers.

"Well, we understand each other and that's all that matters. Take last night, for example. He did something I'm sure he isn't very proud of today. I promised not to tell; but I was with him afterward and I thought to myself, this might be my own Jean-Julien."

"While you're about it," I suggest, "tell them what I did." I turn to Mademoiselle Marthe and the girl. "Drank too much wine and got silly—as a matter of fact I got drunk. Is that so shameful?"

"Depends on why you got drunk, it seems to me," Mademoiselle Marthe puts in drily. "I once got drunk on pure Seltzer water."

Madame Renée shoots her an ugly glance, and she suddenly drops her pretense like a cloak. Anger destroys her manners. She bluntly suggests that it's not too late for Marguerite to take the train back to the City.

The girl looks amused. "But I hate to leave such excellent company, Madame," she protests casually. "I seldom find someone like yourself who can discuss the arts with such authority. Then too, I understood I was to spend the night."

"You wouldn't be comfortable here, Mademoiselle. You can come for dinner again sometime. Our young friend here seems to find life entirely too barren with only us older ladies about."

Marguerite looks at me, her eyes large, and asks innocently, "Is that so, Monsieur? I'm being invited to leave, so you can tell me. Do you find life here barren?"

"Like a desolate plain, dear Mademoiselle," I reply elaborately. "Come, I will accompany you to the station."

"But she can find the way by herself," Madame Renée says irascibly. "She's made the trip alone many times, haven't you, Mademoiselle?"

"Many times, Madame, and always alone."

Laughing, I put on my hat and coat. "In my country, Madame Renée, the gentleman accompanies the lady to the station."

"But you have your work to do," she insists. "I'll take

Mademoiselle Marguerite if she needs company. Or we can all go together, the four of us. I spoke hastily, Marguerite—why don't you spend the night after all?"

Marguerite walks with me to the door. "Impossible, Madame Renée," she says impertinently. "I'll send your adopted son back unharmed as soon as the train leaves."

We quickly step outside before the astounded Madame Renée can collect her wits. We walk arm in arm, and the bridge looms before us against the snow before either of us speaks.

"Poor Monsieur," then laughs Marguerite. "We were shameful, weren't we?"

"Serves the old bat right. She doesn't own me."

"I've known her a long time. You see, this isn't the first time she's asked me to leave. She's a horrible, suspicious woman. I was a young girl studying art in her husband's studio and she got the insane idea there was something between us. Why, he was over seventy years old at the time."

We walk across the bridge. The night is cold and I suggest that we stop at Salesky's and have him drive us to the station. "But don't be surprised at any remarks he might make," I warn her.

The taxi driver answers the bell, wiping his dinner from his mouth with a large towel. He glances at Marguerite and breathes more heavily. "Ooh la la, my friend," he says grinning—and I wink at Marguerite.

"Can you drive us to the station, Salesky? We're in a hurry."

"Sure, get in the car. Be right with you."

We sit alone in the car, very close, and our hands find themselves. There's little time. Placing her hand in my lap I lean against her, and murmur in her ear, "I need you, Marguerite. Won't you help me?"

She doesn't move her hand away. "But we have no time, no place."

"Here and now—I know you want it."

"I'm really a low woman at heart."

"Good! And we'll dedicate it to Madame Renée. May she inspire us to heights!"

Marguerite giggles as fondlings become excitement and spite.

"So," I whisper, "you think I'm just like her Jean-Julien, eh? I'll fix you for that, my precious."

Salesky opens the front door noisily. We sit upright in the back seat, laughing.

"My friend," I tell him gaily, "drive around slowly for half an hour, will you?—and don't look back."

"Aha, M'sieu, as you say." The lecherous smirk on his face shines in the dark.

Wheels crunch slowly through the ice-crusted snow. Salesky whistles to himself. Headlights reflect upward from the rough white ground, upward into the frosty air of night. Lights from the Village fade as we drive into the country and other things more immediate occupy my consciousness: things immediate and warm—for Marguerite is crazed with the need—yet somehow detached. Inner clutchings and desires suddenly become superficial enjoyment of the moment. She bares her breasts. We each become sensations, but my mind can't descend the long curve; it stays in the head. It patiently notices the feel of leather-and-felt upholstery, it hears the tune Salesky whistles softly to himself, it waits half-laughing—and it's pleasant waiting. It's detached. It sees snow from the corner of its eye and feels her hair beneath its cheek and breathes her breath—but it's not there. It waits, calm in frenzy, almost derisive with the growing of pleasure. It thinks of Madame Renée and grows derisive. It thinks of other waiting faces, dumb faces of people standing in line at the bread shop, each waiting his turn to exchange ration tickets for bread. It's that kind of waiting, waiting on floatings and coarse facial pores and liquidness beneath the mouth. Warmth without heat, heat without burning. Calculated waiting in line with a dumb face and an occasional sigh and a cringing from frenzy. The brain refuses to leave the head. Hands draw the bundle closer beneath and, instead of the flesh, feel the roughness of car

378

seat against wrists. Time passes with thought suspended as we take one step, and then another, nearer the end of the line. And there's finally the ultimate in warmth of breathing against cheek, in sounds of lips and wetness on face, and it's a moment not of concentration but of many things. It's the dumb face's turn now, the exchange of its ration tickets. Leather upholstery squeaking and shoes scraping against the rubber floor-mat and Salesky whistling louder for a moment above the rasping rattles of passion. The pressure of drawing closer than close as a reflex, and the waiting to leave. We settle quietly till the gesture of straightening wrinkled clothing gives me permission to go, to move away with a final pat of basic politeness. The arranging of things. The brain settling comfortably and looking out the window, and the one helping the other with hands pulling on clothes and fastening buttons and absent-mindedly dusting wrinkles. The wheels of the car in the snow, and darkness beyond the clear cone of strong headlights. Salesky coughs. I cough in answer and he turns to stare.

"All right, M'sieu?" His voice is saccharine with mocking respect.

"Yes. Take us to the station now."

I move to the far side of the seat and we ride to Town in silence, Marguerite's head resting heavily on my shoulder. At the station I give her a peremptory kiss, but make no offer to get out and wait with her till train time. Without speaking she leaves the car, and I know she's too angry to be hurt.

"We can go back to the Village now," I say to Salesky.

He roars with laughter. "Ah, you treat 'em mean, my friend. Why didn't you go with her?"

"I've got a bellyful of her already," I tell him flatly.

"Wish I had a bellyful of that one myself. Was it good?"

"She's positively fiendish, Salesky."

He hums, "Think I'll just tell Madame Renée about this."

I hum a tune in answer: "You do, you do, and I'll know a few things to run you out of France."

"Ah, but it'd be pretty to watch, eh, M'sieu? What she needs is some of the same thing you gave that girl. Why don't you help her out? She wants it plain enough."

"Don't be a damn' fool. I'd rather take a vow of perpetual chastity than sleep with that."

He stops the cab at my house, charging me too much for the ride. But there's no time to argue. I hastily turn on the light in the hall and check myself in the mirror. Then I walk to Madame Renée's, wondering if she will know, not caring if she does.

The room has been cleared, and Mademoiselle Marthe is gone. Madame Renée is seated by the fire reading the Bible. My entrance brings forth neither a glance nor a word. Her face is granite—expressionless and old and sullen. A rush of pity fills me as I sit down next to her. But she ignores me, reading, turning the pages, reading again.

I ask quietly, "Getting your quota of spiritual uplift for the day?"

"Don't try to be amusing, Monsieur," she says without looking up. "Unless you have some explanation for your conduct, you may go."

"But I haven't done anything," I answer in a hurt tone (I have learned things from her). "What do you expect? You bring a beautiful woman in here, she upsets me terribly, and you blame me."

"You find her beautiful?" Apology creeps into her voice as she finally looks at me.

"Yes, in a way. And of course I don't see many girls here. Makes it sort of hard to take."

"But believe me, Monsieur, I had no idea how abominably she'd act."

"Oh, well . . ." I smile forgivingly, shrugging my shoulders.

"I guess I should have known—yes, of course I should." Her eyes begin to fill with sympathy. "It's not your fault.

380

I saw how she led you on, and after all you're not made of steel."

"It doesn't matter."

"But it does. I shall write her mother about this immediately. And you must forgive me, Monsieur. I know how hard you try and how wonderfully you succeed in living a chaste life here. It's my fault this temptress bothered you. I've done you a terrible wrong."

I shake my head. "Forget it, Madame."

She looks more closely at me. "You're trembling! Let me get you a cup of coffee. Tell me, did Marguerite say anything about me on the way to the station? Or did she make any advances?"

"No, I took her in the taxi," I say innocently, "so we weren't together more than a few moments."

"Then why are you trembling so?"

"I got a little chilled, I guess—a draft on my back."

"Here, stand up, let me see. Why, your shirt tail isn't tucked in properly."

Mustering a nonchalant air, I raise my coat and tuck it in. Madame Renée gazes at me.

"Is the trembling only from chill?" she asks.

I act the callow youth, muttering embarrassedly, "I think so. Perhaps it was her perfume, too, and the fact she sat so close to me in the cab."

Madame Renée's eyes open wide with concern. "Why, that horrible creature. Here, drink this coffee, it'll make you feel better. You poor thing. Now I see you as I thought you were—as a little boy."

I raise the cup to my lips, swallowing the hot liquid to hide my face.

"Do you know if you'd given her the slightest encouragement," my companion goes on, "she'd have been willing to . . . to . . . Well, you know what I mean. And I think she planned the whole thing. I think she planned to try to get you to make love to her, in hopes that if a child came she could force you to marry her. Well, you've had a narrow escape, I can promise you. And I assure you she'll

381

never set foot in my house again. A girl like that just—"

"But don't write her family about it, will you?" I put in. "It could be that I was just imagining things. It might be all my fault, and think how much it would hurt her mother. We may be wrong in suspecting her."

"Wrong in suspecting her? Why, I saw the way she looked at you. She's a tigress, I tell you. The desires stand out on her face. Don't you think so? Don't you think animal sensuality shows in her face? How you could find her beautiful, or even attractive, is beyond me. You don't know much about women like that. Think of it! What if she'd succeeded in her designs? Then you might have been forced to marry her. Incidentally, did you make any plans to see her in the City, or in Paris?"

"No, of course not. And anyway I wouldn't have married her, even if an accident had happened."

"Oh yes, you'd have had to," states Madame Renée dogmatically. "In our country it's a question of honor to make the woman who bears your children honest. I'd have been obliged to see to it that you married her. In any case it didn't happen, and I must forbid you ever to see her again."

"Now just a moment—please." I put down my coffee cup. "I've no intention of seeing her again, but when you start forbidding me to do anything you can be certain I'll do it. You don't run my life."

"I *forbid* you, do you hear?" she says emphatically. "If you should ever see her again and anything happened, and you refused to marry her, then the blame would rest on my shoulders. Unfortunately I'm responsible for bringing you two together, and anything that results from it is as much my affair as it is yours."

"Keep talking like that, Madame, and I go after her."

She becomes frantic, violent, ugly. "You *have* made plans to see her again, haven't you? Very well, Monsieur, I wash my hands of you. It seems I receive nothing but disappointment and pain from those I love."

"I've made *no* plans to see her again," I answer resent-

382

fully. "I tell you that, and you can believe it or not as you please. As for this great love you profess to have for me, you say I'm like another son but you act as though you'd like to make me another slave. I don't know what to make of you."

"Humph!"—staring, flushed with resentment.

"Look at this thing simply," I explain. "What has happened? Nothing, absolutely nothing. I admit this girl might have tempted me, but if I could resist her once I could certainly do it again. I'm not the weakling you seem to think I am. She flirted with me a little and I probably flirted more than my share with her. That's all. She's gone and I'll most likely never see her again. Now, is that any reason for all this emotion?"

"You say you 'most likely' won't see her again. What does that mean? I think too much of you to see you break my heart like Michel has. I'd rather we had nothing else to do with each other unless you're willing to promise me you'll never be with her again. And whether you like it or not, I'll certainly write her mother about this."

"I won't promise anything. She's a woman of thirty and I'm a grown man. What's her mother got to do with it? Now if you really feel about me as you say you do, forget the whole business."

"You're excited, my child," her voice softening, becoming gently sarcastic. "We'll forget it for the moment. You've been through a harrowing experience for one so young, and you've resisted this terrible woman. Your nerves are naturally on edge. Come, let me pour you another cup of coffee. And I'll spoil you—I'll give you two lumps of sugar." She carefully drops the white cubes of sugar into the cup. "She really didn't touch you, did she?" she adds, as though it were an afterthought.

"No, of course not, I'd never allow that." I smile inwardly at the fascination the subject holds for her. "I'm as pure now as I've always been."

Madame Renée stirs my coffee. She laughs and purses her lips, looking at me with amused eyes. She is gay and

383

destructive now. "Marguerite really is fantastic, don't you think? Now please, don't get miffed; let's discuss this thing calmly. Do you know I had to ask her to leave my house once before, several years ago? She was much too friendly with my husband. I could never be sure, of course, but after tonight there's no doubt left in my mind: something went on between them."

"Surely you don't mean to say such things? Your husband's gone now. At least don't accuse him of something he probably never even thought of doing."

"Ha! You men really protect one another, don't you? You can be sure he thought of it, whether or not he ever did it." Remembering, she becomes pensive, forgiving. "Poor thing—if he did do it, it was probably Father Sauvac's fault. My husband detested Father Sauvac." She stirs the fire, making me move back while she adds wood to the stove.

"What's the matter with Father Sauvac?" I ask, placing my empty cup on the table. "I'd think he'd be the type to get along with your husband."

"It's very hard to say, Monsieur, but certainly there's an undercurrent of resentment against him in the Village." She becomes intelligent and assumes the look of the intelligent. "He's very hard—devoted to his flock—but hard and uncompromising. Let me tell you an example. As you know, my Julien was much older than I. He had a son my age by his first marriage. But he was a very passionate man. He died when he was seventy-two, and do you know that up till the time of his death he retained full sexual powers?"

"And you put his son in a monastery!"

She laughs. "Well, he always said he was probably that way because he married a woman so much younger than himself. At any rate, we couldn't be married in the Church until after Julien's first wife's death, which was when Michel was twelve years old. When the ceremony did take place, I naturally confessed and was given the sacraments. It was then I fell under the care of Father Sauvac. He spent a long time trying to build up in me a

384

sense of remorse for past sins. According to him, of course, I had been living in sin with my husband for nearly fifteen years. He succeeded, and I tried to be a good Catholic, I tried very hard. But my husband began to be jealous of the Church. It ruined the Church for him, Monsieur; he didn't understand. You see, he was in his late fifties and we'd decided we could no longer have healthy children. When Father Sauvac questioned me about this, I told him my husband was getting too old to give me children; and Father Sauvac said if there were to be no more children there should be marital chastity. I refused at first, for I had always been able to completely satisfy the needs of my Julien. But Father Sauvac finally persuaded me not to respond to his advances any longer."

I try to keep the disgust from showing on my face, making a pretense of poking the fire; but I say nothing.

"You see," she says after I have replaced the poker, "we hoped to bring Julien to a state of physical purity despite himself. I couldn't refuse his attentions outright, of course. I had to submit to them, but Father Sauvac convinced me I should remain cold to my husband's advances, that I should take no part in satisfying him. We had a terrible time, a most unhappy time, for Julien couldn't understand it at all. He couldn't bear to listen to my reasons for doing it. It drove him into a fury. He felt I no longer loved him, and he detested the Church and Father Sauvac. He said they'd taken me from him—that perhaps I was a good Catholic but that I was certainly a poor wife. I felt sorry for him. I could easily have gone back to my old ways, for I was by nature a warm and loving woman." She pauses. "Now let me see . . . Yes, it was about that time that Marguerite must have started her indiscretions with him." She says this pensively, almost amused.

I stare at her. "I find all this hard to believe," I remark. "I never heard of such a thing. I can't believe Father Sauvac would tell you to be cold to your husband. That's worse than the Inquisition."

"But he did, Monsieur. I know it seems cruel to you,

but I was convinced the act would be sinful unless there was the possibility of children. And I tried (I didn't suffer much except for Julien's anger), I tried for two years to make him confess, to persuade him into keeping a chaste marriage. But I saw it was breaking up my home."

"Your husband should have got himself a mistress. I would have. This is the most heartless thing I ever heard of."

"I know. He aged quickly and our life was pathetic, really. He did everything imaginable to arouse some spark of response in me, and I lay there praying for guidance. It was during the last year of his life that I felt I must change. And despite Father Sauvac's constant reproach I made my husband happy during those last months. I sacrificed much to do it, but he died in peace." A wistful look comes into her eyes. "He would look at me and say, 'My love has finally come home.'" She purses her lips into a reflective smile. "My husband would have liked you. He wasn't a very spiritual man, but he was good—very good. Ah, he'd be sad to see me now—one of our sons lost in the war, the other a traitor to his God. I'm glad he's gone."

"He must have been a very fine man," I force myself to say. "Now, I must—"

"No," she says quickly, "stay and finish this pot of coffee. There's only a little left."

I settle back reluctantly and watch her fill my cup again. The room becomes lonely with corners heavily shadowed beyond the circle of lamplight. We're too intimate here by the fire. There's an uncomfortable conniving fever as her talk becomes more personal. I want to leave it as if it were a sickness. I suddenly want the richness and health of cooler solitude.

"Yes, my Julien was a fine man," she continues. "And I've been a good wife and mother. I've done without food so that my children might eat; and as I told you, I took care of a mother who wouldn't even allow me to attend her funeral, and who left me penniless. But you know, I can't help but believe all the sufferings in my life today are

Julien's fault. He made me live in sin in the eyes of the Church till his first wife died. I can't help but feel my present sufferings are given me by God to pay for my past sins. But it's not right. I was just an innocent young girl. Julien led me into it all the way."

"I really don't think you ought to talk about your husband like that," I tell her. I quickly swallow the last of my coffee. "I appreciate your confidence, but now I really must go. I have work to do."

"Good night, Monsieur—my friend," she laughs warmly. "I wonder if Michel's asleep in Paris now?"

"I imagine so. Good night, Madame." I bow and walk out, closing the door behind me, closing the door on fetid sensations of confusion and disgust made more disgusting by the interest of her story.

My room greets me coolly, in perfect order, with nothing disarranged. I put on pajamas and prepare to work, stopping to remember the pleasure of Marguerite in the back seat of Salesky's taxi: her gaspings for breath, her fury afterward. And Father Clément . . . the dream crashes. How can I tell him this? Any thought of him in the car, no matter how fleeting, would have made me resist—not of myself, not for myself, but for another. I could resist if it meant pleasing Father Clément.

I am sick, sick, sick all the evening. Other considerations become hollow. I must take my ignominy to Father Clément, and read in his face my own guilt. All becomes cacophony in my ears, in my stomach. Remorse, unashamed remorse fills me with memory's first sickness of remorse. The night, the room become a reproach—an abyss of despair and regret.

This, then, is the secret; for sorrow and regret come not from the misdeed, but from the wince of another's face. The strength of morality comes first from without; not from one's feelings, but from one's feelings for another; and eventually, perhaps, from God. That's the meaning of morality. And the hints of last week, the calmness of the long hour in the chapel, the feeling of not being alone with which a few words inundated me, are gone, vanished. And in their place —nothing. And it's not from Father Clément that pardon must come; it's not to him, immediate and present and tangible, that I must apologize for the wrong of this evening; but to something through him, something else. For deep within me I know nothing of it but pleasure. Remorse comes from the pain of another, from the wrong I've done this intangible thing which I shall see written on the face of Father Clément. I must beg him for one more chance, now that I know.

Now, for tonight, there must be a stopping. The sickness of inner turnings must be dissolved in little things: to light a fire, to smoke a cigarette, to turn up all the lights. To hug the fire and smoke a cigarette. To think of friends. But to think of friends is to taste gall in solitude, to feel the deepest and most personal of shames. Humiliation of this malignancy, this inability to overcome the cancer of self. Stagnant rawness, growing with the night.

But it's too cold. The fire dies. I must go to bed. The night is lonely, and in its evil is something wrong. Nights and fires and children and parents and families destroy these things in other worlds. There, after doing what I've done, I should return home to the family, talk of nothing, make excuses, feel hidden delights, and go into the bathroom to wash myself.

Without these things the night gives other balances. Sickness can't be stopped. It takes a swallowing of the throat, until the throat becomes taut and aching with its growth. We need other things to destroy it; and there are no other things when remorse learns its way, when one lives alone with his wrong.

I walk outside before going to bed. Cold clear sky, first brief thawing, the roar of ice breaking on the River. Stars and faraway darkness. It's in such acts as urinating, as taking a drink to satisfy thirst, that we live tonight. These are the things that comfort us. These are desires which can be satisfied without the cramp and fear of guilt. These are platitudes that give a sense of rightness and ease, of

388

security from wrong. They don't change in a world that
grows monstrous as we struggle to understand it. We risk
nothing with the functions; they're a balm. We are cold
in the misery of not knowing, with the despair of outside
guilts and loneliness. We are cold without lights and fires
and children and families and radios to destroy these pri-
vately growing parasites. But we piss as well as we did
before, in the same way, with the same feeling—and it comforts us. That, at least, does not change. It's not affected by
our inner confusions. It's clear and simple and demanding.
It's something constant and concrete from which we can
start again. And we piss on the snow and take courage,
waiting for the morning in order to piss again. It cures
us . . . sets us right . . .

28 january

A sudden feeling of great relief that it's Sunday. There'll be no classes at the Monastery, no townspeople
to come in for the fire, and above all, no necessity of facing
Father Clément today. Turning off my alarm I go back to
sleep. I sleep until a timid knocking at my door recalls me
from this dreamless rest.
   "Yes, who is it?"
   "Monsieur, are you all right?"
   "Yes, Madame Renée. Did you want something?"
   "Did you intend not having lunch today? It's one
o'clock."
   "It is? My Lord, I've slept the clock around. Thanks
for waking me—I'll be there in fifteen minutes."

Hurrying into my clothes, I splash water on my face, straighten the bed, and walk across the deep, hard-topped snow to Madame Renée's little cottage. It is clean and warm, with the impersonal feeling of Sunday. The table is set with the whitest of linen cloths. Sun streams through the curtained lace over the windows, patterning the table. Savory smells arouse sleep-laden senses—a touch of garlic, meat being cooked in a buttered skillet, dampened by the more delicate perfume of red wine in our glasses. The day makes us a part of itself. There's something festive in our feelings, in the setting of the table, in the taste of good food, in our conversation.

We feel comfortable together. Madame Renée gives me a holiday from nagging. No need to be on guard with her. She carefully steers our conversation from dangerous fields. She is charming, and the day is charming and bright. Beyond the window, snow is the color of the reflected sun and afternoon shadows.

"There's something happy about a day like this," observes Madame Renée as we relax with our demitasses, "isn't there, Monsieur?"

"Yes, there is. It's really perfect."

"And I fixed an extra pot of coffee for you. You can take it back with you and enjoy something good and warming. Do you have much work to do this afternoon?"

I groan exaggeratedly. "So much I can't stand to think of it. And the day's so beautiful it seems a shame to stay indoors. What are you going to do?"

"Think I'll walk to the farm for butter and eggs. It'll be a nice afternoon for walking. Like to come along?"

"I'd love to, but I'd better not. After sleeping all morning I've got to prepare my lessons this afternoon."

"I know how tiresome it must be," Madame Renée sympathizes, "to stay cooped up all day. Why don't you run on now and do whatever you feel you must, and then come back for tea and the concert about four?"

"Sounds like a fine idea, Madame—believe I'll do that. I feel more like working now than I will later, anyway."

She is so pleasant today that I'm relieved not to have to spend the afternoon alone.

"Good. I'll fix you a wonderful tea—lots of tasty things —and we'll spend a nice afternoon. Run along now . . . Oh, and will you take this letter from Michel? It came this morning."

"But, Madame—"

"The letter concerns you more than it does me. Whatever you decide will be agreeable with me. Personally I think he rather has a nerve. But you must remember he knows nothing of the ways of the world—he asks you to do for him only what he'd do for you if the situation were reversed. Now, work hard and I'll see you a little later."

In my room I light the fire and open the blinds to early Sunday afternoon. Tile floors reflect the dull light, and there's an air of unfriendliness from the empty rooms about me. A desolation of Sunday calm, like a distant death, makes work at my black table seem impossible. No sound from the countryside. The Village rests at this hour. Slowly the stove heats, with noises of spitting green wood echoing hollowly through the spotless, impersonal rooms. Desk and work forbid, and I take Michel's letter near the window.

DEAREST MAMA,

You see, my luck is good, and God still has a soft spot in his heart for me, for I have, just yesterday, worked the first day in my new job. No one knows that I have been a monk, and I have decided, that it is just as well that way.

But, to tell you the details, I shall be paid 17,000 francs a month, and my work is designing advertising for an airplane company. I know you will be disappointed, as I am, for we had both hoped that I might find something, where my artistic talents could be used a little more seriously, but, this is a beginning, dear Mama, and the pay is very good for a beginner. I consider it only temporary, for I honestly believe, that I am made for more important things, and that the talent which God has given me, cannot end in drawing advertising layouts for airplanes, but I know too much about humility to complain.

My evenings are spent visiting our old friends here, with more invitations, than there are nights in the week, but I do not often accept, for I intend to make my own way in this new

391

life. I must confess, I took a puff from a cigarette the other night, and almost choked to death, and I suppose if I smoked a whole one, it would kill me!!! But, don't worry about me, Mother, my eight years as a monk were not for nothing, and, although I get along wonderfully with the friends I have made here, I lead a life far above theirs. They seem to realize it, too, for they are beginning to come to me, with all sorts of personal problems, and I believe I will be able to carry on God's work, in a very special way, in this outside world.

And the interior life? Why, Mother, I go to Mass every morning, and I pray better than I ever did before. This very morning, I took two of my friends, who live here in the same pension, two young fellows who are pretty wild, to St. Thomas Aquinas Church for Mass, and they both remarked afterward, how much I seemed to know about the Mass, and how beautifully I prayed, and so you see, by setting myself up as an example to these two young fellows, I am doing a great deal of good. They respect me, and the things I stand for, and they turn to me, and instead of going out with girls, as they have always done, they will soon be content to stay here with me, in the evening, and let me make portraits of them, and perhaps even teach them to draw. If you use your head, you can turn energy away from sin, into something much more worth while, and that is what I intend to do.

The other night, I walked about the streets with the younger of these two boys, arguing with him, for he was lonely, and wanted to find a girl. I talked with him as we walked, like an older brother, but it did not seem to change his wishes, so finally, when we got in front of one of those houses, I decided to put it to him squarely, and I said: "If you want to go in there, if you want to commit this sin, then, you will have to knock me down first." As you can imagine, he returned here, to the house, with me. But I find that there is much of this, that I simply know nothing about, and I am wondering if you might send me a good book on the subject, for this will help me to understand their problems, and to talk with a little more authority, in my arguments. You see, Mama, nothing has changed, really, for I still bring all of my problems to you, and you still share in all of my life.

Now, then, I will not cash my pay check, until the end of the month. I know how little money you have, Mama, but I do need better clothes, than this old flying suit of Jean-Julien's, to wear to my work, for my position is fairly important, and I must, of course, dress the part. I wish you could be here, to help me pick out a cloth, and to give the tailor your ideas,

392

for you always had such wonderful taste, when you used to choose Jean-Julien's and Papa's clothes. I am really lost without you, but if you could spare me 5,000 francs, until the first of the month, then I could outfit myself, keeping you always in mind, and trying to select clothes you would like. If you do not have the cash on hand, perhaps you could borrow it from the American boy, whom you write so much about, for, from what you say, I must have an adopted brother in him, and I am so glad. But I cannot understand, why he refuses to come to Paris to see me, for I would be tempted to come there, if only I could spare the 1,000 francs for a ticket, but these things will have to wait. From what you say about him, I feel that I could do a lot for him, for we are about the same age, and, with a little man to man talking, I find that I can do a lot for these young fellows, who are not too impressed by older men, or by priests. So keep after him, until he agrees to come to see me, for I would not let him out of my sight, and I want him to know, that in me, he has a real brother.

And you, Mother darling, I know the torment that you must be suffering, but have faith in me, and know that I have done what is right, for the indult should be here from Rome, within the next few days, and then I will be, officially, in good grace with my Church. Permission from Rome is absolutely certain, and you need not feel ashamed any longer, for I am, in the eyes of God, as good as any of those people there.

You are my dear little Mama, all I have left in the world, and you must be happy, in my choice of this new life. As yet, I have not even looked at a girl who interests me, for, despite my youth, my life in the monastery has made me much more adult, and serious, than most young people. But, there is no hurry, is there? We will find me a fine girl, one day, a girl who is interested in artistic and moral questions, and, with your approval, you will have a daughter, and I will have a wife. Instead of being a Father, with a capital F, I shall be a father, with a small f! (ha, ha!) . . .

The laboriously written letter goes on and on. It's incredible that eight years in a monastery could leave so little imprint. The disgusting revelation of the letter impresses me—the temper and tone of the poorly chosen words. The egoism of his mother, visited in him despite his years of training. His goodness, conniving goodness, and his open-eyed wish to be helpful. His civilian ecstasy during Mass. His desire to find a woman worthy of him and his mother—

393

a wife who can discuss important moral issues and artistic questions, and who is good, like the prayer of Francis Jammes. After reading this disappointing letter I don't wonder at Rome's willingness to be rid of him, to give him whole-hearted permission to leave his monastery.

Other things become clear. Only now do I understand why Dr. Castelar wished to take me to the worst whore he could find, for I should like to do the same thing with this Michel—to kill the rottenness of his goodness with the health, the humiliation of disgust. But he'd probably try to convert the whore.

What is the cure for this pride of self, for this self-adoration, except the destruction of the idol of self? Wouldn't he be better morally if he didn't have such an unblemished temple for the soul? Isn't his pride, his blindness of pride, the most degrading of all conditions? Astonishment, open astonishment to read such lines from a former monk, to deduce how little he must have absorbed from that life.

But he is right in the eyes of the world; in the eyes of the world here is GOODNESS. Goodness in every hidden niche of his being, with just enough of the good fellow in him to look you in the eye and understand the weakness of a character like yours. Even though you're far below him he will love you just the same—and help you. He will slap you on the back and use an inoffensive four-letter word like "damn" to show you he's not shocked, not a prude; for he knows that others, God help them, simply don't have his strength of character. He knows that the only way he can help them is to be sympathetic, to let them see that he has the same inner baseness, that he's human; but that he has achieved this serene inner beauty by conquering sin. Such is the way he thinks Jesus would handle the problem— and after all, isn't he working hand in hand with Jesus? Isn't he constantly bringing new lambs to the fold?

And when he marries, he will sacrifice his purity, his carefully guarded chastity, because God has given him that whispered permission, and because no woman could be expected to understand his flights of mysticism. He will give himself to her because he wants children, and because his wife wants his love. But eventually, in years to come, he will make her as good a Christian as he is; and they will keep a happily chaste bed together except for those rare intervals when they think another child should be brought into the world.

And later they will die, and be mourned and wept over. And they will go to heaven by way of the Helping-Hand Mission, to end up in the Good Fellows' Mansion in paradise. There they will spend eternity laughing, telling happy stories, doing folk dances, grinning, eating apples for the good of their systems, slapping each other on the back, and showing mild surprise at the folly of the world below. They will sing the praises of God made into the image of each: Michel's God will look exactly like Michel, and Mathilde's God will look like a bearded Mathilde. And they will sing together loudly, shaking their heads to urge those who just barely slipped in to sing with a little more gusto.

But they will wonder what ever happened to St. Francis, San Juan de la Cruz, St. Theresa, St. Benedict, and all those other saints. They never show their faces, never drop in at the Good Fellows' Mansion for a neighborly visit, never make appointments.

The Good Fellows console themselves, however, for they have some pretty distinguished company at that. Beethoven is not there, certainly, nor Bach, nor Mozart, nor Chopin. Monteverde and Palestrina are missing too, along with St. Thomas and Fra Angelico. But Massenet and Liszt are present, and Ingres and David. The news of Tchaikovsky and Wagner causes a little tongue-clicking. Wagner, it's rumored, has been put in Cardinal Balue's old cage for a sin against esthetic morality; and Tchaikovsky, that wonderful genius Tchaikovsky whom everyone loved so much on the other plane, has joined Sappho, Gilles de Retz, and Henry III in the ovens, where they are being basted with sauce from the long-since-rendered inhabitants of Sodom and Gomorrah.

I stir the fire in my stove, imagining that it's the one in the ovens—but it's clean and warm and it smells too good. It clears the mind of dreams. My thoughts return to the episode in the taxi without emotion, without regret. I ought to tell Father Clément about it today, but the opportunity hasn't presented itself. I decide not to mention it at all unless he asks a direct question; it's easier not to tell.

But there's a line out of place, a small source of irritation which can't be ignored. Something becomes wrong with the afternoon, something keeps me from working. My enjoyment of the day is destroyed by an involuntary sense of guilt; and I know it will last until I allow it to wear off in silence —or until I confess it to Father Clément and receive my punishment in the form of his speechless rebuke.

The step has been taken. The habit of thought has hardened into a physiological reaction which must either be obeyed and dissolved, or be disobeyed with the nagging dissatisfaction that results when any involuntary reaction is repressed. Until this chain of reaction is destroyed, even if falsely, I will sit here in my silent room unable to go further, unable to know Sunday.

Cursing myself for becoming so entangled in the web of morality, for desiring and seeking the phenomenon of remorse after so-called sin, I decide to alleviate the uneasiness in the only way possible: by telling Father Clément and having done with it.

When I reach the Monastery I'm in a belligerent mood. I find Father Clément in the garden, but I cut his surprised greeting short. "I committed another of your sins of the flesh last night, Father. I got a girl out of spite for Madame Renée, and I possessed her in the meanest way I know—in the back seat of Salesky's taxicab. Now give me the hell I deserve."

The monk stares at me in complete amazement, amazement turning to warmth. He takes my arm and we walk toward the far end of the garden. Below, great chunks of ice float swiftly past in the swollen River. Under the afternoon sun the countryside is naked and bleak, and very quiet.

"If you feel that way, my son," he says slowly, as we walk, "why did you come tell me about it? I do not understand you. You do not have to tell me: since you do not profess our beliefs, there is no obligation for you to answer to anyone but yourself."

"I know, I know," I answer, still disgruntled. "But I couldn't help myself. You may not believe that, but physically I couldn't help coming to you, even though I resent the fact. I never used to be this way—and I was better off then. But now—now if I hadn't come I'd be more miserable than I am already." I look at Father Clément, expectant; but his eyes are on the ground moving beneath our feet, and he says nothing.

"Whatever it is that eases these things," I go on rapidly —"whether it's Divinity, or the mere act of confessing, or the stingy little desire to pay for pleasure, I don't know— but whatever it is it has to be, because I've fallen into this hellish way of thought. I never really wanted to believe like you people; I never wanted to feel that if I slept with a girl I had to run and make my peace with God—but that's just the way it's getting to be. It's getting so I have no control over it." I grow angrier as my words carry me with them, and my voice rises.

Father Clément walks beside me listening carefully; he still says nothing.

. "Up till now I *did* want to understand you—understand how you felt. But I didn't want it to lead to this. Now I want to be rid of it, for it'll ruin my life unless I obey it. I want to be able to do as I please without wondering if I'm committing the sin of pride or avarice or lust or what-have-you. And that's exactly the way I'm beginning to be— always watching every reaction and desire. What a life I've got ahead of me if it keeps up!"

Father Clément stops walking. He turns to me and looks close into my eyes, and a smile breaks over his face—a smile becoming affectionate chuckling.

"What the hell's so funny?" I ask scornfully.

He puts a hand on my shoulder. "Ah, what a superb

397

character you are," he says gently. "Have you quite finished with this little melodrama?"

"Was it that bad, Father? I thought it was pretty good." I stare at my feet in disgust. We begin to walk again.

"You remind me of a spoiled child," he says calmly, "who makes life miserable for his parents until they allow him to ride the merry-go-round. He struggles and kicks and cajoles until they finally put him on it, and then he becomes outraged because they did and because he finds it not what he thought. He resents them, taking out his wrath on them, on the merry-go-round, and on the world in general for something that was entirely his own doing. You have done precisely the same thing, building up in yourself by force a love of God which you never really wanted. I warned you that you were playing with fire, and now that you begin to see what I meant, you start ranting. You are the spoiled child who will have his pleasures without their attendant responsibilities. You want the kind of happiness we have, the kind of love we have, but you do not want to give up any of your little back-seat pleasures. Well, my child, you cannot do it; it does not work that way, ever."

Reaching the end of the garden, we turn back. I can find nothing to say.

"To employ another analogy," Father Clément continues, "you are like the stingy old maid whose house is on fire. She knows she must get out in order to save her very life, but she has to gather up all her trinkets—her knitting needles, her old letters and photographs, and whatever else it is that old maids collect. She must gather up these things even at the risk of losing her life in the flames. She will not leave the danger without the trinkets, for she is a stingy old maid. Now, despite everything you can do, your own house is burning down around your ears. You cannot stop it because you set it afire yourself—you *wanted* it to burn down, as I remember, and you made splendid preparations for a roaring fire. But now that the fire is going good, now that you have knowledge of what a love of God can really be, you want to salvage all your old trinkets at the risk of

398

death—and your death, my son, if you fight this flame, is as certain as the old maid's. If you are wise you will not deny your love, even though you resent it. You will run now and leave your trinkets for those who remain back there where you were, for those who do not set their houses on fire." He studies the snow in which our shoes leave their tracks. "What do you think of all this?" he asks without looking up.

"I think, Father," I falter, lighting a cigarette, "I think—to carry your analogy a little further—that if I'm in love and can't do anything about it, can't put out the fire, then I'm the most miserable man alive. I don't want this thing. To me it's the same as falling in love despite myself with the meanest hag in the world—with Madame Renée, for example." The icy air mingled with cigarette smoke hurts my lungs. Father Clément pulls his cowl closer about his head. Cold cuts through our clothes, cold tells us to hurry, and we walk faster.

"No, you are quite wrong, my son—and you know it, do you not?" He smiles as if I were a child. "I can tell by the expression on your face whenever you mention Madame Renée like that. You make a statement, and in making it you realize how dogmatic it becomes. To fall in love with someone like Madame Renée would simply mean greater unhappiness. You would resent it. You would say to yourself, 'My God, what has caused this terrible thing to happen? What have I done to deserve this?' You confuse the human with the divine. With the love of God—and there must be a hint of it in you, or you would not have *had* to come to see me this afternoon—with the love of God, there is only the most perfect satisfaction once you allow it and accept it. If you reject it, your life can be nothing but discontent and misery." His voice has become a lulling, humming, inner speaking.

I am silent a moment, then, "When I didn't know of God as anything but a beautiful story," I tell him, "I was much happier. It's only since becoming aware of these things that I've been discontented and miserable."

399

"That may be true," he sighs, unconsciously crushing my discarded cigarette in the snow. "But the fact is that that was a happiness of ignorance, of shallowness. You have burned that ignorance, and with it the narcosis of its happiness. With your new knowledge you cannot hope to turn back, to recapture the pleasures of ignorance—no more than can the man who is a connoisseur of fine wines turn back and persuade himself that grape juice is as good as it tasted to him in his youth. Without his growth and experience he would not know the difference; the one would delight him as much as the other. But you cannot deny growth, knowledge, experience. You cannot convince yourself now"—he squints his eyes close to mine, smiling with the wrinkled face of affection—"nor can you ever convince yourself again, that these trinkets of your past life have any worth. You may, you most certainly will, return to them, finding that they still glitter a little like imitation jewelry. One of these jeweled trinkets is your sex life, another your pride, another your anger, and so on. You will probably seek to polish them, to restore some of their former brilliance. You will find another woman, for example, and know her, always in search of the sheen you once saw in it. For a moment you may convince yourself that it is real, that there is neither dullness nor tarnish to it; but as soon as it is over you will know that it was false, and that you were deluding yourself in the hope that the delusion might, by some miracle, become real. It was real before, and it was a source of happiness, almost a reason for being. It will not be that again, my child."

His inexorable logic fills me with gloom. We stop walking, and I kick disconsolately at the snow. The sound is magnified in the still, frozen air of the garden. Father Clément notices my sadness, and smiles.

"Now, my son, there are two things concerning this that will keep you healthy and sane. Either marry as soon as you can, or accept the fact that you can no longer practice licentiousness with impunity. In all things you must now make the choice. You must either do God's bidding and know your rightful bliss in His love, or deny God's will—which you know—and suffer the consequences of today repeated a thousand times. For you can no longer deny God's will peremptorily. The sickness of such denial is rarely the crack of a whip, but rather a slow heaviness that saps you of all energy and, eventually, of all hope. You cannot work when you have this weight on your soul."

The sun remains bright, but we tremble from the chill. The monk takes my arm and we turn to leave the garden.

"You can no longer play the spoiled child or the old maid," he says slowly, impersonally. "You must be willing to give up your little trinkets for something immensely more valuable—and the rewards are a thousand times more wonderful than you can dream. Now," he adds as we enter the courtyard proper, climbing three wide steps to leave the garden, "do you still feel you are falling in love with nothing better than the world's meanest hag, or with Madame Renée?"

I reply, "You have the answer to everything, don't you?" I sigh resignedly. "You don't leave me much choice: both alternatives seem glum to me. The one I can't do; the other I can do well, but with constant remorse. I should never have got so interested."

We step beneath the covering arches of the cloister. Father Clément lowers his cowl and turns to me simply. "I am remembering you in my prayers every day, my son."

"Well, I hope so. After all, you gave me this disease."

He winces at the word "disease."

"I didn't mean it that way, Father," I explain quickly—"didn't mean for it to sound that way. I just don't know what to say or do, I guess." I pause. "You know, I think I'm fundamentally allergic to goodness—to all it implies. I can't get around the feeling that I'm being—well, *forced,* by something more powerful than myself, into the hair shirt and uplifted eyes of the Christian."

"You die hard, my son," mutters Father Clément. "But do not read into this little uneasiness a cataclysmic change in your life. It is more a symptom than anything else. You

401

will not need the hair shirt for some time yet. Use your intelligence; this makes you no different from others. You will continue to live like a normal human being, or I shall be very disappointed in you. Your present life appears to lack balance, and that is dangerous. Remember, my child, God chooses his saints, and they are rare and far apart. You do not seem to understand that sanctity is not a necessary prerequisite for full adherence to a Christian life. There are many intermediate stages between abject, unremorseful sin and the heights of sanctity, but very few limits if you realize these differences. You can no more carry your hair shirt home and bask in the light of God's love than I could play a Brahms concerto without having studied the piano. This is a thing of long training and much courage, and then it cannot be certain. We must take the chance of possible earthly misery in order to assure ourselves of a place with God, both on earth and in heaven."

"Of course, Father," I murmur. "I'm being stupid. I'll return to my house feeling much better."

He looks calmly into my face. "Very well, I wish you would try. We have a rule of thumb that if a man can keep himself completely pure for six months, he can do it forever. You are not happy—why do you not begin again? Ask God for His grace within you, for His help, and see if you cannot do this thing. It is more difficult than you can imagine. We know its difficulty better than others. Our life is not easy, my child, but I honestly believe it to be the happiest life on this earth."

"I remember Marie-Ornoux once mentioned your rule of thumb," I observe. "But six months? Why, that doesn't seem impossible. I've gone almost that long before."

Father Clément shakes his head doubtfully. "No, my son," he says softly but firmly. "Six months is a good testing time, and you have not gone nearly that long since you reached adulthood. If you have gone for a week, or at the most ten days, without some sort of stimulated relief, you have done better than I think. I know you pretty well. Six months will be a gigantic project. Try it—not for me, but for your own personal satisfaction." He coughs, clears his throat. "Now I must run. Do not feel too bad about this. Come to see me when you need help. Try to think before falling into such a situation again. Think of me, and come to see me soon enough next time."

I return to my studies, waiting to take tea with Madame Renée. Day of abortive discontent. My entire being shrivels from the fear of hearing more about her intimate life. For now I know all the words, all the stupid little arguments. And I know that she says them to arouse me, again and again. Hers is a thirst for self-abuse, a perversion debilitating to all who come within her grasp.

I wait. I wait for her to return from the farm. Sunday and Sunday afternoon of beautiful sunlight. The farm. And for the briefest instant I can see the rain-spattered dirt on the grave of the little Chevissier child, piled there by this woman's conniving. And tonight and tomorrow I grow healthy from food paid for by the child. I wait. My fire dies. Finally through the window I see Madame Renée returning, and I walk across to meet her as she enters the gate. Handing me the heavy wicker basket she greets me enthusiastically. Cold has reddened her cheeks and loosened her gray hair; it escapes in a soft aureole about her face. She has been picking among the dead, but the walk back has cheered her, making her beautiful and angelic-looking. Leaning against the gate she forces it open, laughing, unconsciously brushing back her hair.

"The sun must have thawed some of the ice," she says, "and now it's frozen again. The gate sticks in weather like this. Here, I can take the basket now."

"No, I've got it," I answer. "It's heavy—what've you got in here, anyway?"

Opening the door of her house, she turns to let me enter, smiling an open smile. "Food, my young friend, food for the week, so that you can live and keep your strength." She says this in imitation of the way it might be said by the peasants.

"Good! But how you manage it I don't know. You're

403

a genius at finding good things to eat when no one else seems able to." I place the basket on her table.

She becomes serious for a moment as she removes her beret. "As I told you before, it's very simple. I'm friendly with these people. They're good people at heart and they appreciate a kindness. They'll give me anything, Monsieur, because they know I'm their friend. Why, they even come to me for advice."

I look at her closely, and the image of an anguished, red-faced little Papa Chevissier is in my mind. I can't forget what he told me about this woman's exploitation of his family. I search for a sign of guilt in her face, but I find none. "That's really wonderful," I say enthusiastically. "Shall I carry this into the kitchen?"

"Please."

She stirs the coals into a flame, adding more wood. She does all the things one does upon first entering the house—rubs her hands together, removes coat and scarf, runs a comb through her hair—and then goes into the kitchen to boil water for tea. I sit near the fire. Her voice, coming to me from the kitchen, is gay and restful. She is sympathetic, this woman. Despite everything, she is sympathetic and friendly. After a few moments she says, "Did you read Michel's letter?"

"Uh-huh. It was most touching. And it proves you have no real reason to worry about him."

"He wants you to visit him in Paris very much." She comes to the door. Her smile has become petulance. Biting her lower lip, she asks reproachfully, "Why don't you go?"

Echoed warnings of the nerves. A remembered voice: ". . . you will accept Madame Renée as a lesson in humility." No, as a test in patience. She is beginning her campaign, and I'm determined to resist her. "I don't have the time," I say without anger, with finality. "I'm far behind in my work. If Michel wants to see me he can come here. But I'll never make the trip to Paris. That's final."

"But he hasn't the money to come here, you know that," she rejoins angrily; then, regaining composure, "I know

404

you'd make a very fine impression on him. He needs you."

"Then I'll lend him the money to come here. But I really don't have the time to spare for it—and I don't want to be dragged into your affairs with him." I reach into my pocket for a thousand-franc note, and give it to her.

Smiling, warm, soft, she whispers, "You're really very good, Monsieur. You try to hide it, but I know."

"Forget it."

Recovering herself, laughing, she brings tea and buttered tartines with preserves. The tea steams its warm fragrance into my face, and the tartines are fresh. We drink the tea cautiously, for it's very hot: it melts the butter on bread placed next to it. I eat—and as I eat, the anguished red face of little Papa Chevissier returns. I remember his plea for help, and I realize more forcefully that although I condemn Madame Renée for depriving him of food, it's I who grow fat on the results of her evil. My guilt is no—

"Is something the matter, Monsieur?" asks Madame Renée, and I know that my face must show the thoughts brought to mind by her food.

"Nothing, Madame—just a little sleepy, I guess." I thrust from me the image of the little girl's unpainted coffin. "These tartines are marvelous—believe I'll have another one. Are there enough?"

"Oh, of course, Monsieur," she says simply and generously—"plenty."

Our conversation returns to pleasantness. We listen to the concert, and tea becomes supper as cold meats are brought to the table. She talks of many things—of Marguerite, of Michel, of Father Clément. After a while I grow silent, seeking the chance to leave.

"One thing more, Monsieur," she says at last. "If Michel does come here—and I'll see to it that he does—can he stay at your house?"

Ignoring the desire to refuse, I answer wearily, "I suppose so. But why? You have enough room here."

She reddens, looking down. "Despite everything I say, I want to do the right thing for my son. When I'm alone with him I can't help saying things that hurt him. If you're with him, or if he stays with you, I'll be able to hold my tongue. I know I have a bad character, and you can make me behave better than anyone else I know. When you give me those looks I'll hold my tongue."

I rise to leave, a little sickened by her determination to involve me in her most intimate affairs. I feel nothing but coldness and defeat at her deceitful cleverness. Endeavoring to make me stay, she fawns upon me nauseously.

"You know, I don't know why I stand for your treating me like you do. I wouldn't tolerate it from anyone else." She looks at me slyly. The statement is an open demand for discussion.

I let it drop. Bowing, I open the door. "Michel may stay wherever he likes. Now I must go. Good night, Madame, the tea was delicious." And I close the door on a last glimpse of startled redness, of startled half-begun movements that seek another excuse to keep me there. I leave her alone with a tableful of dirty dishes.

Music all evening, nothing but music—on the radio and on my worktable. Pages and pages filled. Calm in my work, desolate in my desire for something I can't know. The Village is quiet this early evening. Surrounded by people who make no sound, my room recedes from me; there's a first feeling of hostility between my fine room and me.

Time and work become night and lateness until the notes in front of me make no more sense. Outside my window, a marvelously clear moonlight. Cold. Now everyone sleeps behind closed shutters. Across the way, smoke from Madame Renée's chimney pours thinly, whitely, rising straight into the frosty night. Her windows are dark.

Fever rises in my cheeks. I close the window and the shutters. The exhaustion of spiritual dissonance makes my legs ache, but I can't go to bed. The bed with its many bright pillows, softened in color by the faintness of my desk lamp, forbids rest. And the terror of new fevers grips my belly.

In desperation I read something familiar, something that
406

will remind me of my country, of things I know: Maurois's *Journal*. Irritating writing. Slightly disguised platitudes. An honest and thoroughly desolating portrait of "young America" after the war. Returned soldiers, heroes, university students—all striving upward, all seeking rightness, all filled with words, clichés, open-faced idealism. All very degrading. Maurois's artistic judgments smell of the Beaux-Arts, and his musical judgments of the Conservatoire.

On the radio the music changes of its own accord. Night goes on toward morning. Fitful sleep, with my head on the desk.

I awaken. I know that I must keep writing, keep moving, for I can't reach the bed now. I must leave the light on in hopes that someone will see it and come help me to bed. If I get to my feet I shall fall.

29 january

And the fever burns. It's impossible to think. Thought becomes perversity when based on the logic of temperature. Early morning carnality of impotent, unsweating heat. The fire is dead.

My table gives up its inventory to dull, sleep-clogged senses: sheaves of music paper, exercises, books, half-smoked packages of Gauloise cigarettes, papers, a Calder exposition folder from Carré in Paris, newspapers, letters.

I sleep again with my head on my hands, leaning over the desk, breathing with great difficulty. Doors and windows are closed against the night, against the rest of this silent, empty house.

407

Bells from the parish church, announcing six o'clock Mass, arouse me from desultory sleep. It's still dark outside as the Villagers begin to stir about. My desk lamp seems tawdry with its diluted rays flickering into dark corners of the room. I haven't moved. Tremblings come in heaves of violence. Still dressed, I sit glued to my desk chair. Light is a torture to my eyes, burning and glassy-feeling with the fevers. Thinking nothing, I wait—wait for someone to find me and put me to bed. May she be young and beautiful, and have sweetness of voice and breasts—and it chokes and becomes hysterical weeping within me.

Sometime later, an eternity later, a whispering voice above house slippers and lace nightgown and gray wool dressing gown. They move in the range of my vision, detached from the voice, framed by the rungs of my table as I gaze at the tiled floor. They belong to Madame Renée. And I laugh, dropping my head to the table; I laugh and cry, for she's not young and beautiful with sweetness of voice and breasts.

Her voice whispers, "Aren't you well, Monsieur? What on earth's the matter?"

"I'm sick, Madame Renée, really sick. Go find help."

I must have talked, for I remember words; and in the half-dream of my delirium I lie here and wonder how a woman could have put me to bed and taken off my clothes—and why she didn't turn off the light when she left.

In the hall, a sound of something falling heavily to the floor. A moaning voice forces me to fight my way back through layers of coma and fever to reality—to a single hawklike image of Madame Renée, still dressed in night clothes, limping back into the room. She falls on a chair, clutching her leg, spitting and complaining about broken teeth in a high falsetto scream.

"Look, look, my teeth! The one beautiful thing left about me! I've always had beautiful teeth." Gasping, sobbing, she gazes at me in horror. "Now they're ruined," she whispers, holding back tears.

With two fingers she opens her bleeding lips to show
408

me the damaged teeth. Clearly, the two front teeth have small pieces chipped out. I look, I gaze drunkenly, and I'm delighted. I swallow wonderful animal words of unspeakable obscenity.

"Be glad—you—didn't—bust—your—" I struggle to get out something, some word so magnificent—But inner laughings make my meaning senseless.

"It's the Lord's doing," she mutters tearfully, ignoring my fine attempt. "I shouldn't have been so proud of my teeth."

Endless struggles with burning fevers. Patches of sanity in an insane quilt of time. I try again to tell her that wonderful sentence: "Be glad—you—didn't—bust—your—"

Darkness. A shimmering chill and fevers running, racking, sinking out of consciousness, struggling to get words out. Then mumbling hurriedly, "B' glad y' di'n' bust y' ASS."

That was it. "ASS," laughing, yelling, screaming before the darkness, before the sinking out of sight. "ASS" spelled in capital letters, shining, glistening from the blackness. And long faraway cacklings of laughter.

Later, my screaming brings me back. From somewhere on the outside I hear the word repeated incessantly—"ASS, ASS, ASS, ASS"—shouted, moaned; and eyes open, wondering who says such beautiful words. Circle of black, beshawled, faceless women knitting, watching me, hearing my splendid obscenity. They wait to help. I am dead. When I speak my voice comes to me from within, but dimly. No, I'm not dead, I'm deaf, not dead but deaf. My voice comes to me dimly from within. I hear nothing through my ears. And when they speak to me I see their lips moving, hear only the roar of silence.

Last vague awareness of a black-robed nun sitting beside me, of hands—strong hands of a woman—taking off my pajama shirt. Wordless protestations. The nun cuts my chest with a small knife, placing leeches on the cuts to bleed me, and turning me on my stomach, repeats the operation. And knowing only that I'm a foreigner, she speaks to me in pidgin French: "You—sick. You—feel—suffer?"

I laugh. I lose consciousness laughing at the funny way she talks. In her own jargon I mimic her: "You—savage—woman. You—cut—man. You—more—beautiful—than—"

Dark nights alone, without fear. Days, the old women waiting for me to have my head cut off by the guillotine. Nightmares of cutting. Mother Nourrie, cross-eyed and giggling, cutting off my prettiness. The nun cutting on chest and back. And now the Revolution, and hags sit and knit, waiting for them to lop off my head so they can applaud and spit and laugh and cackle and return to their knitting until the next head falls. When will the drums start rolling? All a mistake. All a mistake. Name of God, it's a mistake. I, nothing but a poor tailor's apprentice, measuring the length of the nobility's legs, from crotch to ankle. The black women knit.

4 february

Finally, the drunken sleep of sweat and broken fevers. The vague, muffled impression of pouring rivers of perspiration and urine into my bed, of being lifted protestingly out of my nest, of my terror in realizing that they intend bathing me. Voices return, the ones croaking at my embarrassment as they undress and prepare me for the tub, the others lost in a confusion of clean sheets replacing the soiled sheets on my bed.

I can't stand alone. Agony of soap and water and strong hands holding me in place, while women scrub and click their teeth and laugh, cajole, scold. Humiliation of being held vicelike in a half-crouching position by two of them,

410

while another washes soapy water from my behind into the tub. A hazed blushing as they dry me, rubbing hard and hurting, still holding me as they find nothing but a clean shirt for me to wear.

Old Mother Nourrie, flustered, busy, taking command, is resentful that the others have seen. She supports me as another woman buttons my shirt. "There, there, sweet pup," she murmurs soothingly. "Feeling better now, eh? Feels good to be rid of four days' pipi and sweat. Feels good to be clean. Hold still, hold still. Bless him, he's too watery to stand of himself. Here, back to bed. Back to the nice clean sheets. He's my washed young trump, washed and powdered and clean. Hurry and button him, woman. Ah, don't button the bottom one, the child needs his freedom. Now turn over, and zoom! up with the covers. Go to sleep, child. You need to sleep it out, now the poison's left you."

The cracked sweetness of aged voices as they throw out the bath-water and straighten the room. I settle down between the clean, the wondrously clean sheets. Immediate sleep, ever conscious of the newness of fresh bedclothes, of the lightness of my body washed free of filth. Dreamless sleep, lasting forever. Last thought that Madame Renée wasn't there for the bath, that she'll never forgive herself when she learns what has happened. Warmth of gratefulness that it was old Mother Nourrie. Glimpse of her sitting near me, knitting, humming softly to herself, looking well content.

5 february

Again it's daylight, and I am plagued with hunger as wakefulness returns. Voices, instantly recognizable as the circle of old ladies.

"Ah, he's awake. And how does M'sieu feel now?" asks the nameless woman who buttoned me.

"I'm fine," I reply, "thanks to the wonderful care of you good ladies." I glance about the room. "Where is the Sister, the nun?"

"But, child," Mother Nourrie says, as she approaches my bed, "you were so mean to her, she left. And right, too. She had no business here. I told her old Mother Nourrie was more used to you." She chuckles. "You spoke some fine French—good outhouse French. This was no place for her."

"But what day is this?" I ask, worried. "And how was I mean to her? What did I say?"

"Damn! This is Wednesday, child. You've been gone to God for four days. As for that slit-tailed monk, you were rich. Such a tongue! Ha, and you tried to comb her hair."

The old ladies laugh thoughtfully.

"Zut!" Mother Nourrie goes on. "Don't feel bad. Slit-tails shouldn't be running around loose like that."

"I tried to comb her hair?" I inquire frowning.

They become hysterical with laughter. Mother Nourrie's eyes stare at her nose as she slaps herself on the leg. "Sure. You don't know what that means, poor thing. I guess they've got it the same as you and me. You tried to get under her robe."

I listen horrified. "What?"

"That's right, you tried to get under her robe." The old women, led by Mother Nourrie, laugh harder than ever. I look around at them.

"That's enough!" I roar. "If I did what you say, it's unforgivable. You shouldn't be laughing. As soon as I can

412

I'll apologize to her, and I won't tolerate such disrespectful talk in my house again."

They shrug their shoulders and become silent. Mother Nourrie, abashed, leaves the room quietly. Another of the women asks, "Does M'sieu wish us to leave, perhaps?"

"No, no," I say quietly. "I didn't mean to offend you. I'm sorry I spoke like that. But tell me, where is Madame Renée?"

"Alas, the poor woman fell and hurt her leg," she explains. "She's been over to see about you every day till yesterday morning, when Mademoiselle Marthe made her go with her to the City to see the doctor. She hurt her leg pretty bad, M'sieu. She was in awful pain."

Germaine appears from the kitchen, her mother behind her. "Madame Renée asked me to apologize to you for leaving, M'sieu," she says stiffly. "But she left some food in the cellar. Don't you think you should eat something? Maybe a custard, or some eggs?"

"A couple of eggs, please, Germaine," I answer; and seeing Mother Nourrie sulking in the corner, I try to placate her: "And, old Mother, do you think I have some clean pajamas to put on?"

"Sure, sweet." There's a smiling grimace on her mean old face. She turns to her daughter. "Doll, where's the pup's pajamas, eh?"

As Germaine retrieves yesterday's pajamas, now washed and ironed, and goes into the kitchen, I say, "And some coffee too, Germaine, and above all a cigarette."

"I'll get you a cigarette, pup," says Mother Nourrie.

She carefully unbuttons the folded pajamas and hands me the pants. The women make no move to leave or to turn their smiling gazes away. I slip the pants on under the covers, struggle up to sit on the side of the bed, and put on the pajama coat which Mother Nourrie holds for me. Ignoring me again, the women talk of families and Village life while I get back in bed to smoke, waiting for Germaine to prepare the food.

The eggs and coffee are tasteless, hard to swallow. Soon

after I've finished eating, the great boom of Monastery bells announces the end of the day with Vespers. The women leave; they go to their cold houses to prepare food for the evening meal. I let Germaine go too, telling her not to return until morning.

Now the slow recovery, food's digestion, and the return of life—of a reason to live. Once the fever breaks, good feelings return quickly, more quickly than strength.

Quiet evening of music from England. The Bach Concerto in D minor for two violins, played ravishingly by the Ars Rediviva group.

Later, a heavy snow falls outside. My fire burns out, and I feel well. After the fevers and the magnificence of a coma and the breathlessness of a soul-bursting nightmare, I return to the calm of snow, to the awkward, bulky grace of the silence of total solitude—unattached and loveless, gigantic and granitelike, tender and heart-warming. Warming, yes—abstract, unbodied love of warmth—but the body is without strength this night. Choking, growing love for all creatures who sleep alone: the poor, the unwanted, the sick. The snow, muffling sound, releases feelings of rising compassion for those who suffer. Walking weakly about my room, I know a love for those who suffer with no sensation, who are humble with no knowledge of humility; a love for those to whom life has become too raw for them to care, to blush because a strange strong hand washes their behind. Raw, tender, bitter, pure in complete lack of purity —purest of all. Who with all their poverty, their so-called "inferiority," live superbly—struggle, choke, but live. Better than these powdered, anemic, civilized ones who break your heart, who destroy you with the shame and disgust and compassion of their untarnished souls. "I've always had beautiful teeth. Now they're ruined." ". . . with a little man to man talking, I find that I can do a lot for these young fellows . . ." "These tartines are marvelous—believe I'll have another one."

Time wasted, time wasted. I know nothing. I only feel, but the current carries me on.

414

We dare judge; we dare judge a man who breathes, who has a navel, who is lost. Our only superiority is in its denial.

Fateful year in the Valley.

Snow is still falling. I get up to go into the courtyard. The snow pours against my face and neck in slants. It's deep beneath my feet. With no warning I lean forward, giving up my dinner, and the strain of it causes my head to ache again. I know that the fevers are rising once more. I know that unless I hurry, it will be an endless trip back to my room and my bed.

6 february

        In Salesky's taxicab they take me to the hospital in the City.

8 february

        "Hold out your arm." Voice cold and remote. "Not again!" Fear, numb fear, and the turning in bed. A white patch of flesh beneath the short sleeve of a hospital gown. Cold stubby fingers tapping inside the elbow joint. She's big and white, and she's tied with a belt in the middle, like a sack.

Beyond her head is a window. A light, white but sunless, splashes full in my eyes. Dead shining whiteness of the room and her clothes. Frozen polished gleam from the hypodermic syringe. Eyes focus on the patch of white flesh speckled with red pinpoints and blue bruises. She taps and her finger is cold.

"Let me see the other arm." A piece of red rubber hose is tied above the elbow. "Clench your fist."

Her voice sounds dead and remote. From the smooth white patch colors rise, pink congestion and blue veins. The glistening silver point of a needle poised above blue skin; breaking the surface; entering. An inner pop and the vein wall is punctured. Red blood is sucked slowly into the glass syringe. It pains somewhere with an indefinable pain.

Eyes wander. Windows. Hundreds of windows combining into one. Straw hair escapes from her cap and veils the view. All of it fading, pulsing, strong and weak, as concentration centers inside the arm where a sharp point probes vein walls.

Her finger taps frozen against my elbow. "Open your fist."

She releases the rubber band. A wad of alcohol-soaked cotton is folded into my arm. Somewhere out there a white sack tied in the middle shakes blood up and down in a vial. Her movements grow huge in the astigmatic nightmare. Gigantic cocktail in her hands. Arnica-smelling cocktail and everything so cold, so white, so glistening. A clear thin stream of alcohol rolls down my inner arm.

"There you are." She grins. "Hope it's the way you like it." Blood with a head of foam poured thick into a cocktail glass.

"Oof." I drink and grimace. "Not enough sodium cit—" Dazzling lights cloud over and become blackness.

And later, a bare room with four walls and a window. I turn but the window is always in my eyes, wet, wavering, too bright, a liquid blear obsessing my eyes and my mind.

"What're you doing to me?"

Clean white hands soft and moist and cold. A doctor looking clean bends over me. His voice is soft and cold. He smells moist, antiseptic. "We're giving you strong doses of stovarsol—arsenic. Painful but necessary."

"Can't you do something about that window?"

"Of course."

Blackness, and always swallowing nausea, and bending double in bed pressing elbows into my stomach. Vague consciousness that deep in the darkness of warmth under the covers, there's a secret sweating.

"Hey!"

I groan.

"Turn over."

I want to ask what for, but I turn over. On my stomach my eyes find the grimy wooden floor, her shoes, her stockings. My eyes strain upward through the shadows of her uniform. I know it's night because the light is on. She stands soaring into the atmosphere above, a syringeful of clear liquid between her and the light. She pushes with her thumb and a thin stream of the liquid spurts into the air. Chill air on my back as she lifts the covers and parts the hospital gown.

"What're you doing?"

"Some new medicine. I give it in the hip."

"Hip" means buttocks. She grabs a handful of buttock in one hand and with the other applies the giant needle. A long wait.

"All right," and alcohol-soaked cotton like wet ice is rubbed on the spot.

During days, the glaring window and the needle. During nights, the white electricity. During all times, a wood saw ripping across tender intestines and nerves.

14 february

No one knows I'm returning. It's already dark when my bus arrives in the Valley, stopping to let me off at the bridge. I walk slowly across the bridge and enter the Village as rain begins to fall.

The evening is spent alone in my room copying music and lessons missed in the hospital. Happiness of reading my mail.

After a while the rain pours more violently against the window. It's the first warm rain, and after the long frozen winter the steadily falling drops seem an enchantment. The silence is broken only by their delicious sound.

The night quickly passes. Every four hours I stop my work to take a dose of medicine.

Extreme contentment in the early morning hours before dawn as I smoke a final cigarette. Thunder and heavier rain increase the anticipation of sleeping again in my own bed, between clean sheets; sleeping profoundly, dreamlessly; sinking from sight in sleep as the morning air fills my room with dampness.

Monotony of rain, never stopping, inexorable.

Quiet, rhapsodic happiness this night of return.

15 february

"Why didn't you come tell me you were back last night? You know how I've missed you."
418

"I wanted to be alone, Madame Renée."

"Now, that's not very nice. After I've worried so much about you. Michel's arriving tonight." She is in high spirits. She is lying on the chaise longue in her salon, her left leg heavily bandaged.

I sit beside her. "Tell me, is your leg badly hurt?"

"Yes, there's a contusion." She lifts the leg, wincing convincingly. "The doctor says I must stay off my feet as much as possible. So I'm afraid you'll have to go for the provisions if you want to go on eating here."

"Gladly, but can't you send Germaine?"

"If you want to eat, you'll do as I ask!" she answers sharply, almost angrily.

"Well, what brought *that* on?"

"I think it's the least you can do," she pouts. "After all, I hurt my leg in your house because I tried to help you. The doctor says I may be a month getting over this."

"Of course," I mumble, "it was my fault. But were you hurt anywhere else?"

She plumes herself on the couch, looks at her feet, and smiles an inward smile. "No. The doctor examined me thoroughly. He says that despite my age I have the body of a woman of thirty, and that my teeth can be fixed so they'll never show. But of course it will cost money."

My face reddens. "You know I can't afford much," I stammer, "but I suppose it's only right that I pay for everything."

"Don't be ridiculous." She smiles simply. "I wouldn't think of it." Then, more to herself than to me, "Imagine that doctor saying an old hag like me has the body of a woman of thirty."

"You know you're not a hag. You're a remarkably handsome woman."

"And he thinks I should remarry."

"That's a wonderful idea," I say with enthusiasm. "No reason why you shouldn't."

"Don't be silly, Monsieur. What man would have me?" Smiling embarrassedly she looks away.

419

"That's no problem. Anyway, you ought to think about it."

"The only reason I'd do it would be to spite Michel. He adored his father." She says this cautiously, watching for the reaction.

I reply in a normal voice, "That's scarcely a reason for marrying."

"Oh, isn't it?" comes coarsely, like a street woman. "Michel's given no thought whatsoever to his mother's feelings. Why shouldn't I pay him back?"

Fighting to control myself. "Mothers simply don't do things to pay back their children." I pause, lighting a cigarette nervously. "Sometimes I think you say these things just to make me angry."

"Humph. Don't flatter yourself, Monsieur."

I exhale quick short puffs of smoke. She glares at me. Rain drips from the eaves, and the day is dark. After a moment I ask quietly, "You'll be nice to Michel tonight, won't you?"

"Why should I? He's coming here to see you, not me."

"Don't be ridiculous," I retort angrily. "Of course he's coming here to see you. And if you stay in this mood it won't help either of you."

"We'll see." She stretches back, dark, unsmiling. "You can meet him at the station in Town. Tell him his mother is sick and that he can please himself—either come or stay away."

I rise from my chair, flicking cigarette ashes furiously in the direction of the stove. "In that case I'll just tell him to go back to Paris—that he's not welcome either in your house or in mine."

"Why do you insist on taking his side against me?" she asks heatedly, glaring at me with absolute hatred.

"Because you're wrong," I state firmly. "I won't meet the train. He'll come directly to your house. And I warn you, if you don't behave it'll all be over with us."

Burying her head in her hands she begins to sob. I stare at her, forcing my voice to become calm.

420

"I put myself in his place, that's all," I tell her. "I know if my mother talked about me the way you do about Michel, I'd never get over it."

She lifts a tear-streaked face and trembling chin, and looks at me pleadingly. "I'm a godless woman," she moans. "No, I wouldn't really want to hurt my Michel. He's a good boy, you'll see. But he's hurt me so much, so deeply, I can't help myself. Every time I think of the terrible thing he's done, my resentment destroys all my love for him. It'll be better if he marries and goes out of my life forever. But *you* will be good to him, won't you?"

"Of course I will," I answer gently. "Now, that's more like it." I take the lid from her stove and drop a short green log onto the fire. "Try to convince yourself that actually he's done nothing wrong. He's made a mistake that I'll admit I can't understand, but he's corrected it; and now you must hope for his future, not mourn for his past. After all, he's perfectly all right in the eyes of Rome."

She sniffles, following me with her eyes as I resume my seat. "All I know is that when he was a monk he shared his heart with no one but his mother. All his problems were mine. Oh, if you could read the letters he used to write, full of tenderness and love." Her voice falters and tears return. "I hate him for taking that from me," she says resentfully. "Now that I know the truth about him, I wonder how honest his letters really were. He's a sneak, a liar, a weakling." She sobs into her handkerchief. "Other men have remained monks—why couldn't he? My son's a weakling, that's why. How can I be proud of an abortion like that?"

I flinch at the word "abortion." "This is only exciting you," I sigh, rising to leave. "I'd better go."

"No, no!" she cries. "If you leave me now I think I'll lose my mind. Talk to me. Tell me I'm wrong in feeling these things about my son."

Sudden pity fills me. "Well, all you need do, my poor friend, is look at it clearly. How old was Michel when you sent him to monastic school?"

"Just thirteen," she says brokenly. "But you can ask

421

anyone here and they'll tell you that if ever a child had the true monastic vocation, it was Michel. You know what I think? I think the stigma of his birth—the sins of his father who seduced me—are being visited on him."

"No, now," I groan, dropping again into my chair, "you mustn't say that. For the love of heaven be sensible. You put Michel into a monastery school when he was too young to know much. Obviously he developed sexually very late. And when he did develop, he merely discovered that his vocation wasn't strong enough to overcome the desire for a family. Nothing wrong with that. To be perfectly fair you must admit you simply started him on a career of your own choosing, without a vocation—without a real vocation. And you know that without it no man can stand up under the monastic regime."

She looks up sharply and I lean forward.

"It boils down to a couple of things. You're disappointed that Michel wasn't called to God. That can't be helped. But you seem most troubled by the fact he's become man enough not to pour out his heart to you as he did in the past. You should be grateful, for it shows he's developing into a normal human being. No man writes his mother about all his thoughts and desires and disappointments. If he does there's something unhealthy in their relationship."

She begins to weep openly a flood of irritating tears, moaning miserably. I lean back in disgust.

"Ah, you whine like a baby," I say harshly, unthinking.

Breath catches in her throat, and she stifles her sobs. There's a long silence of dripping morning showers and wood catching in the stove. I regret my words.

"Tell me," I say softly at last, "why did you put him in the school so young? Wasn't that a big mistake? Like a lot of parents you wanted something for your child which you wouldn't want for yourself at all. What made you do it?"

"He had such wonderful eyes," she answers eagerly, rapidly. "You couldn't look at him without knowing he was made for God. Such a spiritual look. All that's gone."

422

I smile, stretching. "And for the best, too. Really now, don't you think that's a little too much? Reading a monastic vocation in a pair of childish eyes? All children look spiritual. It's ideals and ignorance and virginity—lots of things that keep a child's eyes clear and stupid."

"You're wrong," she asserts, gritting her teeth. "You're wrong, wrong."

"No, I'm not. You've been responsible for putting Michel through a hell of self-doubts, and now the mistake's become almost irreparable. You want him to continue living your mistake. No man can do that. Don't you see? You must help him correct this mistake instead of being hurt at everything he does. Am I not right?"

She says crossly, "You'll have your way, won't you?" Sitting up, she puts a pillow behind her back. "I tell you, he had the vocation. Something happened. But in any case he owes it to me to listen to what I have to say."

"He's a man, Madame Renée." I shrug my shoulders. "But go ahead—you're only driving him from you."

"Now, be careful what you say, young man," she rejoins with sudden hostility. "I've done nothing to drive him from me. I've been a perfect mother."

"I won't argue with you about it," I sigh, leaning back in my chair.

Neither of us says anything. Madame Renée stares moodily at the ceiling, and I cross and uncross my legs. But after a while she grows calm. Her features begin to relax. And at last, looking at me with affection, she observes, "You know, if Michel were more like you I could bear it. But he's such a naïve oaf, bless his heart. I suppose it's wrong, but I can't help wondering about him. I often wonder what would happen if some woman got hold of him. He'd be putty in her hands."

"That's probably the best thing that could happen to him—to have some woman get hold of him."

"What!" she exclaims. "You don't really mean—?"

I break in, "You don't expect him to remain chaste the rest of his life, do you? Now, don't look sad. It's only

423

natural, and with a young man it really doesn't mean anything."

"Sometimes I don't understand you. How could you want something like that for a boy like Michel? You'd love to see him break his mother's heart, wouldn't you?"

Wearily I get to my feet. "Please, Madame, don't antagonize me any more than you have to. I'm still taking stovarsol—and my nerves can't stand much arguing."

She softens, nodding her head understandingly. "Have you got your bottle of medicine with you?" she asks. "Here, let me read what it says. I want to see what it is they're giving you."

She examines the printing on the label. I know exactly the part she will comment on, the part she will choose to read aloud. And I'm not mistaken. After a moment she glances up, a placid smile on her handsome face.

"Humph," she says, sniffing and blinking her eyes, "listen to this: 'In the event of diarrhea, treatment should be suspended temporarily.'" Her face becomes open piggish smiling, motherly and possessive; she seems delighted to have such an opening.

I wait, knowing what will come.

"So you have to stop taking these pills if you get diarrhea?" she goes on. "I wonder for how long? Did the doctor say? In your weakened condition you couldn't stand much diarrhea, could you? Have you noticed any signs of it yet?"

I roll my eyes heavenward, sick with disgust. "No, I'm all right."

She laughs easily. "I wonder if I could prepare you something special? Or if it does happen, you can tell me and I'll give you a little tea with paregoric in it. Would you like a cup now?"

"No, thank you," I mutter sarcastically.

The tone of my voice takes her eyes from the label. "Why, I'm surprised at you. I do believe you're embarrassed. And I didn't think anything I could do would embarrass you. After all, we've said nearly everything."

424

"Let's not talk about it." I shake my head, looking at her. "Don't you think I've read that? Don't you think I know what to do?"

She hands me the bottle. "You're touchy," she reproves me gently.

I say nothing, replacing the bottle in my pocket.

"I've made out a list of the provisions we need," she says shortly—"but since you suggested it, I'll just send Germaine for them after all." She looks at me gravely. "Hope I'm not getting too much; if I get too tough Michel may not be eating with us . . . Oh, I'm only teasing you," she laughs. "His train gets in at eight. You can walk back together. But before you go for him, would you come help me with my leg bandage? I haven't the strength to wind it as tightly as it should be. Then, when you two boys get back, we'll have a good dinner."

"Fine." I walk to the door.

Snorting, smirking, she asks, "Incidentally, were there any pretty nurses in the hospital?"

"All of them were beautiful," I tell her seriously, "and I violated each one of them twice. Does that satisfy your curiosity?"

"Come now," she admonishes, "you're getting crude."

"Oh, by the way, I completely forgot something. There was a note for me this morning: Mademoiselle Marthe wanted me to have lunch with her today, and I've accepted." I open the door and stare through the misting rain, looking down the dirty street of slush-covered snow.

Madame Renée's voice comes irritatingly from behind me. "Why did you wait so long to tell me? How did she happen to invite you?"

"We're very fond of each other. It'll give you a rest and save you the trouble of cooking for me. I'll drop by this evening before going for Michel."

She doesn't tell me good-bye. I know she is angry and offended at my willingness to take a meal elsewhere—and I am delighted to offend her.

Nerves relax when I step inside the thin gates of the

425

cloister courtyard. The monks seem delighted to have me back, thankful that I'm well again. And after an absence of ten days, the small paleography room welcomes me as a sanctuary. But the hours are short, forming little more than a temporary refuge from compelling outside interests. I am forced to miss Mass in order to catch up with my studies.

I arrive at Mademoiselle Marthe's for an early lunch. In her small, poverty-stricken salon she appears even tinier than before: a quick little thing, of superb intelligence and wit. She has prepared hors d'œuvres, tuna, and potato cakes, accompanied with coffee and a cheap white wine. Moving slowly she serves me with her gnarled hands, bending almost double as she walks.

"And how do you like my cooking, young man?" she inquires. "Are you eating heartily because you're hungry? Or can it possibly be that the food is acceptably prepared?"

I laugh, "Of course it doesn't compare with the sort of thing I'm used to eating, you know that. No one can cook with such skill and grace as Madame Renée—not even the *cordons bleus* of Dijon. But considering the fact it was prepared by a mere mortal like yourself, it's delicious. In fact, if I weren't afraid of committing high heresy, I'd say it was as good as Madame Renée's."

"Hush, child, hush! Name of the Lord, do you want the very heavens to inundate us with wine dregs? I know my cooking lacks a certain—*something.*" She purses her lips comically and holds her hand limply in mid-air. "It hasn't the tone, the bouquet of fine things of the past. You see," she mutters, her aged voice cracking, "I never had the opportunity to learn the culinary arts from innumerable staff cooks in my father's house. Alas"—bowing her head in mock shame—"alas, young man, you're looking upon one of the rarest individuals in this Valley—a poor woman. No, that's not right, poor women aren't rare; but I'm a poor woman who has *never* been rich. Look well, for you won't soon see another. Everyone in the Village who's poor, has at one time been rich and highly cultured."

426

"Except Mother Nourrie," I put in.

"I have doubts even about her," replies Mademoiselle Marthe. "Here, now, finish up this tuna. My father, bless him, never learned to love money or to make it. I've been nothing but a poor university professor. Great is my shame. My only virtue, to which I cling with fierce pride, is my ability to construct a sentence properly."

I put down my fork. "Seriously, Mademoiselle," I moan, "why didn't I know you sooner? Perhaps you'd have let me come here for my meals. I'd gladly pay double what I do now, just to have the peace of a sane woman about me."

"Is it that bad, Monsieur?"

"I'm afraid so," I say sadly. "Lord knows I'm not much good, but somehow that woman brings out the worst in me. You mustn't mention this, but I have a treat in store for tonight—Michel is coming."

Pouring coffee, my hostess clicks her tongue sympathetically. "I thought as much. Madame Renée told me all about Michel when I took her to the City to have her leg treated. He's a dull one, that boy. Try not to get involved with him."

"He's staying at my place, unfortunately."

"It's probably just as well."

"How's that?"

"Madame Renée so bitterly resents what Michel has done, I think it best for them not to be alone together."

"You're right," I sigh. "But I've been wondering how I'll ever handle the situation. I'll be caught right in the middle."

Mademoiselle Marthe nods her head. "Quite true—your position won't be an enviable one." She hesitates a moment, then, "May I say something more?" she asks.

"Please do."

"As difficult as this will be for you, Monsieur, you must resist the desire to wash your hands of the whole affair. Madame Renée's bitterness may lead her to do anything, and you must be there to stop it. You must do all you can

427

to cushion the selfish anger she will direct against Michel."

"What do you think may happen?"

"I think they may break with each other, completely and irreparably. And you are the only one who can possibly prevent it."

"Do you really believe that?" I ask, sipping my coffee.

"I'm convinced of it. And we must never permit such a tragic thing to happen."

"No, of course not."

"Now, shall we discuss something more pleasant? How is your work at the Monastery progressing?"

We converse freely, with the delight of not having to be cautious. We take our chairs near her small cookstove. To stop the cold, Mademoiselle Marthe wraps a blanket around my feet. I have brought my music, and I copy my lessons as we talk. Mademoiselle Marthe is amusing and healthful and very keen. The hunger for such companionship is assuaged in both of us. We discuss Richepin, Sartre, the early mystic poets: clear, precise arguments, interrupted by frequent references to old magazines and books. How gross and bloated seems Madame Renée in her preoccupation with diarrhea, with her beauty, with her thirty-year-old body.

The afternoon soon passes, and I realize how much I've learned from this little wrinkled woman. As I prepare to leave, I decide to ask if I may study with her.

"I lead a lonely life, young man," she answers. "I live now only for my books and for the services at the Monastery —whenever I feel strong enough to attend them. Your company for an hour each day would be most welcome. But what could I teach you?"

"You're joking, Mademoiselle—what *couldn't* you teach me? But I should most like to study the early mystic poets. I'll come each day after Vespers, and I'll pay you fifty francs a day."

"Nonsense."

"Fifty francs a day is all I can afford. It's so little as to be insulting, I know. But you will accept it, won't you?"

"With pleasure, then."

428

"Good." I gather up my work, stacking it neatly together. "Of course," I add, "you realize Madame Renée will be angry? But I want to do it anyway. If she doesn't like it, it's just too bad. I'll brave her if you will, though I don't want to cause a rift between you."

She hands me my coat and scarf. "There's never been anything profound between us, young friend."

"Until tomorrow, then, Mademoiselle. And many thanks for a pleasant afternoon."

It is almost time for Vespers, and I hurry to the Monastery. As I pass through the gatehouse, Father Dutfoy calls to me from the cage where he is sorting papers.

"Monsieur Chevissier is waiting in the parlor to see you, my son."

"Monsieur Chevissier?"

"Yes. He has been here several times the last few days."

"Thanks, Father." I hesitate, uneasiness probing my stomach. It must still be going on, then; and tonight we'll sit at Madame Renée's table and eat death-tainted food. Again the remembered tears, the little coffin, the red face of Papa Chevissier: what can I tell him this time? Without finding an answer, I walk quickly into the parlor.

The little man rises stiffly from an easy chair and greets me warmly. "I've been anxious to see you," he says, "but they told me you were in the hospital. Are you all right, M'sieu?" His voice holds genuine concern.

"Yes, I'm fine now, thanks. Is something wrong?"

"No, not a thing." He smiles happily. "My wife just wanted me to come and thank you."

"Thank me for what? Did our plan work?"

He looks at me in surprise. "No, we didn't need it. Didn't you know? We supposed our good luck was due to you."

"What good luck?"

"Why, Madame Renée came right after she got back from her trip and paid us for the food we'd given her."

"She did?" Amazement and relief begin to dull the sharp uneasiness within me.

429

"Yes—and she begged us to forget her threats, too. Why, we supposed—"

"You can't imagine how glad I am to hear it," I tell him —"but I had nothing to do with it." I control my astonishment as he stares openly.

"You didn't?" he asks incredulously.

"Not a thing. Just like I told you," I explain matter-of-factly, "she's not a bad woman. She recognized her mistake and corrected it of her own accord. You owe me no thanks."

"M'sieu is protecting—"

"No, I'm not," I interrupt. "Not at all. But I appreciate your letting me know. I feel much kinder toward her now."

To my embarrassment he insists on thanking me anyway —again and again. And in parting he invites me to visit him and Madame Chevissier at the farm whenever I can.

After he has gone I stroll out into the garden, bowing low to each monk I pass. My mind rejects an attempt to understand Madame Renée's behavior: the enigma is beyond understanding. The pieces are there, but the pattern is missing.

The River has thawed still more this afternoon. As I look down from the high parapets of the garden wall, the water, curdled with large chunks of ice, moves slowly past. A wind in the trees, and the never-shocking great bells gathering force from silence to announce the beginning of Vespers. Sounds of melting ice dripping from the trees. The ground is ugly slush.

I lean far over the low wall in the empty garden. The first faint noises of an organ prelude from the chapel tell me that Vespers are beginning, but I don't move. Across the wide River, trees and housetops form indistinct designs through afternoon mists. Smoke rises from evening cooking fires and is dissipated in gusts of damp air. The sky remains overcast, dulling all colors in the soaked countryside that stretches flat and empty across the way. Vesper chants float to me on a sudden chilling breeze, then die away.

I think of the day and of the evening to come, formulating answers, trying to plan my actions. Man destroys him-

430

self by associating with those who arouse in him a feeling of repugnance. If I were to follow my desire, my will, I'd never see Madame Renée again. But I know I must swallow my distaste and go back to her, for there's no one to take my place. I try to think of her as good: she did, at least, relent in her demands on the Chevissiers. But it's too late; feelings can never thus change.

When I enter the grilled gate to her cottage yard, it is dusk; but her shutters haven't been drawn and there's no light from the windows. An overwhelming fatigue begins its trembling within me. Wearily, without knocking, I open the door.

A rush of warm dry air, an obscurity of deeply shadowed room. Red from the stove window, magnified, dancing on the wall above Madame Renée's couch. And on the couch, the small movements of her indistinct figure. I whisper, "Are you awake?"—hoping she's not.

"Humph!" is snorted disgustedly; she is awake.

Taking a straight-backed chair from the dining table, I feel my way to sit near her. The warmth and darkness of the room fill me with great loneliness. "How're you feeling this evening?" I ask her.

"Terrible," returns her voice, dolorous, heavy, clumsy, from the dark. "I've been lying here alone all afternoon," she whispers, "and when I'm alone my thoughts turn to Michel and I begin to hate him."

Revulsion, fatigue and the warmth of darkness set me dizzy. Her old, old song doesn't penetrate; like vomit, it seeks to be cast out. The words are rehearsed, like a scene from Racine.

"And you don't help matters much, either, Monsieur."

"*Now* what have I done?"

"Didn't you have lunch with Mademoiselle Marthe? Didn't you spend most of the afternoon with her?"

I say nothing, exhaustion and sickness rising inside me.

"Oh, she's clever, waiting till she knows I can't move to invite you to lunch. Otherwise she'd be obliged to ask me too, wouldn't she? I know it's wrong to suspect you, but is this any way of showing your feelings for me?—running out just when I need you most?"

I stare at the reflection of the stove window dancing on the wall above her head.

"You could've spent the afternoon with me," she moans pathetically, "and then I wouldn't have had time to think about Michel."

"Love of God!" I blurt out suddenly to the impersonal darkness, unable to restrain myself any longer, "I'm tired, tired. Why should I spend any more time with you than necessary? You make my life miserable. If only you'd be *sensible* for a change!" The vomit has been cast out, and I stop.

There's no movement on the couch. Nervously I light a cigarette, the match flame blinding me for a moment. I can find no words with which to apologize. I toss away the match, hearing it strike and bounce on the stone floor in the corner. My hands unconsciously count the cane strands of the chair upon which I sit.

Imperceptibly, as an inner mumbling, her voice drifts into the silence. "It's the medicine that made you say that. You couldn't help it and I'm not blaming you. But don't you see"—her tone turning from dull lifelessness to conniving warmth and the strength of hatred—"Mademoiselle Marthe is a clever woman who's playing you for a dupe. Men are such fools around women. Humph. Did you talk about me, I suppose?"

"Didn't mention you," I lie. "Mademoiselle Marthe is above that sort of thing. You're too suspicious."

Somewhere across the street a light is turned on, pouring instantaneous diluted yellowness into the room. Patterns through lace curtains stand large against the opposite wall. I move my head, and its huge shadow moves on the plaster. Madame Renée looks at me.

"Why, she'd do it just to spite me," she replies with quiet anger. "She knows we're rather close, and women are cats about that sort of thing. She'll try to take you away from me."

432

"But I don't belong to you," I tell her half-laughing. I pause as a log snaps loudly in the stove, briefly intensifying the redness reflected above Madame Renée's head. "You may as well know now," I go on, "that I've asked her to help me with my studies. She's to coach me every afternoon for an hour and I'm to pay her. It'll help the poor woman live."

Madame Renée stares at me in surprise; then her eyes fill with tears and she twists her head away. "Oh, thank you," she sobs, "thank you very much." Turning back to me she props herself on an elbow, her body tense. "Will you tell me one thing?" she says in hoarse fury. "Will you tell me why in God's holy name I always let my affections center on such sorry men? Are you completely faithless, then?"

"What the hell," I exclaim, "are you talking about! Just because you and I are friends doesn't mean I can't work with whom I damn' well please."

She settles back against the pillow, sobs rising again in her throat. "Why couldn't you work with me?" she whines tremulously. "Heaven knows I need the money desperately enough. But no, you take all I have to offer and then go to Mademoiselle Marthe and pay her for doing something I could do as well. Well, it isn't I who'll stop you."

"Thank God," I mutter. The light across the way is turned off and I can no longer see her.

"You're despicable," comes from the darkness. "Why do you upset me like this? Sometimes I think you do it purposely."

"Now look," I say through puffs of smoke, "what have I done? I want to study with Mademoiselle Marthe for two simple reasons: first, she's a professor who knows her field, and second, I'm very fond of her. It's got nothing to do with you, so forget it—and don't think you can make me change my mind. If you hate so much to stay here alone, you might try being a little nicer to people who used to be your friends before I came. Do you realize you've done something to offend each one of them? And all because

433

you didn't want to share me a single minute with anyone."

"That's not true. I—"

"And you might treat Michel a little better—unless you want to drive him away from you too."

"Michel! You only make me *hate* Michel."

"I'm sorry, but if you hate him it's your own fault—it's because your thinking's wrong. And you're intelligent enough to correct that yourself. I refuse to baby you any longer."

"Preach, preach!" she sneers, her voice guttural. "Preach your damned head off! But I'll show you: I'll send my precious Michel packing the minute he sets foot in this house —and you can thank yourself for breaking us up completely. If you weren't so selfish I wouldn't be so upset. Thank yourself for that, and be proud."

"Stop talking nonsense," I interject wearily.

"Get out of my house! Go to your fine Mademoiselle Marthe and tell her what I said; tell her she's succeeded in turning you against me."

I feel my way to the stove and crush out my cigarette on its top. "Why don't we," I suggest dully, ignoring her commands, "try to be a little more pleasant? I'm awfully tired." Finding my chair again, I ask in the most normal tone I can muster, "Did you say you wanted to have dinner after Michel arrives?"

Madame Renée doesn't answer immediately, and when she does, her voice is hollow and melodramatic. "If you want to eat I shall continue to cook for you. You can eat here whenever you like. But I—I shan't eat any more. That way, maybe God will take me from this earth." She hasn't had enough; words are not yet old to her.

I laugh, moving in my chair, hearing my feet scrape on the floor. "In other words you're going to commit suicide?" I look out the window through the curtains: deepening night and hints of wetness.

She snorts, "Ha, no! That wouldn't be Christian. I'll simply quit eating. That'll take care of my life here on earth."

434

"You shouldn't say things like that, Madame Renée," I tell her seriously. "Makes you sound foolish. If you'd ever been hungry enough you'd know that one just doesn't starve to death in the midst of plenty."

"But can't you understand," she groans, making a violent movement on the couch (I imagine that she's shaking her fist at me), "can't you understand, you fool, that I *want* to die?" (For a moment I'm touched; her voice almost loses its falsity.) "What have I to live for?" she continues bitterly. "Not my son, certainly, who's caused me nothing but pain. Not you, whom I've given a mother's love and who disappoints me at every turn with sheer stupidity. You want me to be nothing but your cook—all right, I'll be just that, if it suits you. And we won't talk any more, please." With another sudden movement she shifts her position.

Angrily I walk to the wall and, groping for the switch, flood the room with light. It is brilliant, painful to my squinting eyes. I see that Madame Renée is lying on her side facing the wall. The back of her neck, under the two rolls of poorly combed hair, flames scarlet. She doesn't move.

"What you need," I say harshly, "is a good whack on the behind. You're behaving exactly like a rotten-spoiled child: if we won't play according to your rules, then we won't play at all. I've seen children spanked for less. But children are more original. The trouble with you is, you're too stereotyped—I *always* know what you're going to do next. Right now, for example"—bending over her, trying to find her eyes—"right now's the moment for you to burst into a flood of tears and melt in my arms and make me take back all I've said. Your face is turned from me at just the right angle. But I know your mind is weighing every word I say so you can twist it to your own advantage. Well, all that's finished, do you understand? Two can play at this game. I can act just as well as you can, Madame Duse."

She turns over, and I observe that it hasn't penetrated very deeply; behind her eyes there's only a faint glimmer

435

of curiosity. "What do you mean by that?" she asks sullenly.

"By what?"

"Calling me 'Madame Doozay'? Who was she, one of your mistresses?"

I laugh—a short, quick laugh. "Hardly. Alas, she was a great actress like yourself, only never quite so obvious."

Madame Renée appears old, tear-streaked, tired, but her words are quick: "Perhaps she played to a higher-type audience."

"No doubt," I say acidly.

She stares at her feet. "You do think all this is acting, don't you?" she whispers.

"Isn't it? Aren't you trying to dominate everybody who's within reach?"

"You'll see. I'm a woman out of my time."

I fall into my chair, groaning, "Good Lord!"

"Out of my time," insists Madame Renée. "I belong to the past when emotions were real, young man, not the counterfeit thing you always see nowadays. I shall eat no more," she says heroically, with slightly raised chin, looking up into the light bulb—"I'm announcing that now, simply and calmly. I shall die of starvation. I really can't afford to eat on what you pay me anyhow. And now that Michel is in the world, I'll have to see that he gets what little I have left."

I answer gently, "You've gained at least twenty pounds since I started paying you to cook for me. Look at yourself; your speech is fine, but look at yourself. It'll take some doing to waste you away to nothing."

She sobs, "You can be so unspeakably cruel!"

"I'm sorry, I don't mean to be. Maybe I act like this in hopes of shocking some sense into you. But nothing seems to work with you, and I apologize for acting the way I have. If you'd just realize one simple fact—that you'll never have your way with me."

"I'm a strong woman; no little thing like you can change me."

436

"Good," I reply weakly. "Now it seems we're even. You've treated me as a little thing and a stupid fool. What comes next?"

She moves uncomfortably, blushing, and murmurs pleadingly, "Let's start over, shall we? I don't know why we seem to irritate each other so. I'm always ashamed of it afterward, for I really am fond of you—and I imagine you regret some of the things you say to me. I don't see how you put up with an old woman like me, really. Will you help me with my leg bandage?"

It dissolves; tired and relieved I answer, "Of course."

She pulls the black cotton stocking from her badly discolored lower leg, but she doesn't take it off; her toes remain covered. Handing me some strong muslin gauze, she tells me how to wrap it under her foot and around her ankle and leg, up to the knee. I pass the bandage under the arch for the first turn, but the stocking, rolled about her toes, catches the gauze and hinders my movements. Without thinking, I remove the stocking completely from her foot, and she starts and cries, "No, no, don't expose the toes!"

But it's too late. I have already tossed the stocking to the floor. I gaze dumbly at what it has concealed. The toes are bent far under the foot. Dry, cracked skin peels back from each joint. The bone structure is grotesquely deformed, and curly black hairs sprout from the knobs. Involuntarily I draw back. Madame Renée is deeply embarrassed.

"Oh, I—I'm sorry, Madame," I stammer. "I didn't know your foot was—"

"Such a monstrosity?" she supplies. "You can say it now that you've seen it. Hideous, isn't it?"

"Here," I force out casually, "let me wrap that leg for you."

"No, first"—leaning forward, taking my hand in hers, staring supplication without guile—"first promise me you'll never think of it again. Forget you ever saw my foot. Can you do that? I'd like for you to think only of the finer side of me."

"Of course, Madame."

437

"My feet have always been sources of great shame. Now promise me you'll forget you ever saw this."

"I promise. Don't think anything more about it." Fighting down my revulsion, I begin again to bandage her leg. "There now, does that hurt?"

Her skin is dry like her hands, unpleasant to the touch. Nerves falter as I feel the muscles of her leg move beneath the bruised, feverish skin. I become suddenly aware that she imagines a caress each time I touch her; that she responds to it by contracting the muscles beneath my hand. A redness forms before my eyes: unspeakable natural repugnance. After a moment of this obscene exchange of touches, she stops me and again takes my hand, this time placing it very lightly on her knee. Still holding it, she rubs it gently over a slightly swollen spot until I tremble with the sickness of my disgust. I look at her, swallowing. Her face is flushed. She is magnificent in her piggish affection, smiling inwardly to herself, her lips half-open.

"You see, right there—no, right there. That's another place I was hurt. It's still swollen a little."

I nod my head and return to my task. The innocent process of wrapping an injured leg increases in its perversity. Saliva changes to acid in my mouth. She pushes the leg toward me, ostensibly to make my task easier. The touch becomes alive; the touch becomes a sex act of muscular reflexes. Any physical contact is now a torture of loathing. Old flesh. Old dry skin. No, it's not tight enough, she'll have more of it. And I think of other things. Impersonal in my work, bandaging tightly, careful to touch her as little as possible. I think of Father Clément, of cooler things, of health. Until at last it's finished and I lean back.

"There, Madame," I say lightly, "think that has it. A very professional job. I hope it's all right."

"Just wonderful," she says as she examines it. "It feels better already. Will you be able to do this for me every day? Or perhaps it's distasteful to you?"

"Not at all."

She laughs; she has understood and knows that I understand. Biting her lower lip, she murmurs, "You're really very expert with your hands, you know. Such fine strong hands."

"Thanks, Madame." And to myself I add, "You're quite expert with your legs, too." I rise and walk to the stove, walk away from the bruised leg that has now become so nuptial in character.

"It's almost time," she observes, "for you to go for Michel. You can bring him straight here. And you *will* remember that your fidelity's to me, won't you? Try to remember everything he says so you can tell me later. Are we friends again?"

"Of course, Madame, you know that. And I hope we stay that way." But inside, my disgust hasn't yet drained away. I look at her as I put on my coat and, as it has before, the word "bitch" forms itself in my mind.

"Good-bye, then," she says very quietly, with a strange smile as of things half-done, of propriety over the risk of daring; a smile of the closed mouth, of drawn-together lips in a straight line; a smile of smiling to herself, of looking after me with questions that I'm careful not to answer.

The instant I step outside I feel cleaner and healthier. It's a clear night after the soaking rains, cold, but with a hint of warm currents that blow away contamination. The countryside gives up its odors of smoke and dampness and thawing earth, more pointed in the early evening. The road into Town, following the curved, swollen River, is deserted at this hour, and the long walk becomes repose. Alone, in the midst of a crowded countryside, I am conscious of the hills that can't be seen, rising on either side of the Valley. As I walk, sweats form; and their warming glow is grateful to the senses after the day's spiritual weariness.

At last I arrive at the railroad station: tiny stone buildings clustered together by the tracks, each dimly lighted by a hanging electric lamp. In one of them is the waiting room, where I haven't been since that rainy night months ago when I first arrived in the Valley. I sit down on a hard bench. There are a few scattered people eating sandwiches

439

they have brought from home, surrounded by the wicker baskets which they use as suitcases. The floor is filthy—mealy with mold and ground-in dirts.

A clerk in gray smock and black beret enters with papers under his arm. Important. Busy. He writes on a glass blackboard: "A delay of 15 minutes for the train from Paris south." Dusting the chalk from his hands, he gathers up his sheaf of papers and leaves for other important duties.

I stop him. "Pardon, Monsieur—does that mean the train from Paris will arrive at the station fifteen minutes late, or that it will be loaded for the South fifteen minutes late?"

"It means both, Monsieur," he answers, smiling: flashy, toothy smile, horn-rimmed glasses, and a myopic cordiality.

"Is there a buffet or café on the premises?"

"But yes, Monsieur—come, I'll show you. You can get beer, wine and sandwiches. There—you see?—the building just the other side of the water closets."

I thank him and saunter over to the café. When I open the door, a bell rings somewhere in back. I stand in an empty room with sawdust floors and a bar scarcely four feet in length. Sounds of a chair being pushed back, and odors of garlic and meat as steps approach the curtained doorway behind the bar. A glimpse of the back room as the curtains are drawn aside: three men seated at a table eating.

"Yes, M'sieu?" says a middle-aged woman, tired, color-less, perfunctory. From habit she wipes the bar with a dirty white cloth.

"A glass of beer, Madame—excuse me for interrupting your dinner."

"Oh, that's not important, M'sieu," she says tiredly.

She draws a large glass of pale beer, turns off the spigot to let the foam descend, and finishes filling the glass. I pay her so that she can return to her dinner. The stuff is flat but it can be swallowed, and that's all we expect nowadays. It's a way of passing a few moments, better than sitting on a hard bench in the waiting room watching the others eat their sandwiches. I drink it slowly and smoke a cigarette.

To pass a few more moments I stop at the outhouse, entering the side marked MEN. The damp air inside is heavy with chill. In the separating wall someone has gouged a large peephole that looks into the cubicle reserved for women—but no women are there tonight. The place is empty. Every inch of the wall is covered with pornographic drawings, poems, and scattered requests for girls' telephone numbers and homosexual rendezvous. Some of these are scratched through with crayoned words and phrases like "Shame," "Disgusting," "Go back to Paris," or with Biblical quotations. The stench is abominable.

There's no lock on the door. It opens behind me and I turn, buttoning my pants to leave. I bow low to a bent old man with gray mustaches, wearing wooden shoes and a beret, who holds the door open awaiting his turn.

"M'sieu?" He tips his beret.

"Monsieur?" I bow again and edge out past him, out into the clear fresh night, and follow the graveled path back to the waiting room.

The sandwiches have been finished. Bags are being put in shape to leave. It's time for the train, but the train doesn't arrive. No sound disturbs the silence except an occasional sigh of boredom, along with mumbled vituperation directed at the damnable delays.

The fifteen-minute sign is changed to indicate an additional thirty-minute delay. And the poor clerk has to shake off the curses of those who wait, who place the responsibility for this delay squarely upon his thin shoulders. Tempers are lost, and for a moment we enjoy ourselves. Finally the besieged clerk lifts his hands above his head, and groans, "Ah, but some people can be purgative when they want to."

This elegance is answered by the man with whom he has been arguing, a stockily built middle-aged blond dressed in black. His family is clustered about him, and he answers the "purgative" charge clearly and succinctly and with crushing finality: "Shit, then."

He shrugs his shoulders and returns unruffled to his

seat, followed by the admiring gaze of everyone else in the room. Each of us realizes that here—here is a reply of ideal clarity that has a certain magnificence in its logic. He ignores our attentions, as a great actor or writer might ignore those who stand in rapt appreciation of his skill, but who, nevertheless, bore him with their insipid plaudits. His wife beams at him, takes his left hand in hers, and fingers the wide gold wedding band about his long powerful finger. An old, incredibly tiny woman in the corner struggles to control her delighted laughter, staring at our modest hero with the toothless grin and adoring eyes of age whose faith in youth has been restored.

Satisfied, we wait until the train thunders in around the curve of the track.

To prove that he's consistently a man of pointed clarity, our hero mutters, "God be praised," gathers his luggage and his children and his fine proud wife, and walks heavily to the door as the train comes to a roaring, steam-shedding halt. Unsmiling, with both hands firmly gripping his bag, and a cigarette in his mouth, he turns to his small daughter and roars almost as loudly as the train, "Name of God, Yvette, get out from under my feet!"

We walk out onto the platform. Reaching down, I take Yvette's hand in mine and lead her to the door of the heaving train to wait for her father. His smile is a sneering half-nod of the head.

"Thank you, young man, you're most kind. Now, Yvette, get inside the car and wait for your mother."

Beside the next car a young man dressed elegantly in an overcoat and black homburg hat, bends over his suitcase to check the tag. He straightens up, catches sight of me, and runs to shake my hand. "I'm Michel Renée," he eagerly introduces himself. "Aren't you Mother's friend? Recognized you from her description. She wrote that you'd meet me."

He has a long, thin face, and when he takes off his hat I notice that his hair hasn't yet grown out from his tonsure. He grins openly, and his eyes are wonderfully vital. As we

442

prepare to leave the station he acts and speaks with the verve of a sixteen-year-old. Instinctively I draw back from such openness. I don't offer to help him with his bag.

Hoping to avoid being seen, we walk quickly out of Town. We keep to the side of the road. I say little, listening to Michel's small talk. The distance to the Village is soon covered, and presently the Monastery looms in the starlit night. Down the River to the left, a rising moon, and in the slow-moving waters, a tortured reflection of the Monastery's hulk.

"What a beautiful sight!" whispers my companion, walking more slowly.

"Yes, isn't it?" I reply. We stop for a moment as he admires the view.

"You know, Monsieur," he says after a silence, beginning to walk again, "I was waiting for this. Up to now I couldn't be sure I was right in leaving my monastery; I couldn't be certain I didn't have a real monastic vocation after all. I was terribly anxious to see what my reaction would be when I came back here, where I spent so much of my childhood. But you know, I don't feel a thing—not the slightest desire to go in and say Compline, or to return to my habit." He shakes his head. "No, I'm a civilian and my past life was a mistake." He picks up his steps as we approach the bridge.

I slow him down. "Michel," I caution him, "I must tell you before we get to your house that you should be very careful, and very attentive to your mother. This is a great shock for her, you know. She feels she's losing you. Above all, don't say anything about girls—whether you have any or not. She seems especially sensitive about that."

He coughs and spits to clear his throat. We turn onto the bridge. "All right, Monsieur, I trust your judgment and your friendship for me." He lays a hand on my arm and we pause in the middle of the bridge. "Wait a minute," he says, talking more loudly to be heard above the roar of the water. "Speaking of girls, there's something I may as well tell you right now: I'm planning to get married."

"Already?" I say, peering at his dimly lighted face, con-

443

scious of the black stone battlements beyond. "A little soon for that, isn't it?"

"Well, I don't know—hadn't even thought about it. She's really—"

"How long have you known her, Michel? Your hair hasn't even grown out enough to cover your tonsure."

He laughs shortly, uncomfortably. "I've known her for quite a while," he answers vaguely. "I want to tell you all about it."

"Not now, we don't have time. But you're sleeping at my place, so we can talk later if you like." I begin slowly walking, and he follows.

"Wish I could tell Mother about it," he remarks thoughtfully. "I hate lying."

"But you must realize how peculiar it looks, Michel: here you've been out of the monastery only a few weeks and already you're engaged. We can discuss it later—but remember, no hint of it to your mother. I'll tell you frankly, she's bitter over what she thinks you've done to her. You've *got* to give her time to get used to it before announcing any such plan as marriage."

He laughs, a young boy's laugh. "I guess from what you say, Mama must be pretty ferocious. I'm awfully sorry to cause all this trouble. But don't worry, my friend, I know Mama—I've got around her before. She'll get over it when she sees I'm firm in my decision." We step from the bridge, and our pace becomes even slower.

"I've more or less prepared the way for you," I say to him. "But your mother's a spoiled child, too proud for her own good. Forgive me for saying this—but I don't want us to see her without explaining to you my part in the whole thing. Apparently her letters have given you a false picture of our relationship, for I don't have any special affection for her—what I'm doing for her I'd do for anybody. The only interest I have in her is pity, and—well, I don't want you to make the mistake of considering me one of the family."

He looks at me closely, but I can't see the expression on

444

his face. Somehow I hope that he'll defend his mother, that he'll denounce me for talking this way—but instead he pats me on the shoulder.

"My poor friend," he says sympathetically. "She's been that bad, eh? She can be a hellion when she tries. But we must be patient with her. Above all, let's not lose our tempers."

As we approach the house Michel's voice loses its mellifluous assurance. "Ah, here we are. Wish me luck. Bless her heart, I'll try not to tell her about Madeleine, but I won't lie."

Something false causes me to raise my voice. "You'd better lie if you want any more help from me."

A momentary pause outside the door, followed by a drunken emotion of quick light in our faces as the door is thrown open. Swirls of overcoat and black skirt in a sudden embrace, and a confusion of kisses and hugs and words of endearment between sobs. The mother and son cling to each other. I carry in his bag and put it down near the door.

"Ah, Mama, my dear little Mama," he cries weeping, burying his face in his hands, then kissing her again.

"My child," she croons, "my Michel. There, don't cry. There, there, Michel, my darling sweet son."

Something turns in my stomach. Michel is more clever than I thought; he knows how to handle his mother. An offensive of tears can rarely be ignored by eternal motherhood. But I make myself reject such suspicions and his emotion appears real—and I am ashamed.

We finally calm Michel's heartfelt sobbings, and sit down to dinner. I eat in silence while they chat happily about Paris. Madame Renée's conversation is excited and full of love. Her eyes shine with joy as she looks adoringly at her son, as she laughingly scolds him for eating so fast, as she listens to his fine talk.

"Ah, you do look well, son," she murmurs after a while. "Are you happy to be back here with your mother?"

"You know I am," he says, swallowing—"and happy to get some food like you can get nowhere else in France." He

445

grins, looking at her affectionately, his fork held in mid-air.

"All I want," she says warmly and sincerely, "is your happiness"—and I stare at her open-mouthed.

Dinner is eaten slowly. After the coffee is served, Madame Renée leans forward across the table and pats Michel's hand. "And tell me, my son, how is the spiritual life?"

"Wonderful, Mother. I pray better than I ever have in my life, and Mass is more real to me now than when I was a monk."

"And your love life?" She asks this jokingly, cajolingly, as if she didn't really care.

Michel hesitates, and I shoot him a warning glance. "I have no time for that, Mama," he lies openly. "What with my work and the long distance I have to go on the *Métro* twice a day, I don't have much time to myself."

But he hesitated and his mother saw my glance. She draws back; her face muddies with suspicion. "You're keeping something from me, aren't you?" she says in a strained voice. "I'm honest with you, why can't you be with me?— or is that one of the things you've learned on the outside? Tell me the truth," she demands—"have you slept with a woman?" She pushes her plate to one side; her face is sullen, demanding, changed. "Any woman?"

"There's no woman, Mother," he replies nervously, "and there never has been—and there won't be until I'm married."

Fatal word. She stares haggardly, knowing nothing, detesting the unnerving suggestion. "And have you," she whispers, "any prospects? Surely you're not thinking of marriage, Michel? Not this soon?"

Michel's eyes dart desperately from his mother to me, but I look away. "Well . . ." he mumbles awkwardly, looking at his plate.

"So you are!" she exclaims hoarsely. "You are thinking of marriage!" She shrugs her shoulders and adds bitterly, "Oh, well, I knew it would have to come."

"But, Mama—"

"Look at yourself," she goes on, her voice rising. "Did some woman pick out those clothes you're wearing? Look

446

at that"—pointing to his coat. "Who picked it out for you? Answer me, who picked it out for you?"

Michel's eyes open wide as the onslaught gathers force. My legs ache beneath the table. Madame Renée stares at her son distastefully.

"Madame," I interject feebly, "his jacket is the same material as mine. I think it suits him well."

"But it isn't the same cut," turning to me with unexpected warmth. "You're always dressed in perfect taste, Monsieur. I hadn't wanted to bring this up, but it's too much. My son is best suited to a monk's habit. He only looks like a gigolo in that outfit."

"But, Mother," pleads Michel, "things are different in Paris. Everyone dresses like this."

"What do you know about it?" She rises, impatient, and begins stacking the dishes, shaking her head. "You've been in a monastery for eight years. People of good taste dress the same the world over. You're like a child, trying to follow the herd . . . And that red tie—have you become a communist in addition to your other idiocies? Did she pick that out too?"

Michel protests, "But there *isn't* any girl yet."

"That's right, Madame," I come to his aid. "We talked about it on the way here. Naturally Michel's thinking about marriage, but he hasn't had time to think about finding the girl yet."

She looks at both of us for a moment, then gathers up the dishes. "Well, I still don't like the tie," she says in a softer voice. "I'll find you one of your father's old ties. We'll burn that thing," she adds, carrying the dishes into the kitchen.

Michel looks at me worried, and his lips form the word "Madeleine."

In a loud voice that his mother can hear, I tell him, "Give it to me if you don't want it, Michel."

Madame Renée returns with a fresh pot of coffee. "Very well, you can look any way you please, Monsieur. Give it to him, Michel."

447

He appears relieved. I laugh at Madame Renée, who grudgingly smiles in return. She resumes her seat and pours coffee, asking Michel, "Have you been approached by any street women?"—but the anger has vanished, she says this lightly. "Monsieur here says it's easy to find women in Paris—that sort, I mean."

"No, Mother, not a single time. I suppose they can tell by looking at me that I'm not the kind who'd do such a thing."

She sneers at his self-righteousness. "Humph. You look pretty common to me. How you've changed! Out of your monk's habit you're common—as common as the next man."

I stir my coffee. "Please, Madame Renée, let's not start in on that song tonight."

But she has started, and nothing will stop her. Winking at Michel, I sit back to watch.

"You're common," she repeats—"absolutely common."

There is a muffled gasp in her throat, and suddenly she staggers from her chair in a storm of weeping. Now it's *her* turn to wage an offensive of tears. Falling on the couch she sobs violently, shaking off Michel's frantic caresses, twisting her face away from him, hiding it in her hands. I cross my legs and wait. After a few moments she leans forward, sitting up, with Michel on his knees trying to comfort her. I note the straight line of her neck in profile; I note the straight line of the nape of her neck, from the nebulous mass of gray and black hairs escaping the knots, on down into the collar of her black dress. It reminds me of an animal, and the unruly short hairs on the back of her neck irritate and disgust me. They are caught in the light. They are animal hairs making me lose all feeling for this sobbing woman.

With a gesture she thrusts Michel to his feet, turning half-away and staring dazedly at the fireplace. "My poor Michel," she murmurs, "you see how I suffer, how miserable I am with you. You'd better go back to your life in Paris— perhaps that way we'll both be happier." Her voice becomes quiet, pensive, resonantly sweet. "This thing's too much

for me, Michel. I can't bear to think of it any longer, so—
so we must consider our relationship at an end." (He looks
at her in pained surprise.) "I shall always do what I can
for you," she continues in the same tone, "just as I have
in the past—and you'll be welcome here whenever you care
to return. But you must live your own life—a life I detest.
You'll always make mistakes, and unless I give you up I'll
suffer with you every step of the way. So go live your own
life, but don't ever expect me to accept it." As she speaks
she raises her eyes—dark, retracted, sparkling with tears—
raises her face slowly to the mirror above the fireplace. In
the silent room a rapturous smile-through-tears illuminates
her handsome face, dissolving her son to demoralized
groveling.

He falls again to his knees, buries his head in her lap,
and begs her, weeping like a child, not to say such things,
never to give him up; choking out between sobs how bitterly
sorry he is to disappoint her, how desperately he loves her
and needs her.

Calmly she strokes his head, cradling it in her lap. "No,
my son," she coos, "you've made your choice. Both of us
will suffer this way, but it's the only way."

Perfect picture of mother and son: every gesture, every
word, every intonation. She lifts her eyes, full of love and
compassion, to me as if to say, "I've done it. I've given him
his freedom at the cost of God only knows how much
suffering. Poor child, he'll get over it. But I—I shall live
only to die." She looks at me with self-pitying heroism.

But instead of bursting into tears I grin broadly, leaning
far back in my chair, and pantomime applause with both
hands. As she swells with rage, I whisper, above the uncontrolled sobbing of Michel, "It could have stood another
rehearsal."

"Oh, Mother, Mother," Michel is weeping, head still
buried, "please don't talk like that. I've never touched a
woman, and I never will unless you approve. You're all
I have in the world. Please, please don't give me up."

But the scene has suffered irreparable damage. Madame

Renée no longer caresses her son, no longer listens to his words; for I have touched tendernesses, and she can't go on. When his mother doesn't answer, Michel raises his head to see her glaring coldly at me.

"She won't give you up, Michel," I answer him, my voice calm. "Your mother has proved herself in the past, and she's still the same fine person she was then. She'll see you through all this, even to marriage."

Madame Renée stares at me as if hypnotized.

"And she'll make your children the best grandmother in France. I'm sure of that. You're two of a kind, you and your mother. You're both selfish, and you both insist on turning every emotion into a cheap and tawdry act. You solve every problem in the most melodramatic and roundabout way." I rise, serious; they follow me with their eyes. "Now kiss each other good night—simply, I beg you, and not as if one of you were going to the guillotine in the morning—and let's all go to bed."

I light a cigarette while the celebration of the night's affection is consummated. Multiple, open-mouthed kissing, saliva wetting cheeks, despite my plea.

"You run along, son," Madame Renée dismisses Michel. "I want to speak to Monsieur here a moment." When he has gone she turns on me furiously. "How dare you make me appear so foolish in front of my son!"

"And how dare you," I retort angrily, "appear so foolish in front of me! Don't you know that old renunciation scene went out with the death of Racine? You were fine earlier this evening. I almost thought I was wrong about you—though your questions were a little obvious. Now forget all this and try to act like a human being tomorrow. Good night."

"Wait," she entreats repentantly. "Will you and Michel sit up and talk tonight?"—striving to sound casual.

"I've no idea. I have nothing to talk about, but if Michel wants to, I don't mind. I explained your feelings to him on the way from Town. You can be sure everything I say is in your favor."

450

"Tell him how much he's hurt me. Beg him to go back to the monastery, won't you? And try to find out if there's been a girl."

"All right. Shall I make a list? A list of your son's confidences that I'll later betray to you?"

"Don't forget you and I are friends," she smiles—a smile tinged with guilt. "And you promised. What's my son to you, anyway?"

"I'll do as you ask. And now, good night." At the door I turn. "And please, for the love of God, won't you leave off these exhausting emotional antics tomorrow? Stop acting."

"I was *not* acting—and you were unforgivable tonight."

"No!" I say, feigning surprise. "I thought I behaved very well. I laughed in the funny parts. Well, we'll be over for breakfast in the morning."

She takes my hand, smiling forgivingly of understood things. "Good night. Don't you boys stay up too late."

"I'll send your son to bed early but I'll go to bed when I please."

"You *are* a stubborn one," she laughs.

Outside, the street, the freshness of night air make me realize how sick I am of obvious emotions. They provide momentary health between two sicknesses. I pause before entering my house, before going in to comfort the broken Michel.

He is in the salon searching in his suitcase. Taking out a large envelope, he places it on the table, glances up at me with a whistling smile of relief, and closes the bag. His resilience is apparent: young, boyish, untouched by the scene.

"My poor old man!" he laughs. "How can I apologize for her? She usually doesn't go quite that far."

"I'm used to it," I tell him. "She acts like that nearly all the time now. It's a sad thing to see, when really she has so many fine qualities. She's completely alienated herself from her friends. You know that, don't you?"

"Yes, I've been hearing reports," he says, fumbling with the envelope, bending over my cluttered table. "Marguerite

Désormière came to see me in Paris after her visit here, and she was very positive about her own reactions."

I observe the top of Michel's head. His former tonsure is visible as a faint circle outlined on the crown. He goes on talking, pursing his lips and working his jaw muscles as he struggles with the knot on his envelope.

"She says she'll never have anything to do with Mother again. But then, Marguerite's a little light-headed." He looks up grinning foolishly. "She wanted me to start going with her."

"Did she have anything to say about me, Michel?"

"Ah, there it is"—removing the string. "About you? Only that Mama was terribly jealous of you and that she found you a charming companion. Why're you laughing? Did I say something funny?"

"No—I was thinking of something else. Have you had any dates with her?" I walk to my bed and sit facing the stove.

"Of course not," he answers seriously. "Marguerite's not the sort of girl who interests me. Here, I brought along some snapshots of my fiancée, Madeleine." He sits beside me, holding the photographs in his lap, and begins passing them to me one by one.

I am genuinely surprised at the girl revealed in the pictures. "Why, Michel, she's beautiful," I tell him after a moment. "But how did you find a girl like this so soon? Tell me all about it."

"You won't tell Mother?"

"I never tell 'Mother' anything I can help."

"Well, you know how it is. Last year Mother got permission from my Father Abbot for me to make the pilgrimage with her to England, to visit the grave of my brother Jean-Julien. She's told you about that, I'm sure. When I left the monastery one of my close friends, a young Brother, asked me if I'd take a packet of letters to his sister in Paris. He told me only that she was a Madame Defourque, the mother of two children—there, that's a snapshot of one of her daughters, she's the younger." He leans against me

452

and indicates the figure of a pretty little girl in the picture. "Well, Mother had no objections, so I left the hotel and carried the letters to Madeleine's apartment. Both her daughters were there, and since that was my first time to be out in the world as a grown man—to be in a private home, and see what family life could be—well, I stayed on most of the afternoon. We talked about her brother, and my life in the monastery, and her life there in Paris. Her husband has been dead for eight years. I thought nothing of it except that I hadn't talked with a woman like that in a long time, and I went on to England with Mother. When we returned I decided to visit Madeleine once more, to get the latest news to take back to her brother." Replacing the photographs in the envelope, Michel ties it carefully. "She was lovely," he continues musingly. "We spent the afternoon together and she sent me off with a package of food for the monks. You're smiling—you think I went back there with some idea in mind; well, if I ever told the truth, it's now. I dreamed only of getting back to my cell, to my life as a monk. But, when I came in sight of the monastery— well, something changed in me. That was the first hint. And gradually, the prospect of a lifetime devoted only to God became almost unbearable. The knowledge that I'd never again sit in a comfortable living room—in Madeleine's living room—hit me hard. I never wrote to her, never let her know how unhappy I was. I made a tremendous effort for an entire year. I prayed to God to give me peace, and make me satisfied with the only life I'd ever known. But finally I became obsessed with the idea of a home and a wife and children; and I knew I'd put a bullet through my head if I stayed on. That's how it was. The rest you know. They released me from the monastery and gave me a little money. When I got to Paris, Madeleine found me my job. She's helped me in every possible way—it was she who picked out my clothes. And now she's returned my love and we spend every spare moment together. Can you under-stand, after hearing all this, why I want to bring her here and break the news to Mama, and marry her as soon as possible?" He fingers the envelope nervously, staring at his feet. I offer him a cigarette, which he takes, which he lights and smokes without choking.

I rise, stretching, wanting the interview to end. "Well, Michel, you saw how your mother was tonight. I'll do my best for you, but you must realize it would be unforgivable to break the news to her now."

"I know," he answers, exhaling smoke from nose and mouth. "And of course the fact that Madeleine has two children makes it seem even more impossible. Mother'll think I'm saddling myself with a big family to begin with." He grins up at me. "But when you're in love like this it makes waiting awfully hard." I don't return his smile, and he grows serious, childishly serious. "I'll tell you one thing —if there must be a choice I'll choose Madeleine, even if I have to break with Mother."

"Of course you will, Michel." I walk into the kitchen for a glass of water, calling back, "That's only right. But by waiting a few months you may be able to have your marriage and your mother too. Want a drink?"

"No, thanks."

I return yawning, closing the door behind me. Michel looks at me quickly, uncertainly.

"You say to wait a few months. But that's not possible. I'm willing to go along with you for a few weeks, but it isn't fair to either Madeleine or myself to wait indefinitely."

"You're willing to go along with *me?*" I stare at him angrily. "Why, do you know I wouldn't give a damn if you and your mother went straight to hell this instant? You're not doing me any favors. Make up your mind right now. I'm here on the scene, and I know your mother much better than you do. But if you're going to marry immediately, then don't ask for my help any more. Tell your mother now; go face her—alone. I'm sick of this mess anyway." His eyes quail, and I calm myself. "What difference does a matter of two or three, or perhaps even six months, make?"

"None, I guess," he replies, flicking cigarette ashes onto the top of my stove.

454

For a long moment we find no words. Restlessly I sit again on the bed. He puts his cigarette in his mouth and leaves it there. Then, grinning, he reaches over and pats me on the knee.

"Don't be angry with me, huh?" he says. "You must know how it feels to be in love and want someone so badly you can hardly control yourself. You've been wonderful and I'm not forgetting it. But," he emphasizes, "this is a whirlwind for us. Why, a doctor friend of mine even suggested that if there's any further delay, we go ahead and have physical contact before marriage. What do you think?" His eyes follow me as I lean away from him, lean against my pillows. His eyes are bright, full of life and dumbness. He asks the question seriously, obviously delighted to talk about it.

"I think," I say slowly, "the doctor is a damned fool. But that part of it doesn't interest me. Do as you like—I don't care one way or the other. But I must tell you frankly, Michel, your mother has a lot on her side despite her childish actions. Do you realize how it would look for her, as your mother, if you were to marry almost as soon as you'd grown enough hair to cover your tonsure? And what disrespect for the monks here!"

"Disrespect for the monks?" repeats Michel, surprised. "Why, they're my brothers; they'd be the first to advise a quick marriage. As a matter of fact, my Father Abbot told me I must marry as soon as possible to guard against falling into sin."

"Yes, I understand that. But how will it look here? Here, you're known; your mother must live in this community. The only thing outsiders can think is that a monk leaves his monastery and gets married almost immediately afterward. You and I know this happens very seldom, so seldom as to be nonexistent—and in your case we know it happened because you were put in the monastery too young to make the decision of your own free will. But those on the outside won't know that. They'll say, 'Ah, those monks! What do you suppose really goes on behind the walls?

455

They're a queer bunch. Just show 'em a pretty girl and they go chasing after her.' Don't you see how humiliating that will be for these others whom you call your brothers? There're lots of people on the outside who delight in this sort of thing, who'll change it from something plausible into something filthy. You know that. They'll take your case— an isolated case—and make it a generality. *You* won't be hurt by it; it's the monks and your mother who'll bear the shame. I think you might consider them. As for me, I don't care—but explain the situation to Madeleine. Such things take time; they must be done with a certain discretion."

Michel laughs, "You *are* a good friend"—and I have a desire to take his laugh from him. "Very well, we'll wait till you give the signal, all right? But make it as soon as possible. And tell me, do you think maybe I should try to keep her satisfied in the meantime? I've never had any sexual experience, I'm just asking you."

I sigh disgustedly. "If you've gotten no more than that out of your years in the monastery, go ahead. *I* probably should, but it's disappointing to see a man of your background who'd even consider it. You see, I've grown to know a great love and respect for monks since I've been here. I expect them to be above people like me, and I'm a little sickened when they aren't."

"But," he protests, "I'm not a monk any more. I'm a man like yourself now, with the same problems." He snuffs out his cigarette.

I stare at the ceiling, leaning far back on the pillows. "You threw off the mantle too quickly, Michel," I say bitterly and quietly. "I'm beginning to doubt if you ever really were a monk." I look at him.

He winces, a flush of anger; then immediate control as the eyes become calm. "You're very frank, Monsieur."

"We're not playing games. I learned that sort of frankness from your own monks." The room becomes resentful, and we're two people alone in it.

"But it seems to me you use it as a coward's weapon." His smile is gone. "When frankness turns to insult it loses

456

its value." Under my steady gaze he wavers and looks away.

"I suspect you're right," I tell him evenly. "You see, you and I, who should be the best of friends, who rushed into a quick friendship, appear to have made a mistake. I'll do everything I can for you, and for your mother—but on the whole I find you most unsympathetic. Now let's forget it; it needn't make us angry."

"Please"—turning to me—"you mustn't feel that way about me, I'm not a bad sort. Say we'll be friends—all right?"

"All right, Michel," I agree wearily. "It's late. Let's get to bed."

After I show him to his bedroom upstairs, I return to close the door gratefully against the Michels and Madame Renées and Madeleines of the outside. Alone, I open the window to let cigarette smoke be replaced by fresh night air, and tiredness becomes a healthful desire for sleep. Undressing for bed, I turn on the radio: Poulenc's Mass in G sung by the Chanteurs de Lyon under Commette. A luminous, highly interesting work—still Poulenc, but a Poulenc I've never heard before. But sleep can't be fought; faint notes of the *Kyrie* fade into nothingness.

18 february

Three days of sameness. Days of hearing the same words, the same scenes repeated with a thousand niggardly variations; of seeing a handsome woman colored and ugly with every grandiose expression from suspicion to sneering superiority. At last she has been convinced that her son is still pure, and that he will stay that way for some time to come.

And this morning shortly after midnight, Michel returned to Paris. Tearful, demonstrative parting after dinner last night. Promises and expressions of gratitude. I sat up with Michel till train time, but I let him walk to the station alone.

Steady dosages of arsenic destroy my nerves. I feel a growing desire to avoid scenes of friction, to avoid people, to be alone. Madame Renée's leg doesn't heal, and the bandages must be changed every night. During this rite there exists an ever-increasing sickness of touches and flirting. She transfers her tenderness, her kindness back to me.

6 march

The days have passed quietly; and once again, over two weeks of subtle change and insinuation make themselves felt. Tonight I realize that Madame Renée, with her moral suffering and her inability to move about, demands more and more of my time.

She does everything to make my life pleasant, and in so doing she takes me from my work; but somehow the work gets done. She has assumed a gentle sweetness—but it's too late; I've seen in her too much ugliness to believe that this is more than transitory. In waiting we act gallantly, and there's a welcome peacefulness.

My hours at the Monastery with the monks, and my afternoons with Mademoiselle Marthe, form glad patterns of existence.

458

And over and above and around all this day-to-day life, is felt the pervasive suggestion of spring. It remains cold, but not so cold as winter; and I finger first hints of knotty little buds on the pear trees in my courtyard. The floats of ice are gone from the slow-moving River. The dull browns of pasture lands have taken on the delicate tints of timid greens.

It is a halcyon countryside creating an inner calmness of life and work, with the never-forgetting nag of a feeling akin to nausea. Something within me learns to cast off this dissonance of being, the moment I'm away from Madame Renée; she no longer touches me unless I'm with her. I forget her—but the countryside does not. A part of the picture is out of place. There is a fear, a shadow on otherwise happy exteriors, caused by something we can't even guess. Movements are mean: a meanness of face and action and heart throughout the Valley. Above it all—not obvious, but none the less there—are the red flush of Madame Renée's face and the strings of the many lives which she holds in her hands.

I think it's that—but I don't know. These insinuations of time become fact slowly. But when she appears in the street she receives grudging, almost fearful obeisance from the Villagers. And when I appear there's a mixture of pity and lack of respect—and disappointed reproach.

Michel is rarely mentioned. Madame Renée sits secure and firm on her chaise longue. It's a cycle of quiescence and I wait for it to end, praying that it will never end.

The other feelings don't return. I live and work alone.

21 march

Over a month with no news from Michel,
except short notes which do no more than irritate his mother.
At breakfast she begs me to write to him. I feel that she has
devoted this month of pleasantness to drawing me close to
her—and now in return she begs me to write to her son.

"You see, Monsieur," she says quietly, "it's been only
two months since he left the monastery, and all I get are
these little one-page notes. Tell him not to write me at all
if he can't write as he once did."

I am seated at her dining table. The sun of a cold
windless day makes the room bright. I dip a tartine in a cup
of coffee, looking at it, and say to my cup in impersonal
tones, "But he's busy. I know how that is. I can't write
my mother long letters either, but she doesn't worry about
it."

"I told you I'd lose him," she urges, a grit of impatience
disturbing her voice, "and you wouldn't believe me. He's
already got to where he no longer depends on me for help—
except to ask for money that I don't have to give him. Write
him this morning, will you?" she concludes peremptorily.

"All right," I answer, brushing crumbs from the tartine
into my hand and dumping them in the coffee. "But I'm
sure your fears are groundless."

"*You're* sure!" she groans. "Humph. You can afford
to be."

"Now please, Madame, I haven't slept much these past
few nights—let's not have a scene."

She lingers on the fringe of uncertain tears. "Well, why
don't you get more sleep?"

"Wish I could. I'd like to have more sleep. But I've
been with you every spare moment, and my lessons must be
done at night after I leave here."

"That's right"—commencing her weeping—"that's right,
it's all my—Why, where're you going?"

460

"To the Monastery—today's the Mass for the death of St. Benedict. See you at noon." I walk out, slamming the door behind me, cutting short a scene I can't bear.

As I enter the chapel, Father Dutfoy, rubbing his hands together from the freezing cold, approaches to remind me that this is the first day of spring.

There are only a few in the chapel for the long pontifical Mass. In contrast to the great organs, the choir seems more restrained, more perfectly in balance with the music. At the end of the *Kyrie,* a large group of people enter noisily and fill the empty pews. Their train into Town, I imagine, was late. They quickly settle themselves, and Mass returns to quietness.

After the sleepless night I must stay on my knees to keep awake. Voices grow remote in a nightmare of struggling against sleep in the crowded chapel, as body heats quickly warm. My head drops in a moment of fantastic dreams, till my body jerks back into wakefulness with a shock.

During the sublime *Sanctus* I doze again. Carnal, erotic dreams rouse to disgusts. It's impossible to stay awake. I leave the chapel and return to my house.

An hour's dreamless sleep, and I awake trembling and hungry and uncomfortable. My mouth is filled with a slickness of saliva. I spit from the window and it streams long, refusing to drop. I flick it away with my fingers. Afterward a glass of water, drawn from the kitchen tap, tastes rough and cold.

With a cup of weak coffee and a cigarette, I prepare to write Michel. It is not yet noon. Since I dislike the task, the words come slow. I begin by asking him to write his mother the kind of letters he once did, warning him of her degeneration.

She will either lose her mind or continue in her foolish attempt to starve herself. Her worry has now become a real sickness for which there is only one cure—your paying her more attention.

461

It is a harsh letter full of my disappointment in his treatment of Madame Renée, my disgust at his inexcusable lack
of generosity toward her. I suggest that he return here, or
better still, that he urge her to come to Paris for a short
visit.

> You can't imagine what a nightmare her life is, Michel; if you
> could, you would change your ways. Right now *you* are her
> life—and she should be yours until you can get her well again.
> Do something positive as soon as you receive this letter. For
> the past month she has seemed better, but I suspect that she
> spends most of her nights crying. She is keeping her weight
> although she eats very little. Now, I beg of you, accept your
> responsibilities toward her. If you don't, I can't be responsible
> for what may happen here.

I leave my house and mail the letter, then return to
Madame Renée's for lunch. The table has not been set.
Madame Renée is lying on her couch frowning into space.
I inquire, "Are we to have lunch today?"
"No," without looking at me.
"And may I ask why not?"
"Because," she announces firmly, "there's no more money
in the house." I start to speak and she goes on, "I know
you paid me for the month, but I've already spent it. If
you want to advance me enough to feed you, all right. I'll
eat your scraps."
"I'll advance you the money," I tell her, reaching into
my pocket. "But what did you do with the other?"
"I sent it to Michel, if it's any of your business. You're
as nosy as an old woman."
"I can afford to be nosy about my own money, it seems
to me. I'll give you enough to feed both of us till the first."
"Just give me enough to feed yourself," she pouts. "I
want nothing from you."
Handing her the money, I take a chair near the stove.
"Now what in the name of heaven am I to make of you?
This morning you were all right; at noon you—"
"Then why," she interrupts angrily, "did you walk out
462

on me this morning? Why'd you leave me when I needed you?"

"To avoid a scene. Now look, Madame Renée," I tell her flatly, "either you make up your mind to behave yourself or I go find my food somewhere else. Why get so upset?"

Glaring at me she rises slowly from the couch. "Haven't I been nice to you all month?"

"Yes, you have." I watch her as she turns her back on me, walking away. "You've been so nice I'm determined never to tolerate your caprices again."

Her voice grows coarse. "Did you write Michel?" She stops at the kitchen door.

"Yes, I wrote him a long letter."

"May I see it?" She takes a step back into the room.

"It's already mailed."

"I told you I'd mail it," she returns bitterly. "Why didn't you wait so I could read it? What did you say that I shouldn't read?"

The room is clean, and the sun bright; but the streets are deserted and smallnesses sadden her words. I plead nervously with her, "Now please, don't get excited again. Believe me, I didn't hear you say you'd mail it. I just didn't think, I guess."

"Did you tell Michel how I am?" She approaches my chair.

I glance up at her, standing beside me. "No, I didn't. I simply told him—"

"Don't you *ever* tell him how I am, do you hear? I don't want him to know what he's done to me." Drawing a chair close to mine, she sits beside me and takes my hand, her eyes softening. "I know I'm horrible to you," she whines. "You should've walked out on me long ago. But please— give me your solemn promise you'll never tell Michel about all this? Don't tell him"—sobbing, her voice breaking— "that his mother's dying. I—I prefer him to be notified after I'm gone."

"Very well, if you want it that way." I refuse to argue; I stare at the floor, hoping to keep the scene quiet. "I only told him I didn't think he was being very fair to you—that the least he could do would be to write you all about what he's doing." I raise my head. "But forget about this dying business, won't you? I know how much Michel has hurt you, but he certainly didn't do it intentionally. You're a healthy woman, not yet fifty-five—you have a long life ahead of you and you can do lots of good in this world."

She turns away studiedly, with new-starting tears. "No, no, my life is finished." Her voice is filled with demoralized sadness—irritating, insufferable sadness.

I shrug my shoulders and say nothing.

Quickly facing me again, she whispers, "Are you thinking the same thing I am? You've been so irritable lately, I haven't dared mention it. But don't you see?—we're so close. I'm miserable unless I can share my every thought with you. I think Michel has found himself a girl. No, wait"—gesturing urgently as I start to speak—"if he hadn't, he'd have been writing me all along, wouldn't he? Some woman is taking all his time. He has none left for me. Are you sure he didn't mention some woman when he was here?" She takes my hand and shakes it as though to revive my memory.

"No, he mentioned nothing like that," I assure her, leaving my hand in hers. "But we have no way of knowing if he has a girl or not, so why worry about it till we find out? Still, you ought to be prepared. You've got to realize that he can't go on forever without meeting girls, perhaps even taking them out. It'll come, and you may as well accept it here and now."

Surprisingly, her face becomes calm. "Yes, I know that," she says without emotion. "It will be a horrible day for me, but I know it must come. And do you know, I'll be almost glad when it does." Her voice grows old and tired, and pity feels its way into me. "Glad for Michel," she adds thoughtfully. "Glad to have it over with—to be through with this horrible waiting without knowing."

"I see. You're right. It's bad to—"

"But understand this," she interjects firmly—"when that

464

time does come, I'll break all ties with my son—no, don't interrupt, it has to be that way. I simply cannot share him with another woman, so I shall give him up." She releases my hand. "And nothing you can say will change that," she concludes with finality.

For a moment we sit in silence, listening to the spitting stove. Hunger is forgotten. Bells from the Monastery sound deeply, metallicly, announcing lunch to the monks.

"What a terrible decision for Michel to make," I say as the bells die away—"to have to choose between his mother and a wife. Can't you see that a man needs both? I can certainly understand how much he needs the love of a wife, for I'm beginning to feel the same need myself."

She stares at me in open astonishment. *"You're* beginning to think about a wife? Not *you!"*

"What's so strange about that?" I laugh. "Every man thinks about it at one time or another."

"But you've never mentioned it before," she remarks sullenly. "Have you met someone?"

"No." I bow my head, mocking hurt, and whisper, "I'm still all yours, dear Madame . . . But it will come, and the sooner the better. Since I've been in the Valley my entire outlook has changed. I know now that a man's got to have discipline in his life—some goal toward which to work. I don't know what mine is yet, but I hope to find out."

She hides her concern, but I realize the hatred I've given her; it has set her nerves in motion. "I really believe you're serious," she says calmly enough. "Well, why don't you become a monk? No, now, I'm perfectly sincere in asking you that. You're a fine person. Why don't you consider it?"

"As a matter of fact I have," I reply. "I've hoped that—somehow—I might be chosen for such a vocation. But you know, I imagine everyone who falls under the spell of a monastery must think the same thing; it's easy to convince yourself of a vocation here. I love the monastic life, that's certain. But fundamentally I'm not made for it. If nothing else, though, it's taught me that you've got to accept your responsibilities as a member of society. And to me that

465

means getting married, living decently, and rearing children who'll be a credit to the world."

Madame Renée's face becomes a mocking smile, reddening with distaste. I fumble for words and speak more rapidly, feeling suddenly foolish.

"I know you're laughing at me, but it doesn't matter. I'm the same as anyone else. I need the same love—the love of a wife. I've lived too long as a privileged person without other men's responsibilities." Inwardly I cringe at how absurd my sentiments seem when put into words; and I'm fully aware of what to expect from Madame Renée.

"Wonderful!" she exclaims, giggling meanly. "Sounds just like *Reginald Finds Happiness,* in the little cheap bluebook edition. If you young men only knew how silly you sound! You've all got the same ideals—the same little asinine ideals. I'm disappointed in you, my friend, truly disappointed. I thought you, at least, were above that sort of thing."

"What sort of thing? Wanting a wife?"

"Yes. It cheapens you in a way. You're a scholar—why do you want a woman around your neck? You're made for something better than that. You should let the common herd take care of populating the earth. It's the same with Michel. He has a beautiful life handed him by God and what does he do?—cheapens himself by sniveling after some woman. Humph. You're no better than he is."

I laugh out loud and she looks at me questioningly. "Would it be more distinguished," I ask her sarcastically, "for me to do as I have in the past—to keep a mistress? Since it seems I have no talent for chastity, it's a question either of keeping a mistress or marrying. Before coming here I kept the mistress; that's one of the things that's changed." I shake my head. "And you think it's cheap to want God's way in my life? And in the home I'll make some day? Oh, I know, you've got a certain twisted logic on your side; but it's too weak to matter. Actually I want the same thing Michel does—to do the very best I can with what God has given me. But it's more difficult for Michel,

466

isn't it? And why? Because he has a mother who thinks first of her own happiness. If she can't have her way with her son, then at least she can see to it that he's made unhappy. And in the cruelest way on earth—by taking herself away from him. In order to get a wife he has to lose his mother. How can you be so selfish? So—?"

"Call it what you like," she mutters. "Maybe it's true, but I'm too old to change now. My father spoiled me, my mother hated me, my husband spoiled and perverted me. I've lost one son in the war, and the other one would hurt me less if *he* were dead. I'm too old to change."

There's a silence. Madame Renée moves to the sofa and leans back on the pillows, staring at the ceiling. I light a cigarette and put the match in the stove. I wish I could escape the talk, the mean little miserable talk; but talk is demanded by the quietness of the bright room. Someone walks past whistling in the street.

"But you're not too old, Madame," I protest. "I can't understand you: you profess a great love for both Michel and me, and yet the moment one of us hurts you, you can't rest till you've retaliated in full. I don't believe you've ever known what it is to love someone else—*really* love them. When you love someone, you're not out for revenge—you're anxious to forgive them. And you always place their happiness above your own."

"You're right," she admits. "I don't suppose I ever did love anyone that way. But I was a good wife and mother"—her face deteriorates into bitterness—"and now—now I must die. The sooner the better. But—Michel must never find out."

"Cheap melodrama again!" I roar angrily. "Can't you get out of the acting habit? I'll tell you why you don't want Michel to find out—because you know he'd see through your masquerade and hate you for it; because you know it'd kill all the remorse in him. Well, if you don't make some effort to stop this foolishness, I shall most certainly tell him —that's final. And what's more, if our relationship doesn't become more pleasant I'll be tempted to move back to the

Monastery, now that the weather's warmer. I'm finished."

She flounders into a sitting position, her face tense and ugly. "You do," she forces out between clenched teeth, "and I'll drive you out of the Valley. I know the thing that can do it. I'll see that you leave and never return. That's a promise."

I meet her gaze in silence for a moment, then, "What do you know that could drive me out of the Valley?"

"Ha! I know you killed the Chevissier child. I'd never tell a soul, but believe me," she snarls, "I'll use it against you if you don't do as I ask." She rises from the sofa to stand over me.

Sighing wearily, unbelieving, I look up at her torn face. "So our beautiful friendship is now based on threats of blackmail? I didn't kill the Petite and you know it. She couldn't have been saved. Even the family said that. She died while I was trying to save her." I get up to leave.

Madame Renée follows me to the table, blocks my way by standing close against me. "She'd had those spells before and never died. I found out all about it. Madame Chevissier herself told me you wouldn't let her give the child the enema that might've saved her."

"You people," I tell her, choking with disgust, "have your brains in your intestines. What good would an enema have done? The charge is so ridiculous, so—I won't waste my breath talking about it." I try to move, but she steps in front of me.

"Ah, but it's a charge I can make stick." Her red face stares madly into mine. "Remember that—I can really make you suffer."

I say expressionlessly, "I wouldn't try it if I were you, Madame; you'd never cease regretting it." The room swirls with sunlight and the sordid larding of disgust on disgust.

"Ha! that's good!" She laughs scornfully, looking at me, her eyes sunk far into her head. "Why should I regret it? You're all I have left. After what I've been through, do you think I'd be hurt by losing you too? Good riddance!"

"Such a beautiful friendship," I observe. "One that professes love for me in one breath and perfect willingness to destroy me in the next."

She sneers, "You've never cared anything about me anyway. I can tell." Her voice suddenly becomes sweet. "I'd be doing you a favor by getting you away from me."

"Oh, stop this crazy talk!" I fling my cigarette against the stove. "I *have* cared about you, but I must confess I'm getting damned sick of your whims. You can't drive me from the Valley. For the last time—if you don't stop acting like this I'll write Michel the truth and move back to the Monastery. Is that clear enough?"

Lowering her gaze, she fingers the carved edge of the table and says coldly, "It's clear enough you'll be run out of the Valley for being so damned smart, young man." Her mouth twists into a grin. "And don't try to get out from under it this time." With a sharp movement of her head she looks quickly into my eyes. "You—you with your superiority, your high ideals. All right, so I'm bad—well, I'll be completely bad. You'll find out just how bad I can be. I'll build a case against you that'll make you detested in the Valley, that'll bring the police to your door. Since I'm bad, *bad,* I can embroider the story a little, can't I? I can make it a little worse than it is." She pauses. "Well, why don't you get mad? Why're you standing there so damned cool? And stop looking at me with that cow-eyed pity." She steps closer to me, shaking her fist, and says furiously, "I'll break you down *yet!*"—jerking her hand away.

"You've broken me down," I reply softly, "too much already. I really do pity you. But be quiet a minute—and let go of my coat. I'm wondering where you'll go and what you'll do when *you* leave the Valley? Because don't you see *you're* the one who'll have to leave—and in disgrace, too— if you start this? You'll be exposed as a liar, and possibly something worse. Now let's forget the whole thing. I've excited you, and I'm sorry. But don't threaten me again. You need me—you won't carry out any threats. It makes you—"

She bursts into triumphant laughter. "So you *do* crawl
469

once in a while! You want me to forget what's happened, you're trying to bluff me! Well, come on, come on"—she backs away and, bending down, acts like she's petting a dog —"come on and crawl some more." She straightens up grinning, and I gaze sick with shame and revulsion. "I can promise you one thing," she shouts coarsely—"I'm through with you! I'm sick of you and Michel! I hate you both!"

"No, you don't."

"I'll show you! I'll go to the Prefect of Police and tell him he ought to investigate the Chevissier child's death!"

She starts toward the kitchen, and I spit out the words I can no longer hold: "Tell him to investigate her baptism, too!"

Her head flies back. Deathly silence as she turns to stare at me incredulously, her face immobile from shock. She looks as if she'll faint.

"You see," I go on quietly, sinking tiredly into a chair at the table, "I've known about it all along, but I never meant to tell anyone else. You know I did my best to save the Petite—and I know your intentions in baptizing her were good. But who'd believe that besides me?"

Madame Renée's face, returning to life, falls into her hands: silent, heartbroken weeping.

"I promise never to bring this up again," I assure her. "And don't think I hold it against you or feel differently toward you, because I don't . . . Now let's eat some lunch, shall we?" Trembling, I turn my chair to face the table. She walks very slowly, still crying, into the kitchen.

We eat quietly, with only the sound of silverware. Her face is calm and old. She appears a sick woman, a pitiable figure. I tell her casually of my work at the Monastery and with Mademoiselle Marthe. She follows the conversation with questions about Mademoiselle Marthe and the monks, but without bitterness, without meanness.

After a while she asks, "Tell me one thing more, Monsieur—or perhaps I shouldn't ask?"

"What's that, Madame?"

She half-smiles. "Were you serious when you said you

were thinking of marriage? I mean—will it be soon now?"

"Certainly not soon—I really don't know. I was serious all right, but so far I'm not sure just what I ought to do in the future. I think marriage is the right thing for me, but certainly not soon. I must finish my studies and get started in some sort of work before I can even consider it. I'll talk with Father Clément; he'll know what I should do."

She murmurs, "He'll be disappointed in you, I'm afraid," mopping up gravy with a piece of bread on her fork. "Don't believe I'd mention it to him."

"I don't think he will be. He knows me better than anyone else. He's already suggested once or twice before that I get married. Oh well, you can't tell. I've changed so much already—you can't tell what will happen in a place like this."

Our talk returns to smallness and the quiet sanity of feelings. And soon I leave for my work and the growing thirsts of long corridors. Doors close behind me as I enter the courtyard of the Monastery; the doors click and lock and the outside is once again outside. The morning is swallowed in a profound sigh and in the fatigue of nerves finding their proper liquidness. Resting and floating, calling to rest. Compelling rest and closing eyes. Across the court monks stand on ladders, repairing a crumbling portion of the wall.

Work. Slow, deliberate, eye-focused work. Father G'seau, no longer suffering from intense cold, hums and mentions that tonight at Vespers we are to have a special privilege: Father Abbot has asked a distinguished Dominican to preach. It's a rare thing; we never have sermons in the Monastery.

At the first bells I hurry to the chapel, which is soon crowded for the festival Vespers this anniversary of St. Benedict's death. Once again the half-insanity of exhaustion pulls me toward sleep. I kneel in order to keep myself awake.

Slow movements, exquisite chants, and outer smells of dampness in the obscure chapel.

471

But with the beginning of the sermon, I am lost. The visiting monk walks forward in his white robes, draws forth a sheaf of papers, adjusts his glasses, and speaks over the muffled rustle of the congregation settling itself for the long wait. We listen attentively, but his voice doesn't carry to the back of the chapel. The few disjointed words I hear sound commonplace after the chants—similes and metaphors understandable to the crowded benches of visitors, but explaining nothing, explaining the obvious in a dramatic bargain manner.

We listen, craning necks and straining ears to catch what he says. High mysticism couched in low, unbeautiful language. There shouldn't be any sermon: the liturgy and the music of a past age make contemporary ideals seem incredibly pedestrian in expression. How can a practical voice, glued to the earth, touch people? How dare it speak so entirely out of context with the purity of great art? And the words become falsetto with intense emotion: "Our souls fluttering like wounded birds about the citadel of Christianity." Something we can visualize. Something very feminine. Our souls are uplifted, and my eyes drag me toward sleep. How abominable are the simile and metaphor when used to attach spirituality to practical illustrations!

Madame Renée enters, passes down the aisle without looking in my direction. She stops near the front and, bending down, whispers to a man at the end of a bench. He moves over to make room for her. She kneels to pray.

The Dominican's voice is completely inaudible now, whispering its hypnosis of banality. It causes me to abandon myself to other thoughts—to erotic reminiscences. With eyes closed I sit here ignoring the coughing people, the droning voice of the monk. Images are rejected with a violent shaking of the head—but they can't be rejected; they take me with them till the here and now become nothing. Carnality catalogues past experiences and future desires in the greatest excitement of vividness.

The sermon continues as I bury myself more deeply in the past of liquid images. Drunkenly, fighting a nodding head and limp neck muscles, I think of the phrase, *"Adhaesit in terra venter noster"*—and I laugh at myself seeking to translate it; seeking to translate it into a genteel covering of words. "Our belly is stuck to the earth." No, no, perhaps, "Our sensuality glues us to the earth." Yes, that's more in keeping with our artificial, civilized manner of speaking.

Pursed-lipped embarrassment. Now really, I'm surprised. The female nods, uniting with the male to complement him, to point up his intelligence. My stomach aches with too much swallowed cigarette juice. Airs rise foul in the mouth. I bury my head, dizzy, in my hands. I think of Lucette, missing her, pushing my sensuality against the bench, imagining it's her belly; and after a closer look—eyes against the dark grain of the wood, pores of hands upon which my head rests, magnified—after a closer look, not missing her. I think of the stained breasts of Mexican girls, and of the grace, the intoxicating beauty of woman in youth compared to the dryness, the defense of propriety of woman in age.

Eyes glance up at myriad candles, and at a thunder-voiced priest with uplifted arms, reverberating the word "Love!" to the very back of the chapel. But he says it drily, he says it without juices—as if he were playing a Ravel *Ondine* with a staccato touch, as if he were caressing a woman with gloved hands.

And it's a hurt to the word; the word implies many things that don't change when placed in reference to God. How differently can Claudel and Péguy and Ronsard make you hear the word, even on the printed page! With what warmth does Claudel put it in the mouth of Jeanne d'Arc as she hangs motionless at the stake awaiting death!

And now, after a final "Love!" the Dominican is finished. He makes a large sign of the cross, turns to the altar, and goes to his place amidst noises of moving and shuffling feet. Monks purify the air with a final *Salve Regina*. Then the people move out, genuflecting to the altar. Fathers bend low and speak to their children as they walk to the door. Madame Renée remains alone, rosary beads in her hand.

Father Clément, carrying several books under his arm,

473

meets me at the door of the cloister. "I was just coming to find you, my son," he says warmly. "Are you going to Mademoiselle Marthe's this afternoon?"

"Yes, sir. Want me to take those books?" The Dominican preacher passes, surrounded by a group of monks.

"Please." He smiles happily, his eyes following the Dominican. "And how did you like our sermon? He is a wonderful preacher, is he not?"

"I thought he was terrible, Father."

Father Clément looks back at me in surprise, and asks in a broad accent of disbelief, "You did? What was there about the sermon that displeased you?"

Very carefully I describe my thoughts during Vespers.

"I see, my son," he says when I have finished. "But what about his explanation of our present-day apathy toward the needs of the Church?"

"The fact is, I couldn't hear more than six words of the entire sermon."

"Then how do you know he was terrible?" His voice is tinged with impatience.

"I just don't like preachers," I answer earnestly.

"Wonderful, my son, wonderful—you 'just don't like preachers.' "

"I didn't like the way he said, 'Love!' Sounded like any other word. He made it commonplace. I have a sensitive spirit, Father, easily bruised by humanitarian appeals to the worlds below." I try to keep my face serious.

Father Clément turns quickly away, bending forward to hide his laughter.

"How unmonastic, Father," I mutter in a disgusted tone. "Control yourself."

"I know what you mean," he says softly, still smiling —"and so does the preacher. But if you only knew how precious you sound, how affected."

"I was only joking," I tell him. "But seriously, there's something I wanted to talk to you about."

"Go ahead, my son."

"Well, I've been trying awfully hard to do as you want
474

me to. But my situation at home is becoming unbearable. Madame Renée gets worse every day. She keeps me with her most of the evening, and I have to stay up the rest of the night to prepare my lessons. But that's not the worst of it: I come to the Monastery so sleepy and exhausted I can't pay proper attention to the offices. My mind wanders like it did this afternoon. All I can think of is pure pornography —something I'm really ashamed to admit into the chapel. And the visions are so realistic they—well, they sort of hypnotize me." I look away, embarrassed. Far off, framed by the cloister arch under which we stand, the sun sets in last vivid colors reflected from the River.

Father Clément's voice comes quietly in answer, and I feel the tiredness. "I know the situation, my child," he murmurs. "Every Christian knows it. It is the work of the devil who seeks to play on your weakness, your fatigue, your disgust with Madame Renée. I must tell you, we are quite worried about you here—not because of these things, but because you do not look well. There are great circles under your eyes. It must be hell on earth, this life you are obliged to lead as intermediary between Madame Renée and Michel. I am truly sorry I ever instructed you to accept her."

"I'm not, Father; it'll work out somehow." I sigh. "It's the other that bothers me. Maybe I ought to get married right away."

"Do not worry about these mental images, my son." His voice sounds quiet, normal, human, filling me, as always, with affection for him—and for the sunset and the Valley stretching below the walls. "They are the result of fatigue," he goes on. "They represent the inborn desires in every man. We turn to them to escape the often-unpleasant *now*. Pleasure is immediate, and sometimes the thought of even illicit pleasure can be less evil than the harm you do yourself with this self-imposed fatigue."

"But Madame Renée insists that I stay with her every spare moment."

"Will you tell Madame Renée that I have ordered you to go to bed by midnight every night? And will you honestly

475

try to be in bed and asleep at that hour? You realize, do you not, that this cannot go on?"

"All right, Father Clément, I'll try."

"Good. Now take these books along to Mademoiselle Marthe for me." He hands them to me, and takes my arm; together we walk in silence to the outer gate. "Now, my son," he says in parting, "do everything possible to get some rest. I shall see you in the morning."

When I arrive at Mademoiselle Marthe's, I tell her that I'm too exhausted to work tonight. I drop into a worn felt chair near the open window. Watching the Village become night, I tell her in detail everything that's happened between Madame Renée and me since the beginning—everything except the threats and the story of the baptism. As I talk I realize that something within me exaggerates Madame Renée's meanness, at the same time giving my answers to her a cleverness and a rightness they never possessed in reality. To atone for this I end by defending her, excusing her conduct as natural because of her worry and anxiety concerning Michel. I try to make it sound sincere. After I finish, there's a pause. A wind, cold with hinted warmth, blows in, and I close the window as lights are turned on in houses along the narrow street.

After a moment, Mademoiselle Marthe remarks quietly, "All I can say, young man, is that Madame Renée has found in you a person of such charity and understanding as to be unique for your age. I admire you for taking her side despite her apparently unforgivable conduct." (I cringe inwardly, but I can't bring myself to protest.) "Now, do as Father Clément says," she continues. "Madame Renée dominates you through your pity for her. Get your rest; do your work—and spare her only the time you feel you can. She won't suffer appreciably."

I look across at her, sitting small in a chair opposite me. Her sparse hair catches the light from without, but her face is a nothingness of shadows. She does not turn on the lamp. Like an old Brady photograph she sits there tranquil as the dusk about us, unmoving but not unthinking.

476

"Do you know, young friend," she murmurs after a long silence, her voice old and full of swallowings, "I believe this poor woman has fallen in love with you."

I don't recoil at her words; I only nod and gaze once more out the window at the fast-deepening darkness: it's a thought that has been torturing my own mind these past few weeks.

Somewhere in the street below we hear sounds of heavy wooden footsteps which grow and then fade. Sounds of shutters being closed against the night. We become lonely together in the dark. But I'm content to stay here not speaking, only sensing the miracle of nostalgic life down in the street; content to sit with this aged belly and cracked voice who can now but dimly be seen.

Movements in her chair, and she adds, "Just be careful, my child. Don't permit yourself to be blinded to it."

"Just the thought of her being in love with me," I say without expression, "makes me sick."

"As it would any young man. Shall I turn on the lamp?"

"I prefer the dark, if you don't mind . . . But what can I do?"

"I don't know," she answers slowly, "I really don't know." And then, "Can't you revive some entanglement of the past, or perhaps invent a young girl? Something to divert her mind from this fantastic hope of hers?"

"No," I mutter—"she knows too much about my past already. But surely she can't imagine I'd ever respond to her?"

"We can be sure of nothing. I feel from what you've told me, and from my own knowledge of her, that Madame Renée is a woman literally eaten up with pride: a woman in love with herself. No normal woman could hope for anything but heartbreak from such a liaison, but I don't doubt that Madame Renée imagines herself completely attractive to you. Didn't she tell you that the doctor said she has the body of a woman of thirty? We must think of a way out for you. You must—"

"There's one thing," I put in. "I've been talking to her

477

about my getting married. She didn't like the idea at all, but maybe if I built it up in her mind a little more . . ."

Mademoiselle Marthe sits silently thinking; and when her voice returns from the darkness, it's more tender. "It needn't be a ruse, you know. Marriage would solve your problem. If you're ready to be married, I might help you. I know many girls, and one in particular, who would suit you well."

"Surely you're not serious?" I say hurriedly, surprised. "I know marriages are often arranged in France, but such a thing would never work for me. I couldn't marry a girl without loving her. It's not in my nature."

"I see," she whispers. "It's a shame. We think differently here—or at least we used to. I suppose it's my age. In the old days we didn't believe that a man had to search endlessly for his love. We believed, on the contrary, that without the blindness created by love he could far better find the woman who most suited his needs and his hopes; and that if he carried enough love within himself, he could create a love for his wife after marriage. Nowadays we seek happiness and we seek love; in my day we believed we had to *be* happiness and love. You see," she goes on, her voice droning in the dark, "during my many years as a teacher, I learned to know and to love young people. I know you well, my son—I know you better than you think. You want a home and children and decency, and the love of a woman. You're a worker; you need the tranquillity of completeness within your own household. You need a woman who, while not necessarily sharing your work, shares completely in your ideals. A woman is never happier than when living for another—for a husband and children. It's a serenity of like desires that will make your life and your work fruitful and complete."

I observe, "But she'd have to be a woman who suited me physically."

"Why," asks Mademoiselle Marthe, "must you search frantically for the woman whose nose is just right, or who has the kind of hair you like, or who excites you to bullish-

478

ness? When you find her you imagine you're in love, but you're lost if she happens to be a woman who wants none of the things you want. Suppose she doesn't want children— which many a woman doesn't—or suppose she dislikes to share you with your work? I have the beliefs of the past, my child. Life is too short to make such a mistake. I know that given a certain portion of natural attractiveness, and respect for the sacrament of marriage, almost any two normal people can make a beautiful life together. And if they are tolerant and normal and want love based on the concreteness of family, that love will become a stable and always-healthful partnership. And if it isn't killed—if it is fair and just—it will eventually reach the heights of perfect physical and moral satisfaction. You see, I am old; I can judge youth better than youth can judge itself. I would trust you to want and need such a relationship, and I know the girl—a lovely girl—who would make you just such a mate as I have described. Given an initial meeting and a quick marriage, and tenderness and thoughtfulness and an immediate pregnancy, I'd stake my life on your happiness." She stirs in her chair. "But I'll say no more, my friend; you'll think me a meddling old fool and a marriage broker. But tell me, doesn't what I've said make sense to you? Even though it's foreign to the times and to your way of life?"

"Yes, it does make sense," I reply—"a great deal of sense. I'd trust you, and I dare say you're entirely right, Mademoiselle. But it wouldn't work with me. I have too little control over my physical needs—it'd soon degenerate into a mistress relationship." I light a cigarette, opening the window to throw the match into the street.

"But you're wrong," she chides. "I should hope you *would* want to satisfy your physical desires with her; I hope you're a man of some passion. Any woman understands that and admires it in a man. And if he isn't selfish and thoughtless, it becomes an act of great tenderness—a moral caress. It would be all physical at first. But it would be natural, and soon it would take on the luster of a permanent expression of growing love for each other. The very fact of marriage,

479

my child, the very knowledge that it's a permanent relationship—the desire for children and for freedom to be one with a woman who's not your mistress but your wife—that fact would make an unbelievable difference."

I nod my head. "You almost convince me, Mademoiselle," I tell her. "Perhaps if I were able, I'd ask you to send for this girl you know—if I had the money to marry and start a home. But at any rate I can talk about it before Madame Renée. It'll convince her that she's wrong in feeling as she does."

Mademoiselle Marthe sighs. "I fear it will do no good," she observes. "It was I who asked you to stay with her, and now I feel that you should leave. It's too much to ask of you to submit to such indignity, to the vileness of her lechery."

"It wasn't only you, Mademoiselle Marthe," I say gently. "Both Father Clément and Father Sauvac asked me to stay with her too, you know."

"Why can't you move back to the Monastery?"

"I may do that if things get worse. Right now I don't feel it's the thing to do." Throwing my cigarette through the window, I get stiffly to my feet. "Now I'd better run. Thanks very much for the talk, Mademoiselle—it's helped a lot."

"I hope so, my boy."

I grin. "And don't lose sight of my future wife, eh? If only one of my rich aunts were to pass on . . ."

When I reach my house, Mademoiselle Marthe's laughter still rings in my ears. Across the street Madame Renée's cottage is dark, and the blinds haven't been drawn.

Without turning on the light, I take off my shoes and lie down on the bed. The delight of Mademoiselle Marthe's talk fills me with a newness of sensation: delight in thinking of someone fresh and young, and of a house and a bed and a permanency of clear marriage. Tremblings of excitement, and the sudden rush of a turbulent past: turbulent past when a woman meant nothing more than a quick cleverness of speech and the arousal of verbal advances, with a triumph

480

consummated only in the sex act. Lying in the dark, the pillow cold beneath my cheek, I realize that I've had but little association with such girls as Mademoiselle Marthe described. I bury my face in the pillow. Chivalric protocol of past beds, of tiredness, of loss through gain. It's smart and mean and void. Never have I had a girl without it, and how very much I feel the lack! I think of the possibility of decency in a lasting relationship, and regret and longing turn into something that gives me rest. A newness of thought becomes intense desire—a laughable desire for something above me, for something naïve and old and different. Mademoiselle Marthe's words sing with my dream of tenderness and sweetness and desiring. I sleep fine laughing sleep.

Somewhere in the background the other nights—the other nights of feverish wetness, purple- and black-glistening like a punctured intestine—gyrate torturingly. Past nights revolving slowly, not like a punctured intestine, but like a stillborn embryo not yet dried and shriveled, like the wax embryo of Perotinus; still wet and glutinous and warm to the touch; ugly with veins outside the skin in blacks and purples and reds. Turning in the background without making a sound. I look beyond my sleep and my dreams at it, fascinated, and it rises in me drying, and I vomit at the sight.

Then the dream returns, with fine lines of inner caresses; and in my dreams I sleep live and warm with good odors. It's all new—and it's all mine. Somewhere with a violent jerking movement the embryo is tossed out of sight; in its place is a casket covered with flowers. And I am there trying to act like I'm crying, because my old aunt has died and left me enough for this new thing of giving out and taking in, of laughing and good odors. I am there bowing my head and thanking God for His wanting my old aunt just at that time; and arranging things in the new house her money has bought; and sleeping safe that night and all nights in a growing familiarity with the way another's belly is made . . .

Footsteps in the hall and a knock at the door, and I have to leave all this for later. In protest I sit up and spit off

481

into the dark, in the direction of the fireplace, delighted with my spitting. And then I spit again, wishing I could do all things as beautifully as spit off into the dark in the direction of the fireplace. It makes a loud sound, and it pleases something inside me. I shout, "Who's there?"

"Are you dressed, Monsieur?"—quietly, tenderly, calmly through the closed door: Madame Renée's voice.

"Of course I'm dressed!" I roar, sadly seeing my night and its dream and its spitting fade. "I'm always dressed. I've never been naked in my life. Come in. Come in and turn on all the lights. Come in and sit down."

She opens the door and switches on the light, looking at me strangely, soberly. I calm myself and ask rather foolishly, "Weren't Vespers beautiful this evening?"

"Yes," she answers, nodding, hesitant. "May I speak to you a moment before I go fix your supper?"

"Certainly."

Her face is soft and composed. She finds a seat at my worktable and stares at her hands, which still fondle her rosary beads. She doesn't remove either her worn black coat or her beret. Her escaping hair snares fine lights from the lamp above. I sit on the bed lacing my shoes. In a perfectly modulated, almost impersonal voice she says, "A great deal has happened to me since that—that frightening scene this morning. I believe I've suddenly come to my senses."

I look up. She is gazing at the beads she holds, half-smiling as if she were addressing them.

"You see, Monsieur, I stayed in the chapel and prayed for a long time after Vespers. And then I decided to do something definite. So I asked for your Father Clément to hear my confession. He thinks Michel is doomed—but that can't be helped now, it's Michel's own doing. However, he did say I must see to it that your life is made more restful, that you get more sleep." Smiling sickly, she glances at me and looks away. "Frankly, I admitted that my suffering and my tortured mind were at fault, not you. But we must arrange it now so you can take better care of yourself. It wouldn't be fair to me, you know, if you lost your health while under my care. It'll be better from now on. Soon it will be so warm you won't have to have all those horrible people in your house." She laughs briefly, uneasily. "Ah, Father Clément told me lots of things," she concludes, brushing the hair back from her forehead.

"But he didn't really tell you," I inquire quietly, wary of this change in her, "that Michel is doomed, now did he? I know Father Clément better than that."

"Well, no," she concedes. "Not in so many words. But he did say that since Michel's not prepared to cope with the problems of life on the outside, his life will be difficult." She turns to me pleadingly. "But please, let's not argue. If you're willing to forgive and forget, we'll simply not speak of Michel again. And I'll try to be my old self."

"Do you really mean that?"

"Yes."

I sigh, "If you only knew how that relieves me."

"One thing more"—and her voice becomes insistent— "you know I haven't been entirely to blame. You've always jumped to Michel's defense. As a matter of fact, you argue with everything I say. Now won't you try to be a little more tolerant?"

"Why, of course, Madame."

"I got to thinking, Why should he be so cruel to me?" Her face reddens. "Not because he doesn't like me—he'd simply leave if it were that. No, with all his temper there's a gentleness, a kindness about him. And I suddenly realized that you did it because of your affection for me. I should've realized it earlier. But now that I know, things will be different."

Confusion of sentiments. It's too late; her words repel me. "We've both been under an emotional strain," I say flatly. I walk into the kitchen for a drink, hoping to dissolve this scene in which I can't compete with her.

She follows me hesitantly and stands nearby, silhouetted against the square of light which is the salon door. I drink water in the half-darkness. I can't see her face. She laughs thoughtfully.

483

"You know," she says, "we're too much alike. We're both proud, fiery creatures."

She raises her head, and I imagine that on her face must be an expression of great tenderness. It's not good to stay in the dark. I set the glass loudly on the drainboard and stamp back into the lighted living room.

Again she follows me. "Do you know where I've been?" she remarks, sitting in the same chair. "To the seamstress in Town. I had some wool for Michel, but I took your measurements from a pair of socks and ordered her to make you some of the most beautiful pearl-gray stockings." She shrugs her shoulders, simpering, and then laughs uncertainly. "I suppose Michel will be angry, but he can get his own socks from now on. I much prefer your having them."

"You shouldn't have done that," I tell her. "Such things cost too much, and I don't want them at Michel's expense." I think of the girl and of this capricious woman, and my words are without a hint of gratitude.

"Well, I may let Michel have a few pairs," she teases, "if he changes his way a little. But I want to do something for you too."

I don't answer. She waits for me to say the right thing, and the silence grows long.

"Tell me," she says slowly at last, "have you talked about me to Mademoiselle Marthe?"

"No—only to make conversation when she asks about you. I'd never let myself talk about you behind your back. Why?"

She blushes, her face flaming for a moment. "Well, I must confess: I felt I couldn't go on without some advice, so I—stopped in at Mademoiselle Marthe's on my way back from Town. I told her very simply what had happened, and asked her what I should do to keep you from constantly flaring up at me. I hope you don't mind," she whispers embarrassedly, her face sober and searching, "but I felt this sort of thing couldn't go on. It was making both of us miserable."

"No, I'm glad you went to see her. What did she—?"

484

"Well, I told her how difficult it is for you to control your temper, and asked her if I were to blame. She suggested —and I think this is true—that there's nothing wrong in my actions but that I'm a terrible tease; that I sometimes do and say things to annoy you without meaning any real offense. She suggested I stop joking with you so much"— Madame Renée's face is normal now; she laughs reproachfully—"and start taking you more seriously. It's so simple the way she explains it. I assure you I really will change. A friendship like ours must be based on mutual respect— something which, after all, you haven't shown *me*."

"I understand," I mutter, unbelieving.

"Now it's all settled." She rises gaily from her chair, smiling guilelessly and forgivingly. "Will you come over with me while I fix you a nice supper?"

"No, thanks," I say quickly; then, seizing upon the first logical excuse I can think of, "I left some of my work with Father Clément. I'll run get it and be right back." But my only intention is to go to Mademoiselle Marthe's; I can't wait till tomorrow to tell her about this incredible change, no matter how superficial, which she has wrought in Madame Renée.

"Will you say anything to Father Clément about my confession?" asks Madame Renée.

"If I did he wouldn't answer me. You know a priest can never divulge the secrets of the confessional."

A few moments later I leave her in front of her door; and whistling happily, I walk down the street. I'm filled with gratitude for what Mademoiselle Marthe has done. Taking the steps leading to her room two at a time, I knock exuberantly.

Mademoiselle Marthe's head peers out, astonished and comical. "Well, hello again, young man. Is anything wrong? Come in."

"Just the opposite." I laugh breathlessly, stepping inside and closing the door behind me. "I've just left Madame Renée, and you've really produced a miracle. Since your talk with her this afternoon, she's a completely different

485

person—like her old self and at least half-sane. What on earth did you say to her to make her change so quickly?"

The tiny personification of age stares at me. "I wish I knew," she says slowly, positively. "I haven't had a visit from Madame Renée since Christmas."

A heavy silence as the meaning of her words becomes clear. I feel foolish after my long expression of thanks. "Really," I falter—"you mean she wasn't here this afternoon?"

"No."

"But—why should she tell me she was?"

"I have no idea," replies Mademoiselle Marthe, scratching her head with a stiff-fingered hand of heavy, knotted veins. "Why, she no longer even speaks to me when she passes me on the street. Certainly she'd never lower herself to seek advice concerning her precious American from someone like me."

"Well, Mademoiselle, I'm—" I sigh deeply, not finding the right word to express my astonishment.

"It was rather stupid of her," says Mademoiselle Marthe caustically, "to make such a blunder. Now she'll be terrified every time you come here for fear you may mention her visit—for fear you'll find out she lied."

Taking a chair, I explain, "She thinks I'm at the Monastery now—I told her I had to pick up some work from Father Clément while she fixed dinner. What can we do to keep her from finding out that I know? We don't want to hurt her."

"If she has any brains left, my child, I imagine she'll come to see me tonight. Then she'll know that if you happen to mention her visit, I won't deny having seen her. You'd better get back now. Act as if nothing has happened. Since she thinks you're at the Monastery she may be on her way here this very moment. Return the back way so your paths won't cross—or better still, go on to the Monastery as you'd planned."

Through the darkened streets I walk rapidly to the Monastery, meeting no one. I ask the monk on duty in the

486

gatehouse to lend me a book, and I remain there a few moments talking with him. Then, with the book under my arm as evidence, I casually stroll back to Madame Renée's house.

All the lights are on and the table has been spread with a new linen cloth. For a centerpiece, she has placed a small sprig of greenery in a water glass. The radio is murmuring a newscast from Paris, scarcely audible. I turn it up as she enters from the kitchen with plates of food. We talk quietly and happily. Supper is a feast for the morale as well as for the body—hors d'œuvres, a pork roast with mashed beans and sauce, cheeses, and a sweet cream. Madame Renée eats well and talks well, but always to the same point. I leave the table satisfied.

She clears the table and returns, smiling, with a filter of coffee. I turn the radio dial and take out a cigarette. She sits on the sofa near me.

"Now," she chides gently, "we'll sit and talk over one cup of coffee, and then you must leave me and get your work done. *And* a good night's sleep, eh?" She hands me a cup of coffee and places the sugar bowl on the table beside me, laughing, "Now, you *are* a pig, taking two lumps of sugar. But I suppose this is a celebration for both of us."

I look at the windows, blinded from the outside darkness by green shutters. The night seems faraway. The room is bright—and quiet except for innocuous music from the radio. I switch it off, preferring the intimacy of silence. The room closes us in, but it's not ominous.

"Tell me, Madame," I say to make conversation, "did you visit Paris much? When your husband was alive, I mean?"

Swallowing a mouthful of coffee, she purses her lips absent-mindedly. "Oh, yes, we went to Paris regularly each month—to the opera, concerts, the theater—things we missed in a small town. And how Julien loved them! Of course, I did too. Since we had mutual interests we went quite often." She smiles at the memory of greater nights. "Honestly, you'd have loved my Julien. As you know, he was

487

twenty-nine years my senior"—she chuckles—"and he could never get enough of me. I was a beauty in those days and Julien never tired of showing me off—at parties, balls and the like. And he wasn't a bit jealous. He liked for other men to admire me." Introspectively, she takes another sip of coffee. "He would say, when I complained of something that seemed a little forward, 'But they can't resist my beautiful wife, and I'm proud to have a wife men can't resist.' You know, we used to laugh: I dressed well and I suppose I was as pretty as the next one, and men would always remark, 'Now look at that old Julien Renée—how did he ever get such a beautiful young wife?' But do you know, I never once betrayed my husband. Other women have fallen under similar circumstances, but I never let myself get involved in any scandals. Julien only suspected me once, and that was the time Father Sauvac asked me to discourage his love-making. Julien was too old to give me healthy children, so I turned cold to his advances. And since I'd always been a rather warm-blooded wife, he thought there must be another man. Why, do you know he actually—"

"Yes, Madame Renée," I interrupt gently, "I remember you told me about that."

"Oh, of course. Well, I mustn't keep you any longer— you'd better get to your work."

We walk to the door and shake hands. She clings to my lifeless hand, pulling me to her. Her hand is dry and rough, with little pressures of her fingers in the palm of mine, meaning nothing and everything.

"Is everything all right now?" she whispers intimately. "Did you have enough supper?"

I stare at her and remember almost the same words spoken in the same voice, with the same intonation and the same whisper, when a whore once asked me, "Was that all right?" They are the same, these voices and these words, repeated under not-so-different circumstances; and there's the same questioning on the face, knowing there can be only one answer. The room is quiet. Madame Renée looks at me and asks again if everything is all right, knowing that

I'll answer yes as the whore knew that I'd answer yes. The parallel is too complete. Instinctively I pull away from her, preferring the whore.

For a moment she continues to cling. The closed room surrounds us, makes us alone in the universe of present tense and place. We are conscious only of the life within these four walls. Her voice is unnecessary sweetness as she murmurs, "We won't argue again, will we? Promise?"

"Of course not. Never again."

"Fine. And now good night."

She smiles broadly and breaks away. The room becomes real again, and health returns. Intimacy leaves in a flood of comfortable normalcy. Here is my friend, Madame Renée, and nothing has happened. I owe her no money for the visit, and the bed doesn't need straightening, and the wash-water doesn't have to be thrown out. Nothing has happened, nothing in the least out of the ordinary. My eyes focus on the reality of her as she turns and walks away like an old woman, taking short steps, bending slightly forward. Still smiling she disappears into the kitchen, her hair stirring in a breeze from the open kitchen window. She disappears. The open doorway through which she has passed stares at me emptily; it returns my thirst for young girls of smooth skin and grace of movement, and for an aunt who won't die. Merely to be in their presence, to see their youngness, to watch them. It's an overwhelming desire to know youth again—to drink of young complexions, and talk of young things, and smell the fragrance of youngness about me. The open kitchen door stares back at me, not understanding, empty, revealing the black-bellied stove beyond. Then there's a movement, and Madame Renée steps back into sight and through the door. Her eyes, turned slightly to one side, look at me curiously. I suddenly become conscious that my nose is running, and I sniff and wipe it with a handkerchief. She smiles beautifully and comfortably.

"What are you thinking?" she asks.

"That you should remarry. You're too handsome a woman to live like this." But I stop, swallowing words with

489

the realization that she'll interpret this as an avowal of something to her advantage. Impersonality can and does become personal in her conception of it.

But she knows things. Never rush. Wait and let nature carry it. Store it for later. She knows the rules far better than I. She laughs, letting my remark drop with a casual "Perhaps some day I shall. There may be happiness for me in this world yet. Good night again."

And I leave.

22 march

Impossible to get enough sleep. I struggle up to greet a bright, windy Saturday morning of March. No need for a fire. Classes only until noon, when I return home for lunch, stopping off at Mademoiselle Marthe's. I stand at her door looking idly at the worm-eaten wood of the doorframe.

"I can only stay a moment," I tell her. "But I wanted to find out—did she come?"

"Of course she did. Ah, the poor woman!" Mademoiselle Marthe rolls back her eyes, raising her hands in the air. "And do you know she mentioned you only as being such a lucky person to have her? I had a difficult time holding my tongue. But come in, won't you?"

"No, I can't, thanks—it's time for lunch now. I may drop in this afternoon. I want to tell you what happened last night. She was really most unlike herself."

"Very well, then, if you have time drop in to see old Marthe."

490

I return to my house, walking through the courtyard. The pear trees promise an early blossom, although there is yet no sign of leaves. The buds are full, and a feeling of spring's juices emanates from all living things. The sun is warm, out of the wind. Intoxicating odors of the beginnings of life in the courtyard. At my feet, the first greens of grass shoots. Exhilaration. Heart-poundings of happiness on a day of earth's rite. Feeling that underground saps are rising and will burst into bloom at any moment. Feeling that the long winter is past.

I walk whistling to join Madame Renée for lunch. Her windows are open to the day, and the floor of stone is scrubbed and clean-smelling. On the table next to my plate is a pair of gray knit hose.

"They're beautiful, Madame!" I shout into the kitchen, holding the socks, admiring them. "All my thanks."

She comes in, calm, washed, fragrant in a white dress. I am wrong, lost. Affection for her becomes real.

"My friend," she says tenderly, gravely, "you don't look well. Didn't you sleep again last night? Or is it the other news?"

"I feel wonderful. What other news? Has something happened?"

She sits heavily beside me. "Then you haven't heard?" She looks sadly out the window and says nothing more.

"Well, tell me what it is, won't you?"

"It's—it's hard to tell, to explain how I feel about it." She catches her breath in a sharp, involuntary intake. "But —I suppose I'm the one to break the news. And believe me, I'm very sorry. You can be sure I'm your friend in this. I'll stand by you no matter what happens—and I think none the less of you for it."

Her tone alarms me. Something within me, some dread, causes my voice to break. "For what? Have I done something? I don't know what you're talking about."

She looks at me, so changed in a white dress, she looks at me. "Your Madame Vincent has returned, my friend," she says quietly. "She's taken a room out of the parish, in

491

Town, a room above a grocery store. She's come back. She's already been to the Monastery for six o'clock Mass."

I look at her disgustedly. "Is that all? You're worried about her? Well, let me tell you—"

"You don't understand," she goes on tremulously. "In order to get the room she—she told the proprietor that she's just come from a doctor in Paris. She's sick. She says she needs an operation which she refuses to have."

We forget the room and the windows and the outside; we stare at each other until our thoughts join, until eyes penetrate eyes with disbelief and knowledge, until they half-close with the horror of our thoughts.

I mutter dully, "You don't think—? Oh, no . . ."

She whispers, "I prayed for you this morning, my poor friend. I—I simply don't know. O God, I hope she's not really—pregnant."

The word shimmers like a sudden chill through my body: *Pregnant. Pregnant. Pregnant.*

"She's little more than a whore, that one," says Madame Renée with sudden anger. "Just like her to refuse an operation. Well, I'll help you. I can think of something to drive her away."

"No, no!" and my voice is chokingly dry in my throat. "It can't be. She's a fine woman. It just can't be."

"I hope not," she says distractedly. "But why else would she come back here? We must find out."

"I can't believe it's that. Madame Vincent wouldn't have come back if it were. She'd have written."

"You're so foolish!" Madame Renée says intensely. "She's a whore, I tell you. She's responsible. I hope this teaches you a lesson."

I rise abruptly. "Well, I'll find out—and soon."

"Where're you going?"

"I'm going to find her and ask her, of course."

"But your lunch?" she protests, becoming angry.

"You think I can eat?"

"Let me go with you. She might—"

"Don't be funny. I can trust her as much as I can you.

I don't believe any of this. I don't believe a word of it."

"Very well," sighs Madame Renée, glaring at me. "Very well, Monsieur. One thing, though—what about my money? I've ordered provisions for this afternoon. You'd better give it to me before *she* gets a chance at it."

"I don't have it. I'll bring it this evening. And no more talk like that. I appreciate your standing up for me, but I'll not—"

I slam the door behind me without finishing the sentence. I return to my house for some money. The room, the bed, the day are impossible. My head turns and I fall into a chair. I feel a moment's exultation that my flesh is in the flesh of another's belly—but it's drowned in her age and in threatened disgrace. I will lose consciousness. Half-sobbing, I slam my fist into the wood of the chair, muttering obscenity after obscenity until the pain in my hand causes the other to go away. Something fills my chest with a heavy inner coughing and my mouth with the thick stuff of a cough. It moves about, monstrous and living and sickening, making me struggle for breath as I run to the window to let it drip in a long stream from my mouth. And I imagine it must be this same feeling that fills her belly with me. Dread mingles in counterpoint with the desire that it be true. Fear of the truth no matter what the truth may be. And behind this, the unmoving image of a woman with upswept hair sitting next to a window with ragged lace curtains, and a bathroom with pools of water left on the floor, and a sadness of worn carpet on the dusty floor of the bedroom, and her face looking out the window at a frozen afternoon—untouchable, remote, beyond hope.

Drained of all strength, and the substance of a raw chest burning within me, I go to learn the truth. I walk the miles without thinking, carrying my bruised hand, remembering only a bruised hand and the hurt of it. A wind, the warm wind of afternoon, dries my face, and sweat starts beneath my clothes, wetting them.

They know of Madame Vincent in Town; they tell me where to find her—but she's not there. She has gone somewhere without leaving a message. They can tell me nothing except that she's sick—she was sick this morning after breakfast. They smile knowingly. They don't know just what the trouble is; she hasn't said. But she did get sick after breakfast. Poor woman, she eats with a good appetite but she can't hold her morning meal.

Wanting to rest, I turn into a small café—a small café up a narrow street overlooking the Town square and post office. Cool, sour odors of many wine bottles. I sit at a polished table in a shadowed corner, watching people pass outside in the brilliant sunlight of our first warm day. I drink my wine slowly. The place is scattered with men: Saturday afternoon brings in workers who have just cashed their pay checks. A few play cards or write letters on free stationery, but most of them sit at the small tables and meet their friends and discuss women and the Town and the weather. They talk furtively and calmly, laughing under their breaths. I sit and wait; these men come and stay. It's a way to pass time pleasantly. What they say is of little importance as long as there's talk—honest conversation with the little politenesses of offering and refusing cigarettes, of insisting that a friend take the last one, of offering another glass of wine and fighting to pay the bill. For them the afternoon is long and quiet; the time spent over a drink is never wasted. It's a ritual dear to the hearts of a people who admire leisure as an art.

The waiting calms me. In time, I can go back. Perhaps she'll be there later.

Two young men, comrades, sit down at the next table. They order beer and talk—decent, sincere talk about the lamentable lack of girls in the Town. They are home for a vacation between semesters at school. I listen to them. They worry. They confide in each other as do two people with the same disease—the need of a girl to sleep with. One of them concludes by leaning back in his chair, and smiling sadly, and saying that he really doesn't know what he'll do if something doesn't turn up soon. He takes the check and walks to the door. His friend shouts lazily, "Good luck with . . . you know what!"—and the other turns and grins.

The café fills with people. Old men in wooden shoes deposit burlap sacks of groceries and find places. Young men prance about, talking too loudly. Boys in knee pants urge Father and Grandfather to hurry with their drinks, so they can go. The older men shake off the children and return to adult conversation. Waiters pass carrying trays filled with glasses of beer and wine and cognac.

My postman, looking as uninterested in the world as always, comes through the door and glances about for a seat. Seeing me, he calls a greeting and walks to my table. I offer him a chair and order cognac from a passing waiter.

Leaning against me he asks, "How did you manage to escape, M'sieu?" with great sarcasm. This is followed with other questions, asked as if he doesn't really care to hear the answers.

As we drink and talk, his face becomes redder from the heat. He loosens his collar, smiling, a cigarette hanging from his lips. We drink and talk quietly, sympathetically, and the names of Salesky and Madame Renée enter the conversation. Suddenly he looks me in the face with the hint of a sneer.

"Why do you let her dominate you so, M'sieu? Has she got something on you?"

"No, it's a long story. Not worth telling."

He shrugs his shoulders and swallows the last of his cognac. "All right—but you must know that no one understands why you let her run your life. They like you in the Village but they can't admire you. It's a shame. She's a bad woman, your Madame Renée."

"They don't understand, that's all. Believe me, I'd escape her if I could." I order another cognac for each of us, not caring to discuss her.

"It's your business, M'sieu. I was only—"

"Thanks, my friend. I appreciate your telling me this. But tell me, have you seen or heard from Madame Vincent? I understand she's back." I force my voice to remain casual.

"I haven't seen her—thanks," as he eyes the fresh drink

indifferently—"but she's here somewhere. There's talk she's come back to be near you—but then there's always talk." Smiling, he glances at me sideways. "Would it be that she can't stay away from you?"

"You know better than that. I hear she's sick. What is it, do you suppose?"

"You can't tell," he mutters. "She was supposed to have an operation or something. I don't know what it is. Some sort of female trouble, probably—she's about that age. Anyway, they say she refused to take the chance. Can't blame her. I wouldn't want them opening me up either." He drinks and looks at me. "She's a fine woman, you know. I hope the bitches will leave her in peace this time."

We drink more rapidly and feel better and drunker. "Wish I could see her," I whisper.

His face is sympathetic. "Wish you could too, M'sieu. But if you'll pardon the suggestion, it'd be bad for her if you did."

"Why?"

"Someone would be sure to see you. If she *is* sick, the less talk there is against her the better."

"Of course."

"You know," he says bluntly, impersonally, "I never did much admire you for not helping her when they ran her out of the Valley. If you're seen with her now, they might run her out again."

I look at my glass, turning it between my fingers, and say nothing. Torpor of liquor deadening senses. There's nothing I can say.

The postman leans forward, straightening his pants, and slaps me on the shoulder. "You have a rough time of it, don't you? Going to the dance tonight?"

"What dance?"

"There's going to be a public street ball in front of Madame Rouen's store. Like to see you go. Every girl in the country will be there, and there's not a one of them that'd refuse to go off in the dark with you. If my wife weren't just getting over her pregnancy, I'd be tempted to

496

do a little unbuttoning myself. You really ought to try it."

"Wish I could," I sigh. "But you know I'm too well known here. Might get my face slapped."

"Nonsense—that's what the balls are for, so young bulls can meet young cows. It'd do me good to see you pull this on Madame Renée."

"It's impossible, my friend."

"They're going to have an orchestra."

"Still impossible. I'm getting drunk."

He shakes his head, chuckling. "We're drinking too much, my friend. I don't have any more money."

"I got plenty. I'm sad, my friend. Poor Madame Vincent. Everything I've heard today has been bad."

I drink furiously. My companion drinks very slowly, holding back, one glass to my three. Afternoon becomes late afternoon.

"Here"—and my voice is cracked—"take my wallet, pay the bill. And—call Salesky, won't you? Getting sick. Drank too much."

"You want to vomit?" he asks, alarmed. "I'll take you out back. Might make you feel better if you got rid of it."

"No—hate vomiting. But hurry, will you? Want to get home." Senses swirl brilliantly. I bury my head in my arms on the table, and lose consciousness.

Later, movement and talking, and hands helping me into something that smells like a car. My eyes open to whirling scenery outside the car windows. Laughing and cigarette smoke in the front seat, fading away. Glimpses of the still, photographic woman by the window. Sadness for her. All of it, with the scenery, with the light of day, pulsing brilliant and dim in my consciousness. Momentary returns. Salesky parks in the garage so that no one can see them helping me in.

Pants are pulled from me. Shoes. Underwear. A pajama shirt full of clouds, blue, fluttering before me. Sitting upright on my bed, falling—falling sideways on my pillow. Voices. Friendly voices of friends who understand.

Salesky's voice somewhere near me: "He really does a

job when he gets started. A man couldn't get any drunker."

And the postman's answer: "Poor devil—you can thank Satan's own mother across the street for this."

The money. The bills to pay. Saturday afternoon. Lovely drunk. Wonderful lovely drunk. Dance tonight. Woman at the window. Burning belly. Off in the dark some place. Burning belly rising up. I struggle back to speech: "Give wallet — to — what's that old whore's name? — Madame Renée. Give her—money." Pause. Blinking. Trying to piece the room together. "Tell her I'm drunk—to stay away —for love of God to stay away." Drunken sleep forever. Never to wake up. Dreamless long sleep and smiling.

But Salesky's voice—still there talking to the postman. "He's going to be sick in the morning. Needs to puke, don't you think?"

"I suggested it," the other says softly, "but he hates to puke."

"We better take him out back. He won't know the difference and it'll make him better. There, grab the other arm."

Late afternoon sunlight. I do know the difference. Gray walls around my courtyard and ground reeling beneath me. And hands holding me up. Things seem clearer.

From Salesky—kind voice over my unspoken protest: "Now, you stand behind him. Can you hold him up? And when I stick my finger down his throat, bend him forward so he won't get it on himself. Careful he doesn't fall."

Hands hold me from behind. Salesky's fingers open my lips. I shake my head away and it wobbles crazily on my neck. He pulls it back and opens my mouth. Finger against my tongue. I can feel the texture of the finger. Fine file-like lines and a callous on the side, rough. The nail strikes my palate, and it's rough and broken. Exploring my mouth, it becomes wet. It's finely ridged and the cuticle is dry, hurting my throat. It tastes of copper and sweat and tobacco smoke and the bitterness of not being washed, and it touches a contraction of throat muscles. Other muscles, beginning at the bottom of my stomach, ache, become rigid,

498

and rise in other rigidnesses up, up, hurting all the way as my belly contracts, forcing upward.

Salesky jerks away his dripping finger and mutters, "Bend him forward, here it comes. There, that'll make him feel better."

Eyes closed and face congested from effort. Eyes water as gaspings and swallowings relax, leaning forward. Sick.

"Get a wet cloth"—the postman, grasping me tightly. "Wipe off his face for him."

I hang there waiting. With the gentleness of every man for the helplessness of a drunken brother, Salesky wipes my face and it feels better. I open my eyes, focus them on the ground, see green shoots of grass glistening through the wet lumpy contents of my stomach. See long afternoon shadows.

They take me inside. I feel better. My stomach is empty and my back aches where muscles have fought. I fall asleep thanking them, grateful to them. I never even know when they leave. Consciousness of rest. Totality of rest. Finality of rest . . .

Then, a face above mine, and electric lights—and somewhere outside, the noisy wailing of a faraway saxophone. The face is kind, smiling, tender. It bends low over mine. "Are you all right now?" It's Madame Renée's face and voice.

"Ooh, I'm sore. I'm drunk. So drunk." I shade my eyes from the blinding light.

She laughs at my croaking confession. "You'll feel better in the morning. Will you want anything to eat?"

Stifling new sickness, I mutter elaborately, "Never will another morsel of food pass my lips." Face of unmasked delight. I amuse her, drunk. I grimace again at the thought of food and close my eyes, remembering. "Did you get the money?"

"Uh-huh. I'll go now. Need anything? I'm glad you did this. It'll make things better for you and give you some forced sleep. Did you find out about Madame Vincent? Or can you remember?"

I open my eyes. "You know, you're a very beautiful and kind woman. No, couldn't find her."

Pursing her lips she makes another laughing sound. Intimate, secret. Bends down to look at me more closely, casually putting a heavy hand on my stomach. "Now I know you're drunk, my friend," she chides. "But don't worry, no one else will ever know." Her hand pats my stomach, feels its outline like you'd feel a tomato to see if it's ripe. Pressing, releasing, heavy. Going lower. "Sure I can't get you anything?"

"Nothing," I tell her. Hand on my belly. Hand feeling. Grinning hand and headache lost in pulsing.

Her face bends closer to mine, next to mine. I can smell her breathing and feel it. Skin, pores of skin. And thin gray hair floating in the air near my eye, catching highlights from the lamp. Her face shades mine. Warmth from her. My eyes lower, see the creases of her nose, fine particles of face powder. Hand on my belly and belly moving beneath her answering caress. She makes an intimate sound—small gust of warm air on my cheek. A hair, one fine thin gray hair floating there near my eye. Body in white dress somewhere there above me, near me. And legs, mortal thighs, wide thighs hidden but there somewhere. Face nearer mine. Belly moving under her grasping hand. Heavy hand. My arms go up clumsy, pulling at her body there somewhere, feeling for it. Without opening, lips move against face pores. Spot on the ceiling above her. Eyes turn back to floating hair caught in lamplight. Hands feeling backs of legs. Feeling detached deepness of skin and fats that move. Fingers sinking in, moving up. Two frozen bodies together, waiting for hands to move up to thighs and hips. Hands moving, eyes closed. Softness of flesh changes to rough hard corset staves under white dress. Two frozen bodies. Hesitation of feeling. Again the fumblings. Hinted cringing as mouth opens to taste face, and softness of lips finds fine wrinkles of cheek. Hinted cringing as momentum builds. Her hands moving down on my belly and my hands moving up to feel hardness of covered breasts. Momentum, and

500

her hands touch lowest belly beneath covers. Touch, feel a moment—and it flashes. Light flashes in my eyes as her hands are jerked away, as fine floating hair disappears. As body in white dress becomes motion of brutal tearing-away, as heavy hand slaps hard against my face, and slaps again. Turning of face with the slap. Confusion of spot on the ceiling now that her face is gone. Confused blinking to see the room clearly. She stands there high. Red swollen face. Accusing immobility. I rub my cheek and mouth where the hand struck. And I look at her there. I think of the stiff corset, the hard-packed breasts. I look at her outrage and laugh, and laughter grows uncontrollable. She turns to go, her fine gray hair being arranged with heavy, trembling hands back into a knot of convention atop her head.

My voice brakes her steps to a moment's pause. "So you're like that?" it taunts. "Lead a man on—"

Glimpse of her white skirt, and the door closing against a darkness of hall. The door staring blankly closed. Bells for Compline fill the Valley, loud in the spring night air, and the orchestra down the street sounds louder as Madame Renée opens the front door to go out. Then she closes the door, dimming the sound of bells mixed with sad, screaming dance music.

I sleep fitfully to the accompaniment of the dance music. But its muffled gaiety, coming to me from a distance, can't be fought. It lubricates my thoughts and drags me from bed. Lamps are turned on. I can't fight this intrusion of my solitude, and I resent it. Madame Renée's slap has disorganized my nerves, and her old woman's caress of my belly has filled me with loathing—and with a desire to consummate my excitement in a young girl. Thoughts of Christianne, of the way she moves, of how she would be. I walk about my room. Thoughts become obsession, thoughts of all the women who have insinuated themselves into my life here— Madame Renée, Madame Vincent, Mademoiselle Marthe— and the dreams of Christianne which fight the dreams of an obscurely lighted chapel and of an unknown girl whom I could know in marriage. Laughter comes from outside with

the stopping of the music, and loud talk during the intermission. It grows late, but they'll dance all night. Textures
and tones of voices sound empty on the streets of night.

The music starts again. A polka, badly played. Country
dance band. It's all belly tonight. All physical. Heavy
clouds have covered the sky, and it's dark. Few of them will
return home without having fumbled a frantic little sex
act in the shadows of the parish church. Squeamish, tawdry
satisfaction, hurried by the fear of being caught, pushed by
the dreams of liquidness beneath a partner's belly. Here in
my well-lighted room away from this ugly, masturbatic
dance, how I envy those who at this moment are grunting
pleasure and disgust behind the church or under the bridge,
or perhaps even behind my courtyard wall. They smell of
garlic and wine, and of not having bathed; but in the dark
all this generates heat, arouses, lubricates; not till afterward
do odors and stickiness become repugnant.

To turn aside this growing obsession—the foolhardy desire to join them, to find myself a girl—I switch on the
radio to full volume until the sounds outside are drowned
by those inside: a stupendous performance by Casadesus of
the Beethoven *Emperor* Concerto.

But my mind won't cool to the Adagio. It still dreams
of the possibility of the impossible—of the young flesh of
the young breasts of a young girl in the cool damp night, of
how warm they'd seem. No, no, I can't do it. But there's
loneliness here, and the music is a nausea of other pleasures.
The cleavage between night and day is complete in an aching
empty stomach nourished only with cigarettes.

Without further inner arguments, I walk out into the
street. Ahead, lights have been strung; and there are many
heads moving, heavily shadowed, jogging in rhythm to the
saxophone. I approach quietly, feeling weak from the drunkenness of the afternoon. On the sidewalks several benches
have been placed for the old people. They sit there laughing
and talking and clapping their hands, sipping glasses of red
wine which they buy from a roving vendor. Close above,
a layer of low clouds, murky, moving slowly, reflects the

lights. I stand in a doorway and watch the gaiety of the clumsy dancing, listening to the laughter of those who sit on the benches. Mother Nourrie is there surrounded by friends. She is boisterous, shouting and cackling loudly. I walk over behind her bench.

"Well, old Mother," I say jovially, "why aren't you dancing with some of these fine boys?"

"Ah?" She looks back at me and smiles in delighted, cross-eyed surprise. "So it's you? Didn't expect you here. Well, go on, can't you dance?"

"Not very well. Not like that," I laugh, pointing to a couple nearby. "Here, let me sit with you, I'll buy you a glass of wine."

She is pleased. Between sips of wine she bludgeons me with her roars of laughter at the antics of youth. The band stops again, and she turns to me.

"Don't you know any of these girls?" she asks.

"I recognize one or two. There's the older Chevissier girl, and over there's your Germaine."

"She's no girl," proclaims Mother Nourrie, "she's a woman."

"Oh, sorry. And there's that pretty Christianne."

"Yeah, she's my cousin." The old woman leans her driveling wine-red lips near my ear. "And she's a fiery little bitch. From my side of the family. We got good blood on my side of the family. You look pale tonight—why don't you dance with her? She'll make your stove warm proper." She leans back cackling, nudging me in the ribs. I say nothing, and she cups her hands around her mouth and shouts, "Hey, Christianne! Come over here!" She is ignored by the crowd, many of whom are from other villages in the Valley.

Christianne, the blond sensual Christianne, comes through the colors of lights to join us. Her eyes say the same thing as before. She looks at me, and only her looks warm.

Above the surrounding noise Mother Nourrie says, "My friend wants a dance, Christianne. Give him a fine dance."

The music starts and I stand, swallowing saliva that

503

collects at the sight of her. No one notices us. We dance to the edge of the lights and off down the street without speaking. I feel her against me, her head with its coarse blond hair against my cheek. We dance in the reflected light on the narrow cobblestones, and our shadows dance distortedly, long in pattern, before us. Closed, locked doors stare blankly from each side. A few other dancers straggle in our direction, beyond the strings of feeble red and green electric bulbs.

At last I whisper, "Christianne—that's a nice name," my mouth against her hair, my dry lips tasting her hair.

She hums an inaudible and meaningless answer. I hold her closer, feeling the ridge down the small of her back, the thinness of her dress, the fullness of her breasts lost and tormenting against me. We don't have to talk. She tells me with her dancing, moving tighter against me, making movements against me which I answer as our dancing grows slower and our breathing more labored. Her legs feel strong, pressed to mine. Muscles of her back move beneath my hand.

We dance farther off into the dark. And we move together, fitting close at belly and thigh—straining, torturing animal movements. The saxophone rises in a crescendo that echoes through the dark narrow tunnel of the street. I bend my face down and my lips become wet against her shoulder. She throws back her head, laughing, and we stop dancing. She is full of devil odors and laughter, and it's an easy thing. Her hair falls to the back, away from her face. My lips kiss her under the chin and down the long throat, feeling the smoothness of young flesh. They kiss still lower, into the cut of her dress between her breasts, feeling the crease of her large breasts. Smells from under the dress: smells of sweat and lively odors of exercise. Smells of rutting youngness—rich, animal, intoxicating—tearing me with tremblings. I fondle and fumble and kiss, inhaling risings from her dress. She reaches down, laughing, puts her hand under my chin and lifts my face to hers.

We begin dancing again. Slowness of dance, violent

shaking and violent music. Other odors return, odors of the beginnings of greenery from the pastures about us—waking smells of dampness in the warming earth. We dance a torment of closeness, pressed against a flimsiness of clothing. The sky hangs low, forbidding, and she heats in my arms. She smiles, looking up into my drawn face, and her smile is smells, too—smells of garlic and wine and food digesting below, of white teeth and wetness of inner mouth. I bend down, inhaling these odors, and all about is the burgeoning heaviness of first greens, of earth coming alive after its long sleep. Damp night-odors of earth's rumblings. Thigh straining against thigh. We dance with both arms clasped about each other, arms going lower and lower, pressing lower parts together. The music stops again. Laughing shouts float down the street to us. We don't even think of going back. We continue dancing. And in the dancing, lips find lips, open mouth finds open mouth and inside of mouth, as mouth shakes against mouth laughing and caressing till it engulfs us with its eye-closed dizziness and nose feels warm exhalation from the nose beneath. We stand still. Lips grow rigid. Laughing stops as the hardness of our kiss creates a vacuum of the senses.

A first drop of rain, followed by other scattered drops. A shout of despair from the other dancers. We separate lips and tongues with a noisy wetness. I walk her into the nearest doorway. The rain is light. We stand side by side without speaking until she mutters, "It's blowing on me—I'm getting wet."

"So am I," I laugh. "Here, let me stand in front of you."

Rain falls lightly, wetting the cobblestones. It's a fine mist fogging the streets, catching the reds and greens and oranges of the dance lights. I stand in front of her, against her, protecting her from the rain. Our arms are around each other, and her face is cool with the mist. Noises of water dripping from the eaves about us, and sounds of the River, fill a music-emptied Valley with a flood of moving sound. I stand close to her, clasping her, bending to kiss her eyes, and the rain blows on my back, on my neck and ears. It drips from the roof above, dripping onto my back, wetting my coat and pants. I ignore the coldness of the rain and lean hard against her, pressing her to the locked door behind which someone sleeps never suspecting.

Time and rain and wetness fade. Lips drink of lips. My hands find buttons and undo them, feeling inside. My hands fondle her lightly, a caress to the nakedness of her back and belly and breasts. She trembles violently as blood pounds into the kiss of our joined mouths, as intimacy becomes complete and movements attune themselves to the night and the deserted wet street. I reach up to remove the dress from her shoulders, but her hand against my hand forbids, asks mine to wait.

"Here comes a car," she whispers against my ear. "Don't let them see me."

I stand against her to hide her from the street. The car moves past in a humming of tires on wet pavement, and pulls to a stop. Christianne trembles from the interruption, and rain falls more rapidly. I feel my way into her dress again, but she peers out and whispers, "Why, it's stopped at your house."

"It has?" I turn and look. The taillights glisten redly through the falling rain. And coming from the dark, illuminated in the glare of the headlights, a woman walks rapidly—a glimpse is all, as she gets into the car.

Christianne stares and mutters, "Why, isn't that your lady from Paris?"

"Yes. This may be important. Wait for me here, won't you? I must see her."

"Ah, no—you leave me for her!"

"No, no," I tell her, kissing her hurriedly, "I leave you for no one. But I *must* see her."

The exhaust from the car smokes its acceleration and I leave Christianne unbuttoned, dashing and sliding over the slippery walk, calling for the car to wait. But in the roar of the motor Salesky—for it's his taxi—doesn't hear. The taillights move swiftly away as I reach the gate of my house.

506

Excitement, the effort of running, disappointment. My hair drips water into a trembling and tired face. My desire is gone, but I must go back. Across the way a door opens noisily—Madame Renée's door—and I slip into the house. I am embarrassed that I've called out, and I pray that she won't come to investigate. I am tired. I lean against the wall breathing heavily. After a moment in the near-darkness, I notice a piece of paper lying on the hall table. I pick it up and switch on the light; it contains a message scribbled in pencil: "Meet me on the bridge at 7:30 tomorrow night. I would like to talk." It is unsigned.

I go into the salon and wipe the water from my hair, then wash my hands. The flood of desire has receded dead in me. I think of Christianne waiting in the doorway. I sit down, reread the note, and set it on fire; and feeling the ache of an empty stomach, of passions aroused and unsatisfied and now not wanting satisfaction, I walk sadly to the door. I must finish it for her, for Christianne. The belch of an afternoon's drinking rises sickening me, and my breathing is a cry for sleep. Lights are on at Madame Renée's. I stand in the doorway waiting for them to go off.

The rain slows to a drizzle. Perhaps Christianne will come here. Noises return. The flowing of the River is lost in new noises of laughter and the first chords of band music. The rain stops and the dance begins again. I think of Madame Vincent. I think of her and of tomorrow night and of not knowing till then—and suddenly Christianne, with her needs and her stinks, becomes impossible, nauseating. I don't want her. I am dead with fatigue and I don't want her now.

Reluctantly I slip out, holding the gate bell lest it ring. I go back to a girl who must be my responsibility for a few moments longer, a girl who is waiting with smells and an unbuttoned dress. Lights from the dance reflect in long colors on the wet cobblestones. Clouds, lurid in reflection, hang low above the lights. The night is a turgid night of inverted lusts. I walk to the door where I left her.

And she isn't there. She hasn't waited. I walk on,

breathing relief. Mother Nourrie greets me as I enter the circle of lights.

"Where'd you go, child? Wouldn't my Christianne be nice to you? I'll tell her a thing or two!" She stands close to me, her face serious, concerned.

"It was my fault, old Mother, not hers. She was fine. Where is she now?"

"Just danced off down the street with young Édouard, the sculptor's son. Did she leave you? I'll go get the young slut."

"No, let her go, I'm too tired. But will she be all right, do you think? Will he finish what I started?"

The old hag stares at me, shaking her head. "You look bad, M'sieu. Couldn't you make it go? Should be plenty able from what I've seen. I'm surprised, but I know how it won't go sometimes when you want it to. Try eating boiled celery, they say that helps."

I pat her arm. "It's nothing like that, old Mother. We were interrupted. Something has happened. It's nothing like that."

"Damn! I'm glad to know it. Don't you want me to go for her?"

"No, some other time. I'll leave her for him. Good night."

"Good night, darling boy." She lifts her cheek and I kiss it lightly, smiling to think of the story as Madame Renée will hear it.

I return to my house. The lights are still burning at Madame Renée's. The music screams through the night. I fall asleep immediately, with the saxophone blaring in my consciousness.

Finally in the early morning, the Valley also sleeps. I awaken blissfully happy, knowing that I'll sleep again. There's the beginning of a prayer of thanksgiving, ending in a return to sleep and a vaguely remembered jubilation that nothing has happened; that Madame Vincent saved me from this thing; that the woman with whom I've fallen saved me from the untold remorse of falling again. Thoughts

508

before sleeping of warmth and affection—and the dread of finding out why she returned to the Valley. Last dregs of remembered emotion from two slaps across the face.

23 march

Monastery bells, announcing Sunday High Mass, awaken me. They sound very close. I look up. My window is open to a morning sun. The air is bathed from the night's rain and the earth enters fragrant in my room. I look out. A first white blossom on a pear tree. Greener grasses glistening, still soaked. Fresh odors of Sunday morning, of quietness in the house, of cool warmth.

From the kitchen comes the sound of a broom. Irritated that I can never be left alone, I put on pajamas and go to the door. "Madame Renée?"

"No, M'sieu." It's the voice of Germaine, timid behind the closed door.

"Come in, Germaine."

She opens the door, smiles at my pajamas.

"What are you doing here on Sunday?"

"Well, M'sieu, Madame Renée stopped by my house on her way to Mass. She said you were ill and I should clean the house and open the windows."

"You're a good sort, Germaine, but I know you have better things to do with your day. You know I'm not sick, don't you?"

The big girl, proper, dignified, smiles confusedly. "I did hear some talk that M'sieu might've drunk a little more than he could hold."

"That's right," I laugh—"I was drunk. If you can get me a cup of coffee that'll be all for this morning."

"Yes, M'sieu."

Pots and boiling water in the kitchen. I put on my robe and slippers and join her. Sun streams through the glass doors. The kitchen is spotless, its white and brown tiles newly scrubbed and smelling of strong soap. I sit in a chair at the table, yawning and scratching my head.

"Ah, what a filthy life, Germaine. And it could be such a happy one, too. Do you smoke?"

"No, thank you, M'sieu." Perpetual smile, quietness of voice.

"Tell me, Germaine, the postman says people here resent Madame Renée's dominating me—is that true?"

"I don't know, M'sieu. They don't understand, I guess." She shrugs her shoulders.

"But I feel more or less responsible for her. She wasn't like this before I came."

Germaine turns. "She's always been like this, M'sieu— a mean, vicious woman." Her voice mounts in anger. "If it weren't for you I'd have quit long ago. And even now I feel I can't stay on here much longer."

"But, Germaine—" I exclaim.

She looks at me. "She bullies you," she says bitterly, "just like she did her poor mother and husband. I've known her for years. They say her mother was a mean one. Well, I was her domestic during the war. I can tell you, she was a martyr in her own daughter's house—that I can tell you, for I know. It's shameful the stories Madame Renée's made up against her."

"I can well believe it."

The girl sets a large cup before me and pours coffee. "I shouldn't be telling these things, M'sieu," she whispers.

"That's all right, Germaine. No wonder you hate taking orders from her. But don't quit, things may be better soon. I've had my fill of her too."

"All of us would like to see you rid of her, M'sieu— pardon my saying it, but it's so. Will you want more coffee?"

510

"I can get it. You can go on now—just wait and clean up those dishes tomorrow. And thanks for telling me these things—you can trust me not to mention it to anyone."

After she has gone, I carry my coffee into the salon. I bathe and shave and dress, listening to a radio concert from Paris: the F major Variations of Mozart, followed by the cumbersome Brahms D minor Sonata for violin and piano.

Waiting for Madame Renée to return from Mass, I carry a chair into the sunshine of my courtyard. I sit near the kitchen door with a cup of fresh coffee and the score of the Goudimel Mass, *Le bien que j'ay*. Fragrant, happy music.

The sun grows warm. There's no breeze. The courtyard rests in its brightness and grows green before my eyes. The single white pear blossom hangs still in mid-air. Nothing stirs. I bask in the peace of penetrating warmth, of a clean-washed courtyard. Pools of water, not yet evaporated by the sun, stand between the flagstones.

The sound of bells rises like smoke on the clear air, telling the Valley that Mass is almost over. It is near noon. I think of yesterday—of the clouds, and the drinking smells, and the taste of Salesky's finger down my throat, and the slaps on my face, and the rain last night, and the fumbling into a girl to the accompaniment of a cheap country dance band. The morning becomes brighter, carrying away the yesterdays. The morning is better, much better. It rests lightly on my shoulders. Quietness of waiting, and inner happiness.

The gate bell rings clean, and the gate clangs lightly after it. Nausea tinges my belly. I quickly decide to pretend that I remember nothing that happened during my drunkenness.

"I'm back here," I call out, forcing gladness into my voice.

Madame Renée walks slowly around to join me. Her face is the deep calm of lingering Mass. I rise to give her my chair.

"And how is my sottish friend this morning?" she asks without smiling.

511

"Wonderful, Madame, wonderful!" I exclaim. "Let's sit here in the sun awhile."

I sit on the steps and stretch my legs. She arranges purse and prayer book and rosary beads in her lap. Then she looks at me, and her expression is a mixture of compassion and of having been wronged.

"Now, I want to say this quietly," she begins. "I've given it much thought, and I've decided that if you'll apologize for your outrageous conduct last night, I'll be willing to forgive you for it."

"You mean my getting drunk?" I say innocently. "What's so terrible about that? I've been drunk before."

She rejoins coldly, "You know I wasn't referring to that."

"To tell you the truth," I stammer, "I—I realize there must have been something else. I vaguely remember your slapping me. Please tell me what I did? I was so drunk—"

"You don't know?" Her voice is sharp and suspicious. "Oh, come now."

"Whatever it was, it must have been terrible. But would I pretend I didn't remember if I did? It's frustrating not to remember. If I did something wrong I apologize, but I don't know what it is. Now tell me—what did I do?" I make my eyes look clearly into hers, begging, helpless. And I think of the stiff whalebone staves of her corset, of the heavy hand and tight breasts, of the softness of her upper leg. The disgust of memory apparently makes my expression more poignant.

"I believe you," she says suddenly, her face softening into the most understanding of smiles. "That's all right, I won't embarrass you by telling you what happened"—her gaze embraces me from above; her gaze becomes an intimate soundless chuckling—"but you were pretty terrible." And after a moment during which I crease my forehead in the feigned perplexity of trying to remember, she adds gently, "We won't ever discuss it again. You're young and you had too much liquor, that's all."

We discuss the noise of the dance. Obviously she hasn't heard about my dancing with Christianne, nor about the

512

kiss I gave old Mother Nourrie—nor is there any mention of Salesky's taxi in front of the house last night.

Lunch, long in preparation, is eaten quietly. We listen to her radio and it merges into the beauty of the day. Lazy afternoon, lingering at the table. Visitors walk through the streets—visitors from other villages. They walk slowly past the open, lace-curtained windows. It is afternoon as only Sunday can make it.

Later, the gate to Madame Renée's courtyard clangs; she runs to the window. "Oh, no!" she whispers, turning to me. "It's that unbearable Madame Marceaux. Don't tell me I have to listen to *her* gossip this afternoon."

A knock at the door. I rise. Madame Renée opens, and the two women greet each other delightedly. Madame Marceaux shakes my hand coldly; yes, she remembers me. Her mouth of ill-fitting teeth is sunken at the corners, and her skin is jaundiced and leathery. One has the impression that she's never been touched by man—that her child must have come from some other source.

She and Madame Renée chat bitterly about the ball last night. Neither of them could sleep a wink for the noise of it. And they shake their heads in disgust at the thought of how many illegitimate children will soon appear in the Valley.

Presently, Madame Marceaux looks kindly at me. "And, Monsieur, did you enjoy the ball?"

I glance at Madame Renée; her face flushes with surprise. Smiling, I bow to Madame Marceaux. "Very much, Madame, very much indeed." Then quickly, "But I know you ladies have a lot to discuss," I add, "so if you'll excuse me . . ."

Before they can stop me I walk out the door, turning to look back as it closes. Madame Renée stares after me. She'll learn everything before the afternoon is over—but, somehow, it doesn't matter.

The two women and their prattling have left a bad taste in my mouth. I look about at the Sunday Village, at the Sunday strollers in the street. Nothing seems right. The

day has lost its beauty. Images of yesterday flash again
through my mind; I think once more of Christianne in the
doorway, and of how Madame Vincent saved me from
falling with her. And Father Clément . . . should I tell
him all this? No, there's nothing to confess—nothing happened, really . . . And yet, at the back of my consciousness,
is the hint of something wrong, of something out of place.
Father Clément . . . if nothing else he could explain the
experience to me, tell me what it means. I turn toward the
Monastery, and my steps grow faster; and as I walk, the
desire to talk with him becomes a compulsion. I know
there's no other way: his face will always be there and in
it my eyes must ever read their own judgment, whether of
right or of wrong. But this time it will be easy; at least for
today they can see there, mirrored in the monk's gaunt features, innocence.

I look for him in the Monastery garden, where bright
days always carry him. I find him there alone, walking and
reading his breviary. His hood is pulled back exposing his
perfectly barbered tonsure to the warm afternoon sun.

Closing the book, he listens intently as I quietly relate
the incident with Christianne. I describe our dancing in
the street, and our lust in the doorway, and my later happiness after Madame Vincent had interrupted us. But it's
not the same: somehow in the telling, my complacent innocence dissolves and disappears, and in its place I begin to
notice a deep sense of loss—of guilt that I went even as
far as I did. It's the same feeling I had in Salesky's taxicab
with Marguerite Désormière, only greatly intensified this
afternoon; and I realize that the suffering of remorse will
grow till it can no longer be borne—that there must be a
change.

"What's the cause of this, Father?" I ask, confused.
"Before, these things didn't bother me, but now it seems
I can't do a thing without feeling miserable about it."

The monk takes my arm and we walk for a moment in
silence. "It is very clear to me, my son," he says finally.
"Your virtue last night was nothing, really—you know that.

514

But I wonder if you have noticed the evolution which is clearly taking place within you? It is a significant fact that, although nothing happened, you feel a keen sense of loss. I am happy to see the turn you seem to be taking."

"I don't see any evolution at all," I say disgustedly. "I'm no better than I ever was. It only affects me differently, that's all."

"But that is what I find so encouraging, my son," asserts Father Clément, as we turn to retrace our steps on the garden path. "Let us take just this one sin, the sin of the flesh. Do you remember a few months ago when you fell with Madame Vincent? Do you remember your reactions then? What were they?—a mixture of pride and regret and fear. You regretted forgetting our dried fruits, and you feared being found out. Otherwise I think you were rather pleased with yourself. Now let us examine that fear. You were not afraid of God—you did not give God a thought. And if you were sorry, it was not because you had offended Him. No, your reactions were directed toward your fellow men. You were afraid of the judgment of men—of my judgment, of the other monks', of the Village ladies'. Your concept of morality was purely social."

"I've never thought of that before, Father. I supposed—"

"I know," he says slowly. "So much of our life today is based on this purely social point of view. So much of what we call 'Christian' morality has its basis in social standards of behavior."

"But after all," I protest, "isn't that the function of Christianity? I really don't see the difference."

"But there is a very *great* difference," he sighs, walking more slowly. "Social morality, wherein a man conforms to a certain pattern of behavior because of his fear of another man's opinion, has its place certainly; but it must never be confused with true Christian morality. Look at yourself, for example. After the affair with Madame Vincent you experienced this fear of another man's opinion. But after you had committed another indiscretion, not too long after that,

515

with the girl in Salesky's taxicab, I began to see the change in your reaction. On that occasion there was no reason for you to fear discovery, there was no reason to tell anyone of your misdeed. And yet you felt compelled to come to me. Your fear had changed because, somehow, you felt that you had offended not man, but God. That was the first sign of a true Christian remorse. And today you feel it still more strongly. Your remorse is based not upon any fear of the earthly consequences of your act, but upon a great sense of something wrong in your relations with God. And there you have the primary difference between social remorse and Christian remorse. As long as the misdeed is kept a secret there is no social remorse; but if Christian remorse exists, you will suffer regardless of how carefully the secret is guarded. I believe this sense of loss, of guilt, of something wrong, is growing in you rapidly. Soon you will be able to resist temptation, for soon you will grow to detest the regret consequent to sin. I am very happy to see this in you, my child—happier than you can know."

We have walked to the parapets overlooking the River. Father Clément's words fill me with a sudden longing to do something positive: a longing to leave the world outside and return to the safety of these walls. I tell him of my conviction that Madame Renée is in love with me; and I confess my fear of yet falling with Christianne. "I was wondering," I conclude—"well, I was wondering if perhaps I could return to my old cell?"

Father Clément gazes at the water a long moment before answering. "Well, my child, you must know my affection for you—I am tempted to bring you back here. But my logic as a priest forces me to pause." We walk toward the grove of fruit trees, and he stops to finger a green-budded peach tree. "I do not," he goes on, "think you will fall with Christianne; I have that much confidence in your development. But what makes you think that Madame Renée is in love with you?"

"Well," I hesitate, "I haven't known whether to tell you this or not, Father. Mademoiselle Marthe told me several days ago that she thought Madame Renée was in love with me—but I didn't have proof of it till last night. I got drunk in Town yesterday, and she came over to see me in my room. You may not believe this, but—well, she put her hands all over me, and did everything imaginable to excite me. And then when I did get excited and started making advances, she slapped me. But it was she who led me on, Father. Now I'm glad it didn't happen, of course; but it's made her more repulsive to me than ever. You can't imagine how hard it is for me to be civil to her. All I can think about is her hand on my stomach. How can I do her any good, feeling the way I do?"

Father Clément has released the tree and is absent-mindedly wiping his stained fingers on his robe. "But if you leave Madame Renée now," he reasons, "what intolerable heartache it will cause her—especially if she is in love with you, as she apparently is. You have no affection left for her, agreed—but can you allow yourself to heighten her grief at this particular time of great unhappiness? She is a human being after all, no matter how terrible her actions have seemed to be. We must stop this, but as painlessly as possible and not with such abruptness."

"But, Father, I'm no good for her. Something's wrong with me. I don't help her any—I lose my temper and become something I can't stand. Here with you, there might be some hope of progress. I could finish my work more rapidly and hope that much sooner to make a decent life for myself."

He looks at a newly sawed branch—yellow-grained wood with hints of green; he fingers it and smiles. "I shall be happy to think of you well married, my son, but that is in the future." He shakes his head. "No, your very presence, the fact that you occupy this poor woman's time and thoughts, is the important thing right now. It is her salvation; she told me so herself. We know all about Michel here, and I am sure you know that he is going to be married soon. That will come as a great shock to Madame Renée, and you must not desert her. The two things could combine to drive her to distraction. She is not a profoundly religious

517

person—she needs a much more human support. As a friend I am truly sorry; but as a priest, how can I counsel you differently? Pray for her, my child, pray for her every day. The very act of your prayer will soften the hardness of your feelings toward her." He points to tiny honey-colored drops of sap on the cut wood. "Look at this tree. Did you help Father Gardener prune it? It is bleeding. The countryside is truly beautiful today, is it not?" Leaning forward on tiptoe he smells the branch, and holds it for me to smell. "Yes, the countryside is more aware of God in spring than at any other time, I think. It is alive with the miracle of the rebirth of life. I should have been made the Father Gardener."

"I should have too, Father," I laugh. "I hate to go back to Madame Renée after seeing this garden. Just being here changes a man."

"I must go now," Father Clément tells me. "Stay in the garden as long as you like. Let it give you the courage to turn disgust into acceptance. You have done well. Remember this day and this spot when irritations arise, and perhaps soon you can live here again."

He walks slowly down the path to pass out of sight. The River flows a lulling inevitability through the Valley. I turn back to the newly pruned tree and smell its wood again. Tonight I must meet Madame Vincent. I trust her; whatever it is, I trust her. And my only prayer, alone in this garden, is that she not suffer because of me or my past deeds. A humming quiet about, an answering quiet within. Gradually the scourge of cutting within me disintegrates, finds another outlet.

High Vespers make this acceptance complete. Seeming weakness becomes right and logical and not weak. Hour of lightening all that burdens. Immersion in the familiarity of these chants.

Leaving the Monastery, I begin walking in the country. Past small farmhouses, and by fields stretching away from the River. Slow leisure of aimlessness in the growing dusk. On beside the River, following its course till it leads me

518

where farmhouses are more remote. Goats graze along the road. Crumbling stone walls, covered with moss, separate me from chickens and hogs.

The road forks, and in the fork is a miniature café boasting three outdoor tables. Dusk is here and the tables are deserted. I take a chair and wait for someone to come and take my order. Seated, there's a tiredness. The countryside is calm: chickens, a far-off dog. And inside, sounds of earthenware.

A child brings me white wine. She says it's all they have to serve, but to a dry palate it tastes like champagne. She tells me that her mama is cooking dinner inside. We talk while I drink my wine. I give her a ten-franc tip for which, with a curtsy, she gravely thanks me.

Realization of my immense love for all this: for this country and these people, and for the delicious youngness of this child after the oldness of those who have surrounded me these many months. Realization of the somber cloak with which Madame Renée shrouds my life. But the abhorrence of my having allowed her to insinuate herself into the very core of my being, is countered by the time, the day, the familiarity, the fundamental pity I bear her. Soon I'll be again in her house, in her heats and caprices and loathsomenesses. The fact of her presence commands.

But the spell of Vespers returns. The walk back is long. Trees, walls, first lights in houses are real, in minute detail, along the road. It resolves. All becomes consonance within me. The heart grows soft. Tissues dissolve without tangible images. The smoke of dinner fires and early, early night.

When I come in sight of the bridge, a lone figure is standing at the railing, the vague figure of a woman. She doesn't look up as I walk toward her, my shoes crunching loud on the gravel. I stop at her side and lean on the railing, waiting for her to speak. There's only the liquid murmuring of the River flowing beneath.

When she remains silent, I gaze at the hinted whites of the foaming waters below and find words: "Are you all right?"

"You came. I'm so glad you found my note."

"Of course I came—I've tried to find you ever since I heard you were back."

She doesn't answer. Damp mists rise from the night. I glance at her uneasily. She is staring straight ahead. Her profile, faintly illuminated by lights across the way, is as smooth and poised as that of some ancient marble statue, with the same delicate patina of eternal youngness forever radiating serenity.

"It's good to be with you again," I say clumsily. "Good to have you back."

She lifts her hands to her forehead and draws her finger tips slowly back across her temples. I peer at her through the darkness. She breathes a long sigh, as though she were searching for words with which to tell me something.

"What is it?" I hear myself asking. "What's happened? Why didn't you let them operate?"

A scarcely perceptible pause, then, "The doctors have told me I'm incurably ill."

My sight slowly focuses on her face again. "What?" I mutter dully, not understanding.

"They say it's hopeless."

"Hopeless? But—surely, Madame Vincent, you don't mean—?" On the railing my hand instinctively seeks hers.

"Yes." She nods her head slightly. Her hand in mine is cool and moist, absolutely still. "If they operated I might die on the table. If I lived what would it mean?—only a year or two more. It's not worth the risk. I couldn't stand to die like that—on an operating table, under bright lights."

"I—I had no idea, Madame. I thought it was—" My voice sounds harsh in the soft night. Unreal! It's unreal! *Incurably ill!* My hand tightens about her fingers with such force as to make tendons ache deep inside my arm. Forever the pain of another—and somewhere beyond I begin to hear the lonely raspings of crickets and frogs from the dank depths below. Forever the pain of another and never my own. Forever the night's lonely muffling sounds, dampening, dampening. "Maybe," I say without expression, "maybe

520

the doctors are wrong. Maybe they made a terrible mistake."

The silhouette of her profile changes a little: a flickering softness about the mouth. "No, I'm afraid not. With cancer they know pretty well."

The night shatters, recedes. I am left alone, remote. Unreal! The night towers high, losing all warmth. The night is a vast lonely dome, a hollow skeleton reverberating empty. I fasten my gaze on the black hulk of the Monastery rising out of the River.

"I can't believe it," comes from me, detached, words again heavy and coarse on the silence.

"No, no," she says softly, "you mustn't feel that way."

I fight for control. The stagnant reek of decaying vegetation cuts into my nostrils—acid ash penetrating to the quick—giving lie to the night. My jaws ache as though I'd swallowed vinegar. The poisonous mulch bubbling, vomiting its rot somewhere in the pit of my stomach, and the jaws aching.

"Do you know—? Did they tell you—?" The words hang in my throat, and I force them out: "How long do you have?"

"They give me about two months."

"Two months! But—there must be something, some way—"

"No . . ." the word suspends hesitant, fragile in sound, tentative but starkly final, "there's nothing." For the first time she turns her head to look me full in the face; light glows dully from her upswept blond hair. "Can you understand why I refused the operation? Surely you must. You know what this place means to me. It's so much better to die here where I can hear the Monastery bells. It gives me— I don't know—it gives me a feeling of peace. I can accept here."

I find nothing to say. I am tired. Numb, I gaze at the unchanging Monastery. I release her hand and cross my arms, leaning on the railing.

"I pray well here," she goes on slowly. "Life's an enchantment now. Every day is more perfect than the last.

521

How fortunate I am," she whispers fervently, "to know in time! You must know what it is—what it means to me. I'll have these last weeks of complete happiness, for I live now only to die well prepared, and with the certainty of God's love for me. I've always been afraid I might go suddenly, you know, without being able to . . . Anyway," and her voice becomes almost inaudible, "it's a rare privilege He's given me, to die like this. When it comes I can be glad."

I glance at her. The way in which she speaks of her death is as calm as the night about us. There is no fear, no uncertainty in her voice; *mine* is the only fear. It is death, then, that creates the soft patina of eternal youngness; for she is like a young girl now, filled with the quiet wonderment of life's second great love—this one, which is death, for all time. She is like a young girl tonight, full of whiteness, and made beautiful. And the pulse that fades in her becomes painfully alive in me, throbbing strong in my throat. The poison of fear and revulsion begins to find its antidote, and I feel ashamed. She *wants* to talk of her death; she wants me to agree with her.

"Look," she says, pointing, "isn't that the most beautiful sight on God's earth? That's why I had to come back. Knowing what all that means, it's not possible to be afraid."

Something unspoken passes between us. I look with new eyes. Beneath us, the swirling torrents of the River; to the right, the lights of a neighboring village; and to the left, in an alcove of still waters, the reflection of our Monastery topped by its high silhouette. By some mysterious transference I see through her eyes, seeing as she must be seeing. The sky, with the passing of fragile clouds, becomes luminous with stars mirrored in the black waters of the quiet bay. Standing with her, these things come to startling life. The stagnant putrescence is muted in favor of the delicate sweetness of cooking fires, of spring, of the intangibly hinted moisture of night on the River: permeation of odors. Living sounds from the water's edge: the stippled background of crickets and insects accompanying the deep-throated croaking of frogs, no longer lonely. Early evening is transformed into breathless midnight calm. In a moment of watching, of waiting, this vast scattered night becomes intimate, living with us here and now. A new focus has changed the swift vision of the eyes and the heart. Through her senses, enlivened by death, this woman beside me has lifted a muffling haze from my own senses, deadened by life. Tonight all this becomes a part of us in a bloodless union of infinite completeness, as completely shared as our flesh was once shared. I think of that other night long ago, and of our walk back from Town through the snow; I think of us remote and lonely in the frozen countryside, two shadows evoking the specter of our times. But now, tonight, we stand under a magically transfigured sky; and for an instant it destroys the need of man to huddle against man, of man to protect man. Coolness without mystery. Pools of stars shimmer close above, occasionally falling in sweeps. Lights from the fortresslike Monastery dance on the surface of night's waters. And there's no more fear; the beginnings of sorrow and pity are dissolved in the inundation of tenderness.

I whisper, "I suspect you're more fortunate than I realized, Madame Vincent."

"I know, my friend," she answers simply.

There's a silence of thought as I unconsciously reach for a cigarette.

"It's good to live," she murmurs. "You realize that, when you know death. I ask nothing. I've lived, and now I'll die—and both will be . . ." Her voice trails off.

"Yes," I say gently, and then, "Is there much pain?"

"No, not yet."

I strike a match and light my cigarette, cupping the flame. It illuminates a momentary world in front of my face, glistening in magnified perspective from the moist lines and grooves tooled into the palms of my hands. Astonishing to see this flesh that's alive and full of health, to see this flesh that's torchlit and full of sweats and desires. The heat singes tissues and I quickly toss the match away, overwhelmed at the blatancy of such a sight in the companionship of death. It takes a few moments for my eyes again to accustom themselves to the darkness. I draw deeply on the cigarette and try to forget my hands. I return slowly to the pale flux and flow of darkness cradling the thin line of life and passing time, growing ever thinner. It cools and she's still standing there, ageless and timeless, on the brink of all eternity.

"There's something I must tell you," I say quietly, cringing from the sound of my voice destroying the silence. "When I came here tonight I was afraid you might be pregnant. I came with that one thought. Now I wish—" But something makes me stop.

"I'm so sorry," she whispers. "I should've written you. It never occurred to me that you'd think that, but of course you would. I'm glad it's not that; I'm glad it's this."

Between us flows an undercurrent of tenderness, a liberation of thought freeing us from the need to say things through the cubed filter of living feelings; destroying the need to say what is meaningless merely to fill the silence. She is above such things now.

"You know," I say slowly, "I believe I understand you. I believe I understand how you feel. I don't pity you—nor envy you either, for that matter—but I'm thankful that things have worked out the way you wanted them to." I pause. "Is there anything I can do? May I call on you?"

She doesn't answer.

"I understand," I say after a time.

"Yes," comes softly from the darkness, "I'd like to be alone. I think it will be better that way. Completely alone. This is between God and me now."

Dew has started to form on the bridge railing. The dampness begins to chill. I step close to her, turn to face her, and exhale invisible cigarette smoke. "Of course—it'd ruin it to have all the old ladies in to change your bedclothes and clean your room and feel sorry for you. No reason for them to find out. As for myself, I won't try to see you again."

"Thank you."

524

"Tell me one thing before we separate, though—I must know—are you very sorry about what we did?"

"I'm—really not sure," she replies thoughtfully. "Perhaps I'm sorry, but that part of it's been paid for and seems unimportant now. At any rate I'm glad it made us friends."

"Thank God you feel that way," I tell her. "I'd never forgive myself if I had hurt you . . . I'll leave you now. If you want me—if you find things changed and need me for anything—you know where I live. God bless you. Good night, Madame."

She has turned her back and is gazing again at the Monastery. I drop my cigarette and, feeling very light, I walk swiftly away.

I think of Madame Renée, of the good ladies who will hound Madame Vincent to the grave never knowing the splendor of her; never knowing how great must be her worth in the eyes of God; treating her as a whore. But, somehow, it's to her advantage. Approaching my house, I thrust aside this narcosis of resentment and let myself be filled with thoughts of her on the bridge. Thank God for letting me know her! And within rises the image of her only happiness: the knowledge that somewhere this woman will exist and breathe for a time, given in all her longing to something of the infinite. Profound humility that I could have a part in it, however small. And I murmur a prayer of thanksgiving for her—at first faltering with doubt—then crushing doubt to give thanks again.

On with all the lights, the radio. It's warm enough to bathe in the kitchen sink. Standing high, my head touching the ceiling, I lather with a fresh bar of soap sent from America, then rinse by squeezing a water-soaked sponge over my head. The bath is right for the time: it washes away the things of the past, the last lingering sadness. I dress hurriedly, putting on fresh underwear; and leaving the radio blaring and the lights burning, I walk out into the street.

I look toward the bridge. She is still standing there by the railing. She is another, a no-longer-existing part of my life. Once more I feel a surge of jubilation for her, of gratitude for having known her. And we must go on living. Smells of fresh soap rise on the air. We are glad to go on living, to go on with our existence.

Without knocking I enter Madame Renée's house. It is empty of cooking odors and the table hasn't been set. She is lying on the sofa, weeping; her red face and swollen eyes reveal that she's been weeping all afternoon. I stand at the table looking down at her. Her tears smell of sweat, jarring with the soap-fragrance remaining from my bath. The room is tired, but nothing can dampen moods that smell of soap.

"All right, all right," I shout gaily, "all right, laughing spirit, you can stop now. Madame Vincent's not pregnant. I'm not in disgrace."

She stares up at me. "Why didn't you tell me you were at the dance last night? Madame Marceaux said you danced with Christianne—with a servant girl!"

I laugh. "Madame Marceaux's a bitter old woman; she needs to be violated by an enormous man. Sure, I danced with Christianne. It was a public dance. And if you want to know the rest, Mother Confessor, I played with her too."

"Oh, no!" she moans.

"Don't act so surprised. Both you and Madame Marceaux think it went further than that—and it would have, only we were interrupted. It rained on us."

Renewed, uncontrollable sobbing. "My poor boy . . ."

"Everything's all right. Now will you please get off that mourning bench and fix me some food?"

She sits up, grasping my hands, her cheeks wet. "No, first tell me all about it."

I retort angrily, "Go read yourself a nasty book instead. What happened is between Christianne and me and none of your damned business. Have you been crying all afternoon?"

"I can't help it," she whimpers. "My world is gone."

"Ha!" I sneer, "that's good. So your world can be ruined by the indiscretion of the buttons on my pants! That's really good. Just look at yourself—demoralized because a man on

526

whom you've no claim danced with a servant girl. Why don't you come to your senses? Now get some supper, and let's try to be normal human beings for once."

Glaring at me she releases my hands, slapping them away from her, and opens her mouth to speak.

"And don't try to find out," I add bitterly, "what happened."

"How can I ever trust you again?" she weeps. "How can I be sure Christianne won't be back?"

"You can't," I say loudly—"it's very simple, you can't. But I'll tell you this—I don't want Christianne. You can believe what you like, but I won't *ever* want her. Now get me some supper."

"Very well, you don't have to scream at me." Composing herself, she rises wearily and walks to the kitchen, turning at the door. "What do you want to eat?"

"Perhaps some *crêpes,* and a bottle of red wine. Plenty of *crêpes,* eh?"

"Fine, plenty of *crêpes.* But listen, I wasn't crying about you and Christianne—things just got too much for me." And in a moment, when she has passed out of sight, "Tell me, how'd you find out about Madame Vincent?" she calls back.

"I saw her, of course."

"Oh . . ."

By the time we sit down at the table Madame Renée is exquisite in her submission, and the meal is eaten in peace. In answer to everything she says, I mutter only a skeletal, derisive, bull-like "Yes" or "No."

At the end of the meal, with warming wine inside her, she remarks carefully, sweetly, "Tell me, if Madame Vincent didn't come back here for *that,* don't you think she's a little brazen? After all, we made it obvious enough that she's not wanted here."

"She has as much right here as you."

"Well, she worries those poor monks to death—always in one of their parlors."

"If you tended your own business you wouldn't know

527

that; you wouldn't know a thing about what she does, or—"

"And I'd think," she goes on, ignoring my remark, "I'd think you above all would have no respect for her."

"I'm devoted to her just as the monks are. And what's more, I respect her completely. She's as good as the best of you." I refill my glass with wine, angrily, spilling it on the table.

She says sharply, "Are you trying to put me in the same class with a woman like that?"

"Why not?"

"She's little more than a prostitute."

"What's she done that you haven't done? Or have you forgotten?"

Madame Renée blushes resentment. "Well, at least we got married."

I shrug my shoulders. "Don't talk about Madame Vincent. If you want to know why she returned to the Valley, it's because she's hopelessly ill."

"Well," she sneers, "what's it to me if she's ill? Honestly, after an experience like yours with her I don't see how you can keep any respect for her."

"That experience has nothing to do with it. I dare say she's as clean in the Lord's eyes as you." I drink my wine, furious with myself for having told Madame Vincent's secret.

Madame Renée's eyes soften. "I didn't realize you were that serious about her. If she really is ill I can help her. You don't understand our customs, but don't expect me to feel sorry about it."

"She doesn't need help from any of you fine ladies. Let her alone. Don't be so sticky."

"You're in a real mood, aren't you?" She lowers her head, glaring at me. "Careful you don't overstep yourself, young man. The last time you overstepped yourself you got slapped."

"I'm going over and listen to the radio," I sigh. "Good night, Madame."

"But it's early yet," she objects. "Would you mind if

I came over and listened with you for just a little while?"

"I guess not. Come over when you like."

She smiles understandingly. "I'll powder my nose and fix a pot of coffee. And don't take all this too seriously—you're wrought-up tonight. Ah, that old gossip Marceaux!"

I feel relieved that I won't be alone tonight, even if my companion has to be Madame Renée.

24 march

"Mail for M'sieu, good morning, M'sieu." The postman, standing by my bed, lets the letters fall on my chest one by one, grinning down at me.

"Ah"—I rub my eyes with my knuckles—"this is service. Thanks a lot."

He asks, "Did everything come out all right the other night?" He sits in the chair at my table, feeling in the ash tray for a long cigarette butt.

"When? Oh, that. Sure, not even a hangover. Reach in that drawer, there's a fresh pack of cigarettes. Take the whole pack. I owe you and Salesky a lot more than that for bringing me home."

"Here." He leans forward in the chair, holding a cigarette out to me. "And a light. Ah, you were really drunk, my friend."

"Don't I remember!"

"Drunk enough," he grins, "to . . . uh . . . go after Christianne, from what I hear."

"You don't have to be drunk," I mutter, "to do that. Been wanting her a long time."

529

He squints at me through the smoke of his cigarette, and asks seriously, "How was she, M'sieu? I've always wondered about that one."

"Lord!" I groan, shaking my head appreciatively. "A little animal. I nearly went crazy."

"That good, eh?"

"You can't imagine—she's made for it."

His usual cynical grin is replaced, momentarily, by an expression of benevolent warmth. "I'm glad. Now you'll have her regularly."

"I doubt it. You knew I didn't finish. I only paved the way for Édouard."

"No!" He stares at me. "I knew she was with Édouard too, but I just supposed—"

"I was called away before finishing the job. When I went back she was off in the dark somewhere with him."

"Anyone who'd just walk off and leave something like that . . ." He shakes his head unbelievingly.

"You're right. But I was worried sick about Madame Vincent that night. I was afraid she was pregnant, you know—but I found out she's not."

"Well, I'm glad to hear that, M'sieu. Glad for you," he adds absently, still shaking his head. "You just walked away from Christianne? Left her there?"

"Unbuttoned," I say gravely. I hand him my cigarette to put out. "You think my fooling around with her did me much harm with the gossips?"

"No," he snorts, "probably helped. From what I hear, some of them were beginning to wonder if M'sieu weren't maybe hung like a dove."

"If I wasn't what? You mean . . . Why, they should've known from Madame Vincent it wasn't that."

"Still, it's hard to say. They don't think it's natural for a young man to live like this—in a cage, so to speak, cooped up with an old woman. Has she got to you yet?—not that it's any of my business."

"Not yet, but she—" I hesitate, then decide to say nothing more. The postman looks at me and laughs out loud.

530

I mutter the word "Hell!" and he laughs louder. Apparently the irritation shows in my face, for he rises from the chair and his laughter becomes slightly embarrassed, then fades out. He stretches with an air of nonchalance.

"Well, I must be going. Thanks for the cigarettes, eh?"

"Not at all. Come in any time," I tell him cordially. "I always enjoy talking with you."

When he has gone, I hear noises of dishwashing from the kitchen. "Germaine!" I call.

"Yes, M'sieu?" she answers through the door.

"Is there any coffee?"

"Yes, M'sieu, I'll heat it."

I get out of bed and put on a pair of pajamas. I open the blinds, flooding the room with light. After a few moments Germaine brings a cup of coffee to the door, and I carry it to the table to look over my mail. Letters from Paris and Tours and America—and one from Michel. It is thick. Lighting another cigarette, I take a long swallow of hot coffee. Then, reluctantly, I tear open the envelope.

MY VERY DEAR FRIEND,

Enclosed is a second letter to you, that I thought it best to send, as I know Mama well enough to be certain, that she will want to read my letters to you. Please burn this, as soon as you finish with it, for I have, finally, come to a definite decision, and this is to prepare you for what is to come.

You see, I can see no further advantage in putting off the news of my marriage plans, to a future date, and everything has been written in a letter to Mama, which she should receive, when you receive this one, and so that it won't appear that you have known about it all along, I have written you about it, in the enclosed note.

I think that I know Mama pretty well, well enough to realize, that she will never be any better, but perhaps the shock of finding out this way, aboveboard, from the beginning, will incline her to accept that, which she would never accept otherwise.

Please, as my friend, a new-found friend, but a brother none the less, stand by Mama, and do all that you can for her, for you are young enough to realize, that my impetuosity, the impetuosity of young lovers, cannot be kept a secret. Madeleine and I have decided to be married on the 10th of April, and, of

531

course, that is only a short time away, but the marriage bans have already been published. We feel that we must marry as soon as possible, and you, who have done so much, will surely want to come to Paris, and celebrate the joyous occasion with us.

I know Mama, and she will rave, and weep, and threaten, and I am truly sorry for you, that you have to be subjected to such an ordeal, but this is a final decision, and I have explained everything in my letter to her, begging her to accept, and bless my marriage. But I have, also, made it quite clear that, in any case, she can do nothing to stop it, so be with her when she reads it, if you can, and assure her of my lasting love, and of my gift to her of a daughter, and two new granddaughters. Pray for us, my friend . . .

And on and on. To the very end, he conveniently hides behind the irresponsibility of "young love." In closing he announces his plan to bring Madeleine here on Thursday, to meet his mother. He expresses the hope that I'll do all I can to make the meeting a pleasant one—to put Madame Renée in a receptive mood. The irresponsibility of young love! I'm not surprised at his decision to marry right away— only resentful that he wants to pass the burden of it on to me. But I had expected nothing else, really.

Crumpling the letter, I drop it in the cold stove. With a letter of her own, Madame Renée should be here any minute. I decide not to dress. Instead I finish my coffee and cigarette, and climb back into bed to wait. I pull the covers around me and lie staring at the ceiling. Waiting, dreading. From the kitchen, the clatter of dishes. And outside, the sun of a bright day.

Then, from the courtyard, the imperious clang of the gate bell. Quickly I face the wall and close my eyes, pretending to sleep. The front door opens noisily. Urgent footsteps sound in the hall, and my salon door flies open with such force as to knock plaster from the wall.

"He's got a woman! Wake up, wake up! Michel's got a woman, I tell you! The idiot thinks he'll be married next month. Wake up! We must do something to stop him." The door slams loudly and I hear her fall into a chair.

I turn heavily in bed to glare at her. "How many times,"

I say sharply, "do I have to tell you to knock before coming into my room?"

"Were you asleep?" she asks, her eyes hollow of all expression.

"No, damn it," I admit. "Michel wrote me too. All right, so he's an idiot and so he's getting married. Good riddance!"

She lifts her eyes to the ceiling. "O God! God damn him! God damn his soul for doing this to me! I'll stop it! He can't do it!"

"Oh, yes he can. And try to keep your voice down, Madame, Germaine's in the kitchen."

"I don't care who's in the kitchen. I tell you, he can't do it. I'll stop him if it's the last thing I do."

"You're hysterical. Now get yourself under control and read his letter aloud. Let's see what we can make of it." I sit up in bed.

She is trembling, but with an effort she calms herself. She unfolds the letter and begins reading. I examine the texture of the wool in the brightly patched quilt over my legs. As she reads she emphasizes the wrong words, making sincere passages appear complete hyprocrisy; reads with hatred, making the letter sound like the ravings of an ungrateful son.

"Read it right," I break in harshly after a few lines, not looking at her. "Read it as he wrote it."

Her voice becomes a monotone. I look at the quilt, at the tiled floor, at the walls of the room. She reads to the end without stopping. After a silence she glances up at me, then stares out the window. Her face is a dazed paralysis of expression.

"Very well," I say as normally as I can, "he's found himself a nice girl and they're in love. Nothing bad about that. I'm happy for him, aren't you? You're a fortunate woman to have your son so well mated."

"A widow," she mumbles, "four years his senior, with two daughters. A woman of experience. Is that what I want for my son? He should have a virgin, a girl as pure

533

as himself—a girl who's never been touched by a man."

"God deliver me!" I laugh brutally. "Virginity in a woman is a messy business. Be thankful someone else has already bled her."

"And they're coming here—together—Thursday." Her mouth trembles with distaste. "Apparently she doesn't have the discretion of a maidservant—flaunting her love affair in the faces of these people who don't even know Michel's no longer a monk."

"That *is* bad, isn't it?" I agree. "But after all, it's not terribly important. They only want your consent."

She reddens. "Sure, they want my consent." Her voice grows coarse. "But did Michel ask my consent to court this woman? Will it make any difference if I refuse? Humph. No, it's nothing more than a gesture. But I'll fix her with him," she announces bitterly. "A mother can often show up another woman. I'll make her look like the cheap thing she is, grabbing at the first man who comes along." She snorts, leaning far back in her chair: puffed magnificence of derision.

"You've no right to say that," I answer. "The fact she's been a widow for eight years looks pretty decent to me."

She ignores me. Her hair is disheveled, her face drawn, grinning, black. "I'll explain a few things to them. Why, when Michel's forty-five—in his prime—she'll be used up. He'll probably go out looking for other women. It's madness to marry a woman older than yourself."

The brightness outside seems incongruous. "Maybe she won't be used up," I seek to quiet her. "When she's your age she may still have the body of a thirty-year-old woman, like you have."

"Take his side!" She spits the words into my face. "Take his side! You're just as despicable as he is. Go ahead, everybody line up against me." She begins to cry. "All you're interested in is playing with some country servant girl. You're all *pigs!*"

"Listen, I take nobody's side. I don't owe you blind allegiance when you're wrong. If you want to know what

534

I think, I think Michel's an ass—there's not much choice between you. He's an ass and you're a woman eaten up with selfishness. The combination can never work. I think the girl's too good for him, but their wedding date's been set now. They love each other. Accept it and you'll at least have their affection; reject it and you're alone—completely alone in the world. They'll marry regardless. They *should*. They have every right to."

The loud bitterness of my words sobers her; she pouts, "No one has the right to hurt his mother like this."

"He's a grown man, Madame Renée, doing what grown men have always done—*you're* the one causing the hurt. And why? Because you're too damned selfish to share your son with another woman. Now, let's be sensible about this thing. You're intelligent. When the initial shock wears off you'll realize I'm right; you'll accept Michel's marriage and make a fine mother-in-law. Don't you see? It's a wonderful new beginning for you." My voice has become pleading; and like a pendulum swinging to the other extreme, her voice, her face, her actions become violent.

"Never! I can issue ultimatums too. If he marries this woman I'll never speak to him again. Write him," she commands harshly, "tell him to marry her. But above all, tell them both to stay away from here."

"I will not!" I shout, leaning forward. "Write your own letters."

Weeping, she lowers her head. Veins protrude on the side of her neck. She fumbles in her pocket for a handkerchief. "I'm in no condition to write."

"Any good news you have, you can dictate to me. But I'm through being your go-between, understand? I'm sick of doing your dirty work. I'm sick of the whole rotten mess. Write your own damned letters."

For a moment she weeps loudly, then, "If you don't write them," she gasps, "they'll come Thursday and I won't receive them."

"I don't give a damn," I say coldly. "They're nothing to me. Whether or not you receive them doesn't affect my life

535

in the slightest. You can do what you please. I don't—"

"Good!" She stares at me, a hurt expression competing with the tears. "So now that I'm in trouble, you wash your hands of me."

"I'm ashamed of you, Madame, that's all. There's nothing within reason—nothing honest and right—that I wouldn't help you do. But as for your lying, weak, selfish excuse for a son, I can't get interested in him; I can't get interested in either of you till you decide to do what's right."

"How *dare* you speak of my Michel that way!" She rises furiously from her chair and approaches my bed. "You may get by, insulting a poor old woman like me, but Michel's just as good as *you'll* ever be."

"Ah," I smile, "now that's a little better. Sounds terrible to you when I call him names, doesn't it? Think how much more terrible it sounds to me when his own mother calls him exactly the same names. Do you know this is the first time I've ever heard you defend your son?"

She stands over me, her eyes filled with drying tears and hatred. "It's all right for me—I'm his mother. But you sink pretty low, I must say."

"Forget it."

"Mothers have rights over their children. They bear them, they suffer and give up for them. They should be able to choose for them when the time comes for marriage." She stands majestic.

"That's excellent logic, Madame. It holds true only for male children, I suppose?"

"What do you mean by that?" she asks innocently, her face falling into momentary repose. "A child is a child."

"Then for the love of God!" I roar, making her back away, "for the love of God put yourself in Michel's place! You went through exactly the same thing. You even lived with a man and got pregnant in order to force your parents' consent. Seems to me that Michel is treating you with much more consideration than you treated *your* parents. You married a man below your class, with a son as old as you. If ever a marriage should've failed, that one was it—but it

536

didn't. Think how much better chance Michel's has of succeeding. Think of your own past before condemning your son."

She smiles gravely, amused. Her complexion shines. She sniffs. It's undeniable, all this. There's an unspeakable sordidness in her smile. She bends over me and whispers, "Yes, but my mother disowned me . . . "

"And caused both of you intolerable misery," I rejoin, recoiling from her nearness. "Do you want to make the same mistake with Michel? You want him to hate you like you hated your mother?"

Drawing herself up, she proclaims, "I am right, Michel is wrong—and he will pay."

"Fine!—vengeance, the same as your mother's. Listen, this isn't a game. The world won't justify you; in the eyes of the world you'll be just another mother who couldn't accept the responsibilities of motherhood, who couldn't make the sacrifices. A mother selfish enough to kill her child's love rather than share it. I tell you, you're wrong. Have the decency, I beg you, this one time in your life, to do a generous thing—even if it means humiliating yourself. If you don't I pity you, for the world will leave you—*I* will leave you. The only one to suffer will be *you*—not Michel nor Madeleine nor me nor anyone else. For your own happiness, Madame Renée, you mustn't let this happen." My face aches with the grimace I feel.

"Ah," she groans, "you break my head with so much talk. I can't even think any more. Providence is punishing me for my past sins."

"No, don't think of it that way. Providence is only trying to make your life richer. I'm sorry to have to talk so much, but the solution to all this seems so simple. All you have to do is accept—and love—your new family." She sinks slowly to sit beside me on the bed; I go on, "Now, why not let them come ahead Thursday like they've planned? Let's not condemn this girl without knowing her. Just make her feel welcome, as you would any guest. Then if things are worse than they seem, at least you'll have salvaged your self-respect—you'll have done what's right and decent."

She leans forward, her head in her hands. "It's more than a woman can bear. At least I was in love with my husband."

"I know, but your parents didn't think so. Remember how you yourself felt, and look at Michel's affair from that point of view—will you do that? Who are we to say if Michel's in love or not?"

A deep trembling sigh. "Then you must stay close to me. I—I—don't promise anything, but I'll try. If you leave me alone, though, you know how my mind dwells on these things. And—you must promise not to worry me. Please. You won't see Christianne or Madame Vincent again, will you?"

"Very well," I assure her, "I promise. Now, you must find something to occupy yourself. Stop sitting on that couch all day long doing nothing. Clean your house, wash your own dishes. You can't afford help anyhow, and just doing your work will keep you busy. It'll make things a lot easier."

"You think I'm not trying, don't you? But—don't be angry with me. After all, what can you know of my feelings as a mother?" She pauses. "I suppose you think Michel is absolutely right?"

"I don't know—I don't know what I think. He's certainly going about all this in a crude way. But you can't let that influence you." I draw my legs from behind her and crawl from the bed. "Now go home and we'll let things take their natural course."

She looks up at me in alarm. "No—please. If I go home you must go with me."

"I have to get to my classes in a few moments, Madame."

"No," she mutters, "you can't leave me today. I couldn't bear it. The classes aren't that important."

"I'm sorry—very sorry—but I'm here for the classes, and if I stay away from the Monastery I get too far behind. You mustn't ask me to give up my work." I stand before her in my pajamas, hoping she'll leave.

538

She whispers resentfully, "Easy enough to see how important I am to you."

"That's not true. But let's not waste time arguing. Unless you want to watch me dress, please go in the kitchen for a minute."

I undo the string of my pajama pants. She doesn't move. Filled with disgust, I tie it again.

"What are you waiting for?" I ask. "There's nothing more to say. You know what I think and you don't like it. I'm damned if I'll stay here just to bolster your ego. Maybe Michel wronged you, but I'll never see it the way you do. Now please, let me dress."

She rises, walks to the kitchen door. "Go on, then," she says wearily. "But don't judge me so harshly. We mothers know what's best and we generally end up doing the right thing. I'll stay here and help Germaine. Guess she's heard everything anyway."

As soon as the door is closed, I dress hurriedly. Noises from the kitchen: whisperings intercut at intervals with Germaine's flat-voiced "Yes, Madame." I dress, trying to cast from my mind the glistening image of Michel's adult head attached to the body of a wrinkled red infant, his tiny body in fetal position, his mouth disappearing into the front of his mother's dress, sucking the prune.

As I walk out the door I hear "Yes, Madame," accompanied by a train whistle far away. I step out into the street. Gabled roofs shine blue and gray and rust in the morning sunlight. Once again I hear the faint hint of the train whistle, prolonged like a complaint.

Father Gardener and another monk are pruning fruit trees when I enter the courtyard of the Monastery. Branches fall and are gathered. Sweat is suspended in beads from Father Gardener's scraggly gray eyebrows. He greets me warmly, breathing heavily from the exercise. My own hands and feet are cold, sluggish. The monk rakes his arm across his forehead, pruning shears still in his hand. Suddenly, the prospect of going into the paleography room—of bending over books and manuscripts—seems impossible. I ask Father Gardener if I can work outside with him today. More than anything else I feel the need of exercise, of flowing sweat, as though the sweat would carry off all spiritual poisons. He tells me to join him after lunch.

The prospect of it, the sudden feverish need for it, makes my morning drag endlessly. Every few moments I leave my manuscripts and drift over to the window. The sky is cloudless and infinite and very blue. Below, there are more white blossoms scattered among the trees. Impatiently I wait for distorted Gothic shadows in the courtyard to shorten, wait for afternoon and sweats and an accelerated heartbeat.

At noon I hear monks pass in the corridor on their way downstairs to the refectory. I think of Madame Renée. I think of a shriveled prune exuding thick white milk. Time for lunch. Time to go to her. My stomach trembles uneasily, rejecting the thought of more food cooked in vitriol and tears. I light a cigarette, toss the match out the window into the sparkling green waters of the River below, and decide to miss lunch . . .

I drag a chair close to the window and sit straddling it, my chin resting on my arms folded across its back. I rest here, forcing myself not to think of Madame Renée. Vaguely, I am aware of the two floors of empty cells beneath me, of the silence. Far below I see the black antlike figure of someone riding a bicycle across the bridge. I watch until it disappears behind the gray stone wall of a house. Thoughts idle into nothingness. Beyond my active consciousness, a fragmentary Ave Maria flickers across my mind. I deeply inhale cigarette smoke. The Ave Maria changes into other words, and I hear my voice: "Mary, conceived without sin, pray for us who have recourse to thee." The words are accompanied with puffs of smoke floating out like a knotted rope; for a moment I have the impression that I can see the words rather than hear them. I inhale and do this again and again, staring at the sound, until the cigarette burns my fingers. I exhale a final time without the prayer, and the silence of the smoke surprises me. My chin rests on the back of the chair. I close my eyes to the empty day and feel tenderness become a dizzying ingredient of my blood, flooding, swelling my heart, as the prayer is repeated at all angles of light within me.

Beyond this, on another plane, I realize my aching hunger. I go down to the kitchen and ask for a piece of bread. Their noon meal is over. I wash the bread down with a glass of water, then go out to join Father Gardener and his trees.

He gives me the job of stacking fallen branches into a large pile; and when that is done, I shovel mulched manure around the bases of the trees. The work warms and freshens the blood. The earth is soft, spongy—it invites you to lie down and look at the sky. Muscles react as blood surges into robust activity. After a while I reach up to rake the sweat off my chin and my finger leaves a gritty trail. I look at my hand. The short fingernails are outlined with green stain and dirt, and there's a large pink blister between thumb and forefinger. The sight fills me with unbelievable satisfaction.

Later in the afternoon, we set fire to the wood. It burns slowly, sending thick white smoke into the air, perfuming the high-walled cloister with its fragrance. The air cools rapidly and we stand close to the flames, holding our hands out to them.

The fire has smoldered almost away by the time Vesper bells fill the courtyard. I enter the chapel and kneel on the back bench, puffing from the exercise. Music and prayers lull tired senses to a point near sleep. I rest, my head on the hard wood of the pew in front of me, listening. And the desire to return to this place overwhelms me. Life out of life only a few yards from my other life. The need is to leave all that for the safety of undisturbed peace and health within these walls. I think of the prayers at noon, and some of their warmth returns to me, settling nerves. The chapel grows dark; it becomes gray-and-blue transparence with black shadows. It tells us that outside the sun has set, that it's time to begin cooking suppers, to sit down in lighted rooms and relax.

Here, candles complement the gloom. Coolness of the soul in early evening. My clothes smell strongly of smoke, the sanity of smoke. Noises—a footstep, a prayer desk being moved—reverberate in hollowness to intensify the embracing silence of the chapel. I stay a long time after it's empty; I stay until the blues and grays deepen into candlelit blackness.

The door creaks as I open it, then thumps shut behind me. The early night air is cool to my face, but filled with a lingering warmth from the afternoon. There are no stars. Outside there is activity in the streets. Lights. Doors opening and people going in for the night.

Thunder rumbles in the distance as I make my way to Madame Renée's house. The house is dark, forbidding—the shutters haven't been closed. I put my hand on the gate to open it. In a garish flash of lightning, the house leaps into clear focus—a phosphorescent greenish mask, hideous, its windowed eyes staring blackly. My legs ache with exhaustion, and the peace of the day begins to twang like a taut wire thumbed with dread. I must go in to her. I must step into the putridness, sink in it over my head, and smell its decaying reek.

I hesitate, then turn and cross the street rapidly, unable to make myself face her. Without turning on the lights, I sit on the side of the bed and smoke a cigarette. Exhaustion floats through me as gently as the beginning rain. Nothing matters but sleep now. After a time I finish the cigarette, drop my clothes on the floor, and crawl into bed.

A faint knock on the door awakens me from profound sleep. I hear the knock again, dreamily, distant. Without answering I feel myself sinking back into the thick fog, when I hear the door open. Impossible to fight back the drowsiness. Footsteps approach my bed. Through a drugged veil I'm vaguely aware of a presence hovering over me. The presence waits a long time until my awareness of it fades into returning sleep.

"Are you asleep?"

It seems to me that her words have odors, that they smell
542

of face powder with delicate undertones of sweat. The thought preoccupies me, and I don't answer. I pretend to breathe evenly, filling my lungs with the odor of her words. She stands there forever. The act of breathing so deeply, stimulates my consciousness into heavy, stupid wakefulness. I wonder absently why she doesn't go.

Then I hear a retreating step and breathe easier—until I feel a sagging weight at the foot of the bed. The lightly falling rain outside heightens the silence in the room. Her nearness sets nerves trembling, gathering force gradually. She is dead weight, unmoving, and I know she must be peering at me. The room ricochets back a sort of silent static in the darkness. I feel nerves quake with increasing violence, building in a long arc of ever-greater intensity. Occasionally a prolonged sigh escapes her. Time becomes hypnotic, like a fixed stare. I hold myself tensely still, not moving a muscle; but the bed seems to rock with tremblings.

Time passes. Nerves reach the high point of the curved arc and for a long moment cut into the quick. I close my eyes and concentrate on the weariness that pains dully in all my muscles, and the tremblings begin to shudder away into the distance. But I have felt only the beginnings of warm relaxation when I'm shocked back into wakefulness by a shifting of her weight, as she stretches out along the foot of the bed and then turns on her side, facing me. Through the thick comforter I can feel her heaviness across my ankles. Torturously I control myself as numbness creeps into my feet, where her weight has cut off the circulation. After a time my soles are like sweating ice, and I can bear it no longer. I ease them out from under her, and with my knees drawn up, I turn and face the wall. Thoughts are heavy, thick. I am naked under the covers. Something not right about this. I decide to go sleep in one of the upstairs bedrooms, locking the door—but it's not right to get up and walk naked across the floor, even in the dark, while she is here. Again I feel the bed give as she inches into a more comfortable position, and there is another pressure—this time against the bottoms of my feet. After a while it occurs

543

to me that she has them cradled on her stomach. It's like standing on a soft floor.

My eyes burn. I bury my head deeper in my pillow until I can hear the regular thumping of my heartbeat against my ear. Neither of us moves. I think of two abandoned statues lying in a museum storeroom. Vaguely I feel pity for this softness beneath my feet. A loud snorting snore punctures the silence, and the soft floor begins to move evenly up and down beneath my toes. For a moment I listen to rain dripping from the eaves outside my window and to the accompanying heartbeat in my ear. Gradually, the muffling haze of returning slumber causes all sounds to fade away. I fight it for a brief second; then, because I don't know what else to do, I abandon myself to the gathering pressure of sleep.

25 march

A wasp, feverishly slapping itself against the wall above my bed, awakens me. Warming sunlight pours through the open window. I stretch myself and stir my legs—and suddenly, I jolt into clear reddening wakefulness. The covers are in disarray and only my feet are under them. I pull a quilt over me and glance furiously about the room. A large bowl of coffee, with tartines, is on the table beside me. I take a sip of the coffee; it is cold. I shake my head and try to remember. Was she really here last night? It seems too unreal in the brilliant light of morning. No, I must have dreamt it.

Crawling out of bed, I wave the wasp out the window

and turn back the covers to examine them. On the coarse woolen quilt I see a whitish circle. I bend down and smell the lingering odor of face powder. Close beneath my eyes a silver hair curls upward. I sink onto the bed and finish drinking the coffee. Did I kick the covers off? Irritation of not knowing.

Replacing the coffee cup I reach for my cigarettes. A folded piece of paper flutters to the floor, and I pick it up. A note from Madame Renée: she has gone to Town for provisions and won't be back till late this afternoon. There are, she says, *rillettes* and bread in the kitchen cabinet. She hopes I'll condescend to have dinner with her tonight.

I crumple the paper and throw it in the direction of the stove. The bitch! The damned peeping bitch! But—perhaps I'm wrong. Perhaps I kicked the covers off. The room was warm when I woke up. I *could* have kicked them off.

I think of the prayers I muttered yesterday. They're destroyed today—destroyed as though they'd never been— by the memory of an old woman cradling my feet in her belly, perhaps pulling back covers to gaze at my sleeping nakedness . . .

I shave and dress. Before going to the Monastery I spread *rillettes* thickly between two slices of bread, wrap the sandwich in a torn piece of sack, and carry it with me to eat for lunch.

Hopelessly, I seek today again to recapture the warmth of prayers. I know that their warmth is somewhere close to me—that it can be mine—but it eludes my efforts. I remain in the chapel a long time after Vespers are over; but this evening I am uncomfortable, trespassing. I close my eyes, and instead of suffusing warmth there's a cold pain in my kidneys; instead of escape into rising calm and healthful peace there's the intruding desire, gross and blatant, to urinate, a pinpricking in the bladder. It drives me out, to the shadowed darkness of the nearest tree. Through bare branches I look up at the first pale stars.

Before I get to my house I see that the windows are lighted. The door to my salon is half-open. Madame Renée is lying asleep across the bed, her feet hanging over the edge. The immaculate room floats with emptiness—as neat as a coffin.

I step inside and slam the door behind me. She sits up and begins massaging her eyes. "What's the matter?" I mutter. "Didn't you sleep well last night?" I turn on other lights, cruel to her tear-swollen eyes.

She ignores my question and hoists herself from the bed, stifling a yawn. I look at her ravaged face.

"How're you feeling?" I ask more gently.

She directs a vague smile of affection at me, and I reject the insane thought that I should start undressing. "I'm all—" Her eyes roll far back in her head and she reaches quickly for a chair to keep from falling.

I almost knock over the table getting to her. "Madame! What's the matter?"

Releasing her grasp on the chair, she teeters into my arms.

"Here, here—sit on the bed."

"So tired," she whispers almost inaudibly. Her mouth is rubbery as though the facial muscles can no longer function. A nervous sweat moistens her forehead.

"I know you're tired. Here—just lean back. Like that." I dry her forehead with my handkerchief. "I'll fix you some coffee."

"I'll be all right," she protests weakly. "I—"

"Now, don't move. I'll be right back."

I hurry into the kitchen. Without bothering to heat it I pour her a cupful of the thick black coffee left over from this morning. She is too weak to hold it to her mouth. I support her head with one hand and carefully place the cup to her lips. Beneath half-closed eyelids, her downcast eyes glitter dully. Looking down at her as she swallows, I am shaken with pity. The hair at the crown of her head is disturbed. Absently, I put the coffee cup aside and, with the comb of my fingers, arrange the gray strands.

She raises her gaze to me with an expression of consuming tenderness, and gratefully pats my arm. No longer the

546

face of an old woman: the radiant softness of ageless woman surrendering in a glance the Fallopian pulse of her soul. Irritated, I'm about to move away when she asks for more coffee. As I hold the stained china cup to her lips, it seems to become a jeweled chalice filled with some medieval elixir; and we, two lardy adolescents in a forest exchanging desperately heroic glances, ignoring the fat, checkered, vermilion-tongued serpent coiled around the thick trunk of a tree.

"Thou art the spring," I whisper in mock passion, leaning forward.

"Hm?" she moans, relaxing against my arm.

"Too bad we don't have an orchestral background," I remark, gently weaning the chalice away from her lips.

Muscles tense within her until it seems I'm holding a piece of carved wood. Her face congests with flaming resentment. I release her and rise to my feet, my mouth aching with the grin. She strangles on her fury.

"I'm sorry," I say, "but really now—you're too old to play the maiden-in-distress convincingly."

Her expression becomes apoplectic with loathing, until finally she abandons herself to face-in-hand weeping. Sobs gather momentum, rising in pitch like an untuned harmonium. I stand awkwardly and look down at her, my grin dissolving into despair with myself for being so cruel to her.

"I—I'll fix us some dinner, Madame," I say haltingly. "Look—I don't know what the hell made me say that. Please forget it."

She allows me to bring her a platter of bread and butter and preserves. She eats, her flushed cheeks drawn and wet with tears, her mouth twitching convulsively downward at the corners. A thin, simpering cry escapes her as she drops a preserved peach on the sleeve of her black wool sweater. Dazedly raising the sleeve to her mouth, she licks the peach off. I sit opposite her, watching, my hands folded quietly on the table. She avoids the abject apology of my glance.

After she has eaten all the bread left on the plate, I sigh cautiously and suggest, "Won't you let me take you home now, so you can rest? Being tired only makes things worse."

"I can't sleep," she says dully. "Fine chance I have of resting. You realize they'll be here day after tomorrow?"

"Well, let's not think about it tonight. Try to get some rest and we'll both feel more like working things out tomorrow."

I rise and, reaching down, take her arm to help her up. She pulls away from me with surprising strength. My finger touches the sticky spot on her sleeve where the preserves were dropped.

"Please, Madame Renée, this isn't doing you a bit of good. Let me take you home."

"No . . ." she moans. "Look—I can't bear to go back to my house." She leans forward on the bed, her arms across her lap. "Couldn't I sleep here?" Her voice trembles pathetically near tears. "I can't stand to be alone any more."

I hesitate, then, "Let's not do that again, Madame," I plead gently. "If you sleep here again tonight there's no telling what might—I mean—" My words wither into silence under her sudden glare. "I'm sorry," I say lamely.

"Just what *did* you mean?" she asks, looking back at the floor. Her mouth is pulled in and her eyes are deeply circled.

"Nothing. You know I'm happy to have your company, but I've got to keep my privacy. You understand. What if somebody had walked in here this morning and found us together—with me naked? . . ."

"What?" she asks expressionlessly.

"Well, how would it look? What would *you* think if—?"

"Why, you nasty-mouthed—" Her voice is loud and thick.

"It's the truth, isn't it?" I blurt out. "At least I don't go around peeking at naked old women. I don't—"

A hopeless broken laugh interrupts me. She raises her head, her eyes question insultingly. "You don't?"

"Hell, no!"

"Of course not," she says sweetly, "you're an angel. You

548

prefer tickling their stomachs with your toes, don't you?"

"Well, I'll be damned!" I clamp my teeth together, thoughts tumbling in confusion. I stare at her. "I think you owe me an apology, Madame. I can't—Ah, the hell with it." I let the words die in a tired, dull voice.

She snorts, "I don't apologize to kids," looking away, shrugging her shoulders.

"I think you'd better be going, Madame."

She doesn't move. After a time she says in a flat, harsh voice, "I know all about you—you and Michel. You're just alike. Know what I think? I think you and he worked out his marriage together, behind my back. Didn't you?"

"I've done everything I know to help you," I say sharply, "and you dare accuse me of conspiring against you!"

"Try and make me believe that."

Words seek to puncture and to shock. "Frankly, I don't give a damn *what* you believe."

Madame Renée rises slowly, not taking her eyes off mine; hers are grave and clear. She opens the door and holds it open, standing in the hall. The room quivers in unbroken silence. My shoes creak as I walk around the table to accompany her outside. She doesn't move. Her face is revealed in the full light from my room. Behind her the empty hall is dark. I stand facing her, waiting for her to leave. I study the doorframe stained with dirty fingers.

"Well?" I say coldly.

Madame Renée looks curiously into my face. Her voice taunts, "Tell me something—be honest—what do you really think of me?"

"You wouldn't like it," I say after a long pause.

Her mouth draws up into a tight, wrinkled smile. "Tell me," she whispers.

"Well, if you must know, I think you're the most selfish, false, bad-mannered—Ah, it makes me sick to be with you."

Nodding her head rapidly, she stares with seemingly dilated eyes. "You're right," she whispers, smiling. "You're right. What else?"

I look away from the grinning obscenity. "I'm sorry," I

549

say with genuine regret, "I don't really mean that—but if you'd just act like a human being! Lord!"

Still smiling pleasantly she listens carefully, her head slightly averted.

"No," I go on, "it's mostly my fault. I fight you too much."

"Uh-huh?" she murmurs questioningly.

"What do you want, anyway? I never should—"

She doesn't let me finish; her face clots with rage and she flies at me, shaking her clenched fist under my nose; she screams, "You—you—God, how I *hate* you!"

"Good night, Madame," I say bluntly, my voice quaking in disgust.

She smiles again, uncertainly, and draws back a step. Angrily I reach for the doorknob to shut her out, but she won't move and the door strikes her left shoulder. As I walk away she steps back into the room; she is holding a handful of her left breast, the breast large and cupped in her hand as a lover might hold it.

"You closed the door on my breast," she whines. "You hurt my breast."

The sight of her standing there, grimacing from the imagined pain in her breast, pressing it, squeezing it, pulling down her bodice as though to show me, is more than I can bear. I burst into laughter. "Ah, what a brute I am!" (The insult causes her face to glow with sudden dignity.) "The door didn't touch your breast and you know it. Now, if you want to expose yourself, do it—but for God's sake stop playing with that thing and leave me alone."

"Good night, Monsieur," she says with measured finality.

"I'll see you out, Madame." And I add hastily, repentant, "I'm sorry. There—don't think of this any more. We'll forget it ever happened. Get some sleep, won't you?" I open the front door to cool night air and darkness.

"Pig!" she whispers in a hesitating voice.

"What did you say?"

"Nothing. You realize this is the end, don't you? Unless you come and apologize in the morning, you can find your

550

meals elsewhere." She turns sideways to step out past me.

"But you're the one," I argue, "who owes the apology, Madame. I don't ask it, but I'm certainly not going to bow down to you any more."

Her footsteps move slowly away on the sidewalk.

"If you want to forget it I'm willing. Let's be adults," I tell her, raising my voice. "This isn't a game of all give and no take, you know. Just a good—" Her gate clangs loudly. Frustration of discoursing alone to the darkness of an empty street. Letting the sentence hang in mid-air, I turn back inside.

The place has a lightness about it now that she's gone. The empty house echoes quietness. I turn on my radio and begin to work. I study *Le Chant Grégorien: sa valeur esthétique,* by Fernand Biron. The night draws on and with it my satisfaction in being alone, in being awake while the Village sleeps.

Then, on the radio, Koechlin's *Primavera* played by the Pierre Jamet Quintet. Fresh, clean music. Its melodies are like inner thoughts. I put aside my book and listen to the concluding movement, a movement full of verve and spontaneity. The need for that health in myself. The need for something clear and clean. The spaciousness of a word like *primavera,* verdant, innocent, strangely out of time with this time—strangely out of tone with the virulent tone of Madame Renée's passionate belchings. I listen, carried by the music, and desires begin to clarify themselves—first a desire to escape forever the tired frenetic virtuosity of no heart, no belly. Counterfeit life. Loneliness, forever loneliness in the clammy pallor of cynicism; forever loneliness in the eunuch sheen of silken sneers. Desolation of self, like grit on furniture, irritating to the heart's touch, to the brain's touch.

Escape that in other longings—a longing for the girl who will be my wife. Who will come in from the market red-cheeked and breathless, carrying sacks of water cress and endive for supper. Who will kiss me on the cheek and absently say "Darling" before going on to the kitchen. But that time isn't now; the time now is murky, foul-smelling, filling me with remorse and a colicky conscience. It needs to be on another plane with decency as an ingredient. It needs to be smooth, without pain. It needs to be music and the soft body of a wife beside me, not hurrying, not dropping off to sleep at intermission.

No longer *Primavera;* it disappears and is forgotten. Now, *Tod und Verklärung* of Strauss. The atmosphere of the room is changed. The dying heartbeat. The spattering cry of life. The thrumming strings low in their register, and again the cry above them. No longer the health of Koechlin —the smoke-filled belly of genius that is Strauss.

Above the music, like a sudden toll of silence dampening sound, I feel the muffled vibration of bells. My back is stiff. I straighten up and go outside to listen to the gigantic clanging of the Monastery bells. Absolute stillness in the black night, as wave after wave of metallic sound drifts across the Valley. From across the River, far away, I hear the faint answer of baying hounds.

The enigma of Madame Renée. In her house the lights remain on.

I open my salon door to a smell of tobacco. Warm air gushes out on a triple fortissimo from the orchestra. Noble, soaring melody in the strings.

Exhaustion. Joy mingles with intense sadness in all these things. Confusion of mind and heart. Love and great weariness. All of it ends with the one last hope, which is God, opposed to the persistent selfishness of self not willing to give up the pleasurable narcosis of self, not willing to give up the lust of tortured delight for the greater lust of liberated ravishment. Afraid to make the decision. Afraid to say the great Yes.

26 march

She kneads the black woolen dough of her left breast—"It really did hurt"—and winces with a gentle, forgiving smile.

"I know," I say apologetically, looking at her across the breakfast table.

"I think there's a small knot on the side."

I click my tongue against my teeth regretfully. "I'm sorry." I try not to notice her right hand fondling, but a glistening blemish on the coarsely woven sleeve where the peach preserves congealed into sugar, holds my attention.

"You do have," she says pleadingly, "some affection for me, don't you?"

I glance up. Her eyes are deeply sunk into shadows, haggard eyes that seem never to have known sleep. "Of course I do." My voice is warm. "You know that. I'm terribly sorry about last night. Couldn't sleep for worrying about you."

"That's all right," she says softly. "It was my fault. Afraid I wasn't very nice."

"You weren't feeling well. Let's not—"

"But I'm so worried about Michel."

"I know. And," I add calmly, determined to put her in the best possible mood for her son's arrival, "I haven't been much help, have I? But I'm going to do everything I can to make it easier for you."

Her shoulders relax. She gazes wistfully at the tablecloth covered with bread crumbs. Gradually her hand stops massaging. "Will you really?" she asks me in a throaty, old woman's voice.

"Yes."

We talk on, over coffee and tartines. I deaden all senses, wondering if Michel's marriage isn't less an issue between him and his mother than between his mother and me. Disjointed thoughts attach themselves to the nucleus of hinted coherence. Her craving for intimacy. The touches. Her breast. Thoughts wander into speculation. I place a bare patch of flesh at her disposal and it buys—what? Michel's happiness? I become a whore, then. No, it's not possible . . . but yet, curiously, it's like the whore's "Pssst!"

"Will you do all you can, Madame Renée, to make the visit tomorrow as pleasant as possible—for my sake?"

"If you're going to start that—" she says loudly.

"For my sake," I repeat. "I can't stand all this friction between us. I worry about Michel just as you do; but most of all, I worry about you. I hurt your breast last night when that was the last thing in the world I wanted to do. That's what I mean. Michel's come between us. That's all. Is it bruised?"

She bites her lip pensively, reddening, and closing her eyes she nods that it is—"A little." Her hand begins fondling the breast again, as pleasure bloats her face.

"Hell!" escapes me and I turn away from the sight of her, sick. Catching myself, I'm about to apologize when she lifts herself out of her chair and comes quickly to my side.

"No," she soothes, "you mustn't blame yourself so." Her hand is heavy on my shoulder. "If I'd known you were going to be so upset about it I'd never have mentioned it." She gives me a gentle little shove and laughs warmly. Reaching down, she takes my hand in hers. "Isn't there a little knot—there?"

A shudder of repulsion as she guides my hand into probing softness. "Believe there is," I mumble, struggling against the desire to tear my hand away.

"Listen, stop worrying," she murmurs close to my ear. "It's probably nothing serious."

Her stomach beside me. I'm aware of it as something naked and cavernous. Sensations of a whore. A coin for a caress, submitting to the caress, killing the desire to draw away until the desire flames out and there's only the belly dragging against you. A cheap coin—the price of legitimizing Michel's venereal fevers—cheap. It buys my whorish

554

slaverings and come-ons, my harlot sincerity and warmth.

"Don't feel so bad about it," she goes on, her face brushing against mine. "It doesn't hurt so much now."

I submit, not moving, closing my eyes and seeing her, seeing her swollen into a gigantic serpentine voluptuousness. A vision of strong legs, deep navels, bursting milk-white breasts—insatiable, grasping, choking triangles of pubic grayness before my eyes. Begging to be possessed, wavering slow undulation deep within me, suffocating me. Lost. Irritation of being lost. Touching the table hardness with my hands, fighting the vision. Concentrating against it and carrying it forward, letting it escape into the fog of dreams and desires. Hunger mixing with the deep-etched circular lines inside a woman's navel. I am walking slowly in the navel, on the tiny trails that spiral inside the canyon, looking up, sight-seeing, walking and looking about. Hunger for the taste of maggot-ridden carrion. Veiled redness, glistening. Tremulous building into—

"How about another cup of coffee before you go?"

The flesh on my face feels as if it will burst with the shocked pressure of my blushing. I open my eyes and look feverishly at my hands on the table, then at her. I see a middle-aged woman dressed in black, her face in respectable repose as though nothing had happened, her fine face surrounded with a soft aureole of hair floating silver in the morning sunlight. Nothing *has* happened. Her head is turned to one side, questioningly.

"Coffee? Sure. Fine. I *would* like a cup if there's any left."

"Listen," she says from the kitchen, "I'm going to do what's best for Michel. You can count on that. Mustn't take everything I say so seriously." Her voice is gay.

I lean forward, elbows braced on the table, and hide my face in my hands. Bloods flow back to my heart. Lights shimmer away to darkness, to the great inside blackness, and I accept the cheap coin with honor, convincing myself that it never happened. But in my mind I smell the unbearable reek—the reek of myself, the stench of myself.

555

An odor of strong coffee floats through the room.

Desire to escape—no longer from her, but from myself. I sold the white patch of flesh, sold affection. My conscience is a cloth with a great hole burned out of the center. And in the center swim uneasily the dregs, the sediment of my soul, like vomit that refuses to come out, weighing me down. Unbearable loneliness of my falsity.

I smile and look up as she enters the room with the coffee pot. She glances at me with the tenderest of expressions.

"Just one more cup," she chides, "then you've got to go. I don't want your musty old Fathers to think I'm keeping you from your lessons."

From far away, through a numbing paralysis of self-hatred, I hear her chuckle.

27 march

I listen with growing dread to the noonday Monastery bells, almost inaudible above the roar of rain pelting on the black dome of my umbrella. Michel and Madeleine should have arrived from Paris an hour ago. I slosh reluctantly along the street to my house.

Hanging my coat and hat in the gloom-filled hall, I open the salon door. I'm submerged instantly under the enthusiastic embraces of Michel. He kisses me fervently on each cheek and slaps my back and arms with great friendliness. Then, throwing his arm loosely about my shoulders, he turns me in the direction of the couch.

"And this is Madeleine," he announces expansively, giving my shoulders an eloquent little hug. "Madame Defourque, but we hope she'll soon be Madame Michel Renée."

She takes my hand and looks unwaveringly into my face. "I'm so happy to know you," she smiles.

I shoot an appreciative glance at Michel, then gaze back at his beautiful Parisienne. She is even more attractive than the snapshots indicated. She is dressed in colors, something you never see in the Valley—a gray tweed skirt and red jacket, with a white blouse open at the neck. She gives the impression of freshness and cleanness, with an aristocratic softness of feature. A human face, warm, tender, open.

"How is Mama?" Michel asks, stepping over close to Madeleine. As he leaves my side I note that he's as insignificant-looking as ever—thinner, wearing the same jacket and trousers. His hair has grown out in tight curls.

"Your mother? Pretty touchy, Michel, but I think it'll be all right. Just go easy with her. Does Madeleine know?"

"Yes." He puts his arm around her waist and smiles down at her. "She didn't want to come, but this thing's got to be settled. I know how to handle Mama."

For a moment I'm tempted to tell him the truth about Madame Renée and me, tempted to throw it in his face. I look at him and wonder if he's worth even the cheap coin that has cost me so much. "Maybe you were wise to come on," I sigh, and, to Madeleine, "When she sees you I believe she'll change her mind. You're more—I mean you're not exactly what she expected Michel to bring home, you know. Will you be patient with her?—try to see her side of it too?"

"Of course, Monsieur." She smiles understandingly. "I'll be very careful."

"Good. We'd better go across to her house now."

In the hall, I turn to Madeleine. "I think Michel's mother has outdone herself on the dinner, Madame. Think she wants to show you that we too are people of the world." I laugh, handing the umbrella to Michel. "Let me warn you, though—Madame Renée is unpredictable. She may be a perfect lady, or she may act like a hellion. Whatever she does, don't take her too seriously. She's mostly bluff."

Madeleine disapproves with an embarrassed glance at

557

Michel, but he says nothing. We splash across the street huddled beneath the umbrella. They precede me into the house, passing quickly under the dripping eaves.

Madame Renée, dressed and combed, accepts her son's embrace at the door with a smile of genuine charm. They talk loudly above the rain. I step inside and close the door.

" . . . and this is Madeleine, Mama."

"I'm delighted to know you, Mademoiselle," she says graciously.

I stare at her quickly in disgust—her addressing the girl as "Mademoiselle" is an unexpectedly subtle thrust. But neither Madeleine nor Michel seems to notice.

"Here," she tells Michel, "take Madeleine's things . . . Sit down, Mademoiselle. We'll have a little glass of Montbazillac before lunch. Ah, what terrible weather."

The young Christianne, carrying a silver tray of apéritif glasses, makes her first appearance from the kitchen. She looks at me, smiles warmly. Involuntarily I purse my lips—but Madame Renée catches my glance and smiles sweetly indulgent disapproval, shaking her head.

Michel and Madeleine, apparently overcome with relief, sit on the couch. Madame Renée and I face them in comfortable chairs. Christianne pours the wine. My elbow presses against her leg as she stands next to me. I feel a straining desire to touch her, to cleanse myself of the foul touches of an old woman in the sane touches of young flesh.

Madeleine is radiant. "This apéritif is absolutely delicious," she murmurs. "A treat for us, isn't it, Michel? We can't afford this in Paris."

"I noticed," remarks Madame Renée pleasantly, "how much weight Michel has lost. Is it love, son, or aren't you eating?"

"Too much work, Mama."

We laugh, looking fondly at our boy. Michel gets up to set his glass on the table. His mother rises and stands beside him, putting her arm around his thin waist.

"So my Michel's getting married next month?" She gazes up into his eyes.

"With your permission, Mama."

Rain pours against the windows, darkening the room. I switch on the lamp. Smiling, Madame Renée looks down at Madeleine.

"I imagine you've talked this over," she says cordially, "but as Michel's mother there are certain things I feel I must bring to your attention. Suppose we discuss it fully before sitting down to lunch. Now, we're adult people, and I'm very impressed with my son's choice. Do you mind hearing my side of the story? I want to be fair."

"Of course not, Madame," replies Madeleine warmly, fondling her glass. "We want to know exactly what you think."

Madame Renée resumes her seat and proceeds harmlessly to describe her situation as a poor widow without funds. She explains that she'd hoped for Michel's financial support in her growing age. Her words are sincere and full of dignity.

"We've thought of all that, Madame." Madeleine looks at her tenderly. "I'm sure we can see to it that you're provided for. We want it that way, don't we, Michel?"

Love-laden Michel agrees eagerly, sitting beside her again.

"Another thing that occurs to me," continues his mother gently, "is that Michel took his final vows as a monk, and broke those vows. I'm wondering how you can be sure he won't also break the vows of marriage?" Her voice is soft, perfectly modulated, but the words strike like a physical blow. There's a momentary rain-filled silence, rattling windows. "Knowing this," she adds, "how can you have any faith in such a marriage partner?"

"Mother . . . "

Madeleine doesn't move. She remains perfectly composed except for a slight color rising in her cheeks. From the kitchen, we hear a loud bang as Christianne closes the oven door.

I say quietly, "The parallel doesn't stand up, Madame Renée. You *put* Michel in a monastery school. He took his

559

final vows before he had a chance to find out what he really wanted. But no force has been brought to bear in his engagement to Madame Defourque." Madame Renée glares at me resentfully, accusingly; doggedly I go on, "When he takes the marriage vows he'll be fully accountable, for he knows what he's doing. You can't say that because he broke the one vow, he'll necessarily break the other."

"And, Madame," Madeleine puts in, "do you think I'd go through with this if I weren't sure of your son?"

"Come now, Mademoiselle, let's be honest. You won't be the first widow to marry in order to have a father for her children."

An expression of shocked indignation causes Madeleine's mouth to open in wordless protest. Michel looks nervous, confused.

"Here, a cigarette, Madame Defourque," I say clumsily, seeking to ease the situation.

She refuses, shaking her head. Her shoulders droop listlessly.

Madame Renée wets her upper lip with her tongue. "Oh, go ahead, Mademoiselle, I know all girls smoke nowadays." She pauses. "Now, I have another question. This may seem a little personal, but as Michel's mother I feel justified in finding out. Just how did your first husband meet his death? Michel tells me you've been a widow for eight years, but no one seems to know exactly—"

"My husband, Madame, died of a stroke."

"What caused the stroke?"

"We don't know," Madeleine says coldly. "He died very suddenly."

"That seems a rather—unsatisfactory explanation . . . "

I shake my head, admiring her brutality, her cynicism. Michel squirms miserably, his imploring eyes darting from one to the other.

"What I mean, Mademoiselle," his mother presses her point, "is that if your husband died of some contagious disease . . . "

"If he had, Madame, I should certainly not subject

another man to the same fate. This is absolutely ghoulish. Why, I—"

"You say your husband died eight years ago?" questions the matriarch serenely. "And how old are your daughters? Nine and twelve, I believe Michel wrote. And how long were you married, Mademoiselle?"

"Five years," the other answers in a dull voice.

"Five years. Let's see—that would make—" Madame Renée counts on her fingers.

Madeleine stares at her, and I laugh aloud at this unbelievably insulting gesture. Michel reddens as his mother counts again.

"Both my children are legitimate, if that's what you're insinuating, Madame."

"Now, Madeleine," Michel cajoles pleadingly, "Mama just wants to learn all she can about you."

"Then why doesn't she ask if I can cook or sew? I've never been so insulted, so openly insulted."

The mother feigns mild surprise. "You said you wanted to know how I felt, Mademoiselle. This is perhaps painful to you, but it shouldn't be if you've nothing to hide." With great benevolence she calls for Christianne to bring us another serving of Montbazillac; then she turns back to Madeleine. "You're angry with me. I'm disappointed to see that you anger so easily. After all, Michel's my son and I must see that he lives his life as well as he can. What is he?—an inexperienced child who's captivated by the first woman he meets. Do you blame me for pointing out these obstacles in the hope they'll help you in your final decision? Try to understand. I think you would do as I. Now," she sighs, "I have only a few more things to say and then we can sit down to a good lunch."

The tension in the room seems almost tangible. Madeleine sits motionless. Michel, his hands fingering each other restlessly, gazes at the floor.

"First," Madame Renée continues, "have you thought of the future? In another ten years Michel will be thirty-seven, you'll be forty-one, and your oldest daughter will be

561

twenty-two—in the full bloom of her youthful beauty. I know men, Mademoiselle—it'd be only too natural for Michel to realize that perhaps he was in love with your daughter, and not with you at all."

Madeleine rises slowly, and looks at her hostess with a peculiar softness of expression. "If that's your idea of men, Madame Renée, I must say you've lived among a strange variety. Just what are you trying to do, anyway?"

"I'm trying," Madame Renée says bluntly, "to assure my son's happiness, nothing more. Now, I ask you to consider this. In a few more years Michel, still in the prime of his masculinity, will be married to an already used woman. Oh, I'll admit you look much . . . "

She goes on talking as Madeleine turns to me. For a moment we look at each other, understanding. Then, quietly, she walks to the door and opens it.

". . . but with that considerable age difference, you can readily—Mademoiselle, you're not—?" Madame Renée's voice trails off into silence as the door closes.

Michel, stunned for a time, leaps to his feet and runs to jerk the door open, crying out, "Madeleine! Come back! Come back! Madeleine!" He falters, the conflict tearing at his face; he glances back at his mother's swollen outrage. "That's all right, Mama," he mutters desperately, placatingly, "that's all right—I'll bring her right back." He dashes out into the rain.

Madame Renée faces me triumphantly. I reach up and switch off the lamp, plunging the room into half-shadows.

"Well?" She sinks down on the couch. "What do you think?"

"Nothing." I look out the window at gray noon.

"I didn't say one word that wasn't the truth. And I certainly behaved better than that Madeleine creature, you'll have to admit that."

"You were perfect, Madame. I imagine you succeeded, if you don't mind how you did it."

She chuckles, delighted with her victory. The faults are nebulous, things easily denied. "Oh, I wasn't half-started," she sniggers. "Takes something better than a Parisian strumpet to outwit the old heads. Michel will get over her. He'll see her in a different light now, and be thankful for what I did."

"I expect Madeleine will see *him* in a different light, too. If you ask me, it was she who did the stooping—down to Michel's level."

"You're angry with me, aren't you?" she whispers. "Just a little?"

"No," I answer without expression. "All you've done is ruin two lives. And you're proud of it. I don't get angry at things that low."

"Oh, come now," she says mockingly, "nobody's life is ruined."

Before I can reply, I hear her breath catch in her throat, suddenly, and she runs to the window. She bends forward and parts the lace curtains, peering out. "Look," she calls, half-laughing. "Come here a minute."

I walk over and bend down beside her. A splotch of brilliant red under a transparent raincoat moves down the street. A few feet behind we see the tall figure of bareheaded Michel, gesticulating. They pass on out of our range of vision. Rain spatters into puddles along the street.

"Must be going to catch the one o'clock train back to Paris," I suggest, returning to my chair. "I hope you're satisfied."

She remains at the window, pressing her face against it, twisting her head to one side to see far down the street. "Look at that walk," she chuckles. "Why, she's got hips like a cow."

Finally she straightens up, absently arranging her hair, and looks at me with that expression, sometimes so poignant, that knows a hinted remorse, spontaneous, uncertain. "Don't be angry with me," she whispers, smiling. She comes over and puts a hand on my shoulder.

"All right," I say sharply. "But this is all, you understand. If you start gloating your victory to me . . . "

She pats my cheek. Her fingers, fatty, wrinkled, turn

the gesture into a caress as they explore my lips. In the soft light I see the crust of a small scab on her knuckle—white, scaly. With soothing mumbled sounds, she talks as her fingers move lightly, tracing the ridges of my lips. Faraway pathetic views—pasteled, rain-slaked groves of indolent trees—and her face red and flushed before me, smiling tenderly, possessing me and demanding to be possessed in return. I sit like a defiled statue. From the words of endearment, swirling in confusion with her caresses, other words emerge.

"Why, when I counted on my fingers to see if her children were legitimate, I did it on purpose."

"And I had to bite my tongue to keep from reminding you that both of yours are illegitimate." My lips move against her fingers.

She withdraws her hand resentfully. "Now that's not kind," she pouts. The caress is gone; she acts as though it had never been. Moment of intimacy, experienced but not admitted.

"Not kind!" I snort. "Was anything you said today kind?"

Her face withers into a pleading protest and she approaches me again.

"And for God's sake keep your hands off me for once!"

She stops abruptly, her outstretched hands falling to her sides, and a look of shocked pain distorts her features. We glare at each other with the sudden intimate bluntness of enemies. Nervously I press my hands on the arms of the chair.

"Did you mean that?" she asks coldly.

"You're damn' right."

A strange smile hardens her expression, and her voice becomes almost casual. "Then perhaps you'd better go, Monsieur, until you can learn to—"

"Perhaps I had," I spit out with vehemence. I get to my feet and walk rapidly to the door. I leave without looking back, slamming the door behind me.

I cross to my house, stepping wide across the water-
564

filled gutters. The unutterable silence of drowsing country-side, mournful, deserted, soaked—unbearable accents intensifying the exhaustion of the day. My room is damp. Mists enter the open window. There are hints of frenzied revolt buried, muffled deep within. The hollowness inside me begs to be filled. I sit near the window until the longing for a resurgence of strength becomes desperation. But when I think of her, it's all hollowness; and despite myself her touches create in me a suppressed excitement, tiring, sickening.

The long afternoon, the sadness of wishing all time were past. It ferments quickly in the background of my consciousness until nerves cry out against the decent-faced somberness that converges accusations on me, burying me in confused grief. I walk aimlessly about the room. I bend down and look out the window without seeing anything. I close the window and carefully lock it. I go into the kitchen and wash my hands, taking a long time. The tiles reflect a dull gray light; it reminds me of the open empty gaze of the dead and it drives me back to my room.

Uneasily I finger a package of cigarettes, take one out, then replace it with great care. I stand for a moment, studying nothingness, hesitating. There's the need for activity that will fill the hollowness with comfort. I stand and somehow feel foolish standing, as though I were waiting for something. The silence is disturbed by a dull wooden sound as I open my desk drawer and look inside. Old letters, a fountain pen, a box of matches, scattered stamps—all of it in disarray, all of it speckled with tobacco crumbs. In one corner, wrapped in waxed paper, I see a red-striped chunk of peppermint. It crumbles like chalk when I pick it up. I put a sliver of it in my mouth and throw the rest in the wastebasket. With the back of my hand I shut the drawer. The candy dissolves in my mouth, leaving a sweet, syrupy coating that irritates.

The long afternoon, gray and meaningless. I stand tensed into a desolation that waits, waits for nothing and rejects all thoughts. I ought to be relieved that it's over, but I feel only emptiness—the emptiness one feels after a death.

An image seeps through other images, and for a long moment my soul seems to be a fetus in her belly, waiting to slit the caul and escape, waiting to drink from the exuding prune. Waiting. The fetus struggles to slit the membrane and escape. From somewhere outside this liquid darkness I hear screaming, a hollow, agonized screaming through layers of flesh. I feel muscles, black and glutinous, convulse against me in diapason with the scream, suffocating me. My eyes close against the image as the caul is slit—but there's no escape, for the slit becomes vulvar and draws me back. Clean vulvar slit, reeling in silence now, engulfing me with longing, hopeless. And I feel the stone floor crushing cartilage in my knees. Words flow out to meet the darkness, for there's nothing else to do; pleading, tender words of another love in innocence, a better love, repeated until vertigo makes my head swim: ". . . blessed art thou among women, and blessed is the fruit of thy womb, Jesus. Holy Mary, Mother of God . . ."

Outside, silence roars into focus as lascivious images skitter to the margins of conscience—old images, shriveled images of desire—desire becoming forever the progenitor of my soul's fetus, the two bound together in the caul, waiting.

Words lost to darkness, words of pleading. There is no other cure when you become your own sickness.

After a long time I become aware that my knees are numb with pain. It has stopped raining when I get to my feet. I feel as though I'd just awakened from a long sleep. Hunger scores my intestines with its dull insistent ache. Vaguely, on another level of consciousness, I realize that I want to eat, then to lie down and rest forever.

A thick, turbid gloom, ominous, drives me out into the wet street. Steeply slanted slate roofs glower behind leaden mists, and the narrow sidewalk disappears into opaque density ahead of me. I persuade the storekeeper to sell me three eggs, promising to bring in my ration tickets later.

I walk back to the sound of Vesper bells pealing thickly, muffled by the muggy atmosphere of early twilight. Along the street lights begin to flicker on. As I approach my house, I see a vague shadow angling across to meet me. It is Madame Renée.

"Come," she says without a trace of emotion, "you've not eaten all day. Come have some supper."

Without answering, I follow her into her house. A lamp is burning in the corner. I look warningly at her, but her face is relaxed as though in great fatigue. Her steps are short, tentative, like those of an old woman. Without looking at me she goes into the kitchen, her hands clasped tightly in front of her.

I sit at the table and wait. I hear no pans, no dishes—only the steady monotone of silence. I wait, glancing occasionally toward the kitchen door. The white linen tablecloth before me seems to glow with a ghostly, almost luminous quality. I fold my hands in my lap as thoughts drowse into a vacuum of waiting, aware only of the raw pain of hunger.

Later, I hear a shoe scrape against the stone floor, followed by some indefinable rustle of movement. Movement gathers life and a black woolen shadow enters the room. Madame Renée, an expression of prayerful, resigned calm on her face, carries hors d'œuvres left over from lunch. She holds the silver platter high—and for an instant I have the vivid impression of a venerable, saintly head lying on a charger in the midst of *escargots,* sausages and radishes, and garnished with tastefully arranged beet and onion rings.

She serves my plate and we eat for some time without speaking, avoiding each other's eyes.

"More bread?"

"Please."

Two voices, bodiless, detached, tentatively seeking sound and then sinking back into silence. An atmosphere tense and tired, demanding that even the sounds of silverware against china be cautiously restrained. And yet the need is felt, the need for health of sound.

"Feeling better?" I ask finally.

She nods, a fading smile softening her face. She opens her mouth to speak, falters, and looks away. When she does bring herself to speak, her voice is emotionless, as though she were dictating a telegram with carefully chosen words. "I did what I thought was best. Poor Michel," she sighs guardedly. "As for you, my friend, I know you have some affection for me. I've been thinking about it all afternoon. I intend to do everything possible now, to merit that affection."

"What brought *that* on?" I ask, recoiling in suspicion.

Genuine pain stencils her face; seeming to force the words out, she murmurs, "You don't mean that." Her voice is gentle. "At least you must understand me and respect my intentions. This hasn't been easy for either of us. I realize now that I've dragged you into an affair that really doesn't concern you. But after all," she continues pensively, "our friendship has been so—well, you know, so—Anyway, please believe me. You'll see. Now that this is over I'm going to do everything in my power to make your life here pleasant."

"Do you really mean that?" I say slowly.

She looks at me unwaveringly, her eyes soft and tired, her eyes seeming to ask, "Don't you believe even that?" Guilt in juxtaposition to pain, and over it all an aura of pleading for another chance. "Next week is Holy Week," she whispers resignedly—"a good time to start over. For the time being let's not mention this again."

"All right," I say gravely, wiping my hands on my napkin, "let's forget it. I believe you're really serious this time."

Closing her eyes she nods agreement. Her chin is held high. A crumb of bread sticks to her cheek. "You'll see how I can change. You'll see."

I try to forget the taunting doubts that turn her gesture into a mockery; I try to believe her—but the change seems impossible as the past carries its overtones too vividly into the present. I take more hors d'œuvres on my plate, fighting back a smile.

"I hope," she adds gently, "everything will be all right between us now."

"I'm sure it will, Madame." An uncomfortable pause,

then, "These hors d'œuvres are certainly delicious," I remark to break the silence. "You've never fixed any like this before."

"Really like them, do you? I should've made them for you before, but they're not easy to prepare, you know."

"I imagine not. Where'd you learn to make them?"

"Well, let's see, where *did* I learn to make those? Probably at one of the restaurants in Paris. You know, Julien loved good things, really good things. He used to take me to all the best restaurants in Paris, and when he liked something especially well, I'd learn to make it. Take these *escargots,* for instance—aren't they as good as the ones at Maxim's? Julien thought they were better." She talks on, musing about the past, until suddenly she asks me, "Do you like to dance?"—but there's no malice in her voice. "I know you dance," she adds, "but I can't picture you going to a lot of dances."

"Don't much care for it," I admit.

"Well, Julien and I loved dancing. You know, I was awfully pretty then and he'd take me to all the dances in Paris—just to show me off, I think. He used to say he loved for other men to see me, to see what a beautiful wife old Julien had got himself." She laughs self-consciously. "Why, when I'd complain that all those men kept—you know—flirting with me, he'd tell me—"

"Yes, Madame," I interrupt, "I remember you told me about that. Those were happy times for you, weren't they?"

"Oh, yes. I wish you could've seen me then."

I laugh, "I'd probably have been one of those you complained about flirting with you."

She eyes me coquettishly. "I might not have complained."

"But," I tell her jokingly, "I thought you never did Julien wrong? I'll bet you did him plenty wrong. Now really, didn't you?"

"I certainly did not," she says lightly. "But—"

"But that doesn't mean you didn't want to, eh?" I smile. "If I'd come along about that time—who knows?—Father Sauvac might've heard about me a lot sooner than he did."

"Don't be too sure," she says primly.

I lean back in my chair and burst out laughing.

"You're terrible," she reproaches me gently. "Go on, eat your supper."

Obediently, I dig into a sausage with my fork.

"You're really terrible," she repeats in a chiding voice, reaching across to squeeze my free hand for a moment of exquisite understanding.

The atmosphere is preserved in the syrup of sudden devotion. I feel the consuming affection of her gaze as she watches me eat.

"You know," she says tenderly, "you hurt me this morning."

"How?"

"When you told me not to touch you." I find nothing to say and she goes on, "I know you didn't mean that, did you?"

"Of course not," I mutter without conviction.

Her foot touches mine beneath the table. Neither of us draws back. I feel all concentration centering in the touch, uncomfortable, wanting to move my foot away, somehow not finding the volition. Again, I feel a pulse of warmth as she squeezes my hand. A terrible understanding flows between us with these touches, these gestures, these many intangible hints that combine into vicarious possession. Her foot moves against my ankle in an eloquent and unmistakable caress. Muscles tighten in my leg, and against the top of my foot comes an answering contraction of muscles. I am seized by an almost childish desire for her to remove her foot. After a time, unable to bear the mounting ponderousness of intimacy between us, I seek a distraction. "How's your breast?" I ask loudly.

Her hand flies to it, and the mood is shattered. "A lot better."

"Good," I grunt, drawing my feet back under my chair. "You've got to take care of it. What about bleeding it with leeches?"

"Hush," she smiles. "You're terrible."

"I'm sure the leeches would enjoy it," I say flatly.

"Really, now!"

"Maybe you would too, eh?"

She purses back her delight and the atmosphere is sane once again. "The idea, talking like that to an old woman, an old hag like me."

When I don't reply, a look of disappointment flickers into her eyes.

"You're terrible," she remarks again. "Bet you wouldn't talk that way to a younger woman."

Inside, the urge to be quiet pricks at my mind, but the irresistible answer blunts it. "Ah," I laugh, "with a young one I wouldn't ask questions about her breasts—I'd find out."

A slight expression of hurt crosses her face.

"But don't feel bad," I add. "I found out about yours too—remember?"

"Now listen," she admonishes, as pleasure radiates from her features—"let's not go too far."

I remain silent a moment.

"You need a young girl, don't you?" observes Madame Renée in sympathy.

"Yes," I say with sudden seriousness, "I guess I do."

She whispers, "That animal part can bother all of us. I know how you feel."

Her words cut through me like a chill. The tone of her voice is somehow liquid and promising. I cough and push my plate away. "Good supper," I mutter appreciatively. "I'd better be going."

"But this isn't all," she protests—"only the first course."

I say nothing; it seems to me that we've had enough.

"There's more to come," she adds.

"I know," I grin, forcing out the ambiguous words as embarrassment colors her face.

She falters, "Aren't you—going to finish?" I laugh out loud and her blush deepens.

"Why don't we," I say suggestively, getting to my feet, "have the meat some other time? These hors d'œuvres have

571

just about filled me up for tonight—haven't they you?"

"That's not very funny, Monsieur"—but the reproof is soft and warm. She walks with me to the door, and I turn to her.

"I'm sorry."

"Well, you should be." She takes my arm affectionately. "Anyway I'm glad we had this little talk, aren't you?"

"I certainly am."

"Things will be better for you—you'll see."

She gazes up at me, and for an instant I feel her stomach touching mine. An involuntary tingling of pleasure is perverted by detached uneasiness. I break away and step quickly through the door, closing it behind me with a mumbled "Good night, Madame."

The night is of mists, full of mysterious shadings. Far down the street I see a single light, diffused into a huge formless glow. My shoes make a sucking sound on the wet cobblestones.

In my salon I turn on all the lights, and the glaucoma veil is torn away to reveal bed and chairs in clear detail. The room seems bright and comfortable, suddenly alive. For a moment I lean against the door, overwhelmed with relief that it's over—that the past months have been resolved—that warmth replaces chill.

1 april

Since the day Michel and Madeleine were here, the rains have stopped. The last few days have been clear, with thunderheads hovering above far horizons. This morn-

ing, unable to resist the bright sun, I decide to plant some
lettuce seeds sent from America. With a trowel I prepare a
small bed in the crumbling soil beside my kitchen door. Beneath me the grass is damp and cool. The early morning is
washed with the delicate fragrance of blossoming fruit trees.

As I work I am aware of the pervading quietness all
about me of Holy Week, serenely unobtrusive despite the
influx of pilgrims coming to attend the miraculous services
at the Monastery. The very atmosphere is transformed by
the single purpose in the hearts of all. Aspects are purified
in calmly waiting for the Passion and death of Good Friday,
and for the Resurrection of Easter—not in remembrance, but
in anticipation of these events which, seemingly, will happen
again this week. All emotions are suspended in the partici-
pation of each in the reality of Christ's sacrifice.

Even Madame Renée seems deeply affected. She attends
all the offices and usually remains on her knees long after
the others have gone. A generous tranquillity marks her actions, and she appears content to let the old niggardly prob-
ings lie dormant.

Working slowly, I absorb the morning sun. The courtyard is exquisite with its white pear blossoms—in perfect
harmony with the week. A sense of peace lulls me into
formless daydreams. As from far away the gate bell rings,
and I hear the postman, whistling this morning, enter the
front door of the house. A moment later the bell rings again,
and his whistling fades beyond the next house. Absently,
I'm aware of a troop of girl scouts marching past in the
street, singing Holy Week hymns in their shrill clear voices.

When the seeds are placed I tamp a thin layer of loose
dirt over them, and go inside to dress for the day. I stop in
the kitchen and wash my hands. The clean fresh odor of
soap seems attuned to all feelings within me.

In the salon, I find a stack of mail which the postman
has left on my table. I light a cigarette and sit down. Idly
I look through the letters—until I come to a square blue
envelope with a Paris postmark. A sudden flash of nervous
fear: Michel's scrawled handwriting. I lay aside the other

573

letters and, filled with misgiving, tear open the envelope.

MY DEAR FRIEND,
 After three days of anguish, in which Madeleine refused
to see me, I have, finally, persuaded her to listen to my pleas,
but it has been impossible for me to work, so will you, please,
tell Mama that I cannot send her the money, that she asked for?
 Needless to say, my feelings for Mama are very bitter, and
I see now, that she was unforgivable in her conduct toward
Madeleine, and completely unfair to me, but, I cannot bring
myself to write to her, when I know that she makes a joke of
every real emotion I have. Will you, therefore, tell her that
Madeleine and I will be married, in the Church of St. Thomas
Aquinas, on the 10th as planned?
 Needless to say, we want both you and Mama, to be here
for the great event (!), so, will you do all you can, to make
her see reason? I know that you will find a way, to straighten
things out for us, so, now, make her come, but, above all, don't
show her this note, will you?
 I permit myself to kiss you, as I would a brother.
 MICHEL

I reread the letter slowly as all emotions combine into
a vague, imponderable dread within me. The day disintegrates into a desperation without focus. I fold the letter
resentfully, my happiness for Michel smothered under the
realization that there will have to be more scenes, more
caresses—her hands seeking marasmic comfort, her voice
insinuating its demands for more gorging on my heart and
blood. Nerves tangle into frustration, for I know that despite the dignity of her face and the nobility of her words
these last few days, she still sucks the nipples of dreams.
And after the healthful days of beginning quiescence, the
necessity for this soul-shriveling activity destroys me. It
poisons parts of the brain. This time satiety has been
reached. I can no longer bury my nose in the saliva lake of
her navel. The cost is too much, too venereal, too abnormal.
 I finish dressing. My mind puckers with the sour taste
of mounting uneasiness. Stuffing the letter in my jacket
pocket, I walk across the street, a hopeless fury stirring me.
 Madame Renée, fresh, gay, opens the door. "Did you

hear?" she chuckles. "Madame Salesky had another one of her spells this morning."

"Really?" I say with a show of interest, stepping inside.

"Yes. Some of the men caught her as she came across the bridge in her nightgown. She had a knife in her hand and she screamed she'd kill her husband's mistress. Oh, it was famous, I can tell you. Poor woman. They say Salesky drove off in his taxi and is hiding in Town till they tell him it's all right to come back. And those dear idiotic little girl scouts saw it all. Guess that'll jar them out of their pieties for a while. One thing's sure—they never heard such language before."

We laugh at the story.

"Going to the Monastery this morning?" she asks, looking up into my face.

"Yes . . . Oh, I was about to forget," I remark lightly— "I got a note from Michel this morning."

"You did?" she says unconcernedly. "I suppose he's still angry with his mama. Poor Michel. What did he have to say? Sit down, won't you?"

"No, I must get to the Monastery."

"Well, may I read the letter? After all, you know, he *is* my son."

"Yes, here it is. Now I must go," I tell her abruptly. "See you at noon."

Dropping the letter on the table, she follows me to the door. Her hand finds mine and she whispers, "You know, you're like your old self these past few days. It does me good to see you so—how can I say it?—so peaceful and happy."

"I *am* happy, Madame," I say bluntly. "See you in a few hours."

"What's the matter?" she asks. "You seem peeved about something."

"No—everything's all right. I'll be back for lunch."

"Oh"—she bites her lip—"I couldn't find anything but turnips for lunch. You don't mind, do you?"

"Again?"

"Meat has gone up. I couldn't afford anything else."

"But I just paid you for a month in advance. We can't go on living on turnips. That's all we've had since Michel was here."

"There were some bills I had to meet," she explains good-naturedly. "Now be sensible. I'm doing the best I can. Perhaps Michel will send a little something this month."

When I arrive at the chapel, it is already crowded with pilgrims. I kneel far to the back and close my eyes against the stark black hangings. I concentrate away from thought, away from dread.

Many footsteps in perfect military cadence attract my attention. I look up to see the troop of girl scouts. They march well, their heads held high, ignoring glances from every side. They kneel as one, in a row of seats reserved for them, pray with apparent fervor, rise on a signal from the leader, and sit back to find the office of the day in their prayer books.

The rest of us return to our devotions.

Silently the monks enter. During Holy Week there's no organ music and the chants are unaccompanied. The Mass is skeletal, austere in tone. Above frequent outbursts of reverberant coughing, chant follows chant, creating calm in all hearts. Chants rise to empty spaces above us and lose themselves in bodiless purity.

In the black-shrouded coolness, many of us stay on our knees after the monks have completed Mass. Desire to stay here always. But human sounds eventually destroy the moment, and other awarenesses superpose themselves on prayer.

Dark figures pass, walking slowly down the aisle, stopping to kiss the golden foot of a coldly shadowed St. Peter. Occasionally the rumbling silence is pierced with the sharp clank of a coin being dropped into one of the collection boxes. Someone stands with a booklet in his hand before one of the crypts and whispers explanations to his companions. I stay on my knees, breathing heavily. A phlegm of nausea coats my senses when I think of returning to the outside. The need to stay here, to let morning become afternoon without moving, is physical. I think of Madame Renée's caresses, and all outside things seem to become her fondlings—tempting me, torturing me with suppressed excitement—until I enter the fault and must escape myself rather than her.

Reluctantly I get to my feet, filled with a sensation of loathing. I leave the darkness of polished, empty pews, of smells of dying incense and moldy prayer books. And I walk to her house with the fullness of the past, unable to bear more; unable to bear the inevitable degeneration of myself and of her and of the union of ourselves in anger and despair.

She is prostrate on the couch. Her unblinking eyes are dry and protruding. Fury bursts like obscenity from her lips: "You knew what was in that letter!" It's a dry, catlike sound. "Why'd you leave me?"

"Why should I stay?" I shout back, my voice instinctively seeking to match hers in brutality.

"How could Michel—? Why, that—!" She clenches her fist and draws a mouth of saliva that escapes in gasping.

"Don't start that again!" I command sharply. "I've heard every filthy thing you can say. This morning when you thought you'd won, it was 'poor Michel'—remember? Well, I'm glad he had the—"

"Shut up!" she screams uncontrollably. "For God's sake shut up!"

"You'll *never* see clear!"

She unleashes incoherent groans of anger at the walls. "You—you left me!" she accuses, glaring at me with eyes that seem not to see.

"Listen to me!" I bellow. "Shut up and listen to me! If you promise never to mention this again and to accept Michel's marriage, I'll stay. Otherwise I'm moving out— understand?"

"You left me!" Her chokings become an animal squeal as I turn and walk to the door. "Get out! Get out!"

I step outside and slam the door with all my strength. The street is filled with pilgrims. Quaking with disgust I

577

stump across the street, as Madame Renée screams her loss to the emptiness. Black-dressed people hesitate for a moment, shake their heads, stare curiously at me, and pass on. I see a young man make the sign of the cross on his chest.

In the trembling stillness of my room, I listen until her wails die away. I am soaked with sweat.

The Valley rests silent. Clouds have gathered—violent ominous clouds of Holy Week, obscuring the sun. A peculiar benign stillness, copper-tinted, copper-tasting, terrifies me.

I think coldly on another plane, a detached plane. I think of the past days of quietness, of healthful activity—destroyed abruptly, savagely. Her words, "You left me," sting with the realization that her grief, her madness are due not so much to losing Michel as to my own brutality. A tinge of remorse grows sickening. I think of possessing her —of going to her and possessing her deliberately, in hatred —giving nothing of myself. That's her obsession—why not? Anything to be rid of her. Anything to end this. Go to her now, on the couch; possess her in all the animal heats and hatreds; pay her off and be done with it. But something that Father Clément once told me insinuates itself into my mind: "No end, no matter how important, can justify sinful means." I think that it's late in my life, very late. I laugh at the words but the laughter is its own rebuke, meaningless, aborted.

I stroll aimlessly into the kitchen. In a bowl on the table I see the three eggs I bought the other day. Because there's nothing else to do, I boil an egg for lunch. I sit down at the table and begin to eat it, without thinking, without tasting. The sudden ringing of the gate bell, ominous, makes me pause in the middle of a bite. Again the coppery taste, the shudder of irritation. I get up and go to the salon door.

Calm, sullen, looking as if she can hardly stand, Madame Renée announces quietly, "I have a plan. Want to hear it?"

"Not if it concerns Michel's marriage," I answer, turning away.

578

"No, it's about something else," she says, following me into the kitchen. "I want to go to England, to visit Jean-Julien's grave. But—there's only enough money for the trip. Can you help me clear up my debts here?"

I resume my seat at the table and pick at the egg. "Why not wait till you return to clear them up? I'd let you have the money but I'm down to my last few bills. I'm sorry, Madame."

"What can I do then?" she moans, turning her head away.

"Why not," I suggest with more warmth, "take some sort of a job? Be good for you. After all, everyone works these days."

"What could *I* do?" she says, swallowing.

"Cook, take care of children. You can't imagine how the rest of us would admire you if—"

"You'd like to see me sink to the very bottom, wouldn't you?"

"If you're going to start that—" I glance at her warningly.

"Well, I plan to stay in England," she simpers. "I don't want to be near Michel when he takes his wife, when he loses his purity." She eyes me steadily.

I grunt, "The answer to that's obvious—we won't discuss it. But I think England's a good solution for you. I'll give you all the money I can raise—but you owe me six thousand francs already and I expect to be paid in full for everything I lend you."

She nods, her lips turned down at the corners in a morose smile. I lean my arms on the table and look straight ahead.

"When do you leave?"

"As soon as possible. But you haven't heard the rest of my plan." Her voice becomes soft. "You see, I plan to make sure Michel doesn't marry. I intend to kill myself on Jean-Julien's grave the day before the wedding. I'll save him from that woman after all."

"Good God!" I groan. "What'll you think of next? Now I suppose you think I'll get on my knees and beg you

579

to change your mind. Why don't you grow up? If you think—" My words die as I look up at her sickening grin.

She purses her lips pleasantly. "Are you going to write to Michel?"

"Hell, no."

"No? Why not?"

"Might spoil your plan." Looking at the table, I say wearily, "Can't you understand? I've had all this I can take. What do you want with me, anyway?" Pushing the plate away, I lower my head into the cradle of my arms.

For a moment she doesn't move. Light from the door finds its way through the blue of my shirtsleeve. The room is quiet. Then, above me, I sense a soundless movement, and words are whispered against my ear.

"I'm so sorry," she says in a cracked voice. "I know you. You've needed me and I've failed you. That's what makes you so nervous." Her hand touches the back of my neck, fondles around to my cheek. "Remember the night you got drunk? You wanted me then." A sob breaks her voice. "If —if you'd just be nice to me . . ."

I feel her breath against my face. I sit stunned as her cheek brushes against mine. Unconsciously I arch my head away, but the tingling juncture creates in me a suppressed excitement as hinted animal tangents converge into focused desire. The body knows the possibilities and begins to savor them far in advance of consent. I sit motionless, remembering feelings—the catching of the breath, the flooding of warmth when a whore hisses, when a street girl glances, when body becomes aware of body and stirs its own compulsions. No. I recoil, but muscles and nerves become hypnotized. A faint odor of face powder, musky, stirs my intestines with simultaneous loathing and desire. The taunting possibility—the offer of her body to my body, of her nerves to my nerves in brute slakings of inverse pleasure—is irresistibly compelling. I feel myself relax against her and at the same time stiffen with dread. I feel her hand prowling across my chest, warm and full. A suffocated exhalation rasps loudly from her as her fingers grasp hungrily at my

580

chest and, with a circular motion, caress a wide path to my belt. All feelings, all emotions center in the soft warmth of possibilities contained in her body beside me, repelling, attracting, dragging at me, paralyzing me in suspense while her strong fingers unbuckle my belt and crawl stealthily searching . . . until clothing is no longer a wall and flesh touches living flesh to stimulate engulfing desire. A battery of sensuality is exploded into my belly. Her lips against my face. Through slitted eyes I look downward. The black wool sleeve, disappearing beneath cloth, weaves gently. I hold my breath painfully. For a drunken moment my sight is caught by the glistening stain of coagulated sugar where the preserves were dropped on her sleeve. Her lips trail a pattern of sensation across my cheek and I turn to meet them, closing my eyes. A whimpering sob escapes her as our mouths join and move liquidly, hungrily against each other. Shock as her mouth exudes its warmth onto mine. I struggle to my feet, my legs shaking so that I can scarcely support my weight. I gasp as she withdraws her hand. Her arms snake their way beneath my armpits. We stand pressed together, hands and mouths and groins searching living tumescence.

But passion falters with a caught breath. A thought bolts through my consciousness—a faint protesting plea that warns me of the moment, begs me to break away. Formless plea, vague and meaningless. She rubs against me. She is like a bitch in heat dragging me into her, and tensions build hopelessly against the plea. The plea is a fleck, an irritation flecking mucous union, as groins and bellies become united in overwhelming thirst. Her arms, tentaclelike, tighten around me and we float in feverish embrace as the plea sends words tracing themselves in dreamy sequence, like a curl of smoke, through a faraway consciousness. *Mary, conceived without* . . . I lean back against the table, rejecting the flecked words, and pull her full against me, my hands beneath her buttocks grasping the whale softness. *. . . sin, pray for* . . . Vision alternates with blindness. Suddenly I see a throbbing heartbeat in the hollow of her scarlet throat, then blackness as hands seek intimacy and lips suck lips in hyena laughter. She arches forward, maneuvering until her legs frame my thighs. . . . *pray for us who have* . . . The grit, the irritating grit of pleas, like sand against tender inner flesh. The plea begging me, pumping words against the diaphragm of my craving. Now or never, now or never. Destruction. I feel her hands grasp my head and lower it inexorably to her throat. I taste the flesh and feel her swallowing muscles beneath my lips. *Mary, conceived without sin, pray* . . . Her belly twists with pleasure in a gigantic serpentine voluptuousness, tossing me into a full dream of carnality. But somewhere in the back of my mind, clogged with screaming desire for her, the resisting plea flickers, hesitates, blinks out, pulsates to the fore as bloods pound out visions of strong legs, of distorted buttocks, of insatiable, slavering vaginas. Lost. I lift her higher over me as her hands force my head downward into the opening of her dress. The hard edge of the table bites into my haunches. . . . *without sin* . . . The two images—nakedness full of rich odors struggling against the dim image of words, blotted and blinded. All things—the past, the hopes—combine into ambivalence attracting opposing, striving as all futures and all times become the moment. My hand finds her most intimate warmth and burns with pleasure. The will like an inflexible pole, the will tall and phallic—and something beyond me seeking to bend the will, to change its course for the first time, for the very first time in my life. *Mary* . . . inner sobbing . . . *conceived without sin* . . . forcing the words against all desire . . . *pray for us who have recourse to thee.* Bending the will, distorting the will—until the rack becomes insane and the soul bursts into weeping. Words die in suffocation as a slow undulation knots the entrails with her bitch cravings. I feel her knuckles hard against my chin as she opens her dress. With the other hand she pushes my mouth against the upward slant of her exposed breast, my lips clutching. Concentrating, concentrating, not letting it die. . . . *without sin, pray for us* . . . Insistent, refusing to escape into the fog of dreams. *Mary* . . . like the faded print of an old news-

582

paper, yellowed, mixed with the reek of my saliva on her breast as my mouth is guided hopelessly toward the goal, the detested goal, the nipple. Muscles in my neck resist. The dread of arriving at the prune nipple. Aged flesh, used, but fresh eternally in my cravings. Her hands lock my head, forcing. *Mary* . . . Great exhaustion from struggling against the faded print that now dominates my inner vision. Shaking my head against the lustful snare. Eyes glimpse blue veins beneath transparent white skin, saliva-streaked, saliva-stenched. *Mary* . . . pleading, begging as the nippled goal draws near. *Mary* . . . and the hard warm shriveled bulb against the corner of my mouth. Fighting back the choking rise of vomit, as muscles tense rigid and all concentration divides between the dreaded goal and the words pulsating clearer. *Mary, conceived without sin* . . . And the faded print is suffused slowly with luminous black, and the old newspaper, yellowed, becomes atmosphere shimmering behind words, destroying the other image as I feel the nipple bending to enter my mouth and my mouth rejecting it in a convulsive wrenching as the screeching howling rasping whiteness slithers away to sudden nothingness. I shove her away and stare open-eyed. The room swims wildly. I see her congested face, the exposed breast glistening. Without opening her eyes she flows toward me, arms outstretched. Slowly, dazedly, I lift my arm high in the air and bring my fist smashing down into her face. She crumples to the floor. Dimly I see tiles coming up to meet me as blood-mists float across my eyes. I catch myself against the table, weaving, trying to focus on the whispered *Mary, conceived without sin, pray for us* . . . And far in the distance, out of space, confusions and sicknesses gyrate around the one exultant nucleus: *For the first time. For the very first time.*

Madame Renée, wallowing on the floor, is wrenched with sobs. Slowly, I lower trembling hands to my belt, and stuffing in my shirt tail I buckle my pants. Reeling senses seek their level in the tear-mulched silence. In my legs there's no strength left to support me. I lower myself into the chair and let my head fall forward on the table, inundated with gratitude for the insistent phrase *For the very first time*—abandoning myself to it—*For the very first time.* I am filled with the gentle, floating pain of unbearable relief.

A scuffing sound attracts my attention. I open my eyes and look downward. The table angle gives a triangular view of the floor. Absently I watch, seeing only her sturdy black shoes and the hem of her dress as she gets to her feet. I watch the shoes turn sideways, hesitate, then disappear beyond my range of vision. I don't move for a long time after the front door clicks shut.

I sink into a dreamlike semiconsciousness where all time seems stopped and where awareness becomes superficial observation, seeping around the glowing block of relief. The sun lightens half-shadows into clear divisions. I observe it through some otherworldly antenna, and catalogue it without letting it penetrate. Only the words *For the very first time* penetrate, rocking me in a wave of exultation. Rest, repose, as the body does its own work of settling nerves in patterns of recuperation, as bloods mix with hopes and go their way unaided by me.

Sometime later, quiet voices in the street. For a moment I wonder what time it is—morning, noon, or afternoon. I raise my head to look about. The house seems clean again, mine once more. A sensation of pleasurable emptiness. Everything registers in slow motion. I open the kitchen door and feel warm, soft air against my face. My numbness is lessened by the beautiful spring in the world outside— sober, delicately tinted, sweet-smelling, undisciplined spring.

Thinking of nothing but the moment, I take off my clothes and go to the sink. Vision becomes acute. I notice a bar of soap, white and full of marks like a chunk of driftwood. I wet a large sponge and climb into the sink, and standing upright, I bathe in the cold water. The profound satisfaction of invigorating cleanness, like a confession and absolution of the tainted hide, filters into the spirit. It gives space for a new effort.

I dress unhurriedly, putting on fresh clothes. And when

584

I walk outside, the glory of Holy Week seems to radiate from the earth.

The street is crowded with visitors as more pilgrims enter the Valley by bus, by train, or on foot. They are everywhere, with great wooden walking staves, dusty shoes, and the inevitable packs of food and clothing strapped to tired shoulders.

I follow them into the chapel for Vespers and Tenebrae. The beauty of the offices reduces us to the level, static emotion of pure worship. We are joined, all of us, in a uniform inner calmness, and somehow wrong turns into right.

I stare at the floor, knotted with lumps of mud brought in on heavy shoes. Chants lift thoughts high above, into another realm, and prayers are unleashed within—wordless prayers lost in a silence of the most intense joy. A taste of the quality of innocence, systematically destroyed in me all these years, returns as a new longing. Sudden fatigue with the off-gray tinge of cynicism, the depravity of a sneer. I feel the kneeling-bench cut into my knees, and wavering surprise at myself. Innocence desired as a part of life; abandonment of the comfort of self—these comprise a quality of longing I have always detested. It's as though the gift of self, of logic, were seeking to burn the carefully accumulated garbage from my heart and my brain. But hesitation twists longings in me. I know only the profound solitude of not knowing, of not understanding, of being reduced to formless searching within myself.

Later, I walk back in the dusk, bowing to those I pass in the street. The air is mysterious, full of fragrant balm. I think of Madame Renée, and the thoughts are other confusions. I think of her as the personification of hatred for all she once held dear—and I wonder at the extent of my own fault in hers.

I am torn by a moment of agonizing pity as I look at her house across the way. Windows and shutters are closed. No lights are as yet visible. How desolate she must be, sitting or lying there alone, hearing the street noises of early eve-

585

ning. Understand her there in the darkness. Respect her. But layers of imponderable actions and reactions blanket understanding, blanket knowledge of her and of myself.

My house is somber. Tile floors reflect the last vague light of dusk from the open window. A faint breeze stirs the curtains, and in the gloom of warm evening the room invites rest. There's an intimacy of impersonal half-lights and heavy shadows.

I switch on the radio: at low volume from Paris, the Fauré Requiem. All France bows to the pre-Easter season with music. I take a chair near the window, light a cigarette and wait, savoring the moment of fading daylight. I study the glowing arc of my cigarette as I lift it to my mouth. In the background the chorus murmurs warm, tender harmonies that give life and hope to death. The eternal promise.

Above the jagged silhouette of housetops nearby, a first star appears, spangling and chipped through the stirring curtain. I watch it a moment, then get up and close the blinds. I turn on all the lamps and the room leaps into focus. The spell is broken, but I know now that it will always come back.

Turning, I notice on the table a large envelope. Across its face my name is scrawled in huge letters, underscored with a double line. A new trembling of excitement ripples through my stomach—but it quickly dies. My hands are calm as I pick up the envelope and open it. Somehow I know what it will contain.

MONSIEUR,

When you find this I shall be on the train for Paris, and then England. You will consider it a presumption after this afternoon if I ask you not to follow me, nor to try to stop me, but I ask you none the less.

I might have borne my disappointment in losing Michel, but to lose both you and my son is more than I can be expected to accept; and after your conduct today, I know that you have never been sincere in your feelings for me—and that you never will be. Do not think I hold it against you. When a woman has been so cruelly buffeted by fate as I, she finds it easy to forgive those who do her the greatest harm. My maternal affection has not diminished toward either you or my son. Some day you will realize that my every action was dictated by the unique thought of your welfare and his.

Since you refused me the money, I am leaving debts behind —debts incurred because I fed you better than I could afford to. My consolation for leaving this unfinished business is the knowledge that you are in good health, that you have been well nourished. Tell them that they can sell my belongings to pay what I owe. Later I will inform you of my address in England so that you may send me anything that is left over. For I plan to stay in England permanently. I am breaking off with Michel. He will never again have to worry about his mother's bad conduct.

Remain Michel's friend. It is beyond me to bless this marriage which I know can bring only misery. His children will be poor and his wife may die with the first one. These are things a mother feels. I cannot face it, and so I shall begin a new life far away from him.

Your part in this will be a source of remorse to you. Do not let it grieve you. Know that I forgive you completely.

May God give you a happy life. Yours in Christ.

Adieu

It is unsigned. From the radio a mournful cadence in the chorus dampens the background of sound, as my reactions swing gently between regret and relief. My thoughts go back to the day of the Petite Chevissier's death, to that feeling of infinite sadness mingled with serene happiness that her ordeal was over. And those emotions find duplication at this death of a relationship.

As a final gesture, almost in a dream, I write Michel a brief account of the day, advising him to marry Madeleine as planned, and enclose the note from his mother. Putting a stamp on this last vestige of our life together, I walk to the post office and drop it in the box.

The Village seems cleaner, lighter, as if some oppressive load had been lifted from its conscience. The difference is felt this very night. The cacophony of Madame Renée's domination, gone at last, leaves quietness in its wake.

I walk slowly on the rough cobblestones, following the echo of my footsteps. On each side, lights from shuttered

587

windows tremble crisply in the clean air of night. Dew gathers in the air, and my hand touches wetness as it opens the gatehouse door at the Monastery. A single lamp hangs lonely in the empty room. At my request, the monk on duty leaves to find Father Clément.

Waiting, there is the confusion of all things combined into night. A burden has been lifted, and in its place remains —nothing. I can understand only my desire to escape it. Through the door, open to the cloister gardens, a damp breeze enters and stirs the pages of pious publications on their rack.

Father Clément's face is suddenly there, caught in the light. He shakes my hand and looks at me questioningly.

"She's left, Father," I say flatly.

"Come, my son, let us talk about it outside."

We walk a few steps down the graveled path, following fantastic shadows in front of us. He stops and turns to me. Without looking at him I tell him of the day. I fix my gaze on a low-hanging branch moving in silhouette beside us. I am aware of the black night stirring full of stars.

"You have done what you could, my son," I hear him say when I have finished. "Poor woman." The branch moves, stippling lights and shadows on his wrinkled face. For a long time he remains silent; then finally, "What about you, my son?" he asks. "Now that she has gone, your life outside should be much more pleasant."

I hesitate, swallowing words, wanting to tell him of the things I feel. "I—don't know, Father." My voice sounds hollow, strained.

In the dim glow he peers into my face. "What is the matter, my child?"

"I don't know. It seems like—" My voice falters; I fight the chilling onrush of emotion.

I feel his hand on my arm as he waits for me to go on. At last he says, uneasily, "What are you trying to say?"

I answer dully, "It seems like my life's falling to pieces."

"On account of her, you mean?"

"No," I choke the word out. "You know me better than

588

anyone else in the world. You ought to understand what I mean. It's—well, something's wrong with me." I shuffle my feet on the gravel. "I don't know how to say it, but—I can't stand living like this any more. It has nothing to do with Madame Renée . . . "

"Yes?"

"It's just—me—*inside* me."

"That is indeed gratifying, my son." I jerk my head up in surprise, but he goes on warmly, "I am so glad. If only you knew how much I have longed to hear you say that!"

I am shaken with a sudden chill, a momentary trembling. "I don't understand, Father. I thought I was doing right, but now—I don't even know—"

"How long have you felt like this?"

"A long time. It keeps growing. I feel like everything I do is—well, counterfeit."

"Listen, my son," he whispers rapidly, urgently, "these things are hard to understand. You say I know you—I am not sure whether I do or not."

"But I've told you everything."

"I do not think you know yourself, my son," he says almost tenderly. "No, I think you are just beginning to know yourself." He pauses before going on, as though searching for words. "Is it not true that in each of us there are at least two men, one of whom has the terrible skill of presenting the other with certain favorable characteristics that do not really belong to him? This is done in all sincerity—and there lies the tragedy, my son. I think you have done this with me, unconsciously."

His words touch a deep vein of truth within me. "Then —I've done it with myself too," I mutter.

"I believe you have. During these last few weeks you probably have begun to realize it. It is the shock of seeing yourself in this light that makes you feel as if your life were falling to pieces."

"I've been false even to myself!"

"I know," he says affectionately. "It is a shattering thing, is it not?—a humiliating thing. But just remember that

589

everyone is guilty of it to a certain extent. You must be glad that you discovered your falseness, that you found out in time. Now that you know, you can do something about it. Think of all the people who spend their entire lives in this terrible narcosis of self-delusion!"

I breathe painfully, loathing the sudden image of myself. "Did you know all along that I was doing it, Father?"

"Yes," he murmurs, "I believe I did."

"How could you put up with me?"

"Come now," he protests in an encouraging voice, "you must not feel that way about it." He squeezes my arm reassuringly. "I know how it is. For a while you will hate yourself, you will be disgusted with yourself, you will blame yourself more than you really should. But you must realize, my son, that what seems to you the end is actually only the beginning. You have no reason to be embarrassed with me. I think it wonderful that you found out."

My sigh rasps loudly in the silence. Words seem to formulate themselves, sounding heavy and automatic. "Can I come back here, Father?"

"Do you really want to, my child?"

"Yes," I say tiredly. "I think I almost have to, now. I can't go on—" I shrug my shoulders and look at him.

"I know, my son." He touches my arm again. "Yes, by all means come back if it means that much to you. You may have your old cell this Sunday. I will help you move in."

"Thanks, Father." I turn to go, but falter. "Just one thing more, Father. You knew all this—why didn't you tell me sooner?"

"You had to come to it yourself, my son. You would not have believed it then. But now you can accept your falseness without rebellion—without being driven by pride to take up your defense and to justify yourself. I know how humiliating this is for you, but humiliation is a great purifier, my son. Eventually you will realize that, too."

"Does everybody else—the other monks, I mean—do they know?"

"No," he says quietly. "You must not be ashamed of this.

Think of these things as symptomatic of disease. Take those symptoms to God exactly as you would take physical symptoms to the doctor."

I nod. "I remember Marie-Ornoux and Dr. Castelar once explained that to me."

"The great shame is in not admitting, not accepting the symptoms—in trying to hide them. Once you begin systematically to go about curing the disease, you are on the right track and there need be no more shame."

"Yes, sir."

"Good night, my son."

My footsteps crunch on the cloister path. From the shadows I hear his parting words: "Pray, my son. Pray."

As the gatehouse door clicks shut behind me, deep-toned bells, calling the monks to Compline, vibrate on the still air. Ageless sound of finality, dying to silence. I walk back through the deserted street, watching lights in houses flicker off one by one.

6 april

Movements are slow. Eyes are leaden. Cigarette smoke curls about my face as I unpack the last of my clothes. I open the window of my old cell. The morning smell of distance enters fresh on cool sunlight.

The walls of ancient stone tremble as great bells send metallic discs of sound floating over the countryside. The chapel draws me into its shadowed vastness.

And after the long darkness of Holy Week there are the lightness, the joy of Easter morning in this Monastery.

591

Festive colors and candles and the resounding organs quiet these forty days. And through the texture of morning, the delicate radiance of many and often-chanted Alleluias sung by monks who seem to lift themselves above the earth with the miracle of the Resurrection. On this final day they breathe the chants—sounds made by the human heart, restrained overflowings of joy too profound for jubilation. Through the worshipful hours every fiber of my being listens, listens and feels its first hint of restoration. The long vigil of Lent is past.

I remain kneeling in the chapel as others walk out to the bright accompaniment of a Cabezón Toccata. Sunlight filters through the leaded stained-glass windows. I rest in emptiness. Things long ago . . . in other lives.

The curing charity of solitude. Only alone is there the promise of peace. Alone, the slow turnings of recuperation shake me into belief, ardently desired when I hear with terror and longing the sound of a voice reverberating through cloisters.

I press my forehead against the bench in front of me. Thoughts grate like swinging chains of incense on the migraine hook of my conscience. The lingering obsession with Madame Renée splotches dissonant color on the soul's retina, destroying the hint, forever the hint. The gray hair, the beautiful face shrivel space and time into a knot that can't be swallowed—a knot of my own guilt, a knot of my own hatred. Thought becomes an unbearable weariness closing my eyes and destroying.

Shut out the mystery of her without ever understanding. But words haunt me, whispering back from the mind's crypt, old words never meaningful until now. Pray for the hated. Sink first into chasms of destruction, and in totality of humiliation build again. Know depths first before black hate can find its light of compassion and pity. I search in the dark hole of the past, seeing nothing. But the difference is felt, the great difference. Nothing is clear, nothing can ever be clear again. The soul is its own pit, forever struggling out of its pain.

Pray for her, give thanks for her; for she gave you this—these walls, these ringing silences, these thirsts. As the seed must be bruised from its outer shell before it can grow fruit, so must the soul. Chasms of destruction turn roots to air. The plow kills before it gives life, doing quickly what earth's timeless erosion never accomplished. Her gift was the killing gift of life without which this might never have been.

The atmosphere of stone, then, is changed. The spattering cry of life rising over the dying heartbeat. The time will be long and it will come in little things . . .

And the betweens leave once again. I walk from the chapel stunned with the fantastic thirst for solitude on my lips. The pendulum swings far in the direction of old things returned as new—desolation, warmth, sadness, contentment with sadness. The morning passes, and afternoon grows into lengthening shadows. My fingers absently examine flowering greenery; and inside, the soul cringes and begs for rest.

And later, when Compline is over, I walk in the garden. It is the Great Silence. Magical spring night. Alone. Infinite blackness of silent skies, alive with drifting stars.

I sit in the orchard, and the night grows late. The air is perfumed with blossoming lime and pear trees. Ravishing murmurings from the River below. Across the way, lights in houses disappear one by one. The night cools to its own sounds, giving rest and a first upward-swinging seedling strength nurtured on silence. My footsteps move across wet grasses until my hands touch the parapet, touch mossy fungus damp and gauzelike, touch impersonal dew on rough stones.

And it turns, slowing, this thing within me turns and dissolves in night. Coolness against face. Careening night of hidden sounds rising from the water's edge to float low over the countryside, bringing new life.

I lean on the wall. Fingers idly explore rough seams of mortar where great stones have been joined. But it's dark—living darkness of skies and clouds of stars and earth's purity of resurrected night, of resurrected body.

Now they sleep. In many cells they sleep, and in houses across the way. Winter's stagnant torture becomes the balm of a spring night with lingering coolness late. Garden of the cloister, mysterious forms pervading blackness with bloom. Only I am awake at this hour. The air becomes rarefied and begins to chill. They sleep while I remain awake. It dissolves slowly. Lips taste wetness. Other midnights, other springtimes, other damp nocturnal murmurings. Chords break loose and create freshness. Universality of desires, of loves, of climates of thought this deepening night.

Night of all nativities. Moisture of lateness. Bend low. Lean on the wall. Feel the beginnings of reeling vertigo and—

No. Turn. It can't be borne. Listen for sounds that bring you back. It's too soon, and the weakness too great. Listen. Sifted undertones of crickets' lonely raspings hanging like luminous mists in the Valley below. Beyond, a train going somewhere and soon gone, leaving a greater silence behind. They live out there, outside the high walls; they breathe and sleep and are nourished. And there's no understanding now. It's the mystery of all things. Clutch something there in the dark. Hold to it. The grasses are wet. Hold. Look at the night and beyond to the Source of all nights and of all things, things coming alive in spring and reposing until the light of another day. It is late in our lives, forever late.

Cough. Take a step. God. Let it be not a drunkenness. Let it be not this unbearable dizziness. Let it be the settling of tensions, the flux of respiration seeking rest. Mystery of all mysteries carrying upward, gently. Strength comes slow and it must be in little things. Touch the wall. It must come slow and without the whimpering cries. Spreading, inundating answers to all thirsts, the serene nourishing answer to man's eternal need.

Lamb of God taking away the sins of the world . . . the world sleeps, embracing great silence, healing the darkness.

Move away from the wall. Feel shrubs against your legs as you walk. Walk slow in the night. And the change is deep and not a change to be seen. There must forever be

594

bread and sleep and twisting in a bed of dreams. Let no one see the change. For the smell of soap is better than the smell of mold, and the morning is better than the night. The change is in the greatest of all acceptances. Let it be in quietness, flowing out with its prayer, easily. Let it feel not only the night's scattering stars, but also the warmth following chill; and in solitude know greater lulling textures of richness. For there can be no more loneliness.

Open the door of the cell. Step inside. Let the words flow no longer cramped and stingy, but outward in long undulating waves of easiness. No longer the joyless struggle, but the easy flooding, the peace of sounds and smells and night earth rumbling deep around.

Pray for the hated. Somewhere in the green health of the English countryside a woman dreams distorted dreams. God be with her this night. God cleanse all things this night. God turn the wax embryo and puncture the transcendence of trembling viscera.

The window is opened wide. Pray for the hated. No, there is nothing hated. Greater than that, the night lifts words stratospheres above to all mankind sleeping outside these walls. They soar into tenderness for all the promised and unpromised; for all the sleepy-eyed and wakeful-eyed; for all the predawn coughers and chokers and turners-in-bed; for all the hands clutched soft and feelingless beside faces in sleep; for all the legs moving under covers seeking comfort. All that is mine tonight. And more: the sudden waking pierced with bolts of terror in black rooms; the bloated bellies in dark alleyways; the drunken half-mad horror of sleepless women who finger the ribbed edges of a coin while they become hunks of meat glued to other hunks of meat in a loveless embrace; the sacramental sleep of blessed, cursed, great and ungreat, all seeking, seeking, seeking . . . The world in Thy hands, the world turning in universal sameness forever. Calm the hearts, calm the sleeps and sleep again. Turn in beds and feel quakings die, feel quakings become a long sigh, and before the sigh is completed become slumber,

slumber for all the soft midnight hours. All of that . . .
always . . .

I crawl into my cot, crawl between clean sheets damp
with morning freshness. I pull them close about me in a
cell smelling of stone and dew-filled air from the deep
lands alive.

Night of all nativities. Night of all nights with its
waking morning. Quiet, rhapsodic joy this night of return.

Designed by Gordon W. Smith
Set in Intertype Garamond by F. L. Motheral Co., Fort Worth
Printed and bound by Kingsport Press, Inc., Kingsport, Tennessee